PUDD'NHEAD WILSON
and
THOSE EXTRAORDINARY TWINS

AUTHORITATIVE TEXTS
TEXTUAL INTRODUCTION AND TABLES OF VARIANTS
CRITICISM

A NORTON CRITICAL EDITION

SAMUEL LANGHORNE CLEMENS

PUDD'NHEAD WILSON
and
THOSE EXTRAORDINARY TWINS

AUTHORITATIVE TEXTS
TEXTUAL INTRODUCTION AND
TABLES OF VARIANTS
CRITICISM

Edited by
SIDNEY E. BERGER
MILLIKIN UNIVERSITY

W · W · NORTON & COMPANY
New York   London

Library of Congress Cataloging in Publication Data
Clemens, Samuel Langhorne, 1835–1910.
Pudd'nhead Wilson and Those extraordinary twins.
(A Norton critical edition)
Bibliography: p.
1. Clemens, Samuel Langhorne, 1835–1910.
Pudd'nhead Wilson. 2. Clemens, Samuel Langhorne, 1835–
1910. Those extraordinary twins. I. Clemens, Samuel
Langhorne, 1835–1910. Those extraordinary twins. 1980.
II. Berger, Sidney E. III. Title.
PS1317.B4   1980   813'.4   79-23679
ISBN 0-393-01337-5
ISBN 0-393-95027-1 pbk.

ACKNOWLEDGMENTS

Eberhard Alsen: from *Western American Literature*, 8 (Summer 1972), 2. Used by permission of the publisher.

Frederick Anderson: from the facsimile edition of *Pudd'nhead Wilson* and *Those Extraordinary Twins* published by Chandler Publishing Company, San Francisco. Reprinted by permission of the author.

John M. Brand: from *Western American Literature*, 8 (Summer 1972), 2. Used by permission of the publisher.

Stanley Brodwin: from *Texas Studies in Literature and Language*, 15, 1 (Spring 1973). Reprinted by permission of University of Texas Press and the author.

Richard Chase: from *The American Novel and Its Tradition* by Richard Chase. Copyright © 1957 by Richard Chase. Used by permission of Doubleday & Company, Inc.

Samuel Langhorne Clemens: Hitherto unpublished material included in the Tables of Textual Variants is copyrighted by the University of California Press and is used by their permission. Material previously published by Daniel Morley McKeithan in "The Morgan Manuscript of Mark Twain's *Pudd'nhead Wilson*," *Essays and Studies on American Language and Literature*, No. 12 (Cambridge, Mass.: Harvard University Press, 1961; Uppsala: A.-B. Lundeqvistka Bokhandeln, 1961), is here reprinted by permission of the Mark Twain Foundation. (Specific acknowledgments are given in the Tables of Textual Variants, accompanying the material for which permission is granted.)

James Cox: from *Mark Twain: The Fate of Humor*, copyright © 1966 by Princeton University Press (Princeton Paperback, 1976), pp. 222–46. Reprinted by permission of Princeton University Press.

Bernard De Voto: from *Mark Twain's America*. Copyright 1932 by Bernard De Voto; © renewed 1960 by Avis M. De Voto. Reprinted by permission of the publisher, Houghton Mifflin Company.

Leslie Fiedler: from *The New Republic*, vol. 133, nos. 7–8, issues 2125–2126. Copyright © 1955 by *The New Republic*. Reprinted by permission of *The New Republic*.

Marvin Fisher and Michael Elliott: from *The Southern Review*, 1972. Reprinted by permission of the authors.

John C. Gerber: from *Studies in American Humor*, 2, 1 (April 1975). Reprinted by permission of Jack Meathenia, Editor, *Studies in American Humor*.

Ernest Kroll: from *Poet and Critic*, 7, 2 (1973). Reprinted by permission of *Poet and Critic*.

F. R. Leavis: from *Commentary*, by permission; copyright © 1956 by the American Jewish Committee. Also reprinted from *Pudd'nhead Wilson* published by Chatto & Windus, Ltd., by permission of Chatto & Windus, Ltd., and Dr. F. R. Leavis.

Arthur G. Pettit: from *Mark Twain and the South*. Copyright © 1974 by the University Press of Kentucky. Reprinted by permission of the publishers.

Robert Regan: from *Unpromising Heroes: Mark Twain and His Characters*. Copyright © 1966 by The Regents of the University of California. Reprinted by permission of the University of California Press.

Henry Nash Smith: from *Mark Twain: The Development of a Writer* by Henry Nash Smith (Cambridge, Mass.: The Belknap Press of Harvard University Press). Copyright © 1962 by the President and Fellows of Harvard College. Reprinted by permission of the publisher.

George M. Spangler: from *American Literature*, 42 (1970): 28–37. Copyright 1970 by Duke University Press. Reprinted by permission of the publishers.

Arlin Turner: from *The Southern Review*, IV, n.s. (April 1968). Reprinted by permission of the author.

Edward Wagenknecht: from The Limited Editions Club *Pudd'nhead Wilson*. Reprinted by permission of Russell & Volkening, Inc., as agent for the author. Copyright © 1974.

Robert A. Wiggins: from *Mark Twain: Jackleg Novelist*. Seattle: University of Washington Press, 1964. Reprinted by permission of the publisher.

MARK TWAIN

Bequeathed us
In perpetuity
Himself, a
National park
Of the mind
With a river
Draining him,
Down which
Millions,
Alone,
Together,
Drift on a
Raft as if
It were the
Ark away
From the world.
       —Ernest Kroll

Contents

Preface

When Mark Twain began the composition of what he then called "Those Extraordinary Twins"—some time in 1892—he was fifty-seven years old. He had reached a moment of desperation in his life. His past successes (*The Innocents Abroad* [1869], *Roughing It* [1872], *Tom Sawyer* [1876], *The Prince and the Pauper* [1882], *The Adventures of Huckleberry Finn* [1884], and *A Connecticut Yankee in King Arthur's Court* [1889]) had been followed by three years of what every author fears: literary stagnation —despite his writing of *The American Claimant* (1892), which he must have known was far from being in the same class as his earlier masterpieces.

His desperation came from many sources, not the least of which would have been his own recognition of the low quality of his work. It also came from his precarious financial position. He was sinking a fortune in the Paige typesetting machine, a fantastical creature doomed to failure; and his own publishing house, Charles L. Webster & Company, was—like him—going bankrupt. He was in urgent need of money. He was also traveling with Olivia, his wife, vainly trying to find a spa which would cure her of her ailment. (She suffered from syncope, a fainting disease.) And his extensive travel would have made him hungry for one thing a writer needs as much as he needs inspiration: time.

This desperation can be seen in his writing of the *Claimant*, and his feverish work on *Tom Sawyer Abroad* and the early version of *Those Extraordinary Twins*, all works of dubious literary merit. It can be seen too in his numerous lecture trips, and in his experimentation with dramatized performances of his novels.

The initial conception of the tale—about which he writes in the opening passages of *Those Extraordinary Twins* (preceding Chapter 1)—was that it would be a farce based on the antics and activities of Siamese twins, "a human creature that had two heads, two necks, four arms, and one body, with a single pair of legs attached." (See *Those Extraordinary Twins*, "Emendations of the Copy-Text, Substantives," 124.21–23.) The humor involved here is from Clemens's desperation—from a writer whose imagination had paled with his shaking self-esteem, with his preoccupation with his financial affairs and his wife's health, and with fatigue. That he should introduce David Wilson into the story was a stroke of luck, perhaps, or possibly a stroke of genius. With the introduction of Wilson, Tom Driscoll and Roxana easily followed, and the story "changed itself from a farce to a tragedy while I was going along with it," Clemens says. When he recognized the inappropriateness of a murder in a farce, when he realized that he had two stories and not one, he "pulled one of the stories out by the roots, and left the other one—a kind of literary Caesarean operation." This accounts for the existence of two tales in this volume.

Several things from the author's life influenced his writing of these stories. He had seen Siamese twins on exhibit in 1891. He had been interested in fingerprinting as a means of identification at least as early as 1883 in "A Dying Man's Confession" (Chapter 31) of *Life on the Mississippi*, and had gotten specific details of fingerprinting from Sir Francis Galton's book *Finger Prints* (London, 1892). The topics of slavery and miscegenation (the interbreeding of races) had been with him since his childhood. From his earliest days on the Virginia City *Territorial Enterprise*— as early as 1863—when he adopted the pen name Mark Twain, his own identity had taken on at least two public faces: the humorist writer and the serious reporter. As Frederick Anderson points out, "Identical twins are an obvious and graphic symbol of divided identity and Clemens' preoccupation with them appeared early and was persistent thereafter. In 1869 he had published an account of the 'Personal Habits of the Siamese Twins'—twins possessing many habits and characteristics later to be assigned to the twins, Luigi and Angelo . . ." (see Anderson's essay, below). And he was influenced by his observations of the social evils in his society stemming from man's baseness—a baseness which allowed slavery and its inhumanity to come into being. Finally, Clemens's home town of Hannibal must have served as his model for Dawson's Landing— the name coming from J. D. Dawson, who ran a school in Hannibal. Clemens attended this school, which also served as a model for Dobbin's school in *Tom Sawyer*.

Mark Twain is generally considered a humorist, but his humor throughout this novel—like the idyllic nature of Dawson's Landing —is only on the surface. In *Pudd'nhead Wilson* the humor residual from the excised farce is not the guffawing type; it makes one grin and grimace at the same time. The potential humor from the dialect of the slaves ("'He tuck'n dissenhurrit him.' He licked his chops with relish after the stately word. Roxy struggled with it a moment, then gave it up and said— 'Dissen*whiched* him?'") is undercut by the overall picture we get of slavery and the level of education allowed the slave. This is underscored in the change of babies—another plot element which could yield humor, but ultimately yields a grim situation, with Tom cursing his heritage, and the rightful heir subjected to the pitiful life of a slave. The last words of the story ("the creditors sold him down the river")—emanating as they do from the exchange of babies—make the reader shudder, for we know what that terrible phrase "down the river" means. We have seen Roxy utter it in complete despair (at the end of Chapter 16), and we hear her horror story when she returns from down the river two chapters later.

The humor on the surface that surrounds David Wilson—with his ignominious name and treatment far below what his education, intelligence, and profession deserve—this humor points up the stupidity of all the residents of Dawson's Landing, a pessimistic though perhaps justifiable commentary on the common man. Even Pudd'nhead's own maxims, with their wry humor and satire, make us grimace at how bitter our existence must be, how foolish we all are, how insignificant man is. And the humor in the duel, both for its participants and its observers, is not terribly funny. The seconds get shot. Roxy, observing from afar, gets the skin of her nose shot off. What we have in the duel is Clemens's broad criticism of an entire code of conduct represented by the First Families of Virginia —an antiquated code in a depressingly corrupt South with its fading, outdated aristocracy.

Part of Clemens's attempt to depict the plight of the innocent Negro slave and the corruption of the southern system almost backfires: the murderer, the derelict, the primary source of evil is Tom, who is really Valet de Chambre. Roxy, when she is disturbed at her son's cowardice at his refusal to fight a duel, says of him, "Ain't nigger enough in him to show in his finger-nails, en dat takes mighty little—yit dey's enough to paint his soul." She even says to Tom, ". . . here you is, a slinkin' outen a duel en disgracin' our whole line like a ornery lowdown hound! Yes, it's de nigger in you!" The phrase "our whole line" ostensibly refers to the Essex blood in him, but her final statement redirects our thinking. From the mouth of a character whom we respect we hear that cowardice is a racial matter. Both the southern aristocracy and the Black race suffer here.

For the present edition all versions of the text on which Clemens might have worked have been collated, the variations tabulated, and the copy-text emended so as to produce an authoritative version of the novels. So much revision and outside intervention (in the form of typists, compositors, and editors) took place between the first penning of the story (in the Berg Manuscript) and the final printed texts (the English and American first editions) that I have deemed it proper to show the reader first where the base texts (the Morgan and Berg manuscripts) have been emended, and second what variants exist in these versions which were not used for emendation. Explanations for all categories of editorial selection will be found in the Textual Introduction. The tabular matter includes Emendations of the Copy-Text (Accidentals and Substantives) and Rejected Variants (Substantives). No table of Rejected Variants (Accidentals) has been included, for it would have been many pages long, and would have shown little more than the vagaries of the styles of the printing houses which published the stories. A complete list of rejected accidentals, however, may be obtained from the editor. What may seem to be peculiarities or inconsistencies in punctuation, spelling, or paragraphing are the author's own.

The criticism, arranged chronologically, covers a wide range of approaches—thematic, character study, plot and structure evaluation, humorous and serious elements, literary quality, genre, dialogue, the social and moral commentary of the novel, the entertainment value of the story, the flaws in the novel's construction, and so on. I have not included two "standard" essays on the text (Daniel Morley McKeithan's "The Morgan Manuscript of Mark Twain's *Pudd'nhead Wilson*" and Anne P. Wigger's "The Composition of Mark Twain's *Pudd'nhead Wilson* and *Those Extraordinary Twins*: Chronology and Development"—both cited in the Bibliography) because much of these writers' findings are covered in my own Textual Introduction. However, these two pieces have excellent materials not covered in any of the criticism in this volume, and ought to be consulted by those wishing to know how the novels evolved.

The illustrations accompanying the text are selected from those in the first American edition (Hartford, Conn.: American Publishing Company, 1894). They have been reduced to about 60 percent of their original size, and a few have been slightly cropped. The artists are C. H. Warren and F. M. Senior, whose initials or names can occasionally be seen in the illustrations.

I gratefully acknowledge Greg Bentley, Elyse Blankley, Robert Fitch, Paul J. B. Graham, Mary Hicks, Donna Holt, Carlton Holte, Alice Jurish, Timothy Lulofs, Jeff Meyn, Donald Peri, and Jeannie Rossi for their assistance at various stages of production.

I would also like to thank the people at the J. Pierpont Morgan Library, the Berg Collection of the New York Public Library, and the Mark Twain Papers at the Bancroft Library for making their manuscripts and archives available to me. Thanks are due also to Frederick Anderson and Professors Paul Baender, Warner Barnes, O M Brack, James M. Cox, and G. Thomas Tanselle for their help and encouragement, and to John W. N. Francis, Emily Garlin, and Cynthia Carr of W. W. Norton & Company for their assistance.

Finally, special thanks to Karen J. Ford for her strong coffee and careful proofreading.

SIDNEY E. BERGER

End-of-Line Hyphenation in This Volume

The following table clarifies all ambiguous end-of-line hyphenations in the texts in this volume. The left column shows the page and line number (including lines in the text and in the calendar entries) of the reading in question, and the right column shows how the compound ought to be styled.

3.4	steamboat	**57.16**	anti-rummies
3.10	hollyhocks	**66.22**	watermelon
3.11	old-fashioned	**82.21**	steamboating
4.12	slave-worked	**87.27**	roustabouts
6.16	Simon-pure	**87.39**	outside
7.22	finger-marks	**87.41**	outside
9.32	finger-prints	**89.36**	to-night
14.7	baby-gowns	**98.29**	finger-prints
14.21	tow-linens	**110.39**	finger-marks
20.2	worn-out	**112.22**	effect-collecting
25.26	everybody	**120.20**	lovematch
27.8	undertaker	**121.25**	fireworks
30.12	four-handed	**125.7**	million-voiced
32.36	new-comer	**128.44**	humdrum
33.13	steamboat	**131.29**	dark-complected
34.21	thenceforward	**132.26**	table-room
40.1	to-night	**140.2**	nowdays
49.32	all-around	**159.33**	kind-hearted
51.24	sometimes	**169.2**	stand-still

In most editions of this novel the title is given as *The Tragedy of Pudd'nhead Wilson*. But on the first page of the Morgan manuscript, in Clemens's own hand, the title is simply *Pudd'nhead Wilson, A Tale*. Whether the work is a tragedy, and in what sense it is, are topics of debate among scholars. For the present edition the simple title *Pudd'nhead Wilson* is adopted.

Similarly, the simple title *Those Extraordinary Twins* is used here, though the title page of the first printed edition (American Publishing Company, 1894) says: And the Comedy/THOSE EXTRAORDINARY TWINS. The words "The Tragedy of" and "And the Comedy" are printed in very small type, and seem to be more descriptive than titular.

The Text of
Pudd'nhead Wilson
A Tale

There is no character, howsoever good and fine, but it can be destroyed by ridicule, howsoever poor and witless. Observe the ass, for instance: his character is about perfect, he is the choicest spirit among all the humbler animals, yet see what ridicule has brought him to. Instead of feeling complimented when we are called an ass, we are left in doubt.

—PUDD'NHEAD WILSON'S CALENDAR.

A Whisper to the Reader

A person who is ignorant of legal matters is always liable to make mistakes when he tries to photograph a court scene with his pen; and so, I was not willing to let the law-chapters in this book go to press without first subjecting them to rigid and exhausting revision and correction by a trained barrister—if that is what they are called. These chapters are right, now, in every detail, for they were re-written under the immediate eye of William Hicks, who studied law part of a while in southwest Missouri thirty-five years ago and then came over here to Florence for his health and is still helping for exercise and board in Maccaroni and Vermicelli's horse-feed shed which is up the back alley as you turn around the corner out of the Piazza del Duomo just beyond the house where that stone that Dante used to sit on six hundred years ago is let into the wall when he let on to be watching them build Giotto's Campanile and yet always got tired looking as soon as Beatrice passed along on her way to get a chunk of chestnut-cake to defend herself with in case of a Ghibelline outbreak before she got to school, at the same old stand where they sell the same old cake to this day and it is just as light and good as it was then, too, and this is not flattery, far from it. He was a little rusty on his law, but he rubbed up for this book, and

1

those two or three legal chapters are right and straight, now. He told me so himself.

Given under my hand this second day of January, 1893, at the Villa Viviani, village of Settignano, three miles back of Florence, on the hills—the same certainly affording the most charming view to be found on this planet, and with it the most dream-like and enchanting sunsets to be found in any planet or even in any solar system—and given, too, in the swell room of the house, with the busts of Cerretani senators and other grandees of this line looking approvingly down upon me as they used to look down upon Dante, and mutely asking me to adopt them into my family, which I do with pleasure, for my remotest ancestors are but spring chickens compared with these robed and stately antiques, and it will be a great and satisfying lift for me, that six hundred years will.

MARK TWAIN.

Chapter 1

Tell the truth or trump—but get the trick.
—PUDD'NHEAD WILSON'S CALENDAR.

The scene of this chronicle is the town of Dawson's Landing, on the Missouri side of the Mississippi, half a day's journey, per steamboat, below St. Louis.

In 1830 it was a snug little collection of modest one- and two-story frame dwellings whose whitewashed exteriors were almost concealed from sight by climbing tangles of rose vines, honeysuckles and morning-glories. Each of these pretty homes had a garden in front fenced with white palings and opulently stocked with hollyhocks, marigolds, touch-me-nots, prince's feathers and other old-fashioned flowers; while on the window-sills of the houses stood wooden boxes containing moss-rose plants, and terra cotta pots in which grew a breed of geranium whose spread of intensely red blossoms accented the prevailing pink tint of the rose-clad house-front like an explosion of flame. When there was room on the ledge outside of the pots and boxes for a cat, the cat was there—in sunny weather—stretched at full length, asleep and blissful, with her furry belly to the sun and a paw curved over her nose. Then that home was complete, and its contentment and peace were made manifest to the world by this symbol, whose testimony is infallible. A home without a cat—and a well fed, well petted, and properly revered cat —may be a perfect home, perhaps, but how can it prove title?

All along the streets, on both sides, at the outer edge of the brick sidewalks, stood locust trees, with trunks protected by wooden boxing, and these furnished shade for summer and a sweet fragrance in spring when the clusters of buds came forth. The main street, one block back from the river, and running parallel with it, was the sole business street. It was six blocks long, and in each block two or three brick stores three stories high towered above interjected bunches of little frame shops. Swinging signs creaked in the wind, the street's whole length. The candy-striped pole which indicates nobility proud and ancient, along the palace-bordered canals of Venice, indicated merely the humble barber shop along the main street of Dawson's Landing. On a chief corner stood a lofty unpainted pole wreathed from top to bottom with tin pots and pans and cups, the chief tin-monger's noisy notice to the world (when the wind blew) that his shop was on hand for business at that corner.

The hamlet's front was washed by the clear waters of the great river; its body stretched itself rearward up a gentle incline; its most rearward border fringed itself out and scattered its houses about the base line of the hills; the hills rose high, enclosing the town in a half-moon curve, clothed with forests from foot to summit.

Steamboats passed up and down every hour or so. Those belonging to the little Cairo line and the little Memphis line always stopped; the big Orleans liners stopped for hails only, or to land passengers or freight; and this was the case also with the great flotilla of "transients." These latter came out of a dozen rivers—the Illinois, the Missouri, the Upper Mississippi, the Ohio, the Monongahela, the Tennessee, the Red river, the White river, and so on; and were bound every whither and stocked with every imaginable comfort or necessity which the Mississippi's communities could want, from the frosty Falls of St. Anthony down through nine climates to torrid New Orleans.

Dawson's Landing was a slave-holding town, with a rich slave-worked grain and pork country back of it. The town was sleepy, and comfortable, and contented. It was fifty years old, and was growing slowly—very slowly, in fact, but still it was growing.

The chief citizen was York Leicester Driscoll, about forty years old, Judge of the county court. He was very proud of his old Virginian ancestry, and in his hospitalities and his rather formal and stately manners he kept up its traditions. He was fine, and just, and generous. To be a gentleman—a gentleman without stain or blemish—was his only religion, and to it he was always faithful. He was respected, esteemed, and beloved by all the community. He was well off, and was gradually adding to his store. He and his wife were very nearly happy, but not quite, for they had no children. The longing for the treasure of a child had grown stronger and stronger as the years slipped away, but the blessing never came—and was never to come.

With this pair lived the Judge's widowed sister, Mrs. Rachel Pratt, and she also was childless—childless, and sorrowful for that reason, and not to be comforted. The women were good and commonplace people, and did their duty and had their reward in clear consciences and the community's approbation. They were Presbyterians, the Judge was a free-thinker.

Pembroke Howard, lawyer and bachelor, aged about forty, was another old Virginian grandee with proved descent from the First Families. He was a fine, brave, majestic creature, a gentleman according to the nicest requirements of the Virginian rule, a devoted Presbyterian, an authority on the "code," and a man always courteously ready to stand up before you in the field if any act or word of his had seemed doubtful or suspicious to you, and explain it with any weapon you might prefer, from brad-awls to artillery. He was very popular with the people, and was the Judge's dearest friend.

Then there was Colonel Cecil Burleigh Essex, another F.F.V. of formidable calibre—however, with him we have no concern.

Percy Northumberland Driscoll, brother to the Judge, and younger than he by five years, was a married man, and had had children around his hearthstone; but they were attacked in detail by measles, croup and scarlet fever, and this had given the doctor a chance with his effective antediluvian methods; so the cradles were empty. He was a prosperous man, with a good head for speculations, and his fortune was growing. On the first of February, 1830, two boy babes were born in his house: one to him, the other to one of his slave girls, Roxana by name. Roxana was twenty years old. She was up and around the same day, with her hands full, for she was tending both babies.

Mrs. Percy Driscoll died within the week. Roxy remained in charge of the children. She had her own way, for Mr. Driscoll soon absorbed himself in his speculations and left her to her own devices.

In that same month of February Dawson's Landing gained a new citizen. This was Mr. David Wilson, a young fellow of Scotch parentage. He had wandered to this remote region from his birth-place in the interior of the State of New York, to seek his fortune. He was twenty-five years old, college-bred, and had finished a post-college course in an eastern law school a couple of years before.

He was a homely, freckled, sandy-haired young fellow, with an intelligent blue eye that had frankness and comeradeship in it and a covert twinkle of a pleasant sort. But for an unfortunate remark of his, he would no doubt have entered at once upon a successful career at Dawson's Landing. But he made his fatal remark the first day he spent in the village, and it "gauged" him. He had just made the acquaintance of a group of citizens when an invisible dog began to yelp and snarl and howl and make himself very comprehensibly disagreeable, whereupon young Wilson said, much as one who is thinking aloud—

"I wish I owned half of that dog."

"Why?" somebody asked.

"Because, I would kill my half."

The group searched his face with curiosity, with anxiety even, but found no light there, no expression that they could read. They fell away from him as from something uncanny, and went into privacy to discuss him. One said—

"'Pears to be a fool."

"'Pears?" said another. "*Is*, I reckon you better say."

"Said he wished he owned *half* of the dog, the idiot," said a third. "What did he reckon would become of the other half if he killed his half? Do you reckon he thought it would live?"

"Why, he must have thought it, unless he *is* the downrightest fool in the world; because if he hadn't thought that, he would have wanted to own the whole dog, knowing that if he killed his half and the other half died, he would be responsible for that half, just the same as if he had killed that half instead of his own. Don't it look that way to you, gents?"

"Yes, it does. If he owned one half of the general dog, it would be so; if he owned one end of the dog and another person owned the other end, it would be so, just the same; particularly in the first case, because if you kill one half of a general dog, there ain't any man that can tell whose half if was, but if he owned one end of the dog, maybe he could kill his end of it and—"

"No, he couldn't, either; he couldn't and not be responsible if the other end died, which it would. In my opinion the man ain't in his right mind."

"In my opinion he hain't *got* any mind."

No. 3 said—

"Well, he's a lummux, anyway."

"That's what he is," said No. 4, "he's a labrick—just a Simon-pure labrick, if ever there was one."

"Yes, sir, he's a dam fool, that's the way I put him up," said No. 5. "Anybody can think different that wants to, but those are my sentiments."

"I'm with you, gentlemen," said No. 6. "Perfect jackass—yes, and it ain't going too far to say he is a pudd'nhead. If he ain't a pudd'nhead, I ain't no judge, that's all."

Mr. Wilson stood elected. The incident was told all over the town, and gravely discussed by everybody. Within a week he had lost his first name; Pudd'nhead took its place. In time he came to be liked, and well liked, too; but by that time the nickname had got well stuck on, and it stayed. That first day's verdict made him a fool, and he was not able to get it set aside, or even modified. The nickname soon ceased to carry any harsh or unfriendly feeling with it, but it held its place, and was to continue to hold its place for twenty long years.

Chapter 2

Adam was but human—this explains it all. He did not want the apple for the apple's sake, he only wanted it because it was forbidden. The mistake was in not forbidding the serpent; then he would have eaten the serpent.
—PUDD'NHEAD WILSON'S CALENDAR.

Pudd'nhead Wilson had a trifle of money when he arrived, and he bought a small house on the extreme western verge of the town. Between it and Judge Driscoll's house there was only a grassy yard, with a paling fence dividing the properties in the middle. He hired a small office down in the town and hung out a tin sign with these words on it:

DAVID WILSON

ATTORNEY AND COUNSELOR AT LAW.

SURVEYING, CONVEYANCING, ETC.

But his deadly remark had ruined his chance—at least in the law. No clients came. He took down his sign, after a while, and put it up on his own house with the law features knocked out of it. It offered his services now in the humble capacities of land surveyor and expert accountant. Now and then he got a job of surveying to do, and now and then a merchant got him to straighten out his books. With Scotch patience and pluck he resolved to live down his reputation and work his way into the legal field yet. Poor fellow, he could not foresee that it was going to take him such a weary long time to do it.

He had a rich abundance of idle time, but it never hung heavy on his hands, for he interested himself in every new thing that was born into the universe of ideas, and studied it and experimented upon it at his house. One of his pet fads was palmistry. To another one he gave no name, neither would he explain to anybody what its purpose was, but merely said it was an amusement. In fact he had found that his fads added to his reputation as a pudd'nhead; therefore he was growing chary of being too communicative about them. The fad without a name was one which dealt with people's finger-marks. He carried in his coat pocket a shallow box with grooves in it, and in the grooves strips of glass five inches long and three inches wide. Along the lower edge of each strip was pasted a slip of white paper. He asked people to pass their hands through their hair, (thus collecting upon them a thin coating of the natural oil,) and then make a thumb-mark on a glass strip, following it with the mark of the ball of each finger in succession. Under this row of faint grease-prints he would write a record on the strip of white paper—thus:

"JOHN SMITH, *right hand*"—

and add the day of the month and the year, then take Smith's left hand on another glass strip, and add name and date and the words "left hand." The strips were now returned to the grooved box, and took their place among what Wilson called his "records."

He often studied his records, examining and poring over them with absorbing interest until far into the night; but what he found there—if he found anything—he revealed to no one. Sometimes he copied on paper the involved and delicate pattern left by the ball of a finger, and then vastly enlarged it with a pantagraph so that he could examine its web of curving lines with ease and convenience.

One sweltering afternoon—it was the first day of July, 1830—he was at work over a set of tangled account books in his work-room, which looked westward over a stretch of vacant lots, when a conversation outside disturbed him. It was carried on in yells, which showed that the people engaged in it were not close together:

"Say, Roxy, how does yo' baby come on?" This from the distant voice.

"Fust rate; how does *you* come on, Jasper?" This yell was from close by.

"Oh, I's middlin'; hain't got noth'n to complain of. I's gwyne to come a-court'n you bime by, Roxy."

"*You* is, you black mud-cat! Yah-yah-yah! I got sump'n better to do den 'sociat'n wid niggers as black as you is. Is ole Miss Cooper's Nancy done give you de mitten?" Roxy followed this sally with another discharge of care-free laughter.

"You's jealous, Roxy, dat's what's de matter wid *you*, you huzzy —yah-yah-yah! Dat's de time I got you!"

"Oh, yes, *you* got me, hain't you. 'Clah to goodness if dat conceit o' yo'n strikes in, Jasper, it gwyne to kill you, sho'. If you b'longed to me I'd sell you down de river 'fo' you git too fur gone. Fust time I runs acrost yo' marster, I's gwyne to tell him so."

This idle and aimless jabber went on and on, both parties enjoying the friendly duel and each well satisfied with his own share of the wit exchanged—for wit they considered it.

Wilson stepped to the window to observe the combatants; he could not work while their chatter continued. Over in the vacant lots was Jasper, young, coal-black and of magnificent build, sitting on a wheelbarrow in the pelting sun—at work, supposably, whereas he was in fact only preparing for it by taking an hour's rest before beginning. In front of Wilson's porch stood Roxy, with a local hand-made baby-wagon, in which sat her two charges—one at each end and facing each other. From Roxy's manner of speech, a stranger would have expected her to be black, but she was not. Only one-sixteenth of her was black, and that sixteenth did not show. She was of majestic form and stature, her attitudes were imposing and statuesque, and her gestures and movements distinguished by a noble and stately grace. Her complexion was very fair, with the rosy glow of vigorous health in the cheeks, her face was full of character and expression, her eyes were brown and liquid, and she had a heavy suit of fine soft hair which was also brown, but the fact was not apparent because her head was bound about with a checkered handkerchief and the hair was concealed under it. Her face was shapely, intelligent, and comely—even beautiful. She had an easy, independent carriage—when she was among her own caste—and a high and "sassy" way, withal; but of course she was meek and humble enough where white people were.

To all intents and purposes Roxy was as white as anybody, but the one-sixteenth of her which was black out-voted the other fifteen parts and made her a negro. She was a slave, and salable as such. Her child was thirty-one parts white, and he, too, was a slave, and by a fiction of law and custom a negro. He had blue eyes and flaxen curls, like his white comrade, but even the father of the white child was able to tell the children apart—little as he had commerce with them—by their clothes: for the white babe wore ruffled soft muslin and a coral necklace, while the other wore merely a coarse tow-linen shirt which barely reached to its knees, and no jewelry.

The white child's name was Thomas à Becket Driscoll, the other's name was Valet de Chambre: no surname—slaves hadn't the privilege. Roxana had heard that phrase somewhere, the fine sound of it had pleased her ear, and as she had supposed it was a name, she loaded it onto her darling. It soon got shortened to "Chambers," of course.

Wilson knew Roxy by sight, and when the duel of wit began to play out, he stepped outside to gather in a record or two. Jasper went to work energetically, at once—perceiving that his leisure was observed. Wilson inspected the children and asked—

"How old are they, Roxy?"

"Bofe de same age, sir—five months. Bawn de fust o' Febuary."

"They're handsome little chaps. One's just as handsome as the other, too."

A delighted smile exposed the girl's white teeth, and she said:

"Bless yo' soul, Misto Wilson, it's pow'ful nice o' you to say dat, caze one of 'em ain't on'y a nigger. Mighty prime little nigger, I allays says, but dat's caze it's mine, o' course."

"How do you tell them apart, Roxy, when they haven't any clothes on?"

Roxy laughed a laugh proportioned to her size, and said:

"Oh, I kin tell 'em 'part, Misto Wilson, but I bet Marse Percy couldn't, not to save his life."

Wilson chatted along for a while, and presently got Roxy's fingerprints for his collection—right hand and left—on a couple of his glass strips; then labeled and dated them, and took the "records" of both children, and labeled and dated them also.

Two months later, on the third of September, he took this trio of finger-marks again. He liked to have a "series"—two or three "takings" at intervals during the period of childhood, these to be followed by others at intervals of several years.

The next day—that is to say, on the fourth of September,—something occurred which profoundly impressed Roxana. Mr. Driscoll missed another small sum of money—which is a way of saying that this was not a new thing, but had happened before. In truth it had happened three times before. Driscoll's patience was exhausted. He was a fairly humane man, toward slaves and other animals; he was an exceedingly humane man toward the erring of his own race.

Theft he could not abide, and plainly there was a thief in his house. Necessarily the thief must be one of his negroes. Sharp measures must be taken. He called his servants before him. There were three of these, besides Roxy: a man, a woman, and a boy twelve years old. They were not related. Mr. Driscoll said:

"You have all been warned before. It has done no good. This time I will teach you a lesson. I will sell the thief. Which of you is the guilty one?"

They all shuddered at the threat, for here they had a good home, and a new one was likely to be a change for the worse. The denial was general. None had stolen anything—not money, anyway—a little sugar, or cake, or honey, or something like that, that "Marse Percy wouldn't mind or miss," but not money—never a cent of money. They were eloquent in their protestations, but Mr. Driscoll was not moved by them. He answered each in turn with a stern "Name the thief!"

The truth was, all were guilty but Roxana; she suspected that the others were guilty, but she did not know them to be so. She was horrified to think how near she had come to being guilty herself; she had been saved in the nick of time by a revival in the colored Methodist church a fortnight before, at which time and place she "got religion." The very next day after that gracious experience, while her change of style was fresh upon her and she was vain of her purified condition, her master left a couple of dollars lying unprotected on his desk, and she happened upon that temptation when she was polishing around with a dust-rag. She looked at the money a while with a steadily rising resentment, then she burst out with—

"Dad blame dat revival, I wisht it had a ben put off till tomorrow!"

Then she covered the tempter with a book, and another member of the kitchen cabinet got it. She made this sacrifice as a matter of religious etiquette; as a thing necessary just now, but by no means to be wrested into a precedent; no, a week or two would limber up her piety, then she would be rational again, and the next two dollars that got left out in the cold would find a comforter—and she could name the comforter.

Was she bad? Was she worse than the general run of her race? No. They had an unfair show in the battle of life, and they held it no sin to take military advantage of the enemy—in a small way; in a small way, but not in a large one. They would smouch provisions from the pantry whenever they got a chance; or a brass thimble, or a cake of wax, or an emery-bag, or a paper of needles, or a silver spoon, or a dollar bill, or small articles of clothing, or any other property of light value; and so far were they from considering such reprisals sinful, that they would go to church and shout and pray their loudest and sincerest with their plunder in their pockets. A farm smoke-house had to be kept heavily padlocked, for even the colored deacon himself could not resist a ham when Providence showed him in a dream, or otherwise, where such a thing hung lonesome and longed for some one to love. But with a hundred hanging before him the deacon would not take two—that is, on the same night. On frosty nights the humane negro prowler would warm the end of a plank and put it up under the cold claws of chickens roosting in a tree; a drowsy hen would step onto the comfortable board, softly clucking her gratitude, and the prowler would dump her into his bag, and later into his stomach, perfectly sure that in taking this trifle from the man who daily robbed him of an inestimable treasure—his liberty—he was not committing any sin that God would remember against him in the Last Great Day.

"Name the thief!"

For the fourth time Mr. Driscoll had said it, and always in the same hard tone. And now he added these words of awful import:

"I give you one minute"—he took out his watch—"if at the end of that time you have not confessed, I will not only sell all four of you, *but*—I will sell you DOWN THE RIVER!"

It was equivalent to condemning them to hell! No Missouri negro doubted this. Roxy reeled in her tracks and the color vanished out of her face; the others dropped to their knees as if they had been shot; tears gushed from their eyes, their supplicating hands went up, and three answers came in the one instant:

"I done it!"

"I done it!"

"I done it!—have mercy, marster—Lord have mercy on us po' niggers!"

"Very good," said the master, putting up his watch, "I will sell you *here*, though you don't deserve it. You ought to be sold down the river."

The culprits flung themselves prone, in an ecstasy of gratitude, and kissed his feet, declaring that they would never forget his goodness and never cease to pray for him as long as they lived. They were sincere, for like a god he had stretched forth his mighty hand and closed the gates of hell against them. He knew, himself, that he had done a noble and gracious thing, and he was privately well pleased with his magnanimity; and that night he set the incident down in his diary, so that his son might read it in after years and be thereby moved to deeds of gentleness and humanity himself.

Chapter 3

Whoever has lived long enough to find out what life is, knows how deep a debt of gratitude we owe to Adam, the first great benefactor of our race. He brought death into the world.
—PUDD'NHEAD WILSON'S CALENDAR.

Percy Driscoll slept well the night he saved his house-minions from going down the river, but no wink of sleep visited Roxy's eyes.

A profound terror had taken possession of her. Her child could grow up and be sold down the river! The thought crazed her with horror. If she dozed, and lost herself for a moment, the next moment she was on her feet and flying to her child's cradle to see if it was still there. Then she would gather it to her heart and pour out her love upon it in a frenzy of kisses, moaning, crying, and saying "Dey shant, oh, dey *shan't!*—yo' po' mammy will kill you fust!"

Once, when she was tucking it back in its cradle again, the other child nestled in its sleep and attracted her attention. She went and stood over it a long time, communing with herself:

"What has my po' baby done, dat he couldn't have yo' luck? He hain't done nuth'n. God was good to you; why warn't He good to him? Dey can't sell *you* down de river. I hates yo' pappy; he ain't got no heart—for niggers he haint, anyways. I hates him, en I could kill him!" She paused a while, thinking; then she burst into wild sobbings again, and turned away, saying, "Oh, I got to kill my chile, dey ain't no yuther way,—killin' *him* wouldn't save de chile fum goin' down de river. Oh, I got to do it, yo' po' mammy's got to kill you to save you, honey"—she gathered her baby to her bosom, now, and began to smother it with caresses—"Mammy's got to kill you, —how *kin* I do it! But yo' mammy ain't gwyne to desert you,—no, no; *dah*, don't cry—she gwyne *wid* you, she gwyne to kill herself, too. Come along, honey, come along wid Mammy; we gwyne to jump in de river, den de troubles o' dis worl' is all over—dey don't sell po' niggers down de river over *yonder*."

She started toward the door, crooning to the child and hushing it; midway she stopped, suddenly. She had caught sight of her new Sunday gown—a cheap curtain-calico thing, a conflagration of gaudy colors and fantastic figures. She surveyed it wistfully, longingly.

"Hain't ever wore it yit," she said, "en it's jist lovely." Then she nodded her head in response to a pleasant idea, and added, "No, I ain't gwyne to be fished out, wid everybody lookin' at me, in dis misable ole linsey-woolsey."

She put down the child and made the change. She looked in the glass and was astonished at her beauty. She resolved to make her death-toilet perfect. She took off her handkerchief-turban and dressed her glossy wealth of hair "like white folks;" she added some odds and ends of rather lurid ribbon and a spray of atrocious artificial flowers; finally, she threw over her shoulders a fluffy thing called a "cloud" in that day, which was of a blazing red complexion. Then she was ready for the tomb.

She gathered up her baby once more: but when her eye fell upon its miserably short little gray tow-linen shirt and noted the contrast between its pauper shabbiness and her own volcanic irruption of infernal splendors, her mother-heart was touched, and she was ashamed.

"No, dolling, mammy ain't gwyne to treat you so. De angels is gwyne to 'mire you jist as much as dey does yo' mammy. Ain't gwyne to have 'em putt'n dey han's up 'fo' dey eyes en saying' to David en Goliah en dem yuther prophets, Dat chile is dress' too indelicate fo' dis place."

By this time she had stripped off the shirt. Now she clothed the naked little creature in one of Thomas à Becket's snowy long baby-gowns, with its bright blue bows and dainty flummery of ruffles.

"Dah—now you's fixed." She propped the child in a chair and stood off to inspect it. Straightway her eyes began to widen with astonishment and admiration, and she clapped her hands and cried out, "Why, it do beat all!—I *never* knowed you was so lovely. Marse Tommy ain't a bit puttier—not a single bit."

She stepped over and glanced at the other infant; she flung a glance back at her own; then one more at the heir of the house. Now a strange light dawned in her eyes, and in a moment she was lost in thought. She seemed in a trance; when she came out of it she muttered, "When I 'uz a-washin' 'em in de tub, yistiddy, his own pappy asked me which of 'em was his'n."

She began to move about like one in a dream. She undressed Thomas à Becket, stripping him of everything, and put the tow-linen shirt on him. She put his coral necklace on her own child's neck. Then she placed the children side by side, and after earnest inspection she muttered—

"Now who would b'lieve clo'es could do de like o' dat? Dog my cats if it ain't all *I* kin do to tell t'other fum which, let alone his pappy."

She put her cub in Tommy's elegant cradle and said—

"You's young Marse *Tom* fum dis out, en I got to practice and git used to 'memberin' to call you dat, honey, or I's gwyne to make a mistake some time en git us bofe into trouble. Dah—now you lay still en don't fret no mo', Marse Tom—oh, thank de good Lord in heaven, you's saved, you's saved!—dey ain't no man kin ever sell mammy's po' little honey down de river now!"

She put the heir of the house in her own child's unpainted pine cradle, and said, contemplating its slumbering form uneasily—

"I's sorry for you, honey; I's sorry, God knows I is,—but what *kin* I do, what *could* I do? Yo' pappy would sell him to somebody, some time, en den he'd go down de river, sho', en I couldn't, couldn't, *couldn't* stan' it."

She flung herself on her bed, and began to think and toss, toss and think. By and by she sat suddenly upright, for a comforting thought had flown through her worried mind—

" 'Tain't no sin—*white* folks has done it! It ain't no sin, glory to goodness it ain't no sin! *Dey's* done it—yes, en dey was de biggest quality in de whole bilin', too—*Kings!*"

She began to muse; she was trying to gather out of her memory the dim particulars of some tale she had heard some time or other. At last she said—

"Now I's got it; now I 'member. It was dat ole nigger preacher dat tole it, de time he come over here fum Illinois en preached in de nigger church. He said dey ain't nobody kin save his own self—can't do it by faith, can't do it by works, can't do it no way at all. Free grace is de *on'y* way, en dat don't come fum nobody but jis' de Lord; en *He* kin give it to anybody He please, saint or sinner—*He* don't k'yer. He do jis' as He's a mineter. He s'lect out anybody dat suit Him, en put another one in his place, en make de fust one happy forever en leave t'other one to burn wid Satan. De preacher said it was jist like dey done in Englan' one time, long time ago. De queen she lef' her baby layin' aroun' one day, en went out callin'; en one o' de niggers roun' 'bout de place dat was mos' white, she come in en see de chile layin' aroun', en tuck en put her own chile's clo'es on de queen's chile, en put de queen's chile's clo'es on her own chile, en den lef' her own chile layin' aroun' en tuck en toted de queen's chile home to de nigger quarter, en nobody ever foun' it out, en her chile was de king, bimeby, en sole de queen's chile down de river one time when dey had to settle up de estate. Dah, now—de preacher said it his own self, en it ain't no sin, caze white folks done it. *Dey* done it—yes, *dey* done it; en not on'y jis' common white folks, nuther, but de biggest quality dey is in de whole bilin'. Oh, I's *so* glad I 'member 'bout dat!"

She got up light-hearted and happy, and went to the cradles and spent what was left of the night "practicing." She would give her own child a light pat and say, humbly, "Lay still, Marse Tom," then give the real Tom a pat and say with severity, "Lay *still*, Chambers!—does you want me to take sump'n *to* you?"

As she progressed with her practice, she was surprised to see how steadily and surely the awe which had kept her tongue reverent and her manner humble toward her young master was transferring itself to her speech and manner toward the usurper, and how similarly handy she was becoming in transferring her motherly curtness of speech and peremptoriness of manner to the unlucky heir of the ancient house of Driscoll.

She took occasional rests from practicing, and absorbed herself in calculating her chances.

"Dey'll sell dese niggers to-day fo' stealing' de money, den dey'll buy some mo' dat don't know de chillen—so *dat's* all right. When I takes de chillen out to git de air, de minute I's roun' de corner I's gwyne to gaum dey mouths all aroun' wid jam, den dey can't *nobody* notice dey's changed. Yes, I gwineter do dat till I's safe, if it takes a year.

"Dey ain't but one man dat I's afeard of, en dat's dat Pudd'n-head Wilson. Dey calls him a pudd'nhead, en says he's a fool. My lan', dat man ain't no mo' fool den I is! He's de smartes' man in dis town, less'n it's Jedge Driscoll, or maybe Pem. Howard. Blame dat man, he worries me wid dem ornery glasses o' his'n; *I* b'lieve he's a witch. But nemmine, I's gwyne to happen aroun' dah one o' dese days en let on dat I reckon he wants to print de chillen's fingers agin; en if *he* don't notice dey's changed, I boun' dey ain't nobody gwyne to notice it, en den I's safe, sho'. But I reckon I'll tote along a hoss-shoe to keep off de witch-work."

The new negroes gave Roxy no trouble, of course. The master gave her none, for one of his speculations was in jeopardy, and his mind was so occupied that he hardly saw the children when he looked at them, and all Roxy had to do was to get them both into a gale of laughter when he came about; then their faces were mainly cavities exposing gums, and he was gone again before the spasm passed and the little creatures resumed a human aspect.

Within a few days the fate of the speculation became so dubious that Mr. Percy went away with his brother the Judge to see what could be done with it. It was a land speculation, as usual, and it had gotten complicated with a lawsuit. The men were gone seven weeks. Before they got back Roxy had paid her visit to Wilson, and was satisfied. Wilson took the finger-prints, labeled them with the names and with the date—October the first—put them carefully away, and continued his chat with Roxy, who seemed very anxious that he should admire the great advance in flesh and beauty which the babies had made since he took their finger-prints a month before. He complimented their improvement to her contentment;

and as they were without any disguise of jam or other stain, she trembled all the while and was miserably frightened lest at any moment he—

But he didn't. He discovered nothing; and she went home jubilant, and dropped all concern about this matter permanently out of her mind.

Chapter 4

Adam and Eve had many advantages, but the principal one was, that they escaped teething.
—PUDD'NHEAD WILSON'S CALENDAR.

There is this trouble about special providences—namely, there is so often a doubt as to which party was intended to be the beneficiary. In the case of the children, the bears and the prophet, the bears got more real satisfaction out of the episode than the prophet did, because they got the children.
—PUDD'NHEAD WILSON'S CALENDAR.

This history must henceforth accommodate itself to the change which Roxana has consummated, and call the real heir "Chambers" and the usurping little slave "Thomas à Becket"—shortening this latter name to "Tom," for daily use, as the people about him did.

"Tom" was a bad baby, from the very beginning of his usurpation. He would cry for nothing; he would burst into storms of devilish temper without notice, and let go scream after scream and squall after squall, then climax the thing with "holding his breath" —that frightful specialty of the teething nursling, in the throes of which the creature exhausts its lungs, then is convulsed with noiseless squirmings and twistings and kickings in the effort to get its breath, while the lips turn blue and the mouth stands wide and rigid, offering for inspection one wee tooth set in the lower rim of a hoop of red gums; and when the appalling stillness has endured until one is sure the lost breath will never return, a nurse comes flying and dashes water in the child's face, and—presto! the lungs fill, and instantly discharge a shriek, or a yell, or a howl which bursts the listening ear and surprises the owner of it into saying words which would not go well with a halo if he had one. The baby

Tom would claw anybody who came within reach of his nails, and pound anybody he could reach with his rattle. He would scream for water until he got it, and then throw cup and all on the floor and scream for more. He was indulged in all his caprices, howsoever troublesome and exasperating they might be; he was allowed to eat anything he wanted, particularly things that would give him the stomach ache.

When he got to be old enough to begin to toddle about, and say broken words, and get an idea of what his hands were for, he was a more consummate pest than ever. Roxy got no rest while he was awake. He would call for anything and everything he saw, simply saying "Awnt it!" (want it), which was a command. When it was brought, he said, in a frenzy, and motioning it away with his hands, "Don't awnt it! don't awnt it!" and the moment it was gone he set up frantic yells of "Awnt it! awnt it! awnt it!" and Roxy had to give wings to her heels to get that thing back to him again before he could get time to carry out his intention of going into convulsions about it.

What he preferred above all other things was the tongs. This was because his "father" had forbidden him to have them lest he break windows and furniture with them. The moment Roxy's back was turned he would toddle to the presence of the tongs and say, "Like it!" and cock his eye to one side to see if Roxy was observing; then, "Awnt it!" and cock his eye again; then, "Hab it!" with another furtive glance; and finally, "Take it!"—and the prize was his. The next moment the heavy implement was raised aloft; the next, there was a crash and a squall, and the cat was off, on three legs, to meet an engagement; Roxy would arrive just as the lamp or a window went to irremediable smash.

Tom got all the petting, Chambers got none. Tom got all the delicacies, Chambers got mush and milk, and clabber without sugar. In consequence, Tom was a sickly child and Chambers wasn't. Tom was "fractious," as Roxy called it, and overbearing, Chambers was meek and docile.

With all her splendid common sense and practical every-day ability, Roxy was a doting fool of a mother. She was this toward her child—and she was also more than this: by the fiction created by herself, he was become her master; the necessity of recognizing this relation outwardly and of perfecting herself in the forms required to express the recognition, had moved her to such diligence and faithfulness in practicing these forms that this exercise soon concreted itself into habit; it became automatic and unconscious; then a natural result followed: deceptions intended solely for others gradually grew practically into self-deceptions as well; the mock reverence became real reverence, the mock obsequiousness real obsequiousness, the mock homage real homage; the little counterfeit rift of separation between imitation-slave and imitation-master widened and widened, and became an abyss, and a very real one—and on one side of it stood Roxy, the dupe of her own deceptions, and on the other stood her child, no longer a usurper to her, but her accepted and recognized master.

He was her darling, her master, and her deity, all in one, and in her worship of him she forgot who she was and what he had been.

In babyhood Tom cuffed and banged and scratched Chambers unrebuked, and Chambers early learned that between meekly bearing it and resenting it the advantage all lay with the former policy. The few times that his persecutions had moved him beyond control and made him fight back had cost him very dear at headquarters; not at the hands of Roxy, for if she ever went beyond scolding him sharply for "fogitt'n who his young marster was," she at least never extended her punishment beyond a box on the ear. No, Percy Driscoll was the person. He told Chambers that under no provocation whatever was he privileged to lift his hand against his little master. Chambers overstepped the line three times, and got three such convincing canings from the man who was his father and didn't know it, that he took Tom's cruelties in all humility after that, and made no more experiments.

Outside of the house the two boys were together, all through their boyhood. Chambers was strong beyond his years, and a good fighter; strong because he was coarsely fed and hard worked about the house, and a good fighter because Tom furnished him plenty of practice—on white boys whom he hated and was afraid of. Chambers was his constant body-guard, to and from school; he was present on the play-ground at recess to protect his charge. He fought himself into such a formidable reputation, by and by, that Tom could have changed clothes with him, and "ridden in peace," like Sir Kay in Launcelot's armor.

He was good at games of skill, too. Tom staked him with marbles to play "keeps" with, and then took all the winnings away from him. In the winter season Chambers was on hand, in Tom's worn-out clothes, with "holy" red mittens, and "holy" shoes, and pants "holy" at the knees and seat, to drag a sled up the hill for Tom, warmly clad, to ride down on; but he never got a ride himself. He built snow men and snow fortifications under Tom's direction. He was Tom's patient target when Tom wanted to do some snow-balling, but the target couldn't fire back. Chambers carried Tom's skates to the river and strapped them on him, then trotted around after him on the ice, so as to be on hand when wanted; but he wasn't ever asked to try the skates himself.

In summer the pet pastime of the boys of Dawson's Landing was to steal apples, peaches and melons from the farmers' fruit wagons, —mainly on account of the risk they ran of getting their heads laid open with the butt of the farmer's whip. Tom was a distinguished adept at these thefts—by proxy. Chambers did his stealing, and got the peach stones, apple cores and melon rhinds for his share.

Tom always made Chambers go in swimming with him, and stay by him as a protection. When Tom had had enough, he would slip out and tie knots in Chambers's shirt, dip the knots in the water to make them hard to undo, then dress himself and sit by and laugh while the naked shiverer tugged at the stubborn knots with his teeth.

Tom did his humble comrade these various ill turns partly out of native viciousness, and partly because he hated him for his superiorities of physique and pluck, and for his manifold clevernesses. Tom couldn't dive, for it gave him splitting headaches. Chambers could dive without inconvenience, and was fond of doing it. He excited so much admiration, one day, among a crowd of white boys, by throwing back-summersaults from the stern of a canoe that it wearied Tom's spirit, and at last he shoved the canoe underneath Chambers while he was in the air—so he came down on his head in the canoe-bottom; and while he lay unconscious several of Tom's ancient adversaries saw that their long-desired opportunity was come, and they gave the false heir such a drubbing that with Chambers's best help he was hardly able to drag himself home afterward.

When the boys were fifteen and upwards, Tom was "showing off" in the river one day, when he was taken with a cramp, and shouted for help. It was a common trick with the boys—particularly if a stranger was present—to pretend a cramp and howl for help; then when the stranger came tearing hand-over-hand to the rescue, the howler would go on struggling and howling till he was close at hand, then replace the howl with a sarcastic smile and swim blandly away, while the town-boys assailed the dupe with a volley of jeers and laughter. Tom had never tried this joke as yet, but was supposed to be trying it now, so the boys held warily back; but Chambers believed his master was in earnest, therefore he swam out and arrived in time, unfortunately, and saved his life.

This was the last feather. Tom had managed to endure everything else, but to have to remain publicly and permanently under such an obligation as this to a nigger, and to this nigger of all niggers—this was too much. He heaped insults upon Chambers for "pretending" to think he was in earnest in calling for help, and said that anybody but a blockheaded nigger would have known he was funning and left him alone.

Tom's enemies were in strong force here, so they came out with their opinions quite freely. They laughed at him, and called him coward, liar, sneak, and other sorts of pet names, and told him they meant to call Chambers by a new name after this, and make it common in the town—"Tom Driscoll's Nigger-pappy"—to signify that he had had a second birth into this life, and that Chambers was the author of his new being. Tom grew frantic under these taunts, and shouted—

"Knock their heads off, Chambers! knock their heads off! What do you stand there with your hands in your pockets for?"

Chambers expostulated, and said—

"But Marse Tom, dey's too many of 'em—dey's—"

"Do you hear me?"

"Please, Marse Tom, don't make me! Dey's so many of 'em dat—"

Tom sprang at him and drove his pocket knife into him two or three times before the boys could snatch him away and give the wounded lad a chance to escape. He was considerably hurt, but not seriously. If the blade had been a little longer his career would have ended there.

Tom had long ago taught Roxy "her place." It had been many a day, now, since she had ventured a caress or a fondling epithet in his quarter. Such things, from a "nigger," were repulsive to him, and she had been warned to keep her distance and remember who she was. She saw her darling gradually cease from being her son, she saw *that* detail perish utterly; all that was left was master—master, pure and simple, and it was not a gentle mastership, either. She saw herself sink from the sublime height of motherhood to the sombre deeps of unmodified slavery. The abyss of separation between her and her boy was complete. She was merely his chattel, now, his convenience, his dog, his cringing and helpless slave, the humble and unresisting victim of his capricious temper and vicious nature.

Sometimes she could not go to sleep, even when worn out with fatigue, because her rage boiled so high over the day's experiences with her boy. She would mumble and mutter to herself—

"He struck me, en I warn't no way to blame—struck me in de face, right before folks. En he's allays callin' me nigger wench, en hussy, en all dem mean names, when I's doin' de very bes' I kin. O, Lord, I done so much for him—I lift' him away up to whar he is—en dis is what I git for it."

Sometimes when some outrage of peculiar offensiveness stung her to the heart, she would plan schemes of vengeance, and revel in the fancied spectacle of his exposure to the world as an impostor and a slave; but in the midst of these joys fear would strike her: she had made him too strong; she could prove nothing, and—heavens, she might get sold down the river for her pains! So her schemes always went for nothing, and she laid them aside in impotent rage against the fates, and against herself for playing the fool on that fatal September day in not providing herself with a witness for use in the day when such a thing might be needed for the appeasing of her vengeance-hungry heart.

And yet the moment Tom happened to be good to her, and kind—and this occurred every now and then—all her sore places were healed and she was happy; happy and proud, for this was her son, her nigger son, lording it among the whites and securely avenging their crimes against her race.

There were two grand funerals in Dawson's Landing that fall—the fall of 1845. One was that of Colonel Cecil Burleigh Essex, the other that of Percy Driscoll.

On his death-bed Driscoll set Roxy free and delivered his idolized ostensible son solemnly into the keeping of his brother the Judge and his wife. Those childless people were glad to get him. Childless people are not difficult to please.

Judge Driscoll had gone privately to his brother, a month before, and bought Chambers. He had heard that Tom had been trying to get his father to sell the boy down the river, and he wanted to prevent the scandal—for public sentiment did not approve of that way of treating family servants for light cause or for no cause.

Percy Driscoll had worn himself out in trying to save his great speculative landed estate, and had died without succeeding. He was hardly in his grave before the boom collapsed and left his hitherto envied young devil of an heir a pauper. But that was nothing; his uncle told him he should be his heir and have all his fortune when he died; so Tom was comforted.

Roxy had no home, now; so she resolved to go around and say good-bye to her friends and then clear out and see the world—that is to say, she would go chambermaiding on a steamboat, the darling ambition of her race and sex.

Her last call was on the black giant, Jasper. She found him chopping Pudd'nhead Wilson's winter provision of wood.

Wilson was chatting with him when Roxy arrived. He asked her how she could bear to go off chambermaiding and leave her boys; and chaffingly offered to copy off a series of their finger-prints, reaching up to their twelfth year, for her to remember them by; but she sobered in a moment, wondering if he suspected anything; then she said she believed she didn't want them. Wilson said to himself, "The drop of black blood in her is superstitious; she thinks there's some deviltry, some witch-business, about my glass mystery somewhere; she used to come here with an old horseshoe in her hand; it could have been an accident, but I doubt it."

Chapter 5

Training is everything. The peach was once a bitter almond; cauliflower is nothing but cabbage with a college education.
—PUDD'NHEAD WILSON'S CALENDAR.

Remark of Dr. Baldwin's, concerning upstarts: We don't care to eat toadstools that think they are truffles.
—PUDD'NHEAD WILSON'S CALENDAR.

Mrs. York Driscoll enjoyed two years of bliss with that prize, Tom; bliss that was troubled a little at times, it is true, but bliss nevertheless; then she died, and her husband and his childless sister, Mrs. Pratt, continued the bliss-business at the old stand. Tom was petted and indulged and spoiled to his entire content—or nearly that. This went on till he was nineteen, then he was sent to Yale. He went handsomely equipped with "conditions," but otherwise he was not an object of distinction there. He remained at Yale two years, and then threw up the struggle. He came home with his manners a good deal improved; he had lost his surliness and brusqueness, and was rather pleasantly soft and smooth, now; he was furtively, and sometimes openly, ironical of speech, and given to gently touching people on the raw, but he did it with a good-natured semi-conscious air that carried it off safely and kept him from getting into trouble. He was as indolent as ever, and showed no very strenuous desire to hunt up an occupation. People argued from this that he preferred to be supported by his uncle until his uncle's shoes should become vacant. He brought back one or two new habits with him, one of which he rather openly practiced—tippling —but concealed another, which was gambling. It would not do to gamble where his uncle could hear of it; he knew that quite well.

Tom's eastern polish was not popular among the young people. They could have endured it, perhaps, if Tom had stopped there; but he wore gloves, and that they couldn't stand, and wouldn't; so he was mainly without society. He brought home with him a suit of clothes of such exquisite style and cut and fashion—eastern fashion, city fashion—that it filled everybody with anguish and was regarded as a peculiarly wanton affront. He enjoyed the feeling which he was exciting, and paraded the town serene and happy all day; but the young fellows set a tailor to work that night, and when Tom started out on his parade next morning he found the old deformed negro bellringer straddling along in his wake tricked out in a flamboyant curtain-calico exaggeration of his finery, and imitating his fancy eastern graces as well as he could.

Tom surrendered, and after that clothed himself in the local fashion. But the dull country town was tiresome to him, since his acquaintanceship with livelier regions, and it grew daily more and more so. He began to make little trips to St. Louis for refreshment. There he found companionship to suit him, and pleasures to his taste, along with more freedom, in some particulars, than he could have at home. So, during the next two years his visits to the city grew in frequency and his tarryings there grew steadily longer in duration.

He was getting into deep waters. He was taking chances, privately, which might get him into trouble some day—in fact, *did*.

Judge Driscoll had retired from the Bench and from all business activities in 1850, and had now been comfortably idle three years. He was President of the Freethinkers' Society, and Pudd'nhead Wilson was the other member. The Society's weekly discussions were now the old lawyer's main interest in life. Pudd'nhead was still toiling in obscurity at the bottom of the ladder, under the blight of that unlucky remark which he had let fall twenty-three years before about the dog.

Judge Driscoll was his friend, and claimed that he had a mind above the average, but that was regarded as one of the Judge's whims, and it failed to modify the public opinion. Or, rather, that was one of the reasons why it failed, but there was another and better one. If the Judge had stopped with bare assertion, it would have had a good deal of effect; but he made the mistake of trying to prove his position. For some years Wilson had been privately at work on a whimsical almanac, for his amusement—a calendar, with a little dab of ostensible philosophy, usually in ironical form, appended to each date; and the Judge thought that these quips and fancies of Wilson's were neatly turned and cute; so he carried a handful of them around, one day, and read them to some of the chief citizens. But irony was not for those people; their mental vision was not focussed for it. They read those playful trifles in the solidest earnest, and decided without hesitancy that if there had ever been any doubt that Dave Wilson was a pudd'nhead—which there hadn't—this revelation removed that doubt for good and all. That is just the way, in this world; an enemy can partly ruin a man, but it takes a good-natured injudicious friend to complete the thing and make it perfect. After this the Judge felt tenderer than ever toward Wilson, and surer than ever that his calendar had merit.

Judge Driscoll could be a freethinker and still hold his place in society because he was the person of most consequence in the community, and therefore could venture to go his own way and follow out his own notions. The other member of his pet organization was allowed the like liberty because he was a cipher in the estimation of the public, and nobody attached any importance to what he thought or did. He was liked, he was welcome enough all around, but he simply didn't count for anything.

The widow Cooper—affectionately called "aunt Patsy" by everybody—lived in a snug and comely cottage with her daughter Rowena, who was nineteen, romantic, amiable, and very pretty, but otherwise of no consequence. Rowena had a couple of young brothers—also of no consequence.

The widow had a large spare room which she let to a lodger, with board, when she could find one, but this room had been empty for a year now, to her sorrow. Her income was only sufficient for the family support, and she needed the lodging-money for trifling luxuries. But now, at last, on a flaming June day, she found herself happy; her tedious wait was ended; her year-worn advertisement had been answered; and not by a village applicant, oh, no!—this letter was from away off yonder in the dim great world to the North: it was from St. Louis. She sat on her porch gazing out with unseeing eyes upon the shining reaches of the mighty Mississippi, her thoughts steeped in her good fortune. Indeed it was specially good fortune, for she was to have two lodgers instead of one.

She had read the letter to the family, and Rowena had danced away to see to the cleaning and airing of the room by the slave woman Nancy, and the boys had rushed abroad in the town to spread the great news, for it was matter of public interest, and the public would wonder and not be pleased if not informed. Presently Rowena returned, all aflush with joyous excitement, and begged for a re-reading of the letter. It was framed thus:

> HONORED MADAM: My brother and I have seen your advertisement, by chance, and beg leave to take the room you offer. We are twenty-four years of age and twins. We are Italians by birth, but have lived long in the various countries of Europe, and several years in the United States. Our names are Luigi and Angelo Cappello. You desire but one guest; but dear Madam, if you will allow us to pay for two, we will not incommode you. We shall be down Thursday.

"Italians! How romantic! Just think, ma—there's never been one in this town, and everybody will be dying to see them, and they're all *ours!* Think of that!"

"Yes, I reckon they'll make a grand stir."

"Oh, indeed they will. The whole town will be on its head! Think—they've been in Europe and everywhere! There's never been a traveler in this town before. Ma, I shouldn't wonder if they've seen kings!"

"Well, a body can't tell; but they'll make stir enough, without that."

"Yes, that's of course. Luigi—Angelo. They're lovely names; and so grand and foreign—not like Jones and Robinson and such. Thursday they are coming, and this is only Tuesday; it's a cruel long time to wait. Here comes Judge Driscoll in at the gate. He's heard about it. I'll go and open the door."

The judge was full of congratulations and curiosity. The letter was read and discussed. Soon Justice Robinson arrived with more congratulations, and there was a new reading and a new discussion. This was the beginning. Neighbor after neighbor, of both sexes, followed, and the procession drifted in and out all day and evening and all Wednesday and Thursday. The letter was read and re-read until it was nearly worn out; everybody admired its courtly and gracious tone, and smooth and practiced style, everybody was sympathetic and excited, and the Coopers were steeped in happiness all the while.

The boats were very uncertain, in low water, in those primitive times. This time the Thursday boat had not arrived at ten at night —so the people had waited at the landing all day for nothing; they were driven to their homes by a heavy storm without having had a view of the illustrious foreigners.

Eleven o'clock came; then twelve, and the Cooper house was the only one in the town that still had lights burning. The rain and thunder were booming yet, and the anxious family were still waiting, still hoping. At last there was a knock on the door and the family jumped to open it. Two negro men entered, each carrying a trunk, and proceeded up stairs toward the guest room. Then entered the twins—the handsomest, the best dressed, the most distinguished-looking pair of young fellows the West had ever seen. One was a little fairer than the other, but otherwise they were exact duplicates.

Chapter 6

Let us endeavor so to live that when we come to die even the undertaker will be sorry.
—PUDD'NHEAD WILSON'S CALENDAR.

Habit is habit, and not to be flung out of the window by any man, but coaxed down-stairs a step at a time.
—PUDD'NHEAD WILSON'S CALENDAR.

At breakfast in the morning the twins' charm of manner and easy and polished bearing made speedy conquest of the family's good graces. All constraint and formality quickly disappeared, and the friendliest feeling succeeded. Aunt Patsy called them by their Christian names almost from the beginning. She was full of the keenest curiosity about them, and showed it; they responded by talking about themselves, which pleased her greatly. It presently appeared that in their early youth they had known poverty and hardship. As the talk wandered along the old lady watched for the right place to drop in a question or two concerning that matter, and when she found it she said to the blonde twin, who was now doing the biographies in his turn while the brunette one rested—

"If it ain't asking what I ought not to ask, Mr. Angelo, how did you come to be so friendless and in such trouble when you were little? Do you mind telling? But don't, if you do."

"Oh, we don't mind it at all, madam; in our case it was merely misfortune, and nobody's fault. Our parents were well-to-do, there in Italy, and we were their only child. We were of the old Florentine nobility"—Rowena's heart gave a great bound, her nostrils expanded, and a fine light played in her eyes—"and when the war broke out my father was on the losing side and had to fly for his life. His estates were confiscated, his personal property seized, and there we were, in Germany, strangers, friendless, and in fact paupers. My brother and I were ten years old, and well educated for that age, very studious, very fond of our books, and well grounded in the German, French, Spanish and English languages. Also, we were marvelous musical prodigies—if you will allow me to say it, it being only the truth.

"Our father survived his misfortunes only a month, our mother soon followed him, and we were alone in the world. Our parents could have made themselves comfortable by exhibiting us as a show, and they had many and large offers; but the thought revolted their pride, and they said they would starve and die first. But what they wouldn't consent to do we had to do without the formality of consent. We were seized for the debts occasioned by their illness and their funerals, and placed among the attractions of a cheap museum in Berlin to earn the liquidation money. It took us two years to get out of that slavery. We traveled all about Germany, receiving no wages, and not even our keep. We had to exhibit for nothing, and beg our bread.

"Well, madam, the rest is not of much consequence. When we escaped from that slavery at twelve years of age, we were in some respects men. Experience had taught us some valuable things; among others, how to take care of ourselves, how to avoid and defeat sharks and sharpers, and how to conduct our own business for our own profit and without other people's help. We traveled everywhere—years and years—picking up smatterings of strange tongues, familiarizing ourselves with strange sights and strange customs, accumulating an education of a wide and varied and curious sort. It was a pleasant life. We went to Venice—to London, Paris, Russia, India, China, Japan—"

At this point Nancy the slave woman thrust her head in at the door and exclaimed:

"Ole Missus, de house is plum jam full o' people, en dey's jes' a spilin' to see de gen'lmen!" She indicated the twins with a nod of her head, and tucked it back out of sight again.

It was a proud occasion for the widow, and she promised herself high satisfaction in showing off her fine foreign birds before her neighbors and friends—simple folk who had hardly ever seen a foreigner of any kind, and never one of any distinction or style. Yet her feeling was moderate indeed, when contrasted with Rowena's. Rowena was in the clouds, she walked on air; this was to be the greatest day, the most romantic episode in the colorless history of that dull country town, she was to be familiarly near the source of its glory and feel the full flood of it pour over her and about her, the other girls could only gaze and envy, not partake.

The widow was ready, Rowena was ready, so also were the foreigners.

The party moved along the hall, the Twins in advance, and entered the open parlor door, whence issued a low hum of conversation. The Twins took a position near the door, the widow stood at Luigi's side, Rowena stood beside Angelo, and the march-past and the introductions began. The widow was all smiles and contentment. She received the procession and passed it on to Rowena.

"Good-mornin' Sister Cooper"—hand-shake.

"Good-morning, Brother Higgins—Count Luigi Cappello, Mr. Higgins"—hand-shake, followed by a devouring stare and "I'm glad to see ye," on the part of Higgins, and a courteous inclination of the head and a pleasant "Most happy!" on the part of Count Luigi.

"Good-mornin', Roweny"—handshake.

"Good-morning, Mr. Higgins—present you to Count Angelo Cappello." Handshake, admiring stare, "Glad to see ye,"—courteous nod, smily "Most happy!" and Higgins passes on.

None of these visitors was at ease, but being honest people, they didn't pretend to be. None of them had ever seen a person bearing a title of nobility before, and none had been expecting to see one now, consequently the title came upon them as a kind of pile-driving surprise and caught them unprepared. A few tried to rise to the emergency, and got out an awkward My Lord, or Your Lordship, or something of the sort, but the great majority were overwhelmed by the unaccustomed word and its dim and awful associations with gilded courts and stately ceremony and anointed kingship, so they only fumbled through the handshake, and passed on, speechless. Now and then, as happens at all receptions, everywhere, a more than ordinarily friendly soul blocked the procession and kept it waiting while he inquired how the brothers liked the village, and how long they were going to stay, and if their families were well, and dragged in the weather, and hoped it would get cooler soon, and all that sort of thing, so as to be able to say, when they got home, "I had quite a long talk with them;" but nobody did or said anything of a regrettable kind, and so the great affair went through to the end in a creditable and satisfactory fashion.

General conversation followed, and the twins drifted about from group to group, talking easily and fluently, and winning approval, compelling admiration, and achieving favor from all. The widow followed their conquering march with a proud eye, and every now and then Rowena said to herself with deep satisfaction, "And to think, they are ours—all ours!"

There were no idle moments for mother or daughter. Eager inquiries concerning the Twins were pouring into their enchanted ears all the time; each was the constant centre of a group of breathless listeners; each recognized that she knew now for the first time the real meaning of that great word Glory, and perceived the stupendous value of it, and understood why men in all ages had been willing to throw away meaner happinesses, treasure, life itself, to get a taste of its sublime and supreme joy. Napoleon and all his kind stood accounted for—and justified.

When Rowena had at last done all her duty by the people in the parlor, she went up stairs to satisfy the longings of an overflow meeting there, for the parlor was not big enough to hold all the comers. Again she was besieged by eager questioners and again she swam in sunset seas of glory. When the forenoon was nearly gone, she recognized with a pang that this most splendid episode of her life was almost over, that nothing could prolong it, that nothing quite its equal could ever fall to her fortune again. But never mind, it was sufficient unto itself, the grand occasion had moved on an ascending scale from the start, and was a noble and memorable success. If the twins could but do some crowning act, now, to climax it, something unusual, something startling, something to concentrate upon themselves the company's loftiest admiration, something in the nature of an electric surprise—

Here a prodigious slam-banging broke out below, and everybody rushed down to see. It was the twins knocking out a classic four-handed piece on the piano, in great style. Rowena was satisfied; satisfied down to the bottom of her heart.

The young strangers were kept long at the piano. The villagers were astonished and enchanted with the magnificence of their performance, and could not bear to have them stop. All the music that they had ever heard before seemed spiritless prentice-work and barren of grace or charm when compared with these intoxicating floods of melodious sound. They realized that for once in their lives they were hearing masters.

Chapter 7

One of the most striking differences between a cat and a lie is that a cat has only nine lives.
—PUDD'NHEAD WILSON'S CALENDAR.

The company broke up reluctantly, and drifted toward their several homes, chatting with vivacity, and all agreeing that it would be many a long day before Dawson's Landing would see the equal of this one again. The Twins had accepted several invitations while the reception was in progress, and had also volunteered to play some duets at an amateur entertainment for the benefit of a local charity. Society was eager to receive them to its bosom. Judge Driscoll had the good fortune to secure them for an immediate drive, and to be the first to display them in public. They entered his buggy with him and were paraded down the main street, everybody flocking to the windows and sidewalks to see.

The Judge showed the strangers the new graveyard, and the jail, and where the richest man lived, and the Freemasons' hall, and the Methodist church, and the Presbyterian church, and where the Baptist church was going to be when they got some money to build it with, and showed them the town hall and the slaughter-house, and got out the independent fire company in uniform and had them put out an imaginary fire; then he let them inspect the muskets of the militia company, and poured out an exhaustless stream of enthusiasm over all these splendors, and seemed very well satisfied with the responses he got, for the Twins admired his admiration and paid him back the best they could, though they could have done better if some fifteen or sixteen hundred thousand previous experiences of this sort in various countries had not already rubbed off a considerable part of the novelty of it.

The Judge laid himself hospitably out to make them have a good time, and if there was a defect anywhere it was not his fault. He told them a good many humorous anecdotes, and always forgot the nub, but they were always able to furnish it, for these yarns were of a pretty early vintage, and they had had many a rejuvenating pull at them before. And he told them all about his several dignities, and how he had held this and that and the other place of honor or profit, and had once been to the legislature, and was now president of the Society of Freethinkers. He said the society had been in existence four years and already had two members, and was firmly established. He would call for the brothers in the evening if they would like to attend a meeting of it.

Accordingly he called for them, and on the way he told them all about Pudd'nhead Wilson, in order that they might get a favorable impression of him in advance and be prepared to like him. This scheme succeeded—the favorable impression was achieved. Later it was confirmed and solidified when Wilson proposed that out of courtesy to the strangers the usual topics be put aside and the hour be devoted to conversation upon ordinary subjects and the cultivation of friendly relations and good-fellowship,—a proposition which was put to vote and carried.

The hour passed quickly away in lively talk, and when it was ended the lonesome and neglected Wilson was richer by two friends than he had been when it began. He invited the Twins to look in at his lodgings, presently, after disposing of an intervening engagement, and they accepted with pleasure.

Toward the middle of the evening they found themselves on the road to his house. Pudd'nhead was at home waiting for them and putting in his time puzzling over a thing which had come under his notice that morning. The matter was this. He happened to be up very early—at dawn, in fact; and he crossed the hall which divided his cottage through the centre and entered a room to get something there. The window of the room had no curtains, for that side of the house had long been unoccupiéd, and through this window he caught sight of something which surprised and interested him. It was a young woman—a young woman where properly no young woman belonged; for she was in Judge Driscoll's house, and in the bedroom over the Judge's private study or sitting room. This was young Tom Driscoll's bedroom. He and the Judge, the Judge's widowed sister Mrs. Pratt, and three negro servants were the only people who belonged in the house. Who, then, might this young lady be? The two houses were separated by an ordinary yard, with a low fence running back through its middle from the street in front to the lane in the rear. The distance was not great, and Wilson was able to see the girl very well, the window shades of the room she was in being up, and the window also. The girl had on a neat and trim summer dress patterned in broad stripes of pink and white, and her bonnet was equipped with a pink veil. She was practicing steps, gaits and attitudes, apparently; she was doing the thing gracefully, and was very much absorbed in her work. Who could she be, and how came she to be in young Tom Driscoll's room?

Wilson had quickly chosen a position from which he could watch the girl without running much risk of being seen by her, and he remained there hoping she would raise her veil and betray her face. But she disappointed him. After a matter of twenty minutes she disappeared, and although he stayed at his post half an hour longer, she came no more.

Toward noon he dropped in at the Judge's and talked with Mrs. Pratt about the great event of the day, the levèe of the distinguished foreigners at Aunt Patsy Cooper's. He asked after her nephew Tom, and she said he was on his way home, and that she was expecting him to arrive a little before night; and added that she and the Judge were gratified to gather from his letters that he was conducting himself very nicely and creditably—at which Wilson winked to himself privately. Wilson did not ask if there was a newcomer in the house, but he asked questions that would have brought light-throwing answers as to that matter if Mrs. Pratt had had any light to throw; so he went away satisfied that he knew of things that were going on in her house of which she herself was not aware.

He was now waiting for the Twins, and still puzzling over the problem of who that girl might be, and how she happened to be in that young fellow's room at day-break in the morning.

Chapter 8

The holy passion of Friendship is of so sweet and steady and loyal and enduring a nature that it will last through a whole lifetime if not asked to lend money.
—PUDD'NHEAD WILSON'S CALENDAR.

Consider well the proportions of things. It is better to be a young June-bug than an old bird of paradise.
—PUDD'NHEAD WILSON'S CALENDAR.

It is necessary, now, to hunt up Roxy.

At the time she was set free and went away chambermaiding, she was thirty-five. She got a berth as second chambermaid on a Cincinnati boat in the New Orleans trade, the "Grand Mogul." A couple of trips made her wonted and easy-going at the work, and infatuated her with the stir and adventure and independence of steamboat life. Then she was promoted and became head chambermaid. She was a favorite with the officers, and exceedingly proud of their joking and friendly ways with her.

During eight years she served three parts of the year on that boat, and the winters on a Vicksburg packet. But now for two months she had had rheumatism in her arms, and was obliged to let the wash-tub alone. So she resigned. But she was well fixed—rich, as she would have described it; for she had lived a steady life, and had banked four dollars every month in New Orleans as a provision for her old age. She said in the start that she had "put shoes on one bar'footed nigger to tromple on her with," and that one mistake like that was enough: she would be independent of the human race thenceforth forevermore if hard work and economy could accomplish it.

When the boat touched the levee at New Orleans she bade good-bye to her comrades on the Grand Mogul and moved her kit ashore.

But she was back in an hour. The bank had gone to smash and carried her four hundred dollars with it. She was a pauper, and homeless. Also disabled bodily, at least for the present. The officers were full of sympathy for her in her trouble, and made up a little purse for her. She resolved to go to her birth-place; she had friends there among the negroes, and the unfortunate always help the unfortunate, she was well aware of that; those lowly comrades of her youth would not let her starve.

She took the little local packet at Cairo, and now she was on the home-stretch. Time had worn away her bitterness against her son, and she was able to think of him with serenity. She put the vile side of him out of her mind, and dwelt only on recollections of his occasional acts of kindness to her. She gilded and otherwise decorated these, and made them very pleasant to contemplate. She began to long to see him. She would go and fawn upon him, slave-like—for this would have to be her attitude, of course—and maybe she would find that time had modified him, and that he would be glad to see his long forgotten old nurse and treat her gently. That would be lovely; that would make her forget her woes and her poverty.

Her poverty! That thought inspired her to add another castle to her dream: Maybe he would help her; maybe he would give her a trifle now and then—maybe a dollar, once a month, say; any little thing like that would help, oh, ever so much.

By the time she reached Dawson's Landing she was her old self again; her blues were gone, she was in high feather. She would get along, surely; there were many kitchens where the servants would share their meals with her, and also steal sugar and apples and other dainties for her to carry home—or give her a chance to pilfer them herself, which would answer just as well. And there was the church. She was a more rabid and devoted Methodist than ever, and her piety was no sham, but was strong and sincere. Yes, with plenty of creature comforts and her old place in the amen corner in her possession again, she would be perfectly happy and at peace thenceforward to the end.

She went to Judge Driscoll's kitchen first of all. She was received there in great form and with vast enthusiasm. Her wonderful travels, and the strange countries she had seen and the adventures she had had, made her a marvel and a heroine of romance. The negroes hung enchanted upon the great story of her experiences, interrupting her all along with eager questions, with laughter, exclamations of delight and expressions of applause; and she was obliged to confess to herself that if there was anything better in this world than steamboating, it was the glory to be got by telling about it. The audience loaded her stomach with their dinners and then stole the pantry bare to load up her basket.

Tom was in St. Louis. The servants said he had spent the best part of his time there during the previous two years. Roxy came every day, and had many talks about the family and its affairs. Once she asked why Tom was away so much. The ostensible "Chambers" said:

"De fac' is, ole marster kin git along better when young marster's away den he kin when he's in de town; yes, en he love him better, too; so he gives him fifty dollahs a month—"

"No, is dat so? Chambers, you's a jokin', ain't you?"

" 'Clah to goodness I ain't, mammy; Marse Tom tole me so, his own self. But nemmine, t'ain't enough."

"My lan', what de reason t'ain't enough?"

"Well, I's gwyne to tell you, if you gimme a chanst, mammy. De reason it ain't enough is becase Marse Tom gambles."

Roxy threw up her hands in astonishment, and Chambers went on—

"Ole marse found it out, becase he had to pay two hunderd dollahs for Marse Tom's gamblin' debts, en dat's true, mammy, jes' as dead certain as you's bawn."

"Two—hund'd—dollahs! Why, what is you talkin' 'bout? Two —hund'd—dollahs. Sakes alive, it's mos' enough to buy a tollable good second-hand nigger wid. En you ain't lyin', honey?—you wouldn't lie to yo' ole mammy?"

"It's Gawd's own truth, jes' as I tell you—two hunderd dollahs —I wisht I may never stir outen my tracks if it ain't so. En, oh, my lan', ole Marse was jes' a hoppin! he was bilin' mad, I tell you! He tuck'n dissenhurrit him."

He licked his chops with relish after that stately word. Roxy strugged with it a moment, then gave it up and said—

"Dissen*whiched* him?"

"Dissenhurrit him."

"What's dat? What do it mean?"

"Means he busted de will."

"Bus-ted de will! He wouldn't *ever* treat him so! Take it back, you misable imitation nigger dat I bore in sorrow en tribbilation."

Roxy's pet castle—an occasional dollar from Tom's pocket—was tumbling to ruin before her eyes. She could not abide such a disaster as that; she couldn't endure the thought of it. Her remark amused Chambers:

"Yah-yah-yah! jes' listen to dat! If I's imitation, what is you? Bofe of us is imitation *white*—dat's what we is—en pow'full good imitation, too—Yah-yah-yah!—we don't 'mount to noth'n as imitation *niggers*; en as for—"

"Shet up yo' foolin', 'fo' I knock you side de head, en tell me 'bout de will. Tell me t'ain't busted—do, honey, en I'll never fogit you."

"Well, *t'ain't*—caze dey's a new one made, en Marse Tom's all right agin. But what is you in sich a sweat 'bout it for, mammy? T'ain't none o' your business I don't reckon."

"Tain't none o' my business? Whose business is it den, I'd like to know? Was I his mother tell he was fifteen years old, or wusn't I?—you answer me dat. En you speck I could see him turned out po' en ornery on de worl' en never care noth'n 'bout it? I reckon if you'd ever ben a mother yo'self, Vallet de Chambers, you wouldn't talk sich foolishness as dat."

"Well, den, old Marse forgive him en fixed up de will agin—do dat satisfy you?"

Yes, she was satisfied, now, and quite happy and sentimental over it. She kept coming daily, and at last she was told that Tom had come home. She began to tremble with emotion, and straightway sent to beg him to let his "po' ole nigger mammy have jes' one sight of him en die for joy."

Tom was stretched at his lazy ease on a sofa when Chambers brought the petition. Time had not modified his ancient detestation of the humble drudge and protector of his boyhood; it was still bitter and uncompromising. He sat up and bent a severe gaze upon the fair face of the young fellow whose name he was unconsciously using and whose family rights he was enjoying. He maintained the gaze until the victim of it had become satisfactorily pallid with terror, then he said—

"What does the old rip want with me?"

The petition was meekly repeated.

"Who gave you permission to come and disturb me with the social attentions of niggers?"

Tom had risen. The other young man was trembling, now, visibly. He saw what was coming, and bent his head sideways and put up his left arm to shield it. Tom rained cuffs upon the head and its shield, saying no word; the victim received each blow with a beseeching "Please, Marse Tom!—oh, please, Marse Tom!" Seven blows—then Tom said, "Face the door—March!" He followed behind with one, two, three solid kicks. The last one helped the pure-white slave over the door-sill, and he limped away mopping his eyes with his old ragged sleeve. Tom shouted after him, "Send her in!"

Then he flung himself panting on the sofa again and rasped out the remark, "He arrived just at the right moment; I was full to the brim with bitter thinkings, and nobody to take it out of. How refreshing it was!—I feel better."

Tom's mother entered, now, closing the door behind her, and

approached her son with all the wheedling and supplicating servilities that fear and interest can impart to the words and attitudes of the born slave. She stopped a yard from her boy and made two or three admiring exclamations over his manly stature and general handsomeness, and Tom put an arm under his head and hoisted a leg over the sofa-back in order to look properly indifferent.

"My lan', how you is growed, honey! 'Clah to goodness I wouldn't a knowed you, Marse Tom! 'deed I wouldn't! Look at me good; does you 'member ole Roxy?—does you know yo' ole nigger mammy, honey? Well, now, I kin lay down en die in peace, caze I's seed—"

"Cut it short, damn it, cut it short! What is it you want?"

"You heah dat? Jes' de same old Marse Tom, allays so gay and funnin' wid de ole mammy. I 'uz jes' as shore—"

"Cut it short, I tell you, and get along! What do you want?"

This was a bitter disappointment. Roxy had for so many days nourished and fondled and petted her notion that Tom would be glad to see his old nurse and would make her proud and happy to the marrow with a cordial word or two, that it took two rebuffs to convince her that he was not funning and that her beautiful dream was a fond and foolish vanity, a shabby and pitiful mistake. She was hurt to the heart, and so ashamed that for a moment she did not quite know what to do or how to act. Then her breast began to heave, the tears came, and in her forlornness she was moved to try that other dream of hers—an appeal to her boy's charity; and so, upon the impulse, and without reflection, she offered her supplication—

"Oh, Marse Tom, de po' ole mammy is in sich hard luck, dese days; en she's kinder crippled in de arms en can't work, en if you could gimme a dollah—on'y jes' one little dol—"

Tom was on his feet so suddenly that the supplicant was startled into a jump herself.

"A dollar!—give you a dollar! I've a notion to strangle you! Is *that* your errand here? Clear out! and be quick about it!"

Roxy backed slowly toward the door. When she was half-way she stopped, and said, mournfully—

"Marse Tom, I nussed you when you was a little baby, en I raised you all by myself tell you was most a young man; en now you is young en rich en I is po' en gitt'n ole, en I come heah b'lievin' dat you would he'p de ole mammy 'long down de little road dat's lef' twix her en de grave, en—"

Tom relished this tune less than any that had preceded it, for it began to wake up a sort of echo in his conscience; so he interrupted and said with decision, though without asperity, that he was not in a situation to help her, and wasn't going to do it.

"Ain't you ever gwyne to he'p me, Marse Tom?"

"No! Now go away and don't bother me any more."

Roxy's head was down, in an attitude of humility. But now the fires of her old wrongs flamed up in her breast and began to burn fiercely. She raised her head slowly, till it was well up, and at the same time her great frame unconsciously assumed an erect and masterful attitude, with all the majesty and grace of her vanished youth in it. She raised her finger and punctuated with it:

"You has said de word. You has had yo' chance, en you has tromped it under yo' foot. When you git another one, you'll git down on yo' knees en *beg* for it!"

A cold chill went to Tom's heart, he didn't know why; for he did not reflect that such words, from such an incongruous source, and so solemnly delivered, could not easily fail of that effect. However, he did the natural thing: he replied with bluster and mockery:

"*You'll* give me a chance—*you!* Perhaps I'd better get down on my knees now! But in case I don't—just for argument's sake—what's going to happen, pray?"

"Dis is what is gwyne to happen. I's gywne as straight to yo' uncle as I kin walk, en tell him every las' thing I knows about you."

Tom's cheek blenched, and she saw it. Disturbing thoughts began to chase each other through his head. "How can she know? And yet she must have found out—she looks it. I've had the will back only three months and am already deep in debt again and moving heaven and earth to save myself from exposure and destruction, with a reasonably fair show of getting the thing covered up if I'm let alone, and now this fiend has gone and found me out somehow or other. I wonder how much she knows. Oh, oh, oh, it's enough to break a body's heart! But I've got to humor her—there's no other way."

Then he worked up a rather sickly sample of a gay laugh and a hollow chipperness of manner, and said—

"Well, well, Roxy dear, old friends like you and me mustn't quarrel. Here's your dollar—now tell me what you know."

He held out the wild-cat bill, she stood as she was, and made no movement. It was her turn to scorn persuasive foolery, now, and she did not waste it. She said, with a grim implacability in voice and manner which made Tom almost realize that even a former slave can remember for ten minutes insults and injuries returned for compliments and flatteries received, and can also enjoy taking revenge for them when the opportunity offers—

"What does I know? I'll tell you what I knows. I knows enough to bust dat will to flinders—en more, mind you, *more!*"

Tom was aghast.

"More?" he said. "What do you call more? Where's there any room for more?"

Roxy laughed a mocking laugh, and said scoffingly, with a toss of her head, and her hands on her hips—

"Yes!—oh, I reckon! 'Cose you'd like to know—wid yo' po' little ole rag dollah. What you reckon I's gywne to tell *you*, for?—you ain't got no money. I's gwyne to tell yo' uncle—en I'll do it dis minute, too—he'll gimme *five* dollahs for de news, en mighty glad, too."

She swung herself around disdainfully, and started away. Tom was in a panic. He seized her skirts and implored her to wait. She turned and said, loftily—

"Look-a-here, what was it I tole you?"

"You—you—I don't remember anything. What was it you told me?"

"I tole you dat de next time I give you a chance you'd git down on yo' knees en beg for it."

Tom was stupefied for a moment. He was panting with excitement. Then he said—

"Oh, Roxy, you wouldn't require your young master to do such a horrible thing. You can't mean it."

"I'll let you know mighty quick whether I means it or not! You call me names, en as good as spit on me when I comes here po' en orncry en 'umble, to praise you for bein' growed up so fine en handsome, en tell you how I used to nuss you en tend you en watch you when you was sick en you hadn't no mother but me in de whole worl', en beg you to give de po' ole nigger a dollah for to git her sum'n to eat, en you call me names—*names*, dad blame you! Yassir, I gives you jes' one chance mo', and dat's *now*, en it las' on'y a half a second—you hear?"

Tom slumped to his knees and began to beg, saying—

"You see I'm begging, and it's honest begging, too! Now tell me, Roxy, tell me."

The heir of two centuries of unatoned insult and outrage looked down on him and seemed to drink in deep draughts of satisfaction. Then she said—

"Fine nice young white gen'lman kneelin' down to a nigger wench! I's wanted to see dat jes' once befo' I's called. Now, Gabrel, blow de hawn, I's ready. . . . . . Git up!"

Tom did it. He said, humbly—

"Now Roxy, don't punish me any more. I deserved what I've got, but be good and let me off with that. Don't go to uncle. Tell me—I'll give you the five dollars."

"Yes, I bet you will; en you won't stop dah, nuther. But I ain't gwyne to tell you here—"

"Good gracious, no!"

"Is you feared o' de ha'nted house?"

"N-no."

"Well, den, you come to de ha'nted house 'bout ten or 'leven to-night, en climb up de ladder, caze de star-steps is broke down, en you'll fine me. I's a roostin' in de ha'nted house becaze I can't 'ford to roos' nowher's else." She started toward the door, but stopped and said "Gimme de dollah bill!" He gave it to her. She examined it and said, "Hm—like enough de bank's busted." She started again, but halted again. "Has you got any whisky?"

"Yes, a little."

"Fetch it!"

He ran to his room overhead and brought down a bottle which was two-thirds full. She tilted it up and took a drink. Her eyes sparkled with satisfaction, and she tucked the bottle under her shawl, saying,—

"It's prime—I'll take it along."

Tom humbly held the door for her, and she marched out as grim and erect as a grenadier.

Chapter 9

Why is it that we rejoice at birth and grieve at a funeral? It is because we are not the person involved.
—PUDD'NHEAD WILSON'S CALENDAR.

It is easy to find fault, if one has that disposition. There was once a man who, not being able to find any other fault with his coal, complained that there were too many prehistoric toads in it.
—PUDD'NHEAD WILSON'S CALENDAR.

Tom flung himself on the sofa, and put his throbbing head in his hands and rested his elbows on his knees. He rocked himself back and forth and moaned.

"I've knelt to a nigger wench!" he muttered. "I thought I had struck the deepest deeps of degradation before, but oh, dear, it was nothing to this. . . . . . Well, there is one consolation, such as it is —I've struck bottom this time; there's nothing lower."

But that was a hasty conclusion.

At ten that night he climbed the ladder in the haunted house, pale, weak, and wretched. Roxy was standing in the door of one of the rooms, waiting, for she had heard him.

This was a two-story log house which had acquired the reputation a few years before of being haunted, and that was the end of its usefulness. Nobody would live in it afterward or go near it by night, and most people even gave it a wide berth in the daytime. As it had no competition, it was called *the* haunted house. It was getting crazy and ruinous, now, from long neglect. It stood three hundred yards beyong Pudd'nhead Wilson's house, with nothing between but vacancy. It was the last house in the town at that end.

Tom followed Roxy into the room. She had a pile of clean straw in the corner for a bed, some cheap but well-kept clothing was hanging on the wall, there was a tin lantern freckling the floor with little spots of light, and there were various soap and candle boxes scattered about, which served for chairs. The two sat down. Roxy said—

"Now, den. I'll tell you straight off, en I'll begin to k'leck de money later on; I ain't in no hurry. What does you reckon I's gwyne to tell you?"

"Well, you—you—oh, Roxy, don't make it too hard for me! Come right out and tell me you've found out somehow what a shape I'm in on account of dissipation and foolishness."

"Disposition en foolishness! *No* sir, dat ain't it. Dat jist ain't noth'n at all, 'longside o' what *I* knows."

Tom stared at her, and said—

"Why—Roxy, what do you mean?"

She rose, and gloomed above him like a fate.

"I mean dis—en it's de Lord's truth. You ain't no more kin to ole Marse Driscoll den I is!—*dat's* what I mean!" and her eyes flamed with triumph.

"What!"

"Yassir, en *dat* ain't all! You is a *nigger!*—*bawn* a nigger en a *slave!*—en you's a nigger en a slave dis minute; en if I opens my mouf, ole Marse Driscoll 'll sell you down de river befo' you is two days older den what you is now!"

"It's a thundering lie, you miscrable old blatherskite!"

"It ain't no lie, nuther. It's jes' de truth, en noth'n *but* de truth, so he'p me. Yassir—you's my *son*—"

"You devil!—"

—"en dat po' boy dat you's been a kickin' en a cuffin' to-day is Percy Driscoll's son en yo' *marster*—"

"You beast!"

—"en *his* name's Tom Driscoll en *yo'* name's Vallet de Chambers, en you ain't *got* no fambly name, becaze niggers don't *have* 'em!"

Tom sprang up and seized a billet of wood and raised it; but his mother only laughed at him and said—

"Set down, you pup! Does you think you kin sk'yer me? It ain't in you, nor de likes of you. I reckon you'd shoot me in de back, maybe, if you got a chance, for dat's jist yo' style, *I* knows you, thoo en thoo—but I don't mind gitt'n killed, becaze all dis is down in writin', en it's in safe hands, too, en de man dat's got it knows whah to look for de right man when I gits killed. Oh, bless yo' soul, if you puts yo' mother up for as big a fool as *you* is, you's pow'ful mistaken, I kin tell you! Now den, you set still en behave yo'self; en don't you git up agin till I tell you!"

Tom fretted and chafed a while in a whirlwind of disorganizing sensations and emotions, and finally said with something like settled conviction—

"The whole thing is moonshine—now, then, go ahead and do your worst; I'm done with you."

Roxy made no answer. She took the lantern and started toward the door. Tom was in a cold panic in a moment.

"Come back, come back!" he wailed. "I didn't mean it, Roxy, I take it all back, and I'll never say it again! Please come back, Roxy!"

The woman stood a moment, then she said gravely—

"Dah's one thing you's got to stop, Vallet de Chambers. You can't call me *Roxy*, same as if you was my equal. Chillen don't speak to dey mammies like dat. You'll call me Ma or mammy, dat's what you'll call me—leastways when dey ain't nobody aroun'. *Say* it!"

It cost Tom a struggle, but he got it out.

"Dat's all right. Don't you ever fogit it agin, if you knows what's good for you. Now, den, you has said you wouldn't ever call it lies en moonshine agin. I'll tell you dis, for a warnin': if you ever does say it agin it's de *las'* time you'll ever say it to me; I'll tramp as straight to de Judge as I kin walk, en tell him who you is en *prove* it. Does you b'lieve me when I says dat?"

"Oh," groaned Tom, "I more than believe it, I *know* it."

Roxy knew her conquest was complete. She could have proven nothing to anybody, and her threat about the writings was a lie; but she knew the person she was dealing with, and had made both statements without any doubts as to the effect they would produce.

She went and sat down on her candle-box, and the pride and pomp of her victorious attitude made it a throne. She said—

"Now, den, Chambers, we's gwyne to talk business, en dey ain't gwyne to be no mo' foolishness. In de fust place, you gits fifty dollahs a month; you's gwyne to han' over half of it to yo' ma. Plank it out!"

But Tom had only six dollars in the world. He gave her that, and promised to start fair on next month's pension.

"Chambers, how much is you in debt?"

Tom shuddered, and said—

"Nearly three hundred dollars."

"How is you gwyne to pay it?"

Tom groaned out—

"Oh, I don't know—don't ask me such awful questions."

But she stuck to her point until she wearied a confession out of him: he had been prowling about in disguise, stealing small valuables from private houses; in fact had made a good deal of a raid on his fellow villagers a fortnight before, when he was supposed to be in St. Louis; but he doubted if he had sent away enough stuff to realize the required amount, and was afraid to make a further venture in the present excited state of the town. His mother approved of his conduct, and offered to help, but this frightened him. He tremblingly ventured to say that if she would retire from the town he should feel better and safer, and could hold his head higher—and was going on to make an argument, but she interrupted and surprised him pleasantly by saying she was ready, it didn't make any difference to her where she stayed, so that she got her share of the pension regularly. She said she would not go far, and would call at the haunted house once a month for her money. Then she said—

"I don't hate you so much now, but I've hated you a many a year —and anybody would. Didn't I change you off en give you a good fambly en a good name, en made you a white genl'man en rich, wid store clothes on—en what did I git for it? You despised me all de time; en was allays sayin' mean hard things to me befo' folks, en wouldn't ever let me fogit I's a nigger—en—en—"

She fell to sobbing, and broke down. Tom said—

"But you know, I didn't know you were my mother—and besides —"

"Well, nemmine 'bout dat, now—let it go. I's gwyne to fogit it." Then she added fiercely, "En don't you ever make me remember it agin, or you'll be sorry, *I* tell you."

When they were parting, Tom said, in the most persuasive way he could command—

"Ma, would you mind telling me who was my father?"

He had supposed he was asking an embarrassing question. He was mistaken. Roxy drew herself up, with a proud toss of her head, and said:

"Does I mine tellin' you? No, dat I don't! You ain't got no 'casion to be shame' o' yo' father, *I* kin tell you. He was de highest quality in dis whole town—Ole Virginny stock, Fust Famblies, he was. Jes' as good stock as de Driscolls en de Howards, de bes' day dey ever seed." She put on a still prouder air, if possible, and added impressively, "Does you 'member Cunnel Cecil Burleigh Essex dat died de same year yo' young Marse Tom Driscoll's pappy died, en all de Masons en Odd Fellers en churches turned out en give him de bigges' funeral dis town ever seed? Dat's de man."

Under the inspiration of her soaring complacency the departed graces of her earlier days returned to her, and her bearing took to itself a dignity and state that might have passed for queenly if her surroundings had been a little more in keeping with it.

"Dey ain't another nigger in dis town dat's as high-bawn as you is. Now, den, go 'long! En jes' you hold yo' head up as high as you want to—you has de right, en dat I kin swah."

Chapter 10

All say "How hard it is that we have to die"—a strange complaint to come from the mouths of people who have had to live.
—PUDD'NHEAD WILSON'S CALENDAR.

When angry, count four; when very angry, swear.
—PUDD'NHEAD WILSON'S CALENDAR.

Every now and then, after Tom went to bed, he had sudden wakings out of his sleep, and his first thought was, "O, joy, it was all a dream!" Then he laid himself heavily down again, with a groan and the muttered words, "A nigger!—I am a nigger!—oh, I wish I was dead!"

He woke at dawn with one more repetition of this horror, and then he resolved to meddle no more with that treacherous sleep. He began to think. Sufficiently bitter thinkings they were. They wandered along something after this fashion:

"Why were niggers *and* whites made? What crime did the uncreated first nigger commit that the curse of birth was decreed for him? And why is this awful difference made between white and black? . . . . . . How hard the nigger's fate seems, this morning!—yet until last night such a thought never entered my head."

He sighed and groaned an hour or more away. Then "Chambers" came humbly in to say that breakfast was nearly ready. "Tom" blushed scarlet to see this aristocratic white youth cringe to him, a nigger, and call him "Young marster." He said, roughly—

"Get out of my sight!" and when the youth was gone, he muttered, "He has done me no harm, poor wretch, but he is an eyesore to me, now, for he is Driscoll the young gentleman, and I am a— oh, I wish I was dead!"

A gigantic irruption like that of Krakatoa a few years ago, with the accompanying earthquakes, tidal waves and clouds of volcanic dust, changes the face of the surrounding landscape beyong recognition, bringing down the high lands, elevating the low, making fair lakes where deserts had been, and deserts where green prairies had smiled before. The tremendous catastrophe which had befallen Tom had changed his moral landscape in much the same way. Some of his low places he found lifted to ideals, some of his ideals had sunk to the valleys, and lay there with the sackcloth and ashes of pumice stone and sulphur on their ruined heads.

For days he wandered in lonely places thinking, thinking, thinking—trying to get his bearings. It was new work. If he met a friend he found that the habit of a lifetime had in some mysterious way vanished—his arm hung limp instead of involuntarily extending the hand for a shake. It was the "nigger" in him asserting its humility, and he blushed and was abashed. And the "nigger" in him was surprised when the white friend put out his hand for a shake with him. He found the "nigger" in him involuntarily giving the road, on the sidewalk, to the white rowdy and loafer. When Rowena, the dearest thing his heart knew, the idol of his secret worship, invited him in, the "nigger" in him made an embarrassed excuse and was afraid to enter and sit with the dread white folks on equal terms. The "nigger" in him went shrinking and skulking here and there and yonder, and fancying it saw suspicion and maybe detection in all faces, tones and gestures. So strange and uncharacteristic was Tom's conduct that people noticed it and turned to look after him when he passed on; and when he glanced back—as he could not help doing, in spite of his best resistance—and caught that puzzled expression in a person's face, it gave him a sick feeling, and he took himself out of view as quickly as he could. He presently came to have a hunted sense and a hunted look, and then he fled away to the hill-tops and the solitudes. He said to himself that the curse of Ham was upon him.

He dreaded his meals; the "nigger" in him was ashamed to sit at the white folks' table, and feared discovery all the time; and once when Judge Driscoll said, "What's the matter with you?—you look as meek as a nigger," he felt as secret murderers are said to feel when the accuser says "Thou art the man!" Tom said he was not well, and left the table.

His ostensible "aunt's" solicitudes and endearments were become a terror to him, and he avoided them.

And all the time, hatred of his ostensible "uncle" was steadily growing in his heart; for he said to himself, "He is white; and I am his chattel, his property, his goods, and he can sell me, just as he could his dog."

For as much as a week after this, Tom imagined that his character had undergone a pretty radical change. But that was because he did not know himself.

In several ways his opinions were totally changed, and would never go back to what they were before, but the main structure of his character was not changed, and could not be changed. One or two very important features of it were altered, and in time effects would result from this, if opportunity offered; effects of a quite serious nature, too. Under the influence of a great mental and moral upheaval his character and habits had taken on the appearance of complete change, but after a while with the subsidence of the storm both began to settle toward their former places. He dropped gradually back into his old frivolous and easy-going ways, and conditions of feeling, and manner of speech, and no familiar of his could have detected anything in him that differentiated him from the weak and careless Tom of other days.

The theft-raid which he had made upon the village turned out better than he had ventured to hope. It produced the sum necessary to pay his gaming-debts, and saved him from exposure to his uncle and another smashing of the will.

He and his mother learned to like each other fairly well. She couldn't love him, as yet, because there "warn't nothing *to* him," as she expressed it, but her nature needed something or somebody to rule over, and he was better than nothing. Her strong character and aggressive and commanding ways compelled Tom's admiration in spite of the fact that he got more illustrations of them than he needed for his comfort. However, as a rule, her conversation was made up of racy tattle about the privacies of the chief families of the town (for she went harvesting among their kitchens every time she came to the village), and Tom enjoyed this. It was just in his line. She always collected her half of his pension punctually, and he was always at the haunted house to have a chat with her on these occasions. Every now and then she paid him a visit there on between-days also.

Occasionally he would run up to St. Louis for a few weeks, and at last temptation caught him again. He won a lot of money, but lost it, and with it a deal more besides, which he promised to raise as soon as possible.

For this purpose he projected a new raid on his town. He never meddled with any other town, for he was afraid to venture into houses whose ins and outs he did not know, and the habits of whose households he was not acquainted with. He arrived at the haunted house in disguise on the Wednesday before the advent of the Twins,—after writing his aunt Pratt that he would not arrive until two days later—and lay in hiding there with his mother until toward daylight Friday morning, when he went to his uncle's house and entered by the back way with his own key and slipped up to his room, where he could have the use of mirror and toilet articles. He had a suit of girl's clothes with him in a bundle as a disguise for his raid, and was wearing a suit of his mother's clothing, with black gloves and veil. By dawn he was tricked out for his raid, but he caught a glimpse of Pudd'nhead Wilson through the window over the way and knew that Pudd'nhead had caught a glimpse of him. So he entertained Wilson with some airs and graces and attitudes for a while, then stepped out of sight and resumed the other disguise, and by and by went down and out the back way and started downtown to reconnoitre the scene of his intended labors.

But he was ill at ease. He had changed back to Roxy's dress, with the stoop of age added to the disguise, so that Wilson would not bother himself about a humble old woman leaving a neighbor's house by the back way in the early morning, in case he was still spying. But supposing Wilson had seen him leave, and had thought it suspicious, and had also followed him? The thought made Tom cold. He gave up the raid for the day, and hurried back to the haunted house by the obscurest route he knew. His mother was gone; but she came back, by and by, with the news of the grand reception at Patsy Cooper's, and soon persuaded him that the opportunity was like a special providence it was so inviting and perfect. So he went raiding, after all, and made a nice success of it while everybody was gone to Patsy Cooper's. Success gave him nerve; and even actual intrepidity; insomuch, indeed, that after he had conveyed his harvest to his mother in a back alley, he went to the reception himself, and added several of the valuables of that house to his takings.

After this long digression we have now arrived, once more, at the point where Pudd'nhead Wilson, while waiting for the arrival of the Twins on that same Friday evening, sat puzzling over the strange apparition of that morning—a girl in young Tom Driscoll's bedroom; fretting, and guessing, and puzzling over it, and wondering who the shameless creature might be.

Chapter 11

> *There are three infallible ways of pleasing an author, and the three form a rising scale of compliment: 1, to tell him you have read one of his books; 2, to tell him you have read all of his books; 3, to ask him to let you read the manuscript of his forthcoming book. No. 1 admits you to his respect; No. 2 admits you to his admiration; No. 3 carries you clear into his heart.*
> —PUDD'NHEAD WILSON'S CALENDAR.

> *As to the Adjective: when in doubt, strike it out.*
> —PUDD'NHEAD WILSON'S CALENDAR.

The twins arrived presently, and talk began. It flowed along chattily and sociably, and under its influence the new friendship gathered ease and strength. Wilson got out his Calendar, by request, and read a passage or two from it, which the Twins praised quite cordially. This pleased the author so much that he complied gladly when they asked him to lend them a batch of the work to read at home. In the course of their wide travels they had found out that there are three sure ways of pleasing an author; they were now working the best of the three.

There was an interruption, now. Young Tom Driscoll appeared, and joined the party. He pretended to be seeing the distinguished strangers for the first time when they rose to shake hands; but this was only a blind, as he had already had a glimpse of them at the reception while robbing the house. The Twins made mental note that he was smooth-faced and rather handsome, and smooth and undulatory in his movements—graceful, in fact. Angelo thought he had a good eye, Luigi thought there was something veiled and sly about it. Angelo thought he had a pleasant free-and-easy way of talking, Luigi thought it was more so than was agreeable. Angelo thought he was a sufficiently nice young man, Luigi reserved his decision. Tom's first contribution to the conversation was a question which he had put to Wilson a hundred times before. It was always cheerily and good-naturedly put, and always inflicted a little pang, for it touched a secret sore; but this time the pang was sharp, since strangers were present:

"Well, how does the law come on? Had a case yet?"

Wilson bit his lip, but answered, "No—not yet," with as much indifference as he could assume. Judge Driscoll had generously left the law feature out of the Wilson biography which he had furnished to the Twins. Young Tom laughed pleasantly and said—

"Wilson's a lawyer, gentlemen, but he doesn't practice now."

The sarcasm bit, but Wilson kept himself under control, and said, without passion—

"I don't practice, it is true. It is true that I have never had a case, and have had to earn a poor living for twenty years as an expert accountant in a town where I can't get hold of a set of books to untangle as often as I should like. But it is also true that I did fit myself well for the practice of the law. By the time I was your age, Tom, I had chosen a profession and was soon competent to enter upon it." Tom winced. "I never got a chance to try my hand at it, and I may never get a chance; and yet if I ever do get it I shall be found ready, for I have kept up my law-studies all these years."

"That's it—that's good grit! I like to see it. I've a notion to throw all my business your way. My business and your law-practice ought to make a pretty gay team, Dave," and the young fellow laughed again.

"If you will throw—" Wilson had thought of the girl in Tom's bedroom, and was going to say, "If you will throw the surreptitious and disreputable part of your business my way, it may amount to something," but thought better of it and said, "However, this matter doesn't fit well in a general conversation."

"All right, we'll change the subject—I guess you were about to give me another dig, anyway, so I'm willing to change. How's the Awful Mystery flourishing these days? Wilson's got a scheme for driving plain window-glass out of the market by decorating it with greasy finger-marks and getting rich by selling it at famine prices to the crowned heads over in Europe to outfit their palaces with. Fetch it out, Dave."

Wilson brought three of his glass strips and said:

"I get the subject to pass the fingers of his right hand through his hair, so as to get a little coating of the natural oil on them, and then press the balls of them on the glass. A fine and delicate print of the lines in the skin results, and is permanent if it doesn't come in contact with something able to rub it off. You begin, Tom."

"Why, I think you took my finger-marks once or twice before."

"Yes, but you were a little boy, the last time, only about twelve years old."

"That's so. Of course I've changed entirely since then, and variety is what the crowned heads want, I guess."

He passed his finger through his crop of short hair and pressed them one at a time on the glass. Angelo made a print of his fingers on another glass, and Luigi followed with the third. Wilson marked the glasses with names and date and put them away. Tom gave one of his little laughs and said—

"I thought I wouldn't say anything, but if variety is what you are after, you have wasted a piece of glass. The hand-print of one twin is the same as the hand-print of the fellow-twin."

"Well, it's done, now, and I like to have them both, anyway," said Wilson, returning to his place.

"But look here, Dave," said Tom, "you used to tell people's fortunes, too, when you took their finger-marks. Dave's just an all-around genius, a genius of the first water, gentlemen, a great scientist running to seed here in this village, a prophet with the kind of honor that prophets generally get at home—for here they don't give shucks for his scientifics, and they call his skull a notion-factory—hey, Dave, ain't it so?—but never mind, he'll make his mark some day—finger-mark, you know, he-he! But really, you want to let him take a shy at your palms once, it's worth twice the price of admission or your money's returned at the door. Why, he'll read your wrinkles as easy as a book, and not only tell you fifty or sixty things that's going to happen to you, but fifty or sixty thousand that ain't. Come, Dave, show the gentlemen what an inspired Jack-at-all-science we've got in this town and don't know it."

Wilson winced under this nagging and not very courteous chaff, and the Twins suffered with him and for him. They rightly judged, now, that the best way to relieve him would be to take the thing in earnest and treat it with respect, ignoring Tom's rather overdone raillery; so Luigi said:

"We have seen something of palmistry in our wanderings, and know very well what astonishing things it can do. If it isn't a science, and one of the greatest of them, too, I don't know what its other name ought to be. In the Orient—"

Tom looked surprised and incredulous. He said—

"That jugglery a science? But really, you ain't serious, are you?"

"Yes, entirely so. Four years ago we had our hands read out to us as if our palms had been covered with print."

"Well, do you mean to say there was actually anything in it?" asked Tom, his incredulity beginning to weaken a little.

"There was this much in it," said Angelo; "what was told us of our characters was minutely exact—we could not have bettered it ourselves. Next, two or three memorable things that had happened to us were laid bare—things which no one present but ourselves could have known about."

"Why, it's rank sorcery!" exclaimed Tom, who was now becoming very much interested. "And how did they make out with what was going to happen to you in the future?"

"On the whole, quite fairly," said Luigi. "Two or three of the most striking things foretold have happened since; much the most striking one of all happened within that same year. Some of the minor prophecies have come true; some of the minor and some of the major ones have not been fulfilled yet, and of course may never be—still, I should be more surprised if they failed to arrive than if they didn't."

Tom was entirely sobered, and profoundly impressed. He said, apologetically—

"Dave, I wasn't meaning to belittle that science, I was only chaffing—chattering, I reckon I better say. I wish you would look at their palms. Come, won't you?"

"Why, certainly, if you want me to, but you know I've had no chance to become an expert, and don't claim to be one. When a past event is somewhat prominently recorded in the palm, I can generally detect that, but minor ones often escape me—not always, of course, but often—but I haven't much confidence in myself when it comes to reading the future. I am talking as if palmistry was a daily study with me, but that is not so. I haven't examined half a dozen hands in the last half a dozen years; you see, the people got to joking about it, and I stopped to let the talk die down. I'll tell you what we'll do, Count Luigi: I'll make a try at your past, and if I have any success there—no, on the whole I'll let the future alone; that's really the affair of an expert."

He took Luigi's hand. Tom said—

"Wait—don't look yet, Dave! Count Luigi, here's paper and pencil. Set down that thing that you said was the most striking one that was foretold to you and happened less than a year afterwards, and give it to me so I can see if Dave finds it in your hand."

Luigi wrote a line privately, and folded up the piece of paper and handed it to Tom, saying—

"I'll tell you when to look at it, if he finds it."

Wilson began to study Luigi's plam, tracing life lines, heart lines, head lines, and so on, and noting carefully their relations with the cobweb of finer and more delicate marks and lines that enmeshed them on all sides; he felt of the fleshy cushion at the base of the thumb, and noted its shape; he felt of the fleshy side of the hand between the wrist and the base of the little finger, and noted its shape also; he pains-takingly examined the fingers, observing their form, proportions and natural manner of disposing themselves when in repose. All this process was watched by the three spectators with absorbing interest, their heads bent together over Luigi's palm and nobody disturbing the stillness with a word. Wilson now entered upon a close survey of the palm again, and his revelations began.

He mapped out Luigi's character and disposition, his tastes, aversions, proclivities, ambitions and eccentricities in a way which sometimes made Luigi wince and the others laugh, but both Twins declared that the chart was artistically drawn and was correct.

Next, Wilson took up Luigi's history. He proceeded cautiously and with hesitation, now, moving his finger slowly along the great lines of the palm, and now and then halting it at a "star" or some such landmark and examining that neighborhood minutely. He proclaimed one or two past events, Luigi confirmed his correctness, and the search went on. Presently Wilson glanced up suddenly with a surprised expression—

"Here is record of an incident which you would perhaps not wish me to—"

"Bring it out," said Luigi, good-naturedly, "I promise you it shan't embarrass me."

But Wilson still hesitated, and did not seem quite to know what to do. Then he said—

"I think it is too delicate a matter to—to—. I believe I would rather write it or whisper it to you, and let you decide for yourself whether you want it talked out or not."

"That will answer," said Luigi; "write it."

Wilson wrote something on a slip of paper and handed it to Luigi, who read it to himself and said to Tom—

"Unfold your slip and read it, Mr. Driscoll."

Tom read:

"*It was prophesied that I would kill a man. It came true before the year was out.*" Tom added, "Great Scott!"

Luigi handed Wilson's paper to Tom and said—

"Now read this one."

Tom read.

"*You have killed some one—but whether man, woman or child, I do not make out.*" "Caesar's ghost!" commented Tom, with astonishment. "It beats anything that was ever heard of! Why, a man's own hand is his deadliest enemy! Just think of that—a man's own hand keeps a record of the deepest and fatalest secrets of his life, and is treacherously ready to expose him to any black-magic stranger that comes along. But what do you let a person look at your hand for, with that awful thing printed in it?"

"Oh," said Luigi reposefully, "I don't mind it. I killed the man for good reasons, and I don't regret it."

"What were the reasons?"

"Well, he needed killing."

"I'll tell you why he did it, since he won't say himself," said Angelo warmly. "He did it to save my life—that's what he did it for. So it was a noble act, and not a thing to be hid in the dark."

"So it was, so it was," said Wilson; "to do such a thing to save a brother's life is a great and fine action."

"Now come," said Luigi, "it is very pleasant to hear you say these things, but for unselfishness, or heroism, or magnanimity, the circumstance won't stand scrutiny. You overlook one detail: suppose I hadn't saved Angelo's life, what would have become of mine? If I had let the man kill him, wouldn't he have killed me, too? I saved my own life, you see."

"Yes, that is your way of talking," said Angelo, "but I know you, and I don't believe you thought of yourself at all. I keep that weapon yet that Luigi killed the man with, and I'll show it to you some time. That incident makes it interesting, and it had a history before it came into Luigi's hands which adds to its interest. It was given to Luigi by a great Indian prince, the Gaikowar of Baroda, and it had been in his family two or three centuries. It killed a good many disagreeable people who troubled that hearthstone at one time and another. It isn't much to look at, except that it isn't shaped like other knives, or dirks, or whatever it may be called— here, I'll draw it for you." He took a sheet of paper and made a rapid sketch. "There it is—a broad and murderous blade, with edges like a razor for sharpness. The devices engraved on it are the ciphers or names of its long line of possessors—I had Luigi's name added in Roman letters, myself, with our coat of arms, as you see. You notice what a curious handle the thing has. It is solid ivory, polished like a mirror, and is four or five inches long—round, and as thick as a large man's wrist, with the end squared off flat, for your thumb to rest on; for you grasp it, with your thumb resting on the blunt end—so—and lift it aloft and strike downwards. The Gaikowar showed us how the thing was done when he gave it to Luigi, and before that night was ended Luigi had used the knife and the Gaikowar was a man short by reason of it. The sheath is magnificently ornamented with gems of great value. You will find the sheath more worth looking at than the knife itself, of course."

Tom said to himself:

"It's lucky I came here; I would have sold that knife for a song; I supposed the jewels were glass."

"But go on—don't stop," said Wilson. "Our curiosity is up, now, to hear about the homicide. Tell us about that."

"Well, briefly, the knife was to blame for that, all around. A native servant slipped into our room in the palace in the night, to kill us and steal that knife on account of the fortune encrusted on its sheath, without a doubt. Luigi had it under his pillow; we were in bed together. There was a dim night-light burning. I was asleep, but Luigi was awake, and he thought he detected a vague form nearing the bed. He slipped the knife out of the sheath, and was ready and unembarrassed by hampering bed-clothes, for the weather was hot and we hadn't any. Suddenly that native rose at the bedside and bent over me with his right hand lifted and a dirk in it aimed at my throat, but Luigi grabbed his wrist, pulled him downward and drove his own knife into the man's neck. That is the whole story."

Wilson and Tom drew deep breaths, and after some general chat about the tragedy, Pudd'nhead said, taking Tom's hand—

"Now Tom, I've never had a look at your palms, as it happens; perhaps you've got some little questionable privacies that need—hel-lo!"

Tom had snatched away his hand, and was looking a good deal confused.

"Why, he's blushing!" said Luigi.

Tom darted an ugly look at him and said, sharply—

"Well, if I am, it ain't because I'm a murderer!" Luigi's dark face flushed, but before he could speak or move, Tom added with anxious haste, "Oh, I beg a thousand pardons, I didn't mean that, it was out before I thought, and I'm very, very sorry—you must forgive me!"

Wilson came to the rescue, and smoothed things down as well as he could; and in fact was entirely successful as far as the Twins were concerned, for they felt sorrier for the affront put upon him by his guest's outburst of ill manners than for the insult offered to Luigi; but the success was not so pronounced with the offender. Tom tried to seem at his ease, and he went through the motions

fairly well, but at bottom he felt resentful toward all the three witnesses of his exhibition—in fact he felt so annoyed at them for
having witnessed it and noticed it that he almost forgot to feel
annoyed at himself for placing it before them. However, something
presently happened which made him almost comfortable, and
brought him nearly back to a state of charity and friendliness. This
was a little spat between the Twins; not much of a spat, but still a
spat; and before they got far with it they were in a decided condition of irritation with each other. Tom was charmed; so pleased,
indeed, that he cautiously did what he could to increase the irritation while pretending to be actuated by more respectable motives.
By his help the fire got warmed up to the blazing point, and he
might have had the happiness of seeing the flames show up, in
another moment, but for the interruption of a knock on the door
—an interruption which fretted him as much as it gratified Wilson.
Wilson opened the door.

The visitor was a good-natured, ignorant, energetic, middle-aged
Irishman named John Buckstone, who was a great politician in a
small way, and always took a large share in public matters of every
sort. One of the town's chief excitements just now, was over the
matter of rum. There was a strong rum party and a strong anti-rum
party. Buckstone was training with the rum party, and he had been
sent to hunt up the Twins and invite them to attend a mass meeting of that faction. He delivered his errand and said the clans were
already gathering in the big hall over the market house. Luigi
accepted the invitation cordially, Angelo less cordially, since he dis-
liked crowds, and did not drink the powerful intoxicants of America. In fact, he was even a teetotaler sometimes—when it was judicious to be one.

The Twins left with Buckstone, and Tom Driscoll joined company with them uninvited.

In the distance one could see a long wavering line of torches
drifting down the main street, and could hear the throbbing of the
bass drum, the clash of cymbals, the squeaking of a fife or two, and
the faint roar of remote hurrahs. The tail end of this procession was
climbing the market house stairs when the Twins arrived in its
neighborhood; when they reached the hall it was full of people,
torches, smoke, noise and enthusiasm. They were conducted to the
platform by Buckstone,—Tom Driscoll still following—and were
delivered to the chairman in the midst of a prodigious explosion of
welcome. When the noise had moderated a little, the chair proposed that "our illustrious guests be at once elected, by complimen-
tary acclamation, to membership in our ever glorious organization,
the paradise of the free and the perdition of the slave."

This eloquent discharge opened the flood-gates of enthusiasm again, and the election was carried with thundering unanimity. Then arose a storm of cries:

"Wet them down! wet them down! give them a drink!"

Glasses of whisky were handed to the Twins. Luigi waved his aloft, then brought it to his lips, but Angelo set his down. There was another storm of cries—

"What's the matter with the other one?" "What is the blonde one going back on us for?" "Explain! Explain!"

The chairman inquired, and then reported—

"We have made an unfortunate mistake, gentlemen. I find that the Count Angelo Cappello is opposed to our creed—is a teetotaler, in fact, and was not intending to apply for membership with us. He desires that we reconsider the vote by which he was elected. What is the pleasure of the house?"

There was a general burst of laughter, plentifully accented with whistlings and cat-calls, but the energetic use of the gavel presently restored something like order. Then a man spoke from the crowd and said that while he was very sorry that the mistake had been made, it would not be possible to rectify it at the present meeting. According to the bye-laws it must go over to the next regular meeting for action. He would not offer a motion, as none was required. He desired to apologize to the gentleman in the name of the house, and begged to assure him that as far as it might lie in the power of the Sons of Liberty, his temporary membership in the order would be made pleasant to him.

This speech was received with great applause, mixed with cries of—

"That's the talk!" "He's a good fellow, anyway, if he *is* a teetotaler!" "Drink his health!" "Give him a rouser, and no heel-taps!"

Glasses were handed around, and everybody on the platform drank Angelo's health, while the house bellowed forth in song:

> "For he's a jolly good fel-low,
> For he's a jolly good fel-low,
> For he's a jolly good fe-el-low—
> Which nobody can deny."

Tom Driscoll drank. It was his second glass, for he had drunk Angelo's the moment that Angelo had set it down. The two drinks made him very merry—almost idiotically so—and he began to take a most lively and prominent part in the proceedings, particularly in the music and cat-calls and side-remarks.

The chairman was still standing at the front, the Twins at his side. The extraordinarily close resemblance of the brothers to each other suggested a witticism to Tom Driscoll, and just as the Chairman began a speech he skipped forward and said with an air of tipsy confidence to the audience—

"Boys, I move that he keeps still and lets this human philopena[1] snip you out a speech."

The descriptive aptness of the phrase caught the house, and a mighty burst of laughter followed.

Luigi's southern blood leaped to the boiling-point in a moment under the sharp humiliation of this insult delivered in the presence of four hundred strangers. It was not in the young man's nature to let the matter pass, or to delay the squaring of the account. He took a couple of strides and halted behind the unsuspecting joker. Then he drew back and delivered a kick of such titanic vigor that it lifted Tom clear over the footlights and landed him on the heads of the front row of the Sons of Liberty.

Even a sober person does not like to have a human being emptied on him when he is not doing any harm; a person who is not sober cannot endure such an attention at all. The nest of Sons of Liberty that Driscoll landed in had not a sober bird in it; in fact there was probably not an entirely sober one in the auditorium. Driscoll was promptly and indignantly flung onto the heads of Sons in the next row, and these Sons passed him on toward the rear, and then immediately began to pummel the front-row Sons who had passed him to them. This course was strictly followed by bench after bench as Driscoll traveled in his tumultuous and airy flight toward the door; so he left behind him an ever lengthening wake of raging and plunging and fighting and swearing humanity. Down went group after group of torches, and presently, above the deafen-

---

1. See Textual Notes to *Pudd'nhead Wilson*, 56.18, below.

ing clatter of the gavel, roar of angry voices and crash of succumbing benches, rose the paralyzing cry of

"FIRE!"

The fighting ceased instantly; the cursings ceased; for one distinctly defined moment there was a dead hush, a motionless calm, where the tempest had been; then with one impulse the multitude awoke to life and energy again, and went surging and struggling and swaying, this way and that, its outer edges melting away through windows and doors and gradually lessening the pressure and relieving the mass.

The fire-boys were never on hand so suddenly before; for there was no distance to go, this time, their quarters being in the rear end of the market house. There was an engine company and a hook and ladder company. Half of each was composed of rummies and the other half of anti-rummies, after the moral and political share-and-share-alike fashion of the frontier town of the period. Enough anti-rummies were loafing in quarters to man the engine and the ladders. In two minutes they had their red shirts and helmets on—they never stirred officially in unofficial costume—and as the mass meeting overhead smashed through the long row of windows and poured out upon the roof of the arcade, the deliverers were ready for them with a powerful stream of water which washed some of them off the roof and nearly drowned the rest. But water was preferable to fire, and still the stampede from the windows continued, and still the pitiless drenchings assailed it until the building was empty; then the fire-boys mounted to the hall and flooded it with water enough to annihilate forty times as much fire as there was there: for a village fire company does not often get a chance to show off, and so when it does get a chance it makes the most of it. Such citizens of that village as were of a thoughtful and judicious temperament did not insure against fire, they insured against the fire-company.

Chapter 12

> *Courage is resistance to fear, mastery of fear—not absence of fear. Except a creature be part coward it is not a compliment to say it is brave, it is merely a loose misapplication of the word. Consider the flea!—incomparably the bravest of all the creatures of God, if ignorance of fear were courage. Whether you are asleep or awake he will attack you, caring nothing for the fact that in bulk and strength you are to him as are the massed armies of the earth to a sucking child; he lives both day and night and all days and nights in the very lap of peril and the immediate presence of death, and yet is no more afraid than is the man who walks the streets of a city that was threatened by an earthquake ten centuries before. When we speak of Clive, Nelson and Putnam as men who "didn't know what fear was," we ought always to add the flea—and put him at the head of the procession.*
> —PUDD'NHEAD WILSON'S CALENDAR.

Judge Driscoll was in bed and asleep by ten o'clock on Friday night, and he was up and gone a-fishing before daylight in the morning with his friend Pembroke Howard. These two had been boys together in Virginia when that State still ranked as the chief and most imposing member of the Union, and they still coupled the proud and affectionate adjective "old" with her name when they spoke of her. In Missouri a recognized superiority attached to any person who hailed from Old Virginia; and this superiority was exalted to supremacy when a person of such nativity could also prove descent from the First Families of that great commonwealth. The Howards and Driscolls were of this aristocracy. In their eyes it was a nobility. It had its unwritten laws, and they were as clearly defined and as strict as any that could be found among the printed statutes of the land. The F.F.V. was born a gentleman; his highest duty in life was to watch over that great inheritance and keep it unsmirched. He must keep his honor spotless. Those laws were his chart; his course was marked out on it; if he swerved from it by so much as half a point of the compass it meant shipwreck to his honor; that is to say, degradation from his rank as a gentleman. These laws required certain things of him which his religion might forbid: then his religion must yield—the laws could not be relaxed to accommodate religion or anything else. Honor stood first; and the laws defined what it was and wherein it differed, in certain details, from honor as defined by church creeds and by the social laws and customs of some of the minor divisions of the globe that had got crowded out when the sacred boundaries of Virginia were staked out.

If Judge Driscoll was the recognized first citizen of Dawson's Landing, Pembroke Howard was easily its recognized second citizen. He was called "the great lawyer"—an earned title. He and Driscoll were of the same age—a year or two past sixty.

Although Driscoll was a free-thinker and Howard a strong and determined Presbyterian, their warm intimacy suffered no impairment in consequence. They were men whose opinions were their own property and not subject to revision and amendment, suggestion or criticism, by anybody, even their friends.

The day's fishing finished, they came floating down stream in their skiff, talking national politics and other high matters, and presently met a skiff coming up from town, with a man in it who said:

"I reckon you know one of the new Twins gave your nephew a kicking last night, Judge?"

"Did *what*?"

"Gave him a kicking."

The old Judge's lips paled and his eyes began to flame. He choked with anger for a moment, then he got out what he was trying to say—

"Well—well—go on! Give me the details."

The man did it. At the finish, the Judge was silent a minute, turning over in his mind the shameful picture of Tom's flight over the footlights, then he said, as if musing aloud—

"Hm—I don't understand it. I was asleep at home. He didn't wake me. Thought he was competent to manage his affair without my help, I reckon." His face lit up with pride and pleasure at that thought, and he said with a cheery complacency, "I like that—it's the true old blood—hey, Pembroke?"

Howard smiled an iron smile and nodded his head approvingly. Then the news-bringer spoke again—

"But Tom beat the twin on the trial."

The Judge looked at the man wonderingly, and said—

"The trial? What trial?"

"Why, Tom had him up before Judge Robinson for assault and battery."

The old man shrank suddenly together like one who has received a death-stroke. Howard sprang for him as he sank forward in a swoon, and took him in his arms, and bedded him on his back in the boat. He sprinkled water in his face, and said to the startled visitor—

"Go, now—don't let him come to and find you here. You see what an effect your heedless speech has had; you ought to have been more considerate than to blurt out such a cruel piece of slander as that."

"I'm right down sorry I did it, now, Mr. Howard, and I wouldn't have done it if I had thought; but it ain't a slander, it's perfectly true, just as I told him."

He rowed away. Presently the old Judge came out of his faint and looked up piteously into the sympathetic face that was bent over him.

"Say it ain't true, Pembroke, tell me it ain't true!" he said, in a weak voice.

There was nothing weak in the deep organ-tones that responded—

"You know it's a lie as well as I do, old friend. He is of the best blood of the Old Dominion."

"God bless you for saying it!" said the old gentleman fervently. "Ah, Pembroke, it was such a blow!"

Howard stayed by his friend, and saw him home, and entered the house with him. It was dark, and past supper time, but the Judge was not thinking of supper, he was eager to hear the slander refuted from headquarters, and as eager to have Howard hear it, too. Tom was sent for, and he came immediately. He was bruised and lame, and was not a happy-looking object. His uncle made him sit down, and said—

"We have been hearing about your adventure, Tom, with a handsome lie added to it for embellishment. Now pulverize that lie to dust! What measures have you taken? How does the thing stand?"

Tom answered guilelessly: "It don't stand at all; it's all over. I had him up in court and beat him. Pudd'nhead Wilson defended him—first case he ever had, and lost it. The judge fined the miserable hound five dollars for the assault."

Howard and the Judge sprang to their feet with the opening sentence—why, neither knew; then they stood gazing vacantly at each other. Howard stood a moment, then sat mournfully down without saying anything. The Judge's wrath began to kindle, and he burst out—

"You cur! you scum! you vermin! Do you mean to tell me that blood of my race has suffered a blow and crawled to a court of law about it? Answer me!"

Tom's head drooped, and he answered with an eloquent silence. His uncle stared at him with a mixed expression of amazement and shame and incredulity that was sorrowful to see. At last he said—

"Which of the twins was it?"

"Count Luigi."

"You have challenged him?"

"N-no," hesitated Tom, turning pale.

"You will challenge him to-night. Howard will carry it."

Tom began to turn sick, and to show it. He turned his hat round and round in his hand, his uncle glowering blacker and blacker upon him as the heavy seconds drifted by; then at last he began to stammer, and said, piteously—

"Oh, please don't ask me to do it, uncle! I never could. He is a murderous devil. I-I'm afraid of him!"

Old Driscoll's mouth opened and closed three times before he could get it to perform its office; then he stormed out—

"A coward in my family! A Driscoll a coward! Oh, what have I done to deserve this infamy!" He tottered to his secretary in the corner repeating that lament again and again in heart-breaking tones, and got out of a drawer a paper, which he slowly tore to bits scattering the bits absently in his track as he walked up and down the room, still grieving and lamenting. At last he said—

"There it is, shreds and fragments once more—my will. Once more you have forced me to disinherit you, you base son of a most noble father! Leave my sight! Go—before I spit on you!"

The young man did not tarry. Then the Judge turned to Howard:

"You will be my second, old friend?"

"Of course."

"There is pen and paper. Draft the cartel, and lose no time."

"The Count shall have it in his hands in fifteen minutes," said Howard.

Tom was very heavy-hearted. His appetite was gone with his property and his self-respect. He went out the back way and wandered down the obscure lane, grieving, and wondering if any course of future conduct, however discreet and carefully perfected and watched over, could win back his uncle's favor and persuade him to reconstruct once more that generous will which had just gone to ruin before his eyes. He finally concluded that it could. He said to himself that he had accomplished this sort of triumph once already, and that what had been done once could be done again. He would set about it. He would bend every energy to the task, and he would score that triumph once more, cost what it might to his convenience, limit as it might his frivolous and liberty-loving life.

"To begin," he said to himself, "I'll square up with the proceeds of my raid, and then gambling has got to be stopped—and stopped short off. It's the worst vice I've got—from my standpoint, anyway, because it's the one he can most easily find out, through the impatience of my creditors. He thought it expensive to have to pay two hundred dollars to them for me once. Expensive—*that!* Why, it cost me the whole of his fortune—but of course he never thought of that; some people can't think of any but their own side of a case. If he had known how deep I am in, now, the will would have gone to pot without waiting for a duel to help. Three hundred dollars! It's a pile! But he'll never hear of it, I'm thankful to say. The minute I've cleared it off, I'm safe; and I'll never touch a card again. Anyway I won't while he lives, I make oath to that. I'm entering on my last reform—I know it—yes, and I'll win; but after that, if I ever slip again I'm gone."

Chapter 13

When I reflect upon the number of disagreeable people who I know have gone to a better world, I am moved to lead a different life.
—PUDD'NHEAD WILSON'S CALENDAR.

OCTOBER. *This is one of the peculiarly dangerous months to speculate in stocks in. The others are July, January, September, April, November, May, March, June, December, August, and February.*
—PUDD'NHEAD WILSON'S CALENDAR.

Thus mournfully communing with himself Tom moped along the lane past Pudd'nhead Wilson's house, and still on and on, between fences enclosing vacant country on each hand, till he neared the haunted house, then he came moping back again, with many sighs and heavy with trouble. He sorely wanted cheerful company. Rowena! His heart gave a bound at the thought, but the next thought quieted it—the detested Twins would be there.

He was on the inhabited side of Wilson's house, and now as he approached it he noticed that the sitting-room was lighted. This would do; others made him feel unwelcome sometimes, but Wilson never failed in courtesy toward him, and a kindly courtesy does at least save one's feelings, even if it is not professing to stand for a welcome. Wilson heard footsteps at his threshold, then the clearing of a throat.

"It's that fickle-tempered, dissipated young goose—poor devil, he finds friends pretty scarce to-day, likely, after the disgrace of carrying a personal-assault case into a law-court."

A dejected knock. "Come in!"

Tom entered and drooped into a chair, without saying anything. Wilson said, kindly—

"Why, my boy, you look desolate. Don't take it so hard. Try and forget you have been kicked."

"Oh, dear," said Tom, wretchedly, "it's not that, Pudd'nhead—it's not that. It's a thousand times worse than that—oh, yes, a million times worse."

"Why, Tom, what do you mean? Has Rowena—"

"Flung me? No, but the old man has."

Wilson said to himself, "Aha!" and thought of the mysterious girl in the bed-room. "The Driscolls have been making discoveries!" Then he said aloud, gravely:

"Tom, there are some kinds of dissipation which—"

"Oh, shucks, this hasn't got anything to do with dissipation. He wanted me to challenge that derned Italian savage, and I wouldn't do it."

"Yes, of course he would do that," said Wilson in a meditative matter-of-course way; "but the thing that puzzled me, was, why he didn't look to that last night, for one thing, and why he let you carry such a matter into a court of law at all, either before the duel or after it. It's no place for it. It was not like him. I couldn't understand it. How did it happen?"

"It happened because he didn't know anything about it. He was asleep when I got home last night."

"And you didn't wake him? Tom, is that possible?"

Tom was not getting much comfort here. He fidgeted a moment, then said:

"I didn't choose to tell him—that's all. He was going a-fishing before dawn, with Pembroke Howard, and if I got the Twins into the common calaboose,—and I thought sure I could—I never dreamed of their slipping out on a paltry fine for such an outrageous offense—well, once in the calaboose they would be disgraced, and uncle wouldn't want any duels with that sort of characters, and wouldn't allow any."

"Tom, I am ashamed of you! I don't see how you could treat

your good old uncle so. I am a better friend of his than you are; for if I had known the circumstances I would have kept that case out of court until I got word to him and let him have a gentleman's chance."

"You would?" exclaimed Tom, with lively surprise. "And it your first case! and you know perfectly well there never would have *been* any case if he had got that chance, don't you? and you'd have finished your days a pauper nobody, instead of being an actually launched and recognized lawyer to-day. And you would really have done that, would you?"

"Certainly."

Tom looked at him a moment or two, then shook his head sorrowfully and said—

"I believe you—upon my word I do. I don't know why I do, but I do. Pudd'nhead Wilson, I think you're the biggest fool I ever saw."

"Thank you."

"Don't mention it."

"Well, he has been requiring you to fight the Italian and you have refused. You degenerate remnant of an honorable line! I'm thoroughly ashamed of you, Tom!"

"Oh, that's nothing! I don't care for anything, now that the will's torn up again."

"Tom, tell me squarely—didn't he find any fault with you for anything but those two things—carrying the case into court and refusing to fight?"

He watched the young fellow's face narrowly, but it was entirely reposeful, and so also was the voice that answered:

"No, he didn't find any other fault with me. If he had had any to find, he would have begun yesterday, for he was just in the humor for it. He drove that jack-pair around town and showed them the sights, and when he came home he couldn't find his father's old silver watch that don't keep time and he thinks so much of, and couldn't remember what he did with it three or four days ago when he saw it last; and so when I arrived he was all in a sweat about it, and when I suggested that it probably wasn't lost but stolen, it put him in a regular passion and he said I was a fool —which convinced me, without any trouble, that that was just what he was afraid *had* happened, himself, but did not want to believe it, because lost things stand a better chance of being found again than stolen ones."

"Whe-ew!" whistled Wilson; "score another on the list."

"Another what?"

"Another theft!"

"Theft?"

"Yes, theft. That watch isn't lost, it's stolen. There's been another raid on the town—and just the same old mysterious sort of thing that has happened once before, as you remember."

"You don't mean it!"

"It's as sure as you are born! Have you missed anything yourself?"

"No. That is, I did miss a silver pencil case that aunt Mary Pratt gave me last birth-day—"

"You'll find it's stolen—that's what you'll find."

"No, I shan't; for when I suggested theft about the watch and got such a rap, I went and examined my room, and the pencil-case was missing, but it was only mislaid, and I found it again."

"You are sure you missed nothing else?"

"Well, nothing of consequence. I missed a small plain gold ring worth two or three dollars, but that will turn up. I'll look again."

"In my opinion you'll not find it. There's been a raid, I tell you. Come *in!*"

Mr. Justice Robinson entered, followed by Buckstone and the town constable, Jim Blake. They sat down, and after some wandering and aimless weather-conversation, Wilson said—

"By the way, we've just added another to the list of thefts, maybe two. Judge Driscoll's old silver watch is gone, and Tom here has missed a gold ring."

"Well, it is a bad business," said the Justice, "and gets worse the further it goes. The Hankses, the Dobsons, the Pilligrews, the Ortons, the Grangers, the Hales, the Fullers, the Holcombs, in fact everybody that lives around about Patsy Cooper's has been robbed of little things like trinkets and teaspoons and such-like small valuables that are easily carried off. It's perfectly plain that the thief took advantage of the reception at Patsy Cooper's, when all the neighbors were in her house and all their niggers hanging around her fence for a look at the show, to raid the vacant houses undisturbed. Patsy is miserable about it; miserable on account of the neighbors, and particularly miserable on account of her foreigners, of course; so miserable on their account that she hasn't any room to worry about her own little losses."

"It's the same old raider," said Wilson, "I suppose there isn't any doubt about that."

"Constable Blake doesn't think so."

"No, you're wrong there," said Blake, "the other times it was a man; there was plenty of signs of that, as we know, in the profession, though we never got hands on him; but this time it's a woman."

Wilson thought of the mysterious girl, straight off. She was always in his mind, now. But she failed him again. Blake continued:

"She's a stoop-shouldered old woman with a covered basket on her arm in a black veil dressed in mourning. I saw her going aboard the ferry-boat yesterday. Lives in Illinois, I reckon; but I don't care where she lives, I'm going to get her—she can make herself sure of that."

"What makes you think she's the thief?"

"Well, there ain't any other, for one thing; and for another, some of the nigger draymen that happened to be driving along saw her coming out or going into houses and told me so—and it just happens that they was *robbed* houses, every time."

It was granted that this was plenty good enough circumstantial evidence. A pensive silence followed, which lasted for some moments, then Wilson said—

"There's one good thing, anyway. She can't either pawn or sell Count Luigi's costly Indian dagger."

"My!" said Tom; "is *that* gone?"

"Yes."

"Well, that was a haul! But why can't she pawn it or sell it?"

"Because when the Twins went home from the Sons of Liberty meeting last night, news of the raid was sifting in from everywhere and Aunt Patsy was in distress to know if they had lost anything. They found that the dagger was gone, and they notified the police and pawnbrokers everywhere. It was a great haul, yes, but the old woman won't get anything out of it, because she'll get caught."

"Did they offer a reward?" asked Buckstone.

"Yes—five hundred dollars for the knife, and five hundred more for the thief."

"What a leather-headed idea!" exclaimed the constable. "The thief dasn't go near them, nor send anybody. Whoever goes is going to get himself nabbed, for there ain't any pawnbroker that's going to lose the chance to—"

If anybody had noticed Tom's face at that time, the gray-green color of it might have provoked curiosity; but nobody did. He said to himself, "I'm gone! I never can square up; the rest of the plunder won't pawn or sell for half of the bill. Oh, I know it—I'm gone, I'm gone—and this time it's for good. Oh, this is awful—I don't know what to do, nor which way to turn!"

"Softly, softly," said Wilson to Blake, "I planned their scheme for them at midnight last night, and it was all finished up ship shape by two this morning. They'll get their dagger back, and then I'll explain to you how the thing was done."

There were strong signs of a general curiosity, and Buckstone said—

"Well, you have whetted us up pretty sharp, Wilson, and I'm free to say that if you don't mind telling us in confidence—"

"Oh, I'd as soon tell as not, Buckstone, but as long as the Twins and I agreed to say nothing about it, we must let it stand so. But you can take my word for it you won't be kept waiting three days. Somebody will apply for that reward pretty promptly, and I'll show you the thief and the dagger both very soon afterward."

The Constable was disappointed, and also perplexed. He said—

"It may all be—yes, and I hope it will, but I'm blamed if I can see my way through it. It's too many for yours truly."

The subject seemed about talked out. Nobody seemed to have anything further to offer. After a silence the justice of the peace informed Wilson that he and Buckstone and the constable had come as a committee, on the part of the Democratic party, to ask him to run for mayor—for the little town was about to become a city and the first charter election was approaching. It was the first attention which Wilson had ever received at the hands of any party; it was a sufficiently humble one, but it was a recognition of his début into the town's life and activities at last; it was a step upward, and he was deeply gratified. He accepted, and the committee departed, followed by young Tom.

Chapter 14

The true southern watermelon is a boon apart, and not to be mentioned with commoner things. It is chief of this world's luxuries, king by the grace of God over all the fruits of the earth. When one has tasted it, he knows what the angels eat. It was not a southern watermelon that Eve took: we know it because she repented.
—PUDD'NHEAD WILSON'S CALENDAR.

About the time that Wilson was bowing the committee out, Pembroke Howard was entering the next house to report. He found the old Judge sitting grim and straight in his chair, waiting.

"Well, Howard—the news?"

"The best in the world."

"Accepts, does he?" and the light of battle gleamed joyously in the Judge's eye.

"Accepts? Why, he jumped at it."

"Did, did he? Now that's fine—that's very fine. I like that. When is it to be?"

"Now! Straight off! To-night! An admirable fellow—admirable!"

"Admirable? He's a darling! Why, it's an honor as well as a pleasure to stand up before such a man. Come—off with you! Go and arrange everything—and give him my heartiest compliments. A rare fellow, indeed; an admirable fellow, as you have said!"

Howard hurried away, saying—

"I'll have him in the vacant stretch between Wilson's and the haunted house within the hour, and I'll bring my own pistols."

Judge Driscoll began to walk the floor in a state of pleased excite-

ment; but presently he stopped, and began to think—began to
think of Tom. Twice he moved toward the secretary, and twice he
turned away again; but finally he said—

"This may be my last night in the world—I must not take the
chance. He is worthless and unworthy, but it is largely my fault. He
was entrusted to me by my brother on his dying bed, and I have
indulged him to his hurt, instead of training him up severely and
making a man of him. I have violated my trust, and I must not add
the sin of desertion to that. I have forgiven him once, already, and
would subject him to a long and hard trial before forgiving him
again, if I could live; but I must not run that risk. No, I must
restore the will. But if I survive the duel I will hide it away and he
will not know, and I will not tell him until he reforms and I see
that his reformation is going to be permanent."

He re-drew the will, and his ostensible nephew was heir to a fortune again. As he was finishing his task, Tom, wearied with another
brooding tramp, entered the house and went tip-toeing past the sitting-room door. He glanced in, and hurried on, for the sight of his
uncle had nothing but terrors for him to-night. But his uncle was
writing! That was unusual at this late hour. What could he be writing? A chill anxiety settled down upon Tom's heart. Did that writing concern him? He was afraid so. He reflected that when ill luck
begins, it does not come in sprinkles, but in showers. He said he
would get a glimpse of that document or know the reason why. He
heard someone coming, and stepped out of sight and hearing. It
was Pembroke Howard. What could be hatching?

Howard said, with great satisfaction—

"Everything's right and ready. He's gone to the battle-ground
with his second and the surgeon—also with his brother. I've

arranged it all with Wilson—Wilson's his second. We are to have three shots apiece."

"Good! How is the moon?"

"Bright as day, nearly. Perfect for the distance—fifteen yards. No wind—not a breath; hot and still."

"All good; all first-rate. Here, Pembroke, read this, and witness it."

Pembroke read and witnessed the will, then gave the old man's hand a hearty shake and said—

"Now that's right, York—but I knew you would do it. You couldn't leave that poor chap to fight along without means or profession, with certain defeat before him, and I knew you wouldn't, for his father's sake if not for his own."

"For his dead father's sake I couldn't, I know; for poor Percy—but you know what Percy was to me. But mind—Tom is not to know of this unless I fall to-night."

"I understand. I'll keep the secret."

The Judge put the will away, and the two started for the battle-ground. In another minute the will was in Tom's hands. His misery vanished, his feelings underwent a tremendous revulsion. He put the will carefully back in its place and spread his mouth and swung his hat once, twice, three times around his head, in imitation of three rousing huzzas, no sound issuing from his lips. He fell to communing with himself excitedly and joyously, but every now and then he let off another volley of dumb hurrahs.

He said to himself: "I've got the fortune again, but I'll not let on that I know about it. And this time I'm going to hang on to it. I take no more risks. I'll gamble no more, I'll drink no more, because —well, because I'll not go where there is any of that sort of thing going on, again. It's the sure way, and the only sure way; I might have thought of that sooner—well, yes, if I had wanted to. But now —dear me, I've had a bad scare this time, and I'll take no more chances. Not a single chance more. Land! I persuaded myself this evening that I could fetch him around without any great amount of effort, but I've been getting more and more heavy-hearted and doubtful straight along, ever since. If he tells me about this thing, all right; but if he doesn't, I shan't let on. I—well, I'd like to tell Pudd'nhead Wilson, but—no, I'll think about that; perhaps I won't." He whirled off another dead huzza, and said, "I'm reformed, and this time I'll stay so, sure!"

He was about to close with a final grand silent demonstration, when he suddenly recollected that Wilson had put it out of his power to pawn or sell the Indian knife, and that he was once more in awful peril of exposure by his creditors for that reason. His joy collapsed utterly, and he turned away and moped toward the door moaning and lamenting over the bitterness of his luck. He dragged himself upstairs, and brooded in his room a long time, disconsolate and forlorn, with Luigi's Indian knife for a text. At last he sighed and said:

"When I supposed these stones were glass and this ivory bone, the thing hadn't any interest for me because it hadn't any value and couldn't help me out of my trouble. But now—why, now it is full of interest; yes, and of a sort to break a body's heart. It's a bag of gold that has turned to dirt and ashes in my hands. It could save me, and save me so easily, and yet I've got to go to ruin. It's like drowning with a life-preserver in my reach. All the hard luck comes to me and all the good luck goes to other people—Pudd'nhead Wilson, for instance; even his career has got a sort of a little start at last, and what has he done to deserve it, I should like to know? Yes, he has opened his own road, but he isn't content with that, but must block mine. It's a sordid, selfish world, and I wish I was out of it." He allowed the light of the candle to play upon the jewels of the sheath, but the flashings and sparklings had no charm for his eye, they were only just so many pangs to his heart. "I must not say anything to Roxy about this thing," he said, "she is too daring. She would be for digging these stones out and selling them, and then— why, she would be arrested and the stones traced, and then—" The thought made him quake, and he hid the knife away, trembling all over and glancing furtively about, like a criminal who fancies that the accuser is already at hand.

Should he try to sleep? Oh, no, sleep was not for him; his trouble was too haunting, too afflicting for that. He must have somebody to mourn with. He would carry his despair to Roxy.

He had heard several distant gun shots, but that sort of thing was not uncommon, and they had made no impression upon him. He went out at the back door, and turned westward. He passed Wilson's house and proceeded along the lane, and presently saw several figures approaching Wilson's place through the vacant lots. These were the duelists returning from the fight; he thought he recognized them, but as he had no desire for white people's company he stooped down behind the fence until they were out of his way.

Roxy was feeling fine. She said:

"Whah was you, child? Warn't you in it?"

"In what?"

"In de duel."

"Duel? Has there been a duel?"

"'Cose dey has. De ole Jedge has been havin' a duel wid one o' dem Twins."

"Great Scott!" Then he added to himself, "That's what made him re-make the will; he thought he might get killed, and it softened him toward me. And that's what he and Howard were so busy about. . . . . . Oh, dear, if the Twin had only killed him, I should be out of my—"

"What is you mumblin' 'bout, Chambers? Whah was you? Didn't you know dey was gwyne to be a duel?"

"No, I didn't. The old man tried to get me to fight one with Count Luigi, but he didn't succeed; so I reckon he concluded to patch up the family honor himself."

He laughed at the idea, and went rambling on with a detailed account of his talk with the Judge, and how shocked and ashamed the Judge was to find that he had a coward in his family. He glanced up at last, and got a shock himself. Roxana's bosom was heaving with suppressed passion, and she was glowering down upon him with measureless contempt written in her face.

"En you refuse' to fight a man dat kicked you, 'stid o' jumpin' at de chance! En you ain't got no mo' feelin' den to come en tell me, dat fetched sich a po' low-down ornery rabbit into de worl'! Pah! it make me sick! It's de nigger in you, dat's what it is. Thirty-one parts o' you is white, en on'y one part nigger, en dat po' little one part is yo' *soul*. 'Tain't wuth savin'; 'tain't wuth totin' out on a shovel en tho'in' in de gutter. You has disgraced yo' birth. What would yo' pa think o' you? It's enough to make him turn in his grave."

The last three sentences stung Tom into a fury, and he said to himself that if his father were only alive and in reach of assassination his mother would soon find that he had a very clear notion of the size of his indebtedness to that man and was willing to pay it up in full, and would do it, too, even at risk of his life; but he kept his thought to himself; that was safest, in his mother's present state.

"What ever has 'come o' yo' Essex blood? Dat's what I can't understan'. En it ain't only jist Essex blood dat's in you, not by a long sight—'deed it ain't! My great-great-great-gran'father en yo' great-great-great-great-gran'father was ole Cap'n John Smith, de highes' blood dat Ole Virginny ever turned out; en *his* great-great-gran'mother or somers along back dah, was Pocahontas de Injun queen, en her husbun' was a nigger king outen Africa—en yit here you is, a slinkin' outen a duel en disgracin' our whole line like a ornery low-down hound! Yes, it's de nigger in you!"

She sat down on her candle-box and fell into a reverie. Tom did not disturb her; he sometimes lacked prudence, but it was not in circumstances of this kind. Roxana's storm went gradually down, but it died hard, and even when it seemed to be quite gone it would now and then break out in a distant rumble, so to speak, in the form of muttered ejaculations. One of these was, "Ain't nigger enough in him to show in his finger-nails, en dat takes mighty little —yit dey's enough to paint his soul."

Presently she muttered, "Yassir, enough to paint a whole thimbleful of 'em." At last her rumblings ceased altogether and her countenance began to clear—a welcome sign to Tom, who had learned her moods and knew she was on the threshold of good-humor, now. He noticed that from time to time she unconsciously carried her finger to the end of her nose. He looked closer and said—

"Why, mammy, the end of your nose is skinned. How did that come?"

She sent out the sort of whole-hearted peal of laughter which God has vouchsafed in its perfection to none but the happy angels in heaven and the bruised and broken black slave on the earth, and said:

"Dad fetch dat duel, I ben in it myself."

"Gracious! did a bullet do that?"

"Yassir, you bet it did!"

"Well, I declare! Why, how did that happen?"

"Happen dis-away. I 'uz a sett'n here kinder dozin' in de dark, en *che-bang!* goes a gun, right out dah. I skips along out towards t'other end o' de house to see what's gwyne on, en stops by de ole winder on de side towards Pudd'nhead Wilson's house dat ain't got no sash in it—but dey ain't none of 'em got any sashes, fur as dat's concerned—en I stood dah in de dark en look out, en dah in de moonlight, right down under me 'uz one o' de Twins a-cussin'—not much, but jist a-cussin' soft,—it 'uz de brown one dat 'uz cussin', caze he 'uz hit in de shoulder. En Doctor Claypool he 'uz a workin' at him, en Pudd'nhead Wilson he 'uz a he'pin, en ole Jedge Driscoll en Pem. Howard 'uz a-standin' out yonder a little piece waitin' for 'em to git ready agin. En toreckly dey squared off en give de word, en *bang-bang* went de pistols, en de twin he say 'Ouch!'—hit him on de han' dis time—en I hear dat same bullet go '*spat!*' agin de logs under de winder; en de nex' time dey shoot, de twin say 'Ouch!' agin, en I done it too, caze de bullet glance' on his cheek bone en skip up here en glance on de side o' de winder en whiz right acrost my face en tuck de hide off'n my nose—why, if I'd a ben jist a inch or a inch en a half furder, 'twould a tuck de whole nose en disfigger' me. Here's de bullet; I hunted her up."

"Did you stand there all the time?"

"Dat's a question to ask, ain't it! What else would I do? Does I git a chance to see a duel every day?"

"Why, you were right in range! Weren't you afraid?"

The woman gave a sniff of scorn.

"'Fraid! De Smith-Pocahontases ain't 'fraid o' nothin', let alone bullets."

"They've got pluck enough, I suppose; what they lack is judgment. *I* wouldn't have stood there."

"Nobody's accusin' you!"

"Did anybody else get hurt?"

"Yes, we all got hit 'cep' de blon' twin en de doctor en de seconds. De Jedge didn't git hurt, but I hear Pudd'nhead say de bullet snip some o' his ha'r off."

"'George!" said Tom to himself, "to come so near being out of my trouble, and miss it by an inch. O, dear, dear, he'll live to find me out and sell me to some nigger-trader yet—yes, and he would do it in a minute." Then he said aloud, in a grave tone—

"Mother, we are in an awful fix."

Roxana caught her breath with a spasm, and said—

"Chile! What you hit a body so sudden for, like dat? What's ben en gone en happen'?"

"Well, there's one thing I didn't tell you. When I wouldn't fight, he tore up the will again, and—"

Roxana's face turned a dead white, and she said—

"Now you's *done!*—done forever! Dat's de end. Bofe un us is gwyne to starve to—"

"Wait and hear me through, can't you! I reckon that when he resolved to fight, himself, he thought he might get killed and not have a chance to forgive me any more in this life, so he made the will again, and I've seen it and it's all right. But—"

"Oh, thank goodness, den we's safe agin!—safe! en so what did you want to come here en talk sich dreadful—"

"Hold *on,* I tell you, and let me finish. The swag I gathered won't half square me up, and the first thing we know my creditors —well, you know what'll happen."

Roxana dropped her chin and told her son to leave her alone— she must think this matter out. Presently she said, impressively:

"You got to go mighty keerful now, I tell you! En here's what you got to do. He didn't git killed, en if you gives him de least reason, he'll bust de will agin, en dat's de *las'* time, now you hear me! So—you's got to show him what you kin do in de nex' few days. You's got to be pison good, en let him see it; you got to do everything dat'll make him b'lieve in you, en you got to sweeten aroun' ole Aunt Pratt, too—she's pow'ful strong wid de Jedge, en de bes' frien' you got. Nex', you'll go 'long away to Sent Louis, en dat'll *keep* him in yo' favor. Den you go en make a bargain wid dem people. You tell 'em he ain't gwyne to live long—en dat's de fac', too—en tell 'em you'll pay 'em intrust, en big intrust, too—ten per—what you call it?"

"Ten per cent a month?"

"Dat's it. Den you take en sell yo' truck aroun', a little at a time, en pay de intrust. How long will it las'?"

"I think there's enough to pay the interest five or six months."

"Den you's all right. If he don't die in six months, dat don't make no diff'rence—Providence 'll provide. You's gwyne to be safe —if you behaves." She bent an austere eye on him and added, "En you *is* gwyne to behave—does you know dat?"

He laughed and said he was going to try, anyway. She did not unbend. She said gravely—

"Tryin' ain't de thing. You's gwyne to *do* it. You ain't gwyne to steal a pin—caze it ain't safe no mo'; en you ain't gwyne into no bad comp'ny—not even once, you understand; en you ain't gwyne to drink a drap—nary a single drap; en you ain't gwyne to gamble one single gamble—not one! Dis ain't what you's gwyne to *try* to do, it's what you's gwyne to *do*. En I'll tell you how I knows it. Dis is how. I's gwyne to foller along to Sent Louis my own self; en you's gwyne to come to me every day o' yo' life, en I'll look you over; en if you fails in one single one o' dem things—jist *once*—I take my oath I'll come straight down to dis town en tell de Jedge you is a nigger en a slave—en *prove* it!" She paused, to let her words sink home. Then she added: "Chambers, does you b'lieve me when I say dat?"

Tom was sober enough now. There was no levity in his voice when he answered:

"Yes, mother. I know, now, that I am reformed—and permanently. Permanently—and beyond the reach of any human temptation."

"Den g'long home en begin!"

Chapter 15

Nothing so needs reforming as other people's habits.
    —PUDD'NHEAD WILSON'S CALENDAR.

*Behold, the fool saith, "Put not all thine eggs in the one basket"—
which is but a manner of saying, "Scatter your money and your attention"; but the wise man saith, "Put all your eggs in the one basket
and—*WATCH THAT BASKET."
    —PUDD'NHEAD WILSON'S CALENDAR.

What a time of it Dawson's Landing was having! All its life it had been asleep, but now it hardly got a chance for a nod, so swiftly did big events and crashing surprises come along in one another's wake: Friday morning, first glimpse of Real Nobility, also grand reception at Aunt Patsy Cooper's, also great robber-raid; Friday evening, dramatic kicking of the heir of the chief citizen in presence of four hundred people; Saturday morning, emergence as practising lawyer of the long-submerged Pudd'nhead Wilson; Saturday night, duel between chief citizen and titled stranger.

The people took more pride in the duel than in all the other events put together, perhaps. It was a glory to their town to have such a thing happen there. In their eyes the principals had reached the summit of human honor. Everybody paid homage to their names; their praises were in all mouths. Even the duelists' subordinates came in for a handsome share of the public approbation: wherefore Pudd'nhead Wilson was suddenly become a man of consequence. When asked to run for the mayoralty Saturday night he was risking defeat, but Sunday morning found him a made man and his success assured.

The twins were prodigiously great, now; the town took them to its bosom with enthusiasm. Day after day, and night after night, they went dining and visiting from house to house, making friends, enlarging and solidifying their popularity, and charming and surprising all with their musical prodigies, and now and then heightening the effects with samples of what they could do in other directions, out of their stock of rare and curious accomplishments. They were so pleased that they gave the regulation thirty days' notice, the required preparation for citizenship, and resolved to finish their days in this pleasant place. That was the climax. The delighted community rose as one man and applauded; and when the twins were asked to stand for seats in the forthcoming aldermanic board, and consented, the public contentment was rounded and complete.

Tom Driscoll was not happy over these things; they sunk deep, and hurt all the way down. He hated the one twin for kicking him, and the other one for being the kicker's brother.

Now and then the people wondered why nothing was heard of the raider, or of the stolen knife or the other plunder, but nobody was able to throw any light on that matter. Nearly a week had drifted by, and still the thing remained a vexed mystery.

On Saturday, Constable Blake and Pudd'nhead Wilson met on the street, and Tom Driscoll joined them in time to open their conversation for them. He said to Blake—

"You are not looking well, Blake, you seem to be annoyed about something. Has anything gone wrong in the detective business? I believe you fairly and justifiably claim to have a pretty good reputation in that line, isn't it so?"—which made Blake feel good, and look it; but Tom added, "for a country detective"—which made Blake feel the other way, and not only look it but betray it in his voice—

"Yes, sir, I *have* got a reputation, and it's as good as anybody's in the profession, too, country or no country."

"Oh, I beg pardon, I didn't mean any offence. What I started out to ask, was, only about the old woman that raided the town—the stoop-shouldered old woman, you know, that you said you were going to catch—and I knew you would, too, because you have the reputation of never boasting, and—well, you—you've caught the old woman?"

"Damn the old woman!"

"Why, sho! you don't mean to say you haven't caught her?"

"No, I haven't caught her. If anybody could have caught her, I could; but nobody couldn't, I don't care who he is."

"I am sorry, real sorry—for your sake; because when it gets around that a detective has expressed himself so confidently, and then—"

"Don't you worry, that's all—don't you worry; and as for the town, the town needn't worry, either. She's my meat—make yourself easy about that. I'm on her track; I've got clews that—"

"That's good! Now if you could get an old veteran detective down from St. Louis to help you find out what the clews mean, and where they lead to, and then—"

"I'm plenty veteran enough myself, and I don't need anybody's help. I'll have her inside of a we—inside of a month. That I'll swear to!"

Tom said, carelessly—

"I suppose that will answer—yes, that will answer. But I reckon she is pretty old, and old people don't often outlive the cautious pace of the professional detective when he has got his clews together and is out on his still-hunt."

Blake's dull face flushed, under this gibe, but before he could set his retort in order Tom had turned to Wilson and was saying, with placid indifference of manner and voice—

"Who got the reward, Pudd'nhead?"

Wilson winced slightly, and saw that his own turn was come.

"What reward?"

"Why, the reward for the thief, and the other one for the knife."

Wilson answered—and rather uncomfortably, to judge by his hesitating fashion of delivering himself—

"Well, the—well, in fact nobody has claimed it yet."

Tom seemed surprised.

"Why, is that so?"

Wilson showed a trifle of irritation when he replied—

"Yes, it's so. And what of it?"

"Oh, nothing. Only I thought you had struck out a new idea and invented a scheme that was going to revolutionize the time-worn and ineffectual methods of the—" He stopped, and turned to

Blake, who was happy, now that another had taken his place on the gridiron: "Blake, didn't you understand him to intimate that it wouldn't be necessary for you to hunt the old woman down?"

"B'George, he said he'd have thief and swag both inside of three days—he did, by hokey! and that's just about a week ago. Why, I said at the time, that no thief and no thief's pal was going to try to pawn or sell a thing where he knowed the pawn-broker could get both rewards by taking *him* into camp *with* the swag. It was the blessedest idea that ever *I* struck!"

"You'd change your mind," said Wilson, with irritated bluntness, "if you knew the entire scheme instead of only part of it."

"Well," said the constable, pensively, "I had the idea that it wouldn't work, and up to now I'm right, anyway."

"Very well, then, let it stand at that, and give it a further show. It has worked at least as well as your own methods, you perceive."

The constable hadn't anything handy to hit back with, so he discharged a discontented sniff and said nothing.

After the night that Wilson had partly revealed his scheme at his house, Tom had tried for several days to guess out the secret of the rest of it, but had failed. Then it occurred to him to give Roxana's smarter head a chance at it. He made up a supposititious case and laid it before her. She thought it over, and delivered her verdict upon it. Tom said to himself, "She's hit it, sure!" He thought he would test that verdict, now, and watch Wilson's face; so he said, reflectively—

"Wilson, you're not a fool—a fact of recent discovery. Whatever your scheme was, it had sense in it, Blake's opinion to the contrary notwithstanding. I don't ask you to reveal it, but I will suppose a case—a case which will answer as a starting point for the real thing I'm going to come at, and that's all I want. You offered five hundred dollars for the knife, and five hundred for the thief. We will suppose, for argument's sake, that the first reward is *advertised*, and the second offered by *private letter* to the pawnbrokers and —"

Blake slapped his thigh and cried out—

"By Jackson he's got you, Pudd'nhead! Now why couldn't I or *any* fool have thought of that?"

Wilson said to himself, "Anybody with a reasonably good head would have thought of it. I am not surprised that Blake didn't detect it, I am only surprised that Tom did. There is more to him than I supposed." He said nothing aloud, and Tom went on:

"Very well. The thief would not suspect that there was a trap, and he would bring or send the knife and say he bought it for a song, or found it in the road, or something like that, and try to collect the reward, and be arrested—wouldn't he?"

"Yes," said Wilson.

"I think so," said Tom. "There can't be any doubt of it. Have you ever seen that knife?"

"No."

"Has any friend of yours?"

"Not that I know of."

"Well, I begin to think I understand why your scheme failed."

"What do you mean, Tom?—What are you driving at?" asked Wilson with a dawning sense of discomfort.

"Why, that there *isn't* any such knife."

"Look here, Wilson," said Blake, "Tom Driscoll's right, for a thousand dollars—if I had it."

Wilson's blood warmed a little, and he wondered if he had been played upon by those strangers—it certainly had something of that look. But what could they gain by it? He threw out that suggestion. Tom replied:

"Gain? Oh, nothing that you would value, maybe. But they are strangers making their way in a new community. Is it nothing to them to appear as pets of an Oriental prince—at no expense? Is it nothing to them to be able to dazzle this poor little town with thousand-dollar rewards—at no expense? Wilson, there isn't any such knife, or your scheme would have fetched it to light. Or if there is any such knife they've got it yet. I believe, myself, that they've seen such a knife, for Angelo pictured it out with his pencil too swiftly and handily for him to have been inventing it; and of course I can't swear that they've never had it; but this I'll go bail for—if they had it when they came to this town, they've got it yet."

Blake said,—

"It looks mighty reasonable, the way Tom puts it—it most certainly does."

Tom responded—turning to leave—

"You find the old woman, Blake, and if she can't furnish the knife, go and search the Twins!"

Tom sauntered away. Wilson felt a good deal depressed. He hardly knew what to think. He was loth to withdraw his faith from the Twins, and was resolved not to do it on the present indecisive evidence; but—well, he would think—and then decide how to act.

"Blake, what do you think of this matter?"

"Well, Pudd'nhead, I'm bound to say I put it up the way Tom does. They hadn't the knife; or if they had it they've got it yet."

The men parted. Wilson said to himself:

"I believe they had it; if it had been stolen, the scheme would have restored it, that is certain. And so I believe they've got it yet."

Tom had had no purpose in his mind when he encountered those two men. When he began his talk he hoped to be able to gall them a little and get a trifle of malicious entertainment out of it. But when he left, he left in great spirits, for he perceived that just by pure luck and no troublesome labor, he had accomplished several delightful things: he had touched both men on a raw spot and seen them squirm; he had modified Wilson's sweetness for the Twins with one small bitter taste that he wouldn't be able to get out of his mouth right away; and—best of all—he had taken the hated Twins down a peg with the community; for Blake would gossip around freely, after the manner of detectives, and within a week the town would be laughing at them in its sleeve for offering a gaudy reward for a bauble which they either never possessed or hadn't lost. Tom was very well satisfied with himself.

Tom's behavior at home had been perfect during the entire week. His uncle and aunt had seen nothing like it before. They could find no fault with him anywhere.

On Saturday evening he said to the Judge—

"I've had something preying on my mind, uncle, and as I am going away and might never see you again, I can't bear it any longer. I made you believe I was afraid to fight that Italian adventurer. I had to get out of it on some pretext or other, and maybe I chose badly, being taken unawares, but no honorable person could consent to meet him in the field, knowing what I knew about him."

"Indeed? What was that?"

"Count Luigi is a confessed assassin."

"Incredible!"

"It is perfectly true. Wilson detected it in his hand, by palmistry, and charged him with it and cornered him up so close that he had to confess; but both Twins begged us on their knees to keep the secret, and swore they would lead straight lives here; and it was all so pitiful that we gave our word of honor never to expose them while they kept that promise. You would have done it yourself, uncle."

"You are right, my boy, I would. A man's secret is still his own property, and sacred, when it has been surprised out of him like that. You did well, and I am proud of you." Then he added, mournfully, "But I wish I could have been saved the shame of meeting an assassin on the field of honor."

"It couldn't be helped, uncle. If I had known you were going to challenge him I should have felt obliged to sacrifice my pledged word in order to stop it, but Wilson couldn't be expected to do otherwise than keep silent."

"Oh, no, Wilson did right, and is in no way to blame. Tom, Tom, you have lifted a heavy load from my heart; I was stung to the very soul when I seemed to have discovered that I had a coward in my family."

"You may imagine what it cost *me* to assume such a part, uncle."

"Oh, I know it, poor boy, I know it. And I can understand how much it has cost you to remain under that unjust stigma to this time. But it is all right, now, and no harm is done. You have restored my comfort of mind, and with it your own; and both of us had suffered enough."

The old man sat a while plunged in thought; then he looked up with a satisfied light in his eye, and said: "That this assassin should have put the affront upon me of letting me meet him on the field of honor as if he were a gentleman is a matter which I will presently settle—but not now. I will not shoot him until after election. I see a way to ruin them both before; I will attend to that first. Neither of them shall be elected, that I promise. You are sure that the fact that he is an assassin has not got abroad?"

"Perfectly certain of it, sir."

"It will be a good card. I will fling a hint at it from the stump on the polling-day. It will sweep the ground from under both of them."

"There's not a doubt of it. It will finish them."

"That and outside work among the voters will, to a certainty. I want you to come down here by and by and work privately among the rag-tag and bobtail. You shall spend money among them; I will furnish it."

Another point scored against the detested Twins! Really it was a great day for Tom. He was encouraged to chance a parting shot, now, at the same target, and did it—

"You know that wonderful Indian knife that the Twins have been making such a to-do about? Well, there's no track or trace of it yet; so the town is beginning to sneer and gossip and laugh. Half the people believe they never had any such knife, the other half believe they had it and have got it still. I've heard twenty people talking like that to-day."

Yes, Tom's blemishless week had restored him to the favor of his aunt and uncle.

His mother was satisfied with him, too. Privately, she believed she was coming to love him, but she did not say so. She told him to go along to St. Louis, now, and she would get ready and follow. Then she smashed her whisky bottle and said—

"Dah, now! I's a gwyne to make you walk as straight as a string, Chambers, en so I's boun' you ain't gwyne to git no bad example out o' yo' mammy. I tole you you couldn't go into no bad comp'ny. Well, you's gwyne into my comp'ny, en I's gwyne to fill de bill. Now, den, trot along, trot along!"

Tom went aboard one of the big transient boats that night with his heavy satchel of miscellaneous plunder, and slept the sleep of the unjust, which is serener and sounder than the other kind, as we know by the hanging-eve history of a million rascals. But when he got up in the morning, luck was against him again. A brother-thief had robbed him while he slept, and gone ashore at some intermediate landing.

Chapter 16

If you pick up a starving dog and make him prosperous, he will not bite you. This is the principal difference between a dog and a man.
—PUDD'NHEAD WILSON'S CALENDAR.

We know all about the habits of the ant, we know all about the habits of the bee, but we know nothing at all about the habits of the oyster. It seems almost certain that we have been choosing the wrong time for studying the oyster.
—PUDD'NHEAD WILSON'S CALENDAR.

When Roxana arrived, she found her son in such despair and misery that her heart was touched and her motherhood rose up strong in her. He was ruined past hope, now; his destruction would be immediate and sure, and he would be an outcast and friendless. —That was reason enough for a mother to love a child; so she loved him, and told him so. It made him wince, secretly—for she was a "nigger." That he was one himself was far from reconciling him to that despised race.

Roxana poured out endearments upon him, to which he responded uncomfortably, but as well as he could. And she tried to comfort him, but that was not possible. These intimacies quickly became horrible to him, and within the hour he began to try to get up courage enough to tell her so, and require that they be discontinued or very considerably modified. But he was afraid of her; and besides, there came a lull, now, for she had begun to think. She was trying to invent a saving plan. Finally she started up and said she had found a way out. Tom was almost suffocated by the joy of this sudden good news. Roxana said—

"Here is de plan, en she'll win, sure. I is a nigger, en nobody ain't gwyne to doubt it dat hears me talk. I's wuth six hund'd dollahs. Take en sell me en pay off dese gamblers."

Tom was dazed. He was not sure he had heard aright. He was dumb for a moment; then he said:

"Do you mean that you would be sold into slavery to save me?"

"Ain't you my chile? En does you know anything dat a mother won't do for her chile? Dey ain't nothin' a white mother won't do for her chile. Who made 'em so? De Lord done it. En who made de niggers? De Lord made 'em. In de inside, mothers is all de same. De good Lord He made 'em so. I's gwyne to be sole into slavery, en in a year you's gwyne to buy yo' ole mammy free agin. I'll show you how. Dat's de plan."

Tom's hopes began to rise, and his spirits along with them. He said—

"It's lovely of you, mammy—it's just—"

"Say it agin! En keep on sayin' it! It's all de pay a body kin want in dis worl', en it's mo' den enough. Laws bless you honey, when I's slavin' aroun' en dey 'buses me, if I knows you's asayin' dat, 'way off yonder somers, it'll heal up all de sore places, en I kin stan' 'em."

"I *do* say it again, mammy, and I'll keep on saying it, too. But how am I going to sell you?—you're free, you know."

"Much diffrence dat make! White folks ain't particklar. De law kin sell me now, if dey tell me to leave de State in six months en I don't go. You draw up a paper—bill o' sale—en put it 'way off yonder, down in de middle o' Kaintuck somers, en sign some names to it, en say you'll sell me cheap caze you's hard up; you'll fine you ain't gwyne to have no trouble. You take me up de country a piece, en sell me on a farm—dem people ain't gwyne to ask no questions, if I's a bargain."

Tom forged a bill of sale and sold his mother to an Arkansas cotton planter for a trifle over six hundred dollars. He did not want to commit this treachery, but luck threw the man in his way, and this saved him the necessity of going up country to hunt up a purchaser, with the added risk of having to answer a lot of questions, whereas this planter was so pleased with Roxy that he asked next to none at all. Besides, the planter insisted that Roxy wouldn't know where she was, at first, and that by the time she found out she would already have become contented. And Tom argued with himself that it was an immense advantage for Roxy to have a master who was so pleased with her as this planter manifestly was. In almost no time his flowing reasonings carried him to the point of even half believing he was doing Roxy a splendid surreptitious service in selling her "down the river." And then he kept diligently saying to himself all the time, "It's for only a year—in a year I buy her free again; she'll keep that in mind, and it'll reconcile her." Yes, the little deception could do no harm, and everything would come out right and pleasant in the end, anyway. By agreement, the conversation in Roxy's presence was all about the man's "up-country" farm, and how pleasant a place it was, and how happy the slaves were, there; so poor Roxy was entirely deceived; and easily, for she was not dreaming that her own son could be guilty of treason to a mother who, in voluntarily going into slavery—slavery of any kind, mild or severe, or of any duration, brief or long—was making a sacrifice for him compared with which death would have been a poor and commonplace one. She lavished tears and loving caresses upon him, privately, and then went away with her owner; went away broken-hearted, and yet proud of what she was doing and glad that it was in her power to do it.

Tom squared his accounts, and resolved to keep to the very letter of his reform, and never put that will in jeopardy again. He had three hundred dollars left. According to his mother's plan, he was to put that safely away, and add her half of his pension to it monthly. In one year this fund would buy her free again.

For a whole week he was not able to sleep well, so much the villainy which he had played upon his trusting mother preyed upon his rag of a conscience; but after that he began to get comfortable again and was presently able to sleep like any other miscreant.

The boat bore Roxy away from St. Louis at four in the afternoon, and she stood on the lower guard abaft the paddle-box and watched Tom through a blur of tears until he melted into the throng of people and disappeared; then she looked no more, but sat there on a coil of cable crying, till far into the night. When she went to her foul steerage bunk at last, between the clashing engines, it was not to sleep, but only to wait for the morning; and waiting, grieve.

It had been imagined that she "would not know," and would think she was traveling up stream. She!—why, she had been steamboating for years. At dawn she got up and went listlessly and sat down on the cable-coil again. She passed many a snag whose "break" could have told her a thing to break her heart, for it showed a current moving in the same direction that the boat was going; but her thoughts were elsewhere, and she did not notice. But at last the roar of a bigger and nearer break than usual brought her out of her torpor, and she looked up and her practised eye fell upon that tell-tale rush of water. For one moment her petrified gaze fixed itself there. Then her head dropped upon her breast and she said—

"Oh, de good Lord God have mercy on po' sinful me—*I's sole down de river!*"

Chapter 17

*Even popularity can be overdone. In Rome, along at first, you are full
of regrets that Michelangelo died; but by and by you only regret that
you didn't see him do it.*
— PUDD'NHEAD WILSON'S CALENDAR.

*July 4. Statistics show that we lose more fools on this day than in all
the other days of the year put together. This proves, by the number
left in stock, that one Fourth of July per year is now inadequate, the
country has grown so.*
— PUDD'NHEAD WILSON'S CALENDAR.

The summer weeks dragged by, and then the political campaign
opened—opened in pretty warm fashion, and waxed hotter and
hotter daily. The twins threw themselves into it with their whole
heart, for their self-love was engaged. Their popularity, so general at
first, had suffered afterward; mainly because they had been *too* popular, and so a natural reaction had followed. Besides, it had been
diligently whispered around that it was curious—indeed, *very*
curious—that that wonderful knife of theirs did not turn up—*if* it
was so valuable, or *if* it had ever existed. And with the whisperings
went chucklings and nudgings and winks, and such things have an
effect. The twins considered that success in the election would rein-
state them, and that defeat would work them irreparable damage.
Therefore they worked hard, but not harder than Judge Driscoll
and Tom worked against them in the closing days of the canvass.
Tom's conduct had remained so letter-perfect during two whole
months, now, that his uncle not only trusted him with money with
which to persuade voters, but trusted him to go and get himself
out of the safe in the private sitting-room.

The closing speech of the campaign was made by Judge Driscoll,
and he made it against both of the foreigners. It was disastrously
effective. He poured out rivers of ridicule upon them, and forced
the big mass-meeting to laugh and applaud. He scoffed at them as
adventurers, mountebanks, side-show riff-raff, dime-museum freaks;
he assailed their showy titles with measureless derision; he said they
were back-alley barbers disguised as nobilities, peanut pedlers mas-
querading as gentlemen, organ-grinders bereft of their brother-mon-
key. At last he stopped and stood still. He waited until the place
had become absolutely silent and expectant, then he delivered his
deadliest shot; delivered it with ice-cold seriousness and deliberation, with a significant emphasis upon the closing words: he said he
believed that the reward offered for the lost knife was humbug and
buncombe, and that its owner would know where to find it whenever he should have occasion *to assassinate somebody.*

Then he stepped from the stand, leaving a startled and impressive hush behind him instead of the customary explosion of cheers
and party cries.

The strange remark flew far and wide over the town and made an extraordinary sensation. Everybody was asking, "What could he mean by that?" And everybody went on asking that question, but in vain; for the Judge only said he knew what he was talking about, and stopped there; Tom said he hadn't any idea what his uncle meant, and Wilson, whenever he was asked what he thought it meant, parried the question by asking the questioner what *he* thought it meant.

Wilson was elected, the twins were defeated—crushed, in fact, and left forlorn and substantially friendless. Tom went back to St. Louis happy.

Dawson's Landing had a week of repose, now, and it needed it. But it was in an expectant state, for the air was full of rumors of a new duel. Judge Driscoll's election labors had prostrated him, but it was said that as soon as he was well enough to entertain a challenge he would get one from Count Luigi.

The brothers withdrew entirely from society, and nursed their humiliation in privacy. They avoided the people, and went out for exercise only late at night, when the streets were deserted.

Chapter 18

Gratitude and treachery are merely the two extremities of the same procession. You have seen all of it that is worth staying for when the band and the gaudy officials have gone by.
—PUDD'NHEAD WILSON'S CALENDAR.

THANKSGIVING DAY. *Let all give humble, hearty, and sincere thanks, now, but the turkeys. In the island of Fiji they do not use turkeys; they use plumbers. It does not become you and me to sneer at Fiji.*
—PUDD'NHEAD WILSON'S CALENDAR.

The Friday after the election was a rainy one in St. Louis. It rained all day long, and rained hard, apparently trying its best to wash that soot-blackened town white, but of course not succeeding. Toward midnight Tom Driscoll arrived at his lodgings from the theatre in the heavy downpour, and closed his umbrella and let himself in; but when he would have shut the door, he found that there was another person entering—doubtless another lodger; this person closed the door and tramped up stairs behind Tom. Tom found his door in the dark, and entered it and turned up the gas. When he faced about, lightly whistling, he saw the back of a man. The man was closing and locking his door for him. His whistle faded out and he felt uneasy. The man turned around, a wreck of shabby old clothes sodden with rain and all a-drip, and showed a black face under an old slouch hat. Tom was frightened. He tried to order the man out, but the words refused to come, and the other man got the start. He said, in a low voice—

"Keep still—I's yo' mother!"

Tom sunk in a heap on a chair, and gasped out—

"It was mean of me, and base—I know it; but I meant it for the best, I did indeed—I can swear it."

Roxana stood a while looking mutely down on him while he writhed in shame and went on incoherently babbling self-accusations mixed with pitiful attempts at explanation and palliation of his crime; then she seated herself and took off her hat, and her unkempt masses of long brown hair tumbled down about her shoulders.

"It ain't no fault o' yo'n dat dat ain't gray," she said, sadly, noticing the hair.

"I know it, I know it! I'm a scoundrel. But I swear I meant for the best. It was a mistake, of course, but I thought it was for the best, I truly did."

Roxy began to cry softly, and presently words began to find their way out between her sobs. They were uttered lamentingly, rather than angrily—

"Sell a pusson down de river—*down de river!*—for de bes'! I wouldn't treat a dog so! I is all broke down en wore out, now, en so I reckon it ain't in me to storm aroun' no mo', like I used to when I 'uz trompled on en 'bused. I don't know—but maybe it's so. Leastways, I's suffered so much dat mournin' seem to come mo' handy to me now den stormin'."

These words should have touched Tom Driscoll, but if they did, that effect was obliterated by a stronger one—one which removed the heavy weight of fear which lay upon him, and gave his crushed spirit a most grateful rebound and filled all his small soul with a deep sense of relief. But he kept prudently still, and ventured no comment. There was a voiceless interval of some duration, now, in which no sounds were heard but the beating of the rain upon the panes, the sighing and complaining of the winds, and now and then a muffled sob from Roxana. The sobs became more and more infrequent, and at last ceased. Then the refugee began to talk again:

"Shet down dat light a little. More. More yit. A pusson dat is hunted don't like de light. Dah—dat'll do. I kin see whah you is, en dat's enough. I's gwyne to tell you de tale, en cut it jes' as short as I kin, en den I'll tell you what you's got to do. Dat man dat bought me ain't a bad man, he's good enough, as planters goes; en if he could a had his way I'd a ben a house servant in his fambly en ben comfortable; but his wife she was a Yank, en not right down good lookin', en she riz up agin me straight off; so den dey sent me out to de quarter mongst de common fiel' han's. Dat woman warn't satisfied, even wid dat, but she worked up de overseer agin me, she 'uz dat jealous en hateful; so de overseer he had me out befo' day in de mawnins en worked me de whole long day as long as dey 'uz any light to see by; en many's de lashin' I got becaze I couldn't come up to de work o' de stronges'. Dat overseer 'uz a Yank, too, outen New Englan', en anybody down South kin tell you what dat mean. *Dey* knows how to work a nigger to death, en dey knows how to whale 'em, too—whale 'em till dey backs is welted like a washboard. 'Long at fust my marster say de good word for me to de overseer, but dat 'uz bad for me; for de mistis she fine it out, en arter dat I jist ketched it at every turn—dey warn't no mercy for me no mo'."

Tom's heart was fired—with fury against the planter's wife; and he said to himself, "But for that meddlesome fool, everything would have gone all right." He added a deep and bitter curse against her.

The expression of this sentiment was fiercely written in his face, and stood thus revealed to Roxana by a white glare of lightning which turned the sombre dusk of the room into dazzling day at that moment. She was pleased—pleased and grateful; for did not that expression show that her child was capable of grieving for his mother's wrongs and of feeling resentment toward her persecutors?—a thing which she had been doubting. But her flash of happiness was only a flash, and went out again and left her spirit dark; for she said to herself, "He sole me down de river—he can't feel for a body long; dis'll pass en go." Then she took up her tale again:

"'Bout ten days ago I 'uz sayin' to myself dat I couldn't las' many mo' weeks, I 'uz so wore out wid de awful work en de lashins, en so down-hearted en misable. En I didn't care no mo', nuther—life warn't wuth noth'n to me if I got to go on like dat. Well, when a body is in a frame o' mine like dat, what do a body care what a body do? Dey was a little sickly nigger wench 'bout ten year ole dat 'uz good to me, en hadn't no mammy, po' thing, en I loved her en she loved me; en she come out whah I 'uz workin', en she had a roasted tater, en tried to slip it to me—robbin' herself, you see, caze she knowed de overseer didn't gimme enough to eat—en he ketched her at it, en give her a lick acrost de back wid his stick which 'uz as thick as a broom-han'le, en she drop' screamin' on de groun', en squirmin' en wallerin' aroun' in de dust like a spider dat's got crippled. I couldn't stan' it. All de hell-fire dat 'uz ever in my heart flame' up, en I snatch de stick outen his han' en laid him flat. He laid dah moanin' en cussin', en all out of his head, you know, en de niggers 'uz plum skyerd to death. Dey gethered 'roun' him to he'p him, en I jumped on his hoss en took out for de river as tight as I could go. I knowed what dey would do wid me. Soon as he got well he would start in en work me to death if marster let him; en if dey didn't do dat dey'd sell me furder down de river, en dat's de same thing. So I 'lowed to drown myself en git out o' my troubles. It 'uz gitt'n towards dark. I 'uz at de river in two minutes. Den I see a canoe, en I says dey ain't no use to drown myself tell I got to; so I ties de hoss in de edge o' de timber en shove out down de river, keepin' in under de shelter o' de bluff bank en prayin' for de dark to shet down quick. I had a pow'ful good start, caze de big house 'uz three mile back fum de river en on'y de work mules to ride dah on, en on'y niggers to ride 'em, en *dey* warn't gwyne to hurry—dey'd gimme all de chance dey could. Befo' a body could go to de house en back it would be long pas' dark, en dey couldn't track de hoss en fine out which way I went tell mawnin', en de niggers would tell 'em all de lies dey could 'bout it.

"Well, de dark come, en I went on a spinnin' down de river. I paddled mo'n two hours, den I warn't worried no mo'; so I quit paddlin', en floated down de current, considerin' what I 'uz gwyne to do if I didn't have to drown myself. I made up some plans, en floated along, turnin' 'em over in my mine. Well, when it 'uz a little pas' midnight, as I reckoned, en I had come fifteen or twenty mile, I see de lights o' a steamboat layin' at de bank, whah dey warn't no town en no woodyard, en putty soon I ketched de shape o' de chimbly-tops agin de stars, en de good gracious me, I most jumped out o' my skin for joy! It 'uz de Gran' Mogul—I 'uz chambermaid on her for eight seasons in de Cincinnati en Orleans trade. I slid 'long pas'—don't see nobody stirrin' nowhah—hear 'em a hammerin' away in de engine room, den I knowed what de matter was—some o' de machinery's broke. I got asho' below de boat en turn' de canoe loose, den I goes 'long up, en dey 'uz jes' one plank out, en I step 'board de boat. It 'uz pow'ful hot; deckhan's en roustabouts 'uz sprawled roun' asleep on de fo'cas'l, de second mate, Jim Bangs, he sot dah on de bitts wid his head down, asleep—caze dat's de way de second mate stan' de cap'n's watch!—en de ole watchman, Billy Hatch, he 'uz a noddin' on de companionway;—en I knowed 'em all; en lan', but dey did look good! I says to myself, I wisht old marster'd come along *now* en try to take me—bless yo' heart, I's 'mong frien's, I is. So I tromped right along 'mongst 'em, en went up on de biler deck en 'way back aft to de ladies' cabin guard, en sot down dah in de same cheer dat I'd sot in mos' a hund'd million times, I reckon; en it 'uz jist home agin, I tell you!

"In 'bout an hour I heard de ready-bell jingle, en den de racket begin. Putty soon I hear de gong strike. 'Set her back on de outside,' I says to myself—'I reckon I knows dat music!' I hear de gong agin. 'Come ahead on de inside,' I says. Gong agin. 'Stop de outside.' Gong agin. 'Come ahead on de outside—now we's pinted for Sent Louis, en I's outer de woods en ain't got to drown myself, at all.' I knowed de Mogul 'uz in de Sent Louis trade now, you see. It 'uz jes' fair day light when we passed our plantation, en I seed a gang o' niggers en white folks huntin' up en down de sho', en troublin' deyselves a good deal 'bout me, but I warn't troublin' myself none 'bout dem.

"'Bout dat time Sally Jackson, dat used to be my second chambermaid en 'uz head chambermaid now, she come out on de guard en 'uz pow'ful glad to see me, en so 'uz all de officers; en I tole 'em I'd got kidnapped en sole down de river, en dey made me up twenty dollahs en give it to me, en Sally she rigged me out wid good clo'es, en when I got here I went straight to whah you used to was, en den I come to dis house en dey say you's away but 'spected back every day; so I didn't dast to go down de river to Dawson's, caze I might miss you.

"Well, las' Monday I 'uz pass'n by one o' dem places in Fourth street whah dey sticks up runaway-nigger bills en he'ps to ketch 'em, en I seed my marster! I mos' flopped down on de groun', I felt so gone. He had his back to me, en 'uz talkin' to de man en givin' him some bills—nigger-bills, I reckon, en I's de nigger. He's offerin' a reward—dat's it. Ain't I right, don't you reckon?"

Tom had been gradually sinking into a state of ghastly terror, and he said to himself, now, "I'm lost, no matter what turn things take! This man has said to me that he thinks there was something suspicious about that sale. He said he had a letter from a passenger on the Grand Mogul saying that Roxy came here on that boat and that everybody on board knew all about the case; so he says that her coming here instead of flying to a free State looks bad for me, and that if I don't find her for him, and that pretty soon, he will make trouble for me. I never believed that story; I couldn't believe she would be so dead to all motherly instincts as to come here, knowing the risk she would run of getting me into irremediable trouble. And after all, here she is! And I stupidly swore I would help him find her, thinking it was a perfectly safe thing to promise. If I venture to deliver her up, she—she—but how can I help myself? I've got to do that or pay the money, and where's the money to come from? I—I—well, I should think that if he would swear to treat her kindly hereafter—and she says, herself, that he is a good man—and if he would swear to never allow her to be overworked, or ill fed, or—"

A flash of lightning exposed Tom's pallid face drawn and rigid with these worrying thoughts. Roxana spoke up sharply, now, and there was apprehension in her voice—

"Turn up dat light! I want to see yo' face better. Dah, now— lemme look at you. Chambers, you's as white as yo' shirt! Has you seen dat man? Has he ben to see you?"

"Ye-s."

"When?"

"Monday noon."

"Monday noon! Was he on my track?"

"He—well, he thought he was. That is, he hoped he was. This is the bill you saw." He took it out of his pocket.

"Read it to me!"

She was panting with excitement, and there was a dusky glow in her eyes that Tom could not translate with certainty, but there seemed to be something threatening about it. The handbill had the usual rude wood-cut of a turbaned negro woman running, with the customary bundle on a stick over her shoulder, and the heading, in bold type, "$100 *Reward.*" Tom read the bill aloud—at least the part that described Roxana and named the master and his St. Louis address and the address of the Fourth-street agency; but he left out the item that applicants for the reward might also apply to Mr. Thomas Driscoll.

"Gimme de bill!"

Tom had folded it and was putting it in his pocket. He felt a chilly streak creeping down his back, but said, as carelessly as he could—

"The bill? Why, it isn't any use to you, you can't read it. What do you want with it?"

"Gimme de bill!" Tom gave it to her, but with a reluctance which he could not entirely disguise. "Did you read it *all* to me?"

"Certainly I did."

"Hole up yo' han' en swah to it."

Tom did it. Roxana put the bill carefully away in her pocket, with her eyes fixed upon Tom's face all the while, then she said—

"You's lyin'!"

"What would I want to lie about it for?"

"I don't know—but you is. Dat's my opinion, anyways. But nemmine 'bout dat. When I seed dat man, I 'uz dat s'kyerd dat I could scasely wobble home. Den I give a nigger man a dollah for dese clo'es, en I ain't ben in a house sence, night ner day, till now. I blacked my face en laid hid in de cellar of a ole house dat's burnt down, daytimes, en robbed de sugar hogsheads en grain sacks on de wharf, nights, to git somethin' to eat, en never dast to try to buy noth'n; en I's mos' starved. En I never dast to come near dis place till dis rainy night, when dey ain't no people roun', scasely. But tonight I ben a stannin' in de dark alley ever sence night come, waitin' for you to go by. En here I is."

She fell to thinking. Presently she said—

"You seed dat man at noon, las' Monday?"

"Yes."

"I seed him de middle o' dat arternoon. He hunted you up, didn't he?"

"Yes."

"Did he give you de bill dat time?"

"No, he hadn't got it printed, yet."

Roxana darted a suspicious glance at him.

"Did you he'p him fix up de bill?"

Tom cursed himself for making that stupid blunder, and tried to rectify it by saying he remembered, now, that it *was* at noon Monday that the man gave him the bill. Roxana said—

"You's lyin' agin, sho'." Then she straightened up and raised her finger:

"Now, den! I's gwyne to ast you a question, en I wants to know how you's gwyne to git aroun' it. You knowed he 'uz arter me; en if you run off, 'stid o' stayin' here to he'p him, he'd know dey 'uz somethin' wrong 'bout dis business, en den he would inquire 'bout you, en dat would take him to yo' uncle, en yo' uncle would read de bill en see dat you ben sellin' a free nigger down de river, en you know *him* I reckon! He'd tar up de will en kick you outen de house. Now, den, you answer me dis question: hain't you tole dat man dat I would be sho' to come here, en den you would fix it so he could set a trap en ketch me?"

Tom recognized that neither lies nor arguments could help him any longer—he was in a vise, with the screw turned on, and out of it there was no budging. His face began to take on an ugly look, and presently he said, with a snarl—

"Well, what could I do? You see, yourself, that I was in his grip and couldn't get out."

Roxy scorched him with a scornful gaze a while, then she said—

"What could you do? You could be Judas to yo' own mother to save yo' wuthless hide! Would anybody b'lieve it? No—a dog couldn't! You is de low-downest orneriest hound dat was ever pup'd into dis worl'—en I's 'sponsible for it!"—and she spat on him.

He made no effort to resent this. Roxy reflected a moment, then she said—

"Now I'll tell you what you's gwyne to do. You's gwyne to give dat man de money dat you's got laid up, en make him wait till you kin go to de Jedge en git de res' en buy me free agin."

"Thunder! what are you thinking of? Go and ask him for three hundred dollars and odd? What would I tell him I want with it, pray?"

Roxy's answer was delivered in a serene and level voice—

"You'll tell him you's sole me to pay yo' gamblin' debts, en dat you lied to me en was a villain, en dat I 'quires you to git dat money en buy me back agin."

"Why, you've gone stark mad! He would tear the will to shreds in a minute—don't you know that?"

"Yes, I does."

"Then you don't believe I'm idiot enough to go to him, do you?"

"I don't b'lieve nothin' 'bout it—I *knows* you's a-goin'. I knows it becaze you knows dat if you don't raise dat money I'll go to him myself, en den he'll sell *you* down de river en you kin see how you like it!"

Tom rose, trembling and excited, and there was an evil light in his eye. He strode to the door and said he must get out of this suffocating place for a moment and clear his brain in the fresh air so that he could determine what to do. The door wouldn't open. Roxy smiled grimly, and said—

"I's got de key, honey—set down. You needn't cle'r up yo' brain none to fine out what you gwyne to do—I knows what you's gwyne to do." Tom sat down and began to pass his hands through his hair with a helpless and desperate air. Roxy said, "Is dat man in dis house?"

Tom glanced up with a surprised expression, and asked—

"What gave you such an idea?"

"You done it. Gwyne out to cle'r yo' brain! In de fust place you ain't go none to cle'r, en in de second place yo' ornery eye tole on you. You's de low-downest hound dat ever—but I done tole you dat, befo'. Now den, dis is Friday. You kin fix it up wid dat man, en tell him you's gwyne away to git de res' o' de money, en dat you'll be back wid it nex' Tuesday, or maybe Wednesday. You understan'?"

Tom answered sullenly—

"Yes."

"En when you gits de new bill o' sale dat sells me to my own self, take en send it in de mail to Mr. Pudd'nhead Wilson, en write on de back dat he's to keep it tell I come. You understan'?"

"Yes."

"Dat's all, den. Take yo' umbereller, en put on yo' hat."

"Why?"

"Becaze you's gwyne to see me home to de wharf. You see dis knife? I's toted it aroun' sence de day I seed dat man en bought dese clo'es en it. If he ketched me, I 'uz gwyne to kill myself wid it. Now start along, en go sof', en lead de way; en if you gives a sign in dis house, or if anybody comes up to you in de street, I's gwyne to jam it into you. Chambers, does you b'lieve me when I says dat?"

"It's no use to bother me with that question. I know your word's good."

"Yes, it's diffrent fum yo'n! Shet de light out en move along— here's de key."

They were not followed. Tom trembled every time a late straggler brushed by them on the street, and half expected to feel the cold steel in his back. Roxy was right at his heels and always in reach. After tramping a mile they reached a wide vacancy on the deserted wharves, and in this dark and rainy desert they parted.

As Tom trudged home, his mind was full of dreary thoughts and wild plans; but at last he said to himself, wearily—

"There is but the one way out. I must follow her plan. But with a variation—I will not ask for the money and ruin myself, I will *rob* the old skinflint."

Chapter 19

Few things are harder to put up with than the annoyance of a good example.
—PUDD'NHEAD WILSON'S CALENDAR.

It were not best that we should all think alike; it is difference of opinion that makes horse-races.
—PUDD'NHEAD WILSON'S CALENDAR.

Dawson's Landing was comfortably finishing its season of dull repose and waiting patiently for the duel. Count Luigi was waiting, too; but not patiently, rumor said. Sunday came, and Luigi insisted on having his challenge conveyed. Wilson carried it. Judge Driscoll declined to fight with an assassin—"that is," he added, significantly, "in the field of honor."

Elsewhere, of course, he would be ready. Wilson tried to convince him that if he had been present himself when Angelo told about the homicide committed by Luigi, he would not have considered the act discreditable to Luigi; but the obstinate old man was not to be moved.

Wilson went back to his principal and reported the failure of his mission. Luigi was incensed, and asked how it could be that the old gentleman, who was by no means dull-witted, held his trifling nephew's evidence and inferences to be of more value than Wilson's. But Wilson laughed, and said—

"That is quite simple; that is easily explicable. I am not his doll —his baby—his infatuation: his nephew is. The Judge and his late wife never had any children. The Judge and his wife were past middle age when this treasure fell into their lap. One must make allowances for a parental instinct that has been starving for twenty-five or thirty years. It is famished, it is crazed with hunger by that time, and will be entirely satisfied with anything that comes handy; its taste is atrophied, it can't tell mud-cat from shad. A devil born to a young couple is measurably recognizable by them as a devil before long, but a devil adopted by an old couple is an angel to them, and remains so, through thick and thin. Tom is this old man's angel; he is infatuated with him. Tom can persuade him into things which other people can't—not all things, I don't mean that, but a good many—particularly one class of things: the things that create or abolish personal partialities or prejudices in the old man's mind. The old man liked both of you. Tom conceived a hatred for you. That was enough; it turned the old man around at once. The oldest and strongest friendship must go to the ground when one of these late-adopted darlings throws a brick at it."

"It's a curious philosophy," said Luigi.

"It ain't a philosophy at all,—it's a fact. And there is something pathetic and beautiful about it, too. I think there is nothing more pathetic than to see one of these poor old childless couples taking a menagerie of yelping little worthless dogs to their hearts; and then adding some cursing and squawking parrots and a jackass-voiced macaw; and next a couple of hundred screeching song-birds; and presently some fetid guinea-pigs and rabbits, and a howling colony of cats. It is all a groping and ignorant effort to construct out of base metal and brass filings, so to speak, something to take the place of that golden treasure denied them by Nature, a child. But this is a digression. The unwritten law of this region requires you to kill Judge Driscoll on sight, and he and the community will expect that attention at your hands—though of course your own death by his bullet will answer every purpose. Look out for him! Are you heeled—that is, fixed?"

"Yes; he shall have his opportunity. If he attacks me I will respond."

As Wilson was leaving, he said—

"The Judge is still a little used up by his campaign work, and will not get out for a day or so, but when he does get out you want to be on the alert."

About eleven at night the twins went out for exercise, and started on a long stroll in the veiled moonlight.

Tom Driscoll had landed at Hackett's Store, two miles below Dawson's, just about half an hour earlier, the only passenger for that lonely spot, and had walked up the shore road and entered Judge Driscoll's house without having encountered any one, either on the road or under the roof.

He pulled down his window-blinds and lighted his candle. He laid off his coat and hat, and began his preparations. He unlocked his trunk and got his suit of girl's clothes out from under the male attire in it, and laid it by. Then he blacked his face with a burnt cork and put the cork in his pocket. His plan was, to slip down to his uncle's private sitting room below, pass into the bedroom, steal the safe-key from the old gentleman's clothes, and then go back and rob the safe. He took up his candle to start. His courage and confidence were high, up to this point, but both began to waver a little, now. Suppose he should make a noise, by some accident, and get caught—say in the act of opening the safe? Perhaps it would be well to go armed. He took the Indian knife from its hiding place, and felt a pleasant return of his waning courage. He slipped stealthily down the narrow stair, his hair rising and his pulses halting at the slightest creak. When he was half way down he was disturbed to perceive that the landing below was touched by a faint glow of light. What could that mean? Was his uncle still up? No, that was not likely; he must have left his night-taper there when he went to bed. Tom crept on down, pausing at every step to listen. He found the door standing open, and glanced in. What he saw pleased him beyond measure. His uncle was asleep on the sofa. On a small table at the head of the sofa a lamp was burning low, and by it stood the old man's small tin cash-box, closed. Near the box was a pile of bank notes and a piece of paper covered with figures in pencil. The safe-door was not open. Evidently the sleeper had wearied himself with work upon his finances, and was taking a rest.

Tom set his candle on the stairs, and began to make his way toward the pile of notes, stooping low as he went. When he was passing his uncle, the old man stirred in his sleep and Tom stopped instantly—stopped, and softly drew the knife from its sheath, with his heart thumping and his eyes fastened upon his benefactor's face. After a moment or two he ventured forward again—one step— reached for his prize, and seized it, dropping the knife-sheath. Then he felt the old man's strong grip upon him, and a wild cry of "Help! help!" rang in his ear. Without hesitation he drove the knife home—and was free. Some of the notes escaped from his left hand and fell in the blood on the floor. He dropped the knife and snatched them up and started to fly; transferred them to his left hand and seized the knife again, in his fright and confusion, but remembered himself and flung it from him, as being a dangerous witness to carry away with him.

He jumped for the stair-foot, and closed the door behind him; and as he snatched his candle and fled upward, the stillness of the night was broken by the sound of urgent footsteps approaching the house. In another moment he was in his room, and the Twins were standing aghast over the body of the murdered man!

Tom put on his coat, buttoned his hat under it, threw on his suit of girl's clothes, dropped the veil, blew out his light, locked the room-door by which he had just entered, taking the key, passed through his other door into the back hall, locked that door and kept the key, then worked his way along in the dark and descended the back stairs. He was not expecting to meet anybody, for all interest was centred in the other part of the house, now; his calculation proved correct. By the time he was passing through the back yard, Mrs. Pratt, her servants, and a dozen half dressed neighbors had joined the Twins and the dead, and accessions were still arriving at the front door.

As Tom, quaking as with a palsy, passed out at the gate three women came flying from the house on the opposite side of the lane. They rushed by him and in at the gate, asking him what the trouble was, there, but not waiting for an answer. Tom said to himself, "Those old maids waited to dress—they did the same thing the night Stevens's house burned down next door." In a few minutes he was in the haunted house. He lighted a candle, and took off his girl-clothes. There was blood on him all down his left side, and his right hand was red with the stains of the blood-soaked notes which he had crushed in it; but otherwise he was free from this sort of evidence. He cleansed his hand on the straw, and cleaned most of the smut from his face. Then he burned his male and female attire to ashes, scattered the ashes, and put on a disguise proper for a tramp. He blew out his light, went below, and was soon loafing down the river road, with the intent to borrow and use one of Roxy's devices. He found a canoe and paddled off down stream, setting the canoe adrift as dawn approached, and making his way by land to the next village, where he kept out of sight till a transient steamer came along, and then took deck passage for St. Louis. He was ill at ease until Dawson's Landing was behind him; then he said to himself, "All the detectives on earth couldn't trace me now; there's not a vestige of a clew left in the world; that homicide will take its place with the permanent mysteries, and people won't get done trying to guess out the secret of it for fifty years."

In St. Louis, next morning, he read this brief telegram in the papers—dated at Dawson's Landing:

"Judge Driscoll, an old and respected citizen, was assassinated here about mid-night by a profligate Italian nobleman or barber on account of a quarrel growing out of the recent election. The assassin will probably be lynched."

"One of the twins!" soliloquised Tom; "how lucky! It is the knife that has done him this grace. We never know when fortune' is trying to favor us. I actually cursed Pudd'nhead Wilson in my heart for putting it out of my power to sell that knife. I take it back, now."

Tom was now rich and independent. He arranged with the planter, and mailed to Wilson the new bill of sale which sold Roxana to herself; then he telegraphed his aunt Pratt:

"Have seen the awful news in the papers and am almost prostrated with grief. Shall start by packet to-day. Try to bear up till I come."

When Wilson reached the house of mourning and had gathered such details as Mrs. Pratt and the rest of the crowd could tell him, he took command, as mayor, and gave orders that nothing should be touched, but everything left as it was until Justice Robinson should arrive and take the proper measures as coroner. He cleared everybody out of the room but the Twins and himself. The sheriff soon arrived and took the Twins away to jail. Wilson told them to keep heart, and promised to do his best in their defence when the case should come to trial. Justice Robinson came presently, and with him Constable Blake. They examined the room thoroughly. They found the knife and the sheath. Wilson noticed that there were finger-prints on the knife-handle. That pleased him, for the Twins had required the earliest comers to make a scrutiny of their hands and clothes, and neither these people nor Wilson himself had found any blood-stains upon them. Could there be a possibility that the Twins had spoken the truth when they said they found the man dead when they ran into the house in answer to the cry for help? He thought of that mysterious girl, at once. But this was not the sort of work for a girl to be engaged in. No matter; Tom Driscoll's room must be examined.

After the coroner's jury had viewed the body and its surroundings, Wilson suggested a search up stairs, and he went along. The jury forced an entrance to Tom's room, but found nothing, of course.

The coroner's jury found that the homicide was committed by Luigi, and that Angelo was accessory to it.

The town was bitter against the unfortunates, and for the first few days after the murder they were in constant danger of being lynched. The grand jury presently indicted Luigi for murder in the first degree, and Angelo as accessory before the fact. The Twins were transferred from the city jail to the county prison to await trial.

Wilson examined the finger-marks on the knife handle, and said to himself, "Neither of the Twins made those marks." Then manifestly there was another person concerned, either in his own interest or as hired assassin.

But who could it be? That, he must try to find out. The safe was not open, the cash-box was closed, and had three thousand dollars in it. Then robbery was not the motive, and revenge was. Where had the murdered man an enemy except Luigi? There was but that one person in the world with a deep grudge against him.

The mysterious girl! The girl was a great trial to Wilson. If the motive had been robbery, the girl might answer, but there wasn't any girl that would want to take this old man's life for revenge. He had no quarrels with girls; he was a gentleman.

Wilson had perfect tracings of the finger-marks of the knife handle; and among his glass records he had a great array of the finger-prints of women and girls, collected during the last fifteen or eighteen years, but he scanned them in vain, they successfully withstood every test; among them were no duplicates of the prints on the knife.

The presence of the knife on the stage of the murder was a worrying circumstance for Wilson. A week previously he had as good as admitted to himself that he believed Luigi had possessed such a knife and that he still possessed it notwithstanding his pretence that it had been stolen. And now here was the knife, and with it the Twins. Half the town had said the Twins were hum-bugging when they claimed that they had lost their knife, and now these people were joyful, and said "I told you so!"

If their finger-prints had been on the handle—but it was useless to bother any further about that; the finger-prints on the handle were *not* theirs—that he knew, perfectly.

Wilson refused to suspect Tom; for, firstly, Tom couldn't murder anybody—he hadn't character enough; secondly, if he could murder a person he wouldn't select his doting benefactor and nearest relative; thirdly, self-interest was in the way; for while the uncle lived, Tom was sure of a free support and a chance to get the destroyed will revived again, but with the uncle gone, that chance was gone, too. It was true the will had really been revived, as was now discovered, but Tom could not have been aware of it, or he would have spoken of it, in his native talky unsecretive way. Finally, Tom was in St. Louis when the murder was done, and got the news out of the morning journals, as was shown by his telegram to his aunt. These speculations were unemphasized sensations rather than articulated thoughts, for Wilson would have laughed at the idea of seriously connecting Tom with the murder.

Wilson regarded the case of the Twins as desperate—in fact, about hopeless. For he argued that if a confederate was not found, an enlightened Missouri jury would hang them, sure; if a confederate was found, that would not improve the matter, but simply furnish one more person for the sheriff to hang. Nothing could save the Twins but the discovery of a person who did the murder on his sole personal account—an undertaking which had all the aspect of the impossible. Still, the person who made the finger-prints must be sought. The Twins might have no case *with* him, but they certainly would have none without him.

So Wilson mooned around, thinking, thinking, guessing, guessing, day and night, and arriving nowhere. Whenever he ran across a girl or a woman he was not acquainted with, he got her finger-prints, on one pretext or another; and they always cost him a sigh when he got home, for they never tallied with the finger-marks on the knife handle.

As to the mysterious girl, Tom swore he knew no such girl, and did not remember ever seeing a girl wearing a dress like the one described by Wilson. He admitted that he did not always lock his room, and that sometimes the servants forgot to lock the house doors; still, in his opinion the girl must have made but few visits or she would have been discovered. When Wilson tried to connect her with the stealing-raid, and thought she might have been the old woman's confederate, if not the very thief herself disguised as an old woman, Tom seemed struck, and also much interested, and said he would keep a sharp eye out for this person or persons, although he was afraid that she or they would be too smart to venture again into a town where everybody would now be on the watch for a good while to come.

Everybody was pitying Tom, he looked so quiet and sorrowful, and seemed to feel his great loss so deeply. He was playing a part, but it was not all a part. The picture of his alleged uncle, as he had last seen him, was before him in the dark pretty frequently, when he was awake, and called again in his dreams, when he was asleep. He wouldn't go into the room where the tragedy had happened. This charmed the doting Mrs. Pratt, who "realized now, as she had never done before," she said, what a sensitive and delicate nature her darling had, and how he adored his poor uncle.

Chapter 20

Even the clearest and most perfect circumstantial evidence is likely to be at fault, after all, and therefore ought to be received with great caution. Take the case of any pencil, sharpened by any woman: if you have witnesses, you will find she did it with a knife; but if you take simply the aspect of the pencil, you will say she did it with her teeth.
—PUDD'NHEAD WILSON'S CALENDAR.

The weeks dragged along, no friend visiting the jailed Twins but their counsel and Aunt Patsy Cooper, and the day of trial came at last—the heaviest day in Wilson's life, for with all his tireless diligence he had discovered no sign or trace of the missing confederate. "Confederate" was the term he had long ago privately accepted for that person—not as being unquestionably the right term, but as being at least possibly the right one, though he was never able to understand why the Twins didn't vanish and escape, as the confederate had done, instead of remaining by the murdered man and getting caught there.

The court house was crowded, of course, and would remain so to the finish, for not only in the town itself, but in the country for miles around the trial was the one topic of conversation among the people. Mrs. Pratt, in deep mourning, and Tom with a weed on his hat, had seats near Pembroke Howard the public prosecutor, and back of them sat a great array of friends of the family. The Twins had but one friend present to keep their counsel in countenance, their poor old sorrowing landlady. She sat near Wilson, and looked her friendliest. In the "nigger corner" sat Chambers; also Roxy, with good clothes on and her bill of sale in her pocket. It was her most precious possession, and she never parted with it, day or night. Tom had allowed her thirty-five dollars a month ever since he came into his property, and had said that he and she ought to be grateful to the Twins for making them rich; but had roused such a temper in her by this speech that he did not repeat the argument afterward. She said the old Judge had treated her child a thousand times better than he deserved, and had never done her an unkindness in his life; so she hated these outlandish devils for killing him and shouldn't ever sleep satisfied till she saw them hanged for it. She was here to watch the trial, now, and was going to lift up just one "hooraw" over it if the County Judge put her in jail a year for it. She gave her turbaned head a toss and said, "When dat verdic' comes, I's gwyne to lif' dat *roof*, now, I *tell* you."

Pembroke Howard briefly sketched the State's case. He said he would show by a chain of circumstantial evidence without break or fault in it anywhere, that the principal prisoner at the bar committed the murder; that the motive was partly revenge, and partly a desire to take his own life out of jeopardy, and that his brother, by his presence, was a consenting accessory to the crime; a crime which was the basest known to the calendar of human misdeeds—assassination; that it was conceived by the blackest of hearts and consummated by the cowardliest of hands; a crime which had broken a loving sister's heart, blighted the happiness of a young nephew who was as dear as a son, brought inconsolable grief to many friends, and sorrow and loss to the whole community. The utmost penalty of the outraged law would be exacted, and upon the accused, now present at the bar, that penalty would unquestionably be executed. He would reserve further remark until his closing speech.

He was strongly moved, and so also was the whole house; Mrs. Pratt and several other women were weeping when he sat down, and many an eye that was full of hate was riveted upon the unhappy prisoners.

Witness after witness was called by the State, and questioned at length; but the cross-questioning was brief: Wilson knew they could furnish nothing valuable for his side. People were sorry for Pudd'n-head; his budding career would get hurt by this trial.

Several witnesses swore they heard Judge Driscoll say in his public speech that the Twins would be able to find their lost knife again when they needed it to assassinate somebody with. This was not news, but now it was seen to have been sorrowfully prophetic, and a profound sensation quivered through the hushed court room when those dismal words were repeated.

The public prosecutor rose and said that it was within his knowledge, through a conversation held with Judge Driscoll on the last day of his life, that counsel for the defence had brought him a challenge from the person charged at this bar with murder; that he had refused to fight with a confessed assassin—"that is, on the field of honor," but had added significantly, that he would be ready for him elsewhere. Presumably the person here charged with murder was warned that he must kill or be killed the first time he should meet Judge Driscoll. If counsel for the defence chose to let the statement stand so, he would not call him to the witness stand. Mr. Wilson said he would offer no denial. [Murmurs, in the house—"It is getting worse and worse for Wilson's case."]

Mrs. Pratt testified that she heard no outcry, and did not know what woke her up, unless it was the sound of rapid footsteps approaching the front door. She jumped up and ran out in the hall just as she was, and heard the footsteps flying up the front steps and then following behind her as she ran to the sitting room. There she found the accused standing over her murdered brother—[Here she broke down and sobbed. Sensation in the court.] Resuming, she said the persons entering behind her were Mr. Rogers and Mr. Buckstone.

Cross-examined by Wilson, she said the Twins proclaimed their innocence; declared that they had been taking a walk, and had hurried to the house in response to a cry for help which was so loud and strong that they had heard it at a considerable distance; that they begged her and the gentlemen just mentioned to examine their hands and clothes—which was done, and no blood stains found.

Confirmatory evidence followed, from Rogers and Buckstone.

The finding of the knife was verified, the advertisement minutely describing it and offering a reward for it was put in evidence, and its exact correspondence with that description proven. Then followed a few minor details, and the case for the State was closed.

Wilson said that he had three witnesses, the Misses Clarkson, who would testify that they met a veiled young woman leaving Judge Driscoll's premises by the back gate a few minutes after the cries for help were heard, and that their evidence, taken with certain circumstantial evidence which he would call the court's attention to would in his opinion convince the court that there was still one person concerned in this crime who had not yet been found, and also that a stay of proceedings ought to be granted, in justice to his clients, until that person should be discovered. As it was late, he would ask leave to defer the examination of his three witnesses until the next morning.

The crowd poured out of the place and went flocking away in excited groups and couples, talking the events of the session over with vivacity and consuming interest, and everybody seemed to have had a satisfactory and enjoyable day except the accused, their counsel, and their old-lady friend. There was no cheer among these, and no substantial hope.

In parting with the Twins Aunt Patsy did attempt a good-night with a gay pretence of hope and cheer in it, but broke down without finishing.

Absolutely secure as Tom considered himself to be, the opening solemnities of the trial had nevertheless oppressed him with a vague uneasiness, his being a nature sensitive to even the smallest alarms;

but from the moment that the poverty and weakness of Wilson's case lay exposed to the court, he was comfortable once more, even jubilant. He left the court-room sarcastically sorry for Wilson. "The Clarksons met an unknown woman in the back lane," he said to himself—"*that* is his case! I'll give him a century to find her in—a couple of them if he likes. A woman who doesn't exist any longer, and the clothes that gave her her sex burnt up and the ashes thrown away—oh, certainly, he'll find *her* easy enough!" This reflection set him to admiring, for the hundredth time, the shrewd ingenuities by which he had insured himself against detection—more, against even suspicion.

"Nearly always in cases like this there is some little detail or other overlooked, some wee little track or trace left behind, and detection follows; but here there's not even the faintest suggestion of a trace left. No more than a bird leaves when it flies through the air —yes, through the night, you may say. The man that can track a bird through the air in the dark and find that bird is the man to track me out and find the Judge's assassin—no other need apply. And that is the job that has been laid out for poor Pudd'nhead Wilson, of all people in the world! Lord, it will be pathetically funny to see him grubbing and groping after that woman that don't exist, and the right person sitting under his very nose all the time!" The more he thought the situation over, the more the humor of it struck him. Finally he said, "I'll never let him hear the last of that woman. Every time I catch him in company, to his dying day, I'll ask him in the guileless affectionate way that used to gravel him so when I inquired how his unborn law-business was coming along, 'Got on her track yet—hey, Pudd'nhead?'" He wanted to laugh, but that would not have answered; there were people about, and he was mourning for his uncle. He made up his mind that it would be good entertainment to look in on Wilson that night and watch him worry over his barren law-case and goad him with an exasperating word or two of sympathy and commiseration now and then.

Wilson wanted no supper, he had no appetite. He got out all the finger-prints of girls and women in his collection of records and pored gloomily over them an hour or more, trying to convince himself that that troublesome girl's marks were there somewhere and had been overlooked. But it was not so. He drew back his chair, clasped his hands over his head, and gave himself up to dull and arid musings.

Tom Driscoll dropped in, an hour after dark, and said with a pleasant laugh as he took a seat—

"Hello, we've gone back to the amusements of our days of neglect and obscurity for consolation, have we?" and he took up one of the glass strips and held it against the light to inspect it.

"Come, cheer up, old man, there's no use in losing your grip and going back to this child's play merely because this big sun-spot is drifting across your shiny new disk. It'll pass, and you'll be all right again"—and he laid the glass down. "Did you think you could win always?"

"Oh, no," said Wilson, with a sigh, "I didn't expect that, but I can't believe Luigi killed your uncle, and I feel very sorry for him. It makes me blue. And you would feel as I do, Tom, if you were not prejudiced against those young fellows."

"I don't know about that," and Tom's countenance darkened, for his memory reverted to his kicking; "I owe them no good will, considering the brunette one's treatment of me that night. Prejudice or no prejudice, Pudd'nhead, I don't like them, and when they get their deserts you're not going to find me sitting on the mourners' bench."

He took up another strip of glass, and exclaimed—

"Why, here's old Roxy's label! Are you going to ornament the royal palaces with nigger paw-marks, too? By the date here, I was seven months old when this was done, and she was nursing me and her little nigger cub. There's a line straight across her thumb-print. How comes that?" and Tom held out the piece of glass to Wilson.

"That is common," said the bored man, wearily. "Scar of a cut or a scratch, usually"—and he took the strip of glass indifferently and raised it toward the lamp.

All the blood sunk suddenly out of his face; his hand quaked, and he gazed at the polished surface before him with the glassy stare of a corpse.

"Great Heavens, what's the matter with you, Wilson? Are you going to faint?"

Tom sprang for a glass of water and offered it, but Wilson shrank shuddering from him and said—

"No, no!—Take it away!" His breast was rising and falling, and he moved his head about in a dull and wandering way, like a person who has been stunned. Presently he said, "I shall feel better when I get to bed; I have been overwrought to-day; yes, and overworked for many days."

"Then I'll leave you and let you get to your rest. Good night, old man." But as Tom went out he couldn't deny himself a small parting gibe: "Don't take it so hard; a body can't win every time; you'll hang somebody yet."

Wilson muttered to himself, "It is no lie to say I am sorry I have to begin with you, miserable dog though you are!"

He braced himself up with a glass of cold whisky and went to work again. He did not compare the new finger-marks unintentionally left by Tom a few minutes before on Roxy's glass with the tracings of the marks left on the knife handle, there being no need of that—for his trained eye—but busied himself with another matter, muttering from time to time, "Idiot that I was! Nothing but a *girl* would do me—a man in girl's clothes never occurred to me." First, he hunted out the plate containing the finger-prints made by Tom when he was twelve years old, and laid it by itself; then he brought forth the marks made by Tom's baby fingers when he was a suckling of seven months, and placed these two plates with the one containing this subject's newly (and unconsciously) made record.

"Now the series is complete," he said with satisfaction, and sat down to inspect these things and enjoy them.

But his enjoyment was brief. He stared a considerable time at the three strips, and seemed stupefied with astonishment. At last he put them down and said, "I can't make it out at all—hang it, the baby's don't tally with the others!"

He walked the floor for half an hour puzzling over his enigma, then he hunted out two other glass plates.

He sat down and puzzled over these things a good while, but kept muttering, "It's no use; I can't understand it. They don't tally right, and yet I'll swear the names and dates are right, and so of course they *ought* to tally. I never labeled one of these things carelessly in my life. There is a most extraordinary mystery here."

He was tired out, now, and his brains were beginning to clog. He said he would sleep himself fresh, and then see what he could do with this riddle. He slept through a troubled and unrestful hour, then unconsciousness began to shred away and presently he rose drowsily to a sitting posture. "Now what was that dream?" he said, trying to recall it; "What was that dream?—it seemed to unravel that puz—"

He landed in the middle of the floor at a bound, without finishing the sentence, and ran and turned up his light and seized his "records." He took a single swift glance at them and cried out—

"It's so! Heavens, what a revelation! And for twenty-three years no man has ever suspected it!"

Chapter 21

He is useless on top of the ground; he ought to be under it, inspiring the cabbages.
— PUDD'NHEAD WILSON'S CALENDAR.

April 1. This is the day upon which we are reminded of what we are on the other three hundred and sixty-four.
— PUDD'NHEAD WILSON'S CALENDAR.

Wilson put on enough clothes for business purposes, and went to work under a high pressure of steam. He was awake all over. All sense of weariness had been swept away by the invigorating refreshment of the great and hopeful discovery which he had made. He made fine and accurate reproductions of a number of his "records," and then enlarged them on a scale of ten to one with his pantograph. He did these pantograph enlargements on sheets of white cardboard, and made each individual line of the bewildering maze of whorls or curves or loops which constituted the "pattern" of a "record" stand out bold and black by reinforcing it with ink. To the untrained eye the collection of delicate originals made by the human finger on the glass plates looked about alike; but when enlarged ten times, they resembled the markings of a block of wood that has been sawed across the grain, and the dullest eye could detect at a glance, and at a distance of many feet, that no two of the patterns were alike. When Wilson had at last finished his tedious and difficult work, he arranged its results according to a plan in which a progressive order and sequence was a principal feature, then he added to the batch several pantograph enlargements which he had made from time to time in bygone years.

The night was spent and the day well advanced, now. By the time he had snatched a trifle of breakfast it was nine o'clock and the court was ready to begin its sitting. He was in his place twelve minutes later, with his "records."

Tom Driscoll caught a slight glimpse of the records and nudged his nearest friend and said, with a wink, "Pudd'nhead's got a rare eye to business—thinks that as long as he can't win his case, it's at least a noble good chance to advertise his palace-window decorations without any expense." Wilson was informed that his witnesses had been delayed, but would arrive presently; but he rose and said he should probably not have occasion to make use of their testimony. [An amused murmur ran through the room—"It's a clean back-down! he gives up without hitting a lick!"] Wilson continued—

"I have other testimony,—and better." [This compelled interest, and evoked murmurs of surprise that had a detectible ingredient of disappointment in them.] "If I seem to be springing this evidence upon the court, I offer as my justification for this, that I did not discover its existence until late last night, and have been engaged in examining and classifying it ever since until half an hour ago. I shall offer it presently; but first I wish to say a few preliminary words.

"May it please the court, the claim given the front place, the claim most persistently urged, the claim most strenuously and I may even say, aggressively and defiantly insisted upon by the prosecution, is this—that the person whose hand left the blood-stained finger-prints upon the handle of the Indian knife is the person who committed the murder." Wilson paused, during several moments, to give impressiveness to what he was about to say, and then added, tranquilly, *"We grant that claim."*

It was an electrical surprise. No one was prepared for such an admission. A buzz of astonishment rose on all sides, and people were heard to intimate that the overworked lawyer had lost his mind. Even the veteran Judge, accustomed as he was to legal ambushes and masked batteries in criminal procedure, was not sure that his ears were not deceiving him, and asked counsel what it was he had said. Howard's impassive face betrayed no sign, but his attitude and bearing lost something of their careless confidence for a moment. Wilson resumed:

"We not only grant that claim, but we welcome it and strongly endorse it. Leaving that matter for the present, we will now proceed to consider other points in the case which we propose to establish by evidence, and shall include that one in the chain, in its proper place."

He had made up his mind to try a few hardy guesses, in mapping out his theory of the origin and motive of the murder—guesses designed to fill up gaps in it—guesses which could help if they hit, and would probably do no harm if they didn't.

"To my mind, certain circumstances of the case before the court seem to suggest a motive for the homicide quite different from the one insisted on by the State. It is my conviction that the motive was not revenge, but robbery. It has been urged that the presence of the accused brothers in that fatal room, just after notification that one of them must take the life of Judge Driscoll or lose his own the moment the parties should meet, clearly signifies that the natural instinct of self-preservation moved my clients to go there secretly and save Count Luigi by destroying his adversary.

"Then why did they stay there, after the deed was done? Mrs. Pratt had time, although she did not hear the cry for help, but woke up some moments later, to run to that room—and there she found these men standing, and making no effort to escape. If they were guilty, they ought to have been running out of the house at the same time that she was running to that room. If they had had such a strong instinct toward self-preservation as to move them to kill that unarmed man, what had become of it now, when it should have been more alert than ever? Would any of us have remained there? Let us not slander our intelligence to that degree.

"Much stress has been laid upon the fact that the accused offered a very large reward for the knife with which this murder was done; that no thief came forward to claim that extraordinary reward; that the latter fact was good circumstantial evidence that the claim that the knife had been stolen was a vanity and a fraud; that these details taken in connection with the memorable and apparently prophetic speech of the deceased concerning that knife and the final discovery of that very knife in the fatal room where no living person was found present with the slaughtered man but the owner of the knife and his brother, form an indestructible chain of evidence which fixes the crime upon those unfortunate strangers.

"But I shall presently ask to be sworn, and shall testify that there was a large reward offered for the *thief*, also; that it was offered secretly and not advertised; that this fact was indiscreetly mentioned—or at least tacitly admitted—in what was supposed to be safe circumstances, but may *not* have been. The thief may have been present himself." [Tom Driscoll had been looking at the speaker, but dropped his eyes at this point.] "In that case he would retain the knife in his possession, not daring to offer it for sale, or for pledge in a pawn shop." [There was a nodding of heads among the audience by way of admission that this was not a bad stroke.] "I shall prove to the satisfaction of the jury that there *was* a person in Judge Driscoll's room several minutes before the accused entered it." [This produced a strong sensation; the last drowsy-head in the court room roused up, now, and made preparation to listen.] "If it shall seem necessary, I will prove by the Misses Clarkson that they met a veiled person—ostensibly a woman—coming out of the back gate a few minutes after the cry for help was heard. This person was not a woman, but a man dressed in woman's clothes." Another sensation. Wilson had his eye on Tom when he hazarded this guess, to see what effect it would produce. He was satisfied with the result, and said to himself, "It was a success—he's hit!"

"The object of that person in that house was robbery, not murder. It is true that the safe was not open, but there was an ordinary tin cash-box on the table with three thousand dollars in it. It is easily supposable that the thief was concealed in the house; that he knew of this box, and of its owner's habit of counting its contents and arranging his accounts at night—if he had that habit, which I do not assert, of course; that he tried to take the box while its owner slept, but made a noise and was seized, and had to use the knife to save himself from capture; and that he fled without his booty because he heard help coming.

"I have now done with my theory, and will proceed to the evidences by which I propose to try to prove its soundness." Wilson took up several of his strips of glass. When the audience recognized these familiar mementoes of Pudd'nhead's old-time childish "puttering" and folly, the tense and funereal interest vanished out of their faces and the house burst into volleys of relieving and refreshing laughter, and Tom chirked up and joined in the fun himself; but Wilson was apparently not disturbed. He arranged his records on the table before him, and said—

"I beg the indulgence of the court while I make a few remarks in explanation of some evidence which I am about to introduce, and which I shall presently ask to be allowed to verify under oath on the witness stand. Every human being carries with him from his cradle to his grave certain physical marks which do not change their character, and by which he can always be identified—and that without shade of doubt or question. These marks are his signature, his physiological autograph, so to speak, and this autograph cannot be counterfeited, nor can he disguise it or hide it away, nor can it become illegible by the wear and the mutations of time. This signature is not his face—age can change that beyond recognition; it is not his hair, for that can fall out; it is not his height, for duplicates of that exist; it is not his form, for duplicates of that exist, also, whereas this signature is each man's very own—there is no duplicate of it among the swarming populations of the globe!" [The audience were interested once more.]

"This autograph consists of the delicate lines or corrugations with which Nature marks the insides of the hands and the soles of the feet. If you will look at the balls of your fingers—you that have very sharp eyesight—you will observe that these dainty, curving lines lie close together, like those that indicate the borders of oceans in maps, and that they form various clearly defined patterns, such as arches, circles, long curves, whorls, etc., and that these patterns differ on the different fingers." [Every man in the room had his hand up to the light, now, and his head canted to one side, and was minutely scrutinizing the balls of his fingers; there were whispered ejaculations of, 'Why, it's so—I never noticed that before!'] "The patterns on the right hand are not the same as those on the left." [Ejaculations of 'Why, that's so, too!'] "Taken finger for finger, your patterns differ from your neighbor's." [Comparisons were made, all over the house—even the judge and jury were absorbed in this curious work.] "The patterns of a twin's right hand are not the same as those on his left. One twin's patterns are never the same as his fellow-twin's patterns—the jury will find that the patterns upon the finger-balls of the accused follow this rule."—[An examination of the Twins' hands was begun at once.] "You have often heard of twins who were so exactly alike that when dressed alike their own parents could not tell them apart. Yet there was never a twin born

into this world that did not carry from birth to death a sure identi-
fier in this mysterious and marvelous natal autograph. That once
known to you, his fellow-twin could never personate him and
deceive you."

Wilson stopped, and stood silent. Inattention dies a quick and
sure death when a speaker does that. The stillness gives warning
that something is coming. All palms and finger-balls went down,
now, all slouching forms straightened, all heads came up, all eyes
were fastened upon Wilson's face. He waited yet one, two, three
moments, to let his pause complete and perfect its spell upon the
house; then, when through the profound hush he could hear the
ticking of the clock on the wall, he put out his hand and took the
Indian knife by the blade and held it aloft where all could see the
sinister spots upon its ivory handle; then he said, in a level and pas-
sionless voice—

"Upon this haft stands the assassin's natal autograph, written in
the blood of that helpless and unoffending old man who loved you
and whom you all loved. There is but one man in the whole earth
whose hand can duplicate that crimson sign"—he paused and raised
his eyes to the pendulum swinging back and forth—"and please
God we will produce that man in this room before the clock strikes
noon!"

Stunned, distraught, unconscious of its own movement, the house
half rose, as if expecting to see the murderer appear at the door,
and a breeze of muttered ejaculations swept the place. "Order in
the court!—sit down!" This from the sheriff. He was obeyed, and
quiet reigned again. Wilson stole a glance at Tom, and said to himself, "He is flying signals of distress, now; even people who despise
him are pitying him; they think this is a hard ordeal for a young
fellow who has lost his benefactor by so cruel a stroke—and they
are right." He resumed his speech:

"For more than twenty years I have amused my compulsory leisure with collecting these curious physical signatures in this town.
At my house I have hundreds upon hundreds of them. Each and
every one is labeled with name and date; not labeled the next day
or even the next hour, but in the very minute that the impression
was taken. When I go upon the witness stand I will repeat under
oath the things which I am now saying. I have the finger-prints of
the court, the sheriff, and every member of the jury. There is hardly
a person in this room, white or black, whose natal signature I
cannot produce, and not one of them can so disguise himself that I
cannot pick him out from a multitude of his fellow creatures and
unerringly identify him by his hands. And if he and I should live to
be a hundred I could still do it!" [The interest of the audience was
steadily deepening, now.]

"I have studied some of these signatures so much that I know them as well as the bank cashier knows the autograph of his oldest customer. While I turn my back, now, I beg that several persons will be so good as to pass their fingers through their hair and then press them upon one of the panes of the window near the jury, and that among them the accused may set *their* finger-marks. Also, I beg that these experimenters, or others, will set their finger-marks upon another pane, and add again the marks of the accused, but not placing them in the same order or relation to the other signatures as before—for, by one chance in a million, a person might happen upon the right marks by pure guesswork, *once*, therefore I wish to be tested twice."

He turned his back, and the two panes were quickly covered with delicately-lined oval spots, but visible only to such persons as could get a dark background for them,—the foliage of a tree, outside, for instance. Then, upon call, Wilson went to the window, made his examination, and said—

"This is Count Luigi's right hand; this one, three signatures below, is his left. Here is Count Angelo's right; down here is his left. Now for the other pane: here and here are Count Luigi's, here and here are his brother's." He faced about. "Am I right?"

A deafening explosion of applause was the answer. The Bench said—

"This certainly approaches the miraculous!"

Wilson turned to the window again and remarked, pointing with his finger—

"This is the signature of Mr. Justice Robinson." [Applause.] "This, of Constable Blake." [Applause.] "This, of John Mason, juryman." [Applause.] "This, of the sheriff." [Applause.] "I cannot name the others, but I have them all at home, named and dated, and could identify them all by my finger-print records."

He moved to his place through a storm of applause—which the sheriff stopped, and also made the people sit down, for they were all standing, and struggling to see, of course. Court, jury, sheriff and everybody had been too absorbed in observing Wilson's performance to attend to the audience earlier.

"Now then," said Wilson, "I have here the natal autographs of two children—thrown up to ten times the natural size by the pantograph, so that any one who can see at all can tell the markings apart at a glance. We will call the children A and B. Here are A's finger-marks, taken at the age of five months. Here they are again, taken at seven months." [Tom started.] "They are alike, you see. Here are B's at five months, and also at seven months. They, too, exactly copy each other, but the patterns are quite different from A's, you observe. I shall refer to these again presently, but we will turn them face down, now.

"Here, thrown up ten sizes, are the natal autographs of the two persons who are here before you accused of murdering Judge Driscoll. I made these pantograph copies last night, and will so swear when I go upon the witness stand. I ask the jury to compare them with the finger-marks of the accused upon the window panes, and tell the court if they are the same."

He passed a powerful magnifying glass to the foreman.

One jury man after another took the cardboard and the glass and made the comparison. Then the foreman said to the Judge—

"Your honor, we are all agreed that they are identical."

Wilson said to the foreman—

"Please turn that cardboard face down, and take this one and compare it searchingly, by the magnifier, with the fatal signature upon the knife-handle, and report your finding to the court."

Again the jury made minute examination, and again reported—

"We find them to be exactly identical, your honor."

Wilson turned toward the counsel for the prosecution, and there was a clearly recognizable note of warning in his voice when he said—

"May it please the court, the State has claimed, strenuously and persistently, that the blood-stained finger-prints upon that knife handle were left there by the assassin of Judge Driscoll. You have heard us grant that claim, and welcome it." He turned to the jury: "Compare the finger-prints of the accused with the finger-prints left by the assassin—and report."

The comparison began. As it proceeded, all movement and all sound ceased, and the deep silence of an absorbed and waiting suspense settled upon the house; and when at last the words came—

"*They do not even resemble,*" a thunder-crash of applause followed and the house sprang to its feet, but was quickly repressed by official force and brought to order again. Tom was altering his position every few minutes, now, but none of his changes brought repose nor any small trifle of comfort. When the house's attention was become fixed once more, Wilson said gravely, indicating the Twins with a gesture—

"These men are innocent—I have no further concern with them." [Another outbreak of applause began, but was promptly checked.] "We will now proceed to find the guilty." [Tom's eyes were starting from their sockets—yes, it was a cruel day for the bereaved youth, everybody thought.] "We will return to the infant autographs of A and B. I will ask the jury to take these large pantograph facsimiles of A's, marked five months and seven months. Do they tally?"

The foreman responded—

"Perfectly."

"Now examine this pantograph, taken at eight months, and also marked A. Does it tally with the other two?"

The surprised response was—

"*No—they differ widely!*"

"You are quite right. Now take these two pantographs of B's autograph, marked five months and seven months. Do they tally with each other?"

"Yes—perfectly."

"Take this third pantograph marked 'B, eight months.' Does it tally with B's other two?"

"*By no means!*"

"Do you know how to account for those strange discrepancies? I will tell you. For a purpose unknown to us, but probably a selfish one, somebody changed those children in the cradle."

This produced a vast sensation, naturally; Roxana was astonished at this admirable guess, but not disturbed by it. To guess the exchange was one thing, to guess who did it quite another. Pudd'n-head Wilson could do wonderful things, no doubt, but he couldn't do impossible ones. Safe? She was perfectly safe. She smiled privately.

"Between the ages of seven months and eight months those children were changed in the cradle"—he made one of his effect-collecting pauses, and added—"and the person who did it is in this house!"

Roxy's pulses stood still! The house was thrilled as with an electric shock, and the people half rose, as if to seek a glimpse of the person who had made that exchange. Tom was growing limp; the life seemed oozing out of him. Wilson resumed:

"A was put into B's cradle in the nursery; B was transferred to the kitchen, and became a negro and a slave"—[Sensation—confusion of angry ejaculations]—"but within a quarter of an hour he will stand before you white and free!" [Burst of applause, checked by the officers.] "From seven months onward until now, A has still been a usurper, and in my finger-records he bears B's name. Here is his pantograph, at the age of twelve. Compare it with the assassin's signature upon the knife handle. Do they tally?"

The foreman answered—

"*To the minutest detail!*"

Wilson said, solemnly—

"The murderer of your friend and mine—York Driscoll, of the generous hand and the kindly spirit—sits among you. Valet de Chambre, negro and slave—falsely called Thomas à Becket Driscoll —make upon the window the finger-prints that will hang you!"

Tom turned his ashen face imploringly toward the speaker, made some impotent movements with his white lips, then slid limp and lifeless to the floor.

Wilson broke the awed silence with the words—

"There is no need. He has confessed."

Roxy flung herself upon her knees, covered her face with her hands, and out through her sobs the words struggled—

"De Lord have mercy on me, po' misable sinner dat I is!"

The clock struck twelve.

The court rose; the new prisoner, handcuffed, was removed.

Conclusion

It is often the case that the man who can't tell a lie thinks he is the best judge of one.
—PUDD'NHEAD WILSON'S CALENDAR.

October 12, the Discovery. It was wonderful to find America, but it would have been more wonderful to miss it.
—PUDD'NHEAD WILSON'S CALENDAR.

The town sat up all night to discuss the amazing events of the day and swap guesses as to when Tom's trial would begin. Troop after troop of citizens came to serenade Wilson, and require a speech, and shout themselves hoarse over every sentence that fell from his lips—for all his sentences were golden, now, all were marvelous. His long fight against hard luck and prejudice was ended; he was a made man for good.

And as each of these roaring gangs of enthusiasts marched away, some remorseful member of it was quite sure to raise his voice and say—

"And this is the man the likes of us have called a pudd'nhead for more than twenty years. He has resigned from that position, friends."

"Yes, but it isn't vacant—we're elected."

The Twins were heroes of romance, now, and with rehabilitated reputations. But they were weary of Western adventure, and straightway retired to Europe.

Roxy's heart was broken. The young fellow upon whom she had inflicted twenty-three years of slavery continued the false heir's pension of thirty-five dollars a month to her, but her hurts were too deep for money to heal; the spirit in her eye was quenched, her martial bearing departed with it, and the voice of her laughter ceased in the land. In her church and its affairs she found her only solace.

The real heir suddenly found himself rich and free, but in a most embarrassing situation. He could neither read nor write, and his speech was the basest dialect of the negro quarter. His gait, his attitudes, his gestures, his bearing, his laugh—all were vulgar and uncouth; his manners were the manners of a slave. Money and fine clothes could not mend these defects or cover them up, they only made them the more glaring and the more pathetic. The poor fellow could not endure the terrors of the white man's parlor, and felt at home and at peace nowhere but in the kitchen. The family pew was a misery to him, yet he could nevermore enter into the solacing refuge of the "nigger gallery"—that was closed to him for good and all. But we cannot follow his curious fate further—that would be a long story.

The false heir made a full confession and was sentenced to imprisonment for life. But now a complication came up. The Percy Driscoll estate was in such a crippled shape when its owner died that it could pay only sixty per cent of its great indebtedness, and was settled at that rate. But the creditors came forward, now, and complained that inasmuch as through an error for which *they* were in no way to blame the false heir was not inventoried at that time with the rest of the property, great wrong and loss had thereby been inflicted upon them. They rightly claimed that "Tom" was lawfully their property and had been so for eight years; that they had already lost sufficiently in being deprived of his services during that long period, and ought not to be required to add anything to that loss; that if he had been delivered up to them in the first place, they would have sold him and he could not have murdered Judge Driscoll, therefore it was not he that had really committed the murder, the guilt lay with the erroneous inventory. Everybody saw that there was reason in this. Everybody granted that if "Tom" were white and free it would be unquestionably right to punish him—it would be no loss to anybody; but to shut up a valuable slave for life—that was quite another matter.

As soon as the Governor understood the case, he pardoned Tom at once, and the creditors sold him down the river.

The Text of
Those Extraordinary
Twins

A man who is not born with the novel-writing gift has a trouble-some time of it when he tries to build a novel. I know this from experience. He has no clear idea of his story; in fact he has no story. He merely has some people in his mind, and an incident or two, also a locality. He knows these people, he knows the selected locality, and he trusts that he can plunge those people into those incidents with interesting results. So he goes to work. To write a novel? No—that is a thought which comes later; in the beginning he is only proposing to tell a little tale; a very little tale; a six-page tale. But as it is a tale which he is not acquainted with, and can only find out what it is by listening as it goes along telling itself, it is more than apt to go on and on and on till it spreads itself into a book. I know about this, because it has happened to me so many times.

And I have noticed another thing: that as the short tale grows into the long tale, the original intention (or motif) is apt to get abolished and find itself superseded by a quite different one. It was so in the case of a magazine sketch which I once started to write—a funny and fantastic sketch about a prince and a pauper; it presently assumed a grave cast of its own accord, and in that new shape spread itself out into a book. Much the same thing happened with "Pudd'nhead Wilson." I had a sufficiently hard time with that tale, because it changed itself from a farce to a tragedy while I was going along with it,—a most embarrassing circumstance. But what was a great deal worse was, that it was not one story, but two stories tangled together; and they obstructed and interrupted each other at every turn and created no end of confusion and annoyance. I could not offer the book for publication, for I was afraid it would unseat the reader's reason, I did not know what was the matter with it, for I had not noticed, as yet, that it was two stories in one. It took me months to make that discovery. I carried the manuscript back and forth across the Atlantic two or three times, and read it and studied over it on shipboard; and at last I saw where the difficulty lay. I had no further trouble. I pulled one of the stories out by the roots, and left the other one—a kind of literary Cæsarean operation.

Would the reader care to know something about the story which I pulled out? He has been told many a time how the born-and-trained novelist works; won't he let me round and complete his knowledge by telling him how the jack-leg does it?

Originally the story was called "Those Extraordinary Twins." I meant to make it very short. I had seen a picture of a youthful Italian "freak"—or "freaks"—which was—or which were—on exhibition in our cities—a combination consisting of two heads and four arms joined to a single body and a single pair of legs—and I thought I would write an extravagantly fantastic little story with this freak of nature for hero—or heroes—a silly young Miss for hero-

ine, and two old ladies and two boys for the minor parts. I lav-
ishly elaborated these people and their doings, of course. But the
tale kept spreading along and spreading along, and other people got
to intruding themselves and taking up more and more room with
their talk and their affairs. Among them came a stranger named
Pudd'nhead Wilson, and a woman named Roxana; and presently
the doings of these two pushed up into prominence a young fellow
named Tom Driscoll, whose proper place was away in the obscure
background. Before the book was half finished those three were
taking things almost entirely into their own hands and working the
whole tale as a private venture of their own—a tale which they had
nothing at all to do with, by rights.

When the book was finished and I came to look around to see
what had become of the team I had originally started out with—
Aunt Patsy Cooper, Aunt Betsy Hale, the two boys, and Rowena
the light-weight heroine—they were nowhere to be seen; they had
disappeared from the story some time or other. I hunted about and
found them—found them stranded, idle, forgotten, and permanently useless. It was very awkward. It was awkward all around, but
more particularly in the case of Rowena, because there was a love-
match on, between her and one of the twins that constituted the
freak, and I had worked it up to a blistering heat and thrown in a
quite dramatic love-quarrel, wherein Rowena scathingly denounced
her betrothed for getting drunk, and scoffed at his explanation of
how it had happened, and wouldn't listen to it, and had driven him
from her in the usual "forever" way; and now here she sat crying
and broken-hearted; for she had found that he had spoken only the

truth; that it was not he, but the other half of the freak that had drunk the liquor that made him drunk; that her half was a prohibitionist and had never drunk a drop in his life, and although tight as a brick three days in the week, was wholly innocent of blame; and indeed, when sober, was constantly doing all he could to reform his brother, the other half, who never got any satisfaction out of drinking, anyway, because liquor never affected him. Yes, here she was, stranded with that deep injustice of hers torturing her poor torn heart.

I didn't know what to do with her. I was as sorry for her as anybody could be, but the campaign was over, the book was finished, she was sidetracked, and there was no possible way of crowding her in, anywhere. I could not leave her there, of course; it would not do. After spreading her out so, and making such a to-do over her affairs, it would be absolutely necessary to account to the reader for her. I thought and thought and studied and studied; but I arrived at nothing. I finally saw plainly that there was really no way but one—I must simply give her the grand bounce. It grieved me to do it, for after associating with her so much I had come to kind of like her after a fashion, notwithstanding she was such an ass and said such stupid, irritating things and was so nauseatingly sentimental. Still it had to be done. So at the top of Chapter XVII. I put a "Calendar" remark concerning July the Fourth, and began the chapter with this statistic:

"Rowena went out in the back yard after supper to see the fireworks and fell down the well and got drowned."

It seemed abrupt, but I thought maybe the reader wouldn't notice it, because I changed the subject right away to something else. Anyway it loosened up Rowena from where she was stuck and got her out of the way, and that was the main thing. It seemed a prompt good way of weeding out people that had got stalled, and a plenty good enough way for those others; so I hunted up the two boys and said "they went out back one night to stone the cat and fell down the well and got drowned." Next I searched around and found old Aunt Patsy Cooper and Aunt Betsy Hale where they were aground, and said "they went out back one night to visit the sick and fell down the well and got drowned." I was going to drown some of the others, but I gave up the idea, partly because I believed that if I kept that up it would arouse attention, and perhaps sympathy with those people, and partly because it was not a large well and would not hold any more anyway.

Still the story was unsatisfactory. Here was a set of new characters who were become inordinately prominent and who persisted in remaining so to the end; and back yonder was an older set who made a large noise and a great to-do for a little while and then suddenly played out utterly and fell down the well. There was a radical defect somewhere, and I must search it out and cure it.

The defect turned out to be the one already spoken of—two stories in one, a farce and a tragedy. So I pulled out the farce and left the tragedy. This left the original team in, but only as mere names, not as characters. Their prominence was wholly gone; they were not even worth drowning; so I removed that detail. Also I took those twins apart and made two separate men of them. They had no occasion to have foreign names now, but it was too much trouble to remove them all through, so I left them christened as they were and made no explanation.

The Suppressed Farce

Chapter 1

The conglomerate twins were brought on the stage in Chapter I. of the original extravaganza. Aunt Patsy Cooper has received their letter applying for board and lodging, and Rowena, her daughter, insane with joy, is begging for a hearing of it:

"Well, set down then, and be quiet a minute and don't fly around so; it fairly makes me tired to see you. It starts off so: 'Honored Madam'—"

"I like that, ma, don't you? It shows they're high-bred."

"Yes, I noticed that when I first read it. 'My brother and I have seen your advertisement, by chance, in a copy of your local journal—' "

"It's so beautiful and smooth, ma—don't you think so?"

"Yes, seems so to me—'and beg leave to take the room you offer. We are twenty-four years of age, and twins—' "

"Twins! How sweet! I do hope they are handsome, and I just know they are! Don't you hope they are, ma?"

"Land, I ain't particular. 'We are Italians by birth—' "

"It's so romantic! Just think—there's never been one in this town, and everybody will want to see them, and they're all *ours!* Think of that!"

"— 'but have lived long in the various countries of Europe, and several years in the United States.' "

"Oh, just think what wonders they've seen, ma! Won't it be good to hear them talk?"

"I reckon so; yes, I reckon so. 'Our names are Luigi and Angelo Cappello—' "

"Beautiful, perfectly beautiful! Not like Jones and Robinson and those horrible names."

" 'You desire but one guest, but dear Madam, if you will allow us to pay for two we will not discommode you. We will sleep together in the same bed. We have always been used to this, and prefer it.' And then he goes on to say they will be down Thursday."

"And this is Tuesday—I don't know how I'm ever going to wait, ma! The time does drag along so, and I'm so dying to see them! Which of them do you reckon is the tallest, ma?"

"How do you s'pose I can tell, child? Mostly they are the same size—twins are."

"Well, then, which do you reckon is the best looking?"

"Goodness knows—I don't."

"I think Angelo is; it's the prettiest name, anyway. Don't you think it's a sweet name, ma?"

"Yes, it's well enough. I'd like both of them better if I knew the way to pronounce them—the Eyetalian way, I mean. The Missouri way and the Eyetalian way is different, I judge."

"May be—yes. It's Luigi that writes the letter. What do you reckon is the reason Angelo didn't write it?"

"Why, how can I tell? What's the difference who writes it, so long as it's done?"

"Oh, I hope it wasn't because he is sick! You don't think he is sick, do you, ma?"

"Sick your granny; what's to make him sick?"

"Oh, there's never any telling. Those foreigners with that kind of names are so delicate, and of course that kind of names are not suited to our climate—you wouldn't expect it."

[And so-on and so-on, no end. The time drags along; Thursday comes; the boat arrives in a pouring storm toward midnight.]

At last there was a knock on the door and the family jumped to open it. Two negro men entered, each carrying a trunk, and proceeded up stairs toward the guest room. Then followed a stupefying apparition—a double-headed human creature with four arms, one body, and a single pair of legs!

It—or they, as you please—bowed with elaborate foreign formality, but the Coopers could not respond, immediately; they were paralyzed. At this moment there came from the rear of the group a fervent ejaculation—"My lan'!"—followed by a crash of crockery, and the slave wench Nancy stood petrified and staring, with a tray of wrecked tea things at her feet. The incident broke the spell, and brought the family to consciousness. The beautiful heads of the new comer bowed again, and one of them said with easy grace and dignity—

"I crave the honor, Madam and Miss, to introduce to you my brother, Count Luigi Cappello," (the other head bowed,) "and myself—Count Angelo, and at the same time offer sincere apologies for the lateness of our coming, which was unavoidable;" and both heads bowed again.

The poor old lady was in a whirl of amazement and confusion, but she managed to stammer out—

"I'm sure I'm glad to make your acquaintance, sir—I mean, gentlemen. As for the delay, it is nothing, don't mention it. This is my daughter Rowena, sir—gentlemen. Please step into the parlor and sit down and have a bite and sup; you are dreadful wet and must be uncomfortable—both of you, I mean."

But to the old lady's relief they courteously excused themselves, saying it would be wrong to keep the family out of their beds longer; then each head bowed in turn and uttered a friendly good night, and the singular figure moved away in the wake of Rowena's small brothers, who bore candles, and disappeared up the stairs.

The widow tottered into the parlor and sank into a chair with a gasp, and Rowena followed, tongue-tied and dazed. The two sat silent in the throbbing summer heat, unconscious of the million-voiced music of the mosquitoes, unconscious of the roaring gale, the lashing and thrashing of the rain along the windows and the roof, the white glare of the lightnings, the tumultuous booming and bellowing of the thunder, conscious of nothing but that prodigy, that uncanny apparition that had come and gone so suddenly—that weird strange thing that was so soft spoken and so gentle of manner, and yet had shaken them up like an earthquake with the shock of its grewsome aspect. At last a cold little shudder quivered along down the widow's meagre frame and she said in a weak voice—

"Ugh, it was awful—just the mere look of that phillipena!"[2]

Rowena did not answer. Her faculties were still caked, she had not yet found her voice. Presently the widow said, a little resentfully—

"Always been *used* to sleeping together—in fact, *prefer* it. And I was thinking it was to accommodate me. I thought it was very good of them, whereas a person situated as that young man is—"

"Ma, you oughtn't to begin by getting up a prejudice against him. I'm sure he is good hearted and means well. Both of his faces show it."

"I'm not so certain about that. The one on the left—I mean the one on *its* left—hasn't near as good a face, in my opinion, as its brother."

"That's Luigi."

"Yes, Luigi; anyway it's the dark-skinned one; the one that was west of his brother when they stood in the door. Up to all kinds of

2. See Textual Notes to *Pudd'nhead Wilson,* 56.18, below.

mischief and disobedience when he was a boy, I'll be bound. I lay his mother had trouble to lay her hand on him when she wanted him. But the one on the right is as good as gold, I can see that."

"That's Angelo."

"Yes, Angelo, I reckon, though I can't tell t'other from which by their names, yet awhile. But it's the right-hand one—the blonde one. He has such kind blue eyes, and curly copper hair and fresh complexion—"

"And such a noble face!—oh, it *is* a noble face, ma, just royal, you may say! And beautiful—deary me, how beautiful! But both are that; the dark one's as beautiful as a picture. There's no such wonderful faces and handsome heads in this town—none that even begin. And such hands!—especially Angelo's—so shapely and—"

"Stuff, how could you tell which they belonged to?—they had gloves on."

"Why, didn't I see them take off their hats?"

"That don't signify. They might have taken off each other's hats. Nobody could tell. There was just a wormy squirming of arms in the air—seemed to be a couple of dozen of them, all writhing at once, and it just made me dizzy to see them go."

"Why, ma, I hadn't any difficulty. There's two arms on each shoulder—"

"There, now. One arm on each shoulder belongs to each of the creatures, don't it? For a person to have two arms on one shoulder wouldn't do him any good, would it? Of course not. Each has an arm on each shoulder. Now then, you tell me which of them belongs to which, if you can. *They* don't know, themselves—they just work whichever arm comes handy. Of course they do; especially if they are in a hurry and can't stop to think which belongs to which."

The mother seemed to have the rights of the argument, so the daughter abandoned the struggle. Presently the widow rose with a yawn and said—

"Poor thing, I hope it won't catch cold; it was powerful wet, just drenched, you may say. I hope it has left its boots outside, so they can be dried." Then she gave a little start, and looked perplexed. "Now I remember I heard one of them ask Joe to call him at half after seven,—I think it was the one on the left—no, it was the one to the east of the other one—but I didn't hear the other one say anything. I wonder if he wants to be called, too. Do you reckon it's too late to ask?"

"Why, ma, it's not necessary. Calling one is calling both. If one gets up, the other's *got* to."

"Sho, of course; I never thought of that. Well, come along, maybe we can get some sleep, but I don't know, I'm so shook up with what we've been through."

The stranger had made an impression on the boys, too. They had a word of talk as they were getting to bed. Henry, the gentle, the humane, said—

"I feel ever so sorry for it, don't you, Joe?"

But Joe was a boy of this world, active, enterprising, and had a theatrical side to him.

"Sorry? Why how you talk! It can't stir a step without attracting attention. It's just grand!"

Henry said, reproachfully—

"Instead of pitying it, Joe, you talk as if—"

"Talk as if *what*? I know one thing mighty certain: if you can fix me so I can eat for two and only have to stub toes for one, I ain't going to fool away no such chance just for sentiment."

The Twins were wet and tired, and they proceeded to undress without any preliminary remarks. The abundance of sleeves made the partnership coat hard to get off, for it was like skinning a tarantula, but it came at last, after much tugging and perspiring. The mutual vest followed. Then the brothers stood up before the glass, and each took off his own cravat and collar. The collars were of the standing kind, and came high up under the ears, like the sides of a wheelbarrow, as required by the fashion of the day. The cravats were as broad as a bank bill, with fringed ends which stood far out to right and left like the wings of a dragon-fly, and this also was strictly in accordance with the fashion of the time. Each cravat, as to color, was in perfect taste, so far as its owner's complexion was concerned—a delicate pink, in the case of the blonde brother, a violent scarlet in the case of the brunette—but as a combination they broke all the laws of taste known to civilization. Nothing more fiendish and irreconcilable than those shrieking and blaspheming colors could have been contrived. The wet boots gave no end of trouble—to Luigi. When they were off at last, Angelo said, with bitterness—

"I wish you wouldn't wear such tight boots, they hurt my feet."

Luigi answered with indifference—

"My friend, when I am in command of our body, I choose my apparel according to my own convenience, as I have remarked more than several times already. When you are in command, I beg you will do as you please."

Angelo was hurt, and the tears came into his eyes. There was gentle reproach in his voice, but not anger, when he replied:

"Luigi, I often consult your wishes, but you never consult mine. When I am in command I treat you as a guest; I try to make you feel at home; when you are in command you treat me as an intruder, you make me feel unwelcome. It embarrasses me cruelly in company, for I can see that people notice it and comment on it."

"Oh, damn the people," responded the brother languidly, and with the air of one who is tired of the subject.

A slight shudder shook the frame of Angelo, but he said nothing and the conversation ceased. Each buttoned his own share of the night shirt in silence; then Luigi, with Paine's "Age of Reason" in his hand, sat down in one chair and put his feet in another and lit his pipe, while Angelo took his "Whole Duty of Man," and both began to read. Angelo presently began to cough; his coughing increased and became mixed with gaspings for breath, and he was finally obliged to make an appeal to his brother's humanity:

"Luigi, if you would only smoke a little milder tobacco I am sure I could learn not to mind it in time, but this is so strong, and the pipe is so rank that—"

"Angelo, I wouldn't be such a baby! I have learned to smoke in a week, and the trouble is already over with me; if you would try, you could learn, too, and then you would stop spoiling my comfort with your everlasting complaints."

"Ah, brother, that is a strong word—everlasting—and isn't quite fair. I only complain when I suffocate; you know I don't complain when we are in the open air."

"Well, anyway, you could learn to smoke, yourself."

"But my *principles*, Luigi, you forget my principles. You would not have me do a thing which I regard as a sin?"

"Oh, d-bosh!"

The conversation ceased again, for Angelo was sick and discouraged and strangling; but after some time he closed his book and asked Luigi to sing "From Greenland's Icy Mountains" with him, but he would not, and when he tried to sing by himself Luigi did his best to drown his plaintive tenor with a rude and rollicking song delivered in a thundering bass.

After the singing there was silence, and neither brother was happy. Before blowing the light out Luigi swallowed half a tumbler of whisky, and Angelo, whose sensitive organization could not endure intoxicants of any kind, took a pill to keep it from giving him the headache.

Chapter 2

The family sat in the breakfast room waiting for the Twins to come down. The widow was quiet, the daughter was all alive with happy excitement. She said—

"Ah, they're a boon, ma, just a boon! don't you think so?"

"Laws, I hope so, I don't know."

"Why, ma, yes you do. They're so fine, and handsome, and high-bred, and polite, so every way superior to our gawks here in this village; why, they'll make life different from what it was—so humdrum and commonplace, you know—oh, you may be sure they're full of accomplishments, and knowledge of the world, and all that, that will be an immense advantage to society here. Don't you think so, ma?"

"Mercy on me, how should I know, and I've hardly set eyes on them, yet." After a pause, she added, "They made considerable noise after they went up."

"Noise? Why, ma, they were singing! And it was beautiful, too."

"Oh, it was well enough, but too mixed-up, seemed to me."

"Now, ma, honor bright, did you ever hear 'Greenland's Icy Mountains' sung sweeter—now did you?"

"If it had been sung by itself, it would have been uncommon sweet, I don't deny it; but what they wanted to mix it up with 'Old Bob Ridley' for, I can't make out. Why, they don't go together, at all. They are not of the same nature. 'Bob Ridley' is a common rackety slam-bang secular song, one of the rippingest and rantingest and noisiest there is. I am no judge of music, and I don't claim it, but in my opinion nobody can make those two songs go together right."

"Why, ma, I thought—"

"It don't make any difference what you thought, it can't be done. They tried it, and to my mind it was a failure. I never heard such a crazy uproar; seemed to me, sometimes, the roof would come off; and as for the cats—well, I've lived a many a year, and seen cats aggravated in more ways than one, but I've never seen cats take on the way they took on last night."

"Well, I don't think that that goes for anything, ma, because it is the nature of cats that any sound that is unusual—"

"Unusual! You may well call it so. Now if they are going to sing duets every night, I do hope they will both sing the same tune at the same time, for in my opinion a duet that is made up of two different tunes is a mistake; especially when the tunes ain't any kin to one another, that way."

"But ma, I think it must be a foreign custom; and it must be right, too, and the best way, because they have had every opportunity to know what is right, and it don't stand to reason that with their education they would do anything but what the highest musical authorities have sanctioned. You can't help but admit that, ma."

The argument was formidably strong; the old lady could not find any way around it; so, after thinking it over a while she gave in with a sigh of discontent, and admitted that the daughter's position was probably correct. Being vanquished, she had no mind to continue the topic at that disadvantage, and was about to seek a change when a change came of itself. A footstep was heard on the stairs, and she said—

"There—he's coming!"

"*They*, ma—you ought to say *they*—it's nearer right."

The new lodger, rather shoutingly dressed but looking superbly handsome, stepped with courtly carriage into the trim little breakfast room and put out all his cordial arms at once, like one of those pocket knives with a multiplicity of blades, and shook hands with the whole family simultaneously. He was so easy and pleasant and hearty that all embarrassment presently thawed away and disappeared, and a cheery feeling of friendliness and comradeship took its place. He—or preferably they—were asked to occupy the seat of honor at the foot of the table. They consented with thanks, and carved the beef steak with one set of their hands while they distributed it at the same time with the other set.

"Will you have coffee, gentlemen, or tea?"

"Coffee for Luigi, if you please, madam, tea for me."

"Cream and sugar?"

"For me, yes, madam; Luigi takes his coffee black. Our natures differ a good deal from each other, and our tastes also."

The first time the negro girl Nancy appeared in the door and saw the two heads turned in opposite directions and both talking at once, then saw the commingling arms feed potatoes into one mouth and coffee into the other at the same time, she had to pause and pull herself out of a faintness that came over her; but after that she held her grip and was able to wait on the table with fair courage.

Conversation fell naturally into the customary grooves. It was a little jerky, at first, because none of the family could get smoothly through a sentence without a wobble in it here and a break there, caused by some new surprise in the way of attitude or gesture on the part of the twins. The weather suffered the most. The weather was all finished up and disposed of, as a subject, before the simple Missourians had gotten sufficiently wonted to the spectacle of one body feeding two heads to feel composed and reconciled in the presence of so bizarre a miracle. And even after everybody's mind became tranquilized there was still one slight distraction left: the hand that picked up a biscuit carried it to the wrong head, as often as any other way, and the wrong mouth devoured it. This was a puzzling thing, and marred the talk a little. It bothered the widow to such a degree that she presently dropped out of the conversation without knowing it, and fell to watching, and guessing, and talking to herself:

"Now that hand is going to take that coffee to—no, it's gone to the other mouth; I can't understand it; and now, here is the dark-complected hand with a potatoe on its fork, I'll see what goes with it—there, the light-complected head's got it, as sure as I live!" Finally Rowena said—

"Ma, what is the matter with you? Are you dreaming about something?"

The old lady came to herself, and blushed; then she explained with the first random thing that came into her mind:

"I saw Mr. Angelo take up Mr. Luigi's coffee, and I thought maybe he—shan't I give *you* a cup, Mr. Angelo?"

"Oh, no, madam, I am very much obliged, but I never drink coffee, much as I would like to. You did see me take up Luigi's cup, it is true, but if you noticed, I did not carry it to my mouth, but to his."

"Y-es, I thought you did. Did you mean to?"

"How?"

The widow was a little embarrassed again. She said:

"I don't know but what I'm foolish, and you mustn't mind; but you see, he got the coffee I was expecting to see you drink, and you got a potatoe that I thought he was going to get. So, I thought it might be a mistake all around, and everybody getting what wasn't intended for him."

Both twins laughed, and Luigi said—

"Dear madam, there wasn't any mistake. We are always helping each other that way. It is a great economy for us both; it saves time and labor. We have a system of signs which nobody can notice or understand but ourselves. If I am using both my hands and want some coffee, I make the sign and Angelo furnishes it to me; and you saw that when he needed a potatoe I delivered it."

"How convenient!"

"Yes, and often of the extremest value. Take these Mississippi boats, for instance. They are always overcrowded. There is table-room for only half of the passengers, therefore they have to set a second table for the second half. The stewards rush both parties, they give them no time to eat a satisfying meal, both divisions leave the table hungry. It isn't so with us. Angelo books himself for the one table, I book myself for the other. Neither of us eats anything at the other's table, but just simply works—works. Thus, you see, there are four hands to feed Angelo, and the same four to feed me. Each of us eats two meals."

The old lady was dazed with admiration, and kept saying, "It is *per*fectly wonderful, perfectly wonderful!" and the boy Joe licked his chops enviously but said nothing—at least aloud.

"Yes," continued Luigi, "our construction may have its disadvantages—in fact, *has*—but it also has its compensations, of one sort and another. Take travel, for instance. Travel is enormously expensive, in all countries; we have been obliged to do a vast deal of it—come, Angelo, don't put any more sugar in your tea, I'm just over one indigestion and don't want another right away—been obliged to do a deal of it, as I was saying. Well, we always travel as one person, since we occupy but one seat, so we save half the fare."

"How romantic!" interjected Rowena, with effusion.

"Yes, my dear young lady, and how practical, too, and economical. In Europe, beds in the hotels are not charged with the board, but separately—another saving, for we stood to our rights and paid for the one bed only. The landlords often insisted that as both of us occupied the bed we ought—"

"No, they didn't," said Angelo. "They did it only twice, and in both cases it was a double bed—a rare thing in Europe—and the double bed gave them some excuse. Be fair to the landlords; twice doesn't constitute 'often'."

"Well, that depends—that depends. I knew a man who fell down a well twice. He said he didn't mind the first time, but he thought the second time was once too often. Have I misused that word, Mrs. Cooper?"

"To tell the truth, I was afraid you had, but it seems to look, now, like you hadn't." She stopped, and was evidently struggling with the difficult problem a moment, then she added in the tone of one who is convinced without being converted, "It seems so, but I can't somehow tell why."

Rowena thought Luigi's retort was wonderfully quick and bright, and she remarked to herself with satisfaction that there wasn't any young native of Dawson's Landing that could have risen to the occasion like that. Luigi detected the applause in her face, and expressed his pleasure and his thanks with his eyes, and so eloquently withal, that the girl was proud and pleased, and hung out the delicate sign of it on her cheeks.

Luigi went on, with animation:

"Both of us get a bath for one ticket, theatre seat for one ticket, pew-rent is on the same basis, but at peep-shows we pay double."

"We have much to be thankful for," said Angelo, impressively, with a reverent light in his eye and a reminiscent tone in his voice, "we have been greatly blessed. As a rule, what one of us has lacked, the other, by the bounty of Providence, has been able to supply. My brother is hardy, I am not; he is very masculine, assertive, aggressive, I am much less so. I am subject to illnesses, he is never ill. I cannot abide medicines, and cannot take them, but he has no prejudice against them, and—"

"Why, goodness gracious," interrupted the widow, "when you are sick, does he take the medicine for you?"

"Always, madam."

"Well, I never heard such a thing in my life! I think it's beautiful of you."

"Oh, madam, it's nothing, don't mention it, it's really nothing at all."

"But I say it's beautiful, and I stick to it!" cried the widow, with a speaking moisture in her eye. "A well brother to take the medicine for his poor sick brother—I wish I had such a son," and she glanced reproachfully at her boys. "I declare I'll never rest till I've shook you by the hand," and she scrambled out of her chair in a fever of generous enthusiasm, and made for the twins, blind with her tears, and began to shake. The boy Joe corrected her:

"You're shaking the wrong one, ma."

This flurried her, but she made a swift change and went on shaking.

"Got the wrong one again, ma," said the boy.

"Oh, shut up, can't you!" said the widow, embarrassed and irritated. "Give me *all* your hands, I want to shake them all; for I know you are both just as good as you can be."

It was a victorious thought, a master-stroke of diplomacy, though that never occurred to her and she cared nothing for diplomacy. She shook the four hands in turn cordially, and went back to her place in a state of high and fine exaltation that made her look young and handsome.

"Indeed I owe everything to Luigi," said Angelo, affectionately. "But for him I could not have survived our boyhood days, when we were friendless and poor—ah, so poor! We lived from hand to mouth—lived on the coarse fare of unwilling charity, and for weeks and weeks together not a morsel of food passed my lips, for its character revolted me and I could not eat it. But for Luigi I should have died. He ate for us both."

"How noble!" sighed Rowena.

"Do you hear that?" said the widow, severely, to her boys. "Let it be an example to you—I mean you, Joe."

Joe gave his head a barely perceptible disparaging toss and said—

"Et for both. It ain't anything—I'd a done it."

"Hush, if you haven't got any better manners than that. You don't see the point at all. It wasn't good food."

"I don't care—it was food, and I'd a et it if it was rotten."

"Shame! Such language! Can't you understand? They were starving—actually starving—and he ate for both, and—"

"Shucks! you gimme a chance and I'll—"

"There, now—close your head! and don't you open it again till you're asked."

[Angelo goes on and tells how his parents the Count and Countess had to fly from Florence for political reasons, and died poor in Berlin bereft of their great property by confiscation; and how he and Luigi had to travel with a freak-show during two years and suffer semi-starvation.]

"That hateful black bread! but I seldom ate anything during that time, that was poor Luigi's affair—"

"I'll never *Mister* him again!" cried the widow, with strong emotion, "he's Luigi to me, from this out!"

"Thank you a thousand times, madam, a thousand times! though in truth I don't deserve it."

"Ah, Luigi is always the fortunate one when honors are showering," said Angelo, plaintively, "now what have I done, Mrs. Cooper, that you leave me out? Come, you must strain a point in my favor."

"Call you Angelo? Why, certainly I will; what are you thinking of! In the case of twins, why—"

"But ma, you're breaking up the story—do let him go on."

"You keep still, Rowena Cooper, and he can go on all the better, I reckon. One interruption don't hurt, it's two that makes the trouble."

"But you've added one, now, and that is three."

"Rowena! I will not allow you to talk back at me when you have got nothing rational to say."

Chapter 3

[After breakfast the whole village crowded in, and there was a grand reception in honor of the twins; and at the close of it the gifted "freak" captured everybody's admiration by sitting down at the piano and knocking out a classic four-handed piece in great style. Then the Judge took it—or them—driving in his buggy and showed off his village.]

All along the streets the people crowded the windows and stared at the amazing twins. Troops of small boys flocked after the buggy, excited and yelling. At first the dogs showed no interest. They thought they merely saw three men in a buggy—a matter of no consequence; but when they found out the facts of the case, they altered their opinion pretty radically, and joined the boys, expressing their minds as they came. Other dogs got interested; indeed all the dogs. It was a spirited sight to see them come leaping fences, tearing around corners, swarming out of every by-street and alley. The noise they made was something beyond belief—or praise. They did not seem to be moved by malice, but only by prejudice, the common human prejudice against lack of conformity. If the Twins turned their heads, they broke and fled in every direction, but stopped at a safe distance and faced about, and then formed and came on again as soon as the strangers showed them their back. Negroes and farmers' wives took to the woods when the buggy came upon them suddenly, and altogether the drive was pleasant and animated, and a refreshment all around.

[It was a long and lively drive. Angelo was a Methodist, Luigi was a Freethinker. The Judge was very proud of his Freethinker Society, which was flourishing along in a most prosperous way and already had two members—himself and the obscure and neglected Pudd'nhead Wilson. It was to meet that evening, and he invited Luigi to join; a thing which Luigi was glad to do, partly because it would please himself, and partly because it would gravel Angelo.]

They had now arrived at the widow's gate, and the excursion was ended. The Twins politely expressed their obligations for the pleasant outing which had been afforded them; to which the Judge bowed his thanks, and then said he would now go and arrange for the freethinkers' meeting, and would call for Count Luigi in the evening.

"For you, also, dear sir," he added, hastily, turning to Angelo and bowing. "In addressing myself particularly to your brother, I was not meaning to leave you out. It was an unintentional rudeness, I assure you, and due wholly to accident—accident and preoccupation. I beg you to forgive me."

His quick eye had seen the sensitive blood mount into Angelo's face, betraying the wound that had been inflicted. The sting of the slight had gone deep, but the apology was so prompt, and so evidently sincere, that the hurt was almost immediately healed, and a forgiving smile testified to the kindly Judge that all was well again.

Concealed behind Angelo's modest and unassuming exterior, and unsuspected by any but his intimates, was a lofty pride, a pride of almost abnormal proportions, indeed, and this rendered him ever the prey of slights, and although they were almost always imaginary ones, they hurt none the less on that account. By ill fortune Judge Driscoll had happened to touch his sorest point, *i.e.*, his conviction that his brother's presence was welcomer everywhere than his own; that he was often invited, out of mere courtesy, where only his brother was wanted, and that in the majority of cases he would not be included in an invitation if he could be left out without offence. A sensitive nature like this is necessarily subject to moods; moods which traverse the whole gamut of feeling; moods which know all the climes of emotion, from the sunny heights of joy to the black abysses of despair. At times, in his seasons of deepest depression, Angelo almost wished that he and his brother might become segregated from each other and be separate individuals, like other men. But of course as soon as his mind cleared and these diseased imaginings passed away, he shuddered at the repulsive thought, and earnestly prayed that it might visit him no more. To be separate, and as other men are! How awkward it would seem; how unendurable. What would he do with his hands, his arms? How would his legs feel? How odd, and strange, and grotesque every action, attitude, movement, gesture would be. To sleep by himself, eat by himself, walk by himself—how lonely, how unspeakably lonely! No, no, any fate but that. In every way and from every point, the idea was revolting.

This was of course natural; to have felt otherwise would have been unnatural. He had known no life but the combined one; he had been familiar with it from his birth; he was not able to conceive of any other as being agreeable, or even bearable. To him, in the privacy of his secret thoughts, all other men were monsters, deformities; and during three-fourths of his life their aspect had filled him with what promised to be an unconquerable aversion. But at eighteen his eye began to take note of female beauty, and, little by little, undefined longings grew up in his heart under whose softening influences the old stubborn aversion gradually diminished, and finally disappeared. Men were still monstrosities to him, still deformities, and in his sober moments he had no desire to be like them, but their strange and unsocial and uncanny construction was no longer offensive to him.

This had been a hard day for him, physically and mentally. He had been called in the morning before he had quite slept off the effects of the liquor which Luigi had drunk; and so, for the first half hour had had the seedy feeling, the languor, the brooding depression, the cobwebby mouth and druggy taste that come of dissipation, and are so ill a preparation for bodily or intellectual activities; the long and violent strain of the reception had followed; and this had been followed, in turn, by the dreary sight-seeing, the Judge's wearying explanations and laudations of the sights, and the stupefying clamor of the dogs. As a congruous conclusion, a fitting end, his feelings had been hurt, a slight had been put upon him. He would have been glad to forego dinner, and betake himself to rest and sleep, but he held his peace and said no word, for he knew his brother. Luigi was fresh, unweary, full of life, spirit, energy, he would have scoffed at the idea of wasting valuable time on a bed or a sofa, and would have refused permission.

Chapter 4

Rowena was dining out, Joe and Harry were belated at play, there were but three chairs and four persons that noon, at the home dinner table—the Twins, the widow, and her chum, Aunt Betsy Hale. The widow soon perceived that Angelo's spirits were as low as Luigi's were high, and also that he had a jaded look. Her motherly solicitude was aroused, and she tried to get him interested in the talk and win him to a happier frame of mind, but the cloud of sadness remained on his countenance. Luigi lent his help, too. He used a form and a phrase which he was always accustomed to employ in these circumstances. He gave his brother an affectionate slap on the shoulder and said, encouragingly—

"Cheer up, the worst is yet to come!"

But this did no good. It never did. If anything, it made the matter worse, as a rule, because it irritated Angelo. This made it a favorite with Luigi. By and by the widow said—

"Angelo, you are tired, you've overdone yourself. You go right to bed, after dinner, and get a good nap and a rest, then you'll be all right."

"Indeed I would give anything if I could do that, madam."

"And what's to hender, I'd like to know? Land, the room's yours, to do what you please with! The idea that you can't do what you like with your own!"

"But, you see, there's one prime essential—an essential of the very first importance—which isn't my own."

"What is that?"

"My body."

The old ladies looked puzzled, and Aunt Betsy Hale said—

"Why, bless your heart, how is that?"

"It's my brother's."

"Your brother's! I don't quite understand. I supposed it belonged to both of you."

"So it does. But not to both at the same time."

"That is mighty curious; I don't see how it can be. I shouldn't think it could be managed that way."

"Oh, it's a good enough arrangement, and goes very well—in fact it wouldn't do to have it otherwise. I find that the Teetotalers and the Anti-Teetotalers, hire the use of the same hall for their meetings. Both parties don't use it at the same time, do they?"

"You bet they don't!" said both old ladies in a breath.

"And moreover," said Aunt Betsy, "the Freethinkers and the Babtist Bible class use the same room over the market-house, but you can take my word for it they don't mush-up together and use it at the same time."

"Very well," said Angelo, "you understand it now. And it stands to reason that the arrangement couldn't be improved. I'll prove it to you. If our legs tried to obey two wills, how could we ever get anywhere? I would start one way, Luigi would start another, at the same moment—the result would be a standstill, wouldn't it?"

"As sure as you are born! Now ain't that wonderful! A body would never have thought of it."

"We should always be arguing and fussing and disputing over the merest trifles. We should lose worlds of time, for we couldn't go down stairs or up, couldn't go to bed, couldn't rise, couldn't wash, couldn't dress, couldn't stand up, couldn't sit down, couldn't even cross our legs without calling a meeting first, and explaining the case, and passing resolutions, and getting consent. It wouldn't ever do—now would it?"

"Do? Why, it would wear a person out in a week! Did you ever hear anything like it, Patsy Cooper?"

"Oh, you'll find there's more than one thing about them that ain't commonplace," said the widow, with the complacent air of a person with a property right in a novelty that is under admiring scrutiny.

"Well, now, how ever do you manage it? I don't mind saying I'm suffering to know."

"He who made us," said Angelo, reverently, "and with us this difficulty, also provided a way out of it. By a mysterious law of our being, each of us has utter and indisputable command of our body a week at a time, turn and turn about."

"Well, I never! Now ain't that beautiful!"

"Yes, it is beautiful and infinitely wise and just. The week ends every Saturday at midnight to the minute, to the second, to the last shade and fraction of a second, infallibly, unerringly, and in that instant the one brother's power over the body vanishes and the other brother takes possession, asleep or awake."

"How marvelous are His ways, and past finding out!"

Luigi said—

"So exactly to the instant does the change come, that during our stay in many of the great cities of the world, the public clocks were regulated by it; and as hundreds of thousands of private clocks and watches were set and corrected in accordance with the public clocks, we really furnished the standard time for the entire city."

"Don't tell me that He don't do miracles any more! Blowing down the walls of Jericho with rams' horns warn't as difficult, in my opinion."

"And that is not all," said Angelo. "A thing that is even more marvelous, perhaps, is the fact that the change takes note of longitude and fits itself to the meridian we are on. Luigi is in command this week. Now, if on Saturday night at a moment before midnight we could fly in an instant to a point fifteen degrees west of here, he would hold possession of the power another hour, for the change observes *local* time and no other."

Betsy Hale was deeply impressed, and said with solemnity—

"Patsy Cooper, for detail it lays over the Passage of the Red Sea."

"No, I shouldn't go as far as that," said Aunt Patsy, "but if you're a mind to say Sodom and Gomorrah, I am with you, Betsy Hale."

"I am agreeable, then, though I do think I was right, and I believe parson Maltby would say the same. Well, now, there's another thing. Suppose one of you wants to borrow the legs a minute from the one that's got them, could he let him?"

"Yes, but we hardly ever do that. There were disagreeable results, several times, and so we very seldom ask or grant the privilege, nowadays, and we never even think of such a thing unless the case is extremely urgent. Besides, a week's possession at a time seems so little that we can't bear to spare a minute of it. People who have the use of their legs all the time never think of what a blessing it is, of course. It never occurs to them; it's just their natural ordinary condition, and so it does not excite them at all. But when I wake up, on Sunday morning, and it's my week and I feel the power all through me, oh, such a wave of exultation and thanksgiving goes surging over me, and I want to shout 'I can walk! I can walk!' Madam, do you ever, at your uprising, want to shout 'I can walk! I can walk!' "

"No, you poor unfortunate cretur, but I'll never get out of my bed again without *doing* it! Laws, to think I've had this unspeakable blessing all my long life and never had the grace to thank the good Lord that gave it to me!"

Tears stood in the eyes of both the old ladies, and the widow said, softly—

"Betsy Hale, we have learnt something, you and me."

The conversation now drifted wide, but by and by floated back once more to that admired detail, the rigid and beautiful impartiality with which the possession of power had been distributed between the Twins. Aunt Betsy saw in it a far finer justice than human law exhibits in related cases. She said—

"In my opinion it ain't right now, and never has been right, the way a twin born a quarter of a minute sooner than the other one gets all the land and grandeurs and nobilities in the old countries and his brother has to go bare and be a nobody. Which of you was born first?"

Angelo's head was resting against Luigi's; weariness had overcome him, and for the past five minutes he had been peacefully sleeping. The old ladies had dropped their voices to a lulling drone, to help him steal the rest his brother wouldn't take him up stairs to get. Luigi listened a moment to Angelo's regular breathing, then said in a voice barely audible:

"We were both born at the same time, but I am six months older than he is."

"For the land's sake!—"

" 'Sh! don't wake him up; he wouldn't like my telling this. It has always been kept secret till now."

"But how in the world can it be? If you were both born at the same time, how can one of you be older than the other?"

"It is very simple, and I assure you it is true. I was born with a full crop of hair, he was as bald as an egg for six months. I could walk six months before he could make a step. I finished teething six months ahead of him. I began to take solids six months before he left the breast. I began to talk six months before he could say a word. Last, and absolutely unassailable proof, *the sutures in my skull closed six months ahead of his.* Always just that six months difference to a day. Was that accident? Nobody is going to claim that, I'm sure. It was ordained—it was law—it had its meaning, and we know what that meaning was. Now what does this overwhelming body of evidence establish? It establishes just one thing, and that thing it establishes beyond any peradventure whatever. Friends, we would not have it known for the world, and I must beg you to keep it strictly to yourselves, but the truth is, *we are no more twins than you are.*"

The two old ladies were stunned, paralyzed—petrified, one may almost say—and could only sit and gaze vacantly at each other for some moments; then Aunt Betsy Hale said, impressively—

"There's no getting around proofs like that. I do believe it's the most amazing thing I ever heard of." She sat silent a moment or two, and breathing hard with excitement, then she looked up and surveyed the strangers steadfastly a little while, and added, "Well, it does beat me, but I would have took you for twins anywhere."

"So would I, so would I," said Aunt Patsy with the emphasis of a certainty that is not impaired by any shade of doubt.

"Anybody would—anybody in the world, I don't care who he is," said Aunt Betsy with decision.

"You won't tell," said Luigi, appealingly.

"O, dear no!" answered both ladies promptly, "you can trust us, don't you be afraid."

"That is good of you, and kind. Never let on; treat us always as if we were Twins."

"You can depend on us," said Aunt Betsy, "but it won't be easy, because now that I know you ain't, you don't *seem* so."

Luigi muttered to himself with satisfaction: "That swindle has gone through without change of cars."

It was not very kind of him to load the poor old things up with a secret like that, which would be always flying to their tongues' ends every time they heard any one speak of the strangers as twins, and would become harder and harder to hang on to with every recurrence of the temptation to tell it, while the torture of retaining it would increase with every new strain that was applied, but he never thought of that, and probably would not have worried much about it if he had.

A visitor was announced—some one to see the Twins. They withdrew to the parlor, and the two old ladies began to discuss with interest the strange things which they had been listening to. When they had finished the matter to their satisfaction, and Aunt Betsy rose to go, she stopped to ask a question—

"How does things come on between Roweny and Tom Driscoll?"

"Well, about the same. He writes tolerable often, and she answers tolerable seldom."

"Where is he?"

"In St. Louis, I believe, though he's such a gad-about that a body can't be very certain of him, I reckon."

"Don't Roweny know?"

"Oh, yes, like enough. I haven't asked her lately."

"Do you know how him and the Judge are getting along now?"

"First rate, I believe. Mrs. Pratt says so; and being right in the house, and sister to the one and aunt to t'other, of course she ought to know. She says the Judge is real fond of him when he's away, but frets when he's around and is vexed with his ways, and not sorry to have him go again. He has been gone three weeks this time—a pleasant thing for both of them, I reckon."

"Tom's ruther harum-scarum, but there ain't anything bad in him, I guess."

"Oh, no, he's just young, that's all. Still, twenty-three is old, in one way. A young man ought to be earning his living by that time. If Tom were doing that, or was even trying to do it, the Judge would be a heap better satisfied with him. Tom's always going to begin, but somehow he can't seem to find just the opening he likes."

"Well, now, it's partly the Judge's own fault. Promising the boy his property wasn't the way to set him to earning a fortune of his own. But what do you think—is Roweny beginning to lean any towards him, or ain't she?"

Aunt Patsy had a secret in her bosom; she wanted to keep it there, but nature was too strong for her. She drew Aunt Betsy aside, and said in her most confidential and mysterious manner—

"Don't you breathe a syllable to a soul—I'm going to tell you something. In my opinion Tom Driscoll's chances were considerable better yesterday than they are to-day."

"Patsy Cooper, what *do* you mean?"

"It's so, as sure as you're born. I wish you could a been at breakfast, and seen for yourself."

"You don't mean it!"

"Well, if I'm any judge, there's a leaning—there's a leaning, sure."

"My land! Which one of 'em is it?"

"I can't say for certain, but I think it's the youngest one—Anjy."

Then there were handshakings, and congratulations, and hopes, and so on, and the old ladies parted, perfectly happy—the one in knowing something which the rest of the town didn't, and the other in having been the sole person able to furnish that knowledge.

The visitor who had called to see the Twins was the Rev. Mr. Hotchkiss, pastor of the Baptist church. At the reception Angelo had told him he had lately experienced a change in his religious views, and was now desirous of becoming a Baptist, and would immediately join Mr. Hotchkiss's church. There was no time to say more, and the brief talk ended at that point. The minister was much gratified, and had dropped in for a moment, now, to invite the twins to attend his Bible-class at eight that evening. Angelo accepted, and was expecting Luigi to decline, but he did not, because he knew that the Bible-class and the Freethinkers met in the same room, and he wanted to treat his brother to the embarrassment of being caught in freethinking company.

Chapter 5

[A long and vigorous quarrel follows, between the twins. And there is plenty to quarrel about, for Angelo was always seeking truth, and this obliged him to change and improve his religion with frequency, which wearied Luigi, and annoyed him too; for he had to be present at each new enlistment—which placed him in the false position of seeming to indorse and approve his brother's fickleness; moreover, he had to go to Angelo's prohibition meetings, and he hated them. On the other hand, when it was *his* week to command the legs he gave Angelo just cause of complaint, for he took him to circuses and horse-races and fandangoes, exposing him to all sorts of censure and criticism; and he drank, too; and whatever he drank went to Angelo's head instead of his own and made him act disgracefully. When the evening was come, the two attended the Freethinkers' meeting, where Angelo was sad and silent; then came the Bible-class and looked upon him coldly, finding him in such company. Then they went to Wilson's house, and Chapter XI. of "Pudd'nhead Wilson" follows, which tells

of the girl seen in Tom Driscoll's room; and closes with the kicking of
Tom by Luigi at the anti-temperance mass meeting of the Sons of Liberty;
with the addition of some account of Roxy's adventures as a chambermaid
on a Mississippi boat. Her exchange of the children had been flippantly and
farcically described in an earlier chapter.]

Next morning all the town was a-buzz with great news: Pudd'n-
head Wilson had a law-case!

The public astonishment was so great and the public curiosity so
intense, that when the justice of the peace opened his court the
place was packed with people, and even the windows were full.
Everybody was flushed and perspiring, the summer heat was almost
unendurable.

Tom Driscoll had brought a charge of assault and battery against
the Twins. Robert Allen was retained by Driscoll, David Wilson by
the defence. Tom, his native cheerfulness unannihilated by his
back-breaking and bone-bruising passage across the massed heads of
the Sons of Liberty the previous night, laughed his little customary
laugh, and said to Wilson—

"I've kept my promise, you see: I'm throwing my business your
way. Sooner than I was expecting, too."

"It's very good of you—particularly if you mean to keep it up."

"Well, I can't tell about that, yet. But we'll see. If I find you
deserve it I'll take you under my protection and make your fame
and fortune for you."

"I'll try to deserve it, Tom."

A jury was sworn in; then Mr. Allen said:

"We will detain your honor but a moment with this case. It is
not one where any doubt of the fact of the assault can enter in.
These gentlemen—the accused—kicked my client, at the Market
Hall last night; they kicked him with violence; with extraordinary
violence; with even unprecedented violence, I may say; insomuch
that he was lifted entirely off his feet and discharged into the midst
of the audience. We can prove this by four hundred witnesses—we
shall call but three. Mr. Harkness will take the stand."

Mr. Harkness, being sworn, testified that he was chairman upon
the occasion mentioned; that he was close at hand and saw the
defendants in this action kick the plaintiff into the air and saw him
descend among the audience.

"Take the witness," said Allen.

"Mr. Harkness," said Wilson, "you say you saw these gentlemen,
my clients, kick the plaintiff. Are you sure—and please remember
that you are on oath—are you perfectly sure that you saw *both* of
them kick him, or only one? Now be careful."

A bewildered look began to spread itself over the witness's face.
He hesitated, stammered, but got out nothing. His eyes wandered
to the Twins and fixed themselves there with a vacant gaze.

"Please answer, Mr. Harkness, you are keeping the court waiting. It is a very simple question."

Counsel for the prosecution broke in with impatience:

"Your honor, the question is an irrelevant triviality. Necessarily they both kicked him, for they have but the one pair of legs, and both are responsible for them."

Wilson said, sarcastically:

"Will your honor permit this new witness to be sworn? He seems to possess knowledge which can be of the utmost value just at this moment—knowledge which would at once dispose of what everyone must see is a very difficult question in this case. Brother Allen, will you take the stand?"

"Go on with your case!" said Allen, petulantly. The audience laughed, and got a warning from the court.

"Now, Mr. Harkness," said Wilson, insinuatingly, "We shall have to insist upon an answer to that question."

"I—er—well, of course I do not absolutely *know*, but in my opinion—"

"Never mind your opinion, sir—answer the question."

"I—why, I *can't* answer it."

"That will do, Mr. Harkness. Stand down.

The audience tittered, and the discomfited witness retired in a state of great embarrassment.

Mr. Wakeman took the stand and swore that he saw the Twins kick the plaintiff off the platform. The defence took the witness.

"Mr. Wakeman, you have sworn that you saw these gentlemen kick the plaintiff. Do I understand you to swear that you saw them *both* do it?"

"Yes, sir"—with decision.

"How do you know that both did it?"

"Because I *saw* them do it."

The audience laughed, and got another warning from the court.

"But by what means do you know that both, and not one, did it?"

"Well, in the first place, the insult was given to both of them equally, for they were called a pair of scissors. Of course they would both want to resent it, and so—"

"Wait! You are theorizing, now. Stick to facts—counsel will attend to the arguments. Go on."

"Well, they both went over there—*that* I saw."

"Very good. Go on."

"And they both kicked him—I swear to it."

"Mr. Wakeman, was Count Luigi, here, willing to join the Sons of Liberty last night?"

"Yes, sir, he was. He did join, too, and drank a glass or two of whisky, like a man."

"Was his brother willing to join?"

"No, sir, he wasn't. He is a teetotaler, and was elected through a mistake."

"Was he given a glass of whisky?"

"Yes, sir, but of course that was another mistake, and not intentional. He wouldn't drink it. He set it down." A slight pause, then he added, casually, and quite simply, "The plaintiff reached for it and hogged it."

There was a fine outburst of laughter, but as the justice was caught out, himself, his reprimand was not very vigorous.

Mr. Allen jumped up and exclaimed:

"I protest against these foolish irrelevancies. What have they to do with the case?"

Wilson said:

"Calm yourself, brother; it was only an experiment. Now, Mr. Wakeman, if one of these gentlemen chooses to join an association and the other doesn't; and if one of them enjoys whisky and the other doesn't, but sets it aside and leaves it unprotected," [titter from the audience], "it seems to show that they have independent minds and tastes and preferences, and that one of them is able to approve of a thing at the very moment that the other is heartily disapproving of it. Doesn't it seem so to you?"

"Certainly it does. It's perfectly plain."

"Now, then, it might be—I only say it might be—that one of these brothers wanted to kick the plantiff last night, and that the other didn't want that humiliating punishment inflicted upon him in that public way and before all those people. Isn't that possible?"

"Of course it is. It's more than possible. I don't believe the blonde one would kick anybody. It was the other one that—"

"Silence!" shouted the plaintiff's counsel, and went on with an angry sentence which was lost in the wave of laughter that swept the house.

"That will do, Mr. Wakeman," said Wilson, "you may stand down."

The third witness was called. He had seen the Twins kick the plaintiff. Mr. Wilson took the witness.

"Mr. Rogers, you say you saw these accused gentlemen kick the plaintiff."

"Yes, sir."

"Both of them?"

"Yes, sir."

"Which of them kicked him first?"

"Why—they—they both kicked him at the same time."

"Are you perfectly sure of that?"

"Yes, sir."

"What makes you sure of it?"

"Why, I stood right behind them, and *saw* them do it."

"How many kicks were delivered?"

"Only one."

"If two men kick, the result should be two kicks, shouldn't it?"

"Why—why—yes, as a rule."

"Then what do you think went with the other kick?"

"I—well—the fact is, I wasn't thinking of two being necessary, this time."

"What do you think now?"

"Well, I—I'm sure I don't quite know what to think, but I reckon that one of them did half of the kick and the other one did the other half."

Somebody in the crowd sung out:

"It's the first sane thing that any of them has said."

The audience applauded. The judge said—

"Silence! or I will clear the court."

Mr. Allen looked pleased, but Wilson did not seem disturbed. He said:

"Mr. Rogers, you have favored us with what you think and what you reckon, but as thinking and reckoning are not evidence, I will now give you a chance to come out with something positive, one way or the other, and shall require you to produce it. I will ask the accused to stand up and repeat the phenomenal kick of last night." The Twins stood up. "Now, Mr. Rogers, please stand behind them."

A Voice: "No, stand in front!" [Laughter. Silenced by the court.]

Another Voice: "No, give Tommy another highst!" [Laughter. Sharply rebuked by the court.]

"Now, then, Mr. Rogers, two kicks shall be delivered, one after the other, and I give you my word that at least one of the two shall be delivered by one of the Twins alone, without the slightest assistance from his brother. Watch sharply, for you have got to render a decision without any ifs or ands in it." Rogers bent himself behind the Twins, with his palms just above his knees, in the modern attitude of the catcher at a base-ball match, and riveted his eyes on the pair of legs in front of him. "Are you ready, Mr. Rogers?"

"Ready, sir."

"Kick!"

The kick was launched.

"Have you got that one classified, Mr. Rogers?"

"Let me study a minute, sir."

"Take as much time as you please. Let me know when you are ready."

For as much as a minute Rogers pondered, with all eyes and a breathless interest fastened upon him. Then he gave the word—

"Ready, sir."

"Kick!"

The kick that followed was an exact duplicate of the first one.

"Now, then, Mr. Rogers, one of those kicks was an individual kick, not a mutual one. You will now state positively which was the mutual one."

The witness said, with a crest-fallen look—

"I've got to give it up. There ain't any man in the world that could tell t'other from which, sir."

"Do you still assert that last night's kick was a mutual kick?"

"Indeed I don't, sir."

"That will do, Mr. Rogers. If my brother Allen desires to address the court, your honor, very well; but as far as I am concerned I am ready to let the case be at once delivered into the hands of this intelligent jury without comment."

Mr. Justice Robinson had been in office only two months, and in that short time had not had many cases to try, of course. He had no knowledge of laws and courts except what he had picked up since he came into office. He was a sore trouble to the lawyers, for his rulings were pretty eccentric sometimes, and he stood by them with Roman simplicity and fortitude; but the people were well satisfied with him, for they saw that his intentions were always right, that he was entirely impartial, and that he usually made up in good sense what he lacked in technique, so to speak. He now perceived that there was likely to be a miscarriage of justice here, and he rose to the occasion.

"Wait a moment, gentlemen," he said, "it is plain that an assault has been committed—it is plain to anybody; but the way things are going, the guilty will certainly escape conviction. I cannot allow this. Now—"

"But your honor!" said Wilson, interrupting him, earnestly but respectfully, "you are deciding the case of yourself, whereas the jury—"

"Never mind the jury, Mr. Wilson; the jury will have a chance when there is a reasonable doubt for them to take hold of—which there isn't, so far. There is no doubt whatever that an assault has been committed. The attempt to show that both of the accused committed it has failed. Are they both to escape justice on that account? Not in this court, if I can prevent it. It appears to have been a mistake to bring the charge against them as a corporation; each should have been charged in his capacity as an individual, and—"

"But your honor!" said Wilson, "in fairness to my clients I must insist that inasmuch as the prosecution did not separate the—"

"No wrong will be done your clients, sir—they will be protected; also the public and the offended law. Mr. Allen, you will amend your pleadings, and put one of the accused on trial at a time."

Wilson broke in—

"But your honor! this is wholly unprecedented! To imperil an accused person by arbitrarily altering and widening the charge against him in order to compass his conviction when the charge as originally brought promises to fail to convict, is a thing unheard of before."

"Unheard of *where?*"

"In the courts of this or any other State."

The judge said, with dignity—

"I am not acquainted with the customs of other courts, and am not concerned to know what they are. I am responsible for this court, and I cannot conscientiously allow my judgment to be warped and my judicial liberty hampered by trying to conform to the caprices of other courts, be they—"

"But your honor, the oldest and highest courts in Europe—"

"This court is not run on the European plan, Mr. Wilson; it is not run on any plan but its own. It has a plan of its own; and that plan is, to find justice for both State and accused, no matter what happens to be practice and custom in Europe or anywhere else." [Great applause.] "Silence! It has not been the custom of this court to imitate other courts; it has not been the custom of this court to take shelter behind the decisions of other courts, and we will not begin now. We will do the best we can by the light that God has given us, and while this court continues to have His approval, it will remain indifferent to what other organizations may think of it." [Applause.] "Gentlemen, I *must* have order!—quiet yourselves! Mr. Allen, you will now proceed against the prisoners one at a time. Go on with the case."

Allen was not at his ease. However, after whispering a moment with his client and with one or two other people, he rose and said:

"Your honor, I find it to be reported and believed that the accused are able to act independently in many ways, but that this independence does not extend to their legs, authority over their legs being vested exclusively in the one brother during a specific term of days, and then passing to the other brother for a like term, and so on, by regular alternation. I could call witnesses who would prove that the accused had revealed to them the existence of this extraordinary fact, and had also made known which of them was in possession of the legs yesterday—and this would of course indicate where the guilt of the assault belongs—but as this would be mere hearsay evidence, these revelations not having been made under oath—"

"Never mind about that, Mr. Allen. It may not all be hearsay. We shall see. It may at least help to put us on the right track. Call the witnesses."

"Then I will call Mr. John Buckstone, who is now present; and I beg that Mrs. Patsy Cooper may be sent for. Take the stand, Mr. Buckstone."

Buckstone took the oath, and then testified that on the previous evening the Count Angelo Cappello had protested against going to the hall, and had called all present to witness that he was going by compulsion and would not go if he could help himself. Also, that the Count Luigi had replied sharply that he would *go*, just the same, and that he, Count Luigi, would see to that, himself. Also, that upon Count Angelo's complaining about being kept on his legs so long, Count Luigi retorted with apparent surprise, "*Your* legs!—I like your impudence!"

"*Now* we are getting at the kernel of the thing," observed the judge, with grave and earnest satisfaction. "It looks as if the Count Luigi was in possession of the battery at the time of the assault."

Nothing further was elicited from Mr. Buckstone on direct examination. Mr. Wilson took the witness.

"Mr. Buckstone, about what time was it that that conversation took place?"

"Toward nine yesterday evening, sir."

"Did you then proceed directly to the hall?"

"Yes, sir."

"How long did it take you to go there?"

"Well, we walked; and as it was from the extreme edge of the town, and there was no hurry, I judge it took us about twenty minutes, maybe a trifle more."

"About what hour was the kick delivered?"

"At thirteen minutes and a half to ten."

"Admirable! You are a pattern witness, Mr. Buckstone. How did you happen to look at your watch at that particular moment?"

"I always do it when I see an assault. It's likely I shall be called as a witness, and it's a good point to have."

"It would be well if others were as thoughtful. Was anything said, between the conversation at my house and the assault, upon the detail which we are now examining into?"

"No, sir."

"If power over the mutual legs was in the possession of one brother at nine, and passed into the possession of the other one during the next thirty or forty minutes, do you think you could have detected the change?"

"By no means!"

"That is all, Mr. Buckstone."

Mrs. Patsy Cooper was called. The crowd made way for her, and she came smiling and bowing through the narrow human lane, with Betsy Hale, as escort and support, smiling and bowing in her wake, the audience breaking into welcoming cheers as the old favorites filed along. The judge did not check this kindly demonstration of homage and affection, but let it run its course unrebuked.

The old ladies stopped and shook hands with the Twins with effusion, then gave the judge a friendly nod and bustled into the seats provided for them. They immediately began to deliver a volley of eager questions at the friends around them: "What is this thing for?" "What is that thing for?" "Who is that young man that's writing at the desk?—why, I declare it's Jake Bunce!—I thought he was sick." "Which is the jury?" "Why, is *that* the jury? Billy Price, and Job Turner, and Jack Lounsbury, and—well, I never!" "Now who would ever a thought—"

But they were gently called to order at this point and asked not to talk in court. Their tongues fell silent, but the radiant interest in their faces remained, and their gratitude for the blessing of a new sensation and a novel experience still beamed undimmed from their eyes. Aunt Patsy stood up and took the oath, and Mr. Allen explained the point in issue and asked her to go on, now, in her own way, and throw as much light upon it as she could. She toyed with her reticule a moment or two, as if considering where to begin, then she said:

"Well, the way of it is this. They are Luigi's legs a week at a time, and then they are Angelo's, and he can do whatever he wants to with them."

"You are making a mistake, Aunt Patsy Cooper," said the judge. "You shouldn't state that as a *fact*, because you don't know it to *be* a fact."

"What's the reason I don't?" said Aunt Patsy, bridling a little.

"What is the reason that you do know it?"

"The best in the world—because they told me."

"That isn't a reason."

"Well, for the land's sake! Betsy Hale, do you hear that?"

"*Hear* it?—I should think so," said Aunt Betsy, rising and facing the court. "Why Judge, I was there and heard it myself. Luigi says to Angelo—no, it was Angelo said it to—"

"Come-come, Mrs. Hale, pray sit down, and—"

"Certainly, it's all right, I'm going to sit down presently, but not until I've—"

"But you *must* sit down!"

"*Must!* Well, upon my word if things ain't getting to a pretty pass when—"

The house broke into laughter but was promptly brought to order, and meantime Mr. Allen persuaded the old lady to take her seat. Aunt Patsy continued:

"Yes, they told me that, and I know it's true. They're Luigi's legs this week, but—"

"Ah, *they* told you that, did they?" said the justice, with interest.

"Well, no, I don't know that they *told* me, but that's neither here nor there; I know, without that, that at dinner yesterday, Angelo was as tired as a dog, and yet Luigi wouldn't lend him the legs to go up stairs and take a nap with."

"Did he ask for them?"

"Let me see—it seems to me somehow, that—that—Aunt Betsy, do you remember whether he—"

"Never mind about what Aunt Betsy remembers, she is not a witness; we only want to know what you remember, yourself," said the judge.

"Well, it does seem to me that you are most cantankerously particular about a little thing, Sim Robinson. Why, when I can't remember a thing myself, I always—"

"Ah, *please* go on!"

"Now how *can* she, when you keep fussing at her all the time?" said Aunt Betsy. "Why, with a person pecking at *me* that way, I should get that fuzzled and fuddled that—"

She was on her feet again, but Allen coaxed her into her seat once more while the court squelched the mirth of the house. Then the judge said:

"Madam, do you know—do you absolutely *know*, independently of anything these gentlemen have told you—that the power over their legs passes from the one to the other regularly every week?"

"Regularly? Bless your heart, regularly ain't any name for the exactness of it! All the big cities in Europe used to set the clocks by it." [Laughter, *suppressed by the court.*]

"How do you *know?* That is the question. Please answer it plainly and squarely."

"Don't you talk to me like that, Sim Robinson—I won't have it. How do I know, indeed! How do *you* know what you know? Because somebody told you. You didn't invent it out of your own head, did you? Why, these Twins are the truthfulest people in the world; and I don't think it becomes you to sit up there and throw slurs at them when they haven't been doing anything to you. And they are orphans besides,—both of them. All—"

But Aunt Betsy was up again, now, and both old ladies were talking at once and with all their might, but as the house was wel-

tering in a storm of laughter and the judge was hammering his desk
with an iron paper-weight, one could only see them talk, not hear
them. At last when quiet was restored, the court said—

"Let the ladies retire."

"But your honor, I have the right, in the interest of my clients,
to cross-exam—"

"You'll not need to exercise it Mr. Wilson—the evidence is
thrown out."

"Thrown out!" said Aunt Patsy, ruffled; "and what's it thrown
out, for, I'd like to know."

"And so would I, Patsy Cooper. It seems to me that if we can
save these poor persecuted strangers, it is our bounden duty to stand
up here and talk for them till—"

"There, there, there, *do* sit down!"

It cost some trouble and a good deal of coaxing, but they were
got into their seats at last. The trial was soon ended, now. The
Twins themselves became witnesses in their own defence. They
established the fact, upon oath, that the leg-power passed from the
one to the other every Saturday night at twelve o'clock, sharp. But
on cross-examination their counsel would not allow them to tell
whose week of power the current week was. The judge insisted
upon their answering, and proposed to compel them, but even the
prosecution took fright and came to the rescue then and helped stay
the sturdy jurist's revolutionary hand. So the case had to go to the
jury with that important point hanging in the air. They were out an
hour, and brought in this verdict:

"We the jury do find: 1, that an assault was committed, as
charged; 2, that it was committed by one of the persons accused, he
having been seen to do it by several credible witnesses; 3, but that
his identity is so merged in his brother's that we have not been able
to tell which was him. We cannot convict both, for only one is
guilty. We cannot acquit both, for only one is innocent. Our verdict is that justice has been defeated by the dispensation of God,
and ask to be discharged from further duty."

This was read aloud in court, and brought out a burst of hearty
applause. The old ladies made a spring at the Twins, to shake and
congratulate, but were gently disengaged by Mr. Wilson and softly
crowded back into their places.

The Judge rose in his little tribune, laid aside his silver-bowed
spectacles, roached his gray hair up with his fingers, and said, with
dignity and solemnity, and even with a certain pathos:

"In all my experience on the bench I have not seen Justice bow
her head in shame in this court until this day. You little realize
what far-reaching harm has just been wrought here under the fickle
forms of law. Imitation is the bane of courts—I thank God that

this one is free from the contamination of that vice—and in no long time you will see the fatal work of this hour seized upon by profligate so-called guardians of justice in all the wide circumference of this planet and perpetuated in their pernicious decisions. I wash my hands of this iniquity. I would have compelled these culprits to expose their guilt, but support failed me where I had most right to expect aid and encouragement. And I was confronted by a law made in the interest of crime, which protects the criminal from testifying against himself. Yet I had precedents of my own whereby I had set aside that law on two different occasions and thus succeeded in convicting criminals to whose crimes there were no witnesses but themselves. What have you accomplished this day? Do you realize it? You have set adrift, unadmonished, in this community, two men endowed with an awful and mysterious gift, a hidden and grisly power for evil—a power by which each in his turn may commit crime after crime of the most heinous character, and no man be able to tell which is the guilty or which the innocent party in any case of them all. Look to your homes—look to your property —look to your lives—for you have need!

"Prisoners at the bar, stand up. Through suppression of evidence, a jury of your—our—countrymen have been obliged to deliver a verdict concerning your case which stinks to heaven with the rankness of its injustice. By its terms you, the guilty one, go free with the innocent. Depart in peace, and come no more! The costs devolve upon the outraged plaintiff—another iniquity. The court stands dissolved."

Almost everybody crowded forward to overwhelm the Twins and their counsel with congratulations; but presently the two old aunties dug the duplicates out and bore them away in triumph through the hurrahing crowds, while lots of new friends carried Pudd'nhead Wilson off tavernwards to feast him and "wet down" his great and victorious entry into the legal arena. To Wilson, so long familiar with neglect and depreciation, this strange new incense of popularity and admiration was as a fragrance blown from the fields of paradise. A happy man was Wilson.

Chapter 6

[A deputation came in the evening and conferred upon Wilson the welcome honor of a nomination for mayor; for the village has just been converted into a city by charter. Tom skulks out of challenging the twins. Judge Driscoll thereupon challenges Angelo, (accused by Tom of doing the kicking;) he declines, but Luigi accepts in his place against Angelo's timid protest.]

It was late Saturday night—nearing eleven.

The Judge and his second found the rest of the war party at the further end of the vacant ground, near the haunted house. Pudd'n-head Wlson advanced to meet them, and said anxiously—

"I must say a word in behalf of my principal's proxy, Count Luigi, to whom you have kindly granted the privilege of fighting my principal's battle for him. It is growing late, and Count Luigi is in great trouble lest midnight shall strike before the finish."

"It is another testimony," said Howard, approvingly. "That young man is fine all through. He wishes to save his brother the sorrow of fighting on the Sabbath, and he is right; it is the right and manly feeling and does him credit. We will make all possible haste."

Wilson said—

"There is also another reason—a consideration, in fact, which deeply concerns Count Luigi himself. These Twins have command of their mutual legs turn about. Count Luigi is in command, now; but at midnight, possession will pass to my principal, Count Angelo, and—well, you can foresee what will happen. He will march straight off the field, and carry Luigi with him."

"Why! sure enough!" cried the Judge, "we have heard something about that extraordinary law of their being, already—nothing very definite, it is true, as regards dates and durations of the power, but I see it is definite enough as regards to-night. Of course we must give Luigi every chance. Omit all the ceremonial possible, gentlemen, and place us in position."

The seconds at once tossed up a coin; Howard won the choice. He placed the Judge sixty feet from the haunted house and facing it; Wilson placed the Twins within fifteen feet of the house and facing the Judge—necessarily. The pistol-case was opened and the long slim tubes taken out; when the moonlight glinted from them a shiver went through Angelo. The doctor was a fool, but a thoroughly well-meaning one, with a kind heart and a sincere disposition to oblige, but along with it an absence of tact which often hurt its effectiveness. He brought his box of lint and bandages, and asked Angelo to feel and see how soft and comfortable they were. Angelo's head fell over against Luigi's in a faint, and precious time was lost in bringing him to; which provoked Luigi into expressing his mind to the doctor with a good deal of vigor and frankness. After Angelo came to he was still so weak that Luigi was obliged to drink a stiff horn of brandy to brace him up.

The seconds now stepped at once to their posts, half way between the combatants, one of them on each side of the line of fire. Wilson was to count, very deliberately, "One——two——three ——fire!——stop!" and the duelists could bang away at any time they chose during that recitation, but not after the last word.

Angelo grew very nervous when he saw Wilson's hand rising slowly into the air as a sign to make ready, and he leaned his head against Luigi's and said—

"O, please take me away from here, I can't stay, I know I can't!"

"What in the world are you doing? Straighten up! What's the matter with you?—*you're* in no danger—nobody's going to shoot at you. Straighten up, I tell you!"

Angelo obeyed, just in time to hear—

"One——!"

"Bang!" Just one report, and a little tuft of white hair floated slowly to the Judge's feet in the moonlight. The Judge did not swerve; he still stood, erect and motionless, like a statue, with his pistol-arm hanging straight down at his side. He was reserving his fire.

"Two——!

"Three——!

"Fire!——"

Up came the pistol-arm instantly—Angelo dodged with the report. He said "Ouch!" and fainted again.

The doctor examined and bandaged the wound. It was of no consequence, he said—bullet through fleshy part of arm—no bones broken—the gentleman was still able to fight—let the duel proceed.

Next time, Angelo jumped just as Luigi fired; which disordered his aim and caused him to cut a chip out of Howard's ear. The Judge took his time again, and when he fired Angelo jumped, and got a knuckle skinned. The doctor inspected and dressed the wounds. Angelo now spoke out and said he was content with the satisfaction he had got, and if the Judge—but Luigi shut him roughly up, and asked him not to make an ass of himself; adding—

"And I want you to stop dodging. You take a great deal too prominent a part in this thing for a person who has got nothing to do with it. You should remember that you are here only by courtesy, and are without official recognition; officially you are not here at all; officially you do not even exist. To all intents and purposes you are absent from this place, and you ought for your own modesty's sake to reflect that it cannot become a person who is not present here to be taking this sort of public and indecent prominence in a matter in which he is not in the slightest degree concerned. Now don't dodge again; the bullets are not for you, they are for me; if I want them dodged I will attend to it myself. I never saw a person act so."

Angelo saw the reasonableness of what his brother had said, and he did try to reform, but it was of no use; both pistols went off at the same instant, and he jumped once more; he got a sharp scrape along his cheek from the Judge's bullet, and so deflected Luigi's aim that his ball went wide and chipped a flake of skin from Pudd'n-head Wilson's chin. The doctor attended to the wounded.

By the terms, the duel was over. But Luigi was entirely out of patience, and begged for one more exchange of shots, insisting that he had had no fair chance, on account of his brother's indelicate behavior. Howard was opposed to granting so unusual a privilege, but the Judge took Luigi's part, and added that indeed he himself might fairly be considered entitled to another trial, because although the proxy on the other side was in no way to blame for his (the Judge's) humiliatingly resultless work, the gentleman with whom he was fighting this duel was to blame for it, since if he had played no advantages and had held his head still, his proxy would have been disposed of early. He added—

"Count Luigi's request for another exchange is another proof that he is a brave and chivalrous gentleman, and I beg that the courtesy he asks may be accorded him."

"I thank you most sincerely for this generosity, Judge Driscoll," said Luigi, with a polite bow, and moving to his place. Then he added—to Angelo, "Now hold your grip, hold your *grip*, I tell you, and I'll land him, sure!"

The men stood erect, their pistol-arms at their sides, the two seconds stood at their official posts, the doctor stood five paces in Wilson's rear with his instruments and bandages in his hands. The deep stillness, the peaceful moonlight, the motionless figures, made an impressive picture, and the impending fatal possibilities augmented this impressiveness to solemnity. Wilson's hand began to rise—slowly—slowly—higher—still higher——in another moment—

"*Boom!*"—the first stroke of midnight swung up out of the distance. Angelo was off like a deer!

"Oh, you unspeakable traitor!" wailed his brother, as they went soaring over the fence.

The others stood astonished and gazing; and so stood, watching that strange spectacle until distance dissolved it and swept it from their view. Then they rubbed their eyes like people waking out of a dream.

"Well, I've never seen anything like that before!" said the Judge. "Wilson, I am going to confess, now, that I wasn't quite able to believe in that leg-business, and had a suspicion that it was a put-up convenience between those Twins; and when Count Angelo fainted I thought I saw the whole scheme—thought it was pretext No. 1, and would be followed by others till twelve o'clock should arrive and Luigi would get off with all the credit of seeming to want to fight and yet not have to fight, after all. But I was mistaken. His pluck proved it. He's a brave fellow and did want to fight."

"There isn't any doubt about that," said Howard, and added in a grieved tone, "but what an unworthy sort of Christian that Angelo is—I hope and believe there are not many like him. It is not right to engage in a duel on the Sabbath—I could not approve of that, myself; but to finish one that has been begun—that is a duty, let the day be what it may."

They strolled along, still wondering, still talking.

"It is a curious circumstance," remarked the surgeon, halting Wilson a moment to paste some more court plaister on his chin, which had gone to leaking blood again, "that in this duel neither of the parties who handled the pistols lost blood, while nearly all the persons present in the mere capacity of guests got hit. I have not heard of such a thing before. Don't you think it unusual?"

"Yes," said the Judge, "it has struck me as peculiar. Peculiar and unfortunate. I was annoyed at it, all the time. In the case of Angelo it made no great difference, because he was in a measure concerned, though not officially; but it troubled me to see the seconds compromised, and yet I knew no way to mend the matter."

"There was no way to mend it," said Howard, whose ear was being readjusted now by the doctor; "the code fixes our place, and it would not have been lawful to change it. If we could have stood at your side, or behind you, or in front of you, it—but it would not have been legitimate, and the other parties would have had a just right to complain of our trying to protect ourselves from danger; infractions of the code are certainly not permissible in any case whatsoever."

Wilson offered no remarks. It seemed to him that there was very little place here for so much solemnity, but he judged that if a duel where nobody was in danger or got crippled but the seconds and the outsiders had nothing ridiculous about it for these gentlemen, his pointing out that feature would probably not help them to see it.

He invited them in to take a nightcap, and Howard and the Judge accepted, but the doctor said he would have to go and see how Angelo's principal wound was getting on.

[It was now Sunday, and in the afternoon Angelo was to be received into the Baptist communion by immersion—a doubtful prospect, the doctor feared.]

Chapter 7

When the doctor arrived at Aunt Patsy Cooper's house, he found the lights going and everybody up and dressed and in a great state of solicitude and excitement. The Twins were stretched on a sofa in the sitting room, Aunt Patsy was fussing at Angelo's arm, Nancy was flying around under her commands, the two young boys were trying to keep out of the way and always getting in it, in order to see and wonder, Rowena stood apart, helpless with apprehension and emotion, and Luigi was growling in unappeasable fury over Angelo's shameful flight.

As has been reported before, the doctor was a fool—a kind-hearted and well-meaning one, but with no tact; and as he was by long odds the most learned physician in the town, and was quite well aware of it, and could talk his learning with ease and precision, and liked to show off when he had an audience, he was sometimes tempted into revealing more of a case than was good for the patient.

He examined Angelo's wound, and was really minded to say nothing, for once; but Aunt Patsy was so anxious and so pressing that he allowed his caution to be overcome, and proceeded to empty himself as follows, with scientific relish—

"Without going too much into detail, madam—for you would probably not understand it anyway—I concede that great care is going to be necessary here; otherwise exudation of the aesophagus is nearly sure to ensue, and this will be followed by ossification and extradition of the maxillario superioris, which must decompose the granular surfaces of the great infusorial ganglionic system, thus obstructing the action of the posterior varioloid arteries and precipitating compound strangulated sorosis of the valvular tissues, and ending unavoidably in the dispersion and combustion of the marsupial fluxes and the consequent embrocation of the bi-cuspid populo redax referendum rotulorum."

A miserable silence followed. Aunt Patsy's heart sank, the pallor of despair invaded her face, she was not able to speak; poor Rowena wrung her hands in privacy and silence, and said to herself in the bitterness of her young grief, "There is no hope—it is plain there is no hope;" the good-hearted negro wench, Nancy, paled to chocolate, then to orange, then to amber, and thought to herself with yearning sympathy and sorrow, "Po' thing, he ain' gwyne to las' thoo de half o' dat;" small Henry choked up, and turned his head away to hide his rising tears, and his brother Joe said to himself, with a sense of loss, "The babtizing's busted, that's sure." Luigi was the only person who had any heart to speak. He said, a little bit sharply, to the doctor—

"Well, well, there's nothing to be gained by wasting precious time: give him a barrel of pills—I'll take them for him."

"You?" asked the doctor.

"Yes. Did you suppose he was going to take them himself?"

"Why, of course."

"Well, it's a mistake. He never took a dose of medicine in his life. He can't."

"Well, upon my word, it's the most extraordinary thing I ever heard of!"

"Oh," said Aunt Patsy, as pleased as a mother whose child is being admired and wondered at, "you'll find that there's more about them that's wonderful than their just being made in the image of God like the rest of His creatures, now you can depend on that, *I* tell you," and she wagged her complacent head like one who could reveal marvelous things if she chose.

The boy Joe began—

"Why, ma, they *ain't* made in the im—"

"You shut up, and wait till you're asked, Joe. I'll let you know when I want help. Are you looking for something, doctor?"

The doctor asked for a few sheets of paper and a pen, and said he would write a prescription—which he did. It was one of Galen's; in fact it was Galen's favorite, and had been slaying people for sixteen thousand years. Galen used it for everything, applied it to everything, said it would remove everything, from warts all the way through to lungs—and it generally did. Galen was still the only medical authority recognized in Missouri, his practice was the only practice known to the Missouri doctors, and his prescriptions were the only ammunition they carried when they went out for game. By and by Dr. Claypool laid down his pen and read the result of his labors aloud, carefully and deliberately, for this battery must be constructed on the premises by the family, and mistakes could occur; for he wrote a doctor's hand—the hand which from the beginning of time has been so disastrous to the apothecary and so profitable to the undertaker:

Take of Afarabocca, Henbane, Carpobalsamum, each two Drams and a half; of Cloves, Opium, Myrrh, Cyperus, each two Drams; of Opobalsamum, Indian Leaf, Cinamon, Zedoary, Ginger, Coftus, Coral, Cassia, Euphorbium, Gum Tragacanth, Frankincense, Styrax Calamita, Celtic, Nard, Spignel, Hartwort, Mustard, Saxifrage, Dill, Anise, each one Dram; of Xylaloes, Rheum Ponticum, Alipta Moschata, Castor, Spikenard, Galangals, Opoponax, Anacardium, Mastich, Brimstone, Peony, Eringo, Pulp of Dates, red and white Hermodactyls, Roses, Thyme, Acorns, Penyroyal, Gentian, the Bark of the Root of Mandrake, Germander, Valerian, Bishops Weed,   Bay-Berries, long and white Pepper, Xylobalsamum, Carnabadium, Macodonian, Parsley-seeds, Lovage, the Seeds of Rue, and Sinon, of each a Dram and a half; of pure Gold, pure Silver, Pearls not perforated, the Blatta Byzantina, the Bone of the Stag's Heart, of each the Quantity of fourteen Grains of Wheat; of Sapphire, Emerald, and Jasper Stones, each one Dram; of Hasle-nut, two Drams; of Pellitory of Spain, Shavings of Ivory, Calamus Odoratus, each the Quantity of twenty-nine Grains of Wheat; of Honey or Sugar a sufficient Quantity. Boil down and skim off.

"There," he said, "that will fix the patient; give his brother a dipperful every three-quarters of an hour—"

—"while he survives," muttered Luigi—

—"and see that the room is kept wholesomely hot and the doors and windows closed tight. Keep Count Angelo nicely covered up with six or seven blankets, and when he is thirsty—which will be frequently—moisten a rag in the vapor of the tea-kettle and let his brother suck it. When he is hungry—which will also be frequently —he must not be humored oftener than every seven or eight hours; then toast part of a cracker until it begins to brown, and give it to his brother."

"That is all very well, as far as Angelo is concerned," said Luigi, "but what am I to eat?"

"I do not see that there is anything the matter with you," the doctor answered, "You may of course eat what you please."

"And also drink what I please, I suppose?"

"Oh, certainly—at present. When the violent and continuous perspiring has reduced your strength, I shall have to reduce your diet, of course, and also bleed you, but there is no occasion for that yet awhile." He turned to Aunt Patsy and said: "He must be put to bed, and sat up with, and tended with the greatest care, and not allowed to stir for several days and nights.

"For one, I'm sacredly thankful for that," said Luigi, "it postpones the funeral—I'm not to be drowned to-day, anyhow."

Angelo said quietly to the doctor:

"I will cheerfully submit to all your requirements, sir, up to two o'clock this afternoon, and will resume them after three, but I cannot be confined to the house during that intermediate hour."

"Why, may I ask?"

"Because I have entered the Baptist communion, and by appointment am to be baptised in the river at that hour."

"O, insanity!—it cannot be allowed!"

Angelo answered with placid firmness—

"Nothing shall prevent it, if I am alive."

"Why, consider, my dear sir, in your condition it might prove fatal."

A tender and ecstatic smile beamed from Angelo's eyes and he broke forth in a tone of joyous fervency—

"Ah, how blessed it would be to die for such a cause—it would be martyrdom!"

"But your brother—consider your brother; you would be risking his life, too."

"He risked mine an hour ago," responded Angelo, gloomily; "did he consider me?" A thought swept through his mind that made him shudder. "If I had not run, I might have been killed in a duel on the Sabbath day, and my soul would have been lost—lost."

"O, don't fret, it wasn't in any danger," said Luigi, irritably; "they wouldn't waste it for a little thing like that; there's a glass case all ready for it in the heavenly museum, and a pin to stick it up with."

Aunt Patsy was shocked, and said—

"Looy, Looy!—don't talk so, dear!"

Rowena's soft heart was pierced by Luigi's unfeeling words, and she murmured to herself, "O, if I but had the dear privilege of protecting and defending him with my weak voice!—but alas, this sweet boon is denied me by the cruel conventions of social intercourse."

"Get their bed ready," said Aunt Patsy to Nancy, "and shut up the windows and doors, and light their candles, and see that you drive all the mosquitoes out of their bar, and make up a good fire in their stove, and carry up some bags of hot ashes to lay to his feet—

—"and a shovel of fire for his head, and a mustard plaster for his neck, and some gum shoes for his ears," Luigi interrupted, with a temper; and added, to himself, "damnation, I'm going to be roasted alive, I just know it!"

"Why, Looy! Do be quiet; I never saw such a fractious thing. A body would think you didn't care for your brother."

"I don't—to *that* extent, Aunt Patsy. I was glad the drowning was postponed, a minute ago; but I'm not, now. No, that is all gone by: I want to be drowned."

"You'll bring a judgement on yourself just as sure as you live, if you go on like that. Why, I never heard the beat of it. Now, there-there! you've said enough. Not another word out of you, Looy—I won't have it!"

"But Aunt Patsy—"

"Luigi! Didn't you hear what I told you?"

"But Aunt Patsy, I—why, I'm not going to set my heart and lungs afloat in that pail of sewage which this criminal here has been prescri—"

"Yes you are, too. You are going to be good, and do everything I tell you, like a dear," and she tapped his cheek affectionately with her finger. "Rowena, take the prescription and go in the kitchen and hunt up the things and lay them out for me. I'll sit up with my patient the rest of the night, doctor; I can't trust Nancy, she couldn't make Luigi take the medicine. Of course you'll drop in again during the day. Have you got any more directions?"

"No, I believe not, Aunt Patsy. If I don't get in earlier, I'll be along, by early candle-light, anyway. Meantime, don't allow him to get out of his bed."

Angelo said, with calm determination—

"I shall be baptized at two o'clock. Nothing but death shall prevent me."

The doctor said nothing aloud, but to himself he said, "Why, this chap's got a manly side, after all! Physically he's a coward, but morally he's a lion. I'll go and tell the others about this; it will raise him a good deal in their estimation—and the public will follow their lead, of course."

Privately, Aunt Patsy applauded, too, and was proud of Angelo's courage in the moral field as she was of Luigi's in the field of honor.

The boy Henry was troubled, but the boy Joe said, inaudibly, and gratefully, "We're all hunky, after all; and no postponement on account of the weather."

Chapter 8

By nine o'clock the town was humming with the news of the midnight duel, and there were but two opinions about it: one, that Luigi's pluck in the field was most praiseworthy and Angelo's flight most scandalous; the other, that Angelo's courage in flying the field for conscience sake was as fine and creditable as was Luigi's in holding the field in the face of the bullets. The one opinion was held by half of the town, the other one was maintained by the other half. The division was clean and exact, and it made two parties, an Angelo party and a Luigi party. The Twins had suddenly become popular idols along with Pudd'nhead Wilson, and haloed with a glory as intense as his. The children talked the duel all the way to Sunday school, their elders talked it all the way to church, the choir discussed it behind their red curtain, it usurped the place of pious thought in the "nigger gallery."

By noon the doctor had added the news, and spread it, that Count Angelo, in spite of his wound and all warnings and supplications, was resolute in his determination to be baptised at the hour appointed. This swept the town like wildfire, and mightily reinforced the enthusiasm of the Angelo faction, who said, "If any doubted that it was moral courage that took him from the field, what have they to say now!"

Still the excitement grew. All the morning it was traveling countrywards, toward all points of the compass; and so, whereas before only the farmers and their wives were intending to come and witness the remarkable baptism, a general holiday was now proclaimed and the children and negroes admitted to the privileges of the occasion. All the farms for ten miles around were vacated, all the converging roads emptied long processions of wagons, horses and yeomanry into the town. The pack and cram of people vastly exceeded any that had ever been seen in that sleepy region before. The only thing that had ever even approached it was the time, long gone by, but never forgotten nor ever referred to without wonder and pride, when two circuses and a Fourth of July fell together. But the glory of that occasion was extinguished, now, for good. It was but a freshet to this deluge.

The great invasion massed itself on the river bank and waited hungrily for the immense event. Waited, and wondered if it would really happen, or if the twin who was not a "professor" would stand out and prevent it.

But they were not to be disappointed. Angelo was as good as his word. He came attended by an escort of honor composed of several hundred of the best citizens, all of the Angelo party; and when the immersion was finished they escorted him back home; and would even have carried him on their shoulders, but that people might think they were carrying Luigi.

Far into the night the citizens continued to discuss and wonder over the strangely-mated pair of incidents that had distinguished and exalted the past twenty-four hours above any other twenty-four in the history of their town for picturesqueness and splendid interest; and long before the lights were out and the burghers asleep it had been decided on all hands that in capturing these Twins Dawson's Landing had drawn a prize in the great lottery of municipal fortune.

At midnight Angelo was sleeping peacefully. His immersion had not harmed him, it had merely made him wholesomely drowsy, and he had been dead asleep many hours, now. It had made Luigi drowsy, too, but he had got only brief naps, on account of his having to take the medicine every three-quarters of an hour—and Aunt Betsy Hale was there to see that he did it. When he complained and resisted, she was quietly firm with him, and said in a low voice:

"No-no, that won't do; you mustn't talk, and you mustn't retch and gag that way, either—you'll wake up your poor brother."

"Well, what of it, Aunt Betsy, he—"

"'Sh-h! Don't make a noise, dear. You mustn't forget that your poor brother is sick and—"

"Sick, is he? Well, I wish I—"

"'Sh-h-h! Will you be quiet, Luigi! Here, now, take the rest of it —don't keep me holding the dipper all night. I declare if you haven't left a good fourth of it in the bottom! Come—that's a good boy."

"Aunt Betsy, don't make me! I tell you I feel like I've swallowed a cemetery; I do, indeed. Do let me rest a little—just a little; I can't take any more of the devilish stuff, now."

"Luigi! Using such language here, and him just baptised! Do you want the roof to fall on you?"

"I wish to goodness it would!"

"Why, you dreadful thing! I've a good notion to—let that blanket alone; do you want your brother to catch his death?"

"Aunt Betsy, I've *got* to have it off; I'm being roasted alive; nobody could stand it—you couldn't, yourself."

"Now, then, you're sneezing again—I just expected it."

"Because I've caught a cold in my head. I always do, when I go in the water with my clothes on. And it takes me weeks to get over it, too. I think it was a shame to serve me so."

"Luigi, you are unreasonable; you know very well they couldn't baptise him dry. I should think you would be willing to undergo a little inconvenience for your brother's sake."

"Inconvenience! Now how you talk, Aunt Betsy. I came as near as anything to getting drowned—you saw that, yourself; and do you call this inconvenience?—the room shut up as tight as a drum, and so hot the mosquitoes are trying to get out; and a cold in the head, and dying for sleep and no chance to get any on account of this infamous medicine that that assassin prescri—"

"There, you're sneezing again. I'm going down and mix some more of this truck for you, dear."

Chapter 9

During Monday, Tuesday and Wednesday the Twins grew steadily worse; but then the doctor was summoned south to attend his mother's funeral and they got well in forty-eight hours. They appeared on the street on Friday, and were welcomed with enthusiasm by the new-born parties, the Luigi and Angelo factions. The Luigi faction carried its strength into the Democratic party, the Angelo faction entered into a combination with the Whigs. The Democrats nominated Luigi for alderman under the new city government, and the Whigs put up Angelo against him. The Democrats nominated Pudd'nhead Wilson for mayor, and he was left alone in this glory, for the Whigs had no man who was willing to enter the lists against such a formidable opponent. No politician had scored such a compliment as this before in the history of the Mississippi Valley.

The political campaign in Dawson's Landing opened in a pretty warm fashion, and waxed hotter and hotter every week. Luigi's whole heart was in it, and even Angelo presently developed a surprising amount of interest in it—which was natural, because he was not merely representing Whigism, which was a matter of no consequence to him, he was representing something immensely finer and greater—to wit, Reform. In him was centred the hopes of the whole reform element of the town; he was the chosen and admired champion of every clique that had a pet reform of any sort or kind at heart. He was president of the great Teetotalers' Union and its chiefest prophet and mouthpiece.

But as the canvass went on, troubles began to spring up all around—troubles for the Twins, and through them for all the parties and segments and fractions of parties. Whenever Luigi had possession of the legs, he carried Angelo to balls, rum shops, Sons of Liberty parades, horse races, campaign riots, and everywhere else that could damge him with his party and his church; and when it was Angelo's week he carried Luigi diligently to all manner of moral and religious gatherings, and did his best to get back the ground which he had lost before. As a result of these double performances, there was a storm blowing all the time, and it was an ever rising storm, too—a storm of frantic criticism of the Twins, and rage over their extravagant and incomprehensible conduct.

Luigi had the final chance. The legs were his for the closing week of the canvass. He led his brother a fearful dance.

But he saved his best card for the very eve of the election. There was to be a grand turn-out of the Teetotalers' Union that day, and Angelo was to march at the head of the procession and deliver a great oration afterward. Luigi drank a couple of glasses of whisky—

which steadied his nerves and clarified his mind, but made Angelo drunk. Everybody who saw the march, saw that the Champion of the Teetotalers was half seas over, and noted also that his brother, who made no hypocritical pretentions to extra-temperance virtues, was dignified and sober. This eloquent fact could not be unfruitful at the end of a hot political canvass. At the mass meeting Angelo tried to make his great temperance oration but was so discommoded by hiccups and thickness of tongue that he had to give it up; then drowsiness overtook him and his head drooped against Luigi's and he went to sleep. Luigi apologized for him, and was going on to improve his opportunity with a ringing appeal for a moderation of what he called "the prevailing teetotal madness," but persons in the audience began to howl and throw things at him, and then the meeting rose in a general burst of wrath and chased him home.

This episode was a crusher for Angelo in another way. It destroyed his chances with Rowena. Those chances had been growing, right along, for two months. Rowena had even partly confessed that she loved him, but had begged for time to consider. But now the tender dream was ended, and she frankly told him so, the moment he was sober enough to understand. She said she would never marry a man who drank.

"But I don't drink," he pleaded.

"That is nothing to the point," she said, coldly, "you get drunk, and that is worse."

[There was a long and sufficiently idiotic discussion here, which ended as reported in a previous note.]

Chapter 10

Dawson's Landing had a week of repose, after the election, and it needed it, for the frantic and variegated nightmare which had tormented it all through the preceding week had left it limp, haggard and exhausted at the end. It got the week of repose because Angelo had the legs, and was in too subdued a condition to want to go out and mingle with an irritated community that had come to distrust and detest him because there was such a lack of harmony between his morals, which were confessedly excellent, and his methods of illustrating them, which were distinctly damnable.

The new city officers were sworn in on the following Monday—at least all but Luigi. There was a complication in his case. His election was conceded, but he could not sit in the board of aldermen without his brother, and his brother could not sit there because he was not a member. There seemed to be no way out of the difficulty but to carry the matter into the courts, so this was resolved upon.

The case was set for the Monday fortnight. In due course the time arrived. In the meantime the city government had been at a standstill, because without Luigi there was a tie in the board of aldermen, whereas with him the liquor interest—the richest in the political field—would have one majority. But the court decided that Angelo could not sit in the board with him, either in public or executive sessions, and at the same time forbade the board to deny admission to Luigi, a fairly and legally chosen alderman. The case was carried up and up from court to court, yet still the same old original decision was confirmed every time. As a result, the city government not only stood still, with its hands tied, but everything it was created to protect and care for went a steady gait toward rack and ruin. There was no way to levy a tax, so the minor officials had to resign or starve; therefore they resigned. There being no city money, the enormous legal expenses on both sides had to be defrayed by private subscription. But at last the people came to their senses, and said—

"Pudd'nhead was right, at the start—we ought to have hired the official half of that human phillipene to resign; but it's too late, now; some of us haven't got anything left to hire him with."

"Yes we have," said another citizen, "we've got this"—and he produced a halter.

Many shouted—

"That's the ticket."

But others said—

"No—Count Angelo is innocent; we mustn't hang him."

"Who said anything about hanging him? We are only going to hang the other one."

"Then that is all right—there is no objection to that."

So they hanged Luigi. And so ends the history of "Those Extraordinary Twins."

Final Remarks.

As you see, it was an extravagant sort of a tale, and had no purpose but to exhibit that monstrous "freak" in all sorts of grotesque lights. But when Roxy wandered into the tale she had to be furnished with something to do; so she changed the children in the cradle: this necessitated the invention of a reason for it; this in turn resulted in making the children prominent personages—nothing could prevent it, of course. Their career began to take a tragic aspect, and some one had to be brought in to help work the machinery; so Pudd'nhead Wilson was introduced and taken on trial. By this time the whole show was being run by the new people and in their interest, and the original show was become side-tracked and forgotten; the twin-monster and the heroine and the lads and the old ladies had dwindled to inconsequentialities and were merely in the way. Their story was one story, the new people's story was another story, and there was no connection between them, no interdependence, no kinship. It is not practicable or rational to try to tell two stories at the same time; so I dug out the farce and left the tragedy.

The reader already knew how the expert works; he knows now how the other kind do it.

MARK TWAIN.

Textual Introduction
and
Tables of Variants

Pudd'nhead Wilson and Those Extraordinary Twins:
Textual Introduction

To understand the problems of editing *Pudd'nhead Wilson* and *Those Extraordinary Twins*, one must be familiar with the extant documents which may have some authority in the transmission of the text. Briefly they are:

1) The Berg manuscript (hereafter referred to as BMS)
2) A typescript of the Berg manuscript (TS$_1$)
3) The Morgan manuscript (MMS)
4) The *Century Magazine* serialization (CM)
5) The American Publishing Company edition (APC)
6) The Chatto & Windus edition (C&W)

(Collations of other editions which appeared in Clemens's lifetime prove them to be of no authority, usually deriving from APC, the first printing of *Pudd'nhead Wilson* and *Those Extraordinary Twins* in book form [and the first appearance of *Twins*].)

To this list must be added a typescript made of the MMS; though this typescript is not extant, there is a note in Clemens's letter of February 3, 1893, to Frederick J. Hall that "My book is type-writered and ready for print —'Puddn'head [sic] Wilson—a Tale.' (Or, 'Those Extraordinary Twins,' if preferable.)"[1] (This typescript shall henceforth be referred to as TS$_2$.)

The first manuscript, of about ten thousand words, is in the Berg Collection of the New York Public Library. On page one, Clemens called the story "Those Extraordinary Twins." This manuscript contains Clemens's earliest attempt at writing the story of the Siamese twins, begun some time in 1892. The manuscript is apparently a surviving portion of a longer work, for in a letter dated September 4, 1892, to his junior partner at Charles L. Webster & Company, Fred Hall, Clemens said of the story:

> It is the howling farce I told you I had begun a while back. I laid it aside to ferment while I wrote 'Tom Sawyer Abroad,' but I took it up again on a little different plan lately, and it is swimming along satisfactorily now. I have written about 20,000 words on it, but I can't form any idea of how big a book it is going to make yet. If I keep up my like it will be a book that will *sell* mighty well, I am sure of that. I think all sorts of folks will read it. It is clear out of the common order—it is a

1. Hamlin Hill, *Mark Twain's Letters to His Publishers (MTLP)* (Berkeley and Los Angeles: University of California Press, 1967), pp. 336–337.

fresh idea—I don't think it resembles anything in literature. *I* believe there's a 'boom' in it.[2]

Clemens's word count is apparently accurate, for in a letter to his sister-in-law Sue Crane of September 1, 1892, he says he "took up 'Twins' again, destroyed the last half of the manuscript and then re-wrote it in another form. . . ."[3] At some point—in September or October 1892[4]—the remaining ten thousand word text was typed, and this typescript was later incorporated into the MMS by the author.

Once this typescript was made, Clemens decided to recast the characters of Pudd'nhead Wilson, Tom Driscoll, and Roxy, and had a new burst of creative energies, as can be seen by numerous letters from him to Hall, Vice-Consul-General Hogue in Frankfurt a/M, Chatto & Windus, Clara Clemens, Franklin G. Whitmore, Laurence Hutton, and others, and from some extensive notes on the story in his notebooks of the period. After writing about sixty to eighty thousand words (as his letter to Hall dated December 12, 1892,[5] states) of this new version, Clemens wrote in his notebook, under the date of December 20, 1892:

> Finished 'Pudd'nhead Wilson' last Wednesday, 14th. Began it 11th or 12th of last month, after King girls left. Wrote more than 60,000 words between Nov. 12 & Dec. 14. One day, wrote 6,000 words in 13 hours. Another day wrote 5,000 in 11.

As Frederick Anderson points out, "The bloated book at this stage included all of the fullest expansion of the Siamese-twins farce and the complex variety of serious themes the book now possesses and a drearily facetious foreword about March weather."[6] This new version—the Morgan manuscript (MMS)—was mostly in Clemens's handwriting, except for the pages of the typescript (TS_1) made from the Berg manuscript; these pages were included in the 633½ pages of MMS. Under the same date in the notebook but three pages later is the entry: "Adam and Puddn to type-writer."[7] By March 10, 1893, Fred Hall had received a copy of the "ms" but had "not looked it over yet."[8]

During most of the composition Clemens was in Europe with his wife, Olivia. But in April and May 1893 he was in New York, at which time he apparently visited Hall and retrieved the typescript which he had sent Hall from Florence.[9] After much deliberation, and after gathering much criticism from his wife, Hutton, and Hall about the book, Clemens decided to revise the entire plot, and by July 30 he was able to write to Hall about this new version of the story:

> *This* time "Pudd'nhead Wilson" is a success! . . . I have pulled the twins

2. *MTLP*, p. 319.
3. Copy of letter in Mark Twain Papers (MTP), Berkeley.
4. In an October 14, 1892, letter to Vice-Consul-General Hogue Clemens says, "The closing pages of the Twins have also arrived." (Typescript of letter in MTP.) Presumably he is referring to a typescript.
5. *MTLP*, p. 319.
6. Frederick Anderson, ed., *Pudd'nhead Wilson and Those Extraordinary Twins,* *by Mark Twain, a Facsimile of the First Edition* (San Francisco: Chandler Publishing Company, 1968), p. xiii.
7. A search for an "Adam" typescript has proven fruitless. But in a letter of July 30, 1893, he mentions to Hall that he "shall tackle Adam once more." (*MTLP*, p. 356) Hamlin Hill sees this as a reference to "Adam's Diary."
8. *MTLP*, p. 336, n. 2.
9. As noted above, Clemens had a typist in Florence.

apart & made two individuals of them; I have sunk them out of sight, they are mere flitting shadows, now, & of no importance; *their* story has disappeared from the book. Aunt Betsy Hale has vanished wholly, leaving not a trace behind; aunt Patsy Cooper & her daughter Rowena have almost disappeared—they scarcely walk across the stage. The whole story is centred on the murder and the trial; from the first chapter the movement is straight ahead without divergence or side-play to the murder & the trial; everything that is done or said or that happens is a preparation for those events.

* * *

When I began this final reconstruction the story contained 81,500 words; now it contains only 58,000. I have knocked out everything that delayed the march of the story—even the description of a Mississippi steamboat.[1] There ain't any weather in, & there ain't any scenery—the story is stripped for flight![2]

By mid-August he was ready to send Hall copy for publication.[3]

The copy he sent to Hall was almost certainly a cut, pasted, and revised text of the December 20 typescript (i.e. TS$_2$).[4] In this massive revision he completely rewrote the story, casting characters in new roles, discarding some characters, rearranging the materials of the plot, and separating out the extraordinary twins. This typescript was then sent to Hall,[5] and is almost certainly what was used for printer's copy by the *Century Magazine*. The MMS itself was never used by a printer, for many substantive changes were made in the story which appear in all published versions, but which do not appear in the manuscript. (It is also possible that a carbon copy of TS$_2$ was made.[6]) The first installment appeared in *Century Magazine* for December 1893. Clemens wrote to his wife on September 7, 1893:

I've sold . . . PW to the Century for six thousand five hundred. . . . Story will begin in December number, & be made the "feature."[7]

We learn from one of Clemens's letters to his wife Olivia that on September 21, 1893, he began to read proof for the first installment of the serialization at the *Century* offices; he said that his "deeply thought out, and

1. The passage may be found in "Emendations of the Copy-Text: Substantives (Lengthy Passages)," 33.11, below.
2. *MTLP*, pp. 354–355; the passage about the weather may be found in Appendix 1 of the present edition.
3. We see this in a letter to Hall of August 9, 1893: "I am traveling on the idea that John Brisben Walker will take PW." (*MTLP*, p. 358), and also in another to Hall of August 14, 1893: "I mean to ship PW to you—say tomorrow. It'll furnish me hash for a while I reckon." (*MTLP*, p. 359).
4. Considering how large the text is (over 630 MMS pages), and also considering that almost every passage in the final version of the story is lifted nearly verbatim from the MMS, it is not at all unlikely that Clemens cut and pasted his typescript (TS$_2$) and then added new connecting passages, made his revisions

(especially those concerning the now-separated Siamese twins), and deleted the farcical material—all this being done in TS$_2$. In fact, the printer's copy for the present edition was prepared in just this way, on a typescript of MMS.
5. Anne Wigger claims that Clemens "had a typewritten manuscript mailed to Fred Hall"; see Wigger, "The Composition of Mark Twain's *Pudd'nhead Wilson* and *Those Extraordinary Twins:* Chronology and Development," *Modern Philology*, November 1957, p. 97, note 21. Her arguments are sound, and her discussion of the story is interesting and valuable.
6. See discussion of the Chatto & Windus edition, below.
7. Dixon Wecter, *The Love Letters of Mark Twain* (*LLMT*) (New York: Harper & Brothers, 1949), p. 267.

laboriously perfected" punctuation had been altered by some "imported proof-reader, from Oxford University. . . . I said I didn't care if he was an Archangel imported from Heaven, he couldn't puke his ignorant impudence over *my* punctuation, I wouldn't allow it for a moment. I said I couldn't read this proof. I couldn't sit in the *presence* of a proofsheet where that blatherskite had left his tracks. . . . I'm to return there to-morrow & read the deodorized proof."[8] However, the great number of punctuation changes in the serialization make it highly unlikely that Clemens's wishes as to such styling were respected.

Though he wanted his own printing firm, C. L. Webster & Company, to publish the novel in book form, the nearly bankrupt company was unable to do so; instead he offered it to the American Publishing Company and to Chatto & Windus in England, who contracted to publish it simultaneously. The book was issued on November 28, 1894, by both companies, but in the American publication the farce of *Those Extraordinary Twins* was included. This was done by Clemens mainly for financial reasons, as he sold what he called "refuse matter"[9] (i.e., the deleted Siamese twins story) to the American Publishing Company for $1,500.

For *Pudd'nhead Wilson* the American Publishing Company used CM for its printer's copy; we know this because their edition follows the *Century* consistently in substantives and accidentals.[1] For *Those Extraordinary Twins* the American Publishing Company used "refuse matter" from the cut and pasted typescript (TS$_2$)— material concerning the Siamese twins which was removed from the *Pudd'nhead Wilson* story. Clemens sailed for Europe on March 7, 1894, and was in Paris part of that year, while taking other trips to New York for financial reasons. Distance and financial matters make it unlikely that he had anything to do with the production of the American edition.

It ought to be noted that three distinct states of the printed American text are discernible; chronologically, they are the prospectus,[2] copies in the Library of Congress and Harvard Library, and the first published edition (APC). Further discussion of these states is beyond the scope of this edition.[3]

Chatto & Windus's printer's copy for the first seventeen chapters of *Pudd'nhead Wilson* was undoubtedly CM. Collations along with Chatto & Windus correspondence substantiate this.

Clemens may have been travelling through London on his way back to his family in France at about the time that the *Pudd'nhead Wilson* text was being set and readied for publication at Chatto & Windus, but it is unlikely that the variants between that edition and the other texts came from his pen

8. *LLMT*, pp. 273–274.
9. Typescript of letter to Livy (Olivia Clemens), 4 August 1894; also letter to Henry Huttleston Rogers, February 8–9, 1895 (see Lewis Leary, *Mark Twain's Correspondence with Henry Huttleston Rogers, 1893–1909 [MTHHR]* [Berkeley and Los Angeles: University of California Press, 1969], p. 128).
1. For example, where the MMS has "law-chapters" (5.5–6), both *CM* and APC have the words unhyphenated

(233.i.9 and 15.11 respectively); where the MMS has "was saved" (39.4), the other two have "had been saved" (237.ii.16 and 36.19). See note 5 below for an explanation of the terms "substantives" and "accidentals."
2. In the Yale University Library.
3. See Sidney Berger, "Editorial Intrusion in *Pudd'nhead Wilson*," *Papers of the Bibliographical Society of America*, 70 (1976), 272–76.

on this trip.[4] Some variants, both substantive and accidental in nature,[5] are easily seen as those of a compositor or because of the printing house's style. Thus the Chatto & Windus edition has no authority. A record of its readings has been retained for the present edition.

One feature of the English edition does cause some problems, however: the last five chapters of *Pudd'nhead Wilson* in this edition (chapters 18–21 and the Conclusion) do not follow CM so closely as do all the earlier chapters; in fact, these five chapters have readings which often coincide with MMS where CM varies from that manuscript. For example, where MMS has "man," (509.10), CM (17.i.35) and APC (228.19) have "man;", but the English text has the comma (183.5); where MMS has "mawnins" (510.4), CM (17.ii.45) and APC (229.5) have "mawnin's," but again the English text agrees with the MMS (183.15). The English edition and the manuscript also agree in hyphenations, use of italics, and several other areas of accidentals.

Most perplexing of all, however, is the fact that in substantive readings C&W usually follows CM, but occasionally it does not. And where C&W varies substantively from CM, the English text invariably has MMS readings. For example, where CM has "last" (23.ii.21) MMS and C&W have "past" (559.7 and 207.18). It appears that for these chapters the English printers could not have used CM to set from, but were setting from copy closer to MMS than was CM. The several complex ways of explaining this anomaly are beyond the scope of this edition. It is sufficient to say here that Clemens had no direct hand in the production of the English edition and that this edition hence has no authority.[6]

One further note about the development of the story is in order. When Clemens realized that the complete story (as it existed in MMS) needed to be recast—pulling the twins apart and separating out the farce—he must have initially thought the revision could be made on the Morgan manuscript itself. This thought was necessarily brief, as a glance at the substantive emendations of the copy-text shows. However, there is evidence that he made some revisions in the Morgan manuscript with the concept of separated twins in his mind. At the top of manuscript page 545 he wrote "OVER OVER," and on the back of the sheet he added a paragraph in which he has Luigi, ostensibly alone, going out for a walk (the walk on which he hears the Judge's cries for help). However, when the Morgan manuscript was typed and Clemens made his revisions, he changed "Luigi" to "the twins" (see page 93, line 32, of the present volume), realizing that in the original story the twins were necessarily together everywhere, and that it would be simpler here to have the twins going out for a walk

---

4. The English edition has such variants as "any way" (8.18) where the manuscript has one word (21.35), "asleep;" (111.23) where the other versions have a comma, "down to de" (188.14) where the others have "down de," "by voluntarily" (173.26) where the others have "in voluntarily," and so on.
5. A substantive variant is one in which a word, phrase, or passage in one text varies from that in the other. An accidental variant is a difference in punctuation, capitalization, spelling, hyphenation, italicization, or paragraphing.
6. See Sidney Berger, "Determining Printer's Copy: The English Edition of Mark Twain's *Pudd'nhead Wilson*," *Papers of the Bibliographical Society of America*, 72 (1978), 250–256.

together than to recast the entire murder and trial elements of the story to concern Luigi only.

For *Those Extraordinary Twins* we know that pages of typescript were sent to the American Publishing Company as copy. Clemens simply pieced together the Siamese twins materials which he had excised from *Pudd'n-head Wilson* (i.e., leftover pieces of TS_2), adding bracketed passages as connectors between the various pieces of "refuse matter." Certainly, the American Publishing Company was not setting directly from manuscript, for the farce of the twins still remains embedded, unrevised, in the Morgan manuscript.

Copy-Text

On the simplest level, the term "copy-text" refers to the base text chosen by an editor—the text which the editor emends to create a version closest to the author's final intentions (as well as these intentions can be ascertained). The emendations are drawn from authoritative sources. Once again, it is beyond the scope of the Textual Introduction for a Norton Critical Edition to explain technical bibliographical theories.[7] It is sufficient to say that for the present edition, where there are passages of author's inscription (i.e. his own handwriting), they are used as copy-text. Where—in the final version of the story—there is no inscription, the earliest appearance of the text in print (which presumably most closely resembles the lost typescript) is copy-text. For *Pudd'nhead Wilson* this is the *Century Magazine* text; for *Those Extraordinary Twins* it is the APC printing.

Though the *Century* version of *Pudd'nhead Wilson* represents the first publication of the story in its final order of chapters and passages, and with the characters and plots recast, the correspondence of the individual wording and sentence structure with MMS is close enough that we can see in this manuscript more than merely a rough draft of the story. What the author has done in his massive revision is to use most of his original prose, but he has completely revised it in terms of the order in which his chapters and passages appear, at the same time supplying the necessary new passages to explain additions to and deletions from the plot, and with new transitions where they were needed.

Since the Morgan manuscript text was used nearly verbatim for much of the *Pudd'nhead Wilson* story, it is the best choice for copy-text for much of this edition, whereas the order of the chapters and incidents is taken from the first printed edition: the *Century*. Where there is typescript in MMS (i.e., TS_1), BMS (representing latest authorial inscription) is copy-text; the author's written emendations in TS_1, however, supersede BMS

---

7. The reader who wishes further amplification of the highly complex topic of copy-text may read Greg, W. W., "The Rationale of Copy-Text," *Studies in Bibliography*, III (1950), 19–36; Baender, Paul, "The Meaning of Copy-Text," *Studies in Bibliography*, XXII (1969), 311–318; Bowers, Fredson, "Current Theories of Copy-Text, with an Illustra-tion from Dryden," *Modern Philology*, LXVII (1950), 19–36; Clemens, S. L., *What Is Man and Other Philosophical Writings*, ed. Baender (University of California Press, 1973), pp. 609–613; and Sanderson, Kenneth M. and Stein, Bernard L., eds., *Fables of Man* (University of California Press, 1972), pp. 477–78.

readings. And where new materials not in either manuscript exist, the earliest printed version (the *Century* for *Pudd'nhead Wilson* and the APC for *Those Extraordinary Twins*) is copy-text.

Pudd'nhead Wilson: *Principles of Emendation*

The copy-text has been emended for *Pudd'nhead Wilson* in four distinct ways. 1) The order of the text was made to conform to that of the *Century* edition. 2) Adaptations for the new order of the story are drawn from the *Century*. This, of course, means that passages in the Morgan manuscript which were never printed have been deleted. For example, the end of Chapter 6 in the Morgan manuscript was transferred to the middle of Chapter 1 of *Those Extraordinary Twins*; also, a passage in the Morgan manuscript between pages 92 and 99 concerning Roxy's religion and Jasper's stopping a runaway carriage are found in the Emendations of the Copy-Text. 3) While revising, Clemens occasionally ignored coordinating passages or words which needed changing because of revision. For example, on manuscript page 591 Clemens first decided to end one of David Wilson's speeches after the word "words." But then, after some revision, Wilson continues to speak. Clemens forgot to delete the first closing quotation marks. The emendations of the copy-text in such instances are drawn from the *Century* or are made by the editor. 4) Outright blunders are emended. For example, Clemens ten times spelled "seize" as "sieze."

Clemens's spelling has not been modernized. Forms acceptable (and authorized by contemporary dictionaries) in the 1890s are retained (e.g., "grewsome" or "clew"). Since we have manuscript evidence of authorial punctuation for most of the text, it is safer to retain the author's unevenness in this area than to emend to a more consistent punctuation possibly supplied by the *Century Magazine* editors or compositors.

Clemens was completely indifferent in many of his spellings and word-forms, and to impose a regularity upon his word-forms would be to produce a text which he himself never created.[8] Regularization is a type of modernization, and it produces an anachronistic, non-authorial text. Hence, all of Clemens's inconsistent spellings and punctuation are retained, unless the inconsistency produces an outright blunder (e.g., 519.4 of the Morgan manuscript: the line lacks open quotation marks), a spelling not acceptable in his day, or an instance of punctuation which renders a sentence unintelligible.

A few inconsistent spellings of names have been regularized (e.g. Valet de Chambre/Vallet de Chambers; Capello/Cappello). But, in dialogue, especially in dialect, a sound change might be indicated by a variant spelling (e.g., "jes' "/"jist"/"jis' "); all spelling and punctuation variants have been left to stand as they appear in the manuscripts. There is a great variety in Clemens's use of *a* preceding a verb, where the *a* represents a gerund or replaces "have." For example, he has "a ben," "a had," "a workin'," and

8. For a discussion of the latest views on imposing regularity on the author's accidentals, see the excellent article: Parker, Hershel, "Regularizing Accidentals: The Latest Form of Infidelity," *Proof*, 3 (1973), 1–20.

also "a-court'n," "a-fishing," and "a-yowlin'." These have all been left in the holograph form, even though printed editions frequently add hyphens and make apostrophes more accurately reflect dropped letters.

One word in dialogue, however, has been normalized. Clemens had many times written (for Roxy's dialect) "myself." Several times he slipped and wrote "myseff." In rereading he noticed the slips a few times, and crossed off the lower loop of the first *f* of a few occurrences of the word (e.g., 514.17, 516.7, 519.6). He did not make the correction at 415.21 or 518.2, nor at 424.13 and 535.7 (where the word "seff" is used). These four slips have been emended to his preferred form for Roxy's dialect.

Some of Clemens's habits of writing have been changed with no citation of the change in the tables of emendations. Ampersands have been spelled out. The word "Chapter" has been spelled out, and is followed by Arabic numbers.

The *Century Magazine* readings of italics and exclamation points are assumed to be authorial, and emendations are drawn from the serialization for these two types of accidentals.

One of the problems faced by any editor working directly from a Clemens manuscript is to distinguish between capital and lower case *t*'s, *c*'s, *j*'s, *k*'s, or *m*'s, or perhaps other letters. In *Pudd'nhead Wilson* and *Those Extraordinary Twins* one encounters scores of occurrences of "twins," "court," "church," "judge," "king," and so on, with ambiguous initial letters. For most words the context supplies the answer. But for "twins," "court," "march" (a command, at 201.11 of the manuscript), "mammy" (52.2), and a few others, there is no way of knowing what the author's intention was. In a few instances, however, the word "twins" was clearly written with a lower case *t*, and then—just as clearly—the *t* was capitalized. Hence, in ambiguous cases, when the word "twins" is used to refer directly to Luigi and Angelo, it has been capitalized. Similarly, in ambiguous cases, when "court" refers specifically to the judge it is capitalized. The word "march" (at 201.11 of the manuscript [36.37 of the present edition]) has been capitalized because the context seems to warrant great emphasis. Other instances of ambiguous capital or lower case letters are discussed in the textual notes.

Those Extraordinary Twins: *Copy-Text and Principles of Emendation*

Since printer's copy for the first printing in APC of *Those Extraordinary Twins* was a revised typescript of the Morgan manuscript (TS$_2$), sheets of which were separated from the *Pudd'nhead Wilson* story (see page 176, above), that printer's copy would be the ideal copy-text. However, a situation exists for the *Twins* similar to that for *Pudd'nhead Wilson*: the actual prose of the Morgan manuscript is often closely followed in the final printed form of the *Twins*, though with much rearrangement. In *Those Extraordinary Twins* there has been more revision in the excision of material than there was for *Pudd'nhead Wilson*. Clemens recognized the dreariness and "extravagantly fantastic"[9] nature of the farce, so he has summarized much of the wordiness of the original in brackets in the final printed version of the story.[1]

For this edition the Morgan manuscript is copy-text, with two exceptions: 1) as for *Pudd'nhead Wilson*, the order of the material is adopted from the first printing (APC); and 2) the new prose passages Clemens wrote for APC (often in brackets) to explain the nature of the revision and to condense some passages he has omitted from the Morgan version will be taken from APC. For a few heavily-revised passages copy-text is the first printing of the story. This is so only for passages so heavily revised as to have little semblance to the original from which they were adapted; such passages may be seen as mere rough drafts, not at all representing authorial "final intention."

9. See *Those Extraordinary Twins*, p. 311 of the APC (119.45 of the present edition).

1. See, for example, pages 124, 134, 135(2), 143, 154, 159, and 168 of the present edition.

Pudd'nhead Wilson*

Emendations of the Copy-Text: Substantives

This table lists every substantive emendation of the copy-text, along with all other variant readings. The boldface material represents readings in the present edition; the lightface material contains first the copy-text reading, and second any other variants if there are any. The copy-text reading is for the MMS or the BMS, whichever contains the latest authorial inscription.

"I" after an adopted reading indicates that the emendation is made by the editor. (E.g., at 18.10 "stomach ache" was the author's preferred form, so this spelling is adopted despite the fact that all printed texts have the words hyphenated.)

An asterisk [*] indicates that the reading is discussed in the textual notes.
A caret [∧] is used to show an absence of punctuation.
Where possible, the adopted reading will try to give an indication of context.
Lengthy passages—too long for this table—are listed with an ellipsis [. . .]. They are preceded by a dagger [†], and may be found at the end of the table.
"[n.i.]" indicates a passage not in the copy-text.

†*[n.i.] *CM-C&W To Printer . . . out.*
1.heading *A Whisper to the Reader.* *CM-C&W* Note Concerning the Legal Points.
1.9 here to Florence *CM-C&W* here
1.17 outbreak *CM-C&W* attack
1.19 flattery, far from it. *CM-C&W* flattery.
2.4 three *CM-C&W* two
3.20 were made *CM-C&W* made
4.3 big Orleans liners *CM-C&W* big New Orleans and Cincinnati and Louisville liners
5.29 young Wilson said *CM-C&W* The new-comer, David Wilson, said *BMS* he said *MMS*
5.34 group *MMS-C&W* grouped *BMS*
***6.31 and was to continue to hold its place for twenty long years.** *CM-C&W* and Wilson was still Pudd'nhead Wilson to-day, after all those twenty years. *BMS* and and was to continue to hold its place for twenty long years. Wilson was still Pudd'nhead Wilson to-day, after all those twenty years. *MMS*
6.38 money when he arrived, *CM-C&W* money,
7.12 him such a weary long time *CM-C&W* him twenty years
7.16 into *CM-C&W* in
8.6 come on, *CM-C&W* come
8.8 I's *CM-C&W* I'm
8.11 Is *CM-C&W* Has
8.21 friendly *CM-C&W* good-natured
8.41 even *CM-C&W* perhaps even
8.44 people *CM-C&W* folks
9.7 other *CM-C&W* other kid
9.16 Jasper *CM-C&W* Jim
10.20 had been *CM-C&W* was
12.9 that they *CM-C&W* they

13.6 moaning, crying *CM-C&W* moaning and crying
13.27 it; midway. . . . She had *CM-C&W* it. She
13.38 rather lurid *CM-C&W* pretty loud
14.10 Straightway her *CM-C&W* Her
15.31 to burn wid Satan *CM-C&W* to suffer
15.40 had to *CM-C&W* had a auction to
17.12 providences—namely, there *CM-C&W* providences, see that
18.10 stomach ache. I stomach ache; conse-quently he was hiccuppy beyond reason and a singularly flatulent child. *MMS* stomach-ache. *CM-C&W*
18.31 Roxy would *CM-C&W* Roxy was flying, by now, and would
18.34 delicacies *CM-C&W* delicacies going
18.35 In *CM-C&W* By
19.23 that *CM-C&W* that as
19.30 the person *CM-C&W* the party
19.44 have changed clothes with him, *CM-C&W* have put on his clothes∧
20.4 knees and seat *CM-C&W* knees
20.29 a crowd *CM-C&W* the crowd
20.40 howl *CM-C&W* yell
21.14 to call *CM-C&W* to always call
22.23 was that of *CM-C&W* was
22.24 other that of *CM-C&W* other was
22.42 chambermaiding *CM-C&W* chambermaid
†**22.45 wood.** *CM-C&W* wood. She . . . anyway.
23.4 up *CM-C&W* down
†**23.10 it."** *CM-C&W* it." He wished . . . dat!"
23.35 he rather openly *CM-C&W* he
24.4 Tom *CM-C&W* he
24.9 and after that clothed himself in the local fashion *CM-C&W* and clothed himself after the local fashion after that

---

*In the following tables, the words protected by copyright are reproduced by permission of the University of California Press and the Mark Twain Foundation.

24.24 were now . . . life. *CM-C&W* were . . . life, now.
24.26 before about the dog. *CM-C&W* before.
25.25-25.31 anything. The . . . large. *CM-C&W* anything.
25.35 found *CM-C&W* finds *BMS*
25.36 tedious *CM-C&W* tedious long *BMS*
25.36 was *CM-C&W* is *BMS*
25.36 had *CM-C&W* has *BMS*
25.38 was *CM-C&W* is *BMS*
25.39 was *CM-C&W* is *BMS*
25.39 sat *CM-C&W* sits *BMS*
25.41 it was *CM-C&W* it is *BMS*
25.42 she was *CM-C&W* she is *BMS*
25.43 She had *CM-C&W* She has
25.43 Rowena had *CM-C&W* Rowena has
25.44-45 slave woman *CM-C&W* slave girl *BMS* slave *MMS*
25.45 had *CM-C&W* have
26.1 was *CM-C&W* is
26.3 returned *CM-C&W* returns
__26.3-26 excitement, . . . Here__ *CM-C&W* excitement, and says— ¶ "Do read it again, ma— it's just too lovely for anything! Oh, dear, I *am* so glad!"
__26.34-35 its courtly . . . style, everybody__ *CM-C&W* it, everybody
26.36 Coopers were steeped in happiness *CM-C&W* Coopers swam in seas of glory
__27.4-7 entered the twins . . . duplicates.__ *CM-C&W* entered a human creature that had two heads, two necks, four arms, and one body, with a single pair of legs attached.
27.8-25 Chapter 6. Let . . . rested— *CM-C&W* [n.i.]
27.39-41 languages. Also . . . truth. *CM-C&W* languages.
28.7 attractions *CM-C&W* 'freaks' *BMS* freaks *MMS*
__28.11 bread.__ *CM-C&W* bread. That hateful . . . anywhere."
28.21-24 Venice—to . . . exclaimed: *CM-C&W* Venice—
28.26 to see de gen'lmen!" *CM-C&W* to see— to see—*him—dem!*"
28.26 She *CM-C&W* The slave girl
28.38 also were the foreigners. *CM-C&W* also was Luigi; but Angelo said he would like to go and dress first, and he should think Luigi would prefer that, too. He shot a covert, imploring glance at his brother which said, "Be humane, be generous—don't carry me in there before all those people in this heart-breaking costume, which offends against every canon of harmony in color and will make everybody think we have been brought up among African savages;" but the answering glance said, "We will go just as we are, or we will have a scene here—take your choice." So Angelo sighed, and said he was ready.
28.40-41 and entered the *CM-C&W* toward the
28.41 conversation. *CM-C&W* conversation. When they appeared suddenly before the crowd, every eye flew wide and froze to a glassy stare, there was a universal gasp that chorded itself into a single note, and two or three boys skipped out of the open window like frogs.
29.7 admiring *CM-C&W* devouring
29.9 was *CM-C&W* were

29.15 were overwhelmed *CM-C&W* were knocked cold
29.22 and *CM-C&W* and inquired
29.30 favor from all. *CM-APC* popularity right along. *BMS-MMS* favour from all. *C&W*
29.43 the *CM-C&W* the young
29.45 there *CM-C&W* up there
30.12 twins *CM-C&W* duplicates
30.15-21 The . . . masters. *CM-C&W* [n.i.]
__30.22-24 [maxim] One . . . Calendar.__ *CM-C&W* [n.i.]
30.29-30 to play some duets *CM-C&W* to do the balcony scene in Romeo and Juliet *MMS* [n.i.] *BMS*
30.33 to be *CM-C&W* be
__31.2 see.__ *CM-C&W* see, and a herd . . .
31.6 some *CM-C&W* some of the
31.8 put *CM-C&W* squirt
31.9 fire; then he *CM-C&W* fire, and
31.16 of it *CM-C&W* from it
31.25 Freethinkers. He *CM-C&W* Freethinkers. ¶ This latter fact interested Luigi as much as it discomforted Angelo. The Judge
†*__31.27-29 established. He . . . told__* *CM-C&W* established. Luigi . . . and more. . . . Judge . . . on the way told
31.32 succeeded *CM-C&W* succeeded with Luigi
†**31.32-37 achieved. Later . . . carried.** *CM-C&W* achieved; but with Angelo . . . Wilson's.
31.41-44 presently . . . house. *CM-C&W* [n.i.]
32.15 great, and *CM-C&W* great,
32.18 in *CM-C&W* in alternating
32.22 young Tom *CM-C&W* young
32.33 arrive a little *CM-C&W* arrive
32.40-41 of which she herself was not aware. *CM-C&W* which she was not aware of, herself.
33.9-10 At . . . thirty-five. *CM-C&W* She went away chambermaiding the year she was set free, when she was thirty-five.
†**33.11 Mogul." I** *CM-C&W* Mogul." It was . . . eyesight. Mogul.∧ *CM-C&W*
33.12 made her wonted and easy-going at the work, *CM-C&W* made a wonted and easy-going steamboatman of her,
33.21-22 had banked *CM-C&W* had saved up and banked
33.22 month in New Orleans *CM-C&W* month
33.24 and that *CM-C&W* and
33.39 local packet *CM-C&W* packet
33.40 Time *CM-C&W* At once her memory began to travel back over the long ago, and she found that time
33.41 and *CM-C&W* and that
34.3 upon *CM-C&W* around
34.14 surely *CM-C&W* sure
34.21 would *CM-C&W* should
34.29 expressions *CM-C&W* explosions
34.37 The ostensible "Chambers" *CM-C&W* Chambers
35.16 with *CM-C&W* with complacent
35.26-27 it. Her . . . Chambers: *CM-C&W* it.
36.24 was unconsciously *CM-C&W* was
38.38 a former slave *CM-C&W* a negro ex-slave
__40.17 grieve__ *CM-C&W* weep
40.20-23 [2nd maxim] *CM-C&W* [n.i.]
40.25 Tom *CM-C&W* Then Tom
40.30 lower *CM-C&W* lower than this
40.33 wretched *CM-C&W* tolerably sick
41.33 fambly name *CM-C&W* surname

*41.46–42.1 of disorganizing sensations and CM-C&W of doubt, certainty, fear, derision, and all the other

42.20 it's CM-C&W its

42.30 business CM-C&W cold business

43.2 amount CM-C&W amount on

*44.4–5 [2nd maxim] When angry . . . Calendar. CM-C&W [2nd maxim] Why is it that we rejoice at a birth and weep at a funeral? It is because we are not the person involved.—*Pudd'nhead Wilson's Calendar.*

44.8 groan CM-C&W bitter groan

†44.19 head." CM-C&W head. . . . . I . . . virtue." . . . .

44.25 wretch CM-C&W degraded wretch

44.25 he is an CM-C&W he is white, and for that I could kill him—if I had the courage. Ach! he is an

44.35 ideals, CM-C&W ideals, now,

44.39 work. CM-C&W work; he had not been used to thinking. And it was not easy; his mind was a whirlwind of spinning spirals of dust with elusive rags and fragments of ideas chasing each other through it. But all whirlwinds settle at last, and so did this one; then he had the opportunity to gather his rags and fragments together and put them in order and study the pattern and make out its meaning. ¶ While the whirlwind continued, it furnished him many surprises.

45.5 knew, idol . . . worship, CM-C&W knew,

45.12 passed CM-C&W had passed

45.17–18 He said to himself that the curse of Ham was upon him. CM-C&W The curse of Ham was upon him, he said to himself.

45.25 ostensible "aunt's" CM-C&W aunt's

45.27 ostensible "uncle" CM-C&W uncle

†45.30 dog." CM-C&W dog." ¶ In his . . . rage.

45.41 but after a while CM-C&W but now

45.46 days. CM-C&W days. ¶ Yet a change or two *was* present, and remained. He hated the whites, he would steal from them without shame, and even with a vengeful exultation; he loathed the "nigger" in him, but got pleasure out of bringing this secret "filth," as he called it, into familiar and constant contact with the sacred whites; he privately despised and hated his uncle and all his aristocratic pretensions.

46.19 Occasionally CM-C&W Now and then

46.23 For this purpose he projected a new raid on his town. CM-C&W He projected a new raid on his town in this interest.

46.33 him in a bundle CM-C&W him

46.39 then CM-C&W then he

47.12–13 the valuables of that house CM-C&W that house's valuables

47.16 Twins CM-C&W Twins from the Bible Society

47.19 shameless creature CM-C&W brazen huzzy

47.24 No. 3 CM-C&W but No. 3

47.25 heart. CM-C&W heart with all your clothes on.

47.27–28 [2nd maxim] As to . . . Calendar. CM-C&W [n.i.]

47.29 twins CM-C&W duplicates

47.30–31 influence the . . . strength. CM-C&W influence Angelo cheered up and forgot his late vexations.

47.32 praised CM-C&W complimented

48.6–7 be seeing the . . . time when CM-C&W be startled at the figure the Twins made when

48.24 the law feature CM-C&W this feature

48.32 should CM-C&W would

48.42 Wilson had CM-C&W He had

49.36 notion-factory CM-C&W maggot-factory

49.44 got CM-C&W got here

50.1 chaff CM-C&W raillery

51.27 history CM-C&W past

51.45 it to himself CM-C&W it

52.29 kill him, . . . too? CM-C&W kill Angelo, how many hours would I have survived?

53.18–19 his pillow; we . . . together. CM-C&W our pillow.

53.20 vague CM-C&W dim

53.26 neck. CM-C&W neck. I think he was dead before his spouting blood struck us.

†53.27–28 breaths, and . . . said, CM-C&W breaths, . . . Wilson,

53.28–29 hand— ¶ **"Now Tom, I've** CM-C&W hand, "I've

53.32 had snatched away his hand CM-C&W had drawn his hand away

54.17–18 middle-aged Irishman . . . who was CM-C&W middle-aged man who spoke English with a slight but noticeable Irish accent. When he first came to the town, a few years before, he gave his name as John Buckstone, and added, "formerly Lord Buckstone, author of the Queen's hounds"—meaning master of the Queen's hounds, probably. He was

†54.26–29 Angelo less . . . one. CM-C&W Angelo declined . . . them."

54.33–34 the bass CM-C&W a bass

54.39 and were CM-C&W and

*55.4 were CM-C&W was

55.11 a CM-C&W a pronounced

56.12 side-remarks. CM-C&W side-remarks department of them.

56.14–15 The extraordinarily . . . other suggested CM-C&W The Twins stood with their legs braced slightly apart. Their heads happened to be canted apart, too. Their attitude suggested

*56.18 human philopena CM C&W human pair of scissors

56.20 aptness CM-C&W precision

56.22–25 Luigi's southern . . . took CM-C&W Luigi took

56.26 halted behind CM-C&W was behind

56.27 vigor CM-C&W vigor in the joker's rear

56.28 Tom CM-C&W him

57.21 upon CM-C&W onto

57.24 stampede CM-C&W outpour

57.26–27 to annihilate CM-C&W to have annihilated

58.12 strict CM-C&W stringent

58.40 one of the CM-C&W the

58.42 "Did CM-C&W "They did

59.12 Tom beat the twin on the trial. CM-C&W the trial went against Tom.

59.15 him up CM-C&W them up

59.17–18 The . . . death-stroke. CM-C&W "Oh, my God!" ¶

59.18 for him CM-C&W for his friend,

59.32 ain't . . . ain't CM-C&W isn't . . . isn't

59.37 Dominion." CM-C&W Dominion, and from that blood can spring no such misbegotten son."

59.45 was not CM-C&W not

60.5–8 answered guilelessly . . . assault." CM-C&W answered innocently, with a sheepish little laugh— ¶ "Well, the fact is, it don't stand any way at all. I had them up in court, but they beat me."

60.9 feet with the opening sentence *CM-C&W* feet

†**60.19-24 said— . . . ¶ "You** *CM-C&W* said— . . . responsibility. You

***60.25 it. He** *CM-C&W* it. He was bitterly sorry he had been so premature with his lie. He

*****60.29-30 He is a . . . devil** *CM-C&W* They are . . . devils

60.30 him *CM-C&W* them

60.35 corner∧ *CM-C&W* corner, still

60.37 scattering *CM-C&W* and scattered

61.1 The Count *CM-C&W* He

61.1-2 minutes," said Howard *CM-C&W* minutes."

61.8-9 to ruin *CM-C&W* to rags and ruin

61.17 standpoint *CM-C&W* standpoint it is,

61.18 most easily *CM-C&W* easiest

61.33-36 [maxim] October . . . Calendar. *CM-C&W* [n.i.]

61.39 each *CM-C&W* either

61.40 he came *CM-C&W* came

62.8-9 likely, after . . . law-court. *CM-C&W* likely.

62.13-14 hard. Try and . . . kicked. *CM-C&W* hard. Better luck next time. It's our first lawsuit, and we couldn't both win it, you know. It's your turn next.

62.25 Italian savage *CM-C&W* human lemon-squeezer

62.27 "Yes *CM-C&W* "The Twins—yes

62.41-42 their slipping . . . offense— *CM-APC* there being any doubt about it, such crowds of people saw the assault—never once thought of their slipping out of it the way they did, with their vile double-action and single-action, interchangeable at will when they want to commit crime, and the original Satan himself not able to tell t'other from which when you want to fetch them to book—their slipping . . . offence—*C&W*

63.8-9 being an . . . lawyer *CM-C&W* being on the top wave of legal prosperity

63.19 Italian∧ *CM-C&W* Twins,

64.27 has *CM-C&W* have

66.9 silence *CM-C&W* weighty silence

†**66.9-18 peace . . . Tom.** *CM-C&W* peace . . . been!"

66.25-26 About . . . Pembroke *CM-C&W* It was the gracious watermelon season. All hearts should have been gay and happy, but some were not. About the time that Wilson was saying the words which close the last chapter, Pembroke

†**66.27-40 waiting. ¶ "Well . . . saying—** *CM-C&W* waiting. ∧Howard . . . saying—

67.20 hour. *CM-C&W* hour of the night. It was near eleven—a good hour after his ordinary bed-time.

67.25 sight and hearing *CM-C&W* sight

67.27 Howard said *CM-C&W* Howard had his pistol case with him. He said

67.29 also with his brother. *CM-C&W* also his brother, of course, who is looking indisposed.

68.17 "I *CM-C&W* "Ah, I

68.22 imitation *CM-C&W* mute imitation

68.35-36 getting more . . . doubtful *CM-C&W* getting sicker and sicker

69.1 luck. *CM-C&W* luck. [end of chapter] CHAPTER 22. [maxim] Let us endeavor to so live that when we approach death even the undertaker will be sorry.—*Pudd'nhead Wilson's Calendar.*

69.1-2 He dragged . . . in *CM-C&W* Meantime Tom had been brooding in

69.12 people— *CM-C&W* people. There's

69.13-15 instance; even . . . but he isn't *CM-C&W* instance; his fortune's made, and what has he done to deserve it, I would like to know. Yes, he has made his own fortune, but isn't

69.16 block mine *CM-C&W* ruin mine

69.19 to his *CM-C&W* for his

69.31 and turned westward. *CM-C&W* and just then the Twins whizzed by, on their way home. He wondered what that might mean. Had they seen a ghost at the haunted house?

69.34 duelists returning . . . he *CM-APC* duelists, and he *MMS* duellists returning . . . he *C&W*

69.42-43 wid one o' dem *CM-C&W* wid dat pair o' nutcrackers—dem

69.44 Then he added∧ *CM-C&W* He added,

70.2 Twin I twins twin *CM-C&W*

70.7 Luigi *CM-C&W* Angelo

70.32-33 My great-great-great-gran'father en yo' great-great-great-gran'father *CM-C&W* My father en yo' gran'father

70.33 Cap'n John Smith *CM-C&W* John Randolph of Roanoke

70.36 queen, . . . Africa *CM-C&W* queen

70.43 rumble *CM-C&W* rumble again

71.7 skinned. How *CM-C&W* peeled—how

71.11 on *CM-C&W* in

71.22-23 out, en dah in de moonlight, right I out, en dah I seed everything as plain as day in de moonlight. Right *MMS* out, en dar in de moonlight, right *CM-C&W*

71.23 one o' de *CM-C&W* de

71.23-24 a-cussin' . . . a-cussin' . . . 'uz cussin' *CM-C&W* a-yowlin'. . . . a-yowlin' . . . was yowlin'

71.24 brown *CM-C&W* white

71.25 shoulder. *CM-C&W* shoulder—dat is, I reckon it 'uz his shoulder, dough how he could tell it 'uz his'n, de way dey arms is mixed up do beat me—but anyway he judged it 'uz his'n en so he 'uz doin' de yowlin' till he could fine out.

71.29 twin *CM-C&W* white twin

71.31 de twin *CM-C&W* de white one

71.36 me. *CM-C&W* me. Den dey 'uz a gwyne to shoot agin, but de Twins dey lit out. De white one 'uz gitt'n more'n his sheer, en I reckon it 'uz him dat run. But I don't know—caze 'tother one went too.

71.42 Smith-Pocahontases *CM-C&W* Randolphs

72.2 blon' twin *CM-C&W* nigger-twin

72.2 doctor en de seconds. *CM-C&W* doctor.

73.35 [maxim] Nothing so needs reforming *CM-C&W* Nothing is so injurious

73.37-41 [maxim] Behold . . . Calendar. *CM-C&W* [n.i.]

73.42-74.36 What . . . mystery. *CM-C&W* [n.i.]

75.17 town, the town . . . either. *CM-C&W* town, let the town keep it's shirt on, too.

76.4 B'George *CM-C&W* 'George

76.8 with *CM-C&W* along with

77.1 it. *CM-C&W* it whatever.

77.39 or *CM-C&W* or or

78.10 either *CM-C&W* had either

78.12-13 perfect during . . . week. *CM-C&W* perfect.

78.18 fight that Italian adventurer. *CM-C&W* fight those Twins.

78.20 **unawares,** *CM-C&W* unprepared—
78.21 **meet him . . . about him** *CM-C&W* meet them . . . about them
79.5–22 **enough." ¶ The . . . it."** *CM-C&W* enough." I will cut those Twins when I get the opportunity—one of them ran away from the field, anyway: perhaps both."
79.32 **had restored . . . aunt** *CM-C&W* had made him solid with the aunt
*80.8–12 **[maxim] We . . . Calendar.** *CM-C&W* [n.i.]
80.30 **sudden** *CM-C&W* so sudden
80.35 **dumb** *CM-C&W* speechless
81.11 **"Much** *CM-C&W* "Hm! Much
81.32 **selling** *CM-C&W* sending
83.1–4 **[maxim] Even . . . Calendar.** *CM-C&W* [n.i.]
83.9 **[2nd maxim] Calendar.** *CM-C&W* Calendar. ¶ On Independence Day Rowena went out back to see the fireworks and fell down the well and got drowned. But it is no matter; these things cannot be helped, in a work of this kind.
*83.10–84.19 **The . . . deserted.** *CM-C&W* [n.i.]
84.24–27 **[2nd maxim] Thanksgiving . . . Calendar.** *CM-C&W* [n.i.]
85.13 **I'm** *CM-C&W* I am
86.11 **he said** *CM-C&W* said
86.12 **a deep** *CM-C&W* a deep a deep
*86.20–21 **was only** *CM-APC* was but *MMS, C&W*
*87.21 **Chambermaid** *CM-C&W* head chambermaid
*87.38 **heard** *CM-C&W* hear
*88.9–10 **den I** *CM-C&W* I
*90.14 **de house** *CM-APC* he house *MMS, C&W*
90.29 **effort** *CM-C&W* offer
*91.5 **knows you's a-goin'.** *CM-APC* knows it. *MMS* knows it! *C&W*
92.5 **this** *CM-C&W* that
92.11–16 **[2 maxims] Few . . . Calendar.** *CM-C&W* [n.i.]
†*92.17–20 **Dawson's . . . it. Judge Driscoll declined** *CM-C&W* Dawson's . . . Driscoll. The Judge declined
93.6 **for** *CM-C&W* of
93.17 **howling colony** *CM-APC* harem *MMS, C&W*
93.26 **will** *CM-C&W* shall
93.29 **still a** *CM-C&W* a
*93.32 **the twins** *CM-C&W* Luigi
*93.39 **window-blinds and lighted** *CM-APC* window shades and lit *MMS* window-blinds and lit *C&W*
93.42 **it, and laid it by.** *CM-APC* it. *MMS* it and laid it by. *C&W*
94.16 **old man's small** *CM-C&W* small
94.29 **the notes** *CM-APC* his notes *MMS, C&W*
95.3–4 **had joined** *CM-C&W* were with
95.12 **lighted** *CM-APC* lit *MMS, C&W*
95.16 **most** *CM-APC* the most *MMS, C&W*
95.18 **ashes, scattered the ashes,** *CM-C&W* ashes,
95.28–29 **mysteries, and . . . years."** *CM-C&W* mysteries."
95.33 **profligate Italian nobleman or barber,** *CM-C&W* profligate ex-freak called the Italian Twins
96.1–2 **The assassin will** *CM-C&W* One of them is considered innocent, but the other one will

96.3 **"One of the twins** *CM-C&W* "The Twins
96.4 **him** *CM-C&W* them
*97.10–18 **The coroner's . . . Wilson** *CM-C&W* The coroner's jury found that the homicide was committed by Luigi, and that Angelo was accessory to it. The grand jury indicted Luigi for murder in the first degree and Angelo as accessory. The Twins were transferred from the city jail to the county prison to await trial. ¶ The town was bitter against them, and for the first few days after the murder they were in constant danger of being lynched. ¶ Wilson
97.12 **the unfortunates** *CM-C&W* them
97.14 **jury presently** *CM-C&W* jury
97.15 **accessory before the fact.** *CM-C&W* accessory.
97.33 **last** *CM-APC* past *MMS, C&W*
98.9 **had really** *CM-C&W* had
98.9 **revived, as . . . discovered,** *CM-C&W* revived,
99.18 **Aunt Patsy Cooper** *CM-C&W* the two old aunties
99.33 **one friend** *CM-C&W* two friends
99.33–34 **countenance . . . landlady. She . . . her** *CM-C&W* countenance. These sat near Wilson, and looked their
99.35 **In** *CM-C&W* One was aunt Patsy Cooper, the other was aunt Betsy Hale. In
99.40 **temper** *CM-C&W* fury
*100.1 **these** *CM-C&W* those
100.5 **toss** *CM-C&W* resolute toss
100.12 **his presence** *CM-C&W* his silence
100.29 **budding career** *CM-C&W* new reputation
*100.40 **on** *CM-C&W* in
101.23 **said that** *CM-C&W* said
101.38 **old-lady friend** *CM-C&W* two old-lady friends
101.40 **Aunt Patsy** *CM-C&W* the two old aunties
101.41 **a gay** *CM-C&W* a great and noble
101.42 **finishing.** *CM-C&W* finishing, and went away crying.
101.43–102.33 **Absolutely . . . then.** *CM-C&W* [n.i.]
102.44 **have** *CM-C&W* haven't
103.5 **always?"** *CM-C&W* always, just because you won once?"
103.11–12 **considering the brunette one's** *CM-C&W* considering their odious
103.44–45 **unintentionally left** *CM-C&W* left
104.33 **Heavens** *CM-C&W* Great guns
104.38–40 **[2nd maxim] April . . . Calendar.** *CM-C&W* [n.i.]
104.42 **high** *CM-C&W* tremendous
105.6 **whorls** *CM-APC* sworls *MMS, C&W*
105.20 **was ready** *CM-APC* ready *MMS, C&W*
105.32 **compelled** *CM-C&W* roused immediate
105.33 **evoked** *CM-C&W* also evoked
106.14 **admission.** *CM-C&W* admission as this.
106.19 **said.** *CM-C&W* said. The two old aunties seemed smitten with a collapse.
106.35 **accused brothers** *CM-C&W* accused
106.35–36 **that one of them** *CM-C&W* that they
106.36 **Judge** *CM-C&W* the late Judge
106.36 **lose his** *CM-C&W* lose their
106.38–39 **there secretly . . . adversary.** *CM-C&W* there by night and take their enemy by surprise and save themselves by destroying him.
108.13 **physical marks** *CM-C&W* marks
108.15–16 **physiological autograph** *CM-C&W* autograph

111.3 **pantograph copies** *CM-APC* things *MMS* pantagraph copies *C&W*

111.29 **thunder-crash** *CM-C&W* crash

111.29–30 **followed and** *CM-C&W* followed,

111.30–31 **feet, . . . Tom** *CM-C&W* feet, and the two old ladies flung themselves with hysterical gratitude at the Twins, but were promptly repressed by official force and brought to order along with the rest of the assemblage. Tom

111.33–34 **house's attention . . . more,** *CM-C&W* house was become tranquil again,

112.15–20 **Roxana was . . . privately.** *CM-C&W* Roxana began to fan herself violently, although the fall weather was pleasant; it certainly was not uncomfortably warm, at least.

112.25 **Roxy's . . . still!** *CM-C&W* Roxy collapsed and fell over against her next neighbor, but quickly recovered herself.

*112.41 **sits among you. i** sits in your midst! *MMS* sits in among you. *CM-APC* sits in your midst. *C&W*

113.10–16 **CONCLUSION. [2 maxims]** *CM-C&W* Chapter 32. [no maxims]

113.21–23 **marvelous. His . . . good.** *CM-APC* marvelous. He was a made man for good, this time; nothing could ever shake his foundations again. *MMS* marvellous. His . . . good. *C&W*

113.25 **remorseful** *CM-C&W* remorseful and shame-faced

114.3 **friends** *CM-C&W* boys

114.4 **isn't** *CM-C&W* ain't

*114.5–8 **now, and with . . . Roxy's** *CM-C&W* now, and they came into vast and instant favor again, and aunt Patsy and aunt Betsy's cups of happiness were full. But the restored popularity of the strangers did not last long. . . . Roxy's

†114.14 **solace.** *CM-C&W* solace. ¶ Aunt Patsy . . . kind.

115.2–3 **as through . . . blame the false** *CM-C&W* as the false

115.5 **rightly claimed** *CM-C&W* claimed

115.12 **erroneous inventory** *CM-C&W* dishonest inventory which had suppressed his name

*†115.18 **river.** *CM-C&W* river. ¶ CONCLUSION. . . . sides.

Emendations of the Copy-Text: Substantives
(Lengthy Passages)*

*[n.i.] First entry in Emendations of copy-text, Substantives. (See facsimile, Appendix 1.)

To Printer. Please make fac-similes of those signs, and use them at chapter-tops—one and sometimes two—SLC it is not necessary that they fit the weather of the chapter always.

Key to Signs used in this book.

To save the space usually devoted to explanations of the state of the weather in books of this kind, the author begs leave to substitute a simple system of weather-signs. The hieroglyph at the head of each chapter will instantly convey to the reader's mind a perfect comprehension of the kind of weather which is going to prevail below.

The signs and their meanings here follow:
[Sunny, Pitch Dark, Starlight, Rainy, Moonlight, Snow, Fog—see Appendix 1]

When two or more signs occur together, the ensuing weather is going to be more, or more yet, or still more variable, according to number of signs employed.

When all the signs are used it means Stormy.

When they are doubled it means Extremely Violent and Perilous Weather.

When there is no sign, it means that there is not going to be any weather. It is a mistake to suppose that weather is at all times necessary in a novel. As often as not, it is an inconvenience, and keeps the characters from going out.

22.45   wood. CM-C&W

wood. She had remained a Methodist ever since she first "got religion" and lost two dollars by it; she was a most capable hymn-singer, for she had the rich and sweet and pathetic voice so common to the race which she accepted as hers; she was the best shouter in the "amen corner," and if she wasn't a tough customer in a theological argument, she at least thought she was. Jasper was a Dunker Baptist. He had a pretty robust opinion of his own powers in argument, and was fond of meeting Roxy in that field; consequently the theological fur was quite sure to fly whenever they came together. A chief bone of contention between them was the matter of special providences; they had gnawed it till there was no vestige of meat left on it, but that was no matter, they found it as toothsome without meat as with it. Jasper believed in special providences, Roxy didn't. She believed that whatever happened in this world happened in obedience to a body of well regulated general laws, and that these laws were never set aside by sudden caprice to wet some saint's wilting crop or drown some sinner who went a fishing on the Sabbath.

Three day's [sic] before Roxy's visit, Jasper was

tramping up the "Bluff road," among the hills back of the town. It was a heavy pull, and when he reached what was called Precipice Corner he sat down and hung his heels over the abyss and prepared himself for a rest and a smoke. At his right was a stretch of road as straight as a lance and pretty steep; where he sat, this road made an exceedingly abrupt elbow; between the sheer precipice on the one side and the cut wall of the hill on the other there was not room for two wagons to pass. Whoever drove down the stretch of straight road must turn that elbow cautiously if he would turn it safely.

Presently Jasper heard a noise above him, and glanced up and saw a cloud of gray dust flying down the straight road toward him. It was moving so swiftly that he thought it must be a whirlwind. He jumped up to observe it. But it wasn't a whirlwind.

"By gracious it's somebody's hoss runnin' away wid him! If he whirl's round dis corner at dat gait, somebody got to chink down in de valley en gether him up in a basket."

He took a position, spat in his hands and gave himself a shake as a kind of notice to his vast strength to get ready for business. He was not able to furnish the particulars of what happened after that. He only knew that the next instant the flying horse was upon him and that he grabbed him and stood him upon his hind heels in the air!

Then the dust settled and he had a great and glad surprise, for he saw his young mistress, with her nurse and baby, sitting in the buggy. Jasper led the horse around the elbow and went to examining the harness to see if it was all right. The occupants of the buggy got out, and thought they would walk back to their summer home on the hill for a change of sensations. When the lady turned the elbow she saw her father and mother and the house servants grouped on the precipice and trying to look over; and all were moaning and wailing and ejaculating. The family, standing on the porch, had seen the horse begin to run when he left the gate, and they and the negroes had followed on foot, in the wake of a flight which none imagined could end otherwise than in destruction at the precipice.

"Father, we are not hurt!" The father turned dreamily and incredulously about, at the sound of this voice which he had supposed would never comfort his ear again in this life, and saw his daughter standing unharmed before him, delivered, he knew not by what miracle, from the very grave itself.

There was nothing but wild embracings and incoherent exclamations of gratitude for a little while, then the father said—

"But how was it done? What is the explanation of it?"

---

*Of the sixteen passages cited in this table, only eleven—which have already appeared in print—may be reproduced here in full. These eleven appeared in Daniel Morley McKeithan's essay "The Morgan Manuscript of Mark Twain's *Pudd'nhead Wilson*" (see Bibliography). The other five passages are protected by copyright and may be reproduced only after their publication by the University of California Press.

"Jasper happened to be here, and he siezed [sic] the horse and stopped him."

"That is not possible. No man could do it; ten couldn't. The town will never believe it."

"But Jasper did it, and I saw him."

Jasper was called, and came humbly, with his hat in his hand. His master said—

"Jasper, there is nothing that I can say now—I am too much moved, too much broken up to put rational speech together; but another time—another time I will try to thank you. Put on your hat. Freemen stand in each other's presence in the open air; and you are free, from this hour."

For three days Jasper had been a freed man, a hero, and the talk of the town. He was "laying for" Roxy, all loaded and primed and ready with an argument which he judged would silence her guns for one while, anyway.

23.10 it." CM-C&W

it." He wished her prosperity and a safe return, and turned away, saying—

"You want to modify that highflyer attitude of yours, Roxy, and take your knuckles out of your hips; Jasper's a free citizen and a hero, now, and you must stop putting on airs around him."

The theologians answered with a laugh apiece, and the arguments began to fly. As the fencing went on, Jasper began to lead warily up to his heroic episode; then he set forth the situation: he had to be on that hill, and at that exact spot, at that precise moment of time to the fraction of a minute, or those people's death was an absolutely unpreventable thing. Then he shook a victorious finger in Roxy's face and shouted:

"Dah, now! Dey ain't no special providences, hain't dey? *Who put me dah*?—aha, you answer me dat!"

Roxy's return-blast was instant and disabling:

"Who sent de *hoss* dah in dat shape, you chucklehead? Answer me *dat*!"

*31.27–29 established. He . . . he told CM-C&W
[This passage, of about 960 words, is deleted for copyright reasons. It concerns Luigi's joining the Society of Freethinkers, and Angelo's opposition.]

31.32–37 achieved. Later . . . carried. CM-C&W
[This passage, of about 1,045 words, is deleted for copyright reasons. It concerns the meeting of the Society of Freethinkers, followed immediately by a meeting of the Bible class—both meetings attended by the Twins.]

33.11 Mogul." CM-C&W

Mogul." It was a big steamer for the time—two hundred and fifty feet long. Roxy had never been in a steamer's cabin before—cabin was the western name for the grand salons into which the berthrooms opened, not the berth-rooms themselves. The cabin was like a long, brilliantly lighted tunnel. It was of pine, covered with a highly polished skin of white paint. On every berth-room door of the two far-stretching sides was an oil picture—Mississippi scenery, the subject—with all the known colors in it and some of the unknown, and all the different kinds of drawing in it except good drawing—dreadful pictures, in fact, but very showy and effective. Separating these crimes were fluted white-painted pine pilasters with gilded Corinthian capitals. Overhead the receding stretch of ivory-like ceiling fairly bristled with downpointing wonders of ornamentation done with the jig-saw and the turning-lathe. At fifty-foot intervals there were great pyramidal chandeliers, whose sumptuous fringes of cut-glass prisms, flaming and flashing in the sun, shook out showers of dancing rainbow-flecks upon the white walls and doors in response to the slightest joggle. Tables covered with figured crimson cloths formed a fiery platform down the middle of the tunnel from end to end. Against each wall was backed a stiff rank of windsor chairs, from the bar on the port side and the clerk's office on the starboard clear aft to the piano and the big mirror in the ladies' cabin. And the carpet—the carpet was a revel; not a dream, but a revel, just a revel of bounding and careering great whorls of inflamed scroll-work out on a drunk.

Roxy was entranced. She had often heard of these "floating palaces"—which was the common and quite sincerely-applied name of these museums—but had never been on the inside of one of them before. She moved through it in an ecstasy of bliss. The wilderness of noble furniture amazed her by its magnitude, and its possible cost made all her former notions of wealth seem poor and shabby imaginings; the profusion and richness of the decorations steeped her barbaric soul in delight, and in the glorious insurrection of color she saw her dearest dreams of the splendors of heaven realized. Ah, why hadn't she run away and entered into the joys of this earthly paradise earlier? It grieved her to think she had lost so much time.

Presently passengers began to stream aboard and flock hither and thither in search of their staterooms, inquiring, commanding, exclaiming, and they filled the whole place with inspiriting life and racket and commotion. Ah, it was a thousand times better to be here than in that sleepy dull town.

Soon, a swarm of white-aproned and white-jacketed colored boys burst in from somewhere, and in an instant the red covers were gone and the tables clothed in white! It made Roxy dizzy, the thing was done so suddenly. And she wondered how one mere human establishment could support such a horde of servants. When she came to herself after a couple of seconds, there was another surprise—they had vanished; whither, she didn't know.

Then came a musical kling-kling from a little bell, and they appeared again; they marched in, in a couple of snowy files, and moved down the long cabin, depositing plates and cruets and things as they went, and in a minute the tables stood completely arrayed and ready for the provisions. The last boys in the ranks placed the chairs.

The bell struck again, and again the files entered, some bearing great platters and chafing-dishes of fish, meats and so forth, aloft, and others superb sugar-clad miniature temples, supposed to be made of cake, whereas in truth the finest of them were decorated cheese-boxes, though neither Roxy nor the passengers suspected that.

Then the first gong let go a horrible crash and kept it up two minutes, although there was a passenger behind every chair by the time that the fiend with the gong had hit it the second blow.

At the end of ten minutes the gong broke loose

again, the double file of passengers plunged into their seats, and the havoc began.

To Roxy the prodigious noise and confusion about the stage-planks during the final moments before the boat's departure was a most satisfying delight. Every detail had interest for her: the rushing avalanch of barrels thundering down the stages; the belated passengers skipping perilously among them to win to the forecastle; the clarion voices of the mates discharging volume after volume of the most erudite and versatile and magnificent profanity without a tautological blemish in it anywhere; the yelling of newsboys; the slamming of furnace doors; the screaming of gauge-cocks; the deafening banging and clanging of the everlasting "last bell." Every separate detail had a dulcet charm for Roxy, and the combination constituted bliss.

At last the boat did get away, and went plowing down the Ohio, filling all the heavens with sable smoke; and for seven days and nights she piled States and scenery behind her with a celerity which bewildered the second chambermaid and made her realize as she had never realized before that the white man was in very truth a wonder-compelling creature and a creator of marvelous contrivances. Then she found herself in New Orleans, and when she saw that the wells (cisterns) and the graves were all on top of the ground instead of under it she was sure her excitements had confused her brain and disordered her eyesight.

44.19   head." *CM-C&W*

head. . . . . I am a nigger—a nigger! . . . . . Yesterday I hated nobody very much, but now I hate the whole human race. . . . . If I had the courage, I would kill—somebody—anybody. But she was right—I haven't it. I've only material in me for an assassin. . . . . . Better that than. . . . . . I am so changed, so changed! Yesterday I was ashamed of my thefts—but now, why now, I am not, for I stole from the whites. I will do it again. I will do it whenever I can. . . . . . And that poor lowly and ignorant creature is my mother! . . . . . . Well, she has my respect for one thing—she has never owned a slave. All the white respectability of this town is shabby and mean, beside that one virtue." . . . .

45.30   dog." *CM-C&W*

dog."

In his broodings in the solitudes, he searched himself for the reasons of certain things, and in toil and pain he worked out the answers:

Why was he a coward? It was the "nigger" in him. The nigger *blood*? Yes, the nigger blood degraded from original courage to cowardice by decades and generations of insult and outrage inflicted in circumstances which forbade reprisals, and made mute and meek endurance the only refuge and defence.

Whence came that in him which was high, and whence that which was base? That which was high came from either blood, and was the monopoly of neither color; but that which was base was the *white* blood in him debased by the brutalizing effects of a long-drawn heredity of slave-owning, with the habit of abuse which the possession of irresponsible power always creates and perpetuates, by a law of human nature. So he argued.

But what a totally new and amazing aspect one

or two things, in particular, bore to Tom, now that he found himself looking at them from around on the other side! For instance—nigger illegitimacy, yesterday and to-day. Yesterday, of what consequence could it be to a nigger whether he was a bastard or not? To-day the reflection "I am a bastard!" made the hot blood leap to Tom's very eyelids. Yesterday, if any had asked him, "Which is more honorable, more desirable, and more a matter for a nigger to be proud of—to be a nigger born in wedlock, or a white man's bastard?" he would have thought the questioner was jesting. It was of course an honor to be a white man's bastard, and the highest honor a nigger could have. Who could doubt it? The question would astonish the nigger himself—go ask him and you will see. But to-day—to-day! to be a nigger was shame, but compared with this million-fold obscener infamy it was nothing, it was less than nothing. "And I am a nigger *and* that other thing!" It was only thought, he could not have uttered it, for his throat was dry and his tongue impotent with rage.

53.27-28   breaths, and . . . said, *CM-C&W*

breaths, and Tom said—

"I wonder he was so particular. I should have thought he would kill the first one of you that came handy—or jam his dirk into your mutual body and kill you both."

Angelo colored, and said, rather shame-facedly—

"Well, the truth is, he had a reason, and a good one, for preferring me. He could have killed Luigi without much sin, for Luigi was a freethinker and the fact was known; but he could kill me without any sin at all; and not only that, but it would be a very meritorious and praiseworthy deed, because I had just publicly apostatised from the Mohammedan Church, and this native was a Mohammedan. If he killed Luigi my death would follow, but *he* wouldn't get any credit for it on high, so the knife's gems would be his only reward. Necessarily, common sense moved him to kill me, and get both rewards."

"Well, I *never* should have thought of that ingenious distinction!" exclaimed Tom, with admiration. "That native was no fool, *I* tell you!"

"Now, Tom," said Wilson,

54.26-29   Angelo less . . . one. *CM-C&W*

Angelo declined it as cordially, and called all present to witness that in going with Luigi he was doing it under protest; that he would not go if he could help it; and that he was totally opposed to the principles of the rum party; he added that he was dying of fatigue, and that it was a shameful cruelty to keep him on his legs any longer.

"*Your* legs!" said Luigi indignantly. "I like your impudence. You will go to the meeting—I will see to that. And don't waste any more pathetic speeches here; save them for the temperance meetings—you will probably carry me to enough of them."

60.19-24   said— . . . ¶ "You *CM-C&W*

said—

"So your refuge, the jury, discovered—as we have been informed—that only one of the pair kicked you, but could not determine which one it was? Which one do you think it was?"

Tom had already been to call at the widow Cooper's, and had gathered a strong suspicion there that Rowena was warming toward Angelo and cooling toward him. Without much reflection he framed a lie, now, which gave him a good deal of satisfaction for a moment—

"I don't need to think, I already know which one it was. It was the one named Angelo—the pious one —the one that is to be baptised to-morrow. He was so set-up because he had got the best of me in the trial that he couldn't resist the temptation to crow —so he whispered and told me, going out of court, that he was the one that kicked me."

The way in which the news was received surprised the young fellow, and not pleasantly:

"Ah, that is good! that is splendid!" exclaimed the uncle, beaming with joy. "It locates the responsibility. You have challenged him?"

"N—no," hesitated Tom, turning pale.

"All right, no harm is done. You

66.9–18 peace . . . Tom CM-C&W [This passage, of about 530 words, is deleted for copyright reasons. It concerns a visit to Pudd'nhead Wilson by the town's leading citizens, who offer to back Wilson for election to whatever public office he chooses.]

66.27–40 waiting. ¶ "Well . . . saying— CM-C&W [This passage, of about 1,250 words, is deleted for copyright reasons. It is a discussion between Pembroke Howard and York Leicester Driscoll about Luigi's accepting Driscoll's offer to duel.]

*92.17–20 Dawson's . . . it. Judge Driscoll declined CM-C&W [This passage, of about 160 words, is deleted for copyright reasons. It concerns Luigi's and Angelo's activities after the election.]

114.4 solace. CM-C&W

solace.

Aunt Patsy and Aunt Betsy felt the loss of the Twins deeply, and the scar of that loss remained with them permanently; but their hearts were young and their interests limitless, so they were sufficiently bulwarked against serious unhappiness.

The lads Henry and Joe fell down the well and got drowned. But it is no particular matter, and such things cannot well be provided against in a work of this kind.

115.18 river. CM-C&W

. . . river.

CONCLUSION.

March. Thought by some to be one of the spring months. But this is an error. March is a season by itself, and has not been classified. It was created for some inscrutable, unwise, inexcusable purpose, which we may conjecture about all we want to, but the best plan is to stop there: many a man has died who has been too handy with his opinions about March.

Puddn'head [sic] *Wilson's Calendar.*

[This chapter could not be written, on account of the weather.]

THE END.

Florence, March, 1983.

(Private to "Comp.")

Treble all the weather-signs above "Conclusion," and turn some of them upide [sic] down, and others down on their sides.

Emendations of the Copy-Text: Accidentals

The following table lists every instance in which the copy-text has been emended with an accidental. If the accidental is caused by or coincident with a substantive variation, the word or phrase in question is listed both under accidentals and under substantives.

The boldface words or phrases represent the present text readings and the texts in which those readings appear (indicated by sigla). The lightface material represents the copy-text readings, and any other readings from other texts. The copy-text reading is for the MMS or the BMS, whichever contains the latest authorial inscription.

"I" after an adopted reading indicates that the emendation is made by the editor. An asterisk [*] indicates that the reading is discussed in the textual notes. A squiggle [~] is used to indicate that there is no variant in the word, just in the punctuation. A caret [∧] indicates the lack of punctuation at that point. A paragraph marker [¶] indicates that there is a new paragraph at that point. "[n.i.]" indicates that the word or phrase is not in the text whose abbreviation follows it.

2.1 now. He CM-C&W now, he
2.8 too, CM-C&W ~∧
2.15 Mark Twain CM-APC Mark Twain MMS MARK TWAIN C&W
3.6-7 one- and two-story CM-APC one and two-story MMS one- and two-storey C&W
3.7 frame CM-C&W "-"
3.38 blew)∧ CM-C&W ~),
5.39 'Pears? CM-C&W 'Pears,
5.39 another. "Is CM-C&W another, "is
6.18 I CM-C&W I
7.22 name∧ CM-C&W ~,
8.16 you. CM-APC ~! MMS ~? C&W
8.26 wheelbarrow CM-C&W wheebarrow
*8.43 "sassy" CM-APC "~∧ MMS '~' C&W
*9.16 gather in CM-C&W gather-in
10.7 thief. CM-C&W ~!
11.40 down the river CM-C&W down the river
12.3 it! CM-C&W ~∧
12.6 here CM-C&W here
13.13 you CM-C&W you
13.17 way, CM-C&W ~!
13.18 mammy's got CM-C&W mammy's got
13.21 you, CM, C&W ~! MMS ~∧ APC
13.25 yonder. CM-C&W ~!
13.40 complexion. Then CM-C&W ~, then
14.5 fo' CM-C&W for
14.12 all! CM-C&W ~∧
14.12 lovely. CM-C&W ~!
14.13 bit. CM-C&W ~!
14.19 his'n. CM-C&W ~!
15.10 is, CM-APC ~! MMS ~∧ C&W
15.13 it. CM-C&W ~!
15.44 bilin'. CM-C&W ~!
16.14 fo' CM-C&W for
16.28 sho' CM-C&W sho'
17.23 appalling CM-C&W appaling
18.15 it! CM-C&W ~∧
18.23 "father" CM-C&W ∧~∧
18.25 Like CM-C&W Like
18.27 Awnt CM-C&W Awnt
18.27 Hab CM-C&W Hab

18.28 Take CM-C&W Take
20.32-33 canoe-bottom CM-C&W canoe's bottom
21.6 this nigger CM-C&W this nigger
21.19 Chambers! CM-C&W ~,
21.19 ∧What CM-C&W —what
21.23 hear CM-C&W hear
21.24 me! CM-C&W ~.
21.36 saw that CM-C&W saw that
22.5 it. CM-C&W ~!
22.23 Essex CM-C&W Essex's
22.24 Driscoll CM-C&W Driscoll's
23.11 almond; CM-C&W ~,
23.14 Baldwin's, CM-C&W Baldwin
23.40 couldn't CM C&W couldn't
24.19 did CM-C&W did
25.12 pudd'nhead CM-C&W puddn'head
25.37 no! CM-C&W ~∧
25.39 Louis. CM-C&W ~!
25.41 specially CM-C&W especially
*26.10 Cappello I Capello
*27.24 blonde C&W [n.i.] MMS blond CM-APC
27.26 ought not CM-C&W oughtn't BMS-MMS
*27.35 seized MMS-C&W siezed BMS
27.42 "Our MMS-C&W ∧~ BMS
*28.35 country town, I village, BMS country town. MMS-C&W
*29.7 Cappello." Handshake I ~." ¶ ~ BMS-MMS Capello." Hand-shake CM-APC Capello.' Hand-shake C&W
29.7 ye, CM-C&W ~!
29.33 ours—all ours! CM-C&W ours—~~.
29.36 group MMS-C&W groupe BMS
31.9 fire; CM-C&W ~, BMS-MMS
*31.30 Pudd'nhead CM-C&W Puddn'head
33.11 ∧A CM-C&W ¶ A
33.14 Then she was promoted∧ CM-C&W She was promoted, then,
33.28-30 When the . . . Orleans∧ she bade . . . ashore. CM-C&W She bade . . . ashore∧ when the . . . Orleans.
*34.7 lovely; CM-C&W ~ —

34.7 poverty. *CM-C&W* ~!
34.8 poverty! *CM-C&W* ~.
34.11 much. *CM-C&W* ~!
34.42 so? *CM-C&W* ~!
35.9 dollahs. *CM-C&W* ~!
35.14 tell *CM-C&W* tell
35.22 ever *CM-C&W* ever
35.22 so! *CM-C&W* ~.
35.23 tribbilation. *CM-C&W* ~!
35.28 I's *CM-C&W* I's
36.2 do *CM-C&W* do
36.5 you *CM-C&W* you
36.5-6 mammy? T'ain't *CM-C&W* mammy, t'ain't
36.6 reckon. *CM-C&W* ~?
36.7 my *CM-C&W* my
36.7 is *CM-C&W* is
36.36 Please . . . please *CM-C&W* Please . . . please
37.8 Tom! . . . wouldn't! *CM-C&W* ~, . . . ~.
37.12 short! *CM-C&W* ~.
37.14 mammy. *CM-C&W* ~!
37.15 along! *CM-C&W* ~.
37.30 could *CM-C&W* could
*37.30 dol— *CM-C&W* d—
37.33 you a *CM-C&W* you a
37.34 it! *CM-C&W* ~.
37.35 half-way *CM-C&W* halfway
37.40 he'p *CM-C&W* h'ep
38.1 ever *CM-C&W* ever
*38.3 the *CM-C&W* The
38.11 beg *CM-C&W* beg
38.17 now! *CM-C&W* now.
38.20 you. *CM-C&W* ~!
38.22 she *CM-C&W* she
38.28 knows. I *CM-C&W* ~?
38.43 en more *CM-C&W* en more
39.4 dollah. *CM-C&W* ~!
39.4-5 you ain't *CM-C&W* you ain't
39.9 seized *CM-C&W* siezed
39.20 not! You *CM-C&W* not. You
39.21 me names *CM-C&W* me names
39.28 hear *CM-C&W* hear
39.30 see *CM-C&W* see
39.30 too! *CM-C&W* ~.
39.31 me." *CM-C&W* ~!''
39.37 ready. *CM-C&W* ~!
40.5 bill! *CM-C&W* ~.
40.9 it! *CM-C&W* ~.
*40.32 house, *CM-C&W* ~∧
41.9 me! *CM-C&W* ~.
41.12 dat *CM-C&W* dat
41.13 all *CM-C&W* all
41.15 mean *CM-C&W* mean
41.17-18 You . . . is! *CM-C&W* You . . . is!
41.18 dat's *CM-C&W* dat's
41.21 all! *CM-C&W* ~.
41.22 minute; *CM-C&W* ~!
41.23 sell . . . river *CM-C&W* sell . . . river
41.27 me. *CM-C&W* ~!
41.27 you's my *CM-C&W* you's my
41.29 ¶ —"en I ∧—"~ *MMS* ¶ ∧"En *CM-C&W*
41.30 en yo' *CM-C&W* en yo'
41.33 got *CM-C&W* got
41.35 seized *CM-C&W* siezed
41.37 me *CM-C&W* me
41.40 thoo— *CM, C&W* thoo— *MMS* throo— *APC*
41.40 but I *CM-C&W* but I

41.44 you! Now *CM-C&W* you. Now
41.45 you! *CM-C&W* ~.
42.8 again! Please *CM-C&W* again. Please
42.9 Roxy! *CM-C&W* ~.
42.12 me *Roxy* *CM-C&W* me Roxy
42.13 Ma . . . mammy I *Ma . . . mammy MMS* ma . . . mammy *CM-C&W*
42.20 me *CM-C&W* me
42.22 it. *CM-C&W* ~!
42.23 it. *CM-C&W* ~!
42.39 "How *CM-C&W* ∧~
42.41 I *CM-C&W* I
42.41 questions. *CM-C&W* ~!
43.23 you. *CM-C&W* ~!
43.30 don't! *CM-C&W* ~.
43.38 man. ¶ *CM-C&W* ~!∧
43.42 it. ¶ *CM-C&W* ~·∧
43.44 'long! *CM-C&W* ~.
43.45 right *CM-C&W* right
43.45 swah. *CM-C&W* ~!
44.23 nigger *CM-C&W* nigger
44.27 wish *CM-C&W* wish
45.22 nigger, *CM-C&W* ~!
45.33 himself. ¶ *CM-C&W* ~·∧
45.34 opinions *CM-C&W* opinions
45.36 character *CM-C&W* character
46.13-14 town∧ (for . . . village), *CM-C&W* ~, ∧for . . . village∧,
46.19 St. *CM-C&W* St∧
47.1 and had *CM-C&W* and had
47.23 manuscript *CM-C&W* MS
48.7 hands; *CM-C&W* ~,
48.35 ∧Tom winced.∧ *CM-C&W* [~~.]
48.38 grit! *CM-C&W* ~.
50.14 in *CM-C&W* in
50.34 would *CM-C&W* would
50.35 palms. Come *CM-C&W* palms—come
50.45 Luigi: *CM-C&W* ~—
51.2 alone; *CM-C&W* ~—
51.4 Dave! *CM-C&W* ~.
51.38 quite to *CM-C&W* to quite
52.1 your *CM-C&W* your
52.3 prophesied *CM-C&W* prophecied
52.10 of! *CM-C&W* ~.
52.11 enemy! *CM-C&W* ~.
52.14 along. *CM-C&W* ~!
52.20 I'll *CM-C&W* I'll
53.29 happens; *CM-C&W* ~—
53.31 hel-lo *CM-C&W* Hel-lo
53.40 me! *CM-C&W* ~.
54.32 long wavering *CM-C&W* wavering long
*55.2 cries: *CM-C&W* ~—
56.7 deny. *CM-C&W* ~!
56.19 speech. *CM-C&W* ~!
56.38 them *CM-C&W* them
57.32 absence *CM-C&W* absence
59.1 go *CM-C&W* go
*59.2 the Judge *The Judge*
59.5 didn't *CM-C&W* did not
59.8 that∧— *CM-C&W* ~!—
59.19 arms, *CM-C&W* ~∧
59.32 true! *CM-C&W* ~,
59.36 it's *CM-C&W* it is
60.27 by; *CM-C&W* ~,
60.29 uncle! *CM-C&W* ~.
*60.30 devil *CM-C&W* devils
*60.30 afraid *CM-C&W* afraid
*60.30 him! *CM-C&W* them.
60.35 repeating that lament again and again *CM-C&W* repeating, again and again, that lament

60.41 father! *CM-C&W* ~.
61.20 *that CM-C&W* that
61.21 me *CM-C&W* *me*
61.29 gone. *CM-C&W* ~!
62.6–9 throat. ¶ "It's . . . likely, . . . law-court."
   ¶ A *CM-C&W* throat.∧["It's . . . likely."]∧ A
62.21 discoveries! *CM-C&W* ~.
62.24 dissipation. *CM-C&W* ~!
62.45 you! *CM-C&W* ~.
63.21 Tom! *CM-C&W* ~.
63.22 nothing! *CM-C&W* ~.
63.39 *had CM-C&W* had
63.39 did not *CM-C&W* didn't
63.42 list. *CM-C&W* ~!
64.5 born! *CM-C&W* ~.
64.17 *in CM-C&W* in
64.41 as we *CM-C&W* as *we*
65.10 robbed *CM-C&W* robbed
65.16 *that CM-C&W* that
65.18 was *CM-C&W* was
65.25 Buckstone. *CM-C&W* ~?
65.36 good. *CM-C&W* ~!
65.37 what *CM-C&W* what
65.44 have *CM-C&W* have
66.7 my *CM-C&W* *my*
67.1 think—began *CM-C&W* think. Began
67.20 unusual∧ *CM-C&W* ~—
67.26 could *CM-C&W* could
68.2 apiece." *CM-C&W* ~.∧
68.3 Good! *CM-C&W* ~.
68.31 now *CM-C&W* now
68.40 sure! *CM-C&W* ~.
69.22 then∧— *CM-C&W* then!—
69.44 That's *CM-C&W* That's
70.16 me *CM-C&W* *me*
70.18 nigger *CM-C&W* nigger
70.20 soul. *CM-C&W* soul!
70.30 has *CM C&W* has
70.30 I *CM-C&W* *I*
70.34 his *CM-C&W* his
70.38 nigger *CM-C&W* nigger
70.38 you! *CM-C&W* ~.
71.1 ¶ Presently *CM-C&W* ∧~
71.13 I *CM-C&W* *I*
71.13 myself. *CM-C&W* myseff! *MMS*
71.15 did! *CM-C&W* ~.
71.18 che-bang *CM-C&W* che-bang
71.40 range! *CM-C&W* ~.
71.42 'Fraid *CM-C&W* 'Fraid
71.42 nothin' *CM-C&W* nothin'
71.45 *I* wouldn't *CM-C&W* I wouldn't
72.6 inch. *CM-C&W* ~!
72.8 minute. *CM-C&W* ~!
72.16 Now . . . end. *CM-C&W* Now . . . end!
72.24 *on CM-C&W* on
72.24 you, *CM-C&W* ~!
72.29 I *CM-C&W* *I*
72.29 you! *CM-C&W* ~.
72.32 me! *CM-C&W* me.
73.4 big *CM-C&W* big
73.6 month? *CM-C&W* ~.
73.13 you *is* gwyne *CM-C&W* you's *gwyne*
73.18 once *CM-C&W* once
73.20 one! *CM-C&W* ~.
73.22 self *CM-C&W* seff
75.2 no *CM-C&W* no
75.11 haven't *CM-C&W* haven't
75.19 good! *CM-C&W* ~.
75.20 St. *CM-C&W* St∧
75.24 to! *CM-C&W* ~.

75.30 ¶ Blake's *CM-C&W* ∧~
75.41 that *CM-C&W* *that*
75.43 of *CM-C&W* of
76.5 days∧ *CM-C&W* ~!
76.8 was *CM-C&W* was
76.32 argument's *CM-C&W* arguments
76.35 got *CM-C&W* got
76.36 that? *CM-C&W* ~!
77.6 think I *CM-C&W* think *I*
*77.9 that *CM-C&W* That
77.9 any such knife *CM-C&W* *any such knife*
77.11 dollars *CM-C&W* ~!
77.23 seen *CM-C&W* seen
77.32 Twins! *CM-C&W* ~.
77.36 but *CM-C&W* but
77.40 himself: ¶ *CM-C&W* ~, ∧
78.14 anywhere. ¶ *CM-C&W* ~. ∧
78.22 Indeed? *CM-APC* ~! *MMS* ~. *C&W*
78.37 I *CM-C&W* *I*
79.1 it. *CM-C&W* ~!
*79.6 a while I *CM-C&W* awhile *I*
79.34 ¶ His *CM-C&W* ∧~
79.38 now! *CM-C&W* ~.
79.38 you *CM-C&W* you
81.4 sayin' it! *CM, C&W* ~~∧ *MMS* ~~?
   APC
81.9 *do CM-C&W* do
81.11 law *CM-C&W* *law*
81.12 now *CM-C&W* now
81.17 dem *CM-C&W* dem
82.31 there. Then *CM-C&W* there, then
82.32–33 I's sole down de river *CM-C&W* I's
   sole down de river
85.13 it! *CM-C&W* ~.
85.19 bes' *CM-C&W* bes'
85.20 so! *CM-C&W* ~.
86.9 no mercy *CM-C&W* *no* mercy
86.9 mo'. *CM-C&W* ~!
86.18 was *CM-C&W* was
86.37 stan' it. *CM-C&W* stan' it!
86.39 flat. *CM-C&W* ~!
86.42 me *CM C&W* *me*
87.3 got *CM-C&W* got
87.30 watch! *CM-C&W* ~∧
87.32 myself *CM-C&W* myseff
87.34 I is. *CM-C&W* *I* is!
87.37 home *CM-C&W* home
87.37 I tell *CM-C&W* *I* tell
87.40 dat *CM-C&W* dat
87.44 all.' *CM-C&W* ~.∧
88.3 dem *CM-C&W* dem
88.20 take! *CM-C&W* ~.
88.27 couldn't *CM-C&W* couldn't
88.28 here *CM-C&W* here
88.32 help *CM-C&W* help
88.41 shirt! *CM-C&W* ~.
89.3 me! *CM-C&W* ~.
89.14 bill! *CM-C&W* ~.
89.21 all *CM-C&W* all
89.28 is *CM-C&W* is
90.6 sho." *CM-APC* sho'.∧
90.8 ast you *CM, C&W* ask you *MMS* askyou
   APC
90.25 you *CM-C&W* you
90.26 hide! Would *CM-C&W* hide. *Would*
90.26 it? No∧ *CM-C&W* it! No!
90.26 dog *CM-C&W* dog
90.28 I's *CM-C&W* I is
90.38 gamblin' *CM-APC* gamblin∧ *MMS*
   gambling *C&W*

91.6 you knows *CM-C&W you* knows
91.8 it! *CM-C&W ~.*
91.14 honey—set down. *CM-C&W honey.* Set down!
91.22 tole *CM-C&W tole*
91.31 self *CM-C&W seff*
91.38 en it *CM-C&W en it*
91.42 I *CM-C&W I*
91.44 yo'n! *CM-C&W ~.*
92.8 her *CM-C&W her*
92.9 *rob CM-C&W* rob
92.10 skinflint. *CM-C&W ~!*
93.24 him! *CM-C&W ~.*
93.35 Dawson's, *CM-C&W ~∧*
94.26 seized *CM-C&W siezed*
*****94.29** home—and *CM-C&W ~∧* and
94.32 seized *CM-C&W siezed*
94.35 ¶ He *CM-C&W ∧He*
94.39 man! *CM-APC ~. MMS, C&W*
95.24 St. *CM-C&W St∧*
97.15 degree, *CM-C&W ~∧*
97.28 wasn't *CM-C&W wasn't*
97.44 so! *CM-APC ~. MMS, C&W*
98.4 could *CM-C&W could*
98.9 had *CM-C&W had*
98.12 St. *CM-C&W St∧*
98.20 was *CM-C&W was*
98.25 with *CM-C&W with*
99.12 any . . . any *CM-C&W any . . . any*
99.43 her *CM-C&W her*
100.6 you. *CM-C&W ~!*
*****100.41** added∧ significantly, *CM-C&W ~,~∧*
103.25 face; *CM-APC ~! MMS ~, C&W*
103.42 are! *CM-C&W ~.*
104.3 Nothing *CM-C&W nothing*
104.10 ¶ "Now *CM-C&W ∧ "~*
*****104.19** use; *CM-APC ~, MMS ~ — C&W*
104.28 recall *CM-C&W recal*
104.28 was *CM-C&W was*
104.31 seized *CM-C&W siezed*
104.33 so *CM-C&W so*
104.34 it! *CM-C&W ~.*
*****105.3** his pantograph *CM-APC* his pantagraph *MMS, C&W*
105.22 ¶ Tom *CM-C&W ∧ Tom*
105.30 lick! *CM-C&W ~.*

106.4 words.∧ *CM-C&W ~."*
106.8–10 that . . . murder *CM-C&W that . . . murder*
106.12 *We . . . claim CM-C&W* We . . . claim
107.17 secretly *CM-C&W secretly*
107.19 *not CM-C&W* not
107.25 *was CM-C&W* was
107.26 before *CM-C&W̆ before*
*****107.32** ∧Another *CM-C&W [~*
107.35 "It *CM-C&W '~*
107.35 hit!"∧ *CM-C&W ~.']*
107.43 seized *CM-C&W siezed*
108.22 this *CM-C&W this*
108.23 globe! *CM-C&W ~.*
108.35 that *CM-C&W that*
109.2 autograph. *CM-C&W ~!*
109.2 That *CM-C&W That*
109.25–26 Order . . . down *CM-C&W Order . . . down*
109.44 it! *CM, C&W ~. MMS, APC*
110.5 *their CM-APC* their *MMS, C&W*
110.6 experimenters *CM-C&W experimentors*
110.26–28 Applause [4 times] *CM-C&W Applause* [4 times]
*****110.39** *A . . . B CM-C&W* A . . . B
111.7 ¶ He *CM-C&W ∧ He*
111.16 We . . . honor *CM-C&W We . . . honor*
111.29 *resemble, CM-C&W ~!*
111.39 was *CM-C&W was*
112.4 ¶ "No . . . widely! *CM-APC ¶ "No . . . widely. MMS ∧ "No . . . widely. C&W*
112.11 *By no means! CM-C&W* By no means.
112.14 changed . . . cradle *CM-C&W changed . . . cradle*
112.23–24 and . . . house! *CM-C&W and . . . house.*
112.30–31 Sensation . . . ejaculations *CM-C&W Sensation . . . ejaculations*
112.32–33 Burst . . . officers *CM-C&W Burst . . . officers*
114.1 this . . . us *CM-C&W this . . . us*
114.2 years. *CM-C&W ~!*
114.4 elected. *CM-C&W ~!*
114.25 "nigger gallery" *CM-C&W "nigger" gallery*

Rejected Variants: Substantives

This table contains substantive readings in texts other than the copy-text which are not used for emendation of the copy-text. Page and line numbers indicate present text locations. Any text not cited by sigla in lightface type does not differ from the copy-text reading. An asterisk preceding an entry indicates that the entry is discussed in the textual notes.

For the few instances when the Berg and Morgan manuscripts differ, this fact is emphasized with the citation of sigla in boldface type.

1.10 **Maccaroni and** Macaroni *CM-C&W*
*3.19 **home** house *CM-C&W*
*5.29 **disagreeable, whereupon young Wilson said** *CM-C&W* disagreeable. The new-comer, David Wilson, said *BMS* disagreeble; whereupon he said *MMS*
5.44 **that, he** *BMS* it, he *MMS-C&W*
6.23 **all."** *MMS* all—I ain't no judge." *BMS*
6.29 **was not able** *MMS* never was able *BMS*
11.21 **their loudest** the loudest *APC*
12.13 **he was** was *CM-C&W*
13.4 **feet and** feet *APC*
16.18–19 **if it takes** if it's *CM-C&W*
17.7 **this** the *CM-C&W*
21.39 **deeps** depths *APC*
*22.4 **whar** what *CM-C&W*
25.45 **town** *MMS* village *BMS*
26.3 **aflush** *BMS* ablush *MMS-C&W*
26.29 **Justice Robinson** *MMS* Captain Baldwin *BMS*
26.38 **uncertain, in low water,** *MMS* uncertain *RMS*
26.38 **those** these *CM-C&W*
26.39 **times.** *MMS* times. They took life easy, they were never in a hurry, they arrived early or late, according to circumstances, there was no schedule. *BMS*
*26.43 **came; then twelve, and** *BMS* came; and *MMS-C&W*
26.44 **town** *MMS* village *BMS*
27.1 **on the** *BMS* at the *MMS*
*28.10 **exhibit** *BMS* be exhibited *MMS-C&W*
28.35 **country town** *MMS* village *BMS*
29.15 **the sort** that sort *CM-C&W*
*29.37 **recognized** *BMS* recognizing *MMS* recognised *CM-C&W*
31.24 **now president** *MMS* now local agent of

the packet line, clerk of the county court, chairman of the debating club and president *BMS*
*34.9 **dream: Maybe he would help her;** dream: *CM-C&W*
35.6 **marse** marster *CM-C&W*
*37.12 **damn it** —— it *CM-C&W*
39.24 **you hadn't** hadn't *CM-C&W*
40.12 **deeps** depths *CM-C&W*
42.11 **Dah's** Dat's *APC*
43.22 **don't you** don't *APC*
*46.29 **later—** after— *CM-C&W*
50.11 **jugglery** juggling *CM-C&W*
50.43 **half a dozen years** half dozen years *CM-APC* half-dozen years *C&W*
*52.31–32 **you, and** you∧— *CM-C&W*
*53.17 **that knife** the knife *CM-C&W*
*59.27 **a slander** slander *APC*
*65.9 **out** out of *CM-C&W*
65.12 **lasted for** lasted *CM-C&W*
67.21 **chill** chill of *CM-C&W*
68.32 **bad scare** scare *APC*
71.2 **rumblings** ramblings *CM-C&W*
73.24 **once** one *CM-C&W*
77.43 **had had** had *CM-C&W*
*78.15 **On Saturday** Saturday *CM-C&W*
82.4 **never** never to *CM-C&W*
85.13 **meant** meant it *APC*
91.41 **into** right into *APC*
*93.42 **with a** with *CM-C&W*
94.6 **waning** wandering *APC*
96.11 **prostrated** prostrate *C&W*
98.3 **firstly** first *CM-C&W*
99.24 **didn't** did not *CM-APC*
101.21 **proven** proved *CM-APC*
101.35 **events** event *C&W*
108.18 **the mutations** mutations *APC*
114.26 **that** that it *APC*

197

Textual Notes

[First entry in Emendations of the Copy-Text, Substantives] These first pages in MMS were never used in any printed text of the book. (See the very last entry in Emendations of the Copy-Text: Substantives [Lengthy Passages].) See facsimile, Appendix 1, for this passage about weather signs.

1.9 court A few times the *c* of "court"—referring to a judge and jury—is ambiguous, either upper or lower case. All forms which are ambiguous in the manuscript have been normalized to lower case, the predominant form in the manuscript of unambiguous cases. Unambiguous forms, even when they are capitalized, are not normalized. Below is a table of all ambiguous instances of the word (page and line numbers are those of the present edition):

Pudd'nhead Wilson	TET
106.1	145.14
111.14	147.27
113.9	154.25

3.19 home "house" is probably an eye-skip by the Berg typist to this word a few lines above.

4.12 slave-holding Clemens could not fit the end-of-line hyphen in, so he put it in the left margin before "holding."

4.17 Judge As with the letters *c* and *t*, *j*'s are often written in such a way that they could be either upper or lower case. For the titles "Judge" and "Justice"—when the initial letter is ambiguous—this edition adopts capital letters, since this is the predominant form in the unambiguous cases. The following table lists all ambiguous forms in the present edition:

Pudd'nhead Wilson		TET
4.17	16.23	151.41
4.42	24.29	

What is amusing and perhaps instructive about Clemens's attitudes while he was writing the two parts of the story is that the cluster of lower-case "judges" appears in the farcical "kicking" trial of the twins in *Those Extraordinary Twins*, while in the *Pudd'nhead Wilson* murder trial "judge" appears consistently with a capital *j*, with the single exception of "judge" at 108.39, where the word appears in the phrase "judge and jury."

5.29 disagreeable . . . said Note that here the source of emendation is *CM*, which clearly shows authorial intervention.

6.31–32 and was . . . years. The BMS reading was typed verbatim by the Berg typist; in the MMS Clemens has added with a caret the present text reading, but he has neglected to cross out the other reading, and he also used an extra "and."

8.43 "sassy" House style for C&W called for single quotation marks where all other texts have them double; the practice is consistent throughout the novel and is not recorded in the tables.

9.16 gather in The hyphen in the MMS is not an acceptable form.

10.21 church The MMS reading here and at *TET* 165.6 are ambiguous as to capitalization. More than twenty other instances in the text are unambiguously lower case, so this form is adopted for these two readings.

14.5 fo' Though accidental variations in dialogue are generally not emended in this edition, MMS "for" (and the same form at 16.14) are not characteristic of Roxy's speech. There are many occurrences of her saying "fo'," but only these two of "for."

22.4 whar Clemens's handwriting is somewhat ambiguous in the manuscript, and the typist apparently misread this for "what."

26.3–26.26 excitement, . . . Here The rest of this passage, beginning with "Well, set down," is used in its unrevised BMS form in *Those Extraordinary Twins*, 123.5–124.15 of the present edition. The *CM* version is Clemens's revision of this passage, a passage so revised that the *CM* must be used as the sole authority for *Pudd'nhead Wilson* here. The BMS and MMS readings are identical, except for the word "too" in the deleted passage, which Clemens wrote "two"; the correction was made by the typist.

26.10 Cappello Here and elsewhere there is inconsistency in the spelling of this name. In the BMS, at 13.16, Clemens has written "Capello" and then inserted the second *p* with a caret, clearly showing his preference for this form. The spelling of the name with two *p*'s will be the normal one for this text.

26.34–35 its courtly . . . style, everybody The *CM* has "practiced" spelled "practised," but the passage there is otherwise verbatim with the present edition.

26.43 came; then twelve, and "came; and" is a typist's error in the MMS.

27.24 blonde Though there is no manuscript passage here, and though substantively the C&W text is not authoritative, the present edition adopts "blonde" as the author's sole form. In Clemens's own hand at BMS 26.2 and 32.5 the word is spelled with an *e*. Clemens apparently did not know that this spelling is normally feminine.

27.4–7 entered the twins . . . duplicates See *Those Extraordinary Twins*, 124.21–23.

27.31 child This is a case of carelessness on Clemens's part. The statement (which in *Pudd'nhead Wilson* should have been "children") comes from the original "joined" twins story.

27.35 seized This is one word Clemens uniformly misspelled. The dozen occurrences of it in the MMS are all incorrect, except for the two typed instances, and the corresponding manuscript occurrences of these two in the BMS are also incorrect.

28.10 exhibit "be exhibited" is a typist's error in the MMS.

28.11 bread. The passage removed from the *Pudd'nhead Wilson* story at this point, beginning "That hateful black bread," may be found in *Those Extraordinary Twins* (134.41–135.12 of the present edition).

28.35 country town, In the BMS Clemens wrote "village, she"; the typist changed this to "village. She"; Clemens decided to change "village" to "country town," and in doing so accepted the typist's error. The present text retains the substantive revision but uses the punctuation of the BMS.

28.36 its The MMS typist has incorrectly spelled this word "it's" several times, always using a comma for an apostrophe.

28.40 Twins Many of Clemens's *t*'s can be interpreted as either upper or lower case; context normally helps one decide. But Clemens was inconsistent in his capitalization of "twins," and there are many ambiguous occurrences in both MMS and BMS. This edition normalizes all ambiguous *t*'s to upper case for two reasons: this is the predominant form in the manuscripts in the unambiguous cases, and there are a few cases in the manuscript where a lower case *t* is distinctly changed by the author to a capital letter (but not a single case of the converse). Each ambiguous occurrence in the manuscripts is listed below by page and line number of the present edition. These are not elsewhere recorded.

Pudd'nhead Wilson

28.40	51.25	69.43	79.23	97.15	99.32
28.42	54.23	70.2	79.26	97.19	99.40
29.35	55.4	71.23	94.38	97.42 (2)	100.31
31.12	58.40	77.32	95.4	98.17	101.12
32.42	61.43	77.35	96.19	98.22	101.40
46.28	62.39	78.4	96.20	98.25	108.44
47.32	65.19	78.7	96.26	99.17	111.35
48.25	65.46	78.27	97.2	99.24	114.5
50.2

Those Extraordinary Twins

127.14	144.14	147.32	154.27	165.3
135.31	144.46	147.35	155.15	165.45
137.33	145.24	151.11	155.28	167.1
140.24	146.35	152.40	158.14	167.27
141.30	147.24	153.17	159.26	167.36

Deleted Matter

All these occurrences of "Twins" will appear with a capital *T* in the notes which list passages deleted from the present edition. The page and line number references are to entries in Emendations of the Copy-Text: Substantives.

31.27–29 (3)	62.27	71.36	111.30–31
48.6–7	63.19	78.18	114.14
56.14–15	69.31	79.5–22

29.7 Cappello." Handshake The present edition accepts the paragraphing of the *CM* and the spelling of the manuscripts.

29.37 recognized "recognizing" is an error of the BMS typist. The C&W compositor apparently spotted the need for a past tense, and changed the erroneous reading to "recognised." There is no indication of direct contact with the BMS.

30.22–24 [maxim] One . . . Calendar. This maxim, preceding Chapter 7 of the present edition, does not appear in the manuscripts. Chapter 9 in the MMS—which corresponds to Chapter 7 of the present edition—has no maxim inserted between the typed lines of the page; however, on the preceding page (handwritten, p. 130 of the MMS) the following maxim was inserted. It was not used in the final novel: ¶ "The Creator admired His glittering array of far-stretching solar systems, the work of His hands, but merely pronounced it "good." Considering the modesty of the word, one might think He was describing a village, whereas when you hear a villager describing his village, you think he is describing the solar systems. ¶ —*Pudd'nhead Wilson's Calendar.*" This maxim (at 30.22–24) appears also at the beginning of Chapter 27, Vol. 2, of *Following the Equator*, but beginning, "The principal difference between. . . ."

31.2 see. The continuation of the passage deleted—following the words "a herd"—appears in *Those Extraordinary Twins*, 135.23ff of the present edition.

31.27–29 established. He . . . he told One difficulty in explaining this entry lies in the facts that Clemens has 1) deleted several pages of the manuscript, and 2) linked MMS 135.5 with 161.3. The intervening matter was used for *Those Extraordinary Twins*. Hence, the portion from "Luigi wanted" to "and more" (BMS 84.2–93.19; this is the 960-word passage summarized in the table "Emendations of the Copy-Text: Substantives (Lengthy Passages)" at 31.27–29) is from the BMS; the passage from "Judge" to "told" is from the MMS (MMS 161.1–3, appearing at 31.27–29 of the present edition as "He would . . . told"). The ellipsis in the tabulated passage indicates that the intervening passage ("The hour passed . . . his lodgings") was used elsewhere in *Pudd'nhead Wilson*; see 31.38–41 of the present edition. The typescript of the BMS in the MMS differs from the Morgan typescript in several instances. One accidental and three substantive variants between the BMS and the Morgan typescript are all typist's errors.

31.30 Pudd'nhead Here and at 31.44 Clemens has put the apostrophe in the wrong place. Henceforth this error is silently corrected.

34.7 lovely; Normally the punctuation of the copy-text is retained; however, with two other emendations of an authorial nature in this sentence, the semicolon is adopted as also authorial.

34.9 dream . . . her; The lack of the phrase "Maybe . . . her;" can be seen as a typist's or compositor's eye-skip: the word "maybe" is immediately below "Maybe" in the MMS.

37.12 damn it See textual note to *Those Extraordinary Twins*, 128.22.

37.30 dol— The *CM* reading of "dol—" is much clearer than the MMS "d—"; the former is likely to be authorial.

38.3 the In the MMS the sentence originally began with "The"; Clemens inserted "But now" and forgot to make the *T* of "The" lower case.

39.37 . . . . Git This is one of several instances in the manuscripts in which Clemens used an unusual number of dots (often seven) to represent some kind of pause. *CM* has normalized these to ellipses. C&W uses four dots. The manuscript forms are retained.

40.17–19 [First maxim] This maxim appears in the MMS at the beginning of the following chapter.

40.32 house, Though usually the punctuation of the copy-text is retained, this is one instance in which the comma after "house" is needed for clarity and has thus been adopted.

41.46–42.1 of disorganizing sensations and In the deleted passage, which reads "of doubt, certainty, fear . . . ," Clemens must surely have meant "uncertainty" for "certainty."

44.4–5 [maxim] When angry . . . Calendar. The maxim removed from here ("Why is it . . . involved."), with one substantive change, is moved to Chapter 9, p. 40 of the present edition.

46.29 later— This is most likely an eye-skip to the previous line by the typist.

52.31–32 you, Clemens's ampersand is easily mistaken for a dash in the manuscript.

53.17 that knife The variant reading, "the

knife," is most likely an eye-skip, for the phrase "the knife" appears twice on the manuscript page, once four lines directly above the present reading. The word "the" appears immediately above "knife" in the manuscript.

55.2 cries: A paragraph marker was inserted by the author above the *s* of "cries." Originally the comma would have been adequate; but if the following sentence is made a separate paragraph, the new punctuation characteristic of Clemens's style is called for.

55.4 were The MMS originally had "A glass . . . was"; Clemens emended to "Glasses" but forgot to make the coordinating change of the verb.

56.18 philopena A philopena is "a social game in which each of two persons eats one of the twin kernels of a nut (usually an almond), and one pays a forfeit to the other if first saluted with the word 'philopena' or on other specified conditions" [*A Standard Dictionary of the English Language* (New York: Funk & Wagnalls, 1895), p. 1327]. The picture of the twin kernels apparently prompted Clemens to use this image.

59.2 the Judge The word "the" was originally the first word in the sentence. "At the finish" was inserted with a caret, but Clemens forgot to change "The" to lower case.

59.27 a slander The APC compositor, setting from sheets of the *CM*, probably had an eye-skip to three lines directly above in the dense *CM* column, where the word "slander" appears without "a" before it.

60.30 uncle! . . . him! The phrase "They are murderous devils." was inserted by Clemens with a caret which was at the very end of the line (MMS 343.12). The word "They," above the line, preceded the word "I" in "I never could," so the typist inadvertently reversed the two phrases, typing the one seen first. All printed editions have the phrases in this reverse order, but with Clemens's adaptations for the separated twins.

65.9 out This weakness in grammar is in Constable Blake's speech. He makes many other idiomatic and grammatical errors; the correction would appear to be editorial.

77.9 that This was originally the first word in the sentence. When Clemens added "Why" with a caret, he neglected to make "That" lower case.

78.15 On Saturday In the manuscript Clemens first wrote "Once" and then altered this to "On" by crossing out the *ce*; he clearly wanted "On" even though "Saturday evening" has been inserted with a caret.

79.6 a while The source for this reading, *CM*, has "awhile"; but Clemens clearly preferred the spelling as two words: only twice in the MMS (117.35 and 434.15) does the word appear with no space, while there are twelve occurrences of it as two words.

80.8–12 [maxim] We . . . Calendar. The first maxim of this chapter was transferred here from Chapter 26 of the MMS, which corresponds with Chapter 15 of the present edition.

80.16 friendless.— The punctuation is Clemens's practice of using a dash in the right margin at the end of a sentence where he had no room to write another word; the dash fills the space at the right margin, making it clear that the paragraph was not ending. The dashes at 81.10 ("you?—") and 82.21 ("She!—") are of the same nature.

83.10–84.19 The summer . . . deserted. See 168.24 in "*Those Extraordinary Twins*: Textual Notes," below.

86.20–21 was only For a discussion concerning the agreement of C&W with the MMS, see "Textual Introduction," p. 177, above.

87.21 chambermaid The *CM* compositor could have inadvertently omitted the word "head" in his typesetting. But this reading (without "head," which is the MMS reading) is corroborated by the C&W text. C&W, it should be remembered, is not using *CM* as their printer's copy at this point. If the hypothesis about the two sets of proof sheets of the *CM* printing is correct, then the adopted reading has authority through two separate channels: Clemens's emendations of the first set of proofs which were at the *CM* offices, and the unemended proofs which reflect the emended typescript. Other instances substantiating the hypothesis that there were two sets of proof sheets are noted below.

87.38 heard See note for 87.21.

88.9–10 den I See note for 87.21.

90.14 de house The reading "he house" appears in the MMS and in the C&W printing. C&W is apparently setting from uncorrected proofs of the *CM* printing. The revised proofs yield "de house" for *CM* and APC—a version not available to the C&W compositor.

91.5 knows you's a-goin'. The MMS had "*knows* it." This was changed in Clemens's cut-and-paste job to "knows it!"—the reading on the *CM* proofs. The corrected proofs contain the present reading. The uncorrected proofs yield "knows it!" for C&W.

92.17–21 Dawson's . . . it. Judge Driscoll declined Most of the original paragraph (MMS 539.1–17) has been moved to *Those Extraordinary Twins* (p. 168 of the present edition); Clemens has here rewritten the opening passage of the chapter.

93.32 the twins This sentence was written after Clemens had decided to recast the work with the twins separated; otherwise, he would not have had Luigi going out alone. However, after doing some revision (e.g., on backs of sheets, as in this example), and after having the manuscript typed, he realized that later in the story both Luigi and Angelo are caught at Judge Driscoll's corpse; it was much easier to change "Luigi" to "the twins" (as he has done here) than it would have been to change all the rest of the story to a trial of Luigi alone.

93.36 lonely The word looks like "lovely" in MMS (545.4).

93.39 window-blinds and lighted The C&W text follows the MMS on the word "lit." This is another instance supporting the supposition that two sets of *CM* proofs were being used. When C&W could not get copy for *Pudd'nhead Wilson* further than the fifth installment, despite several requests to Frederick Hall, they directly or indirectly contacted the *CM*, who sent them their house proofs to be set from. [See p. 177 of the "Textual Introduction."]

93.42 with a The "a" was inserted with a caret at the top of the page and was easily not seen by a typist.

94.29 home—and In the MMS Clemens's ampersand looks like a dash. Either the typist typed a dash and supplied the needed "and," or else

Clemens supplied the "and" in this typescript or in the *CM* proofs.

97.10–18 The coroner's . . . Wilson This change was made by the author clearly to show that the twins were separate people.

100.1 these See note for 87.21.

100.40 on See note for 87.21.

100.41 added∧ significantly, With other emendations in this passage which are definitely authorial, this one may be seen also as the author's improvement of his punctuation.

103.32 Take As with "twins," the initial letter of this word is not clearly upper or lower case. See note for 28.40. *CM* and C&W have "take."

104.19 · use; Clemens had "use," in the MMS and changed this in his cut-and-paste job to "use—"; this dash he later changed to a semicolon in correcting proofs, but the uncorrected proofs retained the dash. Hence the C&W reading.

105.3 pantograph Except for the occurrence of this word at 112.1 of the present edition, where the word was spelled correctly (MMS 617.8), the author misspells the word "pantagraph" consistently. The other instances of emendation are at 105.3, 105.4, 105.16, 110.37, 111.41, 112.5, 112.9, and 112.35. The incorrect spelling was caught in proofs at *CM*, but the uncorrected proofs retained this misspelling, which appears in all occurrences of the word in C&W—who even changed Clemens's one correct spelling at 112.1. C&W also has "pantagraph" at 111.3, words not in MMS.

107.32 ∧Another The variant here concerns the use of brackets; however, here and throughout this passage C&W uses parentheses.

107.42 course;∧ In the manuscript a word has been crossed out after the semicolon, and part of the cross-out line looks like a dash. *CM*-APC have the dash.

110.39 *A . . . B* The italicization of the letters *A* and *B* throughout this passage appears in all versions except the manuscript. It is not henceforth recorded.

112.41 sits among you In making the change from "in your midst" to "among you," Clemens probably forgot to cross out the word "in." All printed texts have this slightly awkward phrase: "in among you."

112.41–42 Valet de Chambre Elsewhere in the text (e.g., 36.11, 41.32, and 42.11) the name is spelled "Vallet de Chambers"—in Roxy's dialect, representing her pronunciation. The present spelling represents Wilson's pronunciation.

114.5–8 now, and with . . . Roxy's The passage for MMS represented by the ellipsis in the right column was moved to *Those Extraordinary Twins* (169.1–169.29 of the present edition). Passages deleted in this material and passages revised by the author may be found in the tables for *Those Extraordinary Twins* in this volume.

115.18 river. In the deleted passage, Clemens has accidentally spelled "upside" without the *s*. (See the last entry in "Emendations of the Copy-Text: Substantives [Lengthy Passages]."

Those Extraordinary Twins

Emendations of the Copy-Text: Substantives

This table lists every substantive emendation of the copy-text along with all other variant readings. The material in boldface type represents readings in the present edition; the lightface material contains, first, the copy-text reading, and, second, any other variants, if there are any. The copy-text reading is for the MMS or the BMS, whichever contains the latest authorial inscription. Sigla following the entries indicate the sources of those readings.

"I" after an adopted reading indicates that the emendation is made by the editor.

An asterisk [*] indicates that the reading is discussed in the textual notes.

Where possible, the adopted readings give an indication of context.

Lengthy passages—too long for this table—are printed in lightface type with an ellipsis [. . .]. They are preceded by a dagger [†], and may be found at the end of the table.

"[n.i.]" indicates that a passage is not in the text indicated.

123.15 **"Twins! How sweet! I** *APC* "I
123.30 **you. We** *APC* you, for we
124.15 **expect it.** *APC* expect them to be, yourself, ma." ¶ "Oh, go 'long with such nonsense. If a person's name made him sick, couldn't he rake up another one? You done it yourself." ¶ "Well, if I really thought he *was* sick, I—here
124.21–23 **Then followed . . . legs!** *APC* Then entered a human creature that had two heads, two necks, four arms, and one body, with a single pair of legs attached.
124.34 **Count Luigi** *APC* Luigi
124.35 **Count Angelo** *APC* Angelo
124.42 **into** *APC* in
124.43 **sup** *APC* a sup
125.3–4 **of Rowena's small brothers** *APC* of the boys
125.14 **them** *MMS-APC* them them *BMS*
125.32–33 **one; the . . . door.** *APC* one.
126.2 **trouble** *APC* trouble enough
126.38–39 **the one on the left—no, it was the one to the east of the other one—** *APC* the left-hand one—
127.25 **so far** *APC* as far
127.43 **cruelly** *APC* bitterly
*128.5 **"Whole Duty of Man,"** *MMS-APC* Testament,
128.25 **sing "From Greenland's Icy Mountains"** *APC* sing
130.25 **hands** *APC* arms
131.7 **turned** *APC* turning
131.14 **break** *APC* break in it
131.21 **became** *APC* had become
*131.31 **sure as** *APC* sure's *BMS* sure,s *MMS*
132.21 **both my** *APC* both of my
132.27 **half of the passengers** *APC* half
132.35 **"It is** *APC* "It's
132.39 **has** *APC* it *has*
133.17 **convinced . . . converted** *APC* convicted . . . convinced

133.34 **much less** *APC* less
134.4 **her:** *APC* her, and said—
134.14 **turn cordially** *APC* turn with cordial effusion
134.31 **I'd a et** *MMS* I'd eat *BMS* I'd 'a et *APC*
134.33 **and—"** *APC* and saved his brother's life." ¶ "It ain't anything. If I was starving, you gimme the chance and I'd save a whole family." ¶ "Now you've said enough, Joe, and you can keep still. I never saw such an aggravating boy; the plainer a thing is made to you the more you can't see it." ¶ "Well, anyways, I can see—" ¶ "There!—that'll be
135.12 **three."** *APC* three." ¶ "And you've made it four, and you think *that's* a good argument against a person that's made it three. There, Joe—close your head; when there's any help wanted out of you, I'll let you know. Go on, Angelo, never mind these people; if you wait for *them* to get quiet, you'll never get anywhere."
136.25 **point, i.e.,** *APC* point:
136.44 **point** *APC* point of view
137.10 **influences** *APC* influence
137.22 **the Judge's** *APC* the
*137.31 **[after the chapter heading]** [n.i.] *APC* ¶ It is a mistake to inflate the truth. Dress a fact in tights, not in an ulster. ¶ —*Pudd'nhead Wilson's Calendar.* MMS
137.31 **Joe and Harry** *APC* the brothers
139.23 **regulated** *APC* regulated weekly
139.23 **hundreds** *APC* the hundreds
139.43 **would** *APC* will
*140.9 **Sunday** *APC* a Monday *BMS* a Sunday *MMS*
140.17 **Lord** *APC* God
141.14 **ladies** *APC* people
141.29 **as** *APC* just as
*141.42 **[n.i.]** *APC* ¶ Whenever you find out you have been in error, don't change. This is Consistency. ¶ —*Pudd'nhead Wilson's Calen-*

dar. ¶ When I reflect upon the number of disagreeable people who I know have gone to a better world, I am moved to lead a different life. ¶ *—Pudd'nhead Wilson's Calendar.*

142.22 were doing *APC*   was doing

†**143.9–14 moment, now, to invite . . . company.** *APC*   moment, now, on a . . . controversy.

143.15–144.5 [A long . . . chapter.] *APC*   [n.i. *BMS* or *MMS*]

*****144 [n.i.]** ¶ There are 869 different forms of lying, but only one of them has been forbidden: thou shalt not bear false witness against thy neighbor. ¶ *—Pudd'nhead Wilson's Calendar.*

144.6 Pudd'nhead *APC*   Punk'nhead

144.33 can *APC*   could

144.38 among *APC*   amongst

145.7 said, sarcastically: *APC*   said:

146.26 other *APC*   other one

148.8 man in the world *APC*   man

149.28 for both *APC*   for

150.36 thirteen *APC*   seventeen

151.8 the old favorites *APC*   they

151.15 that young man *APC*   that

151.30 whatever *APC*   what

153.43 head *APC*   sacred head

154.23 injustice *APC*   unjustness

154.34 blown from the fields of paradise *APC*   wafted from paradise

156.31–32 has got nothing to do with it *APC*   has delegated his authority to another

157.17–18 he himself . . . trial, *APC*   he might fairly be considered entitled to another trial himself.

159 [n.i.] [after the chapter heading] *APC*   ¶ He is as conceited as a proverb. ¶ *—Pudd'nhead Wilson's Calendar.*

159.29 and always *APC*   but always

161.15 lungs *APC*   congested lungs

*****161.44 Quantity. Boil down and skim off. I** quantity. Boil down and skim off. *APC*   Quantity. *MMS*

163.32 fractious *APC*   cantankerous

164.2 finger. *APC*   finger; but turning her head to give an order, the finger wandered in reach of Luigi's mouth and he bit it. "Why, you impudent thing!" and she gave him a rap; but she was

flattered, nevertheless, perceiving that it was a love-bite.

164.11–12 prevent me *APC*   prevent it

164.18 proud *APC*   as proud

166.26 goodness *APC*   heaven

166.32 cold *APC*   thundering cold

166.43 infamous *APC*   infernal

†**166.43 prescri—"** ¶ **"There, . . . dear."** *APC*   prescri—" ¶ "Why . . . that."

*****167.27 the Twins I** twins *MMS*   the twins *APC*

†**167.39 canvass. He . . . dance.** *APC*   canvass. He . . . votes.

167.40 he *APC*   Luigi

167.40 best *APC*   greatest

168.1 which steadied his nerves and clarified his mind *APC*   which did not affect him in the least

168.12 persons *APC*   rowdies

*†**168.24 worse."** *APC*   worse." ¶ "Why . . . defeated.

168.37–38 case. His election was conceded, but he *APC*   case. He

169.1–2 fortnight. In due . . . standstill, *APC*   fortnight. The legs were Angelo's for this first week, and the brothers were not on speaking terms, now, but Luigi made no secret anywhere of the fact that there would be a duel when he got possession—either that, or Judge Driscoll would apologize: he could take his choice.

169.3 because without *APC*   ¶ The Twins were heroes of romance, now, and they came into vast and instant favor again, and aunt Patsy and aunt Betsy's cups of happiness were full. But the restored popularity of the strangers did not last long. The city government had been at a stand still ever since election day, because without

169.9 up and up *APC*   up and up and up

169.9 court, yet *APC*   court till it promised to reach the high court of the hereafter, yet

169.29 to that." *APC*   to that." ¶ So the town carried the halter to Luigi, explained its persuasions, and asked him to resign and go to Europe, and not stop anywhere this side. ¶ Luigi accepted the invitation, and took his brother along with him. They never returned. Then a new election was held, and the city got started right, this time.

Emendations of the Copy-Text: Substantives
(Lengthy Passages)*

143.9-14 moment, now, to invite . . . company.
APC [This passage, of about 1,500 words, is deleted for copyright reasons. In it the Twins are invited to join a Bible class, and they have a long discussion about Angelo's hopping from one religion to another, wherever he goes adopting the predominant local creed.]

166.43 prescri—" ¶ "There, . . . dear." *APC*
[This passage, of about 400 words, is deleted for copyright reasons. It is a bantering discussion between Aunt Betsy and Luigi.]

167.39 canvass. He . . . dance. *APC* [This passage, of about 100 words, is deleted for copyright reasons. It concerns Luigi's activities during the canvass—activities which discredited Angelo and lost votes for him.]

*168.24 worse." *APC* [This passage, of about 660 words, is deleted for copyright reasons. It contains (1) a discussion between Angelo and Rowena in which she explains why she cannot marry him (Luigi drinks but Angelo gets drunk on the alcohol, and she refuses to wed anyone who gets drunk); (2) Judge Driscoll's remarks in the political campaign which were intended to discredit the Twins; (3) Wilson's success in becoming Mayor; and (4) Tom's activities in and reactions to the election.]

---

*Because of copyright restrictions, the four passages cited in this table may not be reproduced until they have been published by the University of California Press.

Emendations of the Copy-Text: Accidentals

The following table lists every instance in which the copy-text has been emended with an accidental. If the accidental is caused by or coincident with a substantive variation, the word or phrase in question is listed both under accidentals and under substantives.

The material in boldface type represents the present text readings and the texts in which those readings appear (indicated by sigla). The lightface material represents the copy-text readings and any other readings from other texts. The copy-text reading is for the MMS or the BMS, whichever contains the latest authorial inscription.

"I" after an adopted reading indicates that the emendation is made by the editor. An asterisk [*] indicates that the reading is discussed in the textual notes. A squiggle [~] is used to indicate that there is no variant in the word, just in the punctuation. A caret [∧] indicates the lack of punctuation at that point. A paragraph marker [¶] indicates that there is a new paragraph at that point. "[n.i.]" indicates that the word or phrase is not in the text whose sigil follows it.

123.16　**are!** *APC*　~.
123.18　**so** *APC*　so
123.20　**that!** *APC*　~.
123.21　**"—'but** *APC*　∧—'~
123.23　**ma!** *APC*　~.
123.28　**names.** *APC*　~!
123.34　**ma!** *APC*　~.
123.34　**them!** *APC*　~.
123.39　**I** *APC*　*I*
124.1　**I** *APC*　*I*
124.8　**I** *APC*　*I*
124.10　**hope** *APC*　*hope*
125.13　**weird** *APC*　wierd
125.18　**look** *APC*　*look*
125.22　**I was** *APC*　*I* was
125.29　**on** *its* I　on *it's*
126.10　**say!** *APC*　~.
126.12　**this** *APC*　*this*
126.13　**begin.** *APC*　~!
126.14　**you** *APC*　*you*
126.20　**dizzy** *MMS-APC*　dizz
126.21　**I** *APC*　*I*
126.23　**now.** *APC*　~!
126.27　*They* *APC*　They
127.8　**grand!** *APC*　~.
*127.34　**when** *MMS-APC*　When
127.34　**I am** *APC*　*I* am
127.37　**as you** *APC*　as *you*
128.10　**so strong** *APC*　*so* strong
128.11　**that—"** *APC*　~—∧
128.13–14　**you could** *APC*　*you* could
128.20　*principles* *APC*　principles
128.38　**I don't** *APC*　*I* don't
128.40　**every** *APC*　*every*
128.41　**village;** *APC*　~—
129.4　**I** *APC*　*I*
129.7　**singing!** *APC*　~.
129.9　**ever** *APC*　*ever*
129.9　**'Greenland's Icy Mountains'** *APC*
　　∧~~~∧
129.12–13　**'Old Bob Ridley'** *APC*　∧~~~∧
129.14　**'Bob Ridley'** *APC*　∧~~∧
129.21　*They* *APC*　They

130.1　**I** *APC*　*I*
130.3　**is** *APC*　is
130.14　**coming!** *APC*　~.
131.28　¶ **"Now that** *APC*　∧"Now *that*
131.31　**it—** *APC*　it—
132.4　*you* *MMS-APC*　you
132.13–14　**he . . . he** *APC*　*he . . . he*
132.35　**saying,** *APC*　~∧
132.39　**fact,** *APC*　~∧
133.6　**didn't,** *APC*　~!
133.38　**he** *APC*　*he*
133.40　**never** *APC*　*never*
133.40　**life!** *APC*　~.
133.41　**you.** *APC*　~!
134.2　**hand,** *APC*　~!
134.30　**good** *APC*　good
134.31　**food** *APC*　*food*
134.43　*Mister* *APC*　Mister
134.44　**Luigi** *APC*　*Luigi*
135.6　**certainly** *APC*　*certainly*
135.6　**thinking** *APC*　*thinking*
136.44　**that.** *APC*　~!
137.17　**drunk** *APC*　drank
138.9　**with!** *APC*　~.
138.12　**isn't** *APC*　*isn't*
138.18　**brother's!** *APC*　~.
138.28　¶ **"And** *APC*　∧"~
138.30　**they** *APC*　*they*
139.1　**week!** *APC*　~.
139.7　**do** *APC*　*do*
139.13　**never!** *APC*　~.
139.26　**me** *APC*　*me*
139.44　**borrow** *APC*　*borrow*
140.2　**nowdays** *APC*　now-a-days
140.6　**all** *APC*　*all*
140.8　**does not** *APC*　doesn't
140.10　**such** *APC*　*such*
140.42　**be** *APC*　*be*
141.6　**that,** *APC*　that,
141.12–13　*we . . . are* *APC*　we . . . are
141.14–15　**paralyzed— . . . say—** *APC*　~,. . . ~,
141.21　**anywhere** *APC*　*anywhere* BMS anywhere *MMS*

141.24   *Any*body *APC*   Anybody
141.27   dear *APC*   *dear*
141.33–34   Luigi . . . satisfaction: "That . . . cars." *APC*   *"That . . . cars,"* Luigi . . . satisfaction.
145.10   everyone I   every one *MMS-APC*
145.19   question. *APC*   ~!
145.26   gentlemen *APC*   gentleman
145.32   ¶ The *APC*   ∧~
145.42   it. *APC*   ~!
146.12   they *APC*   *they*
146.24   say it might *APC*   say it *might*
146.26   didn't *APC*   *didn't*
146.28   I *APC*   *I*
147.1   *saw APC*   saw
147.14   said. *APC*   ~!
147.26   A Voice: *APC*   *A Voice.*
147.26–27   Laughter . . . court *APC*   *Laughter . . . court*
147.28   Another Voice: *APC*   *Another Voice.*
147.28–29   Laughter . . . court *APC*   *Laughter . . . court*
148.34   Wilson; ∧the *APC*   ~; "~
149.7   not *APC*   *not*
149.12   unprecedented! *APC*   ~.
149.17   *where APC*   where
149.27   has *APC*   *has*
149.30   Great applause *APC*   *Great* Applause
150.20   impudence! *APC*   ~.
150.21   *Now APC*   Now
151.33   *fact APC*   fact
151.33   *be APC*   be
151.36   do *APC*   *do*
151.40   *Hear APC*   Hear
151.46   down! *APC*   ~.
152.1   *Must APC*   Must
152.8   *they told APC*   they told
152.22   *please go on APC*   please go *on*
152.24   *me APC*   me
152.33   of it! *APC*   ~~.
152.34   Laughter, *APC*   *Laughter—*
153.10   know. *APC*   ~?
154.2   seized *APC*   siezed

154.12   but *APC*   *but*
154.14   gift, *APC*   ~ —
154.19–20   need! ¶ "Prisoners *APC*   ~!∧∧~
154.20   up. *APC*   ~!
154.23   injustice. *APC*   unjustness!
154.24   more! *APC*   ~.
154.28   aunties *APC*   Aunties
155.20   Why! *APC*   ~,
155.44   duelists *APC*   dualists
156.4   can't stay *APC*   *can't* stay
156.6   you're *APC*   you're
156.6–7   at you *APC*   at *you*
156.8   Angelo∧ *APC*   ~,
157.21   was *APC*   *was*
158.3   *Boom APC*   Boom
158.11   that *APC*   *that*
158.11   before! *APC*   ~,
154.24   finish *APC*   *finish*
160.5   maxillario superioris I   *maxillario superioris MMS*   maxillaris superioris *APC*
160.11   populo redax referendum rotulorum *APC*   *populo redax referendum rotulorum*
160.30   can't *APC*   *can't*
160.31   word, *APC*   ~∧
161.8   Joe. *APC*   ~!
161.47   while *APC*   While
162.21   to-day *APC*   *to-day*
163.12   lost. *APC*   ~!
163.18   Looy! *APC*   *Looy!*
163.31   it! *APC*   ~.
163.32   Looy *APC*   *Looy*
163.34   that *APC*   that
163.40   it! *APC*   ~.
163.43   I'm *APC*   *I'*m
164.14   all! *APC*   ~.
164.15   lion. *APC*   ~!
165.4   Pudd'nhead *APC*   Puddn'head
166.16   I— *APC*   *I—*
166.17   Will *APC*   *Will*
166.22   can't *APC*   *can't*
166.40   this *APC*   *this*
169.24   ticket. *APC*   ~!

Rejected Variants: Substantives

This table contains substantive readings in texts other than the copy-text which are not used for emendations of the copy-text. Page and line numbers indicate present text locations. Any text not cited by sigla accompanying the reading given in lightface type does not differ from the copy-text reading. An asterisk preceding an entry indicates that the entry is discussed in the textual notes.

For the few instances when the Berg and Morgan manuscripts differ, this fact is emphasized with the citation of sigla accompanying the boldface material.

124.6 May be Maybe *APC*
124.13 Those These *APC*
*124.18 on the at the *MMS-APC*
*124.18 family anxious family *APC*
124.27 slave wench *MMS* slave girl *BMS* slave-wench *APC*
125.10 lightnings lightning *APC*
127.11 can fix can can fix *MMS*
128.4 in one on one *MMS*
*128.22 d-bosh bosh *APC*
130.15 "They . . . right." [n.i.] *BMS*
*132.7 did not didn't *MMS-APC*
*132.25 these the *MMS-APC*
*132.43 indigestion digestion *MMS*
*133.34 illnesses illness *MMS-APC*
*133.40 "Well "Why *APC*
134.31 a et eat *BMS* 'a et *APC*
136.28 the a *APC*
*137.2 the an *MMS* a *APC*
*137.18 the languor and languor *MMS-APC*
*137.21 long and long *MMS-APC*
*137.32 persons that noon, persons *BMS* persons that noon‸ *APC*

*139.16 shade and fraction shade of a fraction *MMS-APC*
139.39 No Now *APC*
*139.40 you're you've *MMS-APC*
140.9 Sunday a Monday *BMS* a Sunday *MMS*
*141.17 proofs proof *MMS-APC*
*141.35 poor old poor *MMS-APC*
147.34 or ands and and's *APC*
149.9 law laws *APC*
*151.16 Jake Jack *APC*
153.18–19 the one one *APC*
154.3 circumference circumstance *APC*
*154.30 crowds crowd *APC*
159.11 whatsoever whatever *APC*
159.15 about it about *APC*
162.24–25 I cannot cannot *APC*
*163.39 you, Looy you, *APC*
*165.17 and so so *APC*
165.26 ever even *APC*
165.44 the burghers burghers *APC*
166.21 I tell you I I *APC*
*167 [Chapter 9]
*167.31 and his and the *APC*

Textual Notes

124.18 on the "at the" is an error of the typist who typed the BMS. The typed pages are inserted in MMS.

124.18 family This is an eye-skip by the typist. In the deleted matter in the line above this one was the phrase "anxious family."

127.34 when When Clemens inserted words preceding this one in the sentence, he neglected to make this lower case.

128.5 "Whole Duty of Man," The person who typed the BMS accidentally typed "Testament" with a lower case *t*. Clemens has written "Whole Duty of Man" (without the quotation marks) between the lines.

128.22 d-bosh Note that at 37.12 of the present text, the *CM* editors reduced "damn it" to "----it."

128.25 "From Greenland's Icy Mountains" In *Following the Equator* (Vol. 2, Ch. 19) Clemens quotes the lyrics as follows: "From Greenland's icy mountains,/ From India's coral strand,/ Where Afric's sunny fountains/ Roll down their golden sand;/ From many an ancient river,/ From many a palmy plain,/ They call us to deliver/ Their land from error's chain." He then says: "These are beautiful verses, and they have remained in my memory all my life." (*Following the Equator* [New York and London: Harper & Brothers, 1897, 1899], Vol. 2, p. 225.)

131.31 sure as The comma in the rejected reading ("sure,s") is the way it appears in the BMS typescript (i.e., the one embedded in the MMS). The use of the comma for apostrophes by the typist is consistent, and is not henceforth noted.

132.7 did not This is a typist's error.

132.25 these In the BMS Clemens's *se* of "these" was messy and easily taken for an *n*; the typist typed "then"; Clemens, not making any sense of this when he proofread the typescript, crossed off the typist's *n*.

132.43 indigestion The typist erroneously typed "digestion"; someone, seeing the error, inserted a caret before this word in pencil but neglected to insert "in" above the line. (Also, Clemens has had Luigi here ask Angelo not to add any more sugar to his tea, saying it would give him [Luigi] indigestion; this humorous touch is in the wrong brother's mouth, for it is Angelo who is affected by what goes into the stomach.)

133.34 illnesses This is a typist's error.

133.40 "Well This typist's error is an eye-skip to a paragraph above.

137.2 the In BMS "the" is written carelessly; it looks like "an"; the typist typed "an," which form still remains in the MMS. The APC changed "an" to "a."

137.18 the languor "and" is a typist's error.

137.21 long and This is a typist's error.

137.31 [After chapter heading] [n.i.] This maxim, penned into the typed pages of the MMS, was not used in this story.

137.32 persons that noon, "that noon," was added into the MMS by the author in pencil.

139.16 shade and fraction This is a typist's error.

139.40 you're The BMS reading is questionable but appears to be "you're"; the typist read "you've."

140.9 Sunday The "Sun" has been changed in pencil to "Mon"—probably not by Clemens.

141.17 proofs This is a typist's error.

141.35 poor old This omission is a typist's error.

141.42 [n.i.] These two maxims appear on p. 141 of MMS, immediately between the last two paragraphs on p. 141 of the present edition. The words ". . . if he had" originally ended MMS Chapter 10, and the two maxims were headed "Chapter 11." The first of these ["Whenever you find . . ."] was never used. The second ["When I reflect . . ."] heads Chapter 13 of *Pudd'nhead Wilson* (p. 61 of the present edition).

144 [n.i.] This maxim was never used for *Pudd'nhead Wilson*. It appears at the opening of Chapter 19 (Vol. 2) of *Following the Equator*, as part of "*Pudd'nhead Wilson's New Calendar.*" It differs from the MMS version by the inclusion of the word "squarely" before "forbidden."

151.16 Jake This is likely a typist's eye-skip to "Jack Lounsbury" a few lines later.

154.30 crowds This was originally written "crowd," then the comma was changed to an *s* and another comma was inserted. The first comma makes it look as if the *s* is crossed out.

161.44 Quantity. Boil down and skim off. This recipe is pasted into the MMS, cut by Clemens from his article "A Majestic Literary Fossil" in *Harper's New Monthly Magazine*, LXXX (February, 1890), 439–444. This excerpt is on page 444.

163.39 you, Looy "Looy" is inserted with a caret in an area with much authorial revision. It was probably not seen by the typist.

165.17 and so The ampersand is at the end of the line and is followed by a deleted word; thus, it was easily missed by the typist.

167 [Chapter 9] N.B. The published copy of APC has several words deleted from the text as it existed in the earlier form as sent to the Library of Congress. These deletions may be found in Appendix 2.

167.27 the Twins In making a correction, Clemens forgot to include the word "the."

167.31 and his Clemens wrote "& his," and the ampersand could have easily been mistaken for a *t*. The typist or compositor—realizing that the word "this" did not make much sense—evidently changed it to "the."

168.24 worse." Clearly some of this deleted passage refers to the story in *Pudd'nhead Wilson*. But it is recorded here since it is surrounded by the *Those Extraordinary Twins* story, and there was no specific place in *Pudd'nhead Wilson* from which it was deleted. The passage shows how the two stories (the Siamese twins and the murder mystery) were still joined in the MMS. Parts of this deleted passage were substantially rewritten for *Pudd'nhead Wilson*, Chapter 17 (pp. 83–84 of the present edition), though some of it was used verbatim there.

Appendix 1

The Weather Signs Passage Deleted from
*Pudd'nhead Wilson**

To Printer. Please make fac-similes of these signs & use them at chapter-tops — one & sometimes two — She it is not necessary that they but the weather of the chapter always.

Key to Signs used in this book.

To save the space usually devoted to explanations of the state of the weather, in books of this kind, the author begs leave to substitute a simple system of weather-signs. The hieroglyph at the head of each chapter will instantly convey to the reader's mind a perfect comprehension of the kind of weather which is going to prevail below.

The signs & their meanings here follow:

Sunny.
Pitch Dark
Starlight.
Rainy.
Moonlight.
SNOW.
Fog.

When two or more signs occur together, the weather is going to be more, or more yet, or still more variable, according to number of signs employed.

---

*See first entry in "Emendations of the Copy-Text: Substantives (Lengthy Passages)." This "Weather Signs" passage was published by Daniel Morley McKeithan in his essay "The Morgan Manuscript of Mark Twain's *Pudd'nhead Wilson*" (see Bibliography).

4

(Put this paragraph below the succeeding two.)

When there is no sign, it means that there is not going to be any weather. It is a mistake to suppose that weather is at all times necessary in a novel. As often as not, it is an ~~hindrance~~.

inconvenience, & keeps the characters from going out.

When all the signs are ~~used~~ it means Storm. ~~~~

When they are doubled, it means ~~~~ Extremely Violent & Perilous Weather.

(Put it down here.)

Appendix 2

Words Deleted from Chapter 9 of
Those Extraordinary Twins

In the first published version of *Those Extraordinary Twins* (American Publishing Company, 1894) several words were deleted from the text. In the proof copies of this edition sent by the American Publishing Company to the Library of Congress for copyright purposes these words were not deleted. (For an explanation, see Sidney Berger, "Editorial Intrusion in *Pudd'nhead Wilson*," *The Papers of the Bibliographical Society of America*, vol. 70 [1976], pp. 272–276; or see the Textual Introduction, p. 176, above.)

Below is a chart of the present edition readings (those of the MMS and the Library of Congress, printed in boldface type) and the readings in APC (lightface type).

167.16	**hotter and hotter** hotter		**167.35**	**and it was an** an
167.17	**presently developed** developed		**167.37**	**extravagant and** extravagant,
167.18	**interest in it** interest		**168.11**	**a ringing appeal** an appeal
167.19	**which was a** a		**168.14**	**in a general burst of wrath** in wrath
167.20	**him,** him, but		**168.17**	**had even** had
167.24	**Union and** Union,		**168.18**	**but had begged for** but wanted
167.33	**and did his** doing his		**168.18**	**But now** Now
167.33	**to get back** to regain		**168.19**	**she frankly** she
167.33-34	**ground which** ground			

Criticism

Reviews

WILLIAM LIVINGSTON ALDEN

From *The Idler* (August, 1894) †

Puddenhead Wilson, Mark Twain's latest story, is the work of a novelist, rather than of a 'funny man.' There is plenty of humour in it of the genuine Mark Twain brand, but it is as a carefully painted picture of life in a Mississippi town in the days of slavery that its chief merit lies. In point of construction it is much the best story that Mark Twain has written, and of men and women in the book at least four are undeniably creations, and not one of them is over-drawn or caricatured, as are some of the most popular of the author's lay figures. There is but one false note in the picture, and that is the introduction of the two alleged Italian noblemen. These two young men are as little like Italians as they are like Apaches. When challenged to fight a duel, one of them, having the choice of weapons, chooses revolvers instead of swords. This incident alone is sufficient to show how little Italian blood there is in Mark Twain's Italians. But this is a small blemish, and if Mark Twain, in his future novels, can maintain the proportion of only two lay figures to four living characters, he will do better than most novelists. The extracts from 'Puddenhead Wilson's Almanac,' which are prefixed to each chapter of the book, simply 'pizon us for more,' to use Huck Finn's forcible metaphor. Let us hope that a complete edition of that unrivalled almanac will be issued at no distant day.

From *The Athenaeum* (January 19, 1895) ‡

The best thing in *Pudd'nhead Wilson*, by Mark Twain (Chatto & Windus), is the picture of the negro slave Roxana, the cause of all the trouble which gives scope to Mr. Wilson's ingenious discovery about finger-marks. Her gusts of passion or of despair, her vanity, her motherly love, and the glimpses of nobler feelings that

† From *The Idler, an Illustrated Monthly Magazine* (London), Vol. VI, pp. 222–223.
‡ An anonymous review from *The*

Athenæum, a Journal of Literature, Science, The Fine Arts, Music, and the Drama (London), No. 3508, pp. 83–84.

are occasionally seen in her elementary code of morals, make her very human, and create a sympathy for her in spite of her unscrupulous actions. But hers is the only character that is really striking. Her son is a poor creature, as he is meant to be, but he does not arrest the reader with the same unmistakable reality: his actions are what might be expected, but his conversations, especially with Wilson and the Twins, seem artificial and forced. Wilson, the nominal hero, appears to most advantage in the extracts from his calendar which head the chapters, but as a personage he is rather too shadowy for a hero. And what has to be said about the book must be chiefly about the individuals in it, for the story in itself is not much credit to Mark Twain's skill as a novelist. The idea of the change of babies is happy, and the final trial scene is a good piece of effect; but the story at times rambles on in an almost incomprehensible way. Why drag in, for example, all the business about the election, which is quite irrelevant? and the Twins altogether seem to have very little *raison d'être* in the book. Of course there are some funny things in the story—it would not be by Mark Twain if there were not—but the humour of the preface might very well be spared; it is in bad taste. Still, if the preface be skipped the book well repays reading just for the really excellent picture of Roxana.

From *The Critic* (May 11, 1895) †

The literary critic is often puzzled how to classify the intellectual phenomena that come within his ken. His business is of course primarily with *literature*. A work may be infinitely amusing, it may abound even with flashes and touches of genius, and yet the form in which it comes into the world may be so crude, so coarse, so erring from the ways of true classicism, so offensive to immemorial canons of taste, that the critic, in spite of his enjoyment and wonder, puts it reluctantly down in the category of unclassifiable literary things —only to take it up and enjoy it again!

Of such is *Pudd'nhead Wilson*, and, for that matter, Mark Twain in general. The author is a signal example of sheer genius, without training or culture in the university sense, setting forth to conquer the world with laughter whether it will or no, and to get himself thereby acknowledged to be the typical writer of the West. He is the most successful of a class of American humorists whose impulse to write off their rush of animal spirits is irresistible, and who snatch at the first pen within reach as the conductor of their animal electricity. If we look at other national humorists, like Aristophanes, Cervantes, Molière or Swift, we find their humor

† An anonymous review from *The Critic; an Illustrated Monthly Review of Literature, Art, and Life* (New York), Vol. XXVI, pp. 338–339.

expressed in an exquisite literary form, in which a certain polish tempers the extravagance, and annoying metrical (or it may be imaginative) difficulties have been overcome. What wonderful bird-rhythms and wasp melodies and cloud-architecture, so to speak, emerge from the marvellous choral interludes of the Greek comedian; what suave literary graces enclose the gaunt outlines of Don Quixote; in what honeyed verse are Alceste and Tartuffe entangled, and what new, nervous, powerful prose describes the adventures of Gulliver! When we turn our eyes westward we encounter Judge Haliburton, Hosea Biglow, Uncle Remus, Mark Twain—an absolutely new *genre* distinct from what we had previously studied in the line of originalities. The one accomplished artist among these is Lowell, whose university traditions were very strong and controlled his bubbling humor. The others are pure 'naturalists'—men of instinctive genius, who have relied on their own conscious strength to produce delight in the reader, irrespective of classicity of form, literary grace or any other of the beloved conventions on which literature as literature has hitherto depended. This is true in a less degree of Uncle Remus than of Judge Haliburton and Mark Twain.

Pudd'nhead Wilson is no exception to the rule. It is a Missouri tale of changelings 'befo' the wah,' admirable in atmosphere, local color and dialect, a drama in its way, full of powerful situations, thrilling even; but it cannot be called in any sense *literature*. In it Mark Twain's brightness and grotesqueness and funniness revel and sparkle, and in the absurd extravaganza, 'Those Extraordinary Twins,' all these comicalities reach the buffoon point; one is amused and laughs unrestrainedly but then the irksome question comes up: What *is* this? is it literature? is Mr. Clemens a 'writer' at all? must he not after all be described as an admirable after-dinner storyteller—humorous, imaginative, dramatic, like Dickens—who in an evil moment, urged by admiring friends, has put pen to paper and written down his stories? Adapted to the stage and played by Frank Mayo, the thing has met with immediate success.

T. M. PARROTT

From *The Booklover's Magazine* (February, 1904) †

* * *

Pudd'nhead Wilson * * * has an artistic unity which the others lack. Curiously enough this sombre story took shape in the author's mind as a farce, which turned into a tragedy under his very hands.

† From *The Booklover's Magazine* (Philadelphia), Vol. III, pp. 145–154.

In one of the most amusing glimpses of a literary workshop that an author has ever given us, Mr. Clemens tells of his trouble with the tangled story. The farce and the tragedy, he says, obstructed and interrupted each other at every turn, and created no end of confusion and annoyance, until he finally pulled the former up by the roots and left the other, 'a kind of literary Caesarean operation.'

The result of the operation, however, is by no means wholly gratifying. *Pudd'nhead Wilson* is a tragedy, but a very sordid one. There is no trace left of the light-hearted gaiety of *Tom Sawyer*, and very little of the genial humanity of *Huckleberry Finn*. On the contrary, the book is marked by a strong dash of ironical cynicism which finds utterance mainly in the *obiter dicta* of the titular hero, prefixed as mottoes to the various chapters. 'If you pick up a starving dog and make him prosperous, he will not bite you; that is the principal difference between a dog and a man,' says one of these. That is not the sort of thing that the Mark Twain of *Innocents Abroad* would have regarded as a joke, and it runs counter to the experiences of Tom with Muff Potter, and of Huck with 'nigger Jim.' It is, perhaps, a result of this bitter mood that there is no one figure in the book capable of arresting and retaining our sympathies. Tom Driscoll, the slave who takes his master's place, is a monster of meanness, cowardice, and ingratitude; the mulatto, Roxana, is a strongly conceived, but rather repellent character; and Pudd'nhead himself is, till the very close of the book, a mere lay figure on which to hang the author's own philosophizings. And yet the work is by no means devoid of power. It is a strong, direct, and simple piece of narrative; it has an ingeniously constructed plot and a startling climax; and like its predecessors it is a genuine and realistic picture of that phase of American life with which the author is most familiar. Had any one but Mark Twain written such a book it would no doubt have been more generally recognized as the grave and powerful piece of art it really is.

Critical Essays*

BERNARD DE VOTO

[Mark Twain's Presentation of Slavery]†

In "Pudd'nhead Wilson" the institution that had furnished a living background for these other books[1] becomes the active center. In all other places Mark Twain omitted an explicit statement of sexual relationships—though the force of implication is irresistible wherever the squatters are displayed. Here, it may be in all innocence, he states and develops a theme completely tabooed in nineteenth-century American literature, miscegenation. It is so inevitably a part of the book that critical amazement develops only retrospectively. Yet there is an intense artistic courage in this presentation of the slave Roxana, one sixteenth negro, of fair complexion and fine soft hair, and of the son whom she bears to Cecil Burleigh Essex.

Roxy is unique and formidable. Mark's handling of her suffers somewhat from the melodrama and sentimentality that, it should be clear, were inescapable—but does not suffer much. In outline and in detail she is memorably true. She lives: her experiences and emotions are her own, and, being her own, are faithful to the history of thousands. With new instruments at its service and a generation of writers far distant from the reality, literature may make another essay of slavery—but is unlikely to go beyond the superstition, affection, malice, and loyalty of this woman. In her exist, as nowhere else, the experience, the thought, and the feelings of slaves. Even in melodrama she retains her verity. When she forces Valet de Chambre Essex to his knees, she is within reach of the preposterous, but the scene is as true, as inevitable, as her thieving and tippling. It ends with her declaration that "dey ain't another nigger in dis town dat's as high-bawn as you is", and this is grandeur. Gran-

---

* In the critical essays below, the scholars have necessarily quoted from different editions of *Pudd'nhead Wilson* and *Those Extraordinary Twins* than are printed in this new edition. No attempt has been made to make the quoted matter conform to the style of the present edition [*Editor*].

† From Bernard De Voto, *Mark Twain's America* (Boston: Little, Brown and Company, 1932), pp. 293–294.
1. *A Connecticut Yankee, The Prince and the Pauper, Joan of Arc, The Gilded Age, The American Claimant,* and *The Man Who Corrupted Hadleyburg* [*Editor*].

deur of another kind appears in her original crime and, most evidently, in her disgust when she learns that her son has disgraced his father by ratting the duel with Luigi. "En you refuse' to fight a man dat kicked you, 'stid o' jumpin' at de chance! En you ain't got no mo' feelin' den to come en tell me, dat fetched sich a po' lowdown ornery rabbit into de worl'! Poh! it makes me sick! It's de nigger in you, dat's what it is. Thirty-one parts o' you is white, en on'y one part nigger, en dat po' little one part is yo' soul. 'Tain't wuth savin'; 'tain't wuth totin' out on a shovel en throwin' in de gutter." In such passages as this and the mind of Valet de Chambre, slavery finds a profundity and a complexity of expression that it has had nowhere else. . . . It is worth noting that in "Pudd'nhead Wilson", Mark Twain adheres to the artistic necessities of his structure. The tough-minded ending, though clumsily managed, is carried out in its own terms.

Slavery as an institution and Negroes as sharers of the scene are organic in the community to which these novels are devoted. It is a whole community: the effect is totality. Several generations of American experience, a race, an era, and a society, are enregistered.

* * *

LESLIE FIEDLER

"As Free as Any Cretur..."†

The most extraordinary book in American literature unfortunately has not survived as a whole; but its scraps and fragments are to be found scattered through the work of Mark Twain: a cynical comment ascribed to a small-town lawyer and never printed, the wreck of a comic tale framed by apologies and bad jokes, and finally the *Pudd'nhead Wilson* that has come down to us, half melodramatic detective story, half bleak tragedy. What a book the original might have been, before *Those Extraordinary Twins* was detached and Pudd'nhead's *Calendar* expurgated—a rollicking atrocious melange of bad taste and half understood intentions and nearly intolerable insights into evil, translated into a nightmare worthy of America.

All that the surrealists were later to yearn for and in their learned way simulate, Twain had stumbled on without quite knowing it. And as always (except in *Huckleberry Finn*) he paid the price for his lack of self-awareness; he fumbled the really great and mon-

† From *The New Republic*, Vol. CXXXIII, Nos. 7–8, Issues 2125–26 (August 15 and 22, 1955), pp. 130–139.

strous poem on duplicity that was within his grasp. The principle of analogy which suggested to him linking the story of the Siamese Twins, one a teetotaler, the other a drunk, Jekyll and Hyde inside a single burlesque skin—to a tale of a Negro and white baby switched in the cradle finally seemed to him insufficient. He began to worry about broken plot lines and abandoned characters, about the too steep contrast between farce and horror; and he lost his nerve—that colossal gall which was his essential strength as well as his curse. Down the well went the burlesque supernumeraries and finally out of the story; and the poor separated twins remain to haunt a novel which is no longer theirs.

But something in Twain must have resisted the excisions; certainly they were made with a striking lack of conviction, and the resulting book is marred by incomprehensible motivations and gags that have lost their point with the unjoining of the once Siamese twins. The two stories were, after all, one, and the old book a living unity that could not be split without irreparable harm.

Yet *Pudd'nhead Wilson* is, after all, a fantastically good book, better than Mark Twain knew or his critics have deserved. Morally, it is one of the most honest books in our literature, superior in this one respect to *Huckleberry Finn*; for here Twain permits himself no sentimental relenting, but accepts for once the logic of his own premises. The immoral device of Tom's revelation, the fake "happy ending" of *Huck* are avoided in *Pudd'nhead*. It is a book which deals not only with the public issue of slavery, after all, long resolved—but with the still risky private matter of miscegenation, which most of our writers have chosen to avoid; and it creates in Roxy, the scared mulatto mother sold down the river by the son she has smuggled into white respectability, a creature of passion and despair rare among the wooden images of virtue or bitchery that pass for females in American literature. It is a portrait so complex and unforeseen that the baffled illustrator for the authorized standard edition chose to ignore it completely, drawing in the place of a "majestic . . . rosy . . . comely" Roxana—a gross and comic Aunt Jemima.

The scenes between this mother and her unregenerate son, who passes from insolence and cowardice to robbery and murder, and who ends slobbering at the feet of the woman he despises and plots to sell, have the cruelty and magnificence attained only by a great writer telling us a truth we cannot afford to face in a language we cannot afford to forget. It is a book which will be, I am sure, more and more read; certainly it is hard to believe that so rare a combination of wit and the metaphysical shudder will be considered forever of the second rank. Beside this book, *The Mysterious Stranger*, for the last several years a favorite of the writers on Twain, is revealed as the callow and contrived piece of cynicism it is: the best a cultureless man can do when he chooses to "philosophize" rather than dream.

Perhaps the best way to understand *Pudd'nhead* is to read it as a complement to *Huckleberry Finn*, a dark mirror image of the world evoked in the earlier work. Nearly ten years come between the two books, ten years in which guilt and terror had passed from the periphery of Twain's life and imagination to their center. *Huckleberry Finn* also is steeped in horror, to be sure; but it is easier to know this than to feel it. Though the main fable of the earlier book begins with a boy standing off with a rifle, his father gone berserk with the D.T.'s and ends with the revelation of that father's death in a seedy and flooded room scrawled with obscenities, it has so poetic a texture, so genuine though unmotivated a tone of joy—that one finds himself eternally doubting his own sense of its terrible import. In *Pudd'nhead*, however, the lyricism and the euphoria are gone; we have fallen to a world of prose, and there are no triumphs of Twain's rhetoric to preserve us from the revealed failures of our own humanity.

True enough, there is humor in the later book, but on a level of grotesquerie that is more violent and appalling than anything avowedly serious. It is the humor of Dickens' Quilp and Faulkner's idiot Snopes, the humor of the freak. In the chamber of horrors of our recent fiction, the deformed and dwarfed and dumb have come to stand as symbols of our common plight, the failure of everyone to attain a purely fictional norm. Toward this insight, Twain was fumbling almost without awareness, believing all along that he was merely trying to take the curse off of a bitterness he could not utterly repress by being what he liked to think was "funny."

Just as the grotesque in *Pudd'nhead* tends to break free from the humorous, so the tragic struggles to shed the nostalgic which swathes it still in *Huckleberry Finn*. In the earlier book, it is possible to believe that the flight toward freedom and childhood is more than a flight toward isolation and death. There is always waiting in a bend of the river Aunt Sally's homestead: a utopia of childhood visits and Southern homecooking. But Huck rejected this nostalgic Southland at the end of his own book, and in *Tom Sawyer, Detective*, Twain had introduced death and the threat of madness into that Eden itself.

By the time he was attempting to detach *Pudd'nhead* from the wreck of his larger book, Twain had decided that the only unthreatened utopia is death itself; and amid the animal jokes and easy cynicism of the Calendar quotations set at the head of each chapter, rings the sybil's cry: *Let me die*: "Whoever has lived long enough to know what life is knows how deep a debt of gratitude we owe to Adam, the first great benefactor of our race. He brought death into the world." When he writes this, Twain no longer finds in freedom the pat happy ending waiting to extricate his characters from their moral dilemmas and himself from the difficulties of plotting. He does not abandon the theme of liberty, but renders now the full treacherous paradox, only half of which he had acknowledged earlier.

Everyone remembers the climax of *Huckleberry Finn*, at which Tom, "his eye hot, and his nostrils opening and shutting like gills," cries out of Jim: "They hain't no *right* to shut him up. . . . Turn him loose! He ain't no slave; he's as free as any cretur that walks this earth!" As free as any cretur . . . the wry joke is there already, but Twain can no more see it than can Tom; and we are not permitted to see it as readers as long as we remain within the spell of the book. But in *Pudd'nhead Wilson*, the protagonist, who is obviously Tom himself grown older and an outcast but about to be reinstated into the community, rises to answer his own earlier cry, in such a situation as he has always dreamed: "Valet de Chambre, Negro and slave . . . make upon the window the finger-prints that will hang you!" The double truth is complete: the seeming slave is free, but the free man is really a slave.

The resolution of *Pudd'nhead* is, of course, double; and the revelation which brands the presumed Thomas à Becket Driscoll a slave, declares the presumed Valet de Chambre free. We are intended, however, to feel the "curious fate" of the latter as anything but fortunate; neither black nor white, he is excluded by long conditioning from the world of the free, and barred from the "solacing refuge" of the slave kitchens by the fact of his legal whiteness. Really, his is, as Twain himself remarks, quite another story; what is symbolically important is the deposition of Thomas à Becket—and the meaning of this Twain makes explicit in one of the final jottings in his journal, "The skin of every human being contains a slave." We know at last in what bitter sense Tom's earlier boast is true: "As free as any cretur . . ." *Pudd'nhead Wilson* begins and ends in the village where *Huckleberry Finn* began and *Tom Sawyer* was played out, on the banks of the same river and in the same pre-Civil War years. But between "St. Petersburg" and "Dawson's Landing" there is a terrible difference. In the latest book, we see Twain's mythicized Hannibal for the first time from the *outside*; in the two earlier books, we are already inside of it when the action begins, and there is no opportunity to step back and survey it. But Pudd'nhead comes as a stranger to the place of Twain's belonging; and the author himself takes advantage of this occasion to pan slowly into it, giving us an at first misleadingly idyllic description of its rose-clad houses, its cats, its sleepiness, and its fragrance—all preparing for the offhand give-away of the sentence beginning, "Dawson's Landing was a slaveholding town . . ."

The Civil War is the watershed in Twain's life between innocence and experience, childhood and manhood, joy and pain; but it is politically, of course, the dividing line between slavery and freedom. And Twain, who cannot deny either aspect, endures the contradiction of searching for a lost happiness he knows was sustained by an institution he is forced to recognize as his country's greatest shame. It was the best he could dream: to be free as a boy in a world of slavery!

In *Tom Sawyer*, this contradiction is hushed up for the sake of nostalgia and in the name of writing a child's book; in *Huck* it is preserved with all the power of its tensions; in the last book it falls apart into horror. In *Pudd'nhead Wilson*, Hannibal is felt from the beginning not as a Western but as a *Southern* town. The river is no longer presented as the defining edge of the natural world, what America touches and crosses on its way West; but as a passageway into the darkness of the deep South. "Down the river" is the phrase which gives a kind of musical unity to the work—a motif repeated with variations from Roxana's first jesting taunt to a fellow Negro, "If you b'longed to me I'd sell you down the river 'fo' you git too fur gone . . ." to the bleak irony of the novel's final sentence, "the Governor . . . pardoned Tom at once, and the creditors sold him down the river."

A comparison inevitably suggests itself with *Huckleberry Finn* in which the southward motion had served to symbolize (in contempt of fact) a motion toward deliverance. But here the direction of the river that Twain loved is felt only as the way into the ultimate south, the final horror—the absolute pole of slavery. The movement of the plot and the shape of the book are determined by this symbolic motion toward the sea, now transposed from a dream of flight to a nightmare of captivity. It is after she herself has been threatened with such a fate and in order to preserve her son from it, that Roxy switches the children in the cradle. But there is no way to escape that drift downward toward darkness to which the accident of birth has doomed her and her son; by virtue of her very act of evasion she sets in motion the events that bring both of them to the end she had dreaded.

It is not only as a slave-holding town that Dawson's Landing belongs to the South, but also in terms of the code of honor to which everyone in the book subscribes. Patrician and Negro, American and foreigner, freethinker and churchgoer, all accept the notion that an insult can only be wiped out in blood, and that the ultimate proof of manhood is the willingness to risk death in such an attempt. The real demonstration of the unworthiness of the false Tom is his running to the courts for redress in preference to facing a duel. Ironically enough, this very duel was to have been in the book as originally planned a howling travesty of the values of the gentleman; for one of the parties was to have been half of a Siamese twin—and one can see what mad complications would have ensued. The "serious" Twain was, however, as incapable of doubting the code as Tom Sawyer; he could mock it only in pure farce, when he felt it perfectly clear to everyone that he was just kidding. There is in this book no Huck to challenge the many Colonel Sherburnes by rejecting courage as just another temptation—no absolute outcast, armed only with lies, to make it clear that honor is a luxury item for a leisure class. Even Pudd'nhead, for all his skepticism, longs not for bare survival but for style and success—and so he must pay his Tom Sawyerish respects to chivalry.

In *Huckleberry Finn*, the society which Huck finally rejects, his "sivilization," is essentially a world of the mothers, that is to say, of what Christianity has become among the females who sustain it just behind the advancing frontier. It is a sufficiently simple-minded world in which one does not cuss or steal or smoke but keeps clean, wears shoes, and prays for spiritual gifts. Above all, it is a world of those who cannot lie—and the truth, too, Huck finds a virtue beyond his budget. In this world, the fathers appear generally as outcasts and scoundrels, like the Duke and Dauphin and like Pap himself. At best, the paternal is represented by the runaway nigger, the outcast who was never even offered the bait of belonging.

In *Pudd'nhead Wilson*, however, society is defined by the fathers, last defenders of the chivalric code and descendants of the cavaliers. Four in especial represent the world to which Pudd'nhead aspires: York Leicester Driscoll, Percy Northumberland Driscoll, Pembroke Howard and Col. Cecil Burleigh Essex—the names make the point with an insistence that is a little annoying. This is a world continuous with that of Renaissance gallantry, connected with the Court of Elizabeth, which represents for Twain on the one hand a romantic legend, and on the other a kind of lost sexual Eden (celebrated in his privately circulated 1601), whose potency puts to shame a fallen America where the natives "do it onlie once every seven yeares." The religion of such a society is, of course, not Christian at all; of Driscoll, the noble character murdered by the boy to whom he was a benefactor and almost a father, we are told "to be a gentleman was his only religion."

One half of the story of Thomas à Becket Driscoll (really the slave Valet de Chambre) is the account of his failing this world of the fathers, first in gambling and thieving, then in preferring the courts to the field of honor, finally in becoming out of greed and abject rage, a quasi-parricide. Twain spares us, perhaps from some reluctance to surrender to utter melodrama, more probably from lack of nerve, the final horror. The logic of the plot and its symbolic import both demand really that Tom be revealed at last as the bastard of the man he killed; but we are provided instead with a specially invented double of the dead Driscoll as the boy's begetter, a lay figure called Cecil Burleigh Essex.

In all of the book, only a single mother is allowed the center of the stage—the true mother of the false Tom, the slave girl Roxana. Just as in *Huckleberry Finn*, Nigger Jim is played off against the world of Aunt Polly-Aunt Sally-Miss Watson, so in this reversed version a Negress is set against the society defined by Driscoll, Howard, and Essex. This is, of course, a just enough stroke, which satisfies our sense of the historical as well as our desire for the typical. If the fathers of the South are Virginia gentlemen, the mothers are the Negro girls, casually or callously taken in the parody of love, which is all that is possible when one partner to a sexual union is not even given the status of a person.

The second and infinitely worse crime of Tom is the sin against the mother, the black mammy who threatens him with exposure; and the most moving, the most realized sections of the book deal with this relationship. Throughout his career, Twain returned over and over to this theme of the rejection of the mother, the denial by the boy of the woman who has loved him with the purest love Twain could imagine. Of this Tom Sawyer is falsely accused by his Aunt Polly; of this Tom Canty is actually guilty at the tearful climax of *The Prince and the Pauper*, so extravagantly admired by its author. It is as if Mark Twain were trying to exorcise the possibility of himself failing the plea he could never forget, the cry of his own mother, clasping him to her over the death-bed of his father: "Only promise me to be a better boy. Promise me not to break my heart."

In *Pudd'nhead*, this tearful romance of the boy as a heartless jilt, becomes involved with the ambiguous relations of black and white in the United States, with the problems of miscegenation and of "passing," and is lifted out of the sentimental toward the tragic. Twain's own judgment of sexual relations between the races is not explicitly stated; but there seems no doubt that he thought of the union between Roxy and Essex as a kind of fall—evil in itself and the source of a doom on all involved. Paired together, *Huck* and *Pudd'nhead* express both sides of a deep, unthought-out American belief, reflected on the one side of Twain by James Fenimore Cooper and on the other by William Faulkner: that there are two relations, two kinds of love between colored and white, one of which is innocent, one guilty, one of which saves, one damns. The innocent relation can only exist between men, or a man and a boy (Natty Bumppo and Chingachgook, Huck and Jim)—a love unphysical and pure; the other, suspect and impure, tries to join the disjoined in passion, and must end either in frustration and death (Cora and Uncas) or in unhappiness for all (Roxana and Essex).

A further reach of complexity is added to the theme by the symbolic meanings inevitably associated with the colors white and black, meanings which go back through literature (Shakespeare's "Dark Lady," for example) and popular religion (the New England habit of calling the Devil "The Black Man") to the last depths of the folk mind. No matter how enlightened our conscious and rational convictions may be in these matters, we are beset by a buried ambivalence based on this archetypal symbolism of light and dark. Twain himself in this very novel speaks unguardedly of the rain trying vainly to wash soot-blackened St. Louis white; and the implication is clear: black is the outward sign of inward evil. In this sense, the Negro puzzlingly wears the livery of the guilt we had thought the white man's. But *why?* It is a question which rings through the white man's literature in America; and the answer returns in an ambiguity endlessly compounded.

Who, having read it once, can ever forget the terrible exclamation in Melville's "Benito Cereno"—the cry which seems intended to dissolve in irony the problem we had hoped would be resolved in certainty, "It is the Black!" But there are even more terrible lines in *Pudd'nhead*: the lonely and baffled query of Tom (how hard it is to believe that it is not a quotation from Faulkner), "What crime did the uncreated first nigger commit that the curse of birth was decreed for him . . ." and the still more appalling response of Roxy to the news that her son has failed the white man's code, "It's de nigger in you dat's what it is!" The name of their own lot turned insult in the mouth of the offended—beyond this it is impossible to go; and we cannot even doubt that this is precisely what Roxy would have said!

Perhaps the supreme achievement of this book is to have rendered such indignities not in terms of melodrama or as a parochial "social problem" but as a local instance of some universal guilt and doom. The false Tom, who is the fruit of all the betrayal and terror and profaned love which lies between white man and black, embodies also its "dark necessity"—and must lie, steal, kill, and boast until in his hybris he reveals himself as the slave we all secretly are. This tragic inevitability is, however, blurred by the demands of the detective story with which it is crossed. The tragedy of Tom requires that he expose and destroy himself; the melodrama of Pudd'nhead Wilson requires that he reveal and bring to justice the Negro who has passed as white; and Twain decided finally that it was Pudd'nhead's book—a success story. Yet there remains beneath the assertion that a man is master of his fate, the melancholy conviction that to be born is to be doomed, a kind of secularized Calvinism.

We have already noticed that Pudd'nhead is Tom Sawyer grown up, the man who has not surrendered with maturity the dream of being a hero; but it must be added that he wants to be a hero on his own terms, to force himself upon a hostile community without knuckling under to its values; that is to say, he would like still to be as an adult the "good bad boy" who put the finger on Indian Joe. Translated out of the vocabulary of boyhood, this means that he has to become first a rebel and then a detective.

He begins as a pariah, the sage whose wisdom is taken for folly: an outsider in a closed society, a free thinker in a world of conformism, a gadgeteer and crank, playing with palmistry and fingerprints. But he is also, like his creator, a jokester; and, indeed, it is his first quip which earns him a reputation for stupidity and twenty years of exclusion. "I wish I owned half of that dog," he says of a viciously howling beast, "because I would kill my half"—and that is almost the end of him. Yet like his creator he wants to succeed in the world he despises; and he yields to it half-unwittingly even before it accepts him, adjusting to its code of honor, its definition of a Negro—while writing down in private or reading before a two man Free Thinkers' Society his dangerous thoughts.

Typically enough, it is as a detective that he makes his comeback. In three earlier books his prototype, Tom Sawyer, had achieved similar triumphs: exposing Injun Joe, revealing Jim's true status, clearing his half-crazed uncle of the charge of murder; but more is involved than this. Ever since Poe's Dupin, the sleuth has been a favorite guise of the writer in fiction—non-conformist and exposer of evil, the poor man's intellectual. He is the one who, revealing in the moment of crisis "who done it," restores the community (as W. H. Auden has suggested in an acute study of the detective story) to a state of grace.

But Twain has the faith neither of a Chesterton nor a Conan Doyle; and the revelations of David Wilson (the name "Pudd'nhead" is sloughed off with his victory) restore civil peace only between him and the community which rejected him: for the rest, they expose only bankruptcy and horror and shame, and stupidity of our definition of a Negro, and the hopelessness of our relations with him. Wilson's disclosure of Roxy's hoax coalesces with Twain's exposure to America of its own secret self; and the double discovery is aptly framed by Wilson's Calendar entries for two of our favorite holidays.

The chapter which contains the courtroom revelation is preceded by the text, "*April 1*. This is the day upon which we are reminded of what we are on the other three hundred and sixty-four." The implication is clear, whether conscious or not, not fools only but slaves! And it is followed by another, even grimmer, "*October 12, the Discovery*. It was wonderful to find America, but it would have been more wonderful to miss it." The Discovery! It is a disconcerting ending for a detective story, which should have faith in all disclosures; but it is the aptest of endings for an American book, the only last word possible to a member of the Free Thinkers' Society. Beyond such bleak wisdom, there is only the cry of Roxy at the moment of revelation, "De Lord have mercy on me, po' misable sinner dat I is!" But this is forbidden to Mark Twain.

F. R. LEAVIS

Mark Twain's Neglected Classic: The Moral Astringency of *Pudd'nhead Wilson*†

Pudd'nhead Wilson is not faultless—no book of Mark Twain's is that—but it is all the same the masterly work of a great writer. Yet it is very little known. One cannot easily find anyone, English or American, who has read it (at least that is my experience), and it would seem never at any time to have had the beginnings of the recognition that is its due. Its reputation—if it may be said to have a reputation—would not encourage a strenuous search for a copy of the book, unless in an admirer of *Huckleberry Finn* who was curious to look over one of the author's ephemeral productions, one that also dealt in its way with life in Hannibal, Missouri, the village of Mark Twain's childhood.

The explanation, I think, is partly that *Pudd'nhead Wilson* is so very unlike *Huckleberry Finn*. But it is also, I think, that the nature of the greatness of *Huckleberry Finn* itself tends not to be fully recognized. There are, then, two reasons for hoping that *Pudd'nhead Wilson* may come to be appreciated as it deserves: it is a classic in its own right (if an unrecognized classic may be said to *be* one); and, further, for all the unlikeness, it bears a very close relation to *Huckleberry Finn*; a relation of such a kind that to appreciate the lesser work is to have a surer perception of the greatness of the greater.

Huckleberry Finn, by general agreement Mark Twain's greatest work, is supremely the American classic, and it is one of the great

† From *Commentary*, 21 (February 1956), 128–136.

books of the world. The significance of such a work doesn't admit of exhaustive recognition in a simple formula, or in several. Mark Twain himself was no simple being, and the complexity of his make-up was ordinarily manifested in strains, disharmonies, and tormenting failures of integration and self-knowledge. These, in his supreme masterpiece, can be seen to provide the creative drive. There is of course the aspect of return to boyhood, but the relation to complexity and strain represented by *Huckleberry Finn* is not one of escape from them—in spite of the qualities that have established the book as a classic for children (and in spite of Mark Twain's conviction, at times, that its appeal should be as such). It is true that the whole is given through Huck, the embodiment of that Western vernacular, or of the style created out of that, in which the book is written. But that style, perfectly as it renders the illiterate Huck, has been created by a highly sophisticated art to serve subtle purposes, and Huck himself is of course not merely the naive boyish consciousness he so successfully enacts; he is, by one of those triumphant sleights or equivocations which cannot be judiciously contrived, but are proof of inspired creative possession, the voice of deeply reflective maturity—of a life's experience brooded on by an earnest spirit and a fine intelligence. If Mark Twain lacked art in Arnold Bennett's sense (as Arnold Bennett pointed out), that only shows how little art in Arnold Bennett's sense matters, in comparison with art that is the answer of creative genius to the pressure of a profoundly felt and complex experience. If *Huckleberry Finn* has its examples of the unintelligence that may accompany the absence of sustained critical consciousness in an artist, even a great one, nevertheless the essential intelligence that prevails, and from the poetic depths informs the work, compels our recognition—the intelligence of the whole engaged psyche; the intelligence that represents the integrity of this, and brings to bear the wholeness.

For in his supreme creation the complex and troubled Mark Twain did achieve a wholeness; it is manifested in the nature of the creative triumph. The charged significance of *Huckleberry Finn* brings together a strength of naivety and a strength of mature reflective wisdom. Let me quote, with immediate relevance, Mr. Bernard De Voto, most penetrating of the commentators on Mark Twain I am acquainted with: ". . . fundamentally Huck is an expression—a magnificent expression, a unique expression—of the folk mind. The folk mind, that is, in mid-America in the period of the frontier and immediately following, the folk mind shaped for use by the tremendous realities of conquering a hostile wilderness and yet shadowed by the unseen world. He is one of the highest reaches of American fiction.

"But if Huck expresses the folk mind, he is also Mark Twain's surrogate, he is charged with transmitting what that dark, sensitive, and complex consciousness felt about America and the human race. . . . Mark Twain was not a systematic thinker. Customarily, like the creature of fable who was his brother Orion, he held in succession all possible opinions about every subject he tried to analyze, held none of them long, and was able to drive none very deep beneath the surface. Especially as a metaphysician he was as feeble a novice as ever ventured into that stormy sea. But in what he perceived, in what he felt, in the nerve-ends of emotion, in the mysterious ferments of art which transform experience, he was a great mind— there has been no greater in American literature. Be it said once more and ever so wearily: insufficiencies and mental defects prevented him from ever completely implementing the artist throughout the whole course of a book. That does not matter—in *Huckleberry Finn* we get the finest expression of a great artist, the fullest report on what life meant to him."[1]

When Mr. De Voto speaks of the "folk mind" in *Huckleberry Finn* he is making a plainly valid observation; an observation duly offset, as the quoted passage shows, by the recognition of quite other aspects of the book. But insistence on the "folk" element sometimes goes with an attempt to make *Huckleberry Finn* American in a sense that would make it an immeasurably lesser thing than the great work it is. Mr. Van Wyck Brooks, in *The Times of Melville and Whitman*, writes: "He was the frontier storyteller, the great folk writer of the American West, and raised to a pitch unparalleled before him the art of oral story-telling and then succeeded in transferring its effects to paper." Such an account (and there is a formidable representative intention behind it) serves as a license for insisting on the force of the reply—the obvious and unanswerable reply: Mark Twain was something very much more than a folkwriter, and the art of *Huckleberry Finn* is no mere matter of managing effects—suspense, surprise, climax, and so on. One cannot intelligently discuss the art without discussing the complex and reverse of naive outlook it conveys. Mr. Brooks, recognizing, as any reader must, an insistent moral preoccupation in the theme, quotes Paine, Mark Twain's biographer: ". . . the author makes Huck's struggle a psychological one between conscience and the law on one side, and sympathy on the other." But there is more to the moral theme of *Huckleberry Finn* than that suggests. What the book conveys is the drama in a mind in which conscience finds that it is not single, and that the "law" doesn't speak with one voice, and that what Paine calls "sympathy" itself engages a moral imperative. In fact, *Huckleberry Finn* has as a central theme the complexity of

1. From *Mark Twain at Work*.

ethical valuation in a society with a complex tradition—a description that applies (for instance) to any "Christian" society.

The book is a profound study of civilized man. And about its attitude towards civilization as represented by the society depicted in it there is nothing simple or simplifying, either in a "frontier" spirit or in a spirit of reductive pessimism. It is not to the point to adduce such private utterances of Mark Twain's as: "We have no real morals, but only artificial ones—morals created and preserved by the forced suppression of natural and healthy instinct." "Never trust the artist; trust the tale": Lawrence's dictum might have been addressed to Mark Twain's case. *Huckleberry Finn*, the tale, gives us a wholeness of attitude that transcends anything ordinarily attainable by the author. The liberation effected by the memories of youth and the Mississippi was, for the creative genius at his greatest, not into irresponsibility but the reverse. The imaginatively recovered vitality of youth ministered, in sum, no more to the spirit of "Pudd'nhead Wilson's Calendar" than to nostalgia or daydream, but to the attainment of a sure and profound moral maturity. That is, to call *Huckleberry Finn* a great work is not an exaggeration.

I insist in this way because of a tendency in America (and transatlantic fashions regarding American literature tend to be taken over uncritically in England) to suggest that the beginnings of the truly American in literary tradition come from the frontier and the West. According to this view Mark Twain is a more truly American writer than Hawthorne or Henry James. It is a view that, in offering to exalt him, actually denies his greatness, for it makes the attributed advantage in Americanness a matter of his being alienated from English and European tradition as Hawthorne and James are not. Such an alienation could only be an impoverishment: no serious attempt has been made to show that any sequel to disinheritance could replace the heritage lost. Mark Twain is indeed "frontier" and Western, but in being greatly American he bears as close and essential a relation to England and Europe as that which we recognize in Hawthorne or in James (in some ways he strikes an English reader as being less foreign, less positively un-English, than either of them). The Americanness of alienation may be represented by Dreiser, Scott Fitzgerald, and Hemingway: the author of *Huckleberry Finn*, when we think of those writers, seems to belong to another world. Nor as we read the book are we prompted to reflect that he is a fellow countryman of Walt Whitman.

It is not my business here to enforce these observations in a detailed analysis of *Huckleberry Finn*, but, with them in view, to suggest how that book is related to *Pudd'nhead Wilson*, which, different as it is (it makes no show of frontier naivety, but belongs frankly to sophisticated literary tradition), is nevertheless unmistakably by the same hand, develops the same preoccupations and expresses the same moral outlook. With the oral tradition of story-telling, the potent element of recovered boyhood that has so recommended *Huckleberry Finn* is absent too. But the Mississippi *is* there in *Pudd'nhead Wilson*, and its evoked presence occasions a significant expansion:

> The hamlet's front was washed by the clear waters of the great river; its body stretched itself rearward up a gentle incline; its most rearward border fringed itself out and scattered its houses about the base-line of the hills; the hills rose high, inclosing the town in a half-moon curve clothed with forests from foot to summit.
>
> Steamboats passed up and down every hour or so. Those belonging to the little Cairo line and the little Memphis line always stopped; the big Orleans liners stopped for hails only, or to land passengers or freight; and this was the case also with the great flotilla of 'transients.' These latter came out of a dozen rivers—the Illinois, the Missouri, the Upper Mississippi, the Ohio, the Monongahela, the Tennessee, the Red River, the White River, and so on; and were bound every whither and stocked with every imaginable comfort or necessity which the Mississippi's communities could want. . . .

Here, quite plainly, speaks a proud imaginative delight in the memory of the great river; the great river as Mark Twain had known it in boyhood and in his piloting days; and in the memory, or vision, we feel the sense of freedom, beauty, and majesty that informs *Huckleberry Finn*; but there is something further: the passage unmistakably conveys the sense, sanguine and exalted, of an expanding and ripening civilization.

Mark Twain, we are told, was brought up in a frontier society. "Think," it has been written, "of the squalor of those villages, their moral and material squalor, their dim and bounded horizon, their petty taboos: repression at one extreme, eruption at the other, and shiftlessness for a golden mean." But what *Pudd'nhead Wilson* should make us recognize is that "frontier" is an insidious term. It suggests cultural deprivation and loss—a dropping of the heritage in the battle with pioneer hardship. And no doubt it could be argued that the account just quoted fairly describes Dawson's Landing; or that so we should have agreed if we had had to live there. But as a matter of fact this is not the tone, this is not how the stress falls, in *Pudd'nhead Wilson*. After the evocation of the river we read:

> The town was sleepy and comfortable and contented. It was fifty years old, and was growing slowly—very slowly in fact, but still it was growing.

It may have been sleepy, but what Mark Twain conveys with great power is an effect quite other than one of rawness and squalor:

> In 1830 it was a snug little collection of modest one- and two-storey frame dwellings whose white-washed exteriors were almost concealed from sight by climbing tangles of rose-vines, honey-suckles, and morning-glories. Each of these pretty homes had a garden in front, fenced with white palings and opulently stocked with hollyhocks, marigolds, touch-me-nots, prince's feathers and other old-fashioned flowers; while on the window-sills of the houses stood wooden boxes containing moss-rose plants and terra-cotta pots in which grew a breed of geraniums whose spread of intensely red blossoms accented the prevailing pink tint of the rose-clad house-front like an explosion of flame. When there was room on the ledge outside of the pots and boxes for a cat, the cat was there—in sunny weather—stretched at full length, asleep and blissful, with her furry belly to the sun and a paw curved over her nose. Then that house was complete, and its contentment and peace were made manifest to the world by this symbol, whose testimony is infallible. A home without a cat—and a well-fed, well-petted, and properly revered cat—may be a perfect home, perhaps, but how can it prove title?
> All along the streets, on both sides, at the outer edge of the brick sidewalks, stood locust-trees with trunks protected by wooden boxing, and these furnished shade for summer and a sweet fragrance in spring when the clusters of buds came forth.

The comfort, well-being, and amenity evoked here have more than a material significance; they are the outward signs of an inward grace. Provincial as Dawson's Landing may be, it represents a society that has kept its full heritage of civilization. True, it *is* provincial, and Wilson's fate—the "Pudd'nhhead" and the long failure to make way against that estimate—figures for us its attitude towards originality of mind. Moreover an English reader gets what are for him (the human world presented being so essentially unforeign) startling glimpses of mob lawlessness as an accepted social institution. Yet the effect of the opening description of Dawson's Landing remains: this is a civilized community—one qualified to have exacted a very much more favorable report than any brought back by Martin Chuzzlewit.

And further, it is not unaware of its provinciality, and is far from having lost the desire to keep in touch with the remoter centers of its civilization and with its past. This comes out notably in its reception of the twins, the presentment of which illustrates the complex poise of Mark Twain's attitude. The comedy of the reception is not satiric. Dawson's Landing displays, not merely its crudenesses and limitations, but also a touching positive humility, a will to pay homage to something other than provinciality and philistinism and the standards of everyday life. The exhibition of democratic *mœurs* at Aunt Patsy's is finely and subtly done, and quite clear in its significance. These democrats, without being in the least inclined to go back on their democracy, respond imaginatively to their traditional memories and to the sense of ideal values belonging to a richer life that is now remote from them. It is an utterly different thing from snobbery, and, as Mark Twain presents it, something that the social crudity of the occasion sets off as the reverse of trivial or crude:

> None of these visitors was at ease, but, being honest people, they didn't pretend to be. None of them had ever seen a person bearing a title of nobility before, and none had been expecting to see one now, consequently the title came upon them as a kind of pile-driving surprise, and caught them unprepared. A few tried to rise to the emergency, and got out an awkward 'My lord,' or 'Your lordship,' or something of that sort, but the great majority were overwhelmed by the unaccustomed word and its dim and awful associations with gilded courts and stately ceremony and anointed kingship, so they only fumbled through the handshake and passed on, speechless.

Then, significantly, this homage to a glimpsed ideal superiority is followed by the homage to art:

> Here a prodigious slam-banging broke out below, and everybody rushed down to see. It was the twins knocking out a classic four-handed piece on the piano in great style. Rowena was satisfied—satisfied down to the bottom of her heart.
>
> The young strangers were kept long at the piano. The villagers were astonished and enchanted with the magnificence of their performance, and could not bear to have them stop. All the music that they had ever heard before seemed spiritless prenticework and barren of grace or charm when compared with these intoxicating floods of melodious sound. They realized that for once in their lives they were hearing masters.

The poise is beautifully maintained; those first two sentences serve only to enforce the serious and profound significance of the last, the closing one of the chapter.

In its whole attitude towards distinction that appeals to standards other than the "democratic," Dawson's Landing represents a subtler civilization than accounts of "the pioneer community" might suggest. Consider, for instance, the special license accorded Judge Driscoll in an environment that doesn't encourage moral independence or free play of mind. "Judge Driscoll," says Mark Twain, "could be a freethinker and still hold his place in society because he was the person of most consequence in the community, and therefore could go on his own way and follow out his own notions." But York Leicester Driscoll isn't represented as having achieved his leading place by preeminence in the qualities that one would have expected to tell most among pioneering democrats. We are told of him:

> He was very proud of his old Virginian ancestry, and in his hospitalities and his rather formal and stately manners he kept up the tradition. He was fine and just and generous. To be a gentleman—a gentleman without stain or blemish—was his only religion, and to it he was always faithful. He was respected, esteemed, and beloved by all the community.

It is quite unequivocal: he is "respected, esteemed and beloved" (a set of terms that defines something quite different from the attitudes towards the smart and therefore successful man) because he is a "gentleman," representing as such an ideal that doesn't belong to the realm of material "success" and is above the attainment of the ordinary member of the community. And we come here to that complexity of ethical background which I have spoken of as providing a central preoccupation of Mark Twain's, in *Pudd'nhead Wilson* as in *Huckleberry Finn*. I am not thinking merely of the persistence of an aristocratic tradition in a democratic society. That society has also its Christian allegiance, and, while the Judge is "just and generous," the total concept of "gentleman" is decidedly not Christian. When we come to Pembroke Howard, for whom to be a gentleman is *not* his only religion, the situation, with its irony, is focused in the one actor:

> He was a fine, brave, majestic creature, a gentleman according to the nicest requirements of the Virginian rule, a devoted Presbyterian, an authority on the 'code,' and a man always courteously ready to stand up before you in the field if any act or word of his had seemed doubtful or suspicious to you, and explain it with any weapons you might prefer from bradawls to artillery. He was very popular with the people, and was the Judge's dearest friend.

For the gentleman, "honor stood first": the laws of honor "required certain things of him which his religion might forbid him: then his religion must yield—the laws could not be relaxed to accommodate religion or anything else." And the Christian and democratic community, with a complete and exalted conviction, gave its approval.

> The people took more pride in the duel than in all the other events put together, perhaps. It was a glory to the town to have such a thing happen there. In their eyes, the principals had reached the summit of human honor.

There is nothing remarkable about the ability to observe such facts. What is remarkable is the subtlety of the appraising attitude that Mark Twain, in terms of impersonal art, defines towards them —as towards the whole inclusive situation presented in the book. Astringent as is the irony of *Pudd'nhead Wilson*, the attitude here has nothing of the satiric in it (the distinctively satiric plays no great part in the work as a whole). Mark Twain unmistakaly admires Judge Driscoll and Pembroke Howard. And it is important to note that, if they are "fine," the "fineness" is not a mere matter of their being "just and generous." The total attitude where they are concerned is not altogether easy to describe, not because it is equivocal, but because it is not a simple one, and has called for some subtlety of dramatic means to convey it. The two most sympathetic characters in the drama give the "code" itself their active endorsement. It is not for instance suggested that Wilson, in acting as second in the duel, does so with any self-dissociating reservations or reluctance, and he rebukes Tom for not telling his uncle about the kicking and "letting him have a gentleman's choice": "if I had known the circumstances," he says, "I would have kept the case out of court until I got word to him and let him have a gentleman's chance."

"You would?" exclaimed Tom, with lively surprise. "And it your first case! And you know perfectly well there would never have *been* any case if he had got that chance, don't you? And you'd have finished your days a pauper nobody, instead of being an actually launched and recognized lawyer to-day. And you would really have done that, would you?"

"Certainly."

Tom looked at him a moment or two, then shook his head sorrowfully and said:

"I believe you—upon my word I do. I don't know why I do, but I do. Pudd'nhead Wilson, I think you're the biggest fool I ever saw."

This reminder of the circumstances of the rebuke will serve to enforce the point that Wilson, the poised and preeminently civilized moral center of the drama, whom we take to be very close in point of view to Mark Twain, is not, all the same, to be identified with him. Wilson *is* an actor in a dramatic whole that conveys its significances dramatically. The upshot of the drama is to set a high value on the human qualities fostered by the aristocratic code: to endorse the code even as far as Wilson does would be quite a different matter, and no reader of the book can suppose it to be doing that. Against the pride and the allegiance to an ideal of conduct that make personal safety a matter of comparative indifference, we see the ignominy and ugliness of Tom's complete self-centeredness, which is as unchecked by pride or concern for any ideal as by imaginative sympathy. Hearing that the Judge, fighting in *his* cause, has survived the duel, he reflects immediately, with an exasperation untouched by shame, how blessedly all problems would have been solved had the Judge been killed: the duel has been wasted.

The exposure of human nature in Tom Driscoll has an essential part in the total astringency of the book. But it will not do to suggest that human nature, as the book presents it, reduces to Tom. If the Wilson of "Pudd'nhead Wilson's Calendar"is not the Wilson of the drama, neither does he represent the imagination and the sensibility that inform this as a conceived and realized whole. Such utterances of Mark Twain's as this marginal note from a book, characteristic as they are, mustn't be credited with a kind of conclusive authority they certainly haven't:

> What a man sees in the human race is merely himself in the deep and honest privacy of his own heart. Byron despised the race because he despised himself. I feel as Byron did and for the same reason.

The exhibition of Tom's viciousness has its convincing force, no doubt, because *we* recognize in ourselves the potentiality, as Mark Twain did in *him*self. But it would be misleading to say that we despise Tom; that would be to suggest an animus that we do *not* feel when we place him, unequivocally, as contemptible: we are not engaged and involved in that way. The irony of the work as a whole means a very secure poise, and the poise is secure because the author has achieved a mature, balanced, and impersonal view of humanity. He himself is not involved in the personal way that involves animus in condemning.

The attitude of *Pudd'nhead Wilson* is remote from cynicism or pessimism. The book conveys neither contempt for human nature nor a rejection of civilization. It is concerned with the complexities of both human nature and civilization as represented in a historical community—for Dawson's Landing, it may reasonably be said, is one that, at a given time in actual American history, Mark Twain had intimately known.

We are not, by way of dismissing the suggestion of any general contempt, confined to adducing Wilson himself and the "fine, brave, majestic creatures" who uphold the code of the F.F.V. Most impressively, there is Roxy. It is true that her heroic maternal devotion plays against the extremity of mean heartless egotism given us in Tom. But her significance is not exhausted in that irony. We feel her dominating the book as a triumphant vindication of life. Without being in the least sentimentalized, or anything but dramatically right, she plainly bodies forth the qualities that Mark Twain, in his whole being, most values—qualities that, as Roxy bears witness, he profoundly believes in as observable in humanity, having known them in experience. Although born a slave, she is herself a "fine, brave, majestic creature," whose vitality expresses itself in pride, high-spiritedness, and masterful generosity. Her reckless presence at the duel defines Mark Twain's attitude towards the "code" more decisively than Wilson's participation does. When she proudly tells Tom that he is descended from the best blood of Virginia the effect, for all the irony, is not satiric. And her confident and justified reliance on the loyal comradeship, not only of her fellow-"niggers," but also of the officers of the *Grand Mogul*, has its part in the appraisal of human nature conveyed by the book as a whole.

Mr. De Voto makes the point that she represents a frank and unembarrassed recognition of the actuality of sex, with its place and power in human affairs, such as cannot be found elsewhere in Mark Twain. That seems to me true and important. It is an aspect of the general fact, that she is the presence in the book of a free and generous vitality, in which the warmly and physically human manifests itself also as intelligence and spiritual strength. It is this far-reaching associative way in which, so dominating a presence, she stands for—she *is*—triumphant life that gives the book, for all its astringency and for all the chilling irony of the close, its genial quality (to be both genial and astringent is its extraordinary distinction).

How far from satiric the spirit of *Pudd'nhead Wilson* is may be seen in the presentment of the subtleties of conscience and ethical sensibility in Roxy. Consider the episode of the stolen money and the threat to sell the Negro servants down the river. We are no doubt very close to the satiric note in the irony with which the chapter ends—in Percy Driscoll's self-gratulation on his magnanimity: "that night he set the incident down in his diary, so that his son might read it in after years and be thereby moved to deeds of gentleness and humanity himself." But we are remote from satire here:

> The truth was, all were guilty but Roxana; she suspected that the others were guilty, but she did not know them to be so. She was horrified to think how near she had come to being guilty herself; she had been saved in the nick of time by a revival in the colored Methodist Church, a fortnight before, at which time and place she had "got religion." The very next day after that gracious experience, while her change of style was fresh upon her and she was vain of her purified condition, her master left a couple of dollars lying unprotected on his desk, and she happened upon that temptation when she was polishing around with a dust-rag. She looked at the money awhile with a steadily rising resentment, and then she burst out with—"Dad blame dat revival, I wisht it had 'a be'n put off till to-morrow!"

Then she covered the tempter with a book, and another member of the kitchen cabinet got it. She made this sacrifice as a matter of religious etiquette; as a thing necessary just now, but by no means to be wrested into a precedent; no, a week or two would limber up her piety, then she would be rational again, and the next two dollars that got left out in the cold would find a comforter—and she could name the comforter.

Was she bad? Was she worse than the general run of her race? No. They had an unfair show in the battle of life. . . .

In spite of that last phrase, we know that what we have been contemplating is not just an exhibition of Negro traits: "her race" is the human race. These naive and subtle changes and adjustments of conscience and the moral sense we can parallel from our own inner experience. But there is nothing cynically reductive in Mark Twain's study of the moral nature of man; he shows the clairvoyance of a mind that is sane and poised, and the irony that attends the illustration of subtleties and complexities throws no doubt on the reality or the dignity or the effectiveness in human affairs of ethical sensibility.

I have not yet touched on the central irony of the book, the sustained and complex irony inherent in the plot. *Pudd'nhead Wilson* should be recognized as a classic of the use of popular modes—of the sensational and the melodramatic—for the purposes of significant art. The book, I have said, is not faultless, and an obvious criticism lies against the unfulfilled promise represented by the twins— the non-significant play made with them, their history and the sinister oriental dagger. Mark Twain, we can see, had intended to work out some interplay of the two parallel sets of complications: twins and interchanged babies. He abandoned the idea, but didn't trouble to eliminate that insistent focusing of expectation upon the twins. The fault is in a sense a large one, and yet it is not, after all, a very serious one: it doesn't affect the masterly handling of the possibilities actually developed.

The ironic subtleties that Mark Twain gets from the interchange of the babies in their cradles seem, as one ponders them, almost inexhaustible. There is the terrible difference, no more questioned by Roxy than by her master, between the "nigger" and the white. The conventionality of the distinction is figured by the actual whiteness of Roxy, whose one-sixteenth of Negro blood tells only in her speech (with which, indeed, it has no essential relation, as is illustrated later by the inability of "Valet de Chambers," now revealed as the pure-white heir, to shed the "nigger"-speech he learnt in childhood). So awful, ultimate and unchangeable is the distinction that Roxy, as, in order to save her child from the fate hanging over the slave (to be "sold down the river"), she changes the babies in their cradles, justifies herself by the example of God. The rendering is an irresistible manifestation of genius, utterly convincing, and done with a delicate subtlety of ironic significance:

> She flung herself on her bed and began to think and toss, toss and think. By-and-by she sat suddenly upright, for a comforting thought had flown through her worried mind:
>
> "Tain't no sin—*white* folks has done it! It ain't no sin, glory to goodness it ain't no sin! *Dey's* done it—yes, en dey was de biggest quality in de whole bilin', too—*kings!*"
>
> She began to muse; she was trying to gather out of her memory the dim particulars of some tale she had heard some time or other. At last she said:
>
> "Now I's got it; now I 'member. It was dat ole nigger preacher dat tole it, de time he come over here fum Illinois en preached in de nigger church. He said dey ain't nobody kin save his own self—can't do it by faith, can't do it by works, can't do it no way at all. Free grace is de *on'y* way, en dat don't come fum nobody but jis' de Lord; en *he* kin give it to anybody he please, saint or sinner—*he* don't kyer. He do jis' as he's a mineter. He s'lect out anybody dat suit him, en put another one in his place, en make de fust one happy for ever en leave t'other one to burn wid Satan."

There is of course a glance here at the Calvinism of Mark Twain's youth. And it is to be noted that Roxy, while usurping the prerogative of the predestinating Deity, has shown a wholly human compassion, and has invoked a compassionate God in doing so:

> "I's sorry for you, honey; I's sorry, God knows I is—but what *kin* I do, what *could* I do? Yo' pappy would sell him to somebody, some time, en den he'd go down de river, sho', and I couldn't, couldn't, *couldn't* stan' it."

In saving the child from the consequences of the awful distinction that she assumes to be in the nature of things, she demonstrates its lack of any ground but convention; she demonstrates the wholly common humanity of the "nigger" and the white. The father himself cannot detect the fraud: he cannot tell his own child from the other. And—one of the many ironies—it is his cruel, but confidently righteous, severity that imposes the full abjectiveness of slave mentality upon his own child, who becomes the defenseless and rightless servant of the slave's child. On the other hand, Roxy's success in saving Valet de Chambers (the name her proud tribute to an ideal "white" lordliness) from the fate of the slave erects a dreadful barrier between child and mother. Treated as "young Marse Tom," not only does he become that different order of being, the "master"; in Roxy herself the slave attitudes that she necessarily observes towards him find themselves before long attended by the appropriate awe. When at last, outraged by the humiliating and cruel rebuffs that meet her appeal for a little kindness (she is in need) to the old "nigger-mammy," she forgets habit and the ties of motherhood, and pants for revenge, she has to recognize that she has placed him in an impregnable position: no one will believe her tale. A further irony is that, if he has turned out bad, a portent of egocentric heartlessness, that is at least partly due to his spoiling as heir and young master, the lordly superior being.

It is a mark of the poised humanity characterizing the treatment of the themes of *Pudd'nhead Wilson* that, worthless and vicious as "Tom" is, when he has to face the sudden revelation that he is a Negro, we feel some compassion for him; we don't just applaud an irony of poetic justice when he is cornered into reflecting, with an echo of his mother's self-justifying recall of the Calvinistic God:

> "Why were niggers and whites made? What crime did the uncreated first nigger commit that the curse of birth was decreed for him? And why is this awful difference made between black and white?"

Compassion, of course, soon vanishes as the dialectic of utter selfishness unfolds in him. The developments of his incapacity for compassion are done with a convincingness that the creator of Tito Melema would have envied. When Roxy offers to be sold back into slavery in order to save "Tom" from being disinherited, and he, with dreadfully credible treachery, sells her "down the river," the opposite extremes of human nature are brought together in an effect that belongs wholly to the mode of *Pudd'nhead Wilson*, and is equally removed from melodrama and from cynicism. It can hardly be said, when we close the book, that the worst in human nature has not been confronted; yet the upshot of the whole is neither to judge mankind to be contemptible nor to condemn civilization. And it is remarkable how utterly free from animus that astringency is which takes on so intense a concentration in the close:

> Everybody granted that if "Tom" were white and free it would be unquestionably right to punish him—it would be no loss to anybody; but to shut up a valuable slave for life—that was quite another matter.
> As soon as the Governor understood the case, he pardoned Tom at once, and the creditors sold him down the river.

It is an irony of the tale that this, the fate to secure him against which Roxana had committed her crime, is, as an ultimate consequence of that crime, the fate he suffers.

RICHARD CHASE

[The Inadequacy of *Pudd'nhead Wilson*]†

* * *

Two recent essays on *Pudd'nhead Wilson*, one by F. R. Leavis and the other by Leslie Fiedler, make, in their different ways, strong cases for the book. And if neither essay seems quite restrained enough in its praise, they nevertheless make a valuable point of departure. Mr. Leavis, whose passion is generally for the moral quality of literature, is interested in "the complexity of ethical background" which he finds in *Pudd'nhead Wilson*. His essay is eloquent and in many ways exact, but his eloquence rides the impetus of his having discovered a complexity of ethical background to an overestimation of the book. It will probably be a long time before another critic calls Pudd'nhead "the poised and pre-eminently civilized moral center of the drama." This would seem to be high praise for a man who, though undeniably civilized, is only Tom Sawyer grown up and become a conventional and respected citizen of small-town America, after enduring a period of scorn while he was regarded as the village atheist and crank.

Fiedler speaks of *Pudd'nhead Wilson* as barely failing to be "the most extraordinary book in American literature." He sees in *Pudd'n-head Wilson* a book that might have been, but for Mark Twain's revisions, his technical botches, and his indecision about how to dramatize the ultimate ironies he had in mind, "a rollicking, atrocious melange of bad taste and half understood intentions and nearly intolerable insights into evil, translated into a nightmare worthy of America"—the language, obviously, of commendation. In contrast to Fiedler's view that Mark Twain's book lights up the most profound of American moral dilemmas, Mr. Leavis finds the book somehow "English," and oddly remarks (though only parenthetically) that Mark Twain, considered in relation to Hawthorne and James, "in some ways strikes an English reader as being less foreign, less positively un-English, than either of them." All the novels considered in the present study have in one way or another "complexity of ethical background." What is unusual, however, and what interests Leavis, as it must interest us, is that in *Pudd'nhead Wilson* the ethical background is brought into the foreground—that is, it is shown to operate in the observable manners and morals of a certain place at a certain time and thus is rendered in more concrete particularity than is usual in great American novels, of which, one must add, *Pudd'nhead Wilson* is not quite one.

† From Richard Chase, *The American Novel and Its Tradition* (Garden City: Doubleday, 1957), pp. 149–156.

Pudd'nhead is Mark Twain, on the Tom Sawyer but not the Huck Finn side of his personality. He stands at the head of the procession of small-town intellectuals, cranks, and nonconformists that we find in American fiction, especially of the 1920's, although the type continues to be represented—for example, the Gavin Stevens of Faulkner. * * * It is of the essence that Pudd'nhead Wilson is scorned by the citizenry as a crank, a complainer, and an ironist, that he stubbornly takes up a position of aloofness and nonconformity, but that ultimately he shows that he is in no way radically alienated from the conventional ways and in fact dreams of being one of the boys. Pudd'nhead Wilson is finally able to vindicate his Tom Sawyer-like fantasies and crotchets by putting them to direct, socially-approved use. His ingenious mind, his eye for paradox and irony, and his contemned collection of fingerprints reveal in the end that the supposedly aristocratic Tom Driscoll is the son of the mulatto slave girl Roxana and that Chambers, Roxana's supposed son, is actually the legitimate heir of the Driscolls. This mix-up of identities, the effect of which is both enhanced and confused by the improbable arrival of the Italian twins, leads us into the moral complexities of the book and into that nightmare of racial contradiction and paradox which Mark Twain looks at with a tremendous clairvoyance and candor, although it cannot be said that Pudd'nhead himself is much aware of the depths of the racial dilemma in American life.

The most important meanings of *Pudd'nhead Wilson* are suggested by comparing it with *Huckleberry Finn* (which was published nine years before *Pudd'nhead*). Fiedler rightly calls it a prosy book, in which we have "fallen" from the more poetic *Huck* and in which the social realities observed in *Huck* strike us in a different way. Our feelings about justice and injustice are strongly aroused in the earlier book, but they are relatively abstract and universal feelings. In *Pudd'nhead*, we remain through nearly all the book in one small town. Moral issues are ostensibly illustrated in the actions of people in whom we have become interested and in whose fate we feel that we should have a stake. It is not possible "to light out" down the river, if things get hot in Dawson's Landing. Indeed, what happens "down the river" is that there slaves are sold into a far worse servitude than they know in Dawson's Landing, so that throughout the book we think of the Deep South as a kind of mythic but ever-present Hell. The Deep South gives a sinister implication to the small-town treacheries, minor felonies, and social deceptions which more or less sustainedly engage our moral feelings as we read the book. And it comes unmistakably to symbolize that irredeemable slavery—social, psychic, cosmic—to which every human being is in his own way subject. The effect on Mark Twain of the paradox of freedom and slavery is expressed by Mr. Fiedler as follows:

> The Civil War is the watershed in Twain's life between innocence and experience, childhood and manhood, joy and pain; but it is politically, of course, the dividing line between slavery and freedom. And Twain, who cannot deny either aspect, endures the contradiction of searching for a lost happiness he knows was sustained by an institution he is forced to recognize as his country's greatest shame. It was the best he could dream: to be free as a boy in a world of slavery!
>
> In *Tom Sawyer*, this contradiction is hushed up for the sake of nostalgia and in the name of writing a child's book; in *Huck* it is preserved with all the power of its tensions; in the last book it falls apart into horror.

Because the contradiction has indeed fallen apart in *Pudd'nhead Wilson* and also because it is shown to be of the essence of American social life, which consequently has its own fearful capacity to fall apart, Mark Twain's book gives in retrospect a new sense of some of the meanings of *Huckleberry Finn*. The apparently free and open world of the earlier book seems more precarious and more wistfully elusive because, in *Pudd'nhead Wilson*, we have seen its fluid moral life fixed and intensified in power by being expressed in social conventions and institutions.

It is difficult to think of the fluid moral world of *Huckleberry Finn* without recalling how directly it reflects the folkways of Mark Twain's prewar time and place. And indeed *Huck* draws heavily upon folklore for its materials, for the quality of its humor, and for its language. Yet Bernard De Voto was telling only half the story in his general insistence that Mark Twain's art and his intelligence were no more than this folklore organized in book form. Mr. Leavis is correct, of course, in admitting the presence of what he calls the "folk mind" in Mark Twain, and in going on to insist that this must not keep us from seeing also the presence of the mind of Western civilization.

Leavis says that Mark Twain's best writing is the product of "a life's experience brooded on by an earnest spirit and a fine intelligence." And he goes on to say that outside of his best writing Mark Twain still appeals to us as a man of intelligence and inner stress. For he "was no simple being, and the complexity of his make-up was ordinarily manifested in strains, disharmonies, and tormenting failures of integration and self-knowledge."

Yet the folk imagination is always pertinent in considering Mark Twain. In *Pudd'nhead Wilson* there is nothing like the rich store of folk motifs one finds in *Huck*. But there is, as in *Huck*, an imaginative conception at the symbolic heart of the book which before

drawing on Mr. Fiedler to define it one may call a universal "Mani-
chaean" dualism which has been given a special quality, in Mark
Twain, by the Calvinism of his early environment and by the racial
conflict. Fiedler writes that an important dimension of *Pudd'nhead
Wilson* is to be found in

> the symbolic meanings inevitably associated with the colors white
> and black, meanings which go back through literature . . . and
> popular religion . . . to the last depths of the folk mind. No
> matter how enlightened our conscious and rational convictions
> may be in these matters, we are beset by a buried ambivalence
> based on this archetypal symbolism of light and dark. Twain him-
> self in this very novel speaks unguardedly of the rain trying vainly
> to wash soot-blackened St. Louis white; and the implication is
> clear: black is the outward sign of inward evil. In this sense, the
> Negro puzzlingly wears the livery of the guilt we had thought the
> white man's. But *why*? It is a question which rings through the
> white man's literature in America; and the answer returns in an
> ambiguity endlessly compounded.

A book that does as much as *Pudd'nhead Wilson* to objectify
and illustrate the "buried ambivalence," "the archetypal symbolism
of light and dark" that characterize the American imagination cannot be called a failure either artistically or morally. There is always
a sense in which the artistic and the moral elements of a literary
work, especially a not quite perfect one, are separable. And *Pudd'n-
head Wilson* is a book which forces us, more than it can afford to
do, to be conscious of the separation. In considering Mark Twain's
book as an example of the art of the novel, one observes that the
moral truth it asserts is not adequately attached to the characters, or
dramatized by them. In the history of ideas and of American civilization Mark Twain's demonstration of what kind of institutions
those are which objectify in social power the poetic dualism in "the
last depths of the folk mind" is of the first importance. To Mr.
Leavis the fact that this has been done attests to an accomplished
art work—so he appears to affirm when he says that *"Pudd'nhead
Wilson* should be recognized as a classic of the use of popular
modes—of the sensational and the melodramatic—for the purpose
of significant art." Mr. Fiedler finds an artistic success in Mark
Twain's nightmare of racial contradiction. And indeed Mark
Twain's astonishing clairvoyance and honesty have given *Pudd'n-
head Wilson* a strong moral action, an action one can describe as a
radical dilemma turned into a stirring dialogue of traditions, attitudes, and social forces.

But what keeps this book from being a great novel is that the
characters and their relationships are not adequate to the moral action; the split between action and actors runs through the book.
And although this would not necessarily be a flaw in a romance,

even less in a Platonic dialogue, it is in a novel—in a fiction, that is, where the attempt is made to bring forth the ethical background and embody it in the foreground.

Except as something we can ourselves imagine, the putatively tragic action of the book fails, finally, to take on rhythm and form. It is never fully articulated and the book coheres only by its almost geometric demonstration, its true and false equations, its revelation and redistribution of opposites. There are no characters who are capable, either by themselves or in relation to each other, of giving the book a sustained organic life—not even Roxy, who is as vibrantly alive and human as anyone in Mark Twain's books. She is not allowed, by what she says, does, feels, and thinks, to command or permeate the novel, although there are certain scenes—notably the one in the old barn where she contemptuously tells Tom the truth about his parentage—to which she gives dramatic effectiveness. Wilson himself is an original type—but a type still, for we never understand much of what he feels or why he does what he does. We are not told out of what complex of experience and feeling issued his aphorisms in the Calendar, and except for the ones that are mere easy cynicism we do not believe them to have come from him. The fable of overreaching and disaster Mr. Fiedler dimly perceives in the career of Tom Driscoll remains a shadow, a distant imputation of tragedy. And to the mere receptive sense of the reader Mark Twain's novel seems finally, as a work of near-art, to exist as a stiffly dialectic moral action, together with a considerable presentation of manners and morals, into which the breath of life has entered only here and there. Mark Twain's real fictional province is not the novel proper, but the borderland between novel and romance. *Huckleberry Finn* is his one complete triumph, even though the tragic dialogue to which *Pudd'nhead Wilson* almost gives shape will always haunt our minds.

HENRY NASH SMITH

[*Pudd'nhead Wilson* as Criticism of the Dominant Culture]†

* * *

2

* * * The central theme of *Pudd'nhead Wilson* is still the corrupt state of the official culture of Dawson's Landing—that is, Hannibal—and the plot of the novel is focused around two acts which,

† From Henry Nash Smith, *Mark Twain: The Development of a Writer* (Cambridge: The Belknap Press of Har- vard University Press, 1962), pp. 173– 183, 207.

in quite different ways, call attention to evils beneath the apparently placid surface of it. The first act, the slave Roxana's desperate effort to free her son by exchanging him with her master's son in the cradle, is frustrated by the second, which consists in Wilson's detection of Roxy's stratagem more than twenty years later.

*   *   *

* * * Even in this farce,[1] Mark Twain is dramatizing the conflict between propriety and nonconformity that had served him so often before as comic material. The playful fantasy, however, touched off deeper responses—hence the appearance of the three characters who figure in *Pudd'nhead Wilson*. Roxy's son, known as Tom Driscoll during most of the story, is the psychological equivalent of the twins. He is two persons in one: a Negro (according to the definition operative in Dawson's Landing—he "has one thirty-second Negro blood") who appears "white" and is reared as the adopted son of the great man of the town. He is by law a slave but apparently free. The duality of white and Negro introduces the theme of false appearance and hidden reality, which is repeated in Tom's activities as a burglar in the disguise of a woman while he is ostensibly leading the life of the idle young heir to the town's largest fortune.

The material drawn up thus into consciousness is not comic, but intensely serious. When Mark Twain has conceived of Tom Driscoll he is launched upon a fable involving the tragic theme of slavery, with all it implies of hereditary but constantly renewed guilt and of perverted social conventions distorting human fact. For what but a morass of arbitrary assumptions makes Tom originally "black" and enslaved, later "white" and free, then converts him back into a Negro and a slave when the "truth" is revealed? The society of Dawson's Landing imposes upon slaves and masters alike the fictions which sustain the institution of slavery. The training corrupts both: the slave by destroying his human dignity, by educating him to consider himself inferior, by building up in him a ferocious hatred of himself as well as of his rulers; the master by encouraging cruelty toward the human beings he is taught to regard as animals, and thus by blunting his sensibilities and fostering an unwarranted pride of place.

Tom's mixed biological heritage points to the further fact that slavery debases sexual relations. To be sure, Mark Twain handles this topic with marked reticence. From the standpoint of imaginative coherence Judge York Leicester Driscoll is the father of Tom just as clearly as Roxy is his mother. But Mark Twain places the unmentionable fact of sexual intercourse between master and slave at two removes from the actual story—first by making Roxy, Tom's

---

1. *Those Extraordinary Twins* [*Editor*].

mother, the slave of a shadowy brother of Judge Driscoll at the time of Tom's birth; and then by the further precaution of creating an even more shadowy figure, Colonel Cecil Burleigh Essex, to be his biological father.

3

* * *

The problem of tone is often difficult in *Pudd'nhead Wilson*, but Mark Twain's earlier ridicule of Southern aristocratic pretensions in *Life on the Mississippi* and elsewhere strengthens one's suspicion that he intends to caricature Judge Driscoll's pride of ancestry and his equation of honor with readiness to send or accept a challenge. The Judge is unmistakably an object of satire in Chapter 7, when he shows the newly arrived Italian counts the sights of the town— including the slaughter house and the volunteer fire company—and naïvely tells them "all about his several dignities, and how he had held this and that and the other place of honor or profit, and had once been to the legislature." There is some ambiguity in the treatment of the Judge's duel with Luigi; Mark Twain admired physical courage, and the reader is expected to feel contempt for Tom because he is too cowardly to challenge the Count. Yet the duel in *Pudd'nhead Wilson* replaces a farcical encounter in "Those Extraordinary Twins" in which Angelo, physically joined to Luigi and therefore exposed to the Judge's fire against his will, dodges about so violently that he frustrates the efforts of both combatants, and finally assumes control of the twins' common pair of legs to run away. And the bit of slapstick that gives rise to the duel in "Those Extraordinary Twins" is retained in the novel. When Tom directs a sneering jest at Luigi from the platform of an anti-prohibition meeting, Luigi "took a couple of strides and halted behind the unsuspecting joker. Then he drew back and delivered a kick of such titanic vigor that it lifted Tom clear over the footlights and landed him on the heads of the front row of the Sons of Liberty."

Mark Twain's ironic attitude toward the Judge's sense of honor is also indicated by the sequel to the duel. Tom rationalizes his refusal to fight Luigi by declaring that the Count is an assassin. Without asking for particulars, the Judge instantly accepts the explanation, and declares: "That this assassin should have put the affront upon me of letting me meet him on the field of honor as if he were a gentleman is a matter which I will presently settle—but not now. I will not shoot him until after the election [for town officers]. I see a way to ruin them both before; I will attend to that first." The Judge waits until the eve of the election and then, still without any effort to verify Tom's slander, repeats it in a campaign speech. The coup brings about Luigi's defeat.

This incident would be more significant than it is if Judge Driscoll were a fully rounded character. But he is not. Mark Twain is not really interested in him as a person; he merely represents the aristocratic part of Tom Driscoll's heritage, which the writer means to satirize in the composite figure of the four descendants of the First Families of Virginia. Yet there is one odd obscurity of outline in the portrait. Pembroke Howard, the Judge's closest friend, is "a devoted Presbyterian" whereas the Judge is a freethinker. The theological difference is of no consequence in the plot. The Judge's unorthodoxy, like his pride in his Virginian ancestry, seems to be a reminiscence of Samuel Clemens' father, John Marshall Clemens. The parallel is a fleeting reminder that as the story of *Pudd'nhead Wilson* emerged from the farce about the Italian twins it drew into itself buried memories of Mark Twain's childhood—not always to the advantage of the novel.

4

The other half of Tom's heritage is that of his mother, Roxy the slave. The two parts of it are at war with each other. When Tom is but an infant Percy Northumberland Driscoll, Roxy's master, threatens to sell some of his slaves down the river. Although he relents and sells them in the town, Roxy suddenly realizes he has the power to carry out his threat: "Her child could grow up and be sold down the river! The thought crazed her with horror." She says to the sleeping infant: "I hates yo' pappy; he hain't got no heart—for niggers he hain't, anyways. I hates him, en I could kill him!" She is the only articulate enemy of the aristocracy of Dawson's Landing. Just as in some not negligible sense Judge Driscoll takes over the function of the Arthurian aristocracy in representing the values of a society stained by tyranny and cruelty, Roxy takes over Hank Morgan's role as adversary of the dominant class. In doing so, she becomes a successor to the vernacular protagonists of earlier stories.

Of course, there are important differences. Because she is a Negro (however "white" in appearance) and a woman, Mark Twain cannot identify himself with her as he identifies himself with Hank Morgan. And her aggression against the established order is not motivated by a program of reform. Mark Twain has accepted the demonstration in *A Connecticut Yankee* that society cannot be redeemed. Yet in *Pudd'nhead Wilson* he continues his preoccupation with the question of values, stripping down the fictive world of the Matter of Hannibal to the only vestige of affirmation he can find in it: the warmth, the passion of love and of hate, the sheer personal force in this representative of the submerged slave caste.

Roxy thus represents the last trace of unhandseled nature that has survived the perverted training of society in Dawson's Landing. But with a beautiful irony Mark Twain shows that she has adopted many of the values of the white aristocrats: their pride of ancestry, their code of honor, even their contempt for Negroes. Her denunciation of Tom, setting forth Judge Driscoll's sentiments in her heavy dialect, is one of the great passages in this uneven but often powerful book:

> "En you refuse' to fight a man dat kicked you, 'stid o' jumpin' at de chance! En you ain't got no mo' feelin' den to come en tell me, dat fetched sich a po' low-down ornery rabbit into de worl'! Pah! it makes me sick! It's de nigger in you, dat's what it is. Thirty-one parts o' you is white, en on'y one part nigger, en dat po' little one part is yo' *soul*. 'Tain't wuth savin'; 'tain't wuth totin' out on a shovel en throwin' in de gutter. You has disgraced yo' birth. What would yo' pa think o' you? It's enough to make him turn in his grave."

Roxy herself has stood in range of bullets from the duel in order to watch it, and a ricochet shot has tipped her nose. When Tom asks her, "Weren't you afraid?" she invokes in unconscious parody of Judge Driscoll the absurd pedigree she has invented for herself. She believes that "My great-great-great-gran'father en yo' great-great-great-great-gran'father was Ole Cap'n John Smith, de highest blood dat Ole Virginny ever turned out, en *his* great-great-gran'mother or somers along back dah, was Pocahontas de Injun queen, en her husbun' was a nigger king outen Africa." It is a sufficient explanation of her behavior that "De Smith-Pocahontases ain't 'fraid o' nothin', let alone bullets."

Except when she is momentarily under the influence of her "strong and sincere" piety, Roxy is indifferent toward property rights; she offers as a matter of course to help Tom in his burglaries when he needs money to pay his gambling debts. But on the crucial occasion of the theft of money that led her master to sell the guilty slaves, she had overcome temptation herself because she had "got religion" a fortnight before at a revival. Mark Twain is at his comic-ironic best in this scene, culminating in Roxy's exclamation, "Dad blame dat revival, I wisht it had 'a' be'n put off till tomorrow!" Roxy is nevertheless free of the heaviest burden that slavery has imposed on the whites: the sense of guilt. She is not torn by inner conflict, and she conveys the suggestion of subliminal energy, of darkness and mystery, that is attached to women and Negroes in American culture. The aggressiveness of the Judge is controlled by traditional forms, and even on the dueling ground he merely wounds his adversary. But when Roxy, without reference to code or etiquette, conceives the idea of killing her master, or herself and her child, the reader is convinced she is capable of these actions.

There is a haughty grandeur in her character that shines through the degraded speech and manners of a slave, and confers on her an intimation of tragic dignity: "She was of majestic form and stature, her attitudes were imposing and statuesque, and her gestures and movements distinguished by a noble and stately grace." We have seen with what assurance she has imagined an Indian queen and an African king among her ancestors. Mark Twain never conceived a more effective passage than the scene, at once tragic and comic, in which she determines to exchange her son with the Driscoll heir, and justifies the action to herself by a process of reasoning both humble (for she takes for granted the inferiority of the Negro— " 'Tain't no sin—*white* folks has done it!") and arrogant, because she compares herself with royalty and even usurps the divine prerogative of arbitrarily conferring free grace on her child:

> "Now I's got it; now I 'member. It was dat old nigger preacher dat tole it, de time he come over here fum Illinois en preached in de nigger church. He said dey ain't nobody kin save his own self—can't do it by faith, can't do it by works, can't do it no way at all. Free grace is de *on'y* way, en dat don't come fum nobody but jis' de Lord; en *he* kin give it to anybody he please, saint or sinner—*he* don't kyer. He do jis' as he's a mineter. He s'lect out anybody dat suit him, en put another one in his place, en make de fust one happy forever en leave t'other one to burn wid Satan. De preacher said it was jist like dey done in Englan' one time, long time ago. De queen she lef' her baby layin' aroun' one day, en went out callin'; en one o' de niggers roun' 'bout de place dat was 'mos' white, she come in en see de chile layin' aroun', en tuck en put her own chile's clo'es on de queen's chile, en put de queen's chile's clo'es on her own chile, en den lef' her own chile layin' aroun' en tuck en toted de queen's chile home to de nigger-quarter, en nobody ever foun' it out, en her chile was de king bimeby, en sole de queen's chile down de river one time when dey had to settle up de estate."

Roxy's subversive threat to the dominant culture is the only aspect of the material of *Pudd'nhead Wilson* that stirs Mark Twain's imagination. As a result, she is the only fully developed character, in the novelistic sense, in the book. She has a different order of fictional reality from the figures of fable with which she is surrounded. She resembles a portrait in full color set in a black-and-white background.

5

Although Tom Driscoll is evidently the key figure in the imaginative logic of *Pudd'nhead Wilson*, he is, like Judge Driscoll, not so much a character as a complex of themes. He incarnates both the tortured paradox of uncertain identity and the perversions resulting

from generations of the bad training imposed by slavery. He exhibits the worst traits ascribed to both races in this fictive world—the
lax morals and cowardice of the Negro, together with the hatred of
the master that is putatively expressed in his murder of Judge Driscoll; the indolence and affectation of white aristocrats (he is sent to
Yale and returns with mannerisms of dress that are offensive to the
community); the cruelty toward slaves that Mark Twain's latent
respect for the ideal of the Southern gentleman, related to his feeling for John Marshall Clemens, prevents him from attributing
directly to Judge Driscoll. * * *

Tom's most atrocious act, his betrayal of Roxy by selling her
down the river after she has helped him pay his debts by allowing
herself to be sold back into slavery, comes after he is aware that he
is a Negro and himself legally a slave. It is not an expression of aristocratic arrogance but of the unmotivated melodramatic villainy
that Mark Twain ascribes to Tom along with his sociologically
determined traits. While this deed is not inconsistent with Tom's
character, it does not belong to the imaginative fabric of the novel
or even to its idological structure; it represents the infection by stereotypes from popular fiction and the theater to which Mark Twain
was always exposed when he lost control of his materials.

6

The third of the three characters who Mark Twain said "got to
intruding themselves" into his farce about the Italian twins "and
taking up more and more room with their talk and their affairs" was
Pudd'nhead Wilson. Comments in Mark Twain's letters make it
clear that Wilson remained a minor character through the first
drastic revision of the original farce into a "tragedy."[2] Not until
later, when Francis Galton's *Finger Prints* (published in 1892) provided a sound scientific method for establishing the identities of
Tom and Chambers and for proving Tom guilty of the murder of
Judge Driscoll, did Mark Twain undertake the revision that made
Wilson the "chiefest" figure. This version of the novel, incidentally,
has survived in manuscript. Still another revision would be necessary
to dissect out the Siamese-twins motive.

Even when Wilson was given a crucial role in the plot, Mark
Twain did not undertake to characterize him fully. A letter to
Livy in 1894 contains a revealing comment on his intention. A lecturer in New York, he reported, had said that "Pudd'nhead was
clearly & powerfully drawn & would live & take his place as one of
the great creations of American fiction." Mark Twain continued:
"Isn't that pleasant—& unexpected! For I have never thought of

2. Anne P. Wigger, "The Composition
of Mark Twain's *Pudd'nhead Wilson* and
Those Extraordinary Twins: Chronology
and Development," *Modern Philology*,
55:93–102 (November 1957), especially
pp. 93–94.

Pudd'nhead as a *character*, but only as a piece of machinery—a button or a crank or a lever, with a useful function to perform in a machine, but with no dignity above that."[3] Wilson is incarnate analytical intelligence, the personification of science. Mark Twain liked to embody the notion of rational analysis, either farcically or seriously, in a figure borrowed from the newspapers and from popular fiction: the detective. In the later 1870's he had experimented with a novel and a play called "Cap'n Simon Wheeler, the Amateur Detective," traces of which survive in *Tom Sawyer, Detective* (1896); and he makes much of allegedly scientific methods of investigation in *The Stolen White Elephant* (1878) and *A Double Barrelled Detective Story* (1901, containing a burlesque of Sherlock Holmes). Closely tied to the solving of crimes is the sensational effect of the detective's courtroom revelation of the identity of the criminal—a motive that links Wilson retrospectively with Tom Sawyer and proleptically with Wilhelm Meidling, or rather with Satan in the guise of Meidling, in *The Mysterious Stranger*.

These affiliations of Wilson suggest that he has some qualities of transcendence. He does not have the omniscience of the fully transcendent figure: he is deceived by Tom's disguises and is temporarily convinced by Tom's argument that the twins never possessed the valuable dagger they say has been stolen from them. We are also asked to believe that Wilson suffers from his twenty years' isolation and wishes to be accepted as a member of the community, even to the point of being gratified by his popularity after his triumph in the trial scene. But his transcendent traits are unmistakable. He is much better educated and more intelligent than anyone else in the village; he is an outsider who arrives from a great distance and is therefore free from the guilt of slavery that the Virginia gentlemen have brought with them to Dawson's Landing; his mastery of the science of reading palms, like his discovery of the principle of identification through fingerprints, strikes the townspeople as almost miraculous; and he feels no warmth for any human being.[4]

When Wilson reveals in the courtroom that the supposed Tom Driscoll is a bastard, a thief, a murderer, and worst of all a Negro, he demonstrates that the official culture, with its vaunted ideals of honor and chivalry and ancient lineage, is merely a façade for deceit, avarice, and illegitimacy. He also defeats Roxy by frustrating her plan to free her son: Tom suffers precisely the fate of being sold down the river that she had tried to save him from.

* * *

3. New York, 12 January, *The Love Letters of Mark Twain*, ed. Dixon Wecter (New York: Harper, 1949), p. 291.
4. Paul Baender notes transcendent elements in Wilson ("Mark Twain's Transcendent Figure," [unpublished dissertation, University of California, Berkeley, 1956], p. 85).

ROBERT A. WIGGINS

[The Flawed Structure of *Pudd'nhead Wilson*]†

* * * Ordinarily one would say little about *Pudd'nhead Wilson* and move on to other matters, content to have assigned the book a place as a minor partial success. But nearly all who have written about Twain have had good things to say about *Pudd'nhead Wilson*, and at least two critics recently have praised the book extravagantly. * * * This kind of attention given to *Pudd'nhead Wilson* demands that we look more closely at the work.

* * * One cannot properly judge the work as tragedy, but rather must regard it as basically a serious story with some comic overtones.

There are really three plots. The central one concerns Roxana, a slave nurse, who switches her own infant son with the son of her master. The deception is not discovered. Roxy's son, raised as a white boy, becomes a wastrel, and much of the plot is given over to his affairs involving theft, selling his mother, and murdering his benefactor, whose heir he is. The two secondary plots are interwoven with the main plot. One deals with Pudd'nhead Wilson chiefly as a foil for the "damned human race" aspects of the village. His interest in fingerprints provides the device by which the true identities of the two boys are ultimately revealed. The other minor plot, involving the twins, was the plot with which Twain started, but in the final version it was somewhat altered and subordinated.

Pudd'nhead Wilson is a lesser achievement than *Huckleberry Finn*. The humor in the work is of a sardonic sort, taking its tone from *Pudd'nhead Wilson's Calendar*. One redeeming feature is that Twain does finally come close to creating a satisfying full-length female character in Roxana, probably because she was Negro and therefore could be treated as a primitive like Huck, Tom, Jim, Pap, and a lesser gallery of such characters. Not only as a character but in another way, Roxana represents a notable achievement on Twain's part. For the first time, the instituion of slavery had been dealt with relatively objectively and realistically in American fiction. Uncle Tom and Uncle Remus are childishly artificial by comparison. It is a tribute to Twain's art that the theme of miscegenation, daring in his day, was handled unobtrusively—yet without compromising the truth—and did not arouse any objection on the part of his audience. The antipathy toward the institution of slavery is generated almost incidentally to the feeling evoked by the poignant

† From *Mark Twain: Jackleg Novelist* (Seattle: University of Washington Press, 1964), pp. 105–112, 128.

illustration of man's inhumanity to man in Roxana's being sold down the river by her own "white" son.

The incident illustrates Twain's Calvinistic-deterministic belief that man is fundamentally evil and incapable of moral goodness. On the other hand, Roxy represents Twain's emotional desire to affirm mankind's moral responsibility, for although she later reproaches her son, she nonetheless forgives him for his despicable act. The folk mind is nothing if not charitable when one of its principles is involved: blood is thicker than water.

The book's conclusion affirms another of Twain's doctrines, that the individual is not responsible for his character, but is the product of forces outside his control. Tom Driscoll is black-hearted by the circumstances of his birth. Roxy says, "Thirty-one parts of you is white, on'y one part nigger, en dat po' little one part is yo' soul. Tain't wuth savin'; tain't wuth totin' out on a shovel en throwin' in de gutter." And in a scant paragraph Valet de 'Chambre is doomed to a life of misery because he was raised as a slave. He is free, but his conditioning as a slave haunts him the rest of his life. Twain did not see the inconsistency in this conclusion. One is damned because one thirty-second part of him was black, though he was raised as white, and the other damned because he was raised as a black, though all his ancestry was white. On one hand heredity is the factor determining character, and on the other it is environment.

* * *

In such general matters it is not unusual to find Twain at fault. But it is surprising to find Twain remiss in matters of detail. The technical flaws in this work are somewhat more obtrusive than customary in a major work by Twain. We are accustomed to excusing his episodic structure and sometimes lame endings; these are sins of ignorance. But in *Pudd'nhead Wilson*, Twain appears to be careless in the most rudimentary aspects of the storyteller's art.

First of all, Twain was a butcher rather than a surgeon in performing his "literary Caesarian operation." In his preface to *Those Extraordinary Twins*, Twain tells us, "I took those twins apart and made two separate men of them." As normal twins Angelo and Luigi seem a curious pair. Wherever they appear in *Pudd'nhead Wilson*, they are abnormally dependent upon one another. There is only one scene in which clearly they do not stand close together, and this is on the occasion when Luigi steps forward and kicks Tom. There are, however, several places in the book where their words and behavior are indeed puzzling for physically normal men. At the beginning of chapter VI, Angelo tells something of their history. In the course of the narrative he says, "Our parents were well to do, there in Italy, and we were their only child." And a few lines later he tells how, after the death of their parents, the twins were exhibited in a cheap museum in Berlin. In chapter XI, Wilson reads Luigi's palm and discovers that he had once killed a man. Angelo explains that Luigi had done so to protect his brother. But Luigi disclaims any heroic intention by saying, "You overlook one detail; suppose I hadn't saved Angelo's life, what would have become of mine? If I had let the man kill him wouldn't he have killed me, too? I saved my own life, you see."

Such incidents are puzzling until one learns that the twins were originally intended to be Siamese twins. Twain was simply careless in reworking his manuscript to remove these traces of his surgery. Such lapses, however, do not constitute the major flaw with respect to the twins. By his surgery Twain removed the original comic function of the twins, but he appears not to have inquired into what remaining function they performed. It is not a useful one so far as the main plot and theme are concerned. Indeed, the presence of the twins is more than just irrelevant to the central concerns of the book; their behavior is actually distracting. Their exotic personalities are a jarring note on the landscape of Dawson's Landing. The only justification would appear to be that Twain uses them satirically to point up the provincialism and gullibility of the village mentality. And Twain is not even consistent in this, for at the reception for the twins he presents the villagers as honest, simple folk, easily awed by the glamor of the occasion. Their innocence can hardly be held against them.

In his introduction to *Those Extraordinary Twins*, Twain writes of the twins: "They had no occasion to have foreign names now, but it was too much trouble to remove them all through, so I left them christened as they were and made no explanation." Of course Twain was making a joke, but like most jokes, and especially Twain's jokes, there is a large order of truth involved. The evidence suggests an unpardonable carelessness toward the construction of this tale. This tired attitude is conveyed in other ways that invite one to indict the author for not taking advantage of opportunities offered in the plot.

The character of Chambers is a case in point. He had to be invented to provide the occasion for trading places with Tom, but once invented he proved useful dramatically as a foil for Tom. And Twain makes considerable use of him in this role as the boys grow up together. The author must also have had Chambers in mind for the end of the plot, where he is unjustly accused of murder. Certainly Twain knew all this at the beginning, for the business about the fingerprints indicates unmistakably that the trial scene was in Twain's mind at the outset. Chambers' plight as the white heir raised as a Negro offered a ready-made counterplot to Tom's adventures. But what happens? After the first few chapters, Chambers is lost, not even mentioned, until he is resurrected for the concluding trial scene. And even there his role is only a minor one. Twain might well have capitalized on the dramatic possibilities offered by Chambers, for he, not the twins, was really related to the central theme of the book.

The main design of the work involves Wilson, Tom, Chambers, and Roxy. The chapters dealing with the twins that intrude in the body of the novel are there because Twain could not deal with the implications of his theme adequately and was lured away on the trail of farce instead of sticking to the exploration of his main story. It is a promising beginning ironically treating the nature of man's inhumanity to man—not in generalizations, but with two specific instances. One concerns Wilson's reception by the village, a documented case of how a man's reputation may be based upon and fixed by a trivial incident. The other is a particularization in the person of Roxy of the relations between Negro and white, and it too is an ironic examination.

> To all intents and purposes Roxy was as white as anybody, but the one-sixteenth of her which was black outvoted the other fifteen parts and made her a negro. She was a slave, and salable as such. Her child was thirty-one parts white, and he, too, was a slave, and by a fiction of law and custom a negro. He had blue eyes and flaxen curls like his white comrade, but even the father of the white child was able to tell the children apart—little as he had commerce with them—by their clothes; for the white babe wore ruffled soft muslin and a coral necklace, while the other wore merely a coarse tow-linen shirt which barely reached to its knees, and no jewelry.

There is no mistaking the ironic intention, for the method is repeated a number of times throughout the second chapter. Roxy's master discovers the theft of a small sum of money, and the slave servants are suspected. Such petty crimes, Twain tells us, were common and not regarded as sinful by the servants. "They had an unfair show in the battle of life, and they held it no sin to take military advantage of the enemy—in a small way; in a small way, but not in a large one." When the opportunity arose, one of them might take an article of small value, "perfectly sure that in taking this trifle from the man who daily robbed him of an inestimable treasure—his liberty—he was not committing any sin that God would remember against him in the Last Great Day."

To discover the culprit, the master, Percy Driscoll, threatens the slaves with being sold. "He was a fairly humane man toward slaves and other animals; he was an exceedingly humane man toward the erring of his own race." He threatens them further that if the culprit does not confess by the end of a minute all three will be sold down the river. Immediately all three confess. The master then states that they shall be sold locally.

The culprits flung themselves prone, in an ecstacy of gratitude, and kissed his feet, declaring that they would never forget his goodness and never cease to pray for him as long as they lived. They were sincere, for like a god he had stretched forth his mighty hand and closed the gates of hell against them. He knew, himself, that he had done a noble and gracious thing, and was privately well pleased with his magnanimity; and that night he set the incident down in his diary, so that his son might read it in after years, and thereby be moved to deeds of gentleness and humanity himself.

This ironic handling of the theme recurs in the final statement of the book, when Tom has been judged guilty of murder and imprisoned.

> Everybody granted that if 'Tom' were white and free it would be unquestionably right to punish him—it would be no loss to anybody; but to shut up a valuable slave for life—that was quite another matter.
> As soon as the Governor understood the case, he pardoned Tom at once, and the creditors sold him down the river.

The theme is a profoundly moving and serious one of tragic dimensions, but not as Twain handles it. Having done as much as indicated, Twain backs off and does not explore the subject further. Just as gingerly, he treats Roxy as a desirable woman, mistress of a white man, a Virginia gentleman. Saying that this was the first occasion on which the institution of slavery and miscegenation were handled relatively objectively and realistically in fiction is not the same thing as saying they were handled successfully as material for a novel. We may be grateful for what he has done and understand the reasons for his compromise, but if we judge *Pudd'nhead Wilson* fairly, we must recognize that the flawed structure of the work keeps it from being a satisfying novel.

* * *

JAMES M. COX

The Ironic Stranger†

* * *

Written in Europe, *Pudd'nhead Wilson* was Mark Twain's last American novel—the final volume in what we may justly call his Mississippi trilogy. * * *

* * *

† From James M. Cox, *Mark Twain: The Fate of Humor* (Princeton: Princeton University Press, 1966), pp. 222–246.

* * * The novel which remained after the unnatural removal of the farce is not a tragedy. It begins with a seemingly pointless joke, chronicles the history of a crime, and ends as Pudd'nhead Wilson, the stranger and hero, brings to justice the false Tom Driscoll, who has harassed the peace of Dawson's Landing. The hero's triumph over and entry into the society is in the comic rather than the tragic mode. But the facile neatness of the ending, instead of being joyously comic, emphasizes that the problems evoked by the novel have not really been settled so much as swept under the carpet. The triumph of justice, the defeat of the criminal, the success of the long-suffering hero are transparent veils which seem deliberately to expose rather than to conceal the larger doom, the deeper crime, and the final failure of the society which the novel scrutinizes. Coward, thief, and murderer though Tom Driscoll is, his indictment is more disturbing than gratifying. His sale down the river in the closing moment of the novel is a final indictment of the world in which he had his being, a last ironic stroke in this savagely ironic novel. It is ironic for Tom himself, whose career at launching had been pointed toward a raceless utopia only to veer through a series of atrocities culminating in Tom's murder of his white foster father and his selling his mother down the river. But the irony is also directed at the society itself, for Tom's entire career reveals how much he is the instrument of an avenging justice which has overtaken Dawson's Landing.

For Tom is a marked man—a Negro. Yet how different he is from Nigger Jim, whom Huck ultimately saw as "white inside." Tom Driscoll is white *outside*, his white face and white talk hiding the mark within. If Jim was the indulgent slave who wakened Huck's sleeping conscience, Tom Driscoll is the nightmare plaguing the moral sleep of Dawson's Landing. Only one-thirty-second black, he is invisible to his victims, the six generations of white patrimony contributing to his creation having physically equipped him to assume the role of changeling which Mark Twain assigns him. He thus stands always in the foreground as the figure embodying the long history of miscegenation in the background; although this background is not elaborated, the novel is nonetheless the history of a time, a place, and a crime. The narrative is, as Mark Twain insistently terms it, a chronicle.

Since miscegenation can culminate in "passing" the color line, the arbitrary changeling device functions as the comic equivalent of historic possibility and can legitimately dramatize the last phase of a society trapped by its secret history. Although the slaveholding society of Dawson's Landing is built around an aristocracy of Virginia gentlemen who worship honor, the novel discloses that across its coat of arms runs a dark bend sinister, an indelible stain disfiguring the heraldry of every member of the community's ruling class. The first families cannot, of course, see the stain, because they have conditioned themselves not to see it; but the novel exposes it in the person of the false Thomas à Becket Driscoll.

Spawned at the very center of their legalized institution of slavery, he crosses the color line in the white disguise six generations of white blood have given him. He is, after all, the son of white men's casual lust gratified by a series of aggressive sexual acts at the expense of their slaves. Although the masters may have assumed economic responsibility for these actions, their sexual willingness to cross the color line—the legal fiction they have created to define the unbridgeable gulf separating the races—merely underlines their refusal to accept any moral responsibility in the matter. The miscegenation which they have tacitly indulged within the framework of slavery is their own covert affirmation of the inexorable bond between the races. The secret channel carrying white blood steadily down into the area of human life separated and suppressed by slavery, it makes possible the emergence of the false Tom Driscoll into the white world. The dark force he possesses upon his return represents the loss of power sustained by the ruling class.

Pudd'nhead Wilson thus implies a world in which the power of those who rule has been transferred to those who serve, for if the origin of Tom's force is the lust out of which he was created, the immediate source is embodied in the personality of his mother, Roxana, who shifts him into the cradle of the white heir. One of Twain's most interesting creations, she possesses the strength, the passion, and the fertility so strikingly absent in the white women she serves; in fact, her darker, deeper beauty merely emphasizes their frigidity. Mark Twain remarks that on the same day she bore her son she was "up and around," while Mrs. Percy Driscoll "died within the week" of her childbirth confinement. The long logic underlying this chronicle explains Roxana's power, for the submerged lust transfers the passion from the white wives to the slave mistresses. If the transfer bestowed purity upon the white women, it nonetheless left them increasingly impotent. Thus, in the white South of Mark Twain's memory, the Negro women became the Mammies who were the real mothers in a society so obsessed with purity that it divested the ordained mothers of passional vitality. That is why, in the Southern gentleman's idealized version of existence, the white women of privileged classes could not nurse their children and were relieved of the obligation as soon after the travails of childbirth as possible.

In rearing the white man's legitimate children and giving birth to his illegitimate ones, Roxana bears what their honor cannot bear— *the guilt of their repressed desires.* Their guilt is objectified in her repression. Her humiliation (she has no guilt) takes the form of repressed vengeance. Thus, her release of Tom into the white society grows out of her arraignment before Percy Driscoll on the false charge of petty larceny. She acts not in overt vengeance but out of desperation to save him from the fate of being sold down the river. That her ostensibly defensive action constitutes such an aggression against the society discloses how much unconscious power and hostility she actually commands. When Tom Driscoll is finally unmasked, she is the sole person in the society who can assume inward responsibility for the crime of the society. Her cry, "De Lord have mercy on me, po' misable sinner dat I is!" is a stricken cry of acknowledgment in a world given over to repression and confirms the nobility and responsibility she alone possesses. She is, after all, the darkly powerful queen in the society which Mark Twain depicts. Although the "nobles" of the society bear the names of Elizabethan court lovers, the white queens in the New World imitation of the Old remain as remotely in the background of the novel as the real Tom Driscoll who shambles about the slave quarters. Only Roxana has the power to create drama and to become the primary force in the world she serves.

The responsibilities thrust upon her become her critical force, enabling her to vitalize with certain insight the empty illusions which she inherits from the world above her. Reprimanding Tom for his failure to meet the terms of the code duello, she affirms her honor and origins with a summary of the family pedigree.

> "Whatever has become o' yo' Essex blood? Dat's what I can't understan. En it ain't on'y jist Essex blood dat's in you, not by a long sight—'deed it ain't! My great-great-great-granfather en yo' great-great-great-great-granfather was Ole Cap'n John Smith, de highest blood dat Ole Virginny ever turned out, en *his* great-great-granmother or somers along back dah, was Pocahontas de Injun Queen, en her husbun' was a nigger king outen Africa—en yit here you is, a-slinkin' outen a duel en disgracin' our whole line like a ornery low-down hound! Yes, it's de nigger in you!"

Even as she parodies the genealogical obsessions of the first families, she confronts the distinctive heritage of Dawson's Landing and America, the strange and remarkable history which so much defines the New World. Her sketch of her American family tree is the repressed genealogy which upholds the tenuous tracings educed by the First Families of Virginia, at least insofar as the novel implies their genealogies. The self-styled aristocrats of Dawson's Landing, in repressing her genealogy, cut themselves off from the vitality of their own past as well as hers. Denial of their secret history is actually a denial of themselves, and their blood, flowing in that covert tradition, becomes their nemesis in the person of Tom Driscoll.

As long as Tom is ignorant of his identity, he does not direct his inborn hostilities upon his fathers but gratifies his uncontrollable temper with cruel jokes perpetrated on the slaves who serve him, particularly the unfortunate Chambers, his true master, and Roxy his mother. His brutal treatment of Roxy, however, eventually angers her into humiliating him with the facts of his lineage. His discovery of his true mother, though temporarily paralyzing, is nevertheless a self-discovery and a half-conscious realization of his destiny. His casually malevolent will, which has struck blindly downward in indiscriminate aggression, begins to find its fated target. Thus, when Roxy tauntingly asks him what his father would think of his refusal to accept the dueler's challenge, Tom "said to himself that if his father were only alive and in reach of assassination his mother would soon find that he had a very clear notion of the size of his indebtedness to that man, and was willing to pay it up in full, and would do it too, even at risk of his life. . . ." At such a moment, when even Mark Twain's rhetoric assumes Faulknerian aspects, outward and inward action tend to coalesce into social and psychological reality, disclosing that the false Thomas à Becket Driscoll is the avenging agent who carries back across the color line the repressed guilt which has gathered at the heart of slavery. Although he withholds his terrible intention from Roxy, Tom willingly seizes upon his fated mission: the murder of Judge Driscoll. For the Judge, who harbors within his walls the invisible assailant, is not only Tom's foster father and inevitable target of his malice; he is also the living symbol of law and order in the community, and his murder suggests the anarchy which the white society has by its own action released upon itself.

This, then, is the crime which strikes at the heart of Dawson's Landing. The man who finally "sees" Tom Driscoll and restores a semblance of honor and order to the community is quite appropriately the rank outsider, Pudd'nhead Wilson—the stranger who first intruded into Mark Twain's farce about the Siamese twins. Having wandered West from his native New York to seek his fortune, Wilson comes into the community a free agent. His "freedom" places him at the opposite extreme from the fate in which Driscoll is caught. So far apart are they—Wilson on the periphery of the society, Tom at the center—that Mark Twain resorts to arbitrary devices to draw them together. Thus, there is the weakly plotted series of accidents upon which the novel turns: Pudd'nhead arrives in Dawson's Landing during the month in which Tom is born; he is rejected by the society at almost the same time Tom enters it; his rise to fame begins the same moment Tom's honor is questioned. Pudd'nhead even shares character traits with his opposite number. Both are notorious idlers, both are collegiately sophisticated, both are given to droll and cutting irony. Finally, both share a desire for the limelight, and when Wilson exploits the drama of the final courtroom scene, he is merely usurping the role of showman which Tom has played in society. At opposite points on the wheel of fortune, the destinies of the two figures are fatally related, the ascending fortune of Pudd'nhead coming necessarily at the expense of Tom's fall. The novel predictably ends with Wilson standing above his cowering antagonist to pronounce his doom.

In order to show how and why this plot machinery fails to rise above the level of mere mechanical contrivance, it is necessary to recognize the real relationship between Tom Driscoll and Pudd'nhead Wilson which is implied by Mark Twain's insistence on plot symmetries. Wilson's first act upon entering Dawson's Landing is to mutter the joke which isolates him and launches the novel. Hearing an "invisible" dog barking behind the scenes, he expresses to a group of loitering citizens the wish that he owned half the dog. Upon being asked why, Wilson rejoins, "Because I would kill my half." The only response the literal-minded inhabitants can make to this sally is summed up by one of the gullible bystanders, who inquires of his comrades, "What did he reckon would become of the other half if he killed his half? Do you reckon he thought it would live?" Jay B. Hubbell, in a penetrating objection to the novel, contends that the joke is typical of small-town humor and that "the village yokels would have yelled with delight when they heard it."[1] Hubbell feels that at this point in his career Mark Twain had lost his sense of connection with the village of his memory and thus was becoming cut off from the reality of his humor.

In a very particular way Hubbell is right. The joke, an old chestnut in the provinces, should have evoked a warm response. Yet, coming from a total stranger, Pudd'nhead's wisecrack reveals a discomforting familiarity and at the same time betrays a veiled threat. Given the particular province, there is a certain realism in the instinctive withdrawal of the village idlers and their rejection of the strange humorist as a "pudd'nhead." Wilson's subsequent behavior lends a measure of justification to their puzzled distrust, for although he ultimately discloses the invisible assassin in their midst, he is also the one who plants in Roxy's mind the possibility that her son is indistinguishable from the legitimate Driscoll heir. "How do you tell them apart, Roxy, when they haven't any clothes on?" he asks with innocent amusement. Remembering Wilson's observation,

1. Jay B. Hubbell, *The South in American Literature* (Durham, 1954), p. 835.

and assuming that if one so intelligent cannot distinguish the children neither can the dull-witted villagers, Roxy decides to shift her son into the cradle of the legitimate Tom Driscoll.

If Wilson is capable of suggesting the possibility of mistaken identity in the village, he is also visibly engaged in erecting a system of detection which will expose the possibility. Thus, his casual observation to Roxy reveals that personal identity in Dawson's Landing is a matter of mere appearance; and his reliance upon fingerprints as a means of criminal detection undercuts the whole structure of familial identity on which the society stands. His effort to establish a complete fingerprint file of every member of the community is a stratagem for checking personal identity against the one unchanging characteristic of human physiology. Trusting only these "natal autographs," as he calls them, Wilson refuses to rely on names and faces, the conventional hallmarks of identity. His arduous "hobby" is, in fact, based on an essential distrust of the identity of the entire village.

Having precipitated the crisis which only his system can resolve, Wilson's final apprehension of the criminal merely completes and closes the circuit of the plot. For all the detached curiosity with which he surveys the village, he remains singularly blind to the series of incidents set in motion by his own idle remark to Roxy; and although he holds Tom Driscoll's true signature within arm's reach, he is almost as bewildered by the murder case as the dullest citizen in Dawson's Landing. The fatal attraction between detective and criminal is the only thing that finally saves him from failure, despite his foolproof system. For Tom compulsively seeks Wilson out to taunt him for failing to solve the murder of the Judge, only to leave his telltale print on one of Wilson's glass slides. Seeing Wilson's shocked countenance and unaware of his crucial error, Tom grants his host's request to be left in peace but cannot resist a parting jibe: "Don't take it so hard," he says; "a body can't win every time; you'll hang somebody yet." Wilson's reply is a mutter to himself: "It is no lie to say I am sorry I have to begin with you, miserable dog though you are!"

More than being a silent retort to Driscoll's taunt, Wilson's remark is an oblique answer to the joke which initiated his isolated career, for in addition to finding the "invisible dog"—or, as Roxy puts it, the "low down hound"—which disturbed the peace of the community, he has indeed come to own half of it and is ready to assume the role of killer which he first proposed for himself. He demands in the courtroom that Tom make upon the courtroom window the fingerprints which will hang him. But the society into which Wilson is about to be accepted owns the other half and determines not to destroy such a valuable property. The terms of the joke thus become the terms of the novel, and Wilson's casual wish to own half of the unseen dog is realized at the moment he establishes Tom's identity and guilt. As a result of Wilson's detection, Tom reverts from his role of secret agent to the status of property "owned" by the society at the same instant Wilson's twenty-three-year period of rejection is ended and he is welcomed into the community of owners as a reward for his achievement. As the two figures "enter" the social order at the conclusion of the narrative, it becomes evident that they are the *real* twins in this novel which grew around a farce about Siamese twins.

* * *

Thus the character of Pudd'nhead is the "way" or means by which Mark Twain realized his disillusion. He had begun to realize it in Hank Morgan, the stranger whose emergence into the sleepy world of Camelot forecasts Pudd'nhead's entry into Dawson's Landing. But two things caused Mark Twain to lose control over Morgan. First, Morgan's unconverted indignation manifested itself in increasingly bad humor. Second, Morgan's slang could not assimilate the "thought" which Mark Twain increasingly tried to give it. But in the character of Pudd'nhead, Mark Twain solved both these problems. Pudd'nhead is not a vernacular character but a college man and thus can legitimately "say" any thought Mark Twin can give him. More important, the indignation which in effect blows up Morgan, is economized in *Pudd'nhead Wilson* by means of a radically disjunctive irony.

To achieve this irony, Mark Twain moved away from vernacular and back to plot—in the manner of *The Prince and the Pauper* and *Tom Sawyer*. Both these earlier books contain irony, but the emotion on which the irony rests is essentially indulgent. The world depicted is a world of boyhood—particularly is this true in *Tom Sawyer*—and the relationship established between narrative consciousness and action is one of ultimate approval. Even in *Huckleberry Finn*—despite all the bitter knowledge and experience which go into the book—the emotions upon which the humor rides are indulgence and approval. In *A Connecticut Yankee* irony gives way to direct expression, outbursts of anger and spleen, and to a sarcastic tone. In *Pudd'nhead Wilson* a genuine irony is restored—but it is irony without indulgence. Scorn and contempt are the emotions at the heart of this irony. The perspective upon the world of Dawson's Landing is as remote as it was in *Tom Sawyer*, but the world is a world of men, and the narrative consciousness, instead of approving the antics on stage, evokes disapproval of the entire world. There is only one "actor" held in affection by the narrative consciousness: Roxana. The others, even Pudd'nhead, are either held in check or exposed by the sardonic eye of the chronicler.

The strength of Mark Twain's irony is particularly evident in the light of Hank Morgan's slang fiasco; it is a means of keeping the action in focus and control. While its fine edge noticeably diminishes the possibility of "good humor," it nevertheless prevents the intrusion of Mark Twain's anger and bad temper; it is a way of controlling them from the beginning. Speaking from the vantage point of the historian, the chronicler chooses a perspective which allows him to see the events of his history as fatal—to see that the relationships between man, society, and history take precedence over man's individual desires and ambitions. Viewed from such a perspective, man is at once the creator and the creature of fate; he carries out and is the victim of destiny. But in order to achieve this perspective, the plot must be made to *seem* like a part of the destiny. This does not mean that the plot has to be "invisible." Instead, it must be extremely visible, its absolute visibility disclosing that the entire order of the action is an expression or symbolic enactment of fate itself.

* * *

Yet the ironic stranger, whose very irony was a means of releasing order into the chaos left in Hank Morgan's wake, was also repressive—and repressive in two ways. First, his role in the novel is repressive, not liberative. Thus, although his irony ultimately indicts the society his detection has exposed, his immediate concern is to indict the false Tom Driscoll and restore the status quo. But Pudd'nhead is not only repressive within the novel; he is repressive upon it. This would not be true if his character were fully realized, for then his repressive tendencies would be dramatized as character trait. But he is not so realized, and it is just this failure which accomplishes what can be called a completion of the central weakness of the book. For whereas Roxana's character denied her original relation to the plot, Pudd'nhead's plot keeps him from ever really becoming a character. He remains instead little more than a massive plot device. Neither he nor his "twin," the false Tom Driscoll, is ever freed into character; rather, they function as dominant parts of the plot machinery.

Even though Mark Twain confidently asserted that Pudd'nhead came unbidden and "freely" into his creative consciousness, the form which the character imposed upon the action was extremely constrictive—so constrictive that Mark Twain was ironically right in calling the book a tragedy. For the bitter plot of Pudd'nhead overrides the character of Roxana, reducing her vernacular to dialect and severing her humor from the sources of her instinctive power. Exposed by Wilson's detection, that power is reduced to a mere guilty minstrel cry: "De Lord have mercy on me, po' misable sinner dat I is!"

ROBERT REGAN

[An Unpromising Hero]†

* * *

* * * in its published version, most of its self-parodying elements relegated to a sort of oversized appendix,[1] *Pudd'nhead Wilson* is one of Mark Twain's greatest accomplishments; of all his novels, it is the one which faces up to the dilemma of American politics most squarely, and it is the most meaningful of the books in which he employs the Unpromising Hero motif. Pudd'nhead's history, like those of his predecessors, is a success story, but whereas Mulberry Sellers' success and that of the hero of "The £1,000,000 Bank-Note" are financial, Dave Wilson succeeds *politically*.

In *A Connecticut Yankee* and *The American Claimant* Mark Twain both ridiculed aristocratic systems and challenged that view of human perfectibility upon which democratic theory rests. Both books either explicitly or tacitly condemn all the political systems they discuss. *Pudd'nhead Wilson*, in contrast, presents an alternative to aristocracy meaningful for an egalitarian society. Pudd'nhead scatters the proud pseudo-aristocrats of the F.F.V. and, although he makes no attempt to enliven the democratic sentiments of the common people of Dawson's Landing, Missouri, he does use his native superiority to gain for himself the power he helps Fate divest the Virginians of. *A Connecticut Yankee* closes in political despair and *The American Claimant* elects not to give artistic embodiment to the political issues which abound in it; but *Pudd'nhead Wilson* addresses itself directly to the problem of who shall govern and proposes a solution which is realistic and practicable: the hero-leader whose disinterested honesty and personal effectiveness in combating his and society's enemies capture the common imagination—the man, in short, with Dave Wilson's qualities—will be and ought to be followed.

The methods by which the college-bred Easterner Dave Wilson gains respect and a place of leadership in Dawson's Landing, Missouri, are typical of Mark Twain's Unpromising Heroes. Originally, as vestiges in *Those Extraordinary Twins* demonstrate, Pudd'nhead was to have won the applause and votes of his townspeople by demonstrating his admirable rhetorical capacity to prove a lie. Defending one of the Siamese twins against the charge that he had kicked Tom Driscoll, Pudd'nhead demonstrates to the satisfaction of a jury that human reason could never know which of the two heads of the

† From Robert Regan, *Unpromising Heroes: Mark Twain and His Characters* (Berkeley: University of California Press, 1966), pp. 207–219, 240–241.
1. *Those Extraordinary Twins* [Editor].

Italian monstrosity was in control of the offending foot and that a verdict of guilty was consequently impossible. This showy display of sophistry is opposed by Mr. Justice Robinson, a judge little learned in the law but committed irrevocably to plain truth. Nevertheless, Robinson's common sense falls before the rush of Pudd'nhead's rhetoric; the jury returns a verdict of "not guilty" and the admiring courtroom audience conducts Wilson to a tavern to " 'wet down' his great and victorious entry into the legal arena." This scene not only throws an unfavorable light upon the jurors and spectators at the trial, it also denigrates Pudd'nhead at the same time it wins him their admiration: it would appear that, as originally conceived, Wilson was to be the satirized hero, a man who revels in being praised for the wrong reasons by the wrong people. But Mark Twain ultimately showed both the people and their hero clemency: he excised the burlesque trial. In the final version, Pudd'nhead argues his case without sophistry and loses it. We hear of the trial only at second hand, but Pudd'nhead's courtroom performance is, so Mark Twain allows us to conclude, no less effective than it had been in the earlier version; in spite of the loss of the verdict, it wins him the Democratic nomination for mayor. The final and conclusive step in Pudd'nhead's ascent to leadership in Dawson's Landing is another courtroom scene, one in which he employs both rhetoric and science in service of truth and justice. When Pudd'nhead reveals that Tom Driscoll is, first, his supposed uncle's murderer and, second, actually a slave, he causes a courtroom sensation and wins himself a place of unassailable leadership in the town; yet during the triumphant trial scene Pudd'nhead seldom seems to be striving in Hank Morgan's manner or Tom Sawyer's for an "effect." Pudd'nhead succeeds, as Miles Hendon had, without trying: he patiently suffers the contumely of his townspeople during twenty long years; he serves justice and truth when he has an opportunity; he remains aloof from all compromising commitments; and although he does not seek success, success finds him. In proving Tom guilty, Pudd'nhead proves the accused Count Luigi, one of the separated twins, innocent. Once acquitted, Luigi and his brother Angelo, those still extravagant hold-overs from the original extravaganza, become "heroes of romance." But not Pudd'nhead; he is simply "a made man for good" and the first citizen of Dawson's Landing.

Pudd'nhead differs from most of Mark Twain's other Unpromising Heroes in one very significant respect. The kindly and odious attributes of his "fathers" are fused in the F.F.V. aristocrats, four men essentially indistinguishable from one another. Pudd'nhead's attitude toward this group in which the kindly and odious are merged is characterized by tensions and ambiguities. Two celebrated critics, F. R. Leavis and Leslie Fiedler, have indicated what they take to be Mark Twain's intention in his presentation of these Virginia gentlemen translated to the backwash of the Mississippi. Mr. Leavis, arguing persuasively against the once-common myth that Mark Twain's Mississippi River villages were outposts of the American frontier, notes "the persistence of an aristocratic tradition in a democratic society." He accepts at face value Mark Twain's praise of the four aristocrats, " 'the fine, brave, majestic creatures' who uphold the F.F.V."[2] Mr. Fiedler also refuses to be skeptical. He too believes that Mark Twain has endorsed the Virginia aristocracy and, further, that he has caused the hero of the novel to seek preferment in the F.F.V. hierarchy. "In *Pudd'nhead Wilson*," Mr. Fiedler writes, "society is defined by the fathers, last defenders of the chivalric code and descendants of the cavaliers. Four in especial represent the world to which Pudd'nhead aspires: York Leicester Driscoll, Percy Northumberland Driscoll, Pembroke Howard, and Col. Cecil Burleigh Essex—the names make the point with an insistence that is a little annoying."[3] But for Mr. Fiedler's annoyed solemnity and a timely warning from Mr. Leavis that Mark Twain's treatment of the Virginians "has nothing of the satiric about it," and that the author "unmistakably admires Judge Driscoll and Pembroke Howard,"[4] one might be tempted to smile at this plethora of noble names.

For Mark Twain the F.F.V. carried a painfully personal association. His own father, the severe and distant John Marshall Clemens, had considered himself a member of the class. In Pudd'nhead's acceptance of the Democratic party's nomination for mayor, there is a hint that the novel was not intended to propitiate the spirit of the elder Clemens; Judge Clemens was an ardent Whig,[5] and Judge Driscoll and the other Virginians of Dawson's Landing apparently also belong to that party. Because the F.F.V. aristocrats in *Pudd'nhead Wilson* are to so marked a degree fictive realizations of Mark Twain's feelings about his father, a strong element of censorship operates to prevent their portraits from becoming utterly repugnant. The cruel slave-owner whose barbarous and self-righteous treatment of his Negroes triggers the main action of the book conveniently dies at the end of Chapter IV. The lecherous Virginian who begets the white Negro Roxy's slave child also disappears.

---

2. F. R. Leavis, Introduction to the Grove Press edition of *Pudd'nhead Wilson* (New York, 1955), pp. 12, 20, 24. [Reprinted above.—*Editor.*]
3. "As Free as Any Cretur," *The New Republic*, CXXXIII, No. 7 (15 August 1955), 17–19, and No. 8 (22 August 1955), 16–18. The quoted passage is in the second number, pp. 16–17. Mr. Fied-

ler altered the language of these observations when he incorporated the articles in his *Love and Death in the American Novel* (New York, 1960), pp. 385 ff., but the tenor remains unchanged. [The essay is reprinted above.—*Editor.*]
4. Leavis, p. 21.
5. Dixon Wecter, *Sam Clemens of Hannibal* (Boston, 1952), p. 15.

These two unambiguous representatives of the inhuman slave system, Percy Driscoll and Col. Essex, are replaced by Judge Driscoll, Percy's brother, and his friend Pembroke Howard, kindlier representatives of their cast, but this evidence of Mark Twain's censorship does not effectively obscure his point. As Henry Nash Smith has observed,

> From the standpoint of imaginative coherence Judge York Leicester Driscoll is the father of Tom just as clearly as Roxy is his mother. But Mark Twain places the unmentionable fact of sexual intercourse between master and slave at two removes from the actual story—first by making Roxy, Tom's mother, the slave of a shadowy brother of Judge Driscoll at the time of Tom's birth; and then by the further precaution of creating an even more shadowy figure, Colonel Cecil Burleigh Essex, to be his biological father.[6]

And Charles S. Holmes has, in a recent article, inadvertently, but in a sense rightly, referred to Tom Driscoll and Valet de Chambre as "pathetic half-brothers."[7] As was the case with Prince Edward and Tom Canty, the undetected substitution of the one child for the other would be more plausible if they were in fact half-brothers, sons of the same promiscuous father: on some level of Mark Twain's imagination both pairs of boys must have been half-brothers, but the same inhibition operated in the two cases and in each Mark Twain attributed the implausible resemblance of the boys to chance. To such an extent the filial taboo continued to operate in his imagination. It did not, however, alter the essential hostility of his treatment of the fathers.

The four F.F.V. aristocrats of Dawson's Landing represent the old order of authority: they are the collective father-figure for Pudd'nhead, their odious features covered, but only partially, by an attractive disguise of kindly behavior and gracious living. Two of them, Percy Driscoll and Colonel Essex, are dead before the major action of the novel commences. In the middle of the book, Percy's brother is murdered by a mulatto slave he believes to be his nephew. The sole survivor, Pembroke Howard, becomes Pudd'nhead's opposing lawyer in the climactic trial scene. Three issues depend upon the outcome of that trial: the detection of the murderer, the identity of slave and freeman, and the leadership of the community. In settling the first two issues, Pudd'nhead settles the last also. Before his exposés identify criminal, chattel, and leader, the townspeople, characteristically sympathetic to an underdog, are "sorry for Pudd'nhead; his budding career would get hurt by this

6. *Mark Twain: The Development of a Writer* (Cambridge, Mass., 1962), p. 175. [Reprinted above—*Editor*.]
7. "*A Connecticut Yankee in King Arthur's Court:* Mark Twain's Fable of Uncertainty," *South Atlantic Quarterly,* LXI (1961), 468.

trial"; but when the court rises at the conclusion of the trial, the last representative of the Virginia aristocracy, the F.F.V. lawyer who has opposed Wilson, has simply faded from view and Pudd'n-head has begun to act as both defense and prosecuting attorney, as detective and judge, as prophet and king.

Pudd'nhead's rival in the book is, however, not Pembroke Howard or any of the other older aristocrats. His rival is Tom Driscoll, actually a slave but apparently the only F.F.V. of the younger generation and the heir-apparent to leadership in the town. The scheme of the plot would seem to make the supposed slave Chambers (the "real" Thomas à Becket Driscoll) Tom's rival, but in the imaginative shape the novel assumed this is not the case. Again and again through the book Tom and Pudd'nhead are drawn together; in spite of the sharp cleavage between their values, in spite of their often-expressed antagonism for one another, they are together at every crucial turn of the narrative.

Tom Driscoll brings a familiar theme of native American humor into the novel: after his two-years' residence at Yale, he returns to Dawson's Landing considerably dandified, particularly in his dress. The other young men, annoyed by his airs, commission a tailor to produce a costume and Tom soon finds "the deformed negro bell-ringer straddling along in his wake tricked out in a flamboyant curtain-calico exaggeration of his finery, and imitating his Eastern graces as well as he could."[8] Tom surrenders unconditionally; thus the yokels get the best of this slicker, just as their cousins had got the best of Ichabod in "The Legend of Sleepy Hollow," just as other yokels had triumphed over other slickers in hundreds of humorous sketches, including a few of Mark Twain's own. Pudd'n-head also comes to Dawson's Landing from an eastern university, but with a diploma. He does not parade his graces, but he has graces—real ones—which set him apart from the other young men and win him their derision. He does not surrender and ultimately this "slicker" gets the best of the yokels. Pudd'nhead is the obverse of Tom Driscoll, the "stranger," not the "slicker."

The radical, archetypal antagonism between Tom and Pudd'n-head may explain one of the most puzzling flaws in the intellectual structure of the novel, Pudd'nhead's appearing as a partisan of the code duello. This flaw has, not surprisingly, led many commentators to see Pudd'nhead as self-identified with the F.F.V., for the duel is their special ritual, their means of reminding the townspeople that they stand above the ordinary race of men. The life of the novel, its pattern of ideas, lies in its paired opposites, and of these Pudd'nhead and Tom make the most important pair. These two, neither of them rightful and legal heir to the F.F.V., vie for the succession.

8. Wecter quotes the source of this scene in *Sam Clemens of Hannibal*, pp. 143–144.

When Tom disappoints his uncle by avoiding a duel with Count Luigi, it is natural that Pudd'nhead should call him to task; it is natural that he should say, "I don't see how you could treat your good old uncle so. I am a better friend of his than you are." And he is a better friend, a better son, to the Judge than Tom is, but not by as large a margin as his language suggests.

The subsequent duel between Count Luigi and Judge Driscoll, Pudd'nhead standing as second to the Count, verges dangerously on the comic. The Judge is delighted with his opponent, a man as ready as he is to take the field of honor: "He's a darling! Why it's an honor as well as a pleasure to stand up before such a man." The conflict within Mark Twain's mind is apparent: dueling had for years—perhaps since his hasty departure from Nevada—been a special source of irritation to him; it had always been a prime target for his satire. But if Tom Driscoll shunned it, Pudd'nhead was forced into the position of defending it. The only hope under these circumstances lay in making the duel comic and keeping Pudd'nhead's role passive.

From his first action in the novel (taking the fingerprints of the babies Chambers and Tom) to his last (proving that "Tom" is actually the slave Chambers and a murderer) Pudd'nhead's sole concern, conscious or unconscious, his sole objective, is to reveal the hidden truth of the society in which he lives not as a citizen but as a stranger, the truth that in such a society the master is a slave, that both master and slave are degraded, and that for redemption and leadership such a society must look to an outsider. Pudd'nhead is at once the hero and the stranger, the outsider and the leader. But in his characterization there is none of the shifting from one role to another which blurred the features of Hank Morgan: Pudd'nhead is a demonstration of Mark Twain's conviction that only in the stranger, the man who stands aloof, the man who is not implicated in the common guilt, can society find its heroic leader. He demonstrates that stranger and hero are one.[9]

But a disclaimer. For Dave Wilson, whose vision and wit so exceed his townspeople's understanding that for twenty years they take him for a fool and use him as Israel used its prophets, the novel is a success story, a melodramatic fable of an Unpromising Hero complete with happy ending. For the rest of the characters, however, the novel is a tragedy. For Roxy and Chambers, two victims of slavery with whom we sympathize deeply, as well as for the villainous Tom, himself a victim in a subtler sense of the same slave-system, the ending is an unmitigated catastrophe. The Unpromising Hero motif—Dave Wilson's motif—is not the theme

9. The heroes of folktales are often strangers. Rank suggests the psychological significance of this fact in *The Myth of the Birth of the Hero* (New York, 1959), pp. 65–66. See also Lord Raglan, *The Hero* (New York, 1956), pp. 188–189.

774 · *Arlin Turner*

of the novel. The novel's theme is the whole problem of identity—
the identity of the slave and the master, of the Negro and the white
man, of the guilty and the innocent, of the hunter and the hunted,
and of the true and false leader. The history of the Unpromising
Hero Dave Wilson is, in itself, involved with only the last of these
problems of identity, but the actions by which Pudd'nhead makes
himself Mayor Wilson effect (significantly, I believe) the resolution
of all the problems of identity and propound a telling paradox: in a
society in which the chains which bind slave to master and master to
slave call all men's identities in question, only the stranger, the
unfettered outsider, possesses a reliable identity.

* * *

* * * *Pudd'nhead Wilson* presents in the person of its hero the
prophecy—or at least the possibility—that men capable of resolving
the conflicts of democracy will arise in the land. Dave Wilson has
an answer to the question tacitly posed by Huck and his Pap, by
Judge Thatcher and Jim and the "mulatter p'fessor," by the Grangerfords and Shepherdsons and Colonel Sherburn, by the King and
the Duke and the honest, stupid, fallen people of Pikesville, the
question, "Who shall govern?" David Wilson *is* the answer to that
question. Mark Twain's images of the Unpromising Hero had originally arisen in response to his personal anxieties; but his personal
anxieties finally gave place to social concern. If the motive which
gives *Pudd'nhead Wilson* life issues in some measure from the fret-
tings of the nursery, it issues in far greater measure from the mature
meditations of the study. The image of the Unpromising Hero
Dave Wilson epitomizes all of the hope for popular government
which Mark Twain's long years of observation at home and abroad
had allowed him to retain, a hope modified but not vitiated by
experience.

But *Pudd'nhead Wilson*, Mark Twain's most mature and effective fable of the Unpromising Hero, was also his last. The last, at
any rate, of any literary consequence. * * *

ARLIN TURNER

Mark Twain and the South: *Pudd'nhead Wilson*†

Huckleberry Finn paints the world of the lower Mississippi as the
whites see it. To be sure, Huck's level of social vision is little above
Jim's, but his sympathy for Jim is inconstant and may seem to

† From "Mark Twain and the South: *Southern Review,* IV, n.s. (April 1968),
An Affair of Love and Anger," *The*   493–519.

imply an identification which does not exist. The white man's doctrine of race superiority is held up to ridicule, but the victim of that doctrine remains unrealized. The basic situation, Huck and Jim raft-borne in a flight before expected pursuers, led Mark Twain to formulate in this book a sequence of responses to the arguments on slavery and race he had known since childhood but had never before considered seriously. And even here the reader may get the impression that the sequence grew unawares to the author, while his attention was fixed on other elements.

But Mark Twain had long known that not every slave could expect to go rafting down the river to freedom; recollections extending back to his childhood furnished harsh proof to the contrary. He also knew that the doctrines of race which outlived slavery had far greater effects than to form queer ideas in the mind of a boy such as Huck. In 1874 he had published "A True Story," a short narrative telling that he once asked a Negro servant how she could have lived sixty years and "never had any trouble." She answered by recounting how in slave times her husband and seven children were sold away from her and how she met one son by accident during the Civil War. She concluded, "Oh, no, Misto C————, *I* hain't had no trouble. An' no *joy!*" She thus places herself alongside Jim, a Negro employed to pass judgment on the white man's generalized view of race. But the story, in addition, hints that under suitable prompting the author might trace out the human effects of slavery and caste, and might draw full-scale characters in the process.

This hint which may be read in "A True Story" was in a large measure borne out in *Pudd'nhead Wilson*, and the direct promptings under which the novel grew are fully revealed. The author declared that the Negro characters were not in his original plan, and that after he had brought them in for minor roles in the plot, the question of race demanded a hearing without regard to his intentions. When the novel was finished, after extensive recasting, he had treated the dominant Southern issue of his time with more force and realism than elsewhere in his writings—or, for that matter, in any other contemporary writings except Cable's. Here, in a frankness not usual with him, he faced the implications of miscegenation and the psychological effects of racial doctrines on both races. Here, as a consequence, in Roxy, who has one-sixteenth Negro blood, he created his most fully realized female character and through her, in the clearest instance in all his fiction, acknowledged sex to be an element in human relations. As a further consequence, and in spite of inconsistency in the portrait, he achieved in Roxy a level of tragic characterization not present elsewhere in his works. In *Huckleberry Finn* slavery is obscured in the happy ending for Jim, and other aspects of the race question are not broached; *Pudd'nhead Wilson* ends tragically for all the characters, white and black, who are touched by slavery and race.

* * *

The chief need in recasting the story was to adjust the characters Tom Driscoll and Roxy to the new understanding of the race problem the author was approaching. The roles these two had assumed were leading him to understand that slavery and caste shape not only society and its institutions but individuals also, that instead of being merely a social phenomenon, miscegenation is a matter of life and a matter of death among human beings.

As initially introduced, Tom Driscoll is white, with no hint of Negro blood. He is a young man of both innate and cultivated evil, displaying villainy enough to deserve the conviction for crime Pudd'nhead Wilson's fingerprint collection will insure. He embarrasses his friends when he can, robs his neighbors to finance his dissolute life, and gleefully contemplates killing his uncle if that is necessary to hasten his own inheritance.

Such was the character Tom when the author decided to make him a changeling and a Negro. The Tom of the second stage, accustomed to abusing the slaves as members of an inferior race, is grimly embittered to learn that he belongs to that race. In the first draft of the episode in which Roxy tells him who she is, she refuses to identify his father, leaving him consumed by hatred. Vowing to learn the secret from her somehow and to seek out and kill his father, he exults in what he calls his father's death song. He will show what can be expected from "a nigger with a grievance," repeating the word "nigger" in his bitterness. The lowly creature who is his mother, he says, has a nobility beyond anything a slaveholder could ever claim. He is himself both a slave and a white man's bastard. Whatever is base in him may have come from either the white or the black blood, or from both, for it is the product of slavery, through the abuse and degradation experienced by the slaves or through the debasement and tyranny produced in the slaveholder. Tom's resentment inspires in him a raging hatred of all whites and a dedication to revenge which bear overtones of the heroic. His hatred produces the courage he would not otherwise have, and he is capable of murder, not simply assassination. Notebook entries and preserved manuscript scraps show that Mark Twain at one time planned a scene in which Tom confronts his father, hesitates, and then concludes he cannot kill him. But when his father pleads, "O spare me!—I am your father!" Tom cries, "Now for *that*, you shall die," and kills him.

Because the inordinate deceit and meanness and cowardice of the white Tom Driscoll could have no place in this Tom, the author turned back to pages written earlier and modified these aspects of his character. Yet some traits appropriate to the earlier Tom but not this one remained unchanged, and survived in fact to the printed book, such as Tom's goading of Pudd'nhead Wilson about his hobbies and his failure in law practice.

Mark Twain's uncertainty in delineating Tom as the Negro who had been brought up believing he was white suggests that he was exploring his way in areas new to his thought and that more than once he decided he had gone astray in his extemporizing. This Tom Driscoll of hatred and revenge was not acceptable, even after the diabolism of the earlier white man had been diluted. A character who nursed such blind hatred, however many wrongs he might have suffered, seemed to Mark Twain false to the Negro in America, either as a slave or as a freedman. In further—and final—recasting, therefore, Roxy tells Tom he can hold his head high in pride because his father, who died ten years earlier, belonged to one of the First Families of Virginia. Tom's earlier rage against his unknown father now becomes self-pitying analysis of his own weaknesses and a cowering humility in the presence of whites. He is weak, cowardly, given to drink and gambling, incapable of hunting down and killing his father or anyone else. He kills Judge Driscoll when frightened during a robbery rather than by design.

The changes in character Roxy experiences in the sequences of revisions, no less drastic than the changes in Tom, show even more clearly the expansion that was taking place in the author's understanding of Negro character and Negro experiences in America. At her first appearance in the early draft, sick and penniless and whining as she returns from eight years as a chambermaid on the river, Roxy is a stock household Negro, visiting among the servants and living on food they sneak out of the kitchen for her. She has little thought of her son Tom, except that she hopes he will provide for her. Rebuffed in her first pleas to him, she makes a whimpering appeal to his sympathy. Then when she tells Tom who he is and can blackmail him, she becomes a partner in his burglary and frightens him by the risks she will take in her greed. Portions of the early draft show her finally driving Tom, under awesome threats, to steal from Judge Driscoll the money he needs. One manuscript fragment concludes with her saying to Tom: " 'Take yo' choice—hog de money dis night or I tells de Jedge in de mawnin' who you *is*. You'll be on de oction block in 2 minutes.' " Another fragment illustrates Roxy's meanness as she was first drawn. Chambers has been arrested by mistake after Tom's murder of Judge Driscoll. When he has been seized by a lynch mob, Roxy says, "Well twould a ben my son if I hadn't changed 'em."

In the revisions, Roxy's heartlessness and her calculated selfishness are cancelled. She shows genuine affection for Tom when she returns from steamboating, and she is confident he will treat her kindly. When his harshness has convinced her "that her beautiful dream was a fond and foolish vanity, a shabby and pitiful mistake," she has feelings altogether unsuited to the early Roxy: "she was hurt to the heart, and so ashamed that for a moment she did not quite know what to do or how to act." To Tom's continued degrading scorn, she responded as "the heir of two centuries of una-toned insult and outrage," and "the fires of old wrongs flamed up in her breast and began to burn fiercely." Thus the reader of the pub-lished work is prepared to have Roxy take on the role of an aveng-ing angel as she tells Tom who he is. Instead of the scheming woman of the earlier draft who would drive her son to destruction for her own gain, she now goes into slavery to save his fortune. He sells her into what they both know to be the unspeakable horror of slavery "down the river," and after her escape and return she is simply pronouncing on him, in effect, the sentence he has brought upon himself—he must go ask the judge for the money to buy her free. To rob the judge rather than ask for the money is now his decision, not Roxy's. It is worth noting that in the early draft Roxy is normally referred to as a mulatto, a crone, or an old woman, and that in the revisions such designations are replaced by her name or a simple pronoun. In one revision it is said that Roxy's "bearing took to itself a dignity and state that might have passed for queenly if her surroundings had been a little more in keeping with it."

Although slavery and race oppression were introduced late into the plans for *Pudd'nhead Wilson*, in the final version they stand under severe and inclusive charges. The helplessness of the slaves is dramatized in Tom's abuse of Chambers, for example; and the catalog of horrors Roxy experiences after she has been re-sold into slavery gains immediacy and weight from the fact that she describes them to her son, who has betrayed her. The effects of slavery on the slaves, aside from their lot of deprivation and pain, appear in Chambers, when at the end he discovers he is white but cannot recover from the wrenching in both mind and spirit he has received while a slave. After learning that he is in fact a Negro and a slave, Tom finds he can no longer think and act as he did before, even though he and Roxy alone know his identity. In addition, the effect of slavery on the master class becomes clear, as Mark Twain exposes the essential dishonesty entailed by the owning of slaves. Percy Driscoll feels so righteous for selling his three household slaves, not down the river but elsewhere, after they have confessed to petty thievery, that he wants the account to serve his son as an example of moral conduct. Tom, growing up the spoiled heir to a Virginia gen-tleman's estate, develops the cruelty appropriate in that estate to dealings with slaves. His arrogance and his inhumanity as a white man and also his cowardice and meanness later as a slave derive from his own or the experiences of others as slaves or as slave-owners.

* * *

* * * it should be noted that the Negro as a simple comic figure appears also in *Pudd'nhead Wilson*. Jasper, first named Jim in the manuscript, and then Sandy (for a slave in the Clemens household in Hannibal), appears in the second chapter in a bantering dialogue with Roxy. In the initial draft Jasper is a Dunker Baptist and Roxy is a Shouting Methodist, as are also Dan'l and Jinny, and they too argue about divine providence. In marking out the debate of Jasper and Roxy on divine providence, the author reduced the buffoonery of the Negro characters, but the tone of the scene remained slap-stick. Mark Twain's fondness for these characters, with their comical argument, is attested further by their appearance again in a work he left unpublished, *Simon Wheeler, Detective* (1963).

Along with the subject of race, Mark Twain looked more closely in *Pudd'nhead Wilson* than elsewhere in his works at the cult of Southern aristocracy, codes of honor, and the duel, as details of the plot led him from one aspect of the cult to another. Yet he reached no consistent, inclusive attitude, and he displayed a tolerance of slavery as seen from the position of the slaveholders which in the total view is out of keeping with the view of slavery shown through the slaves.

In the past he had thrown many darts at the Sir Walter Scott cult in the South: the naming of children, houses, colleges, and towns from Scott's romances; the importing of unfitting medieval architecture; the revival of the tournament; the awe with which Americans viewed titled Europeans; the taste for medieval romances of adventure; and above all the assumption of class superiority. But Mark Twain acknowledges varying types and grades of aristocracy, and he makes no claim that they are confined within the South. * * * European titled aristocracy stands condemned, but only mildly. The severest strictures are against American pretensions to aristocracy, and much of American life stands indicted through the idealism of the young English nobleman. But his idealism is folly, after all. One man cannot reform an entire social order alone; the sensible course for him is to keep his hereditary station and work for improvement from that as a base.

In *Pudd'nhead Wilson* the First Families of Virginia are represented by Percy Northumberland Driscoll, York Leicester Driscoll, Pembroke Howard, and Tom's father, Colonel Cecil Burleigh Essex. These men, bearing flamboyantly appropriate names, revere their Virginia heritage above all other affiliations, not excluding the loyalties owed to church, state, or family. In this loyalty they are foolish rather than evil, and they possess the virtues of integrity, kindness, and high purpose. Supported by hereditary doctrines of caste, they are unquestioning slaveholders. Kind masters, according to their lights, they would not believe that the slaves suffered under the system or that they were themselves warped through their role as masters. Slavery is under subtler and stronger indictment in the final than in the earlier drafts of the novel. With Roxy becoming more important and the book swinging from farce toward tragedy, greater subtlety was required and greater force in the satire resulted. But the slaveholders do not appear to be responsible for the evils of slavery. Except in the death of Judge Driscoll, they have farcical roles. In the context of the entire plot, Driscoll is destroyed by an agent of the social evil which his proud heritage has fostered, but this larger view is obscured by the surface fact that he falls before Tom's villainy.

Percy Driscoll no doubt owed much of his character and some of his action as a slaveholder to Mark Twain's recollections of his father, and it is probably for this reason that Driscoll is portrayed more absurd than evil and that Tom is left to bear the full curse of slaveholding. Like John Marshall Clemens, Driscoll has come from Virginia, is proud of his gentlemanly heritage, is the soul of generosity toward white men, but applies a different brand of generosity and kindness in dealing with slaves. In an early draft of *Pudd'nhead Wilson* Mark Twain assigned to Judge Driscoll an episode from his father's life. Once journeying south to collect money a friend had long owed him, John Marshall Clemens took along a slave to sell as a way of financing the trip, thoughtless of the sorrow caused the slave and his family. The cutting out of this journey even before the final revision of the novel was probably due in part to the author's reluctance to perpetuate an episode which reflected so unfavorably on his father. In a similar instance, Mark Twain referred in the manuscript of *Following the Equator* (1897) to his father's striking a slave. When his wife objected, he deleted the note.

A key to the author's uncertain way of looking at the cult of Southern aristocracy may be taken from his equivocation in handling the duel. His account of how once in Nevada he came close to engaging in a duel should be noted in this connection. In a passage deleted from the manuscript of *Life on the Mississippi* he remarked that the duel had not quite disappeared in the Southern states but had been "hopefully modified." In New Orleans blood might be drawn now and then, but in Virginia, he added, "the mere flash and smell of powder cure the most acrid wound which can be inflicted upon a statesman's honor." The implication here is that duels are to be condemned, but the direct statement—and the cause for scorn—is that in both New Orleans and Virginia dueling is no more than ritual and pretense, with no real danger to the participants. The same statement and the same scorn dominate two chapters in A *Tramp Abroad*. In one the French political duels are ridiculed as utter sham. Another chapter describes the bloody duels of university students in Germany, detailing the blood, pain, and disfigurement as the serious young Germans hack away at each other. The student duels were genuine, and the author could admire the courage, even though it was displayed in a foolish affair.

The duel recounted in *Pudd'nhead Wilson* as first written, and retained in the supplement, "Those Extraordinary Twins," is broadest farce: one of the conjoined twins has accepted Judge Driscoll's challenge and the other twin is an unwilling close attendant. In the novel proper, with the twins separate, the duel remains farcical—with all those present receiving wounds except the principals—but the episode is less outlandish. Even so, not all is farce. Judge Driscoll and his friend, Pembroke Howard, are shown to be naïve, if not absurd, in their reverence for the code of honor; but they are to be respected for integrity and courage lying beyond all question. In pouring her blistering scorn upon Tom because he has refused to defend his honor in a duel, Roxy in effect condemns rather than defends dueling, for like Huckleberry Finn, she speaks from the false beliefs of the society around her. Yet, the reader notes that Tom refuses to fight not because of any principle but because of his cowardice, and his refusal elicits the derision of Pudd'nhead Wilson, who stands outside the social structure of Dawson's Landing and thus speaks from an uncompromised position.

Dueling on Mark Twain's pages is a silly vestige of an antiquated code which was just as silly when it flourished in remote ages. Still, no one loses more than a drop or two of blood in his version of a Southern duel and no one but a cowardly Tom Driscoll or an other-worldly Italian twin refuses to fight. Like feuds duels are total nonsense, but they are perpetuated by families who bear the best blood and the highest culture of the region. The doctrines supporting race superiority and slavery are false growths from man's greed and his habit of deceiving himself; yet the Driscolls, Miss Watson, and other slaveholders of Mark Twain's fictional world seem to be somehow without responsibility for slavery. They are comical or silly or unaware, but always innocent, at least in intentions. Until *Pudd'nhead Wilson* Mark Twain's fictional slaves knew little of actual slavery; and even in that book the typed stage darky is exploited for comic effect. But under prompting from the characters and the situations he introduced into the plot, he reached understandings of the two races and their influences on each other, both before and after emancipation, which he had not approached before.

In 1894, the year *Pudd'nhead Wilson* appeared, George W. Cable published his last book dealing with the race question in the South, *John March, Southerner*. Cable had found no audience in either North or South for essays or lectures on the subject, and his publishers were urging him to write fiction which would not antago- nize or even disturb anyone. By 1894, the problems explored in *Pudd'nhead Wilson* had grown wearisome in the North as well as the South. More than a decade earlier the political decision had been made that the Southern states should solve the race problem without interference from the national government. As state laws were enacted in the early 1890s which decreed for the former slaves a segregated, non-voting status, no effective protest was voiced in either section. The public, valuing the peace which had been achieved, did not welcome disturbances, even in fiction.

There is something of irony in that, by chance rather than inten- tion, Mark Twain wrote his most perceptive and most impressive attack on racism and related doctrines at a time when his attack could stir no spark in the reading public. It was an irony fitting to the black mood into which he was descending steadily deeper. Roxy, Tom, Chambers, and Judge Driscoll had revealed to him sub- tleties in the race question which in his chuckle-headedness, he might have said, he had not learned from Uncle Dan'l, Aunt Hannah, Jim, or others of the characters he had put into fiction over the preceding twenty years. And his new understanding came at just the time he realized—or might have learned from his friend Cable—that society, in the North no less than in the South, had settled into a pattern of thought which could promise no relief for the victims of race oppression.

Whether Mark Twain was aware that these changes were taking place in the status and the prospects of the former slaves, is not cer- tain—or indeed whether he realized that in *Pudd'nhead Wilson* he had probed more deeply than ever before into the complexities of Southern society. He did not attempt in any of his later works to reconcile the inconsistencies and contradictions which remained in that novel—and in his mind—even after the extensive reworking which accompanied refinements in his understanding. He contin- ued, rather, to speak of the South after his old habit, in affection or disgust, nostalgia or anger, depending on the immediate provocation and his mood at the moment.

FREDERICK ANDERSON

[Mark Twain and the Writing of *Pudd'nhead Wilson*] †

"I am frightened at the proportions of my prosperity. It seems to me that whatever I touch turns to gold." When Mark Twain

† From Frederick Anderson, Introduc- tion to the facsimile of the first Ameri- can edition of *Pudd'nhead Wilson/Those* *Extraordinary Twins* (San Francisco: Chandler, 1968), pp. vii–xxxii.

made this statement in 1885, he was publishing *Huckleberry Finn*. For a man at the peak of his prosperity as author and lecturer, with promising investments in a typesetter and his own publishing company, and an opulent life in an intellectual community in Hartford, such fear might have seemed neurotic. Six years later, Samuel Clemens, at the age of fifty-seven, found his fear had been prophetic. His protracted investment in the Paige typesetter had eroded his fortune, and Charles L. Webster & Co., the publishing house, was headed toward failure. He and his family had retired to economic exile in Europe. The logical salvation for a writer caught in these crises of business failure was to return to the writing which had been the foundation for earlier success.

But the greatest crisis which Mark Twain faced at this time was the assault upon his confidence in himself as a writer. Henry Nash Smith in *Mark Twain: Development of a Writer* and *Fable of Progress* has identified and described the intellectual and moral problems which confronted the author upon discovering the implications of his most recent novel, *A Connecticut Yankee*. "When he found it impossible to show how the values represented by his vernacular protagonist could survive in an industrial society, he lost faith in the value system of that society. Henceforth he worked as a writer in a kind of spiritual vacuum. His imagination was virtually paralyzed."

However afflicted his imagination, Clemens could not afford to be inactive even though the work he produced from 1889 to 1892 shows more evidence of desperate diligence than of creative invention. After having completed the *Yankee*, Clemens published *Merry Tales*, four of whose seven sketches had appeared in previous collections of his work. He had written the feeblest of all his novels, *The American Claimant*, a reworking of dismal material from an abortive play. The novel appeared in serial form throughout 1892. Clemens was also writing *Tom Sawyer Abroad by Huck Finn*, an undistinguished sequel to the earlier books in which those characters had figured. Further evidence of Clemens' willingness to sacrifice literary reputation, and perhaps even self-respect, for financial profit is to be found in the publication of "Esquimau Maiden's Romance" in the rather undistinguished *Cosmpolitan* in November 1893. A month later, however, the first episode of *Pudd'nhead Wilson* appeared in the impeccable *Century Magazine*. The difference in quality between these two stories is even greater than that of the journals in which they appeared.

While Clemens was working on the most challenging novel he had attempted since the *Yankee*, his imagination evidently became active again. Perhaps this recovery was achieved by means of the tension Clemens encountered when, having turned back to the essentially rural and preindustrial society in which he had lived as a boy, he found personal conflict and social evil more intense and more complicated than he had expected. These discoveries provide the substance for *The Tragedy of Pudd'nhead Wilson*.

A man almost equally well known to himself and his friends by two completely different names throughout most of his adult life might have been expected to be concerned with the problem of identity in human character. Questions of personal identity and duality had begun to afflict Samuel Clemens at least as early as 1863 when he felt compelled to adopt "Mark Twain" as a means of distinguishing between his divided roles as comic columnist and serious reporter on the Virginia City *Territorial Enterprise*. Although in those years it was common procedure for reporters to adopt a pen name, the degree to which Clemens became privately identified with his, to himself as well as to others, while remaining almost equally well known by his Christian and family names, is unique. Identical twins are an obvious and graphic symbol of divided identity and Clemens' preoccupation with them appeared early and was persistent thereafter. In 1869 he had published an account of the "Personal Habits of the Siamese Twins"—twins possessing many habits and characteristics later to be assigned to the twins, Luigi and Angelo, in the present book.

Another discovery, although not a wholly new one for Clemens, was his conflicting attitudes toward the border South where a river town full of flowers, cats, and playful boys was also populated by slaves, slaveowners, white trash, and degenerate Virginia gentry. Ideological conflict in Clemens' attitudes toward slavery and the other social institutions of the South must have begun to trouble him by the time he "deserted" the volunteer Marion Rangers, informally organized to support the Confederacy in 1861. His commitment to the Southern cause was ambiguous during the Civil War; but by the end of the decade his disaffection was complete. After 1870, Clemens was a fervent critic in private and in print of the effects of slavery on all participants involved in it.

He was almost equally critical of the corruption and dishonesty which he felt the code of chivalry and the duel, derived as he saw it from the romances of Sir Walter Scott, had imposed upon Southern society and character. The Grangerfords and the Shepherdsons, with names indicative of traditionally opposed occupational loyalties, had been employed in *Huckleberry Finn* to attack the maliciously wasteful folly of the code. Through York Leicester Driscoll and Pembroke Howard, whose names are symbolic of their presumptively corrupt aristocratic origin, Clemens carries on the attack in *Pudd'nhead Wilson*, less brilliantly but with no less determination.

Although the principals in the duels seem to have no direct pro-

totypes in Clemens' childhood experience in the South, less stereo-
typed figures in the story are at least in part based on personal
knowledge. The description of Tom Driscoll's excursion to Yale and
foppish behavior on his return to the village echoes in detail Clemens' factual account of a Hannibal contemporary in "Villagers of
1840–3." Aspects of Pudd'nhead Wilson's character and career, specifically his barren law practice, are based on that of Mark Twain's
brother Orion and the crushing failure he encountered in his
attempt to practice that profession. Roxy, who is by far the most
interesting character in this novel, and one of the most fully realized figures Clemens was ever to create, had been significantly antic-
ipated in "A True Story Repeated Word for Word as I Heard It,"
first published in the November 1874 issue of the *Atlantic
Monthly.* The characterization of Aunt Rachel, the freed-slave narrator in the factual short sketch, incorporates in large measure the
complex qualities of pride, shrewdness, and maternal fury, compounded by the tortures inherent in slavery, which make Roxy into
Mark Twain's most successful female protagonist. Unlike Roxy's,
the stature of Aunt Rachel's heroic martyrdom and dignity was
never diminished. Since these two figures stand alone among Clemens' portraits of women, it appears that he required the distance
provided by color to establish and sustain the vulgar quality of life
in a female character. In *Pudd'nhead Wilson* this unaccustomed
ability to create an unromanticized heroine may have been in part
called forth by the author's recognition that he could not at this
time find his customary satisfaction in developing male characters
whose counterparts in earlier work had provided a sense of artistic
fulfillment.

A final element from Clemens' personal history appears in the
town of Dawson's Landing, which in the opening of the book is as
idealized an evocation of Hannibal as Clemens ever achieved. Its
name is significantly derived from the school kept by J. D. Dawson
which Clemens attended and which had figured prominently as
Dobbin's school in *Tom Sawyer.* As the book progresses, the town
quite literally becomes a school for its inhabitants. The examination
of complicated and tragic institutions and attitudes and the reconstruction of personal history were made additionally awkward by
Mark Twain's irrepressible impulse toward broad burlesque and low
comedy. Before the book which would incorporate these elements
was complete, the author would have to reverse the initial direction
in which his erratic creative imagination led him.

* * *

Such changes as Clemens made in the evolution of the book
seem necessary and wisely motivated. The changes he did not make

are subject to critical comment. In the author's defense it should be pointed out that he was working in a chaos of confusions and demands which contrast forcefully with the serenity of his isolated study at Quarry Farm where he had done most of his imaginative work during leisurely summers. Constant travel and the costly distractions of business and family affairs deducted from the store of creative energy available for literary revision. Evidence of this is the family history of the twins which, apart from internal inconsistencies and unexplained motivations, becomes entirely irrelevant to a description of ordinary twins although it was not removed from the final version of the book.

Mark Twain's fatigue in revision is implicit in his statement after the Siamese twins were separated that they "had no occasion to have foreign names now, but it was too much trouble to remove them all through, so I left them christened as they were and made no explanation."

Nevertheless the author's attempt to avoid such irrelevancies and inconsistencies is effectively illustrated by a sequence of changes in the market-house meeting of the "rum party." At Tom Driscoll's suggestion that "this human philopena snip you out a speech," the audience burst into laughter because of "the descriptive aptness of the phrase." "Philopena" (the matched kernels of a nut) is a resourceful substitute for the "human pair of scissors" which Clemens had used when the Siamese twins had only one pair of legs but the lack of relationship between the new noun and the unrevised verb distinctly diminishes the effect of the phrase. Clemens' recognition of this weakness is demonstrated by replacement of the manuscript's "descriptive precision" with the book's "descriptive aptness." Under more leisurely conditions, Clemens would likely have reconstructed the imagery of the entire passage. But leisure for further revision was absorbed by a demand for returns from his creative investment, whose prospects Clemens' 30 July letter to Hall proceeded to examine:

> Now, then, what is she worth? The amount of matter is but 3,000 words short of the American Claimant, for which the syndicate paid $12,500. There was nothing new in that story, but the finger-prints in this one is virgin ground—absolutely *fresh*, and mighty curious & interesting to everybody.
>
> I don't want any more syndicating—nothing short of $20,000 anyway, & that I can't get—but won't you see how much the Cosmpolitan will stand? At the rate Walker paid for the little story he bought last spring, this one would be worth toward $9,000—say $8,500. At the rate he offered me later for 12 contributions (on any subject) of 2,500 to 3,500 words each (an average of 3,000 each or 36,000 for the 12), the price would be—

well, I don't quite know what. *But*—a 58,000-word story is worth a higher rate than random sketches & contributions, and maybe Walker will stand a raise. Now you just praise the thing up, and get his price and cable me *"Walker offers (so many) dollars."* I will cable *"Accept"* or *"Try elsewhere."*

If I cable the latter, go privately & try the Century. If they won't stand a raise, cable me thus: *"Gilder no better"* or *"Gilder offers* (name sum)*"* & I will return answer.

Do your best for me, for I do not sleep, these nights, for visions of the poor-house. . . .

Throughout this period the Clemens family was living in a 28-room Florentine villa, with a staff of never less than five servants, "with family expenses $1,700 a month, scrimp & economise as we may."

In another reference to imminent business failure and bankruptcy Clemens, rather pathetically, wrote in August to Hall: "I mean to ship 'Pudd'nhead Wilson' to you—say, tomorrow. It'll furnish me hash for a while I reckon. I am almost sorry it is finished; it was good entertainment to work at it, and kept my mind away from things."

* * *

Despite Clemens' reluctance in January and February 1893 to have the book issued by a publisher other than Webster & Co., he realized in the Spring of 1894 that the book would have to be printed and distributed by the American Publishing Co. "on a basis of half of the profits above cost of manufacture." When the last installment appeared in the Summer of 1894 Clemens had become anxious about final arrangements for the book before current interest in the story lagged and in order to take advantage of the Fall and Christmas market for books. But complex negotiations with his creditors concerning the imminent bankruptcy of Clemens and the Webster company led to delays, perhaps to avoid introduction of the additional financial factor of royalties from a new book. H. H. Rogers, a vice-president of Standard Oil who had voluntarily accepted control of Clemens' business affairs, wrote on 1 June:

> I note the willingness of Mrs. Clemens and yourself to allow Mr. Bliss to publish "Pudd'nhead Wilson" by subscription but I hesitate in giving my approval at present, because I am afraid it will not prove satisfactory in the end. However, I am . . . discussing the whole scheme from the many standpoints and hope to reach an intelligent decision.

The many standpoints must have been defined and resolved by discussion, for the few surviving documents leave the reasons for delay cryptic. A contract was signed with Frank Bliss, as president of the American Publishing Company, on 24 August. The terms of the contract called for a $1500 payment by the publisher to the author and one-half of the gross profits from sales in addition to stipulations about manufacturing and distribution procedures including publication of the book "as soon as practicable after the receipt" of the manuscript. *The Tragedy of Pudd'nhead Wilson and The Comedy Those Extraordinary Twins* finally appeared on 28 November 1894.

Critical response to *Pudd'nhead Wilson* was immediately gratifying to the harassed and nearly bankrupt writer. The promise of $6,500 to be paid to Clemens for serial rights in the *Century* had been reinforced by the editors of that journal when they read the manuscript in September. "Gilder and Johnson are vastly pleased with the story, & they say Roxy is a great & dramatic & well-drawn character." Mark Twain's brother Orion wrote shortly after the first installment appeared in the December issue: "Among several complimentary editorials in the [Keokuk, Iowa] Gate City, one speaks of your story in the Century as the flower of your autumn." Clemens was able to write Livy in January 1894:

> Not since Innocents Abroad have I heard so much talk about a book of mine as Pudd'nhead. . . . Professor Powell of the University of Pennsylvania . . . had considerable to say about the serious deeps underlying the humor in my several books, & then said that Puddnhead was clearly & powerfully drawn & would live to take his place as one of the great creations of American fiction.

The first installment evoked further friendly praise: "Mr. Hutton thinks Pudd'nhead opens up in great & fine style. The fact is, I get a great many compliments on that story & the promise holds out to the reader."

The Review of Reviews' January evaluation of the first installment in the *Century* was also enthusiastic and exact in emphasis:

> The feature of the number so far as fiction is concerned is the beginning of Mark Twain's serial novel "Pudd'n Head Wilson," the scene of which is laid in Southwest Missouri thirty-five years ago. The first chapters give but small indication of that humor which made Mr. Clemens' fame. Curiously enough, the plot, if one may presume to prophesy from the first chapters, is going to center around the mixing up of two babies, one of whom is a white child and the other a mulatto with a slight strain of negro blood, the two being under the charge of the fond mulatto mother; so that we may expect to find Mark Twain drawing some healthy moral concerning the race problem before we are through with "Pudd'n Head Wilson."

The Outlook and *The Nation* commented briefly and with less relevance on the "novel detection of crime" which was "humorous" and "genuinely and solidly American in subject and treatment."

Further praise came from one of the most eminent critics of the period: "I was at Brander Matthews's. . . . He said the selling of Roxy down the river is very strong, & the strongest piece of writing I have ever done."

Following the delayed publication of the book, the American reviews were few and cursory. The *New York Times* on 27 January 1895 assumed general knowledge of the story and commented only on the marginal illustrations supplied in profusion for the first edition, chiefly by F. M. Senior,

> an artist who, though he does not draw well, is clever in grasping ideas; the fun and drollery and the comedy and tragedy of two of Mark Twain's most interesting stories have been multiplied many times. Those who have enjoyed "Pudd'nhead Wilson," with nothing but their imaginations to help them picture what sort of man the hero of the story was [although Louis Loeb, a staff artist for the *Century*, had illustrated the serial installments] and what the scenes were in which he acted his part, will be glad to run through the story again along with the artist.

The *Critic* did not notice the book until 11 May 1895, and when it did the reviewer concerned himself almost entirely with an attempt to define Mark Twain's role as "the most successful of a class of American humorists" in contrast to "other national humorists, like Aristophanes, Cervantes, Molière or Swift." The American humorists "are pure 'naturalists'—men of instinctive genius" who, although they "produce delight in the reader, irrespective of classicity of form, literary grace or any other of the beloved conventions on which literature as literature has hitherto depended," are not able to achieve the "wonderful bird-rhythms and wasp melodies and cloud-architecture," the "suave literary graces" and "honeyed verse" of the non-American national humorists.

English reviews of the Chatto & Windus edition of the volume were in general more spacious, more thoughtful, and greater in number than the American. Perhaps the most persuasive explanation for this discrepancy is that the novel had not previously been printed in an English journal whereas it had begun to appear in America a full year before the book was finally issued. An additional possible reason is the characteristic reluctance of American literary journals, largely owned by publishing houses, to endorse by attention the rival subscription publishers' merchandise. An inescapable final consideration is the possible superiority in number and quality of British book reviews.

The earliest English account of the book, printed in *The Idler* (incidentally also published by Chatto & Windus) in August 1894, was presumably based on copies of the *Century* serialization from which the English text was taken. *The Idler* emphasizes that this

"is the work of a novelist, rather than of a 'funny man,' " and proceeds to make a number of critical judgments which should be subjected to impartial examination:

> In point of construction it is much the best story that Mark
> Twain has written, and of men and women in the book at least
> four are undeniably creations, and not one of them is overdrawn
> or caricatured, as are some of the most popular of the author's lay
> figures. There is but one false note in the picture, and that is the
> introduction of the two alleged Italian noblemen. These two
> young men are as little like Italians as they are like Apaches. . . .
> But this is a small blemish, and if Mark Twain, in his future
> novels, can maintain the proportion of only two lay figures to
> four living characters, he will do better than most novelists. The
> extracts from "Puddenhead Wilson's Almanac," which are pre-
> fixed to each chapter of the book, simply "pizon us for more," to
> use Huck Finn's forcible metaphor. Let us hope that a complete
> edition of that unrivalled almanac will be issued at no distant
> day.

The ingenuous public request from the publishing house to itself to
bring out a complete edition of that almanac apparently failed to
attract interest.

Shortly after English publication, *The Bookman* presented a
one-paragraph summary without critical comment in its January
issue. The reader's haste led him to believe that after the exchange
of infants, "one of them, the wrong one, of course, was sold with
the slave mother."

The Athenaeum's reviewer (19 January 1895) read with impressive care and insight:

> The best thing in *Pudd'nhead Wilson* . . . is the picture of the
> negro slave Roxana, the cause of all the trouble which gives scope
> to Mr. Wilson's ingenious discovery about finger-marks. Her
> gusts of passion or of despair, her vanity, her motherly love, and
> the glimpses of nobler feelings that are occasionally seen in her
> elementary code of morals, make her very human, and create a
> sympathy for her in spite of her unscrupulous actions. But hers is
> the only character that is really striking. Her son is a poor crea-
> ture, as he is meant to be, but he does not arrest the reader with
> the same unmistakable reality: his actions are what might be
> expected, but his conversations, especially with Wilson and the
> Twins, seem artificial and forced. Wilson, the nominal hero,
> appears to most advantage in the extracts from his calendar
> which head the chapters, but as a personage he is rather too shad-
> owy for a hero. And what has to be said about the book must be
> chiefly about the individuals in it, for the story in itself is not
> much credit to Mark Twain's skill as a novelist. The idea of the
> change of babies is happy, and the final trial scene is a good piece

of effect; but the story at times rambles on in an almost incomprehensible way. Why drag in, for example, all the business about the election, which is quite irrelevant? and the Twins altogether seem to have very little *raison d'être* in the book. . . . The humor of the preface might very well be spared; it is in bad taste. Still, if the preface be skipped the book well repays reading just for the really excellent picture of Roxana.

Since the English edition appeared without the supplement of "Those Extraordinary Twins," the incomprehensibility of irrelevant survivals from the original story is easily understood.

A paragraph in *The Spectator* (16 March 1895) questions Mark Twain's historical perspective in the use of fingerprints for identification in 1830. However Francis Galton's *Finger Prints* (London, 1892) which had served as Clemens' source for this technical information describes Johannes Evangelista Purkenje's "University Thesis delivered at Breslau in 1823" as a detailed account of the complex variant forms of fingerprints. And although Wilson was compiling his fingerprint "records" as early as 1830, it is not until the trial in 1853 that he makes his dramatic claim and demonstration of the uniquely personal nature of fingerprints. Moreover, Clemens had used the device himself as early as 1883 in an anecdote which purportedly took place during the Civil War, and there appears to have been no critical accusation of anachronism. The author's insistence on the novelty of the literary use of this principle in *Pudd'nhead Wilson* is therefore curiously at odds with fact ("the finger-prints in this one is virgin ground—absolutely *fresh*"). Furthermore, the unique nature of fingerprints was emphasized in *Life on the Mississippi*: "there was one thing about a person which never changed, from the cradle to the grave—the lines in the ball of the thumb; . . . these lines were never exactly alike in the thumbs of any two human beings." The principle is further elaborated and even the concept of preserving a random collection of prints is presented. This passage is illustrated in the first edition with copies of two thumb prints.

Anne E. Keeling, with the perspective of more than four years since book publication, composed the most comprehensively perceptive critical commentary of the period. In her article, "American Humor: Mark Twain" in the July 1899 issue of *The London Quarterly Review*, she ably places *Pudd'nhead Wilson* in the context of Clemens' other writings and the period and place which are its subjects:

> In its unobtrusive way *Pudd'nhead Wilson*—almost the latest performance of its author—is a demonstration of the devilish mischief done by the "peculiar institution," American slavery, as convincing as *Uncle Tom's Cabin*. The indictment is dispassion-

ate as indictment of so monstrous an evil could be; there is little declamation, no exaggeration, and such picturesqueness and grace of old-world dignity and kindliness as could be found among the better sort of slaveholders is touched in with a kind of tender appreciation. But the injury to slave and slave-owner—the distorted morality on both sides, the hopeless degradation of the one, the cruel insolence of superiority in the other—are shown in action with a cogency that is something terrible. Humour there is in almost every scene and every page; but it is such humour as sheds a wild gleam on the greatest Shakespearian tragedies—on the deep melancholy of *Hamlet*, the heart-break of *Lear*.

The characters whose fortunes furnish forth the story are commonplace enough, so is the motive of the action—an exchange of children in their cradles by a slave foster-mother, who, being "only one-sixteenth black and that sixteenth didn't show," could substitute her slave-born boy, thirty-one parts white, fair of face and hair and blue-eyed like his foster-brother, for the son and heir of the lordly master, and so, as she dreamed, ward off from her darling all the horrors of his heritage of woe. How her fraud results in evil such as her poor untaught wit, however shrewd, could never have apprehended as possible, and how her son, thankless, heartless, faithless son to his real and his adoptive parent alike, is branded at last as perjured liar, thief, and murderer, and flung back into the thraldom she had tried to ward off from him—here is the originality in the plot, here the extraordinary power of the story, derived from the situation created for the otherwise insignificant personages and from the consequent evolutions of character. It needs all the quaint inverted wisdom of the citations from "Pudd'nhead Wilson's Kalendar" to waken the familiar laughter that used to convulse Mark Twain's readers in the older days; and even in these there is a note of bitter world-experience. . . . If he does not give us any of those enchantingly gracious pictures of the better side of slave-life which we owe to the creator of *Uncle Remus*, beloved of children, he will not blame the enthralled negroes for the moral defects due to their position. . . .

Piteous, humiliating fruit of injustice and oppression—"twice accursed," hurtful to him who did and him who bore the wrong. Masters themselves had a double code of honour and compassion. "He was a fairly humane man to slaves and other animals; he was an exceedingly humane man towards the erring of his own race."

More recent and therefore more readily available criticism is listed in the Bibliography. The discussions by Leslie Fiedler and James Cox are especially incisive and thorough. Although the relatively small amount of modern criticism is enthusiastic in praise of the book, it cannot fail to take into account the disunity of themes.

Clemens' rather loose grasp of his materials and his willingness in this instance to settle for easy effect is evident in his choice of titles for the variety of pieces presented in a single book. The desirability of preserving publicly *The Comedy Those Extraordinary Twins* is debatable, but the title exactly describes the text. The term "tragedy" in the title of the larger work is not so relevant. Even though the book deals with many aspects of tragedy inherent in slavery, it is not an account of Pudd'nhead Wilson's tragedy since despite his early obscurity he emerges as a triumphant figure. Nor is this book consistently focused on the title character. Clemens himself accurately appraised Wilson's role when he wrote to his wife, "I have never thought of *Puddn'head* [sic Anderson] as a *character*, but only as a piece of machinery—a button or a crank or a lever, with a useful function to perform in a machine, but with no dignity above that." Many years later Clemens again attributed a mechanistic or symbolic function to the nominal protagonist when he told Albert Bigelow Paine:

> Pudd'nhead Wilson came into my mind as an example of that unfortunate type of human being who, misunderstood at the moment of entering a new community, may spend a lifetime trying to live down that blunder, especially if he gets catalogued by some ridiculous nickname. Of course, in my story I brought Wilson out triumphant at the end, but it is not always so in life. Many a man had been labeled a fool, and has died with that label still on him, when the community might very well have gone to him for wisdom and counsel.

Although Clemens' memory of the evolution of emphasis in the book is faulty—or at least variant from the records which survive—he is consistent in identifying Wilson as a device rather than as the central figure of tragedy. Apart from the maxims attributed to him and which bear no evident relationship to the rest of Wilson's actions, there is little attempt to develop the scope of his character. His florid speech and dramatic manner in the courtroom reveal him to be a kind of grown-up Tom Sawyer, but even his prominence in this part of the book does not serve to deepen his character significantly. The impersonality of the nominal hero is reflected in large measure in the static and unrealized portrait of the town which is the setting for the book.

Rarely in *Pudd'nhead Wilson*, as the book was finally presented, do the people of the town live within the community. The "howling farce" which Clemens began, and in this instance preserved through revision, opened with an idyllic description of Hannibal. The town was peopled with the ingratiating widows and aunts and the mischievous boys who stroll along the shaded streets of any of the evocations of the town in which Clemens grew up and which he described in his *Autobiography* as "a little democracy . . . full of liberty, equality, and Fourth of July." But although he started off along this familiar ground, Mark Twain encountered a mixed group of "other people [who] got to intruding themselves and taking up more and more room with their talk and their affairs." The paths of these people were too devious to conform to the geography of the town, and the civic landscape of Dawson's Landing deteriorated to three or four houses and a stretch of open field which are related to each other about as casually as rafts along the river, until the climactic courtroom scene. Here the population of the town and of the surrounding country crowd into the epitome of Southern civic organization, the court house, and characterization and action are replaced by the actors and the contrived suspense of melodrama. At the climax of the trial, Mark Twain's language betrays his seduction by the histrionic impulse which is so often characteristic of Tom Sawyer's performances. At the moment of his triumph in the community Pudd'nhead Wilson descends to the language of the stage. "Valet de Chambre, negro and slave,—falsely called Thomas à Becket Driscoll,—make upon the window the finger-prints that will hang you!" Tom Sawyer never worked up a better "effect." Even Roxy is not permitted to escape an unrealistically sonorous betrayal of her real stature. "The spirit in her eye was quenched, her martial bearing departed with it, and the voice of her laughter ceased in the land. In her church and its affairs she found her only solace." This is a suspiciously easy and even comfortable resolution for a tragic heroine. Samuel Clemens had again abandoned his coveted role as a serious critic of the very real evils he saw in man and society in favor of the almost equally coveted role of writer for the stage. This duality of purpose frustrated his final success in either aspiration, but it is perhaps the dual impulse that in part at least made possible Mark Twain's substantial success in dealing with divided roles as a theme for the present book. His hatred of the enslavement of Negro by white and of man by social institutions with the corollary loss of freedom for all provided the context in which to examine an individual's slavery to his own confused identities.

The intricate manner in which Mark Twain pursued the elaboration of multiple identity may be observed in summary in the roles taken by the protagonist known most consistently as Tom Driscoll. When Roxy exchanged the identity of Valet de Chambre, her son by Colonel Cecil Burleigh Essex, for that of Thomas à Becket Driscoll, "Tom" became the supposed son of Percy Northumberland Driscoll and subsequently the ward of Judge York Leicester Driscoll. Until he became an adult, Tom's duality was the imposed and unconscious one of a Negro presumed to be Caucasian and an impostor in a family to which he did not belong. As an adult, he consciously assumed the symbols of duality in the form of explicit disguises. These are, in sequence, that of a white man with a beard, a young white woman, an old white woman (whose clothes Tom borrows from his Negro mother), a young Negro woman wearing a veil, and finally "a disguise proper for a tramp." He has made multiple interchanges of sex, race, and social position through disguise while maintaining the divided role of a respectable member of the family of the town's leading citizen, and a corrupt and dissolute gambler in St. Louis. When he learns of his Negro heritage he must assume the further role of a Negro passing as white. Roxy also undertakes the role of a transvestite when she escapes from slavery and disguises herself as a man. She is ironically forced to disguise herself further by blackening her face in order to make her skin color conform to her Negro speech. It is during her ostensible change of sex and race that Roxy most forcefully subjects her apparently white son to her domination. Clemens juggled these intricate symbols with brilliant dexterity and concluded the performance with savage irony and icy economy in the concluding sentence of the book. "As soon as the Governor understood the case, he pardoned Tom at once, and the creditors sold him down the river." It is with reluctance that one realizes the sentence is a product of sleight of hand. Tom, exposed as a Negro, could not have been sold down the river to help settle the debts of Percy Driscoll's estate. Judge Leicester Driscoll had bought Percy's slave, in the person of Valet de Chambre, a month before his brother's death in order to save him from that very fate, for "he had heard that Tom had been trying to get his father to sell the boy down the river, and he wanted to prevent the scandal."

To be strictly logical Clemens would have had to end the book with Valet de Chambre, as Judge Driscoll's heir, the owner of Tom. This would have presented the more complicated, but perhaps even more chilling, recognition that master and slave were unable to adopt in fact the roles forced upon them by law. Tom and Valet de Chambre had each become by training and custom enslaved within the character imposed upon him by society. It is this "higher" slavery with which Clemens became increasingly preoccupied during the rest of his life and from which he concluded, as everyone must, there is no Territory into which to flee.

GEORGE M. SPANGLER

Pudd'nhead Wilson: A Parable of Property†

The striking lack of agreement about the merits of Mark Twain's *Pudd'nhead Wilson* is unquestionably related to the equally striking disagreements over interpretation of the novel, related in the crucial sense that all the thematic analyses so far pre-

† From *American Literature*, 42 (March 1970), 1, 28–37.

sented leave important aspects of the novel unaccounted for. The result is that those who are inclined to praise the novel dismiss certain parts as finally inconsequential evidence of Twain's predictably careless technique, while those who have serious reservations about its merits stress its lack of coherence, its lack of an action adequate to embody what appear to be the author's chief concerns. Although interpretations vary widely, ranging from the view that its theme is the conflict between appearance and reality to the assertion that it has "no clear meaning,"[1] two interpretative emphases are most common. First, there are those critics who stress racial themes, especially slavery and miscegenation, and second, those who argue for the centrality of the theme of environmental determinism and see slavery as simply a metaphor for Twain's more general concern with the influence of "training" on the individual.[2]

Although both these approaches yield valuable insights, both are finally unsatisfactory because they leave too many important questions unanswered—except by alluding to Twain's uncertain artistry. If Twain's purpose was to condemn slavery, racism, and miscegenation, why did he grant so much respect and even, at a key point, sympathy to the FFV gentlemen and their code of honor; and why did he allow such sympathetic figures as Wilson and Roxy to accept unquestioningly the values of these leaders of a guilty society? On the other hand, if Tom is the victim and avenger of racial injustice, why did Twain present him as a moral monstrosity, an unmitigated villain throughout the narrative? Why, finally, did Twain allow Roxy's racist explanation of Tom's behavior to go unchallenged? Similarly, the interpretative stress on environmental determinism raises as many questions as it answers. If the novel illustrates the debilitating effects of the training of a corrupt society, why did Twain present Tom as being far beyond the community in viciousness? Why did he present Tom's contempt for the code of honor which the town endorses as major evidence of Tom's baseness? If training is all, Tom should express the values of his environment; but he specifically does not in the key matter of the duel and in his

1. These views are presented respectively in Edgar T. Schell, " 'Pears' and 'Is' in Pudd'nhead Wilson," Mark Twain Journal, XII (Winter, 1964–1965), 12–14, and Warner Berthoff, The Ferment of Realism (New York, 1965), p. 72.
2. The racial interpretation is most elaborately presented in James M. Cox, Mark Twain: The Fate of Humor (Princeton, 1966), pp. 225–246. Racial themes are also stressed in Philip S. Foner, Mark Twain: Social Critic (New York, 1958); Robert A. Wiggins, Mark Twain: Jackleg Novelist (Seattle, 1964); and Barbara A. Chellis, "Those Extraordinary Twins: Negroes and Whites," American Quarterly, XXI (Spring, 1969), 100–112. The case for environmental determinism is best presented in Henry Nash Smith, Mark Twain: The Development of a Writer (New York, 1967), pp. 171–183; and Leslie Fiedler, "As Free as Any Cretur . . . ," in Mark Twain: A Collection of Critical Essays, ed. H. N. Smith (Englewood Cliffs, N.J., 1963), pp. 130–139. Similar emphasis also appears in DeLancey Ferguson, Mark Twain: Man and Legend (Indianapolis, 1963); and Louis J. Budd, Mark Twain: Social Philosopher (Bloomington, Ind., 1962). [The criticism by Cox, Wiggins, Smith, and Fiedler is excerpted above—Editor.]

response to the twins, and in fact generally stands apart from the environment that is supposed to have shaped him. Clearly what is necessary is a thematic analysis that can answer these questions in terms of what is shown in the novel and thus demonstrate a coherence in *Pudd'nhead Wilson* that has too often been denied.

The key to such an analysis is the idea of property, more particularly the obsession with property as a vitiating and reductive influence on human beings. Written when Twain's financial condition was at its worst, *Pudd'nhead Wilson* is a parable dealing with the faults of the Gilded Age, faults of which Twain himself was often guilty. It is a book pervaded from start to finish with the very obsession with property which is its theme, yet fully in control of the revelation it offers about the moral and spiritual consequences of this obsession. At both the beginning and the conclusion of the book the importance of the theme of property is revealed with stark clarity. The basis for the narrative is the fact that human beings may be sold as property, and its starting point is Roxy's recognition, itself the result of an incident involving petty theft, that her master may sell her child down the river at any time. "A profound terror had taken possession of her. Her child could grow up and be sold down the river! The thought crazed her with horror." Her response is to exchange her child and her master's, the fact of plot which is central to the subsequent narrative. Similarly, in the final pages the property theme is underscored, this time through Twain's bitter parody of thinking in terms of property. After Tom is convicted of murder and sentenced to imprisonment for life, the creditors of the Percy Driscoll estate offer their view of the situation.

> They rightly claimed that "Tom" was lawfully their property and had been so for eight years; that they had already lost sufficiently in being deprived of his services during that long period, and ought not to be required to add anything to the loss; that if he had been delivered up to them in the first place, they would have sold him and he could not have murdered Judge Driscoll; therefore it was not he that had really committed the murder, the guilt lay with the erroneous inventory. Everybody saw that there was reason in this.

Inconsistent with the story—if the false heir was not part of the inventory, his substitute certainly was and the creditors had had the benefit of his disposal—this passage defines in the manner of parody what has been the consistent theme of the novel, viz., the distortions of reason, feeling, and mortality that result when economic motives are the primary source of human action. If the creditors' logic is absurd, it is also, in a paradoxical sense, correct, for mistaken attitudes about property are in fact the cause of murder and much other evil in this novel.

In the body of the story Twain's focus is on the false Tom, a character whose increasingly vile acts cannot be understood in terms of race or environmental determinism. Rather Tom makes sense only as a nearly allegorical figure of the obsesssion with property to the exclusion of all other human concerns. Spoiled by too much as a child, threatened by too little as a man, Tom in the end becomes property. His final condition is merely the expression of what his behavior has implied all along: as his singleness of purpose is reductive, so he himself is finally reduced. A nasty child from the start, Tom in his first words makes clear the essence of his bad nature: "He would call for anything and everything he saw, simply saying, 'Awnt it!' (want it), which was a command." When he reaches manhood, his principal vice and the cause of all of his difficulty, gambling, is consistent with his acquisitiveness as a child. Apparently not tempted by sex, alcohol, or other traditional vices, he cannot, on the other hand, resist gambling, even though he knows that the revelation of his losses will cause the judge to disinherit him. Indeed his fear of being disinherited is the crucial emotional fact of his life and the only source of his vows to reform himself. Moreover, his determination to hide his gambling losses leads directly to his overt crimes: the robberies, the betrayal of Roxy, the murder of the judge.

The point is perfectly clear, indeed has the clarity of allegorical pattern: neither when he assumes that he is white nor when he knows that he is legally black does Tom reveal for more than a moment any motive other than the economic one. No moral standard and no personal tie of love, loyalty, or simple gratitude have any force for him. When knowledge of his true birth presents him with a subtle problem of identity, his response is merely a determination to resolve this problem, like all his others, with economic means. Furthermore, in the singleness of his commitment to property values, Tom stands apart from the rest of the community, however deeply it, too, is involved in his kind of thinking. For in the respect it grants to the cosmopolitanism of the visiting Italian twins and to the aristocratic code of honor, Dawson's Landing shows its capacity to appreciate values that are not simply materialistic. Tom, on the other hand, has no such appreciation; he is instinctively hostile to the twins, and his response to Luigi's insult shows that the code of honor is completely unintelligible to him. Twain's characterization of Tom then makes no consistent sense so long as it is seen as embodying some statement about race or training. When, however, this central figure of the parable is recognized as the type of the obsession with property as it reduces human beings and poisons human relations, both characterization and narrative reveal a coherence that they at first may not appear to have.

Structurally the foil to Tom is Pudd'nhead Wilson; as Tom

degenerates morally and is finally convicted of murder and sold into slavery, Wilson gradually gains status in the town and ends as a hero when his file of fingerprints allows him to reveal Tom's true identity. As Tom falls Wilson rises, and in fact the rise of the one depends on the fall of the other. Moreover, this structural contrast has a crucial analogue in the sharp divergence of the values of the two characters. If Tom typifies obsession with property, Wilson is largely dissociated from property, particularly from material success. Wilson is, in fact, long a conspicuous failure, unable to practice law, a profession for which he is well trained. The reason for his lack of success in Dawson's Landing is his fatal display of humor when he first arrives in town. He remarks that he wishes he owned half of a noisy dog so that he could kill his half. His hearers forthwith decide that he is a fool, a pudd'nhead, and the nickname they give him ruins his chances for a successful legal practice. Taken literally, the incident is incredible—Wilson's little joke is of the very sort the town loafers could understand—but in this parable about propery it is clear enough: Wilson's low status is the result of his apparent failure to respect and understand the laws of property. Thus for years Wilson must content himself with the respect of only Judge Driscoll and Roxy (a sign of course of his true merit), until he at last wins favor through his association with the duel between Judge Driscoll and Luigi and becomes a hero through his exposure of Tom.

The contrast between the values of Tom and those of Wilson is fully revealed in their discussion of the legal action Tom brought against Luigi instead of fighting a duel with him. Defending Luigi against Tom's charge was Wilson's first chance to practice his profession in the town and thus perhaps the first step toward at long last establishing himself as a lawyer. Yet when Wilson discovers that Judge Driscoll did not know of Tom's action, he is ashamed of his part in the trial, and he tells Tom that he would have kept the matter out of court until the judge had been informed and had had a "gentleman's chance" to avoid the disgrace of having a member of his family take such a matter to court. Tom finds Wilson's attitude incomprehensible.

> "You would?" exclaimed Tom, with lively surprise. "And it your first case! And you know perfectly well there would never have been any case if he had got that chance, don't you? And you'd have finished your days a pauper nobody, instead of being an actually launched and recognized lawyer today. And you would really have done that, would you?"

What seems incredible to Tom, who has only one standard of value, is matter of fact for Wilson because he has values in the face of which considerations of personal success and status are inconsequential. Himself symbolically dissociated from property, Wilson sees in Tom "a degenerate remnant of an honorable line" who has no other commitment.

Indifferent to material success and respectful of the aristocratic code, Wilson also stands for other values that Tom could not comprehend. Though as well educated as Tom, he is not meanly ambitious in Tom's manner; he is open and frank, not devious like Tom; his sense of humor is kindly, not cutting like Tom's. His interest in fingerprinting and other such scientific advances and his membership with the judge in their two-member Freethinker's Society reveal his intellectual curiosity, which also allows him to appreciate the Italian twins whom Tom only envies. Once again the point is clear: if this tale is primarily an attack on a corrupt community, Twain's sympathetic portrayal of Wilson, who uncritically accepts the values of the community and who is finally and triumphantly accepted into it, is a serious flaw which threatens the coherence of the book. But if *Pudd'nhead Wilson* is above all a protest against exclusively materialistic values, the reason for the status Twain gave Wilson is evident, for it is Wilson, the immaterialist, who stands most apart from and ultimately vanquishes Tom, the figure of unqualified devotion to property.

Unlike Wilson, who serves continuously as a foil to Tom, Roxy becomes deeply involved for a time in her son's economic way of thinking. When she returns to Dawson's Landing after eight years of working on a riverboat, she is the victim of a bank failure which has robbed her of her savings and taught her that "hard work and economy" are not enough to make her secure and independent. Faced with poverty, she pathetically thinks that Tom will give her a little money, "maybe a dollar, once a month, say." But when she discovers what a complete monster he has become, she is willing to blackmail him with the threat that she will reveal his true parentage. Understandably indifferent to property rights, she has no objection to Tom's stealing and is generally willing to aid his plots to remain the heir of the Judge. For a time, that is, economic considerations shape her relation with her son, not simply because of her need, but also because of her desire to be close to a child who does not exist on any other level.

That love is the cause of her apparent acquiescence to Tom's values is movingly suggested in her demand that he recognize her maternity: " 'You'll call me ma or mammy, dat's what you'll call me—leastways when dey ain't nobody aroun'. *Say* it!' " Later, her feeling for Tom becomes patent when she suggests that he sell her in order to pay his gambling debts. Heroic as her sacrifice is, it is still a matter of trying to function at Tom's level, and when she learns

that he has betrayed her trust by selling her *down* the river, her attitude changes greatly. Yet she does not simply denounce him; she
also accepts responsibility for what he is: " 'You is de low-downest
orneriest hound dat was ever pup'd into dis worl'—en I's 'sponsible
for it!' " Moreover, she demands that he tell the Judge the truth
about his debts and ask for money to buy her freedom, even
though, as Tom protests and she realizes, such a confession will
mean disinheritance. Having suffered the consequences of meeting
Tom at his level, she attempts to force him to a higher one where
he will be honest with Judge Driscoll and recognize his obligation
to her. But Tom of course is incapable of such a change; instead he
plans to rob the Judge and ends by murdering him.

Roxy then, despite her temporary acceptance of Tom's standards,
is redeemed by her capacity for love, self-sacrifice, and moral awareness. In comparison to Tom, who has economic motives solely, she
is very heroic indeed. Recognizing a similar sort of comparative
merit is also the key to understanding Twain's attitude toward the
town aristocrats and their code of honor, which has caused commentators so much difficulty. That a problem of ambivalence on
Twain's part exists is evident from two early passages of characterization, which had better be quoted in full. About Judge Driscoll
Twain writes,

> He was very proud of his old Virginian ancestry, and in his hospi-
> talities and his rather formal and stately manners he kept up its
> tradition. He was fine and just and generous. To be a gentleman
> —a gentleman without stain or blemish—was his only religion,
> and to it he was always faithful. He was respected, esteemed, and
> beloved by all the community.

Since the Judge as a freethinker makes no claim to religious ortho-
doxy, the passage must stand as praise unqualified by irony. Yet two
paragraphs later Twain sounds the ironic note in his description of
the Judge's best friend, Pembroke Howard:

> He was a fine, brave, majestic creature, a gentleman according to
> the nicest requirements of the Virginia rule, a devoted Presby-
> terian, an authority on the "code," and a man always courteously
> ready to stand up before you in the field if any act or word of his
> had seemed doubtful or suspicious to you, and explain it with any
> weapon you might prefer from brad-awls to artillery.

The difference of tone between these two passages is not a matter of
distinguishing between the Judge and his friend, for if Twain first
presents the Judge in the language of praise, he subsequently provides evidence for a case against him. For example, the Judge's
swoon when he learns that Tom took an insult to court instead of

the dueling ground has the tone of burlesque. Further, the Judge is not only an aristocrat, he is also a democratic politician and something of a Babbitt. As politician, he is quite willing to buy votes and use innuendo against his opponent, and as Babbitt he escorts the twins around Dawson's Landing, pouring out "an exhaustless stream of enthusiasm" for its paltry "splendors." Finally, he is dozing over his cash and accounts when Tom comes to rob him, a scene which suggests the economic base of his status, one perhaps similar to that of his brother and Tom's presumed father who died a bankrupt because of his speculations in land.

Yet, in spite of these hints, Twain's portrayal of the Judge is not finally negative. Because the sympathetic Roxy and Wilson endorse the duel while the vicious Tom rejects it, the reader is allowed to admire the courage and integrity the Judge displays in the service of his code. More important, just before the duel Twain shows the Judge once more writing a will in Tom's favor, even though he vowed to disinherit Tom after hearing of his cowardice.

> "This may be my last night in the world—I must not take the chance. He is worthless and unworthy, but it is largely my fault. He was entrusted to me by my brother on his dying bed, and I have indulged him to his hurt, instead of training him up severely, and making a man of him. I have violated my trust and I must not add the sin of desertion to that."

Like Roxy, the Judge accepts more responsibility for Tom than is properly his, and also like her, displays an affection which Tom cannot comprehend. Then, to make perfectly sure of his readers' response, the author portrays the Judge's friend Howard fully endorsing the Judge's humane act and, a few pages later, shows Tom, who has overheard the Judge's change of heart, regretting that the Judge has not been killed in the duel. This contrast of attitudes makes perfectly clear the Judge's moral and emotional superiority to Tom. For all his faults, the Judge, like Roxy, has a capacity for feeling and moral judgment that places him far above Tom. His aristocratic code, despite its endorsement of violent foolishness, allows for values far superior to Tom's, and even at its worst, it fosters an integrity that Tom's materialism does not. If it is a dubious center of value for the town, it is also clearly better than the values Tom embodies.[3]

As well, the code is preferable to the democracy the town practices. The townspeople not only accept and admire the aristocratic ways of the Judge, they also make a farce of their practice of

3. F. R. Leavis makes this distinction between the code and certain admirable human qualities it fosters in his introduction to the Grove Press edition of *Pudd'nhead Wilson* (New York, 1955), pp. 9–31.

democracy. Their politics amount to no more than the division between the rum and the antirum parties, and the meeting of the Sons of Liberty ends in a drunken brawl of "raging and plunging and fighting and swearing humanity." The Judge is at his worst, not when he is fighting a duel, but when he runs for office confident that he can win by buying votes and slandering his opponent. The satire of democracy is only a small part of *Pudd'nhead Wilson*, but it is consistent with the main thrust of the book—its relentless attack on the obsession with property. Viewed from this perspective, some of the most striking items in Wilson's *Calendar* become comprehensible.

> July 4. Statistics show that we lose more fools on this day than in all the other days of the year put together. This proves, by the number left in stock, that one Fourth of July per year is now inadequate, the country has grown so.

The irreverence of this reference to Independence Day is repeated in the final and most conspicuous entry in the *Calendar*: "October 12, the Discovery. It was wonderful to find America, but it would have been more wonderful to miss it." Even if it were the only evidence of Twain's attitude available, this book would suggest a Twain writing in reaction to the Gilded Age, in reaction to a period in which democracy seemed to be a failure and obsessive acquisitiveness, of the kind Tom represents, prevailed. In comparison, the ability of Roxy and Judge Driscoll to love, the disinterestedness and immaterialism of David Wilson, and even the aristocratic code—all associated with a bygone age—are very attractive indeed.

Even the extraordinarily unwieldy twins have their place in this parable about property. Representative through their cosmopolitanism and their artistic skills of yet another realm of value that Tom cannot understand, they, too, have experienced financial hardship: "'We were seized for the debts occasioned by their [parents'] illness and their funerals, and placed among the attractions of a cheap museum in Berlin to earn the liquidation money. It took us two years to get out of that slavery.'" It is this kind of slavery that Twain is talking about in *Pudd'nhead Wilson*—slavery to property, to economic motives, which, as in the case of Tom, finally reduces one to property, to slavery.

Biographically related to Twain's own financial distress and historically to an America dominated by robber barons, the book, far from being incoherent or inconsistent, is remarkable among Twain's works for its unity, a unity which derives from its pervasive concern with the theme of property, particularly the perils of an obsession with property to the exclusion of all other human values and needs.

MARVIN FISHER and MICHAEL ELLIOTT

Pudd'nhead Wilson: Half a Dog Is Worse than None†

I

Mark Twain's *Pudd'nhead Wilson* has puzzled and provoked critics who, for various reasons, need to find cause for praise or censure. Some even challenge the appropriateness of the title. Wright Morris, in his introduction to the Signet edition of *Pudd'nhead Wilson*, shrewdly suggests that the last three words of the novel constitute a better title, and he is right that "Down the River" echoes threateningly and ambiguously throughout the novel. It would be no less apt, however, to suggest "A Dog's Life" as an improvement on Mark Twain's title. And there is even a sense in which the more than spectral fear of being sold down the river, the precarious condition of a dog's life, and Wilson's fateful remark solving the problem of a barking dog by killing half are symbolic equivalents.

As we see it, this grotesque and absurd exchange in Chapter I is the most important iconographic clue to the meaning of the novel:

> 'I wish I owned half of that dog.'
> 'Why?' somebody asked.
> 'Because I would kill my half.'

These words have been frequently pointed out but never adequately explained. Usually the incident is dismissed as simply a means of alienating David Wilson from most of the community and blocking him from any meaningful pursuit of his legal career. Both George M. Spangler and James M. Cox, in two of the more illuminating analyses of the novel, cite the rather incredible and unrealistically obtuse reaction of the witnesses to Wilson's capricious, latently vicious remark—witnesses who should have been familiar with this kind of rustic hyperbole.[1] Spangler explains this lapse in terms of his property thesis: "Wilson's low status is the result of his apparent failure to respect and understand the laws of property." He does view the incident symbolically, but discerns its major meaning in Wilson's disregard for the material value of anything he owned. That Wilson cannot comprehend the nature of property seems dubious in view of his demonstrated intelligence, his familiarity with legal and scientific matters, his conventional respect for the town's leading citizens and their spurious values, and his own prolonged quest for acceptance and success. Cox sees the remark as a

† From *The Southern Review*, n.s., 8 (Summer 1972), 3, 533–547.
1. George M. Spangler, "*Pudd'nhead Wilson:* A Parable of Property," *American Literature*, 42 (March, 1970), 28–37;

James M. Cox, *Mark Twain: The Fate of Humor* (Princeton, 1966), pp. 222–46. [The Spangler and Cox pieces are reprinted above—*Editor.*]

veiled and symbolic threat to the values of this slaveholding society and with admirable insight discerns a relationship between the "invisible dog" whose disagreeable barking jarred the tranquility of Dawson's Landing and Tom Driscoll, the "invisible" slave whose flagrant amorality exposes the deceitful morality of the community.

We agree with Mr. Spangler about Mark Twain's concern with those forces that have "a vitiating and reductive influence on human beings," but we see this influence resulting from widespread adherence to any idea that destroys integrity, artificially assigns identity, and breaks up the organic wholeness essential to the survival of almost any living creature or social entity. Common to Mark Twain's characterization of the novel as the result of a literary Caesarian, to his equally complex operation turning the original Siamese twins into the nearly identical dark-haired Luigi and light-haired Angelo, to the easily accomplished exchange of the nearly indistinguishable infants in Roxy's care, and to the innocent but ironic symbolism of Wilson's early remark about an audible but unseen dog, is the sense of sudden separation or violent severance. The book was created by an act of imaginative cutting loose from its sources and draws heavily from Mark Twain's long obsession with twins, intentional imposture, and accidentally confused identities. Deriving also from the dualities of his own psychological tendencies and artistic role, the novel is a semi-serious, semi-comic grotesque, half-revealing, half-concealing the traumatic divisions and gross cruelties of what we have come to call "Middle America." It is a partially intentional, partially intuitive analysis of what can happen when a supposedly organic community maintains a network of social fictions based on an inevitably deadly and socially divisive idea of human fractions.

Although the final version retains elements of the original farce in combination with a distinctly tragic view of the human condition, the meaning can hardly be called unclear when it is so repeatedly reinforced by suggestive description, conscious symbolism, narrative circumstance, and melodramatic characterization.

There are four elements in Wilson's statement that serve a strong structural, symbolic, and thematic function in the novel. Since Spangler has thoroughly examined the element of ownership and property, we would like to focus on the meanings that make up the idea of *dog*, the imaginative function of fractional division conveyed by reference to *half* a dog, and the perverse violence implicit in the overt or covert act of killing a significant fraction of a living entity.

II

There is a marked difference between Mark Twain's use of dogs (and cats) in earlier works and in *Pudd'nhead Wilson*, and the dif-

ference is an indication of the change in his view of human possibilities. In such earlier works as *Roughing It* and *The Adventures of
Tom Sawyer*, there was an exuberant delight in the spontaneous
antics of a dog in church or a cat calculatedly disrupting the genteel formalities of Examination Day at school (and exposing the
false glitter of establishment values by snatching off the toupee
which had concealed the previously gilded surface of the teacher's
bald head). Even the overly proud town dog in Chapter V of
Roughing It participates in a charade wherein his frustrating pursuit
of the wily coyote demonstrates the superiority of unpretentiously
vernacular values over genteel establishment complacency. But there
is an entirely different quality to the "well-fed, well-petted, and
properly revered cat" so evident on many of the flower-laden ledges
of whitewashed houses in Dawson's Landing. This cat has become
an essential feature of the moral inertia of the Southern slaveholding establishment:

> stretched at full length, asleep and blissful, with her furry belly
> to the sun and a paw curved over her nose. Then that house was
> complete and its contentment and peace were made manifest to
> the world by this symbol, whose testimony is infallible.

And the dog also fulfills a symbolic role in the orderly plan of this
pre-Civl War, Middle-American society. He has become the long-
suffering victim of callous and complacent cruelty—infallible testimony to the most helpless and servile aspect of the human condition.

The dog mentioned by garrulous Jim Blaine in the diffuse string
of associations that make up the anecdote of "His Grandfather's
Old Ram" was never in danger of being injured, as was Jim's Uncle
Lem when he broke the fall of an Irishman with a hod full of
bricks, because a dog would never consent to become such an
instrument of Providence. He would not hold still long enough to
become the victim of such a genteel rationalization of divine procedures. Neither in David Wilson's first reference to the unseen dog,
nor in the several circumstances where "dog" is used metaphori-
cally, can the "dog" get out from under the painful role assigned by
social providence. The fate of the dog is throughout the novel a
continuing analogy to the closed-in, helpless state of man—the
victim of complex forces that constitute an irresistible social determinism. Implicit in much of *Pudd'nhead Wilson* is Mark Twain's
recurrent question—What is man?—and the answer—nothing but
a lowly dog—is well on the way to Mark Twain's bitterest image of
man as microbe.

Most of the references linking man's fate and a dog's life draw
from the common reservoir of community values in Dawson's Land-

ing, no matter whether voiced by Roxy, Tom, Wilson, or the ironic narrator, and the epithet "dog" is applied most frequently but not exclusively to Tom Driscoll. One pattern of reference links the help-lessness of a dog owned by a particular master and the similar sub-servience of a slave. The narrator launches this image early in the novel when he describes Percy Driscoll, who is angry about the dis-appearance of a small sum of money, as "a fairly humane man toward slaves and other animals" and "an exceedingly humane man toward the erring of his own race." The attitude thus described is racist in two senses. It does not merely distinguish between black and white human beings; it classifies slaves as part of a different, distinctly inferior species. Further remarks make clear that for vir-tually all members of this community, even the Negroes themselves, the race to which the blacks belonged was not the human race. In describing the consequences of Roxy's substituting her child for that of her master, Mark Twain constructs a passage that not only links the condition of a slave and that of a dog, but also stresses the violent severance of a natural bond and the common fate of slave and dog as victims of a capricious owner—all the elements of Wil-son's cryptic, symbolic, and, as Mark Twain termed it, "his fatal remark":

> She saw her darling gradually cease from being her son, she saw *that* detail perish utterly; all that was left was master—master, pure and simple, and it was not a gentle mastership, either. She saw herself sink from the sublime height of motherhood to the somber depths of slavery. The abyss of separation between her and her boy was complete. She was merely his chattel now, his convenience, his dog, his cringing and helpless slave, the humble and unresisting victim of his capricious temper and vicious nature.

After he learns of his true parentage, Tom Driscoll also sees himself as a helpless figure in the property-slave-dog pattern. Thinking of his foster-father, he tells himself, "He is white; and I am his chattel, his property, his goods, and he can sell me, just as he could his dog."

As Tom applies this term to himself, it connotes self-pity and not condemnation. As others address Tom in terms that connect him with some alleged characteristic of a dog, the meanings escalate in contempt and condemnation. There is even a kind of folk inno-cence in Roxy's exclamation when she first switches the infants' clothes and thereby their identities as well: "Dog my cats if it ain't all I kin do to tell t'other fum which." In a deeper sense, however, "Dog my cats" launches the confusion, the crime, and the chase that form the main plot. The charges that Tom has a viciously inhuman streak in him begin to pick up when Roxy laughs at his attempt to club her in retaliation for her revealing his ancestry to him: "Set down, you pup! Does you think you kin skyer me?" When Judge Driscoll calls Tom "You cur! You scum! You vermin!" he is referring not to Tom's viciousness but to his coward-ice and lack of honor in turning to a court of law rather than the duel required by the F. F. V. code to remedy an insult. Roxy makes the same charge when she concludes her fanciful genealogy linking Tom with his F. F. V. father, John Smith, Pocahontas, and "a nigger king outen Africa": "here you is, a slinkin' outen a duel en disgracin' our whole line like a ornery lowdown hound!"

By the time Tom initiates his plan to save himself by selling his mother, Roxy raises the charge against him from cowardice to superlative viciousness. Her first reaction upon escaping and con-fronting Tom is to detail the cruelties she had been through and try to shame Tom by saying "Sell a pusson down de river—*down de river!* . . . I wouldn't treat a dog so!" But she quickly learns that Tom is beyond shame or redemption, that he intends to profit fur-ther from her third return to slavery, and she charges him with the ultimate betrayal: "You could be Judas to yo' own mother to save yo' wuthless hide! Would anybody b'lieve it? No—a dog couldn't! You is de lowdownest orneriest hound dat was ever pup'd into dis worl'." As if to make sure the trebly made point will not be lost Mark Twain has Roxy repeat the charge a page later: "You's de lowdownest hound dat ever—but I done tole you dat befo'."

The final reference to "dog," like the first, stems from Wilson. Tom has dropped in on Wilson to gloat over what he is certain will be Luigi's impending conviction for the murder Tom has himself committed. Finding Wilson examining slides of fingerprints, Tom picks one up, sees Roxy's name on it, and asks, "Are you going to ornament the royal palaces with nigger paw marks, too?" His next remark is a further attempt to deny his natural relationship to Roxy and to project on to Chambers (the true Tom Driscoll) the subhu-man, animalistic qualities that his mother and foster-father have lev-eled at him: "By the date here, I was seven months old when this was done, and she was nursing me and her little nigger cub." When he hands the slide back to Wilson, he leaves his own fingerprints on it. Wilson recognizes them as matching the set on the murder weapon, realizes the long deception, and solves the current mystery. Tom, mistaking Wilson's sudden excitement for illness, says "Don't take it so hard; a body can't win every time; you'll hang somebody yet," and Wilson's inaudible answer pronounces judgment on Tom and brings the novel full circle to that long forgotten "fatal remark" about an unseen dog: "It is no lie to say that I am sorry I have to begin with you, miserable dog though you are!" The Governor's decision, which concludes the novel, merely implements Wilson's early remark and later judgment, confirming "dog" as the lowest common denominator for "man." In pardoning Tom so that Percy Driscoll's creditors could sell this heretofore invisible piece of property down the river, the Governor has effectively silenced the loud-mouth who had in so many ways disturbed the community, severed him from the identity and status he had so long enjoyed, and upheld the cause of law and order and a kind of justice.

III

Critics who view Wilson as the hero of the story tend to ignore two important factors: first, the inconsistency between the fictional character of Pudd'nhead Wilson in the story and the hazy, transcendent persona responsible for the "Calendar," and second, Twain's own description of what he intended Wilson to be. It would be too much to insist that the bifurcated character of Pudd'n-head Wilson is thematically appropriate to the novel, but it is even less justifiable to view Wilson as a largely sympathetic character reflecting the author's own opinions. Henry Nash Smith has cited Twain's estimate of Wilson as he expressed it in a letter to Livy in 1894: "I have never thought of Pudd'nhead as a *character*, but only as a piece of machinery—a button or a crank or a lever with a useful function to perform in a machine, but with no dignity above that."[2] Wilson may be somewhat sympathetic because of his years of neglect but he is essentially unfeeling and only superficially perceptive. In fact, the Wilson who participates in the action of the story does not seem perceptive enough to have uttered the original remark about killing his half of the dog or to understand the moral consequence of such symbolically charged fractional division.

The maxims of the Calendar reflect an aspect of Wilson we hardly see in the events of the novel. It is scarcely possible to imagine that the Wilson who ostensibly accepts the F. F. V. code and reprimands Tom for not confronting Luigi in a duel could have produced the penetrating combination of disillusioned wit, cynicism, and iconoclasm in the Calendar. And it is scarcely possible to imagine that the Mark Twain who scorned chivalry and dueling in *Life on the Mississippi*, *Huckleberry Finn*, and *A Connecticut Yankee* could admire the spurious nobility of these pretentiously named leading citizens. (In fact such names as Judge York Leicester Dris-coll, Percy Northumberland Driscoll, and Col. Cecil Burleigh Essex recall some of the cast in Mark Twain's pseudo-Elizabethan farce *1601* or his burlesques of Shakespeare.) Wilson wants to be recognized and accepted as part of this village elite, he is "deeply gratified" by the invitation to run for mayor of Dawson's Landing, and he considers this political opportunity "a step upward." In the final

2. *Mark Twain: The Development of a Writer* (Cambridge, 1962), p. 181.

courtroom scene he serves as protector and supporter of the town's most cherished values and institutions—including the system of slavery. For such a man to commemorate Columbus Day by writing "It was wonderful to find America, but it would have been more wonderful to miss it" is inconceivable. Even the one remark about a dog in the Calendar is out of keeping with the meanings attached to "dog" by Wilson or other members of the community, for the Calendar maxim slyly praises virtuous caninity at the expense of brutish humanity: "If you pick up a starving dog and make him prosperous, he will not bite you. This is the principal difference between a dog and a man." Mark Twain has apparently presented us with two rather separate characters in his portrayal of Pudd'n-head Wilson.

As a consequence of this cleavage, he felt the need to supply some exposition to help the reader join the disparate parts of Wilson's character:

> For some years Wilson had been privately at work on a whimsical almanac, for his amusement—a calendar with a little dab of ostensible philosophy, usually in ironical form, appended to each date, and the judge . . . read them to some of the chief citizens. But irony was not for those people; their mental vision was not focused for it. They read those playful trifles in the solidest earnest, and decided without . . . doubt that Dave Wilson was a pudd'nhead.

Quite clearly, this passage, the most extensive of the "unifying" passages, describes the more satanic author of the Calendar, not his notably less visionary counterpart who ultimately thrives so comfortably within the ethos of Dawson's Landing.

And it is in the context of the Calendar that Wilson's original "fatal remark" must be interpreted. We can then treat it as an example of far-reaching, bitterly ironic wisdom—an exposure of what seems at best human folly and at worst the ineradicable evil in man's nature. Like the entries in the Calendar, it is an indictment justified not by any plausible or realistic relationship to the events of the novel, but rather by its moral perception of what makes mankind tick in this Middle-American community and of where the greatest danger to the community lies. When Wilson utters these first significant words, he appears disengaged, not focused on what concerns the citizens he has just met; he speaks "much as one who is thinking aloud." His remark seems to proceed more from the trancelike realm of prophecy than from observation of an immediate situation, as evidenced by its effect on his audience:

> The group searched his face with curiosity, with anxiety even, but found no light there, no expression they could read. They fell

away from him as from something uncanny, and went into privacy to discuss him.

As we know, they wholly misconstrue his meaning. For one thing, they miss his irony and ignore his implication; he *knows* that to kill one half of the dog is to kill the other half too. And as the author of the Calendar he also knows that the citizens are incapable of grasping the moral truth inherent in this graphic image of vivisection—simply that it applies to all aspects of human life, whether physiological, psychological, or social.

The Wilson of the Calendar who can make this point is much closer to Mark Twain than is the unsuccessful lawyer and ardent hobbyist, and only the Calendar character can conceive such a complex analogy wherein for man or for society the whole organism is the fundamental unit of being, and any arbitrary division or artificial quantification for purposes of convenience, profit, or punishment can only mean death. It is doubly ironic that one of the witnesses to Wilson's remark expresses this basic principle when trying to determine Wilson's hypothetical responsibility as a property owner (of his half of the dog): "if he killed his half and the other half died, he would be responsible for that half just the same as if he had killed that half instead of his own." What this man fails to realize is that this idea lies at the heart of Wilson's lesson in fractions. And the society of Dawson's Landing fails to realize that there is little or no moral distinction between the overt violence that can result in physical death and the covert violence that can result in psychic death.

Wilson's "joke," then, describes the essentially destructive effect of division and disunity on certain key, natural relationships symbolically represented in the ideal of the living organism; and the idea behind the joke is closely tied to the twin motif in *Pudd'nhead Wilson*. Even *Those Extraordinary Twins*, the rudimentary farce from which *Pudd'nhead* was extracted, reinforces this suggestion. The story originally centered on a pair of Siamese twins—"a combination consisting of two heads and four arms joined to a single body and a single pair of legs"—a single organism but exhibiting two distinct personalities, often at odds with one another. Twain envisioned various sorts of conflicts between the two "halves" of his twins—fights over deportment, drinking, lovemaking, etc. Of course, certain characteristics of these originals come through in the finished, separated brothers, Luigi and Angelo. Except for the differences in hair color, the two look exactly alike; they travel together and play the piano together. Essentially they exist as one person. As with Wilson's dog, there seems to be no such thing as an experience, relationship, or consequence capable of affecting one half and not the other. When they reveal Luigi's past history and the murder he committed, Angelo asserts: "He did it to save my life, that's what he did it for. So it was a noble act, and not a thing to be hid in the dark." Luigi's explanation reveals even more:

> You overlook one detail; suppose I hadn't saved Angelo's life, what would have become of mine? If I had let the man kill him, wouldn't he have killed me, too? I saved my own life, you see.

Reflected in the concept of brotherhood, and emblematized in the physical fact of twinhood, the ideal of the organism projects itself above the surface of the novel. Luigi knows instinctively that you can't kill half a dog, and his knowledge of this runs deeper than that of the community. (Mark Twain knew this truth instinctively, too. But whether he was *consciously* formulating such a doctrine of organicism is impossible to determine. It is quite likely that his esemplastic[3] imagination, set in motion by a highly charged key image, tended thereafter to operate almost of its own, often producing linked images and ideas whose significance he may not have been fully aware of.)

Though they are not physical brothers, the other twins in the story—Tom and Chambers—might as well be. They look alike; as characters, their respective fathers scarcely differ at all and might just as well have been one person. The nebulous Essex is just Percy Driscoll duplicated and peeled off to avoid the embarrassing situation of the white master's adultery with his black slave, a liaison that would have required Percy Driscoll to vault out of one bed and leap into another in order to father sons born to different mothers on the same day. The fact that there is no apparent physical difference between Tom and Chambers when they are babies allows Roxy, acting out of mother love, to switch them deliberately without detection. Unfortunately, in protecting one twin, she "sells out" the other and so initiates the chain of events that will "dog her cats" inevitably to tragedy. At this point, the theme of disunity and arbitrary division (the clothes seem to make all the difference) becomes connected with the issues of slavery and betrayal. Roxy praises God for the "salvation" of her son: "Oh, thank de good Lord in Heaven, you's saved! Dey ain't no man kin ever sell mammay's po' little honey down de river now!"

Thus the inexorable machinery of the slave society forces Roxy to commit the act that represents the highest form of evil—the betrayal of a close relationship, whether biological or spiritual—in "selling" the real Tom "down the river," figuratively, when she allows him to assume the identity of a slave. Her own son's later actions magnify the betrayal implicit in her own act of radical division and readjustment, and when he is ultimately sold down the

3. Having the function of molding diversified matter into unity; unifying [*Editor*.]

river, the system ironically compensates for her tampering and restores the original arrangement. Either way, however, natural relationships have been sundered and an act of perverse violence has been committed in the killing (or denying the actual existence) of a significant fraction of a living entity.

The act of "killing" one half of the dog, and that of "selling down the river," we are reminded, are symbolic equivalents. Roxy conjoined the two images when she found out that her son had betrayed her: "Sell a pusson down de river—*down de river!* . . . I wouldn't treat a dog so!" The terms are semi-allegorical references to the same species of evil, examples of which saturate the events of the story. Roxy neglects the child in "tow linen" as much for his lack of apparent "class" as the fact of his not being her "real" son. "Tom" abuses "Chambers," whose place he himself would have occupied had Roxy not interfered. Percy mistreats "Chambers," who is actually his own son, unrecognized by his "master." Tom's own nature, which Roxy refers to as "fractious" (a word combining elements of "fractional" and "vicious"), thrives on strife and division among others; he cheers up noticeably when the twins argue, or when Pudd'nhead appears foolish in front of others. He does, however, distribute his hatred evenly: "He hated the one twin for kicking him, and the other for being the kicker's brother." But doubtlessly, the most outrageous incidents of inhumanity and betrayal are the twin acts of sale down the river: Tom sells his mother; the courts of "justice" sell Tom.

The novel suggests further that arbitrary division is by its very nature a form of betrayal which destroys certain fundamental relations based on family, community, and a larger sense of humanity. The society, irrationally and arbitrarily (as it turns out), makes damaging distinctions in regard to race:

> To all intents and purposes Roxy was as white as anybody, but the one sixteenth of her which was black outvoted the other fifteen parts and made her a Negro. She was a slave and salable as such. Her child was thirty-one parts white, and he, too, was a slave, and by a fiction of law and custom a Negro.

The social effect of these distinctions is to cultivate disunity by elevating to quasi-sacred status this communal code, this elaborate fiction of human fractions. By law and custom the identity of an individual could be quantified by fractional division of blood into categories of white and black. In the scheme of Mark Twain's novel, this sort of behavior is a submerged, slow, unconscious moral masochism—a deep, prolonged, unhealing social fracture. The town punishes itself by not only maintaining the false and unnatural distinctions of the slave market, but also by its patently foolish reverence for the F. F. V. pretensions, and their genteel justification of violence. The false Tom, as Henry Nash Smith points out, is really the end-product of Dawson's Landing and, by extension, of the entire region:

> Although Tom Driscoll is evidently the key figure in the imaginative logic of *Pudd'nhead Wilson*, he is . . . not so much a character as a complex of themes. He incarnates both the tortured paradox of uncertain identity and the perversions resulting from generations of the bad training imposed by slavery.

The most evident source of Tom's duality, according to Smith, is in his "divided" background, one half of which is strictly F. F. V. aristocratic—i.e., the part supplied by his father—while the "other half of Tom's heritage is that of Roxy, the slave. The two parts of it are at war with each other."[4]

The politics of the town sustains the image of an organism in internal war with itself, the traditional "diseased body politic" familiar from Shakespeare. The good fellowship of the Sons of Liberty is shown to be only illusory; the members fight over trifles before their meeting is over, and apparently are not averse to the kind of slanderous, brutal campaigning that the Judge sanctions in order to get Wilson elected mayor. The farcical image of the "anti-rummies," in the guise of volunteer firemen, joyfully turning their hoses on their political opponents graphically illustrates the notion of the village as an unbalanced social organism working against its own good health and fated to fall victim to its own internal antagonisms. We should not be amused by the bitter truth that "citizens of that village . . . of a thoughtful and judicious temperament did not insure against fire; they insured against the fire company."

There can be no doubt that *Pudd'nhead Wilson* is a pessimistic book. It moves relentlessly to show that none in "the land of the free" is truly free and the few who are "brave" measure their courage by an inhumane standard. No one is without taint, not the purest descendant of the F. F. V., not the ambitious intellectual, and certainly not the black in bondage. For a variety of reasons and in different ways, the book proves that "the skin of every human being contains a slave." Tom has opportunities along the way to recognize firsthand the essential brutality and inhumanity of accepting and living in accordance with arbitrary labels and divisions. But neither reform nor escape is part of his nature; both have been driven out of him by a devastating combination of corrupt training and his own innate, unyielding temperament. Roxy, who alone attempts to stand against circumstance and the continuing heinous-

4. *Mark Twain*, pp. 176–79.

ness of white domination over her, accepts virtually all of the values and institutions cherished by the slave society in which she finds herself. In the end she fails miserably on all counts, and the novel literally offers no way out, not for the false Tom who gets treated as he was so ready to treat others, nor for the true heir who, despite the fact that he "found himself rich and free" was doubtless doomed to lead a dog's life, for he "could not endure the terrors of the white man's parlor, and felt at home and at peace nowhere but in the kitchen." Mark Twain chooses not to tell this further story, but it is quite clear that if he had, it would be the continuing story of a house divided against itself, some of its inhabitants at home in the parlor, others knowing their place in the kitchen.

That F. R. Leavis should have found *Pudd'nhead Wilson* "a profound study" of an admirable civilization paying homage to art, recognizing excellence in its cultural elite, and exhibiting "the outward signs of an inward grace," is quite incredible.[5] We cannot help feeling some note of condescension here—toward America, toward American literature, and toward Mark Twain as an indigenously American writer. Rather than deny the frequently satirical and occasionally subversive tone of *Pudd'nhead Wilson*, it might be more accurate to view it as a bitter burlesque of what America was supposed to be and a painful depiction of what it had come to be—one nation, under God, infinitely divisible, with a mockery of justice for all.

JOHN M. BRAND

The Incipient Wilderness: A Study of *Pudd'nhead Wilson*†

It is hardly an understatement to suggest that Mark Twain would not have appreciated the use of any works of Cooper to throw light on one of his own. Nevertheless, one way of making entry into *Pudd'nhead Wilson* is through *The Prairie*, where the aged Natty Bumppo warns travellers who have left the settlement and ventured deep into the uncharted wilderness:

> 'Why then do you venture in a place where none but the strong should come?' he demanded. 'Did you not know that when you crossed the big river you left a friend behind you that is always bound to look to the young and feeble like yourself?'
> 'Of whom do you speak?'

5. Introduction to *Pudd'nhead Wilson* (New York: Grove Press, 1955), pp. 13–19. [Reprinted above—*Editor.*]

† From *Western American Literature*, 8 (Summer 1972), 2, 125–34.

'The law—'tis bad to have it, but I sometimes think it is worse to be entirely without it. Age and weakness has brought me to feel such weakness at times. Yes—yes, the law is needed when such as have not the gifts of strength and wisdom are to be taken care of. I hope, young woman, if you have no father you have at least a brother.'[1]

The sense of tension which we get from parts of *The Prairie* stems from the repeatedly helpless wanderings of just these people, who in reaching that area have entered an ethical no-man's-land where law, the ordering force of the settlement, is non-existent, and wayfarers must create their rules as they go along. The loftiness of Natty Bumppo and Ishmael Bush in large measure emerges from their ability to exist in that very situation.

Pudd'nhead Wilson lacks the zest and flair of Cooper's novel. A great river has been crossed, but the crossing was made so a settlement could occur. Just west of the Mississippi River, Dawson's Landing is anything but spectacular. Neither, for that matter, will its hero dazzle us, for David Wilson's primary resources in attacking challenges are his wit, wisdom and patience. Compared to the likes of Natty and Bush, Wilson is prosaic. So is the novel as a whole. Its plot, for example, is stationary, as few characters go anywhere; the action occurring does so within the rather puny confines of Dawson's Landing. But to say the novel is stationary is not to label it static, because it has its own dynamics and in its own way is akin to *The Prairie*. For granted the prosaic and even hum-drum quality of life in Dawson's Landing, a kinship with Cooper's world arises when existing law proves insufficient to reorder a threatened society. In fact, from the beginning of his novel, Twain traces the inexorable process by which the lawlessness of the wilderness slowly permeates the settlement. It is true that, unlike the situation in Cooper's novel, law does exist in Dawson's Landing. However, instead of being based on something like natural rights or Christian ethics, it is shakily rooted in custom and tradition, in this case, white prejudices against black people. Law is thus impotent in caring for "the young and feeble" like Roxy, a white woman who, because of a tiny part of her, is judged legally black by her community. Frustrated by the enduring unfairness of things, and thus goaded into rebellion, she switches her white, but legally black child with the child of her master and therein sets in motion forces which further disorder the life of Dawson's Landing. For her real son Tom, becoming well-versed in the ways of the young white master, eventually turns in his scorn upon both black and white humanity, in this case, his own step-father, who he murders. Because the disgraced Italian twins,

---

1. James Fenimore Cooper, *The Prairie* (New York, 1964), p. 28.

Luigi and Angelo, are the first to arrive at the murder scene, and because the people have a handy grudge they would like to exercise, they are only too eager to use the law to convict and dispose of the two. In effect they are doing what they must, since, through their shackling of the law to custom and tradition, they have no other way of arriving at the truth. Law in Dawson's Landing is in effect non-existent. Since it is largely a vehicle of a people's prejudices, it cannot transcend their tormented subjectivity. It has no way of objectively sighting and correcting the wrong in a people's midst, no way of discerning and disclosing the fact that the primary cause inciting Roxy to action was precisely this limited and narrow force, the law itself. But this is not to suggest that absolute Truth exists at any point in Twain's world, because a major reason for this society's bondage to its own norms is the absence of any transcendent power or pattern. There is nothing Eternal underneath society. So social stability will always be short-lived because it is fragile to begin with, and is so in Dawson's Landing because these citizens compound cosmic insecurity with crippling value systems, making absolute those values that at best are relative, and surely have a questionable place in the West. But even assuming their willingness to scrutinize and reorder their own premises, it is not likely that any more stable culture will emerge. Even granting a desire to raise standards a certain degree, towards what abiding Ideal may citizens move? Does such a spiritual or moral realm or power exist? And if it does, if, for example, the Heavenly City can be perceived and emulated, who stands among them to set their sights towards it? Here then is a chilling look at life in the Secular City, where we experience the anguish of an age lacking not only such giants as Bumppo and Bush, but also the gods Cooper envisioned underlying even the savage wilderness. It is significant that in *Pudd'nhead Wilson* the great river is used for a crossing, but little else. The dark but undeniable river god of *Huck Finn* is ignored, in part because the piety of Dawson's Landing is sheer religiosity, but also because Twain himself is already heading towards the despair that produced *The Mysterious Stranger* and *Letters from the Earth*. He thus creates in this novel a society with no objective pattern by which it may order itself, a society passionate about social stability, but lacking a Torah or Logos upon which to base it. *Pudd'nhead Wilson* thus demonstrates the manner in which any settlement can become a wilderness again, and how one man brings "law and order" back to his time.

The dynamics of *Pudd'nhead Wilson* begin as soon as Twain places his novel. He gives us the settlement of Dawson's Landing, just west of which is the wilderness. The wilderness is wide open both spatially and ethically. It is open to all codes because it is friendly to none. It is barren and crusty, and will crush certain codes attempting to take root there, while reshaping others. Yet this vast nothingness exerts a compelling dynamics of its own. It is there and is there to be crossed and, hopefully, conquered in the form of settlements. As long as it is there people will strive to subdue it. They or their seed must do so sooner or later, since having once severed the spatial ties between them and their old home, they lack the enduring rootage of their ancestors.

Sitting atop what was once sheer open space, Dawson's Landing is just this conquest. It exudes the confident and serene mood that the journey is over and that it is a blessing indeed to get settled. It is this illusory settled quality that Twain is satirizing as he opens his novel. The houses he mentions make up a "snug little collection of modest one- and two-story frame dwellings." Hardly nomadic, the citizenry intend to stay, and proceed to develop and maintain their property, even to the point of adding a touch of luxury, the flower garden. The apparently fixed quality of life there is manifested in the household cat outside, "stretched at full length, asleep and blissful, with her furry belly to the sun and a paw curved over her nose. Then that house was complete, and its contentment and peace were made manifest to the world by this symbol, whose testimony is infallible."

Unfortunately, Dawson's Landing lives on the assumption that people can migrate without losing or having to alter old codes. If they accept the necessity of changing certain ways, they do so with the strong hope that one change will be enough. Without knowing it, settlers are living between codes, the one they left behind and the one in process of being born in the westward movement. It is during this period of stress that the dynamics of the wilderness are most prone to rupture the settlement and precipitate disorder. What is being tested is thus a people's ability to live between these codes. Some, like Percy Northumberland Driscoll, are quite vulnerable to this pressure. Driscoll will succumb to the pressure of change by envisioning a hyper-extension of the old code, and will be willing, if pressed, to exert it to its most logical and grotesque conclusion, the sending of slaves down the river. He is representative of those white supremists who either try, or are willing to try, to perpetuate the Virginia tradition, but who have to do so in a different situation, and lack the concern for the weaker that kept slavery in some places from becoming a total monstrosity. Tom Driscoll is vulnerable to the wilderness in another sense. As he moves into the future, he hardly looks back at all. His adaptation to his surroundings has been final. He belongs among those who think current, and thus engages in a hasty acceptance of what is new, in this case, the profligate activity he finds available in the glittering city of St. Louis to the north. Therefore, lacking such inner resources as love to curb tendencies to grotesque extremes, Percy Driscoll is an atavist, while Tom is an anarchist. The father's behavior will stem from his passion to maintain old ties and customs in their primal forms, whereas the son's vagrancy will stem from his refusal to honor any ties at all. The exterior Twain thus gives us of Dawson's Landing is akin to the prosaic tone permeating much of the novel, for the novel's rather drab superstructure hides a turbulent substructure, just as the settlement of Dawson's Landing sits atop inevitably eruptive forces. The settlement is an incipient wilderness, where the center never holds.

Twain dramatizes this tension between the wilderness and the settlement by placing most important events just west of town, where things not only happen, but where, because of the compelling pressure being exerted on the town, things simply have to happen.

For example, after telling the joke that alienates him from the townspeople, Wilson is next seen inhabiting the western fringe of town. It is suggestive that because of the citizens' insensitivity and lack of vision, this above-average newcomer is deprived of the chance to practice law. His house is thus an indication of the direction he conceivably could take towards spiteful rebellion, since just west of it is the haunted house Roxy and Tom use as their headquarters, whereas beyond this house is nothing. As they meet in the haunted house, Tom and Roxy, succumbing to the attraction of the wilderness, foment trouble that disrupts the whole community. Wilson, on the other hand, remains a model citizen while in his house, and turns to the hobby that will in effect help him and his townspeople better move westwards. His hobby is finger-printing, a new science that will better insure the detection and control of crime, and thus the stability of Dawson's Landing. Neither atavist nor anarchist, Wilson brings to his town the virtues of Franklin; curious, he is ready to make certain adaptations to a new environment which men like Percy Northumberland Driscoll are unwilling to make; disciplined, he will not succumb to lawlessness with Tom Driscoll. Painstaking and disciplined curiosity is thus Wilson's response to the attraction of the West.

But before Wilson can act as deliverer, he must act as dupe. Twain next creates a series of situations where the actual truth about Dawson's Landing is being disclosed, but ineffectually, since these disclosures in no way alter the diseased condition of the community. There is disclosure, but is no such thing as that revelation which eventuates in repentance. Twain thus skillfully reenacts the plight of any age undergoing the loss of God, or regenerating myth or ethic. With nothing Beyond to look to, people inevitably take the easy course of making their own norms sacrosanct. They soon get used to short-sightedness, so that even when the truth about themselves appears, they fail to see and understand. Wilson himself is flawed in this respect.

One afternoon as he works on his books, in a room looking "westward over a stretch of vacant lots," he hears joking going on between two slaves, a black man named Jasper and the white slave Roxy. Their goading is idle, but still betrays the extent to which Dawson's Landing stands under the shadow of the wilderness, since Roxy is jesting about abolishing ties: " 'If you b'longed to me, I'd sell you down de river 'fo' you git too fur gone.' " Hers is followed by Wilson's idle chatter, in which he innocently asks the question that eventuates in the chaotic reality of the novel: " 'How do you tell them apart, Roxy, when they haven't any clothes on?' " It is later when Roxy, under the threat of being sold down the river, anxious about the welfare of her baby, and perhaps in response to Wilson's question, actually switches the babies, marvelling, " 'Now who would b'lieve clo'es could do de like o' dat' "?[2] The only possible foil to her plot is Wilson, who, Roxy muses, " 'worries me wid dem ornery glasses o' his'n; I b'lieve he's a witch.' " But her worries are unnecessary, since Wilson is unable to spot the switch when she takes the infants right by him. Hence Wilson is unknowingly instrumental in helping launch the ruin Roxy begins with the switch. For the sake of her son, she deliberately severs ties whose endurance are at the heart of a healthy culture. To aid her own son, she in effect casts him out of her presence. She then adopts Driscoll's son as her own and assumes the responsibility of rearing him, but does so only after violating that child's relationship to his own father. Her behavior thus discloses the extent to which the settlement is becoming the wilderness, a fact known only to the reader.

The extent to which these ties have been severed is borne out in the confrontation occurring later between Tom and Roxy in the haunted house. Tom is now a young man and quite adept in assuming the role of the young white master. He renders Roxy a deep hurt when she approaches him in the Driscoll home after years of separation. Eager to receive affection from him, and just as eager to get part of the fifty dollars he is receiving monthly from Judge Driscoll just to stay out of town and out of sight, she approaches him and is hastily rebuffed. Roxy reacts with sheer force, threatening to expose Tom's dark secret, his black identity. He thinks she is referring to his gambling, a fact the threatened disclosure of which is sufficient to frighten him into submission. The two meet later to talk the situation over, and do so in what the town calls "*the* haunted house. It was getting crazy and ruinous now, from long

2. James M. Cox, *Mark Twain: The Fate of Humor* (Princeton, 1966), p. 234.

neglect. It stood three hundred yards beyond Pudd'nhead Wilson's house, with nothing between but vacancy. It was the last house in the town at that end." Only there is Tom's actual identity first made known to him. The mother is actually telling him that he belongs to her: " 'Yassir—you's my *son*—.' " But her disclosure serves only to widen the distance between them. What follows is mutual violation, since Roxy uses her knowledge of Tom's secret to blackmail him, while Tom will get back at her by selling her down the river. This mother and son probably embody the dynamics of the wilderness to a greater extent than any other characters in the novel. At any rate, the resurgence of the wilderness is a fact no one is present to witness. The truth is being made known, but to nobody's benefit.

Twain carefully connects with this episode another disclosure of the truth, this one managed by the astute Wilson in his own home and concerning the past of Luigi and Angelo. By reading Luigi's palm, Wilson detects a blemish in the man's past and learns that he has killed somebody. His procedure in making this discovery foreshadows the use to which he puts his disciplined ingenuity in solving the crime. Taking Luigi's hand, he "began to study . . . tracing life lines . . . noting carefully their relations . . . he felt of the fleshy side of the hand . . . he painstakingly examined the fingers, observing their form . . . entered upon a close survey of the palm again, and his revelations began." Wilson's work looms as an initial counterforce to the destructive developments we have been witnessing. Unlike the other people of Dawson's Landing, he does not arrive easily at binding decisions on the basis of unenlightened custom or haphazard emotion; and unlike Roxy, he does not disclose truth for purpose of harsh mastery. His motives and his methods are more disinterested, foreshadowing the kind of objectivity that should enable people in an advancing nation to explore, understand and order their surroundings. But this is not to suggest that Pudd'nhead Wilson has escaped the threat of the wilderness, for while his efforts here do not seem to add to the encroaching disorder around him, they in no way arrest it either. Aside from the fact that his discovery is a bit theatrical, it is flawed mainly because it is as much off the center of things as Roxy's shattering disclosure to Tom. Discovering Luigi's mystery benefits no one, while the real mystery concerning the corruption of Dawson's Landing remains undetected. Wilson, however, should be appreciated for trying. For just as his activity begins to emerge as a way of countering current wrong, respectable men like the Judge engage in activity that outshines Wilson's theatrics but is even less to the point. The duel is the old way of settling grievances, and can but enact the wills of those who have no way or desire to see beneath the surface of things. It is not a search for truth, since participants have already decided that each has the truth and now must proceed to prove it. The Judge's and Luigi's combat barely disrupts the order of the community, and as a device to redress wrongs, fails to settle such atrocities as slavery. The duelists are thus on the harmless, however spectacular, fringe of things. The Judge can win and feel more confident both of his humor and his manhood, and yet remain unconscious of the fact that his stepson Tom is legally a black man. A winner and full of more repute than ever, the Judge remains ignorant of the canker in everybody's soul, the sign of which is the gleeful Roxy, who, without being noticed, views the proceedings from the window of the haunted house. In addition, the Judge is ignorant of the frailty of the very code he embodies. For it is Tom who will not defend himself, forcing the Judge to duel and uphold the family honor. And it is the same Tom who, when caught looting to pay off his gambling debts, actually kills the Judge. The occurrence of the duel west of town is thus an indication of the extent to which even this esteemed old custom is existing under the destructive spell of the wilderness.

The murder of Judge Driscoll finally forces townspeople to reckon with their own sickness. Instead, they react blindly and, because the twins were the first to arrive at the scene of the murder, readily jump to the pleasing conclusion that the two are the culprits. Enter Pudd'nhead Wilson again and finally.

While he is no Natty Bumppo or Dupin, Wilson is nevertheless a hero of his time, and probably of ours. Like many today, he has a marked distaste for disturbances in his community, and longs to put his talents to use in "bringing things back to normal." Wilson is also akin to us because of his unspectacular qualities. He evokes a response from us because he is one of us more than is Natty or Dupin. His time, after all, is prosaic to the point of being drab. Its crises are of lesser make and intensity than those of the wilderness, and are made to order for his unglamorous plod. And along with his plod is sheer luck. From the beginning the truth has stood under his own nose. It was he who failed to detect the switch Roxy made, he who possessed from the first the evidence in the prints that would illuminate the mystery, and he again who even discussed the crime at some length with Tom Driscoll. An unlikely Dupin, Wilson never has the situation completely under his control, and it is only after he has misjudged situations, or neglected them altogether, that he finally arrives at the truth, and he does this as much through Tom's bravado as his own ingenuity. Still, in spite of his ugly duckling qualities, Wilson keeps emerging as a man of some stature. As Twain describes him at work on the evidence, we find glimpses of a modern deliverer, the unspectacular researcher, who learns to keep subjective considerations under control for the sake of discovery. For we are told that Wilson's initial speculations about Tom's innocence "were unemphasized sensations rather than articulated thoughts, for Wilson would have laughed at the idea of seriously connecting Tom with the murder." What he learns to do is to temper his subjective judgments with more objective evidence. In this respect he is admirable, for with his plod and finally his flash of insight, he does put things together and forces a disclosure of the truth. His usefulness thus stems from his placing law in Dawson's Landing on a less subjective basis than before. His fingerprinting procedures put an end to the legality of sheer emotion. This action climaxes in the court house, dramatizing the momentous step Dawson's Landing has taken back east, away from the chaos of the wilderness. Wilson thus begins to turn the wilderness back into the settlement.

Nevertheless, this does not mean that he achieves an objective reordering of his society, for his truth is used by a slave-holding culture needing increasing support in guaranteeing its survival; his justice is used to relegate Tom back to slave status and then on down the river. Wilson then improves the periphery, but not the center of his society; its surface, but not its underlying rottenness. A partial deliverer, he sees "through a glass darkly."

It is for this reason that much irony arises from Wilson's use of the terminology of religious experience to designate his activity. A favorite word of his is "revelation." As we view him at work, we see a man engaged in tackling a problem with all the resources he has at his disposal. But from some of his statements, we may be led to believe that another force is at work the same time. Addressing the baffling evidence at hand, he remarks, " 'There is a most extraordinary mystery here,' " which then points to his moment of discovery, " 'It's so! Heavens, what a revelation! And for twenty-three years no man has ever suspected it!' " But the closer we look, the more convinced we become that the supernatural is going to have no part at all in Wilson's discovery, and is not about to force a renovation of life in Dawson's Landing. Hence the impact of this "revelation" will be infinitely removed from the experience of St. Paul or Rilke, to whom the ecstatic experience also brought the admonition, "you must change your life."[3] There can be no abiding constructive change in Wilson's world, because there is no Center to fix it to, no Divine Law serving as the source and pattern of societal law. But even if such Law existed, it is doubtful that even Wilson, the best of his community, would have eyes to see and the will to apply it. His range of perception is too narrow, and his desire to transcend the morés of Dawson's Landing with another standard, even if such cannot be absolute, is essentially nil.

3. Rainer Maria Rilke, "Torso of an Archaic Apollo," from *Rilke: Selected Poems*, trans. C. F. MacIntyre (Berkeley, 1959), p. 93.

This novel is therefore anything but Twain's celebration of such Yankee virtues as diligence and common sense. To the contrary, while he foresees and sanctions the kind of wisdom that will be brought to bear upon the issues of increasingly complex societies, Twain is too deeply aware of what to him is the godless human predicament, and the hold human evil has over all forms of civilization, to forget that while strides by such mortals may be taken, never will they be giant ones, and never will they eradicate yesterday's wrongs or obviate tomorrow's. The grain of hope in this novel is thus mixed with Twain's dark and ruthless honesty, for he is noting a culture's increasing propensity to try to right wrongs without sighting and challenging their bases. When this is the case, those moving mankind into its future may be only a little less subjective than their predecessors; for, even when we have the best of intentions to put our talents to use in the service of society, this service will be at best a modified version of the wrongs plaguing our time, if our disinterestedness is blighted like Wilson's. Lacking any way, or having a way but lacking the will to evaluate the presuppositions of our own culture, and hence allowing our so-called "objectivity" to work only this side of our sacred presuppositions, like the earnest but deluded Wilson, we will continue to make a wilderness out of the settlement we wish to preserve.

EBERHARD ALSEN

Pudd'nhead Wilson's Fight for Popularity and Power†

Let us be thankful for the fools. But for them the rest of us could not succeed.
—PUDD'NHEAD WILSON'S CALENDAR.

Mark Twain's *Pudd'nhead Wilson* is generally considered an unsuccessful novel because of its alleged lack of coherence and consistency in the development of its several thematic concerns. In 1970, however, George M. Spangler presented a thematic analysis which convincingly argues that "the book, far from being incoherent or inconsistent, is remarkable among Twain's works for its unity, a unity which derives from its pervasive concern with the theme of property, particularly the perils of an obsession with property to the exclusion of all other human values and needs."[1]

† From *Western American Literature*, 7 (Summer 1972), 2, 135–143.
1. George M. Spangler, "*Pudd'nhead* Wilson: A Parable of Property," *American Literature*, 42 (Mar. 1970), 37. [Reprinted above—*Editor*.]

This interpretation points out a very important and hitherto over-looked aspect of the novel and it provides a good explanation of the motivations and attitudes of Tom Driscoll, Roxy, and the townspeople of Dawson's Landing; but it does not do justice to the character of David Wilson and to the role he plays in the book.

Mr. Spangler bases his thesis on the assumption that the focus of the novel is on Tom Driscoll rather than on David Wilson. He sees Driscoll as an almost allegorical representation of the obsession with property and Wilson merely as Driscoll's foil. He argues that Wilson "has values in the face of which considerations of personal success and status are inconsequential"; that Wilson is "not meanly ambitious in Tom's manner"; that he is "open and frank, not devious like Tom"; and that he is "respectful of the aristocratic code" and "uncritically accepts the values of the community."[2]

But the novel's chief concern, from the first to the last chapter, is not with Tom Driscoll's exploits but with David Wilson's rise to the mayorality of Dawson's Landing. This is supported by what Twain has established about the character and motivation of his protagonist. A close examination of the text will show that—contrary to Mr. Spangler's contentions—David Wilson is extremely interested in personal success and status; that he is even more ambitious and devious than Tom Driscoll; and that he is opposed to the aristocratic code and the values of the community.

And although the concern with property unquestionably serves to unify the novel, it is not the central theme. The central theme, it seems to me, evolves out of David Wilson's twenty-three year fight for popularity and power, a fight in which his chief weapons are his superior intelligence and his astute knowledge of human nature, both hidden behind his mask of irony.[3]

When Twain first introduces David Wilson, he makes sure to explain that the young man has left his native New York and has come to Missouri "to seek his fortune." And at the end of the novel we find that Wilson has succeeded in his objective, even if it has taken him twenty-three years; for Twain stresses in the last chapter that "He was a made man for good."

Like many ambitious young men of the period, Wilson obviously felt that he would be able to make "his fortune" much more easily and quickly in the West than in the East. But his first attempt at making friends with the townspeople of Dawson's Landing and establishing himself as a popular fellow backfires. The townspeople cannot appreciate the humor in the remark that Wilson makes

2. Spangler, p. 33.

3. I would like to express my gratitude to the students of my American Literature Seminar, Fall 1970, whose responses to the novel helped me develop the thesis of this article. I am particularly indebted to Judith Rand, who took it upon herself to synthesize the results of our discussions in her term paper.

about an obnoxious dog: "I wish I owned half of that dog." "Why?" "Because I would kill my half." This remark earns Wilson the title of the town's "pudd'nhead" and spoils his chances of quickly becoming a successful lawyer. But Wilson does not give up his dream of success, for, as Twain points out, "with Scotch pluck and patience he resolved to make his way into the legal profession yet." Wilson soon finds out that his fight for success is going to be a protracted one, but he uses his time well.

Under the cover of his reputation as pudd'nhead, Wilson begins his campaign for success and power by systematically finding out everything he can about the townspeople of Dawson's Landing. While his interest in palmistry and fingerprinting further convinces the people that he is indeed a fool, Wilson establishes his "records," a collection of fingerprints of every person and child in the town. Characteristically, he "would not explain to anybody what its purpose was," and instead he misleads the townspeople by claiming that "it was an amusement."

Wilson's studies of palmistry and fingerprinting are undoubtedly motivated by his realization of the often ironic discrepancy between what people seem to be and what they really are. He doesn't trust appearances and wants to discover the true identities of the people of Dawson's Landing. Wilson's behavior indicates that he realizes that by finding out about people's secrets he can gain control and power over them. But in order to succeed, he has to carry on his detective work secretly, under the disguise of the harmless fool.

A good illustration of Wilson's interest in other people's private affairs and of his secretiveness is the incident involving the mysterious girl in Tom Driscoll's bedroom. Wilson has long suspected Driscoll to be a scoundrel, and when he accidentally observes a strange girl in Tom's bedroom, he approaches Judge Driscoll's sister, Mrs. Pratt, and carefully questions her in order to find out about the identity of the girl. When he discovers that Mrs. Pratt knows nothing about the girl's existence, Wilson "went away satisfied that he knew things that were going on in her house of which she herself was not aware." Wilson never mentions his observation to anyone because he wants to find out the precise nature of the wrongdoings of which he suspects Driscoll. As it turns out, Wilson's secretiveness pays off, for his observation of the mysterious girl later provides him with the clue he needs to bring about Driscoll's downfall and his own triumph.

Only the two smartest people in Dawson's Landing, Roxy and the Judge, realize that David Wilson is not really a pudd'nhead, but neither of them is aware of the significance of his "records," nor do they suspect that Wilson is just waiting for an opportunity to use his secret knowledge to his advantage.

This opportunity does not present itself for twenty-three years. All this time Wilson is, as Twain makes us aware, "toiling in obscurity at the bottom of the ladder." But Twain also shows that Wilson has never given up his dream of success. We are reminded of Wilson's ambition when Tom Driscoll needles him in front of the newly arrived Italian twins and jokes about the fact that Wilson has never had the opportunity to practice law. Twain explains that Tom's mischievous banter "touched a *secret sore*" [my italics] in Wilson. Wilson's reply to Tom Driscoll is also telling. He says that if he ever should get the chance to practice law, he "shall be found ready," for he has "kept up [his] studies all these years."

Wilson gets his chance when Luigi, one of the Italians hauled into court by Tom Driscoll on an assault and battery charge, selects David Wilson as his defense attorney. Significantly, this occurs on a day when the town's first citizen, Tom's uncle, Judge Driscoll, is absent from Dawson's Landing. Although Luigi is found guilty and Wilson loses his first case, Wilson is at last launched on his professional career. That same evening the Democratic Party asks Wilson to run for mayor in the upcoming charter elections, and Twain underlines the significance of this invitation by commenting that this "was a recognition of his debut into the town's life and activities at last; it was a step upward, and he was deeply gratified."

When Tom Driscoll appears at David Wilson's house that evening and tells him that his uncle, the Judge, has disinherited him for not challenging Luigi to a duel, as the code of the First Families of Virginia dictates, Wilson says:

> "Tom, I am ashamed of you! I don't see how you could treat your good uncle so. I am a better friend of his than you are; for if I had known the circumstances I would have kept that case out of court until I got word to him and let him have a gentleman's chance."

This statement reveals Wilson's deviousness. He pays lip service to the code of the F.F.V. not only because he wants to deceive Tom —for during their conversation he subtly tries to make Tom give away the secret of the mysterious girl that he had observed in Tom's bedroom—but also because he has to uphold this code if he wants to assure his popularity with the people of Dawson's Landing.

Careful analysis of the text proves that Wilson is lying when he tells Tom that he would have kept the case out of court "if [he] had known the circumstances." For one thing, he is definitely not surprised about Tom's behavior, nor is he ashamed for him. For when he sees Driscoll walk toward his house that evening, Wilson makes a comment to himself that shows that he has been aware all along of the fact that Tom disgraced his family in the eyes of the Judge and the rest of the townspeople. Hearing Driscoll's footsteps on his porch, Wilson says: "It is that fickle-tempered, dissipated young goose—poor devil, he finds friends pretty scarce today, likely, after the disgrace of carrying a personal assault case into a law court." When Driscoll tells him how upset his uncle is about his behavior, Wilson feigns surprise and pretends he didn't know about the "circumstances" and would have kept the case out of court had he known what the Judge's reaction would be.

Tom's response to Wilson's declaration is very revealing:

> "You would?" exclaimed Tom, with lively surprise. "And it your first case! And you know perfectly well there never would have *been* any case if he [the Judge] had got that chance, don't you? And you'd have finished your days a pauper nobody, instead of being an actually launched and recognized lawyer today. And you would really have done that, would you?"

Twain apparently phrased Tom's statement the way he did in order to direct the reader's attention to David Wilson's true motivation. For Tom's doubts are quite legitimate. If Wilson had really been concerned about the Judge's sense of family honor, he certainly would have kept the case out of court until the Judge returned from his hunting trip later that same day. It seems that, on the contrary, Wilson was extremely interested in getting the case into court before the Judge could interfere and spoil his chance to practice law at last, a chance for which he had been waiting for twenty-three years.

Despite the fact that Wilson did, in fact, nothing to keep the case out of court, he is able to assuage Driscoll's doubts and to convince him of the purity of his motivations. For Driscoll says:

> "I believe you—upon my word I do. I don't know why I do, but I do. Pudd'nhead Wilson I think you're the biggest fool I ever saw."

Why does the otherwise shrewd Tom Driscoll believe Wilson? The reason is of course that Wilson does an extremely convincing job in acting out the role of the self-effacing fool and vociferous supporter of the aristocratic code.

An entry from Pudd'nhead Wilson's Calendar provides further proof that Wilson does not really support the aristocratic code but only pretends to do so because he knows that this will help his career. This calendar entry precedes the chapter which explains the code of honor of the F.F.V. and then describes the Judge's reaction to Tom's "cowardice." In this entry, Wilson celebrates the flea as "incomparably the bravest of all creatures of God," thus undercut-ting the entire chapter. With this calendar entry Twain clearly serves notice that we should not accept at face value David Wilson's chastising of Tom Driscoll for his lack of "courage."

Despite his disdain for the code of the F.F.V., Wilson later volunteers to serve as Luigi's second when the Judge himself challenges the Italian to the duel that Tom should have fought. It seems that Wilson's decision is motivated not so much by his friendship with Luigi as by his realization that he will greatly rise in the regard of the townspeople by participating in the affair. Twain hints at Wilson's motivation when he explains that the townspeople take tremendous pride in the duel and that "even the duelists' subordinates came in for a handsome share of public approbation; *wherefore Pudd'nhead Wilson was suddenly become a man of consequence.*" (My italics.)

Another aspect of the deviousness with which David Wilson pursues his campaign for popularity and power is the fact that he has no scruples about sacrificing the interests of his friends to his own ambition. Wilson's unwillingness to protect the family honor of his friend, the Judge, by not keeping Tom's personal-assault case out of court might be excusable if one considers how much was at stake for Wilson and how little he respected the aristocratic code. But there can be no excuse for his letting down the twins when the Judge publicly impugns their character and hints that Luigi is guilty of a murder. Although Wilson knows these accusations to be false, he fails to come to the twins' defense. When asked to explain what the Judge meant by his insinuation, Wilson merely "parried the question by asking the questioner what *he* thought it meant."

The reason Wilson does not publicly defend his two friends is quite clear. The Judge's allegations are made during the election campaign. Wilson himself is running for mayor, and if he opposes the Judge he will certainly lose votes. Moreover, Twain points out that the twins' "popularity, so general at first, had suffered afterward," and that the Judge's campaign against them "was disastrously effective." To stick up for the twins at this time would obviously seriously hurt Wilson's chances for success. Wilson's strategy once more pays off, for he wins the election.

Although David Wilson has been elected mayor of Dawson's Landing, and although he has begun to practice law, Twain does not end the story here but shows Wilson's continued progress to the top of the social ladder. To get there, Wilson has to replace Judge Driscoll as the "chief citizen" of Dawson's Landing and he has to cancel out the popularity and power of the only other remaining member of the F.F.V., "the great lawyer," Pembroke Howard.

Wilson gets his chance to assume the position of ultimate popularity and power one week after his election to the mayorality, when
Judge Driscoll is murdered. The twins are mistakenly charged with
the murder, and Wilson, knowing them to be innocent because
their fingerprints do not match those on the murder weapon, undertakes their defense.

During the trial, Wilson reveals to the stunned townspeople that
his studies of fingerprinting and his keeping of records were not
merely a foolish "amusement" as he had let them believe, but that
his research allows him to positively establish the true identity of
each one of them:

> "There is hardly a person in this room, white or black, whose
> natal signature I cannot produce, and not one of them can so dis-
> guise himself that I cannot pick him out from a multitude of his
> fellow creatures and unerringly identify him by his hands. And if
> he and I should live to be a hundred I could still do it."

Because of the "records" he has kept and the detective work that
he has carried on under his disguise as pudd'nhead, Wilson is now
able to identify Tom Driscoll as the mysterious female burglar and
the murderer of his uncle, and he can furthermore prove that Tom
is not the rightful heir to the Driscoll estate but an impostor.

Naturally, Wilson's disclosures produce "a vast sensation," but
Wilson is not content with merely presenting the facts in the case.
Throughout his presentation he cleverly manipulates his audience.
Witness his "effect collecting pauses," his dramatic announcement
that he will identify the murderer "in this room before the clock
strikes twelve," and his concluding statement which forces the criminal to confess precisely on the stroke of noon.

It seems to me that Twain makes Wilson manipulate the audience's reactions not so much because he loves theatrical effects, but
because he wants Wilson to impress upon the townspeople his
unquestionable professional superiority over Pembroke Howard.
This Wilson manages to do so well that even Judge Robinson feels
compelled to comment that Wilson's performance "certainly
approaches the miraculous." By roundly defeating Pembroke
Howard and so demonstrating his superiority over the only remaining member of the F.F.V., Wilson increases and secures his popularity with the townspeople and thereby firmly establishes his power
as the mayor and new "chief citizen" of Dawson's Landing.

The trial has thus brought David Wilson to the top of the social
ladder, to the pinnacle of popularity and power. But that does not
mean that he accepts the values of the community. There are, in
fact, several indications that he does not subscribe to the codes and
customs of Dawson's Landing. After the Judge has refused to fight

Luigi a second time "on the field of honor," Wilson tries to explain to the Italian what this refusal means. His ironic tone indicates his negative attitude toward the customs of the area:

> "The unwritten law of this region requires you to kill Judge Driscoll on sight, and he and the community will expect that attention at your hands—though of course your own death by his bullet will answer every purpose."

Wilson manifests the same disdainful attitude toward the values and attitudes of his community during the trial when he ruminates about the fact that the murder weapon belongs to the twins while the fingerprints on it are clearly someone else's:

> Wilson regarded the case of the twins as desperate—in fact, about hopeless. For he argued that if a confederate was not found, *an enlightened Missouri jury* would hang them, sure; if a confederate was found, that would not improve the matter but would simply furnish one more person for the sheriff to hang. [My italics.]

Wilson's irony indicates that he has little faith in the people who have elected him mayor. His and their mentality, attitudes, and levels of intelligence are worlds apart.

So David Wilson has been successful in his fight for popularity and power. He has made it to the top of the heap and he has made his fortune; but can he be content with his achievement? The only people that were able to appreciate the quality of his intellect, his humor, and his irony, Judge Driscoll and the twins, are gone; and so Wilson finds himself at the head of an unenlightened community whose values he despises but cannot change (witness the absurdity of the logic that makes them decide to sell Tom Driscoll as a slave). The ultimate futility of Wilson's success seems to be the final irony of the novel. It suggests that he is a pudd'nhead after all.

The theme that this reading of the novel points out is not contradictory but in fact complementary to that discovered by Mr. Spangler. The protagonist's quest for popularity and power and the antagonist's quest for property create the novel's central conflict, and the outcome of this conflict is the rise of David Wilson from pudd'nhead to mayor, a rise that is paralleled by Tom Driscoll's fall from aristocrat to slave. These two thematic concerns provide an interesting commentary on the social and political conditions in mid-nineteenth century America and give the novel an additional historical significance.

The action of the novel begins in 1830, when Dawson's Landing is ruled by the aristocratic First Families of Virginia. It ends in 1853, when the town "was about to become a city" and "the first charter elections" are being held. These elections and the events immediately following them result in a shift of power from the old aristocracy to the Democratic Party with David Wilson at its head. The novel can therefore be seen as a chronicle of the social and political change that occurred in America just previous to the Civil War, a change from a society in which the power depended on property to one in which the power is based on popularity.

The two major themes of the novel, the theme of power which evolves out of the story of the protagonist and the theme of property which evolves out of the story of the antagonist, thus mutually support and clarify each other. This structural and thematic symmetry proves that *Pudd'nhead Wilson* is far from incoherent and inconsistent in its development, that it is, on the contrary, Mark Twain's most tightly constructed novel.

STANLEY BRODWIN

Blackness and the Adamic Myth in Mark Twain's *Pudd'nhead Wilson*†

Shortly after completing A *Connecticut Yankee in King Arthur's Court* (1889), Mark Twain wrote to W. D. Howells that he had left many things out of that book, and they still "burn in me; & they keep multiplying & multiplying; but now they can't ever be said. And besides, they would require a library—& a pen warmed-up in hell."[1] In later works like *Pudd'nhead Wilson* (1894), "The Man That Corrupted Hadleyburg" (1899), *The Mysterious Stranger* manuscripts,[2] and several shorter, darkly satirical works attacking God, the Bible, imperialism, and war,[3] Mark Twain indeed wrote with a pen warmed up in hell. But of all the novels and stories of his last years of despair, *Pudd'nhead Wilson* is his most classically conceived "tragedy" and the epitome of his deterministic view of reality in the novel form. Like most of Mark

† From *Texas Studies in Literature and Language*, 15 (1973–74), 167–176.
1. *Mark Twain—Howells Letters*, ed. H. N. Smith and W. M. Gibson (Cambridge, Mass., 1960), II, 613.
2. Since the publication of *Mark Twain's Mysterious Stranger Manuscripts*, ed. with an Introduction by William M. Gibson (Berkeley and Los Angeles, 1969), it seems to me that critics can no longer make the traditionally accepted Paine-Duneka version the definitive one for critical analysis.
3. For example, see Mark Twain, *Letters from the Earth*, ed. Bernard DeVoto (New York, 1962); "Reflections on Religion," ed. Charles Neider, *Hudson Review*, 16 (1963), 329–352; and an excellent anthology, *Mark Twain on the Damned Human Race*, ed. with an Introduction by Janet Smith (New York, 1962), containing such pieces as "To the Person Sitting in Darkness" (1901), "The War Prayer" (1905, 1916), and "The United States of Lyncherdom" (1901). Even his *Personal Recollections of Joan of Arc* (1896) must be considered as a "symbol of despair" since it deals with innocence betrayed and destroyed while holding fast to the possibility that man could overcome evil on earth.

Twain's work in this period it deals with failure, betrayal, and damnation—innocence lost even as it gives the illusion of man's capacity to triumph over the fate of the damned human race.[4] *Pudd'nhead Wilson* is, therefore, not merely a "novel of ideas," but a theological study of man's nature whose intrinsic pattern is modeled on the myth of the fall of man. Temptation, pride, banishment, and damnation, dramatized in biblical terms, provide the key to the novel's meaning and help us to resolve some of the critical questions raised by its archetypal and tragi-satirical form.[5]

Yet, characteristically, in a letter to Fred J. Hall, Mark Twain judged *Pudd'nhead Wilson* as a story whose ostensible interest "centered on the murder and the trial; from the first chapter the movement is straight ahead without divergence . . . to the murder and the trial. . . . Therefore, 3 people stand up high . . . and only 3—Pudd'nhead, 'Tom' Driscoll, and his nigger mother, Roxana. . . ."[6] In the same letter, however, Mark Twain writes that unless he can finish a new work he will "tackle Adam once more, and do him in a kind of a friendly and respectful way that will commend him to the Sunday schools. I've been thinking out his first life-days today and framing his childish and ignorant impressions and opinions for him."[7] This was to be "Extracts from Adam's Diary," published that year (1893), and the first of a group of works that included "Eve's Diary" (1905) and "That Day in Eden" (1923). Apart from the very obvious humor Mark Twain extracts from his anachronistic treatment of Adam and Eve, these works deal in comic and tragic terms with the theme of man's fall from innocence—a

4. For Mark Twain, man was "damned" in the precise theological sense. He wrote in the margin of a book by an optimistic evolutionist that man "was made to suffer and be damned." Quoted in Roger B. Salomon, *Twain and the Image of History* (New Haven, 1961), p. 50. And in a speech he gave on his "Seventieth Birthday," he talked seriocomically about the "sin microbes" in man. See *Mark Twain's Speeches* (New York, 1910), p. 433. Finally, Joseph Twichell chided Mark Twain for being "too orthodox on the Doctrine of Total Human Depravity"; Joseph Twichell to Mark Twain, September 5, 1901, as quoted by Kenneth R. Andrews, *Nook Farm: Mark Twain's Hartford Circle* (Cambridge, Mass., 1950), pp. 47, 253. Indeed, there are a great many references in Mark Twain's works to man's sinfulness, his fall, and the demonic God who punishes him for it.

5. Several of the best studies of *Pudd'nhead Wilson* have commented on the book's structural tightness and its evocation of a sense of genuine doom, praising its depth, though criticizing the mechanical quality of its structure and the

flaw of mixing a tragic racial theme with a detective story. I hope to answer some of these objections in my study. But see James M. Cox, *"Pudd'nhead Wilson*: The End of Mark Twain's American Dream," *South Atlantic Quarterly,* 58 (1959), 351–363; Leslie Fiedler, "As Free as Any Cretur . . . ." in *Mark Twain, A Collection of Critical Essays,* ed. H. N. Smith (Englewood Cliffs, N.J., 1963); F. R. Leavis, "Mark Twain's Neglected Classic: The Moral Astringency of *Pudd'nhead Wilson," Commentary,* 21 (1956), 128–136; George M. Spangler, *"Pudd'nhead Wilson*: A Parable of Property," *American Literature,* 42 (1970), 28–37; and Barbara A. Chellis, "Those Extraordinary Twins: Negroes and Whites," *American Quarterly,* 21 (1969), 100–112, for a variety of different, but excellent approaches to the book. [The Fiedler, Spangler, and Leavis essays are reprinted above—*Editor.*]

6. *Mark Twain's Letters,* ed. A. B. Paine (New York, 1917), II, 590–591.

7. Ibid., 591–592. For a study of Mark Twain's Adamic references see Allison Ensor, *Mark Twain and the Bible* (Lexington, 1970).

fall that is inevitable because man cannot transcend his machine-like nature. Man, burdened with the "Moral Sense," chooses a congenial or attractive evil rather than an uncongenial "good" or agonizing truth.[8] Thus, despite Mark Twain's interest in the melodramatic murder and trial, the combination of his erupting pessimism and long preoccupation with the Adamic myth found its way into the form and meaning of Pudd'nhead Wilson.

The basic technique by which Mark Twain achieves artistic and philosophic unity in this novel is to make the leading characters become victims of forces both outside and within themselves. Two linked tragedies are therefore developed. One is concerned with man's sin and fall, and the other with the fall of America. Pudd'n-head satirically points to the latter in his calendar entry, entered just after he makes his discovery of the identities of Tom and Chambers: "October 12, the Discovery. It was wonderful to find America, but it would have been more wonderful to miss it." For the American dream has become vitiated by slavery. Its grass-roots mentality drives intellectuals like Pudd'nhead underground, and its cultural provincialism is exposed by the Italian twins, Luigi and Angelo. Knowledge through irony is wasted upon the people of Daw-son's Landing, as when Judge Driscoll tries to read Pudd'nhead's calendar to them: "But irony was not for those people; their mental vision was not focused for it. They read those . . . trifles in . . . ear-nest, and decided . . . that if there had ever been any doubt that Dave Wilson was a pudd'nhead—which there hadn't—this revela-tion removed that doubt. . . ." Pudd'nhead's ironic joke about the dog, from which he gained his nickname, can now be seen as only the first in a series of ironies that fail to enlighten, indicating the impotence of humor in raising a fallen world. But behind this account of America's failings lurks the more significant and unifying theme of original sin. The proper setting is Eden, of which Daw-son's Landing is yet another avatar.[9] The town is described as a "snug little collection of modest . . . dwellings whose white-washed exteriors were almost concealed from sight by climbing tangles of rose vines, honeysuckles, and morning-glories." The names of the flowers suggest the lush, yet homey, quality of the place that was "sleepy and comfortable and contented." But Dawson's Landing is also a "slave-holding town, with a rich slave-worked grain and pork country back of it." Herein lies the metaphorical serpent in this apparent Eden. For the slavery is not only evil in itself—the

8. This is one of the fundamental ideas in What is Man? (1906). For a good study of the Moral Sense in Mark Twain's thought, see Coleman O. Par-sons, "The Devil and Samuel Clemens," Virginia Quarterly Review, 23 (1947), 582–606. See also my study, "The

Humor of the Absurd: Mark Twain's Adamic Diaries," Criticism, 14 (1972), 49–64.
9. See Henry Nash Smith, "Mark Twain's Image of Hannibal: From St. Petersburg to Eseldorf," Texas Studies in English, 37 (1958), 3–23.

National Sin—but is the condition that leads to a variety of crimes: miscegenation, betrayal, murder, and tampering with the lives of innocent infants. A whole range of man's sinful impulses is dramatically realized. From this fact springs the essential, mythic tragedy of the book.

The initial agents of the tragedy are Percy Northumberland Driscoll and Colonel Cecil Burleigh Essex, two of the honor-worshiping aristocrats of the town. It is they who sire two sons, one born to Driscoll and his wife, who dies in childbirth, the other to Essex and Driscoll's slave Roxana, who is only one-sixteenth black.[1] Miscegenation becomes the first of several blood-sins, offenses against primal taboos. These sins pollute the earth, bring suffering or death to all, and demand retribution as in the stories of Cain and Oedipus.

Added to Essex's sins of fleshly pollution, so common and held in such abhorrence in the South, is Driscoll's original, spiritual sin—pride. For Driscoll, power over slaves is power over life and death, Heaven and Hell. He can sell slaves "down the river," which, writes Twain, "was equivalent to condemning them to hell!" In this way Driscoll terrifies a group of slaves into confessing a petty theft. Driscoll relents and says he will sell them at Dawson's Landing. The slaves kiss his feet in gratitude. Then follows a passage that captures in a coldly ironic style the act of pride. And it begins fittingly and grandly, with a biblically shaped line:

> They were sincere, for like a god he had stretched forth his mighty hand and closed the gates of hell against them. He knew, himself, that he had done a noble and gracious thing, and was privately well pleased with his magnanimity; and that night he set the incident down in his diary, so that his son might read it in after years, and be thereby moved to deeds of gentleness and humanity himself.

Mark Twain's use of irony is masterful here and may be regarded as a stylistic paradigm of the novel as a whole. The biblical line at the same time widens the vision of the incident by its suggestive allusion to the serpent's lure to Eve: "Ye shall be as gods" (Gen. 3:5). Driscoll behaves like a "god" and thus personifies fallen man trapped not only in pride but in pride's twin, blind self-deceit. And

1. In developing the character of Roxy, Mark Twain owed much to the long-standing stereotype of the tragic mulatto in American writing. The problems of "passing," double identity, and the melodramatic revelations are all standard fare and are all used in *Pudd'nhead Wilson*. Indeed, the tragic mulatto was one stereotype exploited by antislavery writers for propaganda purposes. No doubt Mark Twain learned much about anti-slave fiction from Harriet Beecher Stowe and George Washington Cable as well as from his general literary apprenticeship. Still, Mark Twain is often able to give a visceral human quality to his "types" as witness Jim, Roxy, and the Mammy in "A True Story" (1874). But see Sterling A. Brown, "Negro Character as Seen by White Authors," *Journal of Negro Education*, 2 (1933), 180–201.

these are the qualities that he transmits to his new "son" who becomes Thomas à Becket Driscoll. These traits become manifest in Thomas and not in Percy's legitimate son, who becomes a humble, ignorant slave, because the culture of white supremacy brings them out of Thomas and suppresses them in Valet de Chambre. Man is seen as an "over-determined" creature, controlled by both his intrinsic nature and an environment that reinforces that nature. Pudd'nhead's calendar entry for chapter II crystallizes the determinism that the action of the chapter plays out:

> Adam was but human—this explains it all. He did not want the apple for the apple's sake, he wanted it only because it was forbidden. The mistake was in not forbidding the serpent; then he would have eaten the serpent.

Perhaps even more directly, this aphorism, with its trenchant humor, applies to Pudd'nhead himself. For in this chapter the now rejected "college-bred" Pudd'nhead turns to his hobbies of palmistry and fingerprinting.[2]

It is a standard criticism of the novel that Pudd'nhead's concern for fingerprints and his use of them in solving a crime represent the "popular" and vulgar melodrama of the novel that Mark Twain never quite integrated with the tragedy of Roxy and her son.[3] But it seems fairly clear from the juxtaposition of the aphorism and the description of fingerprinting that there is some fundamental thematic connection, and that this is the necessity of the fall of man. Adam had to fall, and his destiny is stamped in man from birth. When Pudd'nhead takes the fingerprints of the two babies and Roxy, more than a melodrama of crime detection is being prepared. Pudd'nhead is actually translated into an instrument of God whose task it is to teach man the nature of his fate, a role concerning which Roxana has some intimations:

> Blame dat man, he worries me wid dem ornery glasses o' his'n; I b'lieve he's a witch. But nemmine, I's gwine to happen aroun' dah one o' dese days en let on dat I reckon he wants to print de chillen's fingers ag'in; en if *he* don't notice dey's changed . . . den I's safe, sho'. But I reckon I'll take along a hoss-shoe to keep off de witch work.

2. For information on Mark Twain's interest in fingerprinting, see Anne P. Wigger, "The Source of Fingerprint Material in Mark Twain's *Pudd'nhead Wilson* and *Those Extraordinary Twins*," *American Literature*, 28 (1957), 517–520.

3. See, for example, Richard Chase, *The American Novel and Its Tradition* (New York: Anchor Books, 1957), p. 155. He writes, "the characters and their relationships are not adequate to the moral action; the split between action and actors runs through the book." And Leslie Fiedler, who recognizes in the story a "local instance of some universal guilt and doom," also remarks that the "tragic inevitability" is "blurred by the demands of the detective story with which it is crossed"; in "Free as Any Cretur . . . ," p. 137. [Reprinted above— *Editor.*] I am arguing, however, for the organic relationship between the philosophic and detective elements in the book on the grounds that the fingerprinting functions as a theological symbol of man's fall.

For Roxana, Pudd'nhead is a kind of witch-priest who is really the "smartes' man in dis town." Her magic fails because Pudd'nhead's magic represents the truth about man, locked in the whorls of his fingertips.

Pudd'nhead, with all his aphorisms about Adam, functions as the servant of God who rules over a deterministic world. He accepts this world with bitter humor and, like Mark Twain himself, comes to see that the result of the Fall has its own ironic consolation. The entry for chapter III is:

> Whoever has lived long enough to find out what life is, knows how deep a debt of gratitude we owe to Adam, the first great benefactor of our race. He brought death into the world.

Apart from expressing Pudd'nhead's own spiritual character, the aphorism relates—as all the calendar entries do—to the specific action of the chapter. And the action in chapter III is Roxy's trick of exchanging the destinies of the two infants. The link is again clear. Roxy, ironically playing God as her master did, commits an act of pride that brings tragedy and death (the murder of Judge Driscoll by Thomas, Roxy's son) into the world. But first she must justify her act, and this she does by telling herself that *"white* folks has done it! It ain't no sin, glory to goodness it ain't no sin!" To bolster her rationalization on an even deeper level, she invokes the Calvinist doctrine of the Elect expounded by a traveling preacher:

> He said dey ain't nobody kin save his own self—can't do it by faith, can't do it by works, can't do it no way at all. Free grace is de *on'y* way, en dat don't come fum nobody but jis' de Lord; en *he* kin give it to anybody he please, saint or sinner—*he* don't kyer. He do jis' as he's a mineter. He s'lect out anybody dat suit him, en put another one in his place, en make de fust one happy forever en leave t'other one to burn wid Satan.

Thus, if destiny—or Free Grace—offers her a chance to save her child from slavery, then, reasons Roxana, she must take the opportunity presented to her. She herself becomes an agent of Election or Grace. But though she has great provocation for what she does, and the reader must partially sympathize with her, her action injures many innocent people and cannot finally be justified. Indeed, almost immediately, Roxana begins to suffer. Her child, now her master, becomes a sickly and pernicious person who takes particular delight in treating Roxana with open contempt. With characteristic irony, Mark Twain shows how Roxana loses the pleasure she sought in seeing her son master. Her "mock reverence" to Tom becomes "real reverence . . . the mock homage real homage." In short, she becomes the "dupe of her own deceptions." Punishment follows swiftly on the heels of sin.

Even more quickly does the essential pattern of the book assert itself: the two boys follow fixed paths. Spoiled and pampered beyond limit, Tom becomes an egotist without moral backbone. Given a chance to be a free and purposeful human being, he fails to live up to the expectations of his mother and his "uncle," Judge Driscoll, who takes him in hand after his "father," Percy Driscoll, dies. His betrayal consists of two terrible crimes: selling his mother down the river after she reveals his true origin to him, and murdering his "uncle." A lesser, but still significant betrayal is demonstrated when Tom, rather than answering Count Luigi's challenge to a duel, takes the affair to court, thereby blemishing the aristocratic honor-code held by his family and the town's leading citizens. Much of what Tom does is explained by his "training," but the deepest quality of his soul's evil, and its cause, reveals itself in the great "discovery" scenes between Roxana and Tom. Roxana, free for many years now, returns to Dawson's Landing to see her son once again. Asking him for some money, she receives only humiliation. Her proud character rebels; she becomes determined to reveal the truth to him. Shattered, Tom listens to the truth in impotent rage. Then, he utters the lament that is the tragic core of the novel, a lament that makes the social tragedy of slavery part of the cosmic tragedy of original sin: "Why were niggers *and* whites made? What crime did the uncreated first nigger commit that the curse of birth was decreed for him? And why is this awful difference made between white and black?"

For an explanation of the awful racial problem, Tom can only fall back on a theological concept of primal guilt. Tom feels that "the curse of Ham" is upon him. Here, Mark Twain, though in sympathy with the Negro, recognizes the persuasiveness of this biblical apologetic in the South. The Negro is *doomed* to suffer. To generations—North and South—saturated with biblical thought and seeking answers in vast cosmic solutions, whether through the Bible or Darwinism or through the fixed power of a vague "Providence," such an answer would have its impact—and its believers. For Mark Twain, the tragedy is not in being born black, but in being born black into a white world. That is the agony. Man's punishment lies in the very fragmentation of his physical as well as moral nature. The contrast between white and black with all its symbolic and cosmic connotations of struggle and strife lives in the flesh of man.

There is the momentary hope that a perception of such tragic depth could, and would, alter character. But the hope flickers and dies. Tom is afflicted with guilt for being black—he hears the biblical accusation "Thou art the man" that Nathan hurled at David (2

Sam. 12:7). Slowly but surely Tom responds with such intensity to the idea of being black that his manners and behavior take on the aspect of a slave. "But," writes Mark Twain, "the main structure of his character was not changed, and could not be changed." Soon after, Tom commits his crimes. A child of miscegenation, he embodies the doom of guilt and suffering for being a Negro, with the rich white man's vices of gambling, contempt for inferiors, egotism, and self-indulgence. The main line of the plot is simply a demonstration of the consequences of this fate.

It is Roxana's fate to be both creator and victim of Tom at one and the same time. This is what makes her the protagonist as well as the emotional center of the novel. It is she who is most aware of the tragically ironical world around her, and it is she who tries to struggle out of the trap she has created for herself. The burden of Tom's failure to succeed in the white man's world falls on her shoulders. While she tries to save her son from debts and disinheritance, she is also called upon to condemn him when he fails to answer Luigi's challenge to a duel:

> "It's de nigger in you, dat's what it is. Thirty-one parts o' you is white, en on'y one part nigger, en dat po' little one part is yo' *soul*. 'Tain't wuth savin'; 'tain't wuth totin' out on a shovel en throwin' in de gutter. You has disgraced yo' birth. What would yo' pa think o' you? It's enough to make him turn in his grave."

The terrible irony of a Negro condemning her own race is, indeed, an "appalling response,"[4] as Leslie Fiedler has termed it. This, for Mark Twain, is the ultimate tragedy of the Negro. His mind and soul have been literally and figuratively "whitewashed," so that he sometimes assumes the point of view of the slaveholder and despises himself for being a slave and black. It is the final stage of degradation in slave-psychology. Roxy even goes so far as to invoke the white man's racism on the basis of the distorted Christian reading of the Bible that makes the tribe of Ham inherently guilty. Thus, she and her white masters join together in condemning blacks on the grounds of a kind of original sin, though the sin itself can never be clearly articulated in theological terms. For the sin of Ham, "the father of Canaan" who "saw the nakedness of his father," Noah (Gen. 9:22), is neither the sin of pride nor lust nor any of the other major sins against God. The biblical text, in fact, does not suggest that Ham entered the tent in order to see the nakedness of his father. The implication is clearly that Ham entered by chance. Accident or not, in the severely patriarchal society of the Hebrews, beholding the genitalia of the father was a terrible trans-

---

4. Leslie Fiedler, "As Free as Any Cretur . . . ," p. 137.

gression against the sexual mores. The punishment is for Canaan to be a "servant of servants" (Gen. 9:25). The biblical passage is etiological and attempts to degrade the Canaanites (who were not Negroid) because of the conflict the Hebrews were to have with them later, recounted in The Book of Judges and Samuel 1 and 2. The historical irony, as it was developed in the South, and reflected in *Pudd'nhead Wilson*, is that the white sons of Noah punished the sons of Ham by degrading them sexually. But Roxana is proud, ironically, of being used by the aristocratic Essex, who, like many of the white masters who used their slaves sexually, unconsciously degraded himself. Tom, the spawn of such an act, becomes its spiritual incarnation. And he knows that this doom has been foisted on him. That is why, after listening to Roxy's condemnation, Tom wishes that his white father were alive so that he could kill him. As it is, he kills his surrogate father, Judge Driscoll, though ostensibly for money.

Roxy, however, is the more tragic figure, for she is the self-deceived one, trying to escape her destiny through her child, yet having to turn on her child with her master's religious and racial attitudes. Clearly, Mark Twain is sympathizing with her and agonizing over her destiny.[5] He is delineating the tragedy of the Negro rather than accepting Roxy's own judgment of her race. This point must be emphasized,[6] for on the surface it might appear that Mark Twain implicitly accepted the "original" inferiority of the Negro by making Tom evil and Chambers good. But such a view would miss the tragic religious, social, and sexual ironies that permeate the novel. For Mark Twain the tragedy lies in the fact that Tom, by "training" a white slaveholder with the white slaveholder's vices, is blamed for these vices because of his Negro birth. Chambers, goodness and humility personified, has been conditioned by his Negro

5. Yet Philip Butcher in his article "Mark Twain Sells Roxy down the River," *CLA Journal*, 8 (1965), 228, writes that Roxy is a "ludicrous grotesque, a shadow signifying nothing except Twain's inability . . . to rise above popular notions about the Negro's instability and lack of profound feeling." I feel that this criticism is unjustifiable. While Roxy is, as I have pointed out, part of a tradition of Negro stereotypes, Mark Twain humanizes her. He shows her to be driven to her actions by the oppression of slavery and the loss of a genuine womanhood and motherhood. These actions are "believable" because they derive from an authentic despair. Butcher also writes in the same passage that Mark Twain "seems to forget how little 'Negro blood' flows in Roxy's veins and to lend support to the shabby opin-

ion that any 'taint' of Negro ancestry . . . was 'remote' and could not account for her 'irrational, ignoble behavior.' " But Mark Twain is not forgetting that in the South any "taint" of Negro blood was enough to condemn a person to racist oppression. He is not justifying it; he is commenting on the tragedy of such a condition. *Pudd'nhead Wilson* is a masterly, ironic delineation of the racial traps both black man and white man are caught in.
6. See, for example, Anne T. Wigger, "The Composition of Mark Twain's *Pudd'nhead Wilson* and *Those Extraordinary Twins*: Chronology and Development," *Modern Philology*, 55 (1957), 93–102. Miss Wigger argues that Tom's function is "unclear—almost as if innately corrupt due to his Negro blood" (p. 98).

training that teaches him to know his place and accept his lot, yet that goodness is assumed to be the result of his being white. Such is the terrible irony and confusion about race and character with which the South (and, by extension, America) was burdened. And the tragedy is compounded because of the irrevocability of training, the attitudes it creates, and the universal nature of man himself. Man could not reform. Once fallen, he must stay fallen. That is the essence of Mark Twain's pessimistic determinism.

The idea is made explicit at the end of this scene between Roxy and Tom. Roxy terrifies Tom into behaving well so that Judge Driscoll will make a new will leaving him his fortune. Tom says, "I know, now, that I am reformed—and permanently. Permanently—and beyond the reach of any human temptation." To underscore the resolution, Mark Twain writes that there was "no levity in his voice." But the result of Tom's reformation is contained in Pudd'nhead's calendar entry for the next chapter: "Nothing so needs reforming as other people's habits." Tom is robbed of his stolen loot by a thief and so the plot is hatched whereby he will recoup his loss by selling his mother down the river. This occurs in the next chapter, whose calendar entry is: "If you pick up a starving dog and make him prosperous, he will not bite you. This is the principal difference between a dog and a man." Once again the point is driven home that a man cannot reform.

Roxy eventually escapes, but shortly thereafter Tom commits the murder with which the twins are charged. The stage is set for the courtroom scene in which Pudd'nhead will emerge from relative obscurity to produce his grand "effect." The calendar entry is: "*April 1*. This is the day upon which we are reminded of what we are on the other three hundred and sixty-four." And the chapter heading is the melodramatic but Calvinistic "Doom." The doom and the tragedy that come with Tom's exposure involve white and Negro, American life as a whole. Roxy cries, "De Lord have mercy on me, po' misable sinner dat I is!" She is not merely lamenting, nor does Mark Twain suggest that it is only a lament. Truly, she has sinned. But she has been more sinned against. She has played God, and she has been used by men playing God. If she and her son are punished, so is the white society that shaped their fate. The miscegenation, an act of intimacy, has only torn the white man and Negro further apart, creating provocation to other sins. Tom is, indeed, sent down the river in the novel's final crushing irony, but he has left death behind and a clear condemnation of the white man's values that had corrupted him. The "triumph" of Pudd'nhead is weak compensation for such a tragedy and, in his way, Pudd'nhead realizes this in his bitterly ironic remark that it would have been more wonderful for Columbus to miss discovering America.[7] In the end, there is only the realization that man is tricked by God or Providence and his own sinful nature into thinking that through choice (Roxana) or through the saving grace of ironic humor (Pudd'nhead) he could change destiny and reform the world and himself. And it is this realization that Mark Twain consciously embraced, allowing it to dominate the mood and content of the work of his remaining years.

EDWARD WAGENKNECHT

[Development of Plot and Character in *Pudd'nhead Wilson*]†

Though it is not usually regarded as anything like a perfect work of art, *Pudd'nhead Wilson* has maintained a comparatively prominent place among Mark Twain's more important fictions—and has done so with what may seem under the circumstances a somewhat surprising ease. In its own time the dramatic version by Frank Mayo probably contributed to the book's fame, but this can hardly have influenced modern critics. Mayo's success on the road, early in 1896, roused Mark Twain's hopes that the play might turn out to be another perennial like Joseph Jefferson's *Rip Van Winkle*; but in June the actor unexpectedly died, and though his son Edwin later tried reviving the play, he met with little sucess.

* * *

Mark Twain's interest in the related themes of twinship, disguise, and switched identity (which he employed most successfully in *The Prince and the Pauper*) was very old. Problems of identity and self-realization seem to have been very important to him, and Justin Kaplan has acutely suggested that the idea of twinship may have helped him to objectify a "steadily deepening sense of internal conflict and doubleness" in his own personality. In 1868 or 1869 he wrote a piece, now included in *Sketches New and Old*, about the famous Siamese (actually half-Chinese) twins, Chang and Eng

7. That is why *Pudd'nhead Wilson* is not a "success story"—despite Pudd'nhead's ostensible triumph—as Fiedler characterizes it. There is no real "assertion that man is master of his fate." Pudd'nhead is simply an instrument of Divine Justice, however impersonal. He brings retribution after the fall. What Fiedler states as the underlying theme—"that to be born is to be doomed"—is true, but it is not worked out in "secularized" Calvinistic terms. Rather it is structured in genuinely biblical tropes, with the clear implication that man has sinned against an impersonal God who does not allow tampering with the fixed order of things; see Fiedler, "As Free as Any Cretur . . . ," p. 137.

† From the Introduction to *Pudd'nhead Wilson* (Avon, Ct.: The Limited Editions Club, 1974), pp. v–xiii.

(1811–1874), who came to this country for exhibition purposes in 1828 and finally settled in North Carolina. But Chang and Eng were two bodies joined to one another "by a short tubular cartilaginous band," while Mark Twain's "freak" consisted of a single body with two heads and four arms. Robert A. Wiggins was able to find only one corresponding real-life monstrosity, Giovanni and Giacomo Tocci, born in Italy in 1875, who toured the United States in 1891, and he makes it seem very likely that Mark Twain saw the picture and the description of them which *Scientific American* published in December; the parallels between Mark's own twins (to whom he gave Italian names) and those described in the periodical seem too close to be accidental.

This, then, was probably the beginning of *Those Extraordinary Twins*, but it was certainly not the only "source." Never quite sane on the subject of novelty, Mark Twain was tremendously excited about the "virgin ground" he was exploring for fiction with the fingerprinting business, and though he had been interested in this subject before, both his knowledge and his interest were greatly increased when he read Sir Francis Galton's book on the subject soon after it was published in 1892. Galton's influence upon *Pudd'nhead Wilson* seems clear, as Mark Twain had originally intended to use footprints.

* * *

Mark Twain has been credited with having introduced the miscegenation theme to American fiction, but this is a view which shows little knowledge of his predecessors and contemporaries. Roxy's talk makes it difficult to remember that she is only one-sixteenth black and her son one-thirty-second; indeed, an early illustrator, E. W. Kemble, forgot it so completely that he depicted her as a perfect Negro "mammy." The Swedish translation of *Pudd'nhead Wilson* carries the interesting title: *En Droppe Negerblod*.

The point is of course that that "droppe" was all the American legal fiction required to classify a person as black, just as, under the Third Reich, a comparable "droppe" made a Jew. Both sides of her inheritance speak through Roxy, depending upon her position and the particular situation by which she is confronted when she sounds off. It is the fifteen-sixteenths white part of her that speaks when she denounces her recreant son as a "nigger"; or if not that, then she expresses the point of view that her white masters have forced upon her through the circumstances of her life, but the really important thing to remember is that she does not speak for the book or for its author.

It has been objected that in his portrayal of the two boys Mark Twain vacillates between a belief in heredity and a belief in environment. In itself this would not be wonderful—nearly all human beings do the same. Mark Twain was not noted for consistency; though he professed, toward the end of his life, to see man as a machine, he never ceased to admire those who were "good" and to condemn those who were "bad." Chambers, the false "Tom," is "bad" clear through; before his fall, he behaves like a thoroughly vicious young Southern aristocrat-wastrel; later he simply adds the bitterness, the unscrupulousness, and the determination of the underdog to seize upon any advantage that may present itself to him. The real Tom, on the other hand, wholly white but reared as a slave, and with a slave's outlook, is unable to throw it off even after her has learned the truth about himself.

The book, then, does not seem to deny that some people (presumably in all races) are "born bad," but in it conventional "black" and "white" characteristics are determined by conditioning. The thought is quite as good as the reality; "if you believe it, it's so." Only, it is not being black that contaminates, but being a slave, and there is nothing in nature itself to account for the conventional identification of blackness with slavery in this country, which is an accident of geography, economics, and social conditions.

All this is even clearer in the Morgan Library manuscript of *Pudd'nhead Wilson*, which represents an earlier stage of the revision than the one we have in print, but it is clear enough here. Roxy is no authority on ethics, but it is impossible not to sympathize with her (or to believe that her creator sympathized with her) when she justifies her exchange of the babies on the ground that only thus can she, as a slave, save her own child from what would be worse than death (in a quite different sense from that posited in the old melodramas).

On the other hand, Mark Twain offers no shadow of justification for what the white people and the white government do to Chambers at the end, waiving even the claims of justice out of sheer greed for money. Even the final act of violence does not quite refuse to fit into the picture. As an individual the Judge did not deserve his fate; neither could the thoroughly evil "Tom" very well qualify as an avenger of the race to which only one-thirty-second of him belonged. Yet without the slave system and the sexual abuses inevitably connected with it, the Judge could not have met the fate meted out to him. And Mark Twain seems as well aware of all these things as even William Faulkner was to be.

Pudd'nhead Wilson himself is a kind of *deus ex machina* character, and certainly more convincing than most such; but it is generally agreed that the triumph of the book is Roxy, and most of the critics dust off all their superlatives for her. Thus Lynn calls her Mark Twain's finest character with the single exception of Huckleberry Finn, and Henry Seidel Canby thought her "the only completely real woman" in Mark Twain's books. To me, even after having made all reasonable allowances for her primitivism, her Negro psychology or what Mark Twain may have supposed to be that, and for the complications necessarily involved in the presentation of a character who is required to be both wicked and heroic, she changes toward her son too radically, too suddenly, and too often to be wholly convincing. And I would have to add that to make even her comic excursions into genealogy—and her story about the "nigger" who stole the Queen of England's child—a part of Mark Twain's serious design in the book, and to adjust them neatly into an overall conception of his views about race and his patterns of characterization (as one scholar has attempted), is to put much too heavy a strain upon Mark Twain's humor and to think of him not so much as a greater artist than he was but certainly as a different kind.

Whether or not we can figure out an underlying consistency in Roxy's behavior, if we try hard enough, is really beside the point. Impressions of character that you have to argue about in literature really do not matter, and probably the most devastating thing ever said about "modern art" was the statement of Maxfield Parrish that it consisted of one-fourth God-knows-what with three-fourths explanation. In art what *seems* is always more important than what *is*, and everybody knows that the least convincing characters in literature are those which have been transferred without alteration to the printed page, out of the writer's own direct experience.

It does not matter one whit whether the great characters of Shakespeare could have existed in "real life" or not; they exist triumphantly as art, and carry direct conviction there, and that is all we can ask of them. As I have said elsewhere, Mark Twain's faculty for *evoking* character was very great, but he had considerably less skill in *constructing* it. Roxy is a combination of sometimes magnificent parts, but it would be too much to say that they cohere into a completely convincing whole.

For Mark Twain she was nevertheless a remarkable achievement. He was, it is now the fashion to say, sentimental about women, though it might be more accurate to say that he was idealistic toward them. Whatever it be called, his attitude prevented him from seeing them whole, as he saw men and boys. For all his love for little girls, nobody would pretend that he could ever have created a girl worthy to stand beside Huck and Tom; indeed he could not have given us even such a thoroughly "nice" girl as Louisa May Alcott gave us in Jo or Kate Douglas Wiggin in Rebecca. Well, Roxy is not a "nice" woman, nor even a good one, judged by the standards Mark Twain applied to women. He glosses over none of her faults (indeed, he uses the stock whisky-bottle prop somewhat too freely), but for all her contradictions he still presents her as capable, at her best, of a kind of grandeur that most "nice" women never achieve. When, at the end,

> Roxy flung herself upon her knees, covered her face with her hands, and out through her sobs the words struggled:
> "De Lord have mercy on me, po' misable sinner dat I is!"

few of us can remain unmoved. This is Mark Twain's triumph of comprehension and compassion, and these things are more precious even than perfectly wrought art.

ARTHUR G. PETTIT

The Black and White Curse: *Pudd'nhead Wilson* and Miscegenation†

You's a *nigger!—bawn* a nigger en a *slave!* . . .
   Thirty-one parts o' you is white, en on'y one part nigger, en dat po' little one part is yo' *soul.*
                                          —*Pudd'nhead Wilson* (1894)

   I have no race prejudices, and . . . no color prejudices . . . [Black Africans] should have been crossed with the Whites. It would have improved the Whites and done the Natives no harm. . . . Nearly all black and brown skins are beautiful, but a beautiful white skin is rare. . . .
   Where dark complexions are massed, they make the whites look bleached out, unwholesome, and sometimes frankly ghastly.
                                          —*In Defense of Harriet Shelley* (1893)
                                          Following the Equator (1897)[1]

Notwithstanding his fondness for black culture and causes, by the 1890s Mark Twain had a serious, even shattering color problem. On the one hand he had persuaded himself that persons of dark skin were physically more attractive than those of white skin, and he said so. Moreover he was convinced that the greater tragedy of the South was not miscegenation, but the curse that white Southerners had placed upon it. *The Tragedy of Pudd'nhead Wilson* is Mark Twain's most eloquent declaration of conscience on these two subjects.

   Yet Clemens also had a private, more or less conscious craving to find a credible sexual being in that most incongruous and puzzling of all places in the nineteenth century, namely a *white* woman. The result was an extraordinary amount of color confusion in his private thinking and in his art, culminating in Mark Twain's two-toned portrait of the mulatto slave woman Roxana in *Pudd'nhead Wilson.* At the same time that Roxana's small drop of black blood

† From Arthur G. Pettit, *Mark Twain and the South* (Lexington, Ky.: The University Press of Kentucky, 1974), pp. 139–155, 207–210.
1. *Harriet Shelley*, p. 264; *Following the Equator*, 1:247; 2:51.

made the point about the tragedy of racial mixture in a slave society, Mark Twain's Victorian teachings demanded that her skin be white. By painting this woman in a baffling black-and-white collage he tried to have it both ways: to satisfy the requirements of the Victorian code, while calling down the curse of the South. The ultimate outcome was chaos; but in the process of making a shambles of Roxana, Mark Twain let slip some revealing opinions about color. The purpose of this chapter is to trace the curiously shaded patterns that ripple over this woman and to place them in the context of Mark Twain's changing notions of skin color and of miscegenation.

*   *   *

Mark Twain was not the first to explore the plight of the Tragic Mulatto: Cable, Melville, Stowe, and Howells were there before him.[2] But sometime in the 1880s Mark Twain also began to sense the pathos in the subject. Possibly inspired by conversations with Cable before and during their lecture tour, he sketched a four-page outline for a story about the misfortunes of a mulatto man who has the same amount of Negro blood as Roxana in *Pudd'nhead Wilson*. Although the story is rough and incomplete, it is Mark Twain's most compact and explicit statement about miscegenation, and it merits full quotation:

> Before the War he is born—1850
> The Accident—Mrch or Apl—1860
> The Sale, April, 1860.
>
> The War.
>
> The Wanderings.
> (His father his master & mean.)
> ==

Does not deny but speaks of his n [sic] blood. His struggles—education—advertises & hunts for his mother & sister—at last gives them up. At last, seeing even the best educated negro is at a disadvantage, besides always being insulted, clips his wiry hair close, wears gloves always (to conceal his telltale nails,) & passes for a white man, in a Northern city.

Makes great success—becomes wealthy.

Falls in love with his cousin, 7 years younger than himself—he used to "miss" her, on the plantation.

2. For the similarities between Roxana and the mulatto slave woman Cassy in *Uncle Tom's Cabin*, see Kenneth S. Lynn, *Mark Twain and Southwestern Humor* (Boston: Little, Brown, 1960), pp. 265–266. Clemens read Cable's *The Grandissimes*, which deals in part with miscegenation, and may have borrowed part of the plot for *Pudd'nhead Wilson* from Cable's *Madame Delphine*, which deals with a quadroon mother who renounces her daughter so she may enter the white world. Howells' *Imperative Duty*, about a white man and a very white octoroon woman who have trouble deciding whether they should marry, was published one year before *Pudd'nhead Wilson*.

She & her father are very poor; he blows & gasses & talks blood
& keeps up the lost cause fires, & she supports him. She is a very
fine & every way noble & lovely girl; but of course the moment
the revelation comes that he is 1/16 negro, she abhors him. Her
father & she wears [sic] fictitious names, to indulge his pride, &
he makes a mystery of their former history—which enables him to
aggrandize it & at the same time prevents either of them from
saying anything which would lead XX to recognize them.

XX keeps his early history a secret, of course—& it is the only
secret which he has from *her*. All the towns people try to dig out
his secret, but fail.

At the climax when his mother & sister (who is waiting on the
table) expose his origin & his girl throws him & her cousin
(proud, poor, & not sweet), voices *her* horror, he is at least able
to retort, "Well, rail on; but there is one fact which Atlantics of
talk cannot wash away; & that is, that this loathsome negro is
your *brother*.

At time of the climax he is telling the stirring tale of the heroic
devotion of a poor negro mother to her son—of course not
mentioning that he was the son & that *his* is the mother who
bears the scar which he has described. Then she steps forward &
shows the scar she got in saving him from his own father's brutality. So this gassy man is *his* [sic, whoever XX is] father, & it is
his niece whom XX loves, & who with (perhaps) his daughter,
supports him.[3]

Apparently the mulatto boy was sold by his master-father directly
after the unknown "accident," which may have been the blow suffered by his mother in attempting to protect him. Freed by the war,
he courts and perhaps marries the cousin he used to address as
"Miss" on the antebellum plantation, but whom he does not now
recognize. The girl soon learns that he is part Negro, but she is too
ashamed to reveal her knowledge to him. This leaves the way open
for the mulatto to be dramatically exposed by his long-lost, and now
freed, mother and sister. From there the genealogical ramifications
of the plot grow more confusing, but they include the revelation
that other people who had been under the illusion that they were
all-white are also tainted.

In this brief sketch Mark Twain uncovered the fear, doubt,
hypocrisy, and guilt of white feelings about mixing with blacks. The
implications of this unfinished story become fully explicit only in
the light of *The Tragedy of Pudd'nhead Wilson,* Mark Twain's last
American novel and his last published outcry against the American

3. DV 128, MTP. ["DV . . . MTP" references are to a typescript on file in the
Mark Twain Papers (U.C. Berkeley)
under De Voto.] Paine dates the story
in the 1880s.

South. That the story turned out to be so anti-Southern was more accidental than planned.[4] Having begun with the notion of chronicling the absurd adventures of an extraordinary pair of Siamese twins—one virtuous and fair, the other vicious and swarthy—Mark Twain was chagrined to find that a stranger named Pudd'nhead Wilson, a mulatto woman named Roxana, and another mulatto named Tom Driscoll were taking over the story. Dimly aware that the plot was veering from comedy toward tragedy, he attempted to solve the problem of his hybrid creation by performing what he called a "literary Caesarian operation," yanking out the Siamese twins altogether. The extraction, though physically complete, was artistically incomplete and the novel remains a semiserious, semi-comic grotesque—a hodgepodge of characters and events which somehow still reveal the traumatic divisions and cruelties that Mark Twain had come to associate with the antebellum South.

* * *

From the beginning this novel is a chronicle of interracial crime and punishment. The true *Tragedy of Pudd'nhead Wilson* is not the lawyer David Wilson's quarter-century of social exile in Dawson's Landing,[5] but the two centuries of white exploitation of black —the South's great self-inflicted wound. By the end of the story one harmless aristocrat, Judge York Leicester Driscoll, has been killed by the mulatto Tom Driscoll. Roxana, after two decades of sacrifice to protect her son from exposure, is condemned by a court of law for enslaving a white aristocrat in order to free a mulatto slave. And the all-white aristocrat Chambers is so bent and stifled from shuffling around the slave quarters all those years that he can be "liberated" only into a life of genteel misery: "He could neither read nor write, and his speech was the basest dialect of the negro quarter. His gait, his attitudes, his gestures, his bearing, his laugh— all were vulgar and uncouth; his manners were the manners of a slave. . . . The poor fellow could not endure the terrors of the white man's parlor, and felt at home and at peace nowhere but in the kitchen. The family pew was a misery to him, yet he could never-more enter into the solacing refuge of the 'nigger gallery.'"

The most eloquent commentary on Southern chauvinism over interracial intercourse comes from its least sympathetic victim.

4. I do not intend to summarize or to cite critical discussions of *Pudd'nhead Wilson*. Numerous listings are available.
5. David Wilson is condemned to twenty-three years of social exile in Dawson's Landing for remarking on his arrival in the village that if he owned half of a dog that was yelping, he would kill his half. The villagers promptly label him a pudd'nhead ("What did he reckon would become of the other half if he killed his half?") and boycott his law practice. In his leisure Wilson takes fingerprints of most of the citizens, including the mulatto Tom Driscoll, whom he ultimately exposes as the murderer of Judge Driscoll.

Coward, thief, and murderer though he is, the mulatto Tom Driscoll reaches a more profound understanding of the tragedy of racial mixture in a racially unequal society than any other character in Mark Twain's writing. When this villain learns that the mammy who wet-nursed him as a child is actually his mother, the shock almost destroys him. For the next quarter of the novel Driscoll suffers through an excruciating crisis of identity: he too is one of the despised race. In his person he gives the lie to white distaste for black and reveals the philistinism of a society that privately tolerates miscegenation, then publicly punishes its victims. In an unpublished portion of the manuscript Driscoll asks himself which in fact is the higher or the lower in him, the white or the black, and has the perception to see that "the high is either color, when undegraded by slavery." In the published version of the novel he pursues the agonizing inquiry farther: "Why were niggers *and* whites made? What crime did the uncreated first nigger commit that the curse of birth was decreed for him? And why is this awful difference made between white and black? . . . How hard the nigger's fate seems [now]."

Yet, for all his perception, Tom Driscoll's insight is wasted on a scoundrel. The reader who comes to this novel expecting to learn how a part-black man, given the privileges of passing as a white, will prove himself worthy of this rare opportunity is in for a surprise: Driscoll proves thoroughly unregenerate. Although Mark Twain implies that the mulatto may have been warped by six generations of decadent FFV blood rather than by his drop of Negro blood, Driscoll's mother Roxana is convinced that her son's wickedness flows from his invisible mark of blackness—a color irony which is compounded when we compare *Pudd'nhead Wilson* to *Huckleberry Finn*. Huck believes that Nigger Jim must be "white inside"; but Tom Driscoll is white on the *outside*. His whiteness thoroughly conceals both his wickedness *and* his blackness, until his bad behavior exposes them both.[6]

For all his heartfelt ruminations on the plight of niggers, Tom Driscoll's insight leads not to reformation but to recovery of his old vicious self. Self-pity soon gives way to more typical trains of thought, including future villainies which are directly spawned by his discovery that he is not who he thought he was. Before the revelation of his race Driscoll was a liar, gambler, and petty thief. He continues these activities but now expands his evil doings to include selling his mother Roxana down the river and murdering his foster

6. James M. Cox, *Mark Twain: The Fate of Humor*, (Princeton: Princeton University Press, 1966), p. 228. [Reprinted above—*Editor.*]

father,[7] thus becoming Mark Twain's first, but not his last, mulatto avenger.[8] Although Driscoll gets his comeuppance by being sold down the river himself into the same slave fate he had decreed for his mother,[9] this facile ending of the story is not very satisfying, for it reminds us that the main problems posed by the novel have not been resolved. The defeat of the mulatto criminal at the hands of a depraved white society seems deliberately to extenuate rather than to lessen the larger crimes of slavery and of color discrimination. By declaring Tom Driscoll to be a black slave and hence a valuable piece of property to be sold rather than jailed, the court of Dawson's Landing denies Driscoll the dignity of human punishment and acts as the instrument of an avenging justice which ought itself to be punished. Blackguard though he is, Tom Driscoll's fate is more disturbing than gratifying, for it leaves us with the suspicion that the worse offender is not the mulatto avenger, but the white South.

That the innocent Judge Driscoll must bear the full white burden of "black" revenge in *Pudd'nhead Wilson*, while the aristocrat who started the trouble, Essex, dies unpunished, compounds the irony. There is, Mark Twain implies, no such thing as a "free" Southerner. All Southerners, innocent and guilty, will suffer for the sins of slavery and concubinage. And the suffering will go on until emancipation from both slavery *and* the stigma of miscegenation brings remission to black and white alike.

More than any character in the novel Roxana embodies this suffering and gives it enormous power and poignancy. Herself a fourth-generation product of interracial union, she adds one more. And more than any character in Mark Twain's writing she suffers the consequences.

Unlike her son, who is accepted as white and free until proven otherwise, Roxana is a slave. She too, however, has a color problem, though a very different one. Dawson's Landing had no difficulty deciding she was a mulatto, but her creator did. Mark Twain in effect wound up with two Roxanas: a near-white one, carefully adjusted to the proper shade for white readers, and a much darker

7. In the working notes for the novel Mark Twain made Judge Driscoll himself the father of Tom. But in the finished work he shied from such intimacy, possibly because his own father, Marshall Clemens, resembled the aristocrats in the story. Marvin Fisher and Michael Elliott, in *"Pudd'nhead Wilson:* Half a Dog Is Worse than None," *Southern Review* 8 (1972):544, point out that Percy Driscoll would have had "to vault out of one bed and leap into another in order to father sons born to different mothers on the same day." [The Fisher-Elliott essay is reprinted above.—*Editor.*]

8. The mulatto Jasper, discussed in the next chapter, is Mark Twain's superlative portrait of the black avenger.

9. Mark Twain originally had Tom Driscoll hang himself with his suspenders after David Wilson finds him guilty of murder. By changing Tom's fate to being sold down the river, Mark Twain completes the cycle of Tom earlier selling Roxana down the river.

Roxana who may have figured more prominently in Mark Twain's imagination. The public Roxana is, for all intents and purposes, an all-white Southern belle: "Only one-sixteenth of her was black, and that sixteenth did not show. She was of majestic form and stature, her attitudes were imposing and statuesque, and her gestures and movements distinguished by a noble and stately grace. Her complexion was very fair . . . her eyes were brown and liquid, and she had a heavy suit of fine soft hair which was also brown. . . . Her face was shapely, intelligent, and comely—even beautiful."

Roxana's drop of blackness seems important at first only as a reminder that miscegenation did in fact take place in the South and to explain why this lovely white woman is a slave. For Roxana, however, it has always been disastrous. It dictates her mudsill position in white society and it explains why she despises all niggers, who remind her of her own invisible mark. Indeed much of Roxana's credibility is based on prejudice and hatred. Rejected by one race and hardly wishing to be embraced by the other, she resorts to almost any means of redress for the vast injustice that is her life. She lies, steals,[1] cajoles, threatens, and flatters. She never questions slavery, except as it applies to herself and her son; and she repeatedly attempts to catapult herself into the highest order of whites. When Tom Driscoll first learns he is tainted and timidly asks who his father was, Roxana launches into the sort of trumped-up family genealogy we customarily associate with white Southerners: "You ain't got no 'casion to be shame' o' yo' father, I kin tell you. He wuz the highest quality in dis whole town—ole Virginny stock. Fust famblies, he wuz. . . . Does you 'member Cunnel Cecil Burleigh Essex. . . . Dat's de man. . . . Dey ain't another nigger in dis town dat's as high-bawn as you is."[2]

As with Nigger Jim before her, much of Roxana's credibility is founded on her fallibility, especially the extent to which she has picked up white prejudices. When her son refuses to challenge a white man to a duel for a petty insult, Roxana denounces him by way of one of the more confusing family pedigrees in American literature. The passage is a fine piece of irony, and it momentarily places this mulatto woman in company with the poor-white Huck as a naive, and therefore merciless, reporter of bloated Southern notions of ancestry. In one spasm of specious reasoning Roxana manages not only to make a sharp distinction between superior African blacks and loathsome New World niggers, but to parrot one of

1. Mark Twain made it clear that for slaves robbed of their freedom, stealing was not immoral. According to Kenneth M. Stampp, adult slaves "doubtless detected the element of hypocrisy in white criticism of their moral laxity" (*The Peculiar Institution; Slavery in the Ante-Bellum South.* [New York: Alfred A. Knopf, 1956], p. 350).
2. Roxana's genealogical pretensions are strikingly similar to Aunt Rachel's in "A True Story," as Roxana herself is similar to Rachel in every detail but color. ["A True Story" was published by Clemens in the *Atlantic* in 1874—*Editor.*]

the white South's favorite clichés about the desirability of mixing a smidgen of *red* with white:

"You has disgraced yo' birth. What would yo' pa think o' you? . . . Yo' great-great-great-great-gran'father was Ole Cap'n John Smith, de highest blood dat Ole Virginny ever turned out, en his great-great-gran'mother or somers along back dah, was Pocahontas de Injun queen, en her husbun' was a nigger king outen Africa—en yit here you is, a-slinkin' outen a duel en disgracin' our whole line like a ornery low-down hound! Yes, it's de nigger in you! . . . Ain't nigger enough in [you] . . . to show in [your] . . . finger-nails . . . yit dey's enough to paint [your] . . . soul."[3]

Yet for all her efforts to bolster her whiteness with nigger prejudices and genealogical fantasies, Roxana is a good deal darker than her physical appearance would lead us to believe. In the course of the story her whiteness is the one thing about her that we tend to ignore or to forget: her speech and manners, strength and endurance, shrewdness and passion are qualities that Mark Twain usually reserved for black women. In every characteristic except color Roxana is an exact duplicate of the female slaves and servants Clemens knew as a boy in Missouri and as a wealthy Yankee employer of black domestic help. Like Aunt Hanner of Quarles Farm, the Clemens's slave girl Jenny in Hannibal, Aunty Cord in Elmira who became Aunt Rachel in "A True Story," and Aunty Phyllis in "Refuge of the Derelicts," Roxana is statuesque, good-looking, courageous, arrogant, strong, and smart.[4] First introduced as a new mother, back on her feet caring for her white mistress's newborn child a few hours after giving birth to her own, Roxana is the archetypal black matriarchal figure—the combination of mistress and wet nurse who rears the white man's legitimate children and bears his bastards.

The one thing wrong with Roxana is that she is neither black nor white long enough at a stretch to be entirely convincing. The problem is not that she is, literally, a mulatto but that Mark Twain had trouble deciding which Roxana is the real one: the one who looks white or the one who acts black. Even *as* a black Roxana changes roles with bewildering speed. At times she is a loving, warm-hearted, pious and simple Black Mammy. At other times she is just as black but cunning and ruthless. When she meets her son for the first time in several years, Roxana first behaves like a doting mammy.

3. Thomas Jefferson, among others, elaborated on the desirability of mixing red with white as opposed to black with white in *Notes on the State of Virginia*, ed. William Peden (Chapel Hill, 1955), pp. 58–64, 100–102, 140. For an excellent account of Jefferson's racial feelings and fantasies, see Winthrop D. Jordan, *White Over Black: American Attitudes toward the Negro, 1550–1812* (Chapel Hill, 1968), pp. 475–81.

4. Jenny, Marshall Clemens's slave in Hannibal, is described by both Mark Twain and Paine as young, handsome, arrogant, stubborn, insolent, and statuesque. Later, like Roxana, she was sold down the river and became a chambermaid on a steamboat.

Then, with incredible swiftness, she turns herself into a vengeful bitch, exulting over the "fine nice young gen'l'man kneelin' down to a nigger wench" and taking swigs from a whiskey bottle more in the manner of a black shrew than the tragic mother figure Mark Twain had carefully constructed up to this point.

The problem with this woman is not that she lacks qualities of character but that she has too many of them. Wandering back and forth between comedy and tragedy, between all-white Southern belle and all-black mammy, Roxana is the victim of Mark Twain's own color confusion. When obviously black, she is a creature of rare beauty and passion, courage and dignity, vitality and fertility, with an immense capacity to love, hate, and forgive. When near-white she is tepid. Alternately bleached and blackened too often and too haphazardly, Roxana ultimately fails to transcend the sentimentality she evokes and loses much of her identity and, therefore, much of her credibility.

Mark Twain's color confusion over Roxana was in part the result of a collision between his attraction to persons of dark skin and his bondage to white social and sexual values. Indeed it is not too much to say that he consciously used blacks and mulattoes to express sexual feelings that were prohibited by white standards of propriety, especially feelings about miscegenation. Concubinage was, after all, an accepted part of the social system of the antebellum South;[5] and Mark Twain, who was quite reticent about sexual relations between whites,[6] never tried to conceal the obvious fact of Southern interracial intercourse. There were a number of mulattoes in Hannibal and even in St. Petersburg white, mulatto, and Negro children patronize the town pump to which Tom flees from his whitewashing job. In his *Autobiography* Mark Twain remembered that Wales McCormick, a fellow newspaper apprentice in Hannibal, "was constantly and persistently and loudly and elaborately making love" to a mulatto girl and that "by the customs of slaveholding communities it was Wales's right to make love to that girl if he wanted to." Four years after he left Hannibal, while working on a Cincinnati paper, young Clemens placed one of his first

5. W. J. Cash wrote that black women, "taught an easy complaisance for commercial reasons," were "to be had for the taking" and that white boys "inevitably learned to use" them. *The Mind of the South* (New York, 1940), p. 87. Bernard De Voto speaks sweepingly of the "forbidden world of slaves," with its black concubines ready to initiate "their quota of pubescent boys" into manhood. *Mark Twain's America* (Boston, 1932), pp. 64–65. Kenneth M. Stampp, using specific evidence, concludes that "sexual contacts between the races were not the rare aberrations of a small group of depraved whites but a frequent occurrence involving whites of all social and cultural levels." *The Peculiar Institution*, pp. 350–51.

6. The Beinecke Rare Book and Manuscript Library at Yale University has some verses by Mark Twain about lost virility, and his speech to the Stomach Club on "The Science of Onanism." There is of course *1601*, and Mark Twain's late remarks about white female sexuality in *Letters from the Earth*, ed. Bernard De Voto (New York, 1962), pp. 16–17, 50–53.

fictional characters, Thomas Jefferson Snodgrass, in an embarrassing predicament. Snodgrass is approached on the street by a fashionably dressed white woman, who asks him to hold a basket for her for a moment, then disappears. When the lady does not return Snodgrass opens the basket and finds he has become foster father to a mulatto child. Then there was the furor in Virginia City launched by Mark Twain's ill-considered suggestion that some local charity funds had been turned over to a miscegenation society in the East; and as late as 1872 Clemens told Howells that he was so uplifted by Howells's favorable review of *Roughing It* that he felt like "a mother who has given birth to a white baby when she was awfully afraid it was going to be a mulatto."[7]

Neither serious nor malicious, these early remarks about miscegenation are playful flights of fancy by a humorist who liked to test the limits of public tolerance and of private taste. The same can be said for the commonplace jokes about black sexuality that Clemens set down in his notebooks. In 1882, on his trip down the river, he recorded a dialogue he supposedly overheard on board the *Gold Dust* between two black laundresses, who chit-chat about wayward nigger employees who "takes up with everybody and anybody that comes along." One laundress explains that if she were young again she would change her habits and refuse to sleep with strangers. While Clemens listened (or so he made it appear in his notebook), the laundress illustrated her technique by withstanding the advances of a brash "young colored chap" who happened along at that moment. Though she permitted the man to come "pretty close to it," the laundress made it clear that that was "just as close as I allows one of them young fellows to go." If she was going to go farther at her age, she was going to go with "a *man*."[8]

Given Clemens's imaginative and vernacular powers, this "conversation" is at least as suspect as the "dialogue" between the two black deckhands about God being responsible for man's sins—recorded on board the same boat, in the same river notebook, and on the same journey. At the very least the part pertaining to the young colored chap probably gained in elaborateness as Clemens warmed to his subject. Other notebook jottings, especially those made after Livy died, are almost certainly fictitious:

She. I cain't dance wid you. I don't know who you is.
He. Plenty knows me en dey kin tell you. My name's Clapp.
She. Oh yes. Is you de genlmn dat start de epidermic in de Babtis' chu'ch?

7. Albert Bigelow Paine, ed., *Mark Twain's Autobiography* (New York and London: Harper & Brothers, 1924), 2 vols., 2:276–77; MTHL, 1:7. Dixon Wecter discusses Hannibal's brothels and prostitutes and concludes that Clemens, "with a taste for the 'low company' of the Blankenships, and tutelage in several newspaper offices," was probably well-acquainted with the town's "seamy side" (*Hannibal*, pp. 147, 174–75, 214–15).

8. Typescript Notebook 16a, pp. 26–28, MTP [Mark Twain Papers—*Editor*].

After this entry Clemens added a telephone conversation, in which a black woman accepts a proposition with, "Yas—but who *is* you, anyhow?"[9]

Taken separately these jokes are not compelling evidence of preoccupation with black sex. Clemens's notebooks are sprinkled with mild smut about animal copulation, masturbation, scatology, and heterosexual intercourse, most of it set down after Livy died.[1] Moreover, since it was taboo to write about white female sexuality, it was taken for granted by many whites that black females gave an extra excitement to sex jokes—a common prejudice which Clemens was willing to foster. Yet when taken together these "jokes" suggest that Clemens may have been sexually troubled in his late years, and that race came into it as an expression of his repression. The most revealing example is a dream Clemens said had been bothering him for a long time before he finally set it down in 1897:

> In my dream last night I was suddenly in the presence of a negro wench who was sitting in grassy open country, with her left arm resting on the arm of one of those long park-sofas that are made of broad slats with cracks between, & a curve-over back. She was very vivid to me—round black face, shiny black eyes, thick lips, very white regular teeth showing through her smile. She was about 22, & plump—not fleshy, not fat, merely rounded & plump; & good-natured & not at all bad-looking. She had but one garment on—a coarse tow-linen shirt that reached from her neck to her ankles without a break. She sold me a pie; a mushy apple pie —hot. She was eating one herself with a tin teaspoon. She made a disgusting proposition to me. Although it was disgusting it did not surprise me—for I was young (I was never old in a dream yet) & it seemed quite natural that it should come from her. It was disgusting, but I did not say so; I merely made a chaffing remark, brushing aside the matter—a little jeeringly—& this embarrassed her & she made an awkward pretence that I had mis-understood her. I made a sarcastic remark about this pretence, & asked for a spoon to eat my pie with. She had but the one, & she took it out of her mouth, in a quite matter-of-course way, & offered it to me. My stomach rose—there everything vanished.[2]

The sixty-one-year-old man who dreamed this dream had grown up in a slaveholding society which had among its commonest insti-

9. Typescript Notebook 38, p. 14, MTP.

1. Justin Kaplan, *Mr. Clemens and Mark Twain*, (New York: Simon and Schuster, 1966), pp. 222, 323, offers a few titillating examples of Mark Twain's sex jokes, but omits the more numerous and mild examples, such as a couple copulating under a bridge; a girl who goes to a doctor to be vaccinated, is raped, and asks "to be vaccinated again"; and a "procrastitute," who is defined as "a woman who promises & then fools along & doesn't perform." In the last notebook there is some very bad verse about lovers returning a buggy with "a grease-spot on the cushion/And I think there's been some pushing,/For there's boot-tracks on the dashboard upside down," and a comparison between Standard Oil being slapped with a heavy fine and the June bride who "expected it but didn't suppose it would be so big." Typescript Notebook 38, pp. 17–19, MTP.

2. Paine, *Mark Twain's Notebook*, pp. 348–52.

tutions black wet nurses and black concubinage. The dream is open to numerous interpretations, but the least farfetched is the possibility that Clemens found the woman, who was "not at all bad-looking," less repulsive than the proposition itself, which was disgusting because it violated Clemens's code of *conduct*, not of color. The woman's blackness simply made her sexuality possible. Being non-white, she could behave in a manner that, for black women, was "quite natural." Being white, Clemens could not behave in such a manner, and he went to considerable pains to dissociate himself from this woman. Since most of his dreams, by his own admission, were shaped by guilt[3] and since he was rarely able or willing to untangle the dream from the reality, Clemens sought release from the haunting mystery of the black woman by insisting that the rational and responsible wide-awake Clemens had no physical or psychological resemblance whatever to the self of his dreams. By denying emphatically that the one had any knowledge of the other, he could disown any disturbing symbolic meanings he may have seen in his dreams. If the two Clemenses were wholly unknown and wholly unrelated, then how on earth could the real Clemens be held accountable for the actions or thoughts of his dream self?

This is precisely where Mark Twain boxed himself into a corner with Roxana in *Pudd'nhead Wilson*. For here, in full consciousness, is a near-*white* hussy; acting provocatively when seemingly black, yet white on the outside nonetheless. By combining disguised blackness with surface whiteness, Mark Twain managed to endow Roxana with the uninhibited mannerisms of his black dream woman, while at the same time satisfying the popular demand for the Tragic Mulatto who must appear to be white.

Always his own most rigid censor, Mark Twain approached Roxana's sexual behavior with great caution and delicacy. In her first appearance in the novel this off-white woman does not actually "appear" at all; instead she is introduced offstage as an invisible, seemingly all-black voice which exchanges a series of sexual sallies with a coal-black slave named Jasper, who plans to court her as soon as she has recovered from childbirth. Though Roxana makes it clear that she does not mix "wid niggers as black as you is," she teases Jasper ("how does *you* come on, Jasper? . . . Is ole Miss Cooper's Nancy done give you de mitten?") and comes off as a "high and sassy," plainly provocative woman. Only *after* this scene do we learn that Roxana looks white: Mark Twain's careful description of Roxana's physical appearance comes only after we have been led to believe she is black.

It is the invisible black mark that gives Roxana her marvelously

3. "I go to unnameable places. I do un-principled things; and every vision is vivid, every sensation—physical as well as moral—is *real*" (Kaplan, *Mr. Clemens and Mark Twain*, pp. 340–46).

uninhibited manner. White women simply do not behave this way in Mark Twain's writing, either because he was unwilling to break the bonds of convention or because he was constitutionally unable, until late in life, even to imagine the possibility of white women behaving in an overtly sexual manner.[4] The pity is that he failed to maintain the color dichotomy consistently. When obviously all-white, Roxana is anemic. When obviously part-black, she is a fascinating mixture of white pathos and black boldness. Indeed in her finest moments Roxana transcends the prototypical heroine of the age to become that rarest of nineteenth-century creatures, a white woman who acts "black." For all the color confusion that ultimately crippled her credibility, this woman, at her "blackest," is the one convincing female character in Mark Twain's writing who is not an adolescent, a widow, or a middle-aged aunt. Although Mark Twain failed to stick to a single image of Roxana, the very *idea* of such a woman, capable of running the full range of human passions, was a far more original and daring experiment than either the all-white Tragic Mulatto she finally turned out to be or the predictably disgusting and hardly original black wench who haunted Clemens in his dreams.

Roxana is more than a bewildering mixture of black and white, however. She is also the most poignant example in Mark Twain's writing of his conviction that the greater crime of the South was not miscegenation but the white Southerners' unwillingness to admit that mulattoes were, after all, the products of their own lust.[5] Since mulattoes offered visible evidence of a covert bond between the races, that bond had to be overtly denied at all costs. The price of such deceit was bound to be paid by Southerners of every hue: all-white aristocrats like Chambers, mistaken for black; supposedly all-white Southerners who must worry whether the stig-

4. Joan of Arc was, for Clemens, an idealization of nonsexual and, as he understood it, constitutionally nonnubile young womanhood. In his copy of Jules Michelet's *Jeanne d'Arc* (1853), opposite a passage citing the testimony of Domrémy women that Joan had never menstruated, Clemens wrote: "The higher life absorbed her and suppressed her physical (sexual) development" (*Mr. Clemens and Mark Twain*, p. 315). In a courtship letter to Livy, Clemens described her "as pure as snow . . . untainted, untouched even by the impure thoughts of others." March 1869, in Dixon Wecter, ed., *The Love Letters of Mark Twain* (New York: Harper & Brothers, 1949), p. 76. Howells called Livy "heavenly white," and Mrs. James T. Fields described Livy as especially "white and delicate and tender." *Atlan-*

tic Monthly, 130 (1922):342–48. When told of the alarming amount of venereal disease among British troops in India, Clemens wrote that clean native women "subject to rigid inspection ought to be kept for these soldiers," so the soldiers would not subsequently infect the "fresh young English girls" they married. Paine, *Mark Twain's Notebooks*, pp. 280, 286.
5. In 1906, in response to William Lecky's remarks in his *History of European Morals, from Augustus to Charlemagne*, 2 vols. (New York, 1903; Clemens's copy in MTP), that "the chastity of female slaves was sedulously guarded by the Church," Clemens scrawled in the margin: "This is better than the Southern Protestant Church of America ever did, *nicht wahr?*"

mata might not turn out to be theirs also; mulattoes like Roxana who are recognized as contaminated; mulattoes like Tom Driscoll who pass the color line only to be brought back across into slavery and blackness. No amount of deceit or dissimulation can guarantee permanent protection from discovery. After twenty-three years of indoctrination into white manners, speech, and decorum, the fair-skinned Tom Driscoll can still be declared tainted. And, conversely, after twenty-three years of indoctrination into black manners, speech, and decorum, the fair-skinned Chambers is beyond redemption. Neither environment *nor* heredity can match Southern prejudice.[6]

In its exposure of the Southern racial trauma, *Pudd'nhead Wilson* anticipates one of the obsessive themes of Southern writing in the twentieth century. The legacy of slavery and concubinage is one of fear, suspicion, false accusation, hypocritical exoneration, and guilt—a legacy that can be wiped out only by putting an end not to miscegenation but to discrimination. In a society of mixed blood in which the central preoccupation is with purity of blood, denial of the dignity and worth of blacks and mulattoes becomes, inevitably, a denial of the self. If some blacks are partly white, then some whites must be partly black. If some whites are slaves, then some blacks must be free. Who are they? And how many? And how long is this self-defeating denial going to go on? The fear and the hypocrisy seem endless: by rejecting blackness by day and embracing it by night, white Southerners have planted a lie in the soul of their progeny, cut themselves off from a vital part of their past, and locked themselves into a dilemma which will last as long as the blood curse itself.

For Mark Twain this was the central tragedy of the Southern experience—the curse of blood. The problem was not one of racial mixture, but the destructive emphasis on purity of blood of *any* sort. Injustice toward blacks springs from intraracial as well as interracial discrimination. The whole business of "born a gentleman, always a gentleman," or Marshall Clemens's efforts to compensate for poverty by assuring his family they were "blood-pure," or the blood feud of the Grangerfords, or Pap Finn's hatred of black skin when his own was "a white to make a body's flesh crawl," or Roxana bragging to her mulatto son about his FFV blood—all this adds up to an intolerable burden imposed by white on black, white

---

6. Robert Wiggins, in *Mark Twain: Jackleg Novelist* (Seattle, 1964), p. 107, points out that Mark Twain is inconsistent when he argues that environment (what he called training) determines human behavior exclusively. With Chambers, Mark Twain's deterministic theory is convincing: slavery ruins him. But Tom Driscoll is carefully shown to be wicked *before* his white training has the opportunity either to uplift or to damage him. With Chambers, environment is the determining factor; with Driscoll, both environment and heredity (including six generations of white blood) could be said to determine his behavior.

on white, and black on black. Tainted blood goes far beyond color; indeed it may have nothing whatever to do with race. But from blood consciousness springs the stultifying pride of those who believe they are pure and the paralyzing fear of those who believe they are not. Southern pride in blood and Southern fear of miscegenation are two sides of the same sword and the sword cuts black and white alike. More than any nineteenth-century novel except Cable's *The Grandissimes, The Tragedy of Pudd'nhead Wilson* implies that the greater tragedy of the South is not miscegenation but the curse that white Southerners have placed upon it; and, therefore, upon themselves.

JOHN C. GERBER

Pudd'nhead Wilson as Fabulation†

Criticism of *Pudd'nhead Wilson* seems to have come to a dead end. What one critic finds admirable, another deplores. Robert Rowlette writes a monograph in praise of the book's design;[1] Robert A. Wiggins thinks the design is a failure.[2] Henry Nash Smith believes that Roxy is "the only fully developed character, in the novelistic sense, in the book,"[3] but Arthur Pettit argues that she is just another example of the "tragic mulatto" type and not a very good example at that, for she is really two persons—a black and a white—and is neither black nor white long enough at a stretch to be entirely convincing.[4] F. R. Leavis finds *Pudd'nhead Wilson* "a classic in its own right,"[5] and Leslie Fiedler variously calls it "the most extraordinary book in American literature" and "a fantastically good book."[6] Richard Chase, however, believes that in considering *Pudd'nhead Wilson* "as an example of the art of the novel, one observes that the moral truth it asserts is not adequately attached to the characters, or dramatized by them."[7] Rowlette summarizes the situation rather well when he writes, "If critics now generally agree that *Pudd'nhead Wilson* has artistic stature—even while disagreeing about how much, or what accounts for it—they

† From *Studies in American Humor*, 2, 1 (April 1975), 21–31.
1. *Twain's "Pudd'nhead Wilson": The Development and Design* (Bowling Green, Ohio: Bowling Green University Popular Press, 1971).
2. *Mark Twain: Jackleg Novelist* (Seattle: University of Washington Press, 1964), pp. 108–112.
3. *Mark Twain: The Development of a Writer* (Cambridge: Harvard University Press, 1962), p. 179.
4. *Mark Twain and the South* (Lexington: University Press of Kentucky, 1974), p. 149.
5. Introduction to the Grove Press edition of *Pudd'nhead Wilson* (New York, 1955), p. 9.
6. " 'As Free as Any Cretur . . .' " *New Republic*, 133 (15 August 1955), 17.
7. *The American Novel and Its Tradition* (Garden City, N.Y.: Doubleday, 1957), p. 155.

also agree that the novel is seriously flawed."[8] So here we have a book that has artistic stature but is seriously flawed, a book that critics admire though they cannot agree on the reasons for their admiration.

At the risk of compounding the confusion, I should like to suggest that almost all of the criticism proceeds from the wrong premise, namely that *Pudd'nhead Wilson* is a novel and therefore must be measured primarily by the standards of realism.[9] I would suggest that the basic question is not to what degree is it a success or failure as a novel but is it a novel at all? Can it appropriately be read in the tradition of *Madame Bovary, A Modern Instance, The Portrait of a Lady,* and *Sister Carrie?* Or is the question of realism irrelevant, and should the book be read in an altogether different tradition?

Not unexpectedly, my answer is that it *should* be read in another tradition. The appropriate one, it seems to me, is the great story-telling tradition that stretches from Cervantes, Fielding, Smollett and Sterne to such writers of our own day as Heller, Vonnegut, and Hawkes. Robert Scholes in his valuable little volume entitled *The Fabulators* refers to the works in this tradition as *fabulations.*[1] The term is a good one for my purpose here because it so plainly places the emphasis on the fable or story, not on careful documentation of the outer world or on detailed analyses of the characters' inner worlds. Like the novel the fabulation is a species of the genus narrative, but unlike the novel it does not depend for its success upon the objectivity of its author and the realism of its subject matter and its presentation. The fabulator is more like the oral story-teller than the novelist. Concerned primarily with the design and effects of his story, he cheerfully ignores the realism of both subject matter and presentation when it serves his purpose to do so. Yet by keeping his fantasy ethically controlled he puts forth a story that paradoxically comments upon actual human life at the same time that it seems to be flouting that life.

As a fabulation *Pudd'nhead Wilson* holds a rather remarkable position between the great stories of the eighteenth century and those of our own time. Like *Tom Jones* and *Humphry Clinker,* for example, it has an omniscient author who is immediately and pervasively present, a story told in dramatic episodes and without worry for coincidence, and an approach to the material that is essentially ironic. Additionally, like *Catch 22* and *Cat's Cradle,* Pudd'nhead

8. Rowlette, p. viii.
9. See Chapter Two in Wayne C. Booth, *The Art of Fiction* (Chicago: University of Chicago Press, 1961) in which he demonstrates that modern critics almost to a person share the belief that novels by definition must create the illusion of reality.

1. *The Fabulators* (New York: Oxford University Press, 1967), pp. 3–6. Although I have not quoted him exactly I am greatly indebted to Professor Scholes for his discussion of fabulations and fabulators.

Wilson pictures a bizarre world in which the characters play necessary roles in what can only be called a cruel and on-going Joke. Not so sweeping and imaginative as the great fabulations before it, nor so witty and wildly absurd as those of our own time, Pudd'nhead Wilson nevertheless shares characteristics of both groups and occupies a midpoint in their tradition.

Like the great stories of the eighteenth century, Pudd'nhead Wilson is the work of an author who never for a moment relinquishes his authority—or lets you forget his presence. Consider how carefully Mark Twain establishes his control as narrator in the first chapter. From the very first we are conscious that it is an imaginative story and that a narrator called Mark Twain is the story teller. The opening sentence of the novel is more formal than "Once upon a time" but the actual words—"The scene of this chronicle"—have much the same effect. In true story-telling fashion Mark Twain then starts off with the setting and with an introduction of several of the major characters. Clearly, we are going to see only what the narrator wants us to see, and to react the way he wants us to react. Every detail, for example, is carefully selected to make Dawson's Landing seem pretty and quaint: white-washed cottages concealed in part by rose-vines, honeysuckles, and morning glories; white paling fences and flower gardens; brick sidewalks lined with locust trees; the front of the hamlet washed by the clear waters of the river. So that we do not miss the effect desired, the descriptive passage is pulled together with the generalization that "the town was sleepy and comfortable and contented."

We are not permitted to judge for ourselves about the characters either. We are told explicitly, for example, that Judge York Leicester Driscoll is "fine and just and generous," that Pembroke Howard is "a fine, brave, majestic figure," and that Percy Northumberland Driscoll is "a propserous man, with a good head for speculations." When Mark Twain wishes us to understand that several of his characters are completely unimportant he labels them No. 3, No. 4, No. 5 and No. 6. His omniscience and hence his control are further demonstrated when he looks into the future and tells us that Pudd'nhead Wilson's nickname is "to continue to hold its place for twenty long years."

William Dean Howells had inveighed, doubtless at times in Mark Twain's presence, against author intrusion, holding that it destroys the illusion of reality. But Mark Twain gives no indication in Pudd'nhead Wilson that he is attempting to create such an illusion. Throughout the book he feels free to intrude both as commentator and narrator, just as Fielding and Smollett and Sterne had felt free to do. As commentator he writes, "A home without a cat may be a perfect home, but how can it prove title?" "Childless people are not difficult to please." "An enemy can partly ruin a man, but it takes a good-natured injudicious friend to complete the thing and make it perfect." He even addresses the reader directly in statements such as: "Then there was Colonel Cecil Burleigh Essex, another F.F.V. of formidable calibre; however, with him we have no concern." At the very end of the book, to take another example, he says of Tom: "But we cannot follow his fate further—that would be a long story."

This persisting presence of Mark Twain as story-teller, despite the fact that the story is told in the third person, has several happy effects. Mark Twain himself becomes an appealing and interesting character, or, more accurately, presence. He is lively, witty, and shrewd. He is "good" because he hates social injustice, a "regular guy" because he can enjoy buffoonery as well as irony. He has an enthusiasm for his own story that is infectious. His personality is so strong, indeed, that it gives the work a rhetorical unity that holds it together even when the action seems to be exploding in three ways at once.

With all of these appealing qualities the Mark Twain who is the narrator of *Pudd'nhead Wilson* can nevertheless be faulted. He seems not to be so learned, so careful with details, so chary of melodrama and burlesque as we might like. Worse, he does not seem interested enough in his characters. He is too predictable in his response to goodness and evil, and his descriptions of joy and sorrow are so exaggerated that we feel he is not moved by either. Nothing stops him if he senses possibilities for humor; he even makes fun of Roxy as he has her preparing to commit suicide. In fine, one becomes more aware than he should of the author as manipulator, of the way he moves his characters at will for such purposes as climax, irony, humor, and pathos.

Another matter of crucial importance to the fabulation is action or plot. For over a hundred years, now, the realists have been telling us that plot must be muted, that it must be subservient to revelation of character. But just the reverse has been true of the great adventure and picaresque novels. If Tom Jones emerges as an appealing and individualized character, so much the better. But Fielding did not write the book to give us a character analysis; *Tom Jones*, he held, was to be a comic epic—a mode in which the action is central. Furthermore, almost all of the great story-writers have had a devil-may-care attitude about holding the action tightly in check. If new characters keep pouring in, and the action keeps getting more and more convoluted, so what? And well might we agree, so what? What would *Tom Jones* be without its bizarre coincidences and cross-currents of adventure, or *Tristram Shandy* without its fantastic turns and surprises, or to move into the nineteenth century, *David Copperfield* without its huge panoply of characters?

Mark Twain evinces something of the same cavalier attitude toward his story line. In a frequently-quoted passage he wrote:

> narrative should flow as flows the brook down through the hills and leafy woodlands, its course changed by every bowlder it comes across and by every grass-clad gravelly spur that projects into its path; its surface broken, but its course not stayed by rocks and gravel on the bottom in the shoal places; a brook that never goes straight for a minute, but *goes*, and goes briskly, sometimes ungrammatically, and sometimes fetching a horseshoe three-quarters of a mile around, and at the end of the circuit flowing within a yard of the path it traversed an hour before; but always *going*, and always following at least one law, always loyal to that law, the law of *narrative*, which *has no law*.[2]

Mark Twain *did* attempt to eliminate some of the chaos of the first version of the story. It began as a "howling farce" about an Italian freak with two heads, four arms, and a single pair of legs. In addition there was a "silly young miss" for a heroine, and two old ladies and two boys for the minor parts.

> But the tale kept spreading along, and spreading along, and other people got to intruding themselves and taking up more and more room with their talk and their affairs. Among them came a stranger named Pudd'nhead Wilson, and a woman named Roxana; and presently the doings of these two pushed up into prominence a young fellow named Tom Driscoll, whose proper place was away in the obscure background. Before the book was half finished those three were taking things almost entirely into their own hands and working the whole tale as a private venture of their own—a tale which they had nothing at all to do with, by rights.[3]

At first, or so he tells us, Mark Twain simply tried to drown the characters that were getting lost by having them fall down a well. Then he realized that he had two stories in one, a farce and what he called a tragedy. So he pulled out the farce by a literary "Caesarian operation" and called it "Those Extraordinary Twins."

> This left the original team in, but only as mere names, not as characters. Their prominence was wholly gone; they were not even worth drowning; so I removed that detail. Also I took those twins apart and made two separate men of them. They had no

2. *Mark Twain's Autobiography*, ed. Albert Bigelow Paine (New York: Harper & Brothers, 1924), I, 237.
3. Samuel L. Clemens, *The Writings of Mark Twain*. Definitive Edition. (New York: Gabriel Wells, 1928), XVI, 209. [See paragraph 4 of Clemens's introduction to *Those Extraordinary Twins*, p. 120 of the present edition—*Editor*.]

occasion to have foreign names now, but it was too much trouble
to remove them all through, so I left them christened as they
were and made no explanation.[4]

In a letter to his publisher he bragged:

> When I began this final reconstruction the story contained
> 81,500 words; now it contains only 58,000. I have knocked out
> everything that delayed the march of the story—even the descrip-
> tion of a Mississippi steamboat. There ain't any weather in, and
> there ain't any scenery—the story is stripped for flight![5]

The extant manuscripts in the Berg Collection of the New York
Public Library and in the J. Pierpont Morgan Library corroborate
Mark Twain's contention that he performed a massive revision
before sending the tale to the *Century Magazine* where it was published in seven installments from December 1893 to June 1894.
The point to be stressed here, however, is that though he strove to
give the work design, Mark Twain calls it throughout a "tale" or
"story," and never once suggests that in his revisions he was attempting to achieve anything like a self-contained illusion of reality. On
the contrary he seems to have deleted the descriptive passages that
best tended in that direction. Furthermore, in a silly "Whisper" to
the reader affixed to the last draft he even lays open to question the
realism of his climactic court scene by saying that it was rewritten
under the immediate eye of William Hicks, "who studied law part
of a while in southwest Missouri thirty-five years ago and then came
over here to Florence for his health and is still helping for exercise
and board in Macaroni Vermicelli's horse-feed shed. . . ."[6]

So for Mark Twain it was the story that counted—just as it
should in a fabulation. Even with the revisions, though the tale
remains so loose that by turn it follows the affairs of Pudd'nhead
Wilson, those of Roxy and her son, and those of Angelo and Luigi,
the Italian twins (who are still referred to on one page as though
they are Siamese).[7] Somehow, Mark Twain manages to bring the
three story lines together at the end when Pudd'nhead through
fingerprints discovers Roxy's son to be guilty of the murder the
town has pinned on Luigi.[8] But along the way when the story lines
drift apart, Mark Twain with the aplomb of an experienced racon-
teur simply tells us that he is dropping one line and taking up
another. At the beginning of Chapter 8, for example, he amiably

4. *Writings*, XIV, p. 212 [P. 122 of
the present edition—*Editor*.]
5. *Mark Twain's Letters to His Publishers*, ed. Hamlin Hill (Berkeley: University of California Press, 1967), p. 355.
6. *Writings*, V, xix. [See p. 1 of the
present edition—*Editor*.]
7. See, for example, early in Chapter 6:
"Our parents were well to do, there in
Italy, and we were their only child."
8. Robert Rowlette examines in great detail what he calls "Twain's structural
achievement of integrating the novel's
three apparently disparate themes and
the plots that dramatize them: slavery,
detection, and twinhood." *Op. cit.*, p. ix.

announces, "It is necessary now to hunt up Roxy." And at the end of Chapter 10 he says, "After this long digression, we have now arrived once more at the point where Pudd'nhead Wilson . . . sat puzzling over the strange apparition of that morning—a girl sitting in Tom Driscoll's bedroom. . . ." (Pudd'nhead has been sitting there for over twenty-five pages.)

The implausibilities that are the curse of realistic fiction but part of the charm of fabulation abound in *PW*. Pudd'nhead Wilson, who has to his credit not only a college degree but a year's postgraduate work in an Eastern law school, settles in Dawson's Landing of all places *to seek his fortune*. Furthermore, this handsomely educated fortune hunter, despite the fact that he gets no legal business because of his nickname, stays in Dawson's Landing for twenty years! By chance Roxy and the Percy Driscolls have babies on the same day, and the babies look so much alike that only Roxy can tell them apart. Mrs. Driscoll conveniently dies within the week of the birth of her baby so that Roxy can take care of both children—and exchange their clothes and cradles. Roxy plans to establish herself in New Orleans, but the bank fails in which she has her money invested, and so she has to return to Dawson's Landing. By chance the false Tom, Roxy's son, sees the cashbox of his "uncle" open and available, a circumstance that leads to both theft and murder. And it is the same false Tom who inadvertently calls attention to the glass strip that carries the fingerprints which eventually convict him. It is a world of make-believe in which excitement, suspense, and ingenuity are more important than probability.

Typically, too, a great part of the action is physical. The young babies start off by cuffing and banging and scratching each other. As they grow older, the false Tom continues to kick and maul the real Tom. Eventually, and obviously with satisfaction, the narrator tells how in turn the false Tom in a town meeting receives a kick of such titanic vigor that he is lifted clear over the footlights and is landed on the heads of the Sons of Liberty seated in the front row of the auditorium. There follow a riot and fire of epic proportions. Thefts, a duel, murder, they are all here, one fracas following hard on the heels of another.

Whether an incident involves physical violence or not, however, Mark Twain plays it for climax. Chapters almost invariably end with dramatic tableaux or startling revelations, especially those in which Roxy is the central character. In her first really dramatic scene (Chapter 8), the one in which her son, the proud false Tom, kneels to her, Roxy finishes off the confrontation by taking a drink and with the bottle tucked under her shawl marches out the door "as grim and erect as a grenadier." (One can almost see the curtain drop and hear the applause.) In her next big scene (Chapter 9) she tells the false Tom that she is his mother and that his father is "Cunnel Cecil Burleigh Essex."

Under the inspiration of her soaring complacency the departed grades of her earlier days returned to her, and her bearing took to itself a dignity and state that might have passed for queenly if her surroundings had been a little more in keeping with it.

"Dey ain't another nigger in dis town dat's as high-bawn as you is. Now den, go 'long! En jes you hold yo' head up as high as you want to—you has de right, en dat I can swah." (Curtain and great applause)

In her third big scene (Chapter 14) she cautions her son that he must reform and live a Moral Life. In true stage fashion he replies, " 'Yes, mother, I know, now, that I am reformed—and permanently. Permanently—and beyond the reach of any human temptations.' " And Roxy replies: " 'Den g'long home en begin!' " (Curtain and tremendous applause)

Her fourth and fifth scenes (Chapters 16 and 21) are potentially more poignant. Having sold herself back into slavery to obtain money for her son, she is led on a boat that she has been told is going upstream from St. Louis. But soon her "practiced eye fell upon that telltale rush of water" and her head drops upon her breast, and she cries, " 'Oh, de good Lord God have mercy on po' sinful me—I's *sole down de river!*' " (Curtain, tears, and applause.) Finally, when the false Tom is disclosed in court as Roxy's son, she flings herself on her knees, covers her face with her hands, and sobs, " 'De Lord have mercy on me, po' misable sinner dat I is.' " Whereupon the clock strikes twelve, the court rises, and the new prisoner is removed. (Curtain, general weeping, and thunderous applause.)

Readable as it is, *Pudd'nhead Wilson* nevertheless falters as story, chiefly because of Mark Twain's dependence upon stock situations. The good boy saves the bad boy from drowning. Babies are exchanged so that the offspring of the doting mother will have honor and riches. The chief concern of the villain is over a will that will make him either a prince or a pauper. The virtuous slave is sold down the river by the villain. The aristocratic gentleman has nothing but contempt for a son who when insulted fails to challenge the offender to a duel. Capping the stock situations are the stock scenes: the son on his knees before his mother, the worried villain sitting on a sofa with his throbbing head between his hands, the murderer finally convicting himself by fainting when the facts are offered in court. In sum, the overlay of nineteenth-century melodrama is too great to allow the narrative to come through freshly and vigorously. To say this is not to downgrade the book for lack of realism, but to fault its narrator for failing to portray his fictive world with enough imagination. The story is weaker than it should be, not because it departs from life but because in departing from life it stays too close to other stories.

For the modern reader the most interesting aspect of *Pudd'nhead Wilson* is its social satire or commentary, that component of fabulation that keeps it in touch with actual life, however wildly the author otherwise indulges himself in fantasy. Since this aspect has already been examined at considerable length by others, my task here is simply to suggest how the intellectual freight of the work relates it to the tradition of fabulation. Most obviously, the ironic treatment of the characters recalls the tone and treatment of characters in the fabulations of the eighteenth and nineteenth centuries. There is the same range in irony from affectionate amusement to sharp disdain. The characters are similarly discovered to be naive, gullible, fickle, pretentious, and hypocritical. And the reader experiences the same heightening of enjoyment and insight.

If we move, however, from Mark Twain's treatment of the particular men and women of Dawson's Landing to his consideration of man as species, we suddenly find ourselves contemplating concepts that are not at all implied in the works of earlier writers. The earlier writers, especially those of the eighteenth century, assumed a rational universe in which people get into difficulties because of their own imprudence or unreason, the operations of malevolent persons or forces, and bad luck. Despite widespread evils, reform in the world of these books seems wholly possible; indeed one is led to expect that in due time reform will undoubtedly come to pass.[9] There are no such encouraging assumptions in *Pudd'nhead Wilson*.

Since it was based on a tissue of false assumptions, the slave culture of the South offered Mark Twain ideal material for exposing what he considered to be the irrationality of man. *Pudd'nhead Wilson* exhibits a surprising number of those assumptions: slavery as an unquestionably acceptable social institution; the superiority of the blood of the white race and hence of the race itself; the black as anyone with a black ancestor, no matter how remote; the right of white males to fornicate with black women without incurring any responsibility for the issue of such action; the grave importance of honor, and the duel as the proper way of settling questions of honor; the identification of ability and virtue with such matters as birth, social station, and manners.[1] Of all of these Mark Twain

9. My colleague, W. R. Irwin, has been most helpful in commenting upon this essay, especially those portions of it dealing with the narrative tradition.
1. I do not mean to imply in this section that Mark Twain's thematic interests supersede or damage his story—as they do at times in *A Connecticut Yankee*.

Those critics who by their preoccupation with theme give the impression that *Pudd'nhead Wilson* is primarily a solemn examination of slavery, miscegenation, and/or determinism seem to me to have lost their sense of balance, if not their sense of humor.

chose to deal most explicitly and vividly with the assumption about the superiority of "white" blood. Roxy is his major instrument. Before we see her, we hear her jabbering away with someone called Jasper in slave dialect. Then Twain stuns us by describing her as "fair," indeed so fair that she cannot be distinguished from a white Southern belle. Why is she a slave? Because she had a great, great grandparent who was black. For Dawson's Landing (and the South), we learn, the one sixteenth of black blood "outvotes" the fifteen sixteenths of white blood and degrades Roxy below the most thick-witted of the whites. To reinforce the point, Twain immediately thereafter introduces her son, a blue-eyed, flaxen haired baby, whose background is white except, of course, for one great, great, great grandparent. No one but Roxy can distinguish him from the baby son of the Percy Driscolls. All of the crimes and tragedies that follow in the story, Mark Twain makes evident, result directly or indirectly from the fact that the Southern whites cling perversely to the myth about blood instead of accepting the evidence of their senses.

The basic conflict in the tale, thus, is not between the moral and the immoral, or between a sound heart and a deformed conscience, but between the rational thought of the author and the irrational thought of man as represented by the people of Dawson's Landing. As a counter to the unscientific thought of his characters Mark Twain opposes his own brand of science, mechanical determinism. "Training—training is everything," he had written in A Connecticut Yankee several years before. And by training he meant not only the shaping of the personality by society but also its shaping as a result of the cumulative social pressure represented in heredity.[2] In *Pudd'nhead Wilson* the concept is most simply dramatized in the real Tom, Thomas à Becket Driscoll. After Roxy exchanges him for her own son he is raised a slave. Knowing nothing but hard work and abuse, he grows up quite unspoiled. But when freed because of the discovery of Roxy's crime, he is wholly unable to reenter white society because of his training as a slave. This story has about it a parable-like clarity: we are what our training makes us. Unfortunately Mark Twain blurs his point with the false Tom who, pampered as a youth, grows up to be selfish and arrogant as one might expect. But he also turns out to be cowardly and not even above killing his benefactor and selling his mother down the river —traits that are not inevitable because of the training. Nevertheless, though Mark Twain may botch a demonstration now and then (usually to answer the siren calls of melodrama and burlesque) his belief in determinism emerges clearly in the book as a whole. The blacks are obviously trapped by their training, but the whites do not

2. Henry Nash Smith makes this point in his *Mark Twain: The Development of a Writer*, p. 172.

escape. They are the products of the myths, prejudices, and false assumptions that have been drilled into them since childhood. Possibly the ultimate in entrapment is that none of the characters even remotely suspects that he is trapped. Life as depicted in *Pudd'nhead Wilson*, then, is a purposeless absurdity in which the men and women simply play out their destined roles.

But even this evidence of metaphysical truth does not justify evaluating the work in the realistic tradition. *Cat's Cradle*, *Catch 22*, *The Lime Twig*, and *Clockwork Orange* have their metaphysical truth also, but no one praises them for holding up the mirror to life —or denigrates them for their failure to do so. Like these fabulations of our own time, *Pudd'nhead Wilson* locates its truth in a bizarre tale in which the irrational is the norm, and coincidence the expected. Even the farce, on reflection, turns out to be bitter. *Pudd'nhead Wilson* ends with Roxy's son, convicted of murder, being freed because execution would result in loss of property to his owners. In its absurdity, its satiric bite, and the sweep of its implications the detail is not unlike the ending of Vonnegut's *Cat's Cradle* in which Bokonen writes of lying on his back, frozen stiff from *ice-nine*, grinning horribly, and thumbing his nose at You Know Who.

BARRY WOOD

Narrative Action and Structural Symmetry in *Pudd'nhead Wilson*†

As any student of Mark Twain soon discovers, serious critical attention to his work is not apparent until the middle of the twentieth century. In the case of *Pudd'nhead Wilson* (1894), the watershed dates from essays by Leslie Fiedler in 1955 and F. R. Leavis in 1956.[1] Since that time there have been a surprising number of studies of the novel, all of them useful in unravelling one or another aspect of the work without presenting in total more than a mosaic of motifs and themes. Without attempting to present a detailed summary of scholarship, I would like to point to a few of the issues in the novel around which the thematic interpretations have been built.

First, there is the racial theme centering on miscegenation and

† Previously unpublished essay.

1. Leslie Fiedler, "As Free as Any Cretur . . . ," *Mark Twain: A Collection of Critical Essays*, ed. Henry Nash Smith (Englewood Cliffs, N.J.: Prentice-Hall, 1963), pp. 130–39; F. R. Leavis, "Mark Twain's Neglected Classic: The Moral Astringency of *Pudd'nhead Wilson.*" *Commentary*, 21 (February 1956), 128–36. [Both essays are reprinted above —*Editor*.]

the disastrous results of interbreeding at Dawson's Landing, the small Missouri settlement on the west bank of the Mississippi south of St. Louis where the major action is set.[2] A second theme derives from the notion of environmental determinism, a concept specifically linked to the realism and naturalism so central to the writings of the later nineteenth century.[3] As a key to human behavior, environmental determinism has been brought forward to explain the fortunes of Roxana's two infant charges after she has exchanged their roles, placing her own Negro son into the white environment of the First Families of Virginia. A third theme, set forth persuasively by Edgar T. Schell, also focusses on the changeling motive but adds to it the succession of hidden or disguised identities in the story, arguing that the confusion between appearance and reality provides the central organization of the book. The resolution of the book, says Schell, occurs when Pudd'nhead Wilson discovers "the perspective from which appearance and reality are the same."[4] A fourth approach, emphasized in an important article by George Spangler, interprets the story as "a parable of property," showing how the actions principally of Tom, partially of Roxana, and peripherally of Wilson derive from their single-minded concern (or lack of it) for property. The thrust of this study centers on "the obsession with property as a vitiating and reductive influence on human beings."[5] A fifth approach, set forth by Eberhard Alsen, argues that the property theme reduces Wilson to "the foil to Tom," and therefore neglects the centrality of the title character—particularly the important effects on the story of his twenty-three year "fight for popularity and power."[6]

The variations in these thematic approaches and the very different data in the novel to which they address themselves illustrate the fundamental critical problem of the book. As with studies of many literary works, a number of studies of *Pudd'nhead Wilson* are true, in the sense of demonstrable, without being particularly satisfactory. Each one either omits important events or issues in the book or interprets them as servants to a thesis. At the same time, certain features are simply not taken seriously. The tendency is to treat the Italian twins, Luigi and Angelo, as vestigia from *Those Extraordi-*

2. See Thomas W. Ford, "The Miscegenation Theme in *Pudd'nhead Wilson*," *Mark Twain Journal*, 10:1 (1955), 13–14; and Barbara A. Chellis, "Those Extraordinary Twins: Negroes and Whites," *American Quarterly*, 21 (1969), 100–112.

3. See Leslie Fiedler, "As Free as Any Cretur"; also Henry Nash Smith, *Mark Twain: The Development of a Writer* (Cambridge, Mass.: Harvard University Press, 1962), pp. 171–84. [The Smith essay is reprinted above—*Editor.*]

4. Edgar T. Schell, " 'Pears' and 'Is' in *Pudd'nhead Wilson*," *Mark Twain Journal*, 12:3 (Winter 1964–65), 14.

5. George M. Spangler, "*Pudd'nhead Wilson*: A Parable of Property," *American Literature*, 42:1 (1970), 29. [Reprinted above—*Editor.*]

6. Eberhard Alsen, "Pudd'nhead Wilson's Fight for Popularity and Power," *Western American Literature*, 7:2 (1972), 135–43. [Reprinted above—*Editor.*]

nary Twins or as examples of Twain's fascination with doubles;[7] to eliminate Wilson's palmistry and fingerprinting as cheap motifs from Victorian melodrama;[8] and to ignore all but a handful of entries from *Pudd'nhead Wilson's Calendar* which are easily recognized as satiric commentary on the story.[9]

Difficulties in almost every case would appear to derive from an almost exclusively thematic emphasis with the underlying assumption that Twain was attempting, through the medium of the novel, to say something, satirize something, or criticize something. These assumptions, often accurate in the context of realism where art so often spills over into social commentary, can easily lead to the kind of dismissal registered by Warner Berthoff, who finds no "significant art," a "crude and forced" compositional design, and a "profound archetypal symbolism—black and white, guilt and innocence" which "composes, in *Pudd'nhead Wilson*, no clear meaning."[1] The fact of the matter is, however, that the narrative movement of the book has been so consistently ignored, or limited to plot summary in the service of theme, that almost any intelligent commentary should open up new areas of understanding. What I propose to consider is the narrative movement of the book based on the notion that narrative action begins with, and consists of, a disruption of equilibrium and ends when some form of equilibrium has been restored.[2]

A cursory glance at the opening chapter of *Pudd'nhead Wilson* reveals an apparent equilibrium before the narrative action begins:

> Dawson's Landing was a slaveholding town, with a rich slave-worked grain and pork country back of it. The town was sleepy

7. See George Feinstein, "Vestigia in *Pudd'nhead Wilson*," *Twainian* (May 1942), 1–3; and Robert Rowlette, "Mark Twain and Doubles," Chapter 4 of *Mark Twain's Pudd'nhead Wilson: The Development and Design* (Bowling Green, Ohio: Bowling Green University Popular Press, 1971), pp. 62–82.
8. See "Mark Twain and the Detective," Chapter 3 in Rowlette.
9. This is not to overlook the valuable suggestions in Jim W. Miller, "'Pudd'nhead Wilson's Calendar'," *Mark Twain Journal*, 13:3 (1967), 8–10; and useful remarks in more general studies such as James M. Cox, "*Pudd'nhead Wilson:* The End of Mark Twain's American Dream," *The South Atlantic Quarterly*, 57 (1959), 351–63, and Stanley Brodwin, "Blackness and the Adamic Myth in Mark Twain's *Pudd'nhead Wilson*," *Texas Studies in Literature and Language*, 15:1 (1973), 167–76. [The Brodwin essay is reprinted above—*Editor*.]
1. Warner Berthoff, *The Ferment of Realism: American Literature, 1884–1919*

(New York: The Free Press, 1965), p. 72. A useful study which nicely counters the realist dismissal is John C. Gerber, "*Pudd'nhead Wilson* as Fabulation," *Studies in American Humor*, 2:1 (April 1975), 21–31. Gerber locates the major critical shortcoming as I have in the approach through theme: "Those critics who by their preoccupation with theme give the impression that *Pudd'nhead Wilson* is primarily a solemn examination of slavery, miscegenation, and/or determinism seem to me to have lost their sense of balance, if not their sense of humor" (p. 31, n. 19). [See Gerber's essay, above.—*Editor*.]
2. This approach to narrative action is based on suggestions in Sheldon Sacks, *Fiction and the Shape of Belief: A Study of Henry Fielding, With Glances at Swift, Johnson and Richardson* (Berkeley: University of California Press, 1964), and Robert Scholes and Robert Kellogg, *The Nature of Narrative* (New York: Oxford University Press, 1966), especially Chapter 6.

and comfortable and contented. It was fifty years old, and was growing—very slowly, in fact, but still it was growing.

One can hardly avoid the irony implicit in this summation after two pages devoted to the whitewashed houses hidden behind lush gardens, brick sidewalks, tree-lined streets, and the occasional outstretched cat—"symbol" says Twain of "contentment and peace." The irony rests in the fact, nowhere mentioned, that there is—there must be—a line of demarcation between slaveholders and slaves, presumably corresponding to the color line between white and black. Later we learn of a deeper irony: the blurring of this color line through a long history of miscegenation. Roxana, for instance, who looks white, is a slave because one-sixteenth of her blood is black. It is worth emphasizing that Roxana's diluted black blood is the result of four cases of miscegenation in four successive generations; her son's dilution to one thirty-second is the further result of her secret union with Colonel Cecil Burleigh Essex—the fifth successive occurrence. Yet nothing is disturbed. The regular crossing of the color line for the purpose of gratifying white lust is by now an established institution, completely integrated into the equilibrium of the community. Twain emphasizes this when he outlines the important citizens of the town: "Then there was Colonel Cecil Burleigh Essex, another F.F.V. of formidable calibre—however, with him we have no concern."

Miscegenation, then, while often discussed as an important theme of *Pudd'nhead Wilson*, is simply a point of interest in the book; but it plays no part in the disruption of the equilibrium which starts the narrative action. At the same time, the history of miscegenation symbolizes the underlying tension persisting at Dawson's Landing—a tension, however, which has no resolution within the context of the quiet town. The duality of slaveholder and slave, "white" and "black," exists in a finely tuned balance. This situation points out the purpose of the narrative action: the introduction of some disruptive element into the town can, or may, unmask the tension by carrying it to a different arena such that the tension will be rooted out and perhaps resolved.

The disruption occurs with the arrival in Dawson's Landing of David Wilson with his "fatal remark." This occurrence may be regarded as mechanical or wooden, but could hardly be otherwise, given the completeness of the equilibrium into which he moves. His arrival, however, begins the narrative action by translating the rooted contradictions of the town into new terms. His remark—"I wish I owned half of that dog. . . . I would kill my half"—not only isolates him from the community but reveals precisely what kind of tension Dawson's Landing *cannot* tolerate. Clearly there are profound differences among the citizens of the town, but the disinterested intellect is not a difference that the town can absorb. Both slaveholders and slaves reject him, label him a "pudd'nhead," turn him into an outsider, and banish him to the fringes of social life. The hiding of Pudd'nhead's intellect behind the mask of the fool, paradoxically, allows for his acceptance and partial integration into the life of the town. Meanwhile, unable to practice his legal profession, he remains an intellectual isolate for more than twenty years. His presence constitutes an instability which can only be corrected when Dawson's Landing finally assimilates into itself the qualities Wilson represents: intellect, in its purest sense; law, the practical application of intellect; and perhaps wisdom. I say perhaps because this side of Wilson, it turns out, is never successfully integrated into the community at the end. The fact that many entries in his *Calendar* have no apparent bearing on events of the story may function symbolically as an indication of a degree of wisdom quite beyond the comprehension of the town, at the beginning and later.[3]

Wilson's isolation in itself is not enough to create a major sequence of narrative events, partially because the town finds a way to absorb him through his "humble capacities of land-surveyor and expert accountant." The result is that he appears initially to slip into an incidental position in the story. Nevertheless, the particular qualities which lead to his isolation create a kind of polar opposite in the person of Thomas Driscoll. Wilson's penetrating observation of life touches the spring that sets off this action. Roxana, of course, is extremely intelligent, but primarily in cases where she is forcibly confronted with a specific problem to be solved—and her solutions are often ingenious. But her intelligence is derivative rather than original, so that she is, by herself, incapable of a highly creative action such as the exchange of babies. It requires Wilson's perceptive remarks about the similarity between the babies and his suggestive question "How can you tell them apart, Roxy, when they haven't any clothes on?" to initiate and ratify her thinking. Given the problem arising the next day—Percy Driscoll's threat to sell not only the thief of his household but *all* his slaves down the river, Roxana is able to turn Wilson's revealing question into her own private solution for the problem. Even so, she has to justify her actions with the communally accepted rationale of her Calvinist religion: "He [de Lord] s'lect out anybody dat suit him, en put another one in his place, en make de fust one happy forever en leave t'other one to burn wid Satan." By giving her own son the Driscoll name she launches him into the white world with everything that membership in it entails. The false Thomas Driscoll thus becomes the polar

3. This suggestion seems more plausible to me than the assumption of artistic failure.

opposite for Pudd'nhead Wilson, precisely because his identity poses problems that no one else in Dawson's Landing has the intellectual prowess to solve. Like Wilson, Tom's true identity is masked; the revelation of his real identity by Wilson at the end of the book constitutes a double unmasking.

Thomas' secret identity creates a new tension in the community, though not a tension that will manifest itself immediately. However, as he grows up, he develops a distinctive pattern of behavior which is traceable neither to his white environment nor to his Negro blood. Roxana argues once that "It's de nigger in you, dat's what it is"; but more likely the source of Tom's scorn for white values and his slippage into a series of crimes can be blamed on the situation created by an exchange of identities while Roxana, his real mother, continues her maternal care in the guise of a Driscoll slave. Any definitive explanation for his moral corruption is out of reach, of course, and Twain appears to have intended that it remain so. What does seem clear, however, is that Twain created in Tom a new variety of isolation—and a precise opposite of Wilson's. Thus Tom represents that disruption of community life that comes with persistent crime and outright lawlessness, exactly balancing the isolated power of law represented by Wilson. Moreover, Tom's progressive alienation turns his behavior into a combination of personal greed and untrammelled passion, the polar opposite of Wilson's methodical precision of mind. This dramatic polarity constitutes a transformation of the balanced equilibrium at the beginning of the novel—a transformation whereby the deeply masked contradictions of the society are now more explicitly expressed and therefore capable of being discovered and rooted out. The subsequent narrative action of the novel, revolving around these polarized varieties of isolation, can be seen as a movement toward a new equilibrium. George Spangler's notion of the novel as "a parable of property" applies specifically to Tom's criminal attempts to obtain Judge Driscoll's inheritance at all costs, thus bringing an end to his own isolation from the propertied white community. Similarly, Eberhard Alsen's perceptive account of Pudd'nhead Wilson's fight for popularity and power describes Wilson's attempts to end his own isolation and win communal acceptance for himself, specifically in terms of his professional and avocational skills, law and fingerprinting.

The real ironies of Dawson's Landing, intensified in these polar characters, are now clear. What is hidden behind the gardens and sunlit homes of the town is not so much a racial dichotomy, nor even a history of miscegenation: these are only symptoms. What Wilson's lonely vigil from his little house "on the extreme western verge of the town" reveals is that the community has no place for intelligence, wisdom, or procedural law.[4] What Tom's repeated crimes reveal is that the original harmony of the town rests on a fabric of fundamental lawlessness and passion. The fact of persistent miscegenation through generations—without a visible tremor—serves as fundamental evidence. That Judge Driscoll, the highest legal authority, abhors the idea of a courtroom trial and resorts to the aristocratic code of the duel reinforces it.

The ostensible harmony of the town thus turns out to be a mask obscuring fundamental inconsistencies and profound ironies. The novel unfolds as the discovery of what the community really *is*. The metaphorical action accompanying this discovery is the action of identity concealed and revealed. Who people are becomes the real key to discovering what the community is. As people hide their identity behind masks appearances take on the status of reality, leading to multiple levels of irony.[5] Roxana appears to be white but is really a slave according to the arbitrary definition of Dawson's Landing. Her son is likewise "black" but his whiteness allows for the substitution of appearance for reality—engineered by the exchange of babies. Thenceforward, Roxana, who is really the mother of Tom, assumes the *appearance* of a family slave (which, paradoxically, she *is*), while Tom confuses her appearance for reality. Twain is explicit about the effects of this confusion:

> Roxy was a doting fool of a mother. She was this toward her child—and she was also more than this: by the fiction created by herself, he was become her master; the necessity of recognizing this relation outwardly and of perfecting herself in the forms required to express the recognition, had moved her to such diligence and faithfulness in practicing these forms that this exercise soon concreted itself into habit; it became automatic and unconscious; then a natural result followed: deceptions intended solely for others gradually grew practically into self-deceptions as well; the mock reverence became real reverence, the mock obsequiousness real obsequiousness, the mock homage real homage; the little counterfeit rift of separation between imitation-slave and imitation-master widened and widened, and became an abyss, and a very real one. . . . In her worship of him she forgot who she was and what he had been.

The description is emblematic of the novel as a whole, for it traces exactly the way in which the realities of life in Dawson's Landing have been hidden beneath multiple layerings of fictions, deceptions,

---

4. A study that bears on this point, though obliquely, is John M. Brand's "The Incipient Wilderness: A Study of *Pudd'nhead Wilson*," *Western American Literature*, 7:2 (1972), 125–34. [Reprinted above—*Editor*.]

5. Edgar T. Schell, already cited, has worked out the notion of appearance and reality in strictly thematic terms without placing it in the context of the larger narrative action.

counterfeitings, and imitations until these patterns have been legitimized as habit.

At the death of Percy Driscoll Roxana is set free. Years later, after a bank failure in New Orleans which leaves her penniless, she returns to Dawson's Landing in order to obtain money from Tom —whose role is now that of former master. Tom is away in St. Louis, but Roxana learns of his gambling from Valet de Chambre, who is really white but appears to be a slave because of Roxana's exchange of sons. "Take it back, you mis'able imitation nigger dat I bore in sorrow en tribbilation" she shouts at him, her words containing levels of irony of which even she is unaware. The reply of her "son" is equally layered: "If I's imitation, what is you? Bofe of us is imitation *white*—dat's what we is—en pow'ful good imitation, too." The deepest irony, of course, is the unquestioned acceptance by Roxana and Valet de Chambre of the arbitrary logic according to which someone with Negro blood diluted to one thirty-second is still a "nigger" and thus only "imitation white."

When Tom returns Roxana humbly requests money from him; he refuses, and she threatens to tell Judge Driscoll "what I knows. I knows enough to bu'st dat will to flinders—en more, mind you, more!" What she really knows is the secret of his identity; what she appears to know is the facts of his gambling. Begging Roxana not to require her young master to do the "horrible thing" of humiliating himself before her, Tom finally slumps to his knees and begs her not to expose him—an action which he feels has plummeted him to "the deepest depths of degradation." In reality, of course, the son has bowed before the mother, his single noble action in the book. The appearance of this act to him, however, is an index of the twisted masks worn by this apparently harmonious community.

From this point on the ironies of lost or hidden identity take on even more explicit form. In order to conceal his identity during his robberies in Dawson's Landing, Tom adopts the disguise of a Negro woman; later, when he attempts to rob Judge Driscoll, he blackens his face to look like a Negro slave. After Tom sells Roxana down the river she returns, disguised as a Negro tramp. These disguises represent a kind of masochistic wish fulfillment, as Roxana and her son assume the appearance of precisely what Dawson's Landing has arbitrarily defined them to be. Tom's robbery of the Judge in the guise of a Negro functions symbolically for the generalized robbery he has been engaged in for years while really a Negro disguised as a white. The fact that disguises which are identical to the underlying reality serve as the perfect way to *hide* one's identity is germane to the larger contradictions in the community where all of this takes place.

Pudd'nhead Wilson is then a labyrinth of lost identities or secret identities, appearances which look real, disguises which symbolize reality. David Wilson is given an identity on the day he arrives in the community; what he has been given serves thereafter as a disguise concealing his real shrewdness. Disguised as a fool, Wilson uses his spare time for more than twenty years developing a foolproof test for *identity*. Each glass slide containing the "physiological autograph" of someone in Dawson's Landing allows for the penetration of any disguise adopted by a citizen of the town. The sum total of Wilson's slides constitutes the infallible test for the identity of the town itself.

Pudd'nhead's unmasking of Tom is a case of truly multiple discoveries of identity in which Tom is simultaneously revealed as Negro, a false heir to the Driscoll estate, a thief, the real face behind the disguise of a girl, and a murderer. In the same moment, Wilson is unmasked and revealed for what he is, a brilliantly competent lawyer, a carefully observant scientist, and a capable leader for the community. Dawson's Landing, too, is unmasked, though— one must add—not reformed. The real Thomas Driscoll, now "rich and free," continues to be victimized by the masks he has worn, while the false Thomas is inventoried as part of the Driscoll estate and sold down the river. Indeed, the tragedy of the free slave and the blatant illogic of the final economic solution serve as indices of the real Dawson's Landing, quite unapparent in the idyllic scenery of the opening pages. The new equilibrium which occurs, even though it now includes the lawlessness of Tom brought under the control of Wilson's legal intellect, reveals the deeper ironies of a slaveholding civilization; for even the most powerful penetration of deception and the unveiling of truth make no lasting mark on this society.

We have then a double narrative action, which may be diagrammed by two intersecting curves. The widest distance at the center of their arcs suggests the point of complete communal disruption, caused by the masking within the community of Wilson's intellect and Tom's greed. At one end (the left), before the intersection occurs, we have the harmonious equilibrium of a town even though it is divided between slaveholders and slaves. At the other end (the right), we have the harmonious equilibrium of the town recovered—though now revealed for what it really is. Wilson's isolation is represented by the downward curve while Tom's career is represented by the upper. The upward curve diagrams Tom's entry into the white community after Roxana's exchange of babies; the downward curve projects Wilson's isolation from the white community to the periphery of the town and its life. The relative positions of these curves, with Tom's lawlessness soaring *above* Wilson's law, with greed quite out of reach of intellectual control, poses the dilemma of Dawson's Landing in dramatic terms, and suggests the kind of reversal of values that a new equilibrium will require.

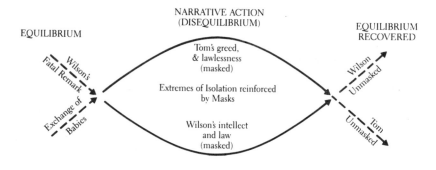

The reversal occurs in the final courtroom scene when Wilson, through the application of intellect and legal reasoning, regains supremacy over the lawlessness and passion of Tom. Twain has simplified the issues, but for a gain rather than a loss of emphasis. As James M. Cox has put it, "the arbitrary neatness of the ending serves only to remind us that the problem has not been finally settled; the triumph of justice, the defeat of the criminal, the success of the long-suffering hero are thin masks which seem deliberately to reveal the larger doom, the deeper crime, the final failure to which we have been exposed."[6]

This kind of structural picture of the novel can help to put several things into focus—the proliferation of themes that critics have unfolded during the last twenty years, for instance. Certain themes, like the property theme or the emphasis on fingerprinting, are confined to one or another of the curves, touching the other only at the moment of intersection. Miscegenation is operative but primarily as a fact within the equilibrium of Dawson's Landing before the action begins and after it has ended; it does not in itself generate the action of the story—providing only the *possibility* for mistaken identity. The double curves, diagramming the careers of the two principal characters, serve to show the double genre of the book,

6. Cox, *"Pudd'nhead Wilson:* The End of Mark Twain's American Dream," 353.

which is partly comic and partly tragic.[7] At the same time, the machinery operating between these poles modifies both genres considerably. Thus, for instance, some of Wilson's demonstrations—his palmistry, and the elaborately staged and timed trial at the end of the book—tend to cast what is normally the curve of comedy into burlesque. Similarly, many aspects of Tom's career—the exchange of roles, the adoption of disguises, the elaborate playacting he performs as a girl before the spying Wilson, the use of a haunted house for laying plans, the selling of his mother, and above all his murder of Judge Driscoll with an elaborately carved dagger which is then dropped at the scene of the crime with bloody fingerprints—all of this redefines the usual tragic curve in terms of melodrama. No single theme dominates the structure; instead various serious themes are played off against one another in a tightly controlled structure of burlesque and melodrama. This is not to say that the book is perfectly realized; it is rather to point out that apparently incongruous themes and tones are unified within a double narrative action.

The mistake is, of course, to regard the novel in strictly thematic terms. From such a vantage point the farce and the melodrama, the use of fingerprinting and other devices from the popular detective story, seem ruinous to the serious intention of the book. An approach through narrative, however, reveals how the narrative action operates to dramatize what cannot otherwise be rooted out —the hidden lawlessness penetrating every facet of life at Dawson's Landing.[8] But, more important, a look at the unfolding narrative restores what seems to have been forgotten about *Pudd'nhead Wilson*: that the novel is also to be enjoyed. Symmetry and balance, tension and harmony, are always essential ingredients of esthetic pleasure. One cannot help thinking about the Italian twins, for instance, in esthetic terms; they remain in the mind long after one has set the book aside as a kind of analogy for the symmetry of the story. They reinforce and echo the other set of handsome look-alikes whose exchange sets up repeated doublings of identity; they tantalize us with the mystery of differences hidden between same-

---

7. That *Pudd'nhead Wilson* is comedy has been recognized by several critics, among them Henry Nash Smith, *Mark Twain, The Development of a Writer* (Cambridge, Mass.: Harvard Univ. Press, 1962), who sees the book as a comedy of manners; and James M. Cox, *Mark Twain: The Fate of Humor* (Princeton, N.J.: Princeton Univ. Press, 1966), who notes that "the hero's triumph over and entry into the society is in the comic rather than the tragic mode" (p. 228). A recent study which sees the book as both comedy and trag-edy is Clark Griffith's "*Pudd'nhead Wilson* as Dark Comedy," *ELH*, 43:2 (Summer 1976), 209–26.

8. The relevance of this approach through narrative action understood as disequilibrium is apparent in "The Man That Corrupted Hadleyburg" (1899), a work which is purely comic though more heavily ironic. Approximately the same thing happens: an initial equilibrium is disrupted by the incursion of an outsider who ultimately unmasks the hidden corruption of the town.

ness of appearance which is so germane to the story. At the other extreme we have Pudd'nhead Wilson's "whimsical almanac . . . a calendar, with a little dab of ostensible philosophy, usually in ironical form, appended to each date." Because the people of Dawson's Landing possess only a single, literal view of things, "irony was not for those people"; Wilson alone has the gift of double vision. The excerpts from his *Calendar* printed at the head of each chapter give a tonal reinforcement to the dramatic polarities of the story itself. They reinforce the more profound man which the community has masked as a fool. At the same time, if *Pudd'nhead Wilson's Calendar* seems to fly free of direct commentary on the situation this is after all the irony of its author's isolated intellect.

A great deal is left out of any thematic interpretation of this novel, if only because a thematic approach searches for singleness of idea beneath variations in event. Esthetically, however, everything makes sense when seen within the context of the narrative action and symmetry of the novel. Here, indeed, form is wedded to content. At the same time, we need to recognize and admit that the mixture of motifs and genres in this book often verges on the bizarre. But critics often act as though the novelist who mixes too daring a brew ought to be punished by authoring a poor book which is soon forgotten. As Wilson puts it in his *Calendar*, "Few things are harder to put up with than the annoyance of a good example."

Selected Bibliography

Articles reprinted in this edition are not included in the bibliography.

MARK TWAIN: GENERAL

Allen, Jerry. *The Adventures of Mark Twain.* Boston: Little, Brown, 1954.

Andrews, Kenneth R. *Nook Farm: Mark Twain's Hartford Circle.* Cambridge: Harvard University Press, 1950.

Asselineau, Roger. *The Literary Reputation of Mark Twain From 1910 to 1950; A Critical Essay and Bibliography.* Paris: M. Didier, 1954.

Baetzhold, Howard G. *Mark Twain and John Bull.* Bloomington: Indiana University Press, 1970.

Baldanza, Frank. *Mark Twain: An Introduction and Interpretation.* New York: Barnes & Noble, 1961.

Bellamy, Gladys C. *Mark Twain As a Literary Artist.* Norman: University of Oklahoma Press, 1950.

Berthoff, Warner. *The Ferment of Realism, American Literature, 1884–1919.* New York: Free Press, 1965.

Blair, Walter. *Horse Sense in American Humor.* Chicago: University of Chicago Press, 1942.

———. *Native American Humor: 1800–1900.* New York: American Book, 1937.

Blues, Thomas. *Mark Twain and the Community.* Lexington: University of Kentucky Press, 1970.

Branch, Edgar M. *The Literary Apprenticeship of Mark Twain, with Selections from His Apprentice Writing.* Urbana: University of Illinois Press, 1950.

Brashear, Minnie M. "Formative Influences in the Mind and Writings of Mark Twain." Dissertation, University of North Carolina, 1930.

———. *Mark Twain, Son of Missouri.* Chapel Hill: University of North Carolina Press, 1934.

Brooks, Van Wyck. *The Ordeal of Mark Twain.* Revised Edition. New York: E. P. Dutton, 1933.

Budd, Louis J. *Mark Twain: Social Philosopher.* Bloomington: Indiana University Press, 1962.

Canby, Henry S. *Turn West, Turn East: Mark Twain and Henry James.* Boston: Houghton Mifflin, 1951.

Clemens, Clara. *My Father, Mark Twain.* New York: Harper & Brothers, 1931.

Covici, Pascal, Jr. *Mark Twain's Humor, The Image of a World.* Dallas: Southern Methodist University Press, 1962.

Cox, James M. *Mark Twain: The Fate of Humor.* Princeton: Princeton University Press, 1966.

De Voto, Bernard. *Mark Twain at Work.* Cambridge: Harvard University Press, 1942.

———. *Mark Twain's America.* Boston: Little, Brown, 1932.

Dreiser, Theodore. "Mark the Double Twain." *English Journal,* 24 (1935), 615–27.

Ferguson, DeLancey. *Mark Twain: Man and Legend.* Indianapolis: Bobbs-Merrill, 1943.

Foner, Philip S. *Mark Twain: Social Critic.* New York: International Publishers, 1958.

Geismar, Maxwell. *Mark Twain: An American Prophet.* Boston: Houghton Mifflin, 1970.

Grant, Douglas. *Twain.* Writers and Critics Series. New York: Grove Press, 1963.

Harnsberger, Caroline Thomas. *Mark Twain, Family Man.* New York: Citadel Press, 1960.

Hill, Hamlin. *Mark Twain: God's Fool.* New York: Harper & Row, 1973.

———, ed. *Mark Twain's Letters to His Publishers.* Berkeley: University of California Press, 1967.

Howells, William Dean. *My Mark Twain: Reminiscences and Criticisms.* New York: Harper and Brothers, 1910.

Kaplan, Justin. *Mr. Clemens and Mark Twain, A Biography.* New York: Simon and Schuster, 1966.

Leary, Lewis. *Mark Twain.* Minneapolis: University of Minnesota Press, 1960.

———, ed. *Mark Twain's Correspondence with Henry Huttleston Rogers, 1893–1909.* Berkeley: University of California Press, 1969.

Long, E. Hudson. *Mark Twain Handbook.* New York: Hendricks House, 1958.

Lynn, Kenneth S. *Mark Twain and Southwestern Humor.* Boston: Little, Brown, 1960.

Macy, John A. *The Spirit of American Literature.* New York: Doubleday, Page, 1913.

McKeithan, Daniel Morley. *Court Trials in Mark Twain and Other Essays.* The Hague: M. Nijoff, 1958.

Moore, Olin Harris. "Mark Twain and Don Quixote." *Publications of the Modern Language Association,* 37 (1922), 324–46.

Paine, Albert Bigelow. *Mark Twain: A Biography. The Personal and Literary Life of Samuel Langhorne Clemens.* 3 vols. New York: Harper and Brothers, 1912.

———, ed. *Mark Twain's Autobiography.* New York: Harper and Brothers, 1924.

Pochmann, Henry A. "The Mind of Mark Twain." Dissertation, University of Texas, 1924.

Quinn, Arthur H., ed. *The Literature of the American People.* New York: Appleton-Century-Crofts, 1951.

Regan, Robert. *Unpromising Heroes: Mark Twain and His Characters.* Berkeley: University of California Press, 1966.

Rodney, Robert M. "Mark Twain in England: A Study of the English Criticism of and Attitude Toward Mark Twain, 1867–1940." Dissertation, University of Wisconsin, 1945.

Rourke, Constance M. *American Humor: A Study of National Character.* New York: Harcourt, Brace, 1931.

Salomon, Roger B. *Mark Twain and the Image of History.* New Haven: Yale University Press, 1961.

Scott, Harold P. "Mark Twain's Theory of Humor: An Analysis of the Laughable in Literature." Dissertation, University of Michigan, n.d.

Sloane, David Edward Edison. "Mark Twain as a Literary Comedian: The Heritage of Artemus Ward in the 1860's." Dissertation, Duke University, 1970. (Especially chapter 6 on *Pudd'nhead Wilson.*)

Smith, Henry Nash. *Mark Twain: The Development of a Writer.* Cambridge: Harvard University Press, 1962.

Spiller, Robert E., *et al.,* eds. *Literary History of the United States.* New York: Macmillan, 1948.

Stone, Albert E. *The Innocent Eye; Childhood in Mark Twain's Imagination.* New Haven: Yale University Press, 1961.

Trent, W. P., *et al.,* eds. *Cambridge History of American Literature.* New York: G. P. Putnam's Sons, 1922.

Van Doren, Carl. "Mark Twain." In *Dictionary of American Biography* (1928).

Wagenknecht, Edward. *Mark Twain: The Man and His Work.* New Haven: Yale University Press, 1935.

Wecter, Dixon. *Sam Clemens of Hannibal.* Boston: Houghton Mifflin, 1952.

———, ed. *The Love Letters of Mark Twain.* New York: Harper & Brothers, 1949.

MARK TWAIN: *PUDD'NHEAD WILSON* AND *THOSE EXTRAORDINARY TWINS*

Anderson, Frederick, ed. *Pudd'nhead Wilson and Those Extraordinary Twins.* San Francisco: Chandler Publishing Company, 1968. (Facsimile of edition published by American Publishing Company, 1894.)

Aspiz, Harold. "The Other Half of Pudd'nhead's Dog." *Mark Twain Journal,* 17 (Summer 1975), 4, 10–11.

Berger, Sidney E. "New Mark Twain Items." *The Papers of the Bibliographical Society of America,* 68 (1974), 331–335.

———. "Editorial Intrusion in *Pudd'nhead Wilson.*" *The Papers of the Bibliographical Society of America,* 70 (1976), 272–276.

———. "Determining Printer's Copy: The English Edition of Mark Twain's *Pudd'nhead Wilson.*" *The Papers of the Bibliographical Society of America,* 72 (1978), 250–256.

Butcher, Philip. "Mark Twain Sells Roxy Down the River." *CLA Journal,* 8 (1965), 225–233.

Chapin, Henry B. "Twain's *Pudd'nhead Wilson*, Chapter VI." *Explicator*, 21 (April 1963), Item 61.
Chellis, Barbara A. "Those Extraordinary Twins: Negroes and Whites." *American Quarterly*, 21 (Spring 1969), 1, 100–112.
Coburn, Mark D. " 'Training Is Everything': Communal Opinion and the Individual in *Pudd'nhead Wilson*." *Modern Language Quarterly*, 31 (March 1970), 1, 209–219.
Cronin, Frank C. "The Ultimate Perspective in *Pudd'nhead Wilson*." *Mark Twain Journal*, 16 (Winter 1971–72), 1, 14–16.
D'Avanzo, Mario L. "In the Name of Pudd'nhead." *Mark Twain Journal*, 16, 2, 13–14.
Eschholz, Paul A. "Twain's *The Tragedy of Pudd'nhead Wilson*." *Explicator*, 31 (April 1973), Item 67.
Feinstein, George. "Vestigia in *Pudd'nhead Wilson*," *Twainian* (May 1942), 1–3.
Ford, Thomas W. "The Miscegenation Theme in *Pudd'nhead Wilson*." *Mark Twain Quarterly*, 10 (1955–58), 13–14.
Freimarck, John. "*Pudd'nhead Wilson*: A Tale of Blood and Brotherhood." *The University Review* (Kansas City), 34 (June 1968), 4, 303–306.
Gargano, James W. "*Pudd'nhead Wilson*: Mark Twain as Genial Satan." *South Atlantic Quarterly*, 74 (Summer 1975), 365–375.
Griffith, Clark. "*Pudd'nhead Wilson* as Dark Comedy." *Journal of English Literary History*, 43:2 (Summer 1976), 209–226.
Haines, James B. "Of Dogs and Men: A Symbolic Variation on the Twin Motif in *Pudd'nhead Wilson*." *Mark Twain Journal*, 18 (Winter 1976–77), 3, 14–17.
Hughes, Langston. Introduction to *Pudd'nhead Wilson*. New York: Bantam Books, 1964. Pp. vii–xiii.
Jeffries, William B. "The Montesquiou Murder Case: A Possible Source for Some Incidents in *Pudd'nhead Wilson*." *American Literature*, 31 (1959–60), 488–490.
Kolin, Philip C. "Mark Twain, Aristotle, and Pudd'nhead Wilson." *Mark Twain Journal*, 15 (Summer 1970), 2, 1–4.
Leiter, Louis H. "Dawson's Landing: Thematic Cityscape in Twain's *Pudd'nhead Wilson*." *Mark Twain Journal*, 13 (Winter 1965–66), 1, 8–11.
Lewis, Stuart A. "Pudd'nhead Wilson's Election." *Mark Twain Journal*, 15 (Winter 1970), 1, 21.
Mann, Carolyn. "Innocence in *Pudd'nhead Wilson*." *Mark Twain Journal*, 14 (Winter 1968–69), 3, 18–21, 11.
Mann, Karen B. "Pudd'nhead Wilson: One Man or Two?" *Research Studies*, 42 (1974), 175–181.
McKeithan, Daniel Morley. "The Morgan Manuscript of Mark Twain's *Pudd'nhead Wilson*." In *Essays and Studies on American Language and Literature*, No. 12. Cambridge, Mass.: Harvard University Press, 1961; Uppsala: A.-B. Lundeqvistka Bokhandeln, 1961, 1–64.
Miller, Jim Wayne. "Pudd'nhead Wilson's Calendar." *Mark Twain Journal*, 13 (Winter 1966–67), 3, 8–10.
Rose, Marilyn Gaddis. "*Pudd'nhead Wilson*: A Contemporary Parable." *Mark Twain Journal*, 13 (Summer 1966), 2, 5–7.
Ross, Michael L. "Mark Twain's *Pudd'nhead Wilson*: Dawson's Landing and the Ladder of Nobility." *Novel*, 6, 244–256.
Rowlette, Robert. *Twain's Pudd'nhead Wilson: The Development and Design*. Bowling Green, Ohio: Bowling Green University Popular Press, 1971.
Schell, Edgar T. " 'Pears' and 'Is' in *Pudd'nhead Wilson*." *Mark Twain Journal*, 12 (Winter 1964–65), 3, 12–15.
Schleiner, Louise. "Romance Motifs in Three Novels of Mark Twain." *Comparative Literature Studies*, 13: 330–347.
Smith, Laura. "Fictive Names in Mark Twain's *Pudd'nhead Wilson*." In *Love and Wrestling, Butch and O.K.*, ed. Fred Tarpley. South Central Names Institute, Publication No. 2. Commerce, Tex.: Names Institute Press, 1973.
Wheelock, C. Webster. "The Point of Pudd'nhead's Half-a-Dog Joke." *American Notes and Queries*, viii (June 1970), 10, 150–151.
Wigger, Anne P. "The Composition of Mark Twain's *Pudd'nhead Wilson* and *Those Extraordinary Twins*: Chronology and Development." *Modern Philology*, 55 (November 1957), 93–102.